WILKIE COLLINS

GREAT CLASSIC LIBRARY

WILKIE COLLINS

THE MOONSTONE

THE HAUNTED HOTEL

MY LADY'S MONEY

CHANCELLOR
PRESS

The Moonstone was first published in 1868
The Haunted Hotel was first published in 1879
My Lady's Money was first published in 1879

This collected volume first published in Great Britain in 1994
by Chancellor Press
an imprint of Reed Consumer Books Ltd
Michelin House
81 Fulham Road
London SW3 6RB
and Auckland, Melbourne, Singapore and Toronto

Design and arrangement © 1994 Reed International Books Ltd

ISBN 1 85152 719 2

A CIP catalogue record for this title is available
at the British Library

Printed and bound in Great Britain by Cox & Wyman

Contents

THE MOONSTONE

AUTHOR'S PREFACES

IN SOME OF MY FORMER NOVELS, the object proposed has been to trace the influence of circumstances upon character. In the present story I have reversed the process. The attempt made, here, is to trace the influence of character on circumstances. The conduct pursued, under a sudden emergency, by a young girl, supplies the foundation on which I have built this book.

The same object has been kept in view, in the handling of the other characters which appear in these pages. Their course of thought and action under the circumstances which surround them, is shown to be (what it would most probably have been in real life) sometimes right, and sometimes wrong. Right, or wrong, their conduct, in either event, equally directs the course of those portions of the story in which they are concerned.

In the case of the physiological experiment which occupies a prominent place in the closing scenes of *The Moonstone*, the same principle has guided me once more. Having first ascertained, not only from books, but from living authorities as well, what the result of that experiment would really have been, I have declined to avail myself of the novelist's privilege of supposing something which might have happened, and have so shaped the story as to make it grow out of what actually would have happened – which, I beg to inform my readers, is also what actually does happen, in these pages.

With reference to the story of the Diamond, as here set forth, I have to acknowledge that it is founded, in some important particulars, on the stories of two of the royal diamonds of Europe. The magnificent stone which adorns the top of the Russian Imperial Sceptre, was once the eye of an Indian idol. The famous Koh-i-Noor is also supposed to have been one of the sacred gems of India; and, more than this, to have been the subject of a prediction, which prophesied certain misfortune to the persons who should divert it from its ancient uses.

Gloucester Place, Portman Square, *June* 30, 1868.

*

The circumstances under which *The Moonstone* was originally written, have invested the book – in the author's mind – with an interest peculiarly its own.

While this work was still in course of periodical publication in England, and in the United States, and when not more than one third of it was completed, the bitterest affliction of my life and the severest illness from which I have ever suffered, fell on me together. At the time when my mother lay dying in her little cottage in the country, I was struck prostrate, in London; crippled in every limb by the torture of rheumatic gout. Under the weight of this double calamity, I had my duty to the public still to bear in mind. My good readers in England and in America, whom I had never yet disappointed, were expecting their regular weekly instalments of the new story. I held to the story – for my own sake, as well as for theirs. In the intervals of grief, in the occasional remissions of pain, I dictated from my bed that portion of *The Moonstone* which has since proved most successful in amusing the public – the 'Narrative of Miss Clack.' Of the physical sacrifice which the effort cost me I shall say nothing. I only look back now at the blessed relief which my occupation (forced as it was) brought to my mind. The Art which had been always the pride and the pleasure of my life, became now more than ever 'its own exceeding great reward.' I doubt if I should have lived to write another book, if the responsibility of the weekly publication of this story had not forced me to rally my sinking energies of body and mind – to dry my useless tears, and to conquer my merciless pains.

The novel completed, I awaited its reception by the public with an eagerness of anxiety, which I have never felt before or since for the fate of any other writings of mine. If *The Moonstone* had failed, my mortification would have been bitter indeed. As it was, the welcome accorded to the story in England, in America, and on the Continent of Europe was instantly and universally favourable. Never have I had better reason than this work has given me to feel gratefully to novel-readers of all nations. Everywhere my characters made friends, and my story roused interest. Everywhere the public favour looked over my faults – and repaid me a hundred-fold for the hard toil which these pages cost me in the dark time of sickness and grief.

I have only to add that the present edition has had the benefit of my careful revision. All that I can do towards making the book worthy of the readers' continued approval has now been done.

W.C.

May, 1871.

⋘PROLOGUE⋙

The Storming of Seringapatam (1799)

Extracted from a Family Paper

I

I ADDRESS THESE LINES – WRITTEN IN India – to my relatives in England.

My object is to explain the motive which has induced me to refuse the right hand of friendship to my cousin, John Herncastle. The reserve which I have hitherto maintained in this matter has been misinterpreted by members of my family whose good opinion I cannot consent to forfeit. I request them to suspend their decision until they have read my narrative. And I declare, on my word of honour, that what I am now about to write is, strictly and literally, the truth.

The private difference between my cousin and me took its rise in a great public event in which we were both concerned – the storming of Seringapatam, under General Baird, on the 4 May 1799.

In order that the circumstances may be clearly understood, I must revert for a moment to the period before the assault, and to the stories current in our camp of the treasure in jewels and gold stored up in the Palace of Seringapatam.

II

One of the wildest of these stories related to a Yellow Diamond – a famous gem in the native annals of India.

The earliest known traditions describe the stone as having been set in the forehead of the four-handed Indian god who typifies the Moon. Partly from its peculiar colour, partly from a superstition which represented it as feeling the influence of the deity whom it adorned, and growing and lessening in lustre with the waxing and waning of the moon, it first gained the name by which it continues to be known in India to this day – the name of The Moonstone. A similar superstition was once prevalent, as I have heard, in ancient Greece and Rome; not applying, however (as in India), to a diamond devoted to the service of a god, but to a semi-transparent stone of the inferior order of gems, supposed to be affected by the lunar influences – the moon, in this latter case also, giving the name by which the stone is still known to collectors in our own time.

The adventures of the Yellow Diamond begin with the eleventh century of the Christian era.

At that date, the Mohammedan conqueror, Mahmoud of Ghizni, crossed India; seized on the holy city of Somnauth; and stripped of its treasures the famous temple, which had stood for centuries – the shrine of Hindoo pilgrimage, and the wonder of the eastern world.

Of all the deities worshipped in the temple, the moon-god alone escaped the rapacity of the conquering Mohammedans. Preserved by three Brahmins, the inviolate deity, bearing the Yellow Diamond in its forehead, was removed by night, and was transported to the second of the sacred cities of India – the city of Benares.

Here, in a new shrine – in a hall inlaid with precious stones, under a roof supported by pillars of gold – the moon-god was set up and worshipped. Here, on the night when the shrine was completed, Vishnu the Preserver appeared to the three Brahmins in a dream.

The deity breathed the breath of his divinity on the Diamond in the forehead of the god. And the Brahmins knelt and hid their faces in their robes. The deity commanded that the Moonstone should be watched, from that time forth, by three priests in turn, night and day, to the end of the generations of men. And the Brahmins heard, and bowed before his will. The deity predicted certain disaster to the presumptuous mortal who laid hands on the sacred gem, and to all of his house and name who received it after him. And the Brahmins caused the prophecy to be written over the gates of the shrine in letters of gold.

One age followed another – and still, generation after generation, the successors of the three Brahmins watched their priceless Moonstone, night and day. One age followed another, until the first years of the eighteenth Christian century saw the reign of Aurungzebe, Emperor of the Moguls. At his command, havoc and rapine were let loose once more among the temples of the worship of Brahmah. The shrine of the four-handed god was polluted by the slaughter of sacred animals; the images of the deities were broken in pieces; and the Moonstone was seized by an officer of rank in the army of Aurungzebe.

Powerless to recover their lost treasure by open force, the three guardian priests followed and watched it in disguise. The generations succeeded each other; the warrior who had committed the sacrilege perished miserably; the Moonstone passed (carrying its curse with it) from one lawless Mohammedan hand to another; and still, through all chances

4

and changes, the successors of the three guardian priests kept their watch, waiting the day when the will of Vishnu the Preserver should restore to them their sacred gem. Time rolled on from the first to the last years of the eighteenth Christian century. The Diamond fell into the possession of Tippoo, Sultan of Seringapatam, who caused it to be placed as an ornament in the handle of a dagger, and who commanded it to be kept among the choicest treasures of his armoury. Even then – in the palace of the Sultan himself – the three guardian priests still kept their watch in secret. There were three officers of Tippoo's household, strangers to the rest, who had won their master's confidence by conforming, or appearing to conform, to the Mussulman faith; and to those three men report pointed as the three priests in disguise.

III

So, as told in our camp, ran the fanciful story of the Moonstone. It made no serious impression on any of us except my cousin – whose love of the marvellous induced him to believe it. On the night before the assault on Seringapatam, he was absurdly angry with me, and with others, for treating the whole thing as a fable. A foolish wrangle followed; and Herncastle's unlucky temper got the better of him. He declared, in his boastful way, that we should see the Diamond on his finger, if the English army took Seringapatam. The sally was saluted by a roar of laughter, and there, as we all thought that night, the thing ended.

Let me now take you on to the day of the assault.

My cousin and I were separated at the outset. I never saw him when we forded the river; when we planted the English flag in the first breach; when we crossed the ditch beyond; and, fighting every inch of our way, entered the town. It was only at dusk, when the place was ours, and after General Baird himself had found the dead body of Tippoo under a heap of the slain, that Herncastle and I met.

We were each attached to a party sent out by the General's orders to prevent the plunder and confusion which followed our conquest. The camp-followers committed deplorable excesses; and, worse still, the soldiers found their way, by an unguarded door, into the treasury of the Palace, and loaded themselves with gold and jewels. It was in the court outside the treasury that my cousin and I met, to enforce the laws of discipline on our own soldiers. Herncastle's fiery temper had been, as I could plainly see, exasperated to a kind of frenzy by the terrible slaughter through which we had passed. He was very unfit, in my opinion, to perform the duty that had been entrusted to him.

There was riot and confusion enough in the treasury, but no violence that I saw. The men (if I may use such an expression) disgraced themselves good-humouredly. All sorts of rough jests and catchwords were bandied about among them; and the story of the Diamond turned up again unexpectedly, in the form of a mischievous joke. 'Who's got the Moonstone?' was the rallying cry which perpetually caused the plundering, as soon as it was stopped in one place, to break out in another. While I was still vainly trying to establish order, I heard a frightful yelling on the other side of the court-yard, and at once ran towards the cries, in dread of finding some new outbreak of the pillage in that direction.

I got to an open door, and saw the bodies of two Indians (by their dress, as I guessed, officers of the palace) lying across the entrance, dead.

A cry inside hurried me into a room, which appeared to serve as an armoury. A third Indian, mortally wounded, was sinking at the feet of a man whose back was towards me. The man turned at the instant when I came in, and I saw John Herncastle, with a torch in one hand, and a dagger dripping with blood in the other. A stone, set like a pommel, in the end of the dagger's handle, flashed in the torchlight, as he turned on me, like a gleam of fire. The dying Indian sank to his knees, pointed to the dagger in Herncastle's hand, and said, in his native language: – 'The Moonstone will have its vengeance yet on you and yours!' He spoke those words, and fell dead on the floor.

Before I could stir in the matter, the men who had followed me across the courtyard crowded in. My cousin rushed to meet them, like a madman. 'Clear the room!' he shouted to me, 'and set a guard on the door!' The men fell back as he threw himself on them with his torch and his dagger. I put two sentinels of my own company, on whom I could rely, to keep the door. Through the remainder of the night, I saw no more of my cousin.

Early in the morning, the plunder still going on, General Baird announced publicly by beat of drum, that any thief detected in the fact, be he whom he might, should be hung. The provost-marshal was in attendance, to prove that the General was in earnest; and in the throng that followed the proclamation, Herncastle and I met again.

He held out his hand, as usual, and said, 'Good morning.'

I waited before I gave him my hand in return.

'Tell me first,' I said, 'how the Indian in the armoury met his death, and what those last words meant, when he pointed to the dagger in your hand.'

'The Indian met his death, as I suppose, by a mortal wound,' said Herncastle. 'What his last words meant I know no more than you do.'

I looked at him narrowly. His frenzy of the previous day had all calmed down. I determined to give him another chance.

'Is that all you have to tell me?' I asked.

He answered, 'That is all.'

I turned my back on him; and we have not spoken since.

IV

I beg it to be understood that what I write here about my cousin (unless some necessity should arise for making it public) is for the information of the family only. Herncastle has said nothing that can justify me in speaking to our commanding officer. He has been taunted more than once about the Diamond, by those who recollect his angry outbreak before the assault; but, as may easily be imagined, his own remembrance of the circumstances under which I surprised him in the armoury has been enough to keep him silent. It is reported that he means to exchange into another regiment, avowedly for the purpose of separating himself from *me*.

Whether this be true or not, I cannot prevail upon myself to become his accuser – and I think with good reason. If I made the matter public, I have no evidence but moral evidence to bring forward. I have not only no proof that he killed the two men at the door; I cannot even declare that he killed the third man inside – for I cannot say that my own eyes saw the deed committed. It is true that I heard the dying Indian's words; but if those words were pronounced to be the ravings of delirium, how could I contradict the assertion from my own knowledge? Let our relatives, on either side, form their own opinion on what I have written, and decide for themselves whether the aversion I now feel towards this man is well or ill founded.

Although I attach no sort of credit to the fantastic Indian legend of the gem, I must acknowledge, before I conclude, that I am influenced by a certain superstition of my own in this matter. It is my conviction, or my delusion, no matter which, that crime brings its own fatality with it. I am not only persuaded of Herncastle's guilt; I am even fanciful enough to believe that he will live to regret if, if he keeps the Diamond; and that others will live to regret taking it from him, if he gives the Diamond away.

THE STORY

FIRST PERIOD

The Loss of the Diamond (1848)

**The Events related by Gabriel Betteredge,
House-Steward in the service of Julia, Lady Verinder**

❧ ONE ❧

IN THE FIRST PART OF *Robinson Crusoe*, at page one hundred and twenty-nine, you will find it thus written:

'Now I saw, though too late, the Folly of beginning a Work before we count the Cost, and before we judge rightly of our own Strength to go through with it.'

Only yesterday, I opened my *Robinson Crusoe* at that place. Only this morning (May twenty-first, Eighteen hundred and fifty), came my lady's nephew, Mr Franklin Blake, and held a short conversation with me, as follows: –

'Betteredge,' says Mr Franklin, 'I have been to the lawyer's about some family matters; and, among other things, we have been talking of the loss of the Indian Diamond, in my aunt's house in Yorkshire, two years since. Mr Bruff thinks, as I think, that the whole story ought, in the interests of truth, to be placed on record in writing – and the sooner the better.'

Not perceiving his drift yet, and thinking it always desirable for the sake of peace and quietness to be on the lawyer's side, I said I thought so too. Mr Franklin went on.

'In this matter of the Diamond,' he said, 'the characters of innocent people have suffered under suspicion already – as you know. The memories of innocent people may suffer, hereafter, for want of a record of the facts to which those who come after us can appeal. There can be no doubt that this strange family story of ours ought to be told. And I think, Betteredge, Mr Bruff and I together have hit on the right way of telling it.'

Very satisfactory to both of them, no doubt. But I failed to see what I myself had to do with it, so far.

'We have certain events to relate,' Mr Franklin proceeded; 'and we have certain persons concerned in those events who are capable of relating them. Starting from these plain facts, the idea is that we should all write the story of the Moonstone in turn – as far as our own personal experience extends, and no farther. We must begin by showing how the Diamond first fell into the hands of my uncle Herncastle, when he was serving in India fifty years since. This prefatory narrative I have already got by me in the form of an old family paper, which relates the necessary particulars on the authority of an eye-witness. The next thing to do is to

11

tell how the Diamond found its way into my aunt's house in Yorkshire, two years ago, and how it came to be lost in little more than twelve hours afterwards. Nobody knows as much as you do, Betteredge, about what went on in the house at that time. So you must take the pen in hand, and start the story.'

In those terms I was informed of what my personal concern was with the matter of the Diamond. If you are curious to know what course I took under the circumstances, I beg to inform you that I did what you would probably have done in my place. I modestly declared myself to be quite unequal to the task imposed upon me – and I privately felt, all the time, that I was quite clever enough to perform it, if I only gave my own abilities a fair chance. Mr Franklin, I imagine, must have seen my private sentiments in my face. He declined to believe in my modesty; and he insisted on giving my abilities a fair chance.

Two hours have passed since Mr Franklin left me. As soon as his back was turned, I went to my writing-desk to start the story. There I have sat helpless (in spite of my abilities) ever since; seeing what Robinson Crusoe saw, as quoted above – namely, the folly of beginning a work before we count the cost, and before we judge rightly of our own strength to go through with it. Please to remember, I opened the book by accident, at that bit, only the day before I rashly undertook the business now in hand; and, allow me to ask – if *that* isn't prophecy, what is?

I am not superstitious; I have read a heap of books in my time; I am a scholar in my own way. Though turned seventy, I possess an active memory, and legs to correspond. You are not to take it, if you please, as the saying of an ignorant man, when I express my opinion that such a book as *Robinson Crusoe* never was written, and never will be written again. I have tried that book for years – generally in combination with a pipe of tobacco – and I have found it my friend in need in all the necessities of this mortal life. When my spirits are bad – *Robinson Crusoe*. When I want advice – *Robinson Crusoe*. In past times, when my wife plagued me; in present times, when I have had a drop too much – *Robinson Crusoe*. I have worn out six stout *Robinson Crusoes* with hard work in my service. On my lady's last birthday she gave me a seventh. I took a drop too much on the strength of it; and *Robinson Crusoe* put me right again. Price four shillings and sixpence, bound in blue, with a picture into the bargain.

Still, this don't look much like starting the story of the Diamond – does it? I seem to be wandering off in search of Lord knows what, Lord knows where. We will take a new sheet of paper, if you please, and begin over again, with my best respects to you.

∽ TWO ∾

I SPOKE OF MY LADY A line or two back. Now the Diamond could never have been in our house, where it was lost, if it had not been made a present of to my lady's daughter; and my lady's daughter would never have been in existence to have the present, if it had not been for my lady who (with pain and travail) produced her into the world. Consequently, if we begin with my lady, we are pretty sure of beginning far enough back. And that, let me tell you, when you have got such a job as mine in hand, is a real comfort at starting.

If you know anything of the fashionable world, you have heard tell of the three beautiful Miss Herncastles. Miss Adelaide; Miss Caroline; and Miss Julia – this last being the youngest and the best of the three sisters, in my opinion; and I had opportunities of judging, as you shall presently see. I went into the service of the old lord, their father (thank God, we have got nothing to do with *him*, in this business of the Diamond; he had the longest tongue and the shortest temper of any man, high or low, I ever met with) – I say, I went into the service of the old lord, as page-boy in waiting on the three honourable young ladies, at the age of fifteen years. There I lived, till Miss Julia married the late Sir John Verinder. An excellent man, who only wanted somebody to manage him; and, between ourselves, he found somebody to do it; and what is more, he throve on it, and grew fat on it, and lived happy and died easy on it, dating from the day when my lady took him to church to be married, to the day when she relieved him of his last breath, and closed his eyes for ever.

I have omitted to state that I went with the bride to the bride's husband's house and lands down here. 'Sir John,' she says, 'I can't do without Gabriel Betteredge.' 'My lady,' says Sir John, 'I can't do without him, either.' That was his way with her – and that was how I went into his service. It was all one to me where I went, so long as my mistress and I were together.

Seeing that my lady took an interest in the out-of-door work, and the farms, and such like, I took an interest in them too – with all the more reason that I was a small farmer's seventh son myself. My lady got me put under the bailiff, and I did my best, and gave satisfaction, and got promotion accordingly. Some years later, on the Monday as it might be, my lady says, 'Sir John, your bailiff is a stupid old man. Pension him liberally, and let Gabriel Betteredge have his place.' On the Tuesday as it might be, Sir John says, 'My lady, the bailiff is pensioned liberally; and Gabriel Betteredge has got his place.' You hear more than enough of married people living together miserably. Here is an example to the contrary. Let it be a warning to some of you, and an encouragement to others. In the meantime, I will go on with my story.

Well, there I was in clover, you will say. Placed in a position of trust and honour, with a little cottage of my own to live in, with my rounds on the estate to occupy me in the morning, and my accounts in the afternoon, and my pipe and my *Robinson Crusoe* in the evening – what more could I possibly want to make me happy? Remember what Adam wanted when he was alone in the Garden of Eden; and if you don't blame it in Adam, don't blame it in me.

The woman I fixed my eye on, was the woman who kept house for me at my cottage. Her name was Selina Goby. I agree with the late William Cobbett about picking a wife. See that she chews her food well, and sets her foot down firmly on the ground when she walks, and you're all right. Selina Goby was all right in both these respects, which was one reason for marrying her. I had another reason, likewise, entirely of my own discovering. Selina, being a single woman, made me pay so much a week for her board and services. Selina, being my wife, couldn't charge for her board, and would have to give me her services for nothing. That was the point of view I looked at it from. Economy – with a dash of love. I put it to my mistress, as in duty bound, just as I had put it to myself.

'I have been turning Selina Goby over in my mind,' I said, 'and I think, my lady, it will be cheaper to marry her than to keep her.'

My lady burst out laughing, and said she didn't know which to be most shocked at – my language or my principles. Some joke tickled her, I suppose, of the sort that you can't take unless you are a person of quality. Understanding nothing myself but that I was free to put it next to Selina, I went and put it accordingly. And what did Selina say? Lord! how little you must know of women, if you ask that. Of course she said, Yes.

As my time drew nearer, and there got to be talk of my having a new coat for the ceremony, my mind began to misgive me. I have compared notes with other men as to what they felt while they were in my interesting situation; and they have all acknowledged that, about a week before it happened, they privately wished themselves out of it. I went a trifle further than that myself; I actually rose up, as it were, and tried to get out of it. Not for nothing! I was too just a man to expect she would let me off for nothing. Compensation to the woman when the man gets out of it, is one of the laws of England. In obedience to the laws, and after turning it over carefully in my mind, I offered Selina Goby a feather-bed and fifty shillings to be off the bargain. You will hardly believe it, but it is nevertheless true – she was fool enough to refuse.

After that it was all over with me, of course. I got the new coat as cheap as I could, and I went through all the rest of it as cheap as I could. We were not a happy couple, and not a miserable couple. We were six of one and half-a-dozen of the other. How it was I don't understand, but we always seemed to be getting, with the best of motives, in one another's way. When I wanted to go upstairs, there was my wife coming down; or when my wife wanted to go down, there was I coming up. That is married life, according to my experience of it.

After five years of misunderstandings on the stairs, it pleased an all-wise Providence to relieve us of each other by taking my wife. I was left with my little girl Penelope, and with no other child. Shortly afterwards Sir John died, and my lady was left with her little girl, Miss Rachel, and no other child. I have written to very poor purpose of my lady, if you require to be told that my little Penelope was taken care of, under my good mistress's own eye, and was sent to school, and taught, and made a sharp girl, and promoted, when old enough, to be Miss Rachel's own maid.

As for me, I went on with my business as bailiff year after year up to Christmas, 1847, when there came a change in my life. On that day, my lady invited herself to a cup of tea alone with me in my cottage. She remarked that, reckoning from the year when I started as page-boy in the time of the old lord, I had been more than fifty years in her service, and she put into my hands a beautiful waistcoat of wool that she had worked herself, to keep me warm in the bitter winter weather.

I received this magnificent present quite at a loss to find words to thank my mistress with for the honour she had done me. To my great astonishment, it turned out, however, that the waistcoat was not an honour, but a bribe. My lady had discovered that I was getting old before I had discovered it myself, and she had come to my cottage to wheedle me (if I may use such an expression) into giving up my hard out-of-door work as bailiff, and taking my ease for the rest of my days as steward in the house. I made as good a fight of it against the indignity of taking my ease as I could. But my mistress knew the weak side of me; she put it as a favour to herself. The dispute between us ended, after that, in my wiping my eyes, like an old fool, with my new woollen waistcoat, and saying I would think about it.

The perturbation in my mind, in regard to thinking about it, being truly dreadful after my lady had gone away, I applied the remedy which I have never yet found to fail me in cases of doubt and emergency. I smoked a pipe and took a turn at *Robinson Crusoe*. Before I had occupied myself with that extraordinary book five minutes, I came on a comforting bit (page one hundred and fifty-eight), as follows: 'To-day we love, what to-morrow we hate.' I saw my way clear directly. To-day I was all for continuing to be farm-bailiff; to-morrow, on the authority of *Robinson Crusoe*, I should be all the other way. Take myself to-morrow while in to-morrow's humour, and the thing was done. My mind being relieved in this manner, I went to sleep that night in the character of Lady Verinder's farm-bailiff, and I woke up the next morning in the character of Lady Verinder's house-steward. All quite comfortable, and all through *Robinson Crusoe*!

My daughter Penelope has just looked over my shoulder to see what I have done so far. She remarks that it is beautifully written and every word of it true. But she points out one objection. She says what I have done so far isn't in the least what I was wanted to do. I am asked to tell the story of the Diamond, and, instead of that, I have been telling the story of my own self. Curious, and quite beyond me to account for. I wonder whether the gentlemen who make a business and a living out of writing books, ever find their own selves getting in the way of their subjects, like me? If they do, I can feel for them. In the meantime, here is another false start, and more waste of good writing-paper. What's to be done now? Nothing that I know of, except for you to keep your temper, and for me to begin it all over again for the third time.

⇛ THREE ⇚

THE QUESTION OF HOW I AM to start the story properly I have tried to settle in two ways. First, by scratching my head, which led to nothing. Second, by consulting my daughter Penelope, which has resulted in an entirely new idea.

Penelope's notion is that I should set down what happened, regularly day by day, beginning with the day when we got the news that Mr Franklin Blake was expected on a visit to the house. When you come to fix your memory with a date in this way, it is wonderful what your memory will pick up for you upon that compulsion. The only difficulty is to fetch out the dates, in the first place. This Penelope offers to do for me by looking into her own diary, which she was taught to keep when she was at school, and which she has gone on keeping ever since. In answer to an improvement on this notion, devised by myself, namely, that she should tell the story instead of me, out of her own diary, Penelope observes, with a fierce look and a red face, that her journal is for her own private eye, and that no living creature shall ever know what is in it but herself. When I inquire what this means, Penelope says, 'Fiddlesticks!' I say, Sweethearts.

Beginning, then, on Penelope's plan, I beg to mention that I was specially called one Wednesday morning into my lady's own sitting-room, the date being the twenty-fourth of May, Eighteen hundred and forty-eight.

'Gabriel,' says my lady, 'here is news that will surprise you. Franklin Blake has come back from abroad. He has been staying with his father in London, and he is coming to us to-morrow to stop till next month, and keep Rachel's birthday.'

If I had had a hat in my hand, nothing but respect would have prevented me from throwing that hat up to the ceiling. I had not seen Mr Franklin since he was a boy, living along with us in this house. He was, out of all sight (as I remembered him), the nicest boy that ever spun a top or broke a window. Miss Rachel, who was present, and to whom I made that remark, observed, in return, that *she* remembered him as the most atrocious tyrant that ever tortured a doll, and the hardest driver of an exhausted little girl in string harness that England could produce. 'I burn with indignation, and I ache with fatigue,' was the way Miss Rachel summed it up, 'when I think of Franklin Blake.'

Hearing what I now tell you, you will naturally ask how it was that Mr Franklin should have passed all the years, from the time when he was a boy to the time when he was a man, out of his own country. I answer, because his father had the misfortune to be next heir to a Duke-dom, and not to be able to prove it.

In two words, this was how the thing happened:

My lady's eldest sister married the celebrated Mr Blake – equally famous for his great riches, and his great suit at law. How many years he went on worrying the tribunals of his country to turn out the Duke in possession, and to put himself in the Duke's place – how many lawyers' purses he filled to bursting, and how many otherwise harmless people he set by the ears together disputing whether he was right or wrong – is more by a great deal than I can reckon up. His wife died, and two of his three children died, before the tribunals could make up their minds to show him the door and take no more of his money. When it was all over, and the Duke in possession was left in possession, Mr Blake discovered that the only way of being even with his country for the manner in which it had treated him, was not to let his country have the honour of educating his son. 'How can I trust my native insti-tutions,' was the form in which he put it, 'after the way in which my native institutions have behaved to *me*?' Add to this, that Mr Blake disliked all boys, his own included, and you will admit that it could only end in one way. Master Franklin was taken from us in England, and was sent to institutions which his father *could* trust, in that superior country, Germany; Mr Blake himself, you will observe, remaining snug in England, to improve his fellow-countrymen in the Parliament House, and to publish a statement on the subject of the Duke in possession, which has remained an unfinished statement from that day to this.

There! thank God, that's told! Neither you nor I need trouble our heads any more about Mr Blake, senior. Leave him to the Dukedom; and let you and I stick to the Diamond.

The Diamond takes us back to Mr Franklin, who was the innocent means of bringing that unlucky jewel into the house.

Our nice boy didn't forget us after he went abroad. He wrote every now and then; sometimes to my lady, sometimes to Miss Rachel, and sometimes to me. We had had a transaction together, before he left, which consisted in his borrowing of me a ball of string, a four-bladed knife, and seven-and-sixpence in money – the colour of which last I have not seen, and never expect to see again. His letters to me chiefly related to borrowing more. I heard, however, from my lady, how he got on abroad, as he grew in years and stature. After he had learnt what the institutions of Germany could teach him, he gave the French a turn next, and the Italians a turn after that. They made him among them a sort of universal genius, as well as I could understand it. He wrote a little; he painted a little; he sang and played and composed a little – borrowing, as I suspect, in all these cases, just as he had borrowed from me. His mother's fortune (seven hundred a year) fell to him when he came of age, and ran through him, as it might be through a sieve. The more money he had, the more he wanted: there was a hole in Mr Franklin's pocket that nothing would sew up. Wherever he went, the lively, easy way of him made him welcome. He lived here, there, and everywhere; his address (as he used to put it himself) being, 'Post Office, Europe – to be left till called for.' Twice over, he made up his mind to come back to England and see us; and twice over (saving your presence), some unmentionable woman stood in the way and stopped him. His third attempt succeeded, as you know already from what my lady told me. On Thursday the twenty-fifth of May, we were to see for the first time what our nice boy had grown to be as a man. He came of good blood; he had a high courage; and he was five-and-twenty years of age, by our reckoning. Now you know as much of Mr Franklin Blake as I did – before Mr Franklin Blake came down to our house.

The Thursday was as fine a summer's day as ever you saw: and my lady and Miss Rachel (not expecting Mr Franklin till dinner-time) drove out to lunch with some friends in the neighbourhood.

When they were gone, I went and had a look at the bedroom which had been got ready for our guest, and saw that all was straight. Then, being butler in my lady's establishment, as well as steward (at my own particular request, mind, and because it vexed me to see anybody but myself in possession of the key of the late Sir John's cellar) – then, I say, I fetched up some of our famous Latour claret, and set it in the warm summer air to take off the chill before dinner. Concluding to set myself in the warm summer air next – seeing that what is good for old claret is equally good for old age – I took up my beehive chair to go out into the back court, when I was stopped by hearing a sound like the soft beating of a drum, on the terrace in front of my lady's residence.

Going round to the terrace, I found three mahogany-coloured Indians, in white linen frocks and trousers looking up at the house.

The Indians, as I saw on looking closer, had small hand-drums slung in front of them. Behind them stood a little delicate-looking light-haired English boy carrying a bag. I judged the fellows to be strolling conjurors, and the boy with the bag to be carrying the tools of their trade. One of the three, who spoke English, and who exhibited, I must own, the most elegant manners, presently informed me that my judgment was right. He requested permission to show his tricks in the presence of the lady of the house.

Now I am not a sour old man. I am generally all for amusement, and the last person in the world to distrust another person because he happens to be a few shades darker than myself. But the best of us have our weaknesses – and my weakness, when I know a family plate-basket to be out on a pantry table, is to be instantly reminded of that basket by the sight of a strolling stranger whose manners are superior to my own. I accordingly informed the Indian that the lady of the house was out; and I warned him and his party off the premises. He made me a beautiful bow in return; and he and his party went off the premises. On my side, I returned to my beehive chair, and set myself down on the sunny side of the court, and fell (if the truth must be owned), not exactly into a sleep, but into the next best thing to it.

I was roused up by my daughter Penelope running out at me as if the house was on fire. What do you think she wanted? She wanted to have the three Indian jugglers instantly taken up; for this reason, namely, that they knew who was coming from London to visit us, and that they meant some mischief to Mr Franklin Blake.

Mr Franklin's name roused me. I opened my eyes, and made my girl explain herself.

It appeared that Penelope had just come from our lodge, where she had been having a gossip with the lodge-keeper's daughter. The two girls had seen the Indians pass out, after I had warned them off, followed by their little boy. Taking it into their heads that the boy was ill-used by the foreigners – for no reason that I could discover, except that he was pretty and delicate-looking – the two girls had stolen along the inner side of the hedge between us and the road, and had watched the proceedings of the foreigners on the outer side. Those proceedings resulted in the performance of the following extraordinary tricks.

They first looked up the road, and down the road, and made sure that they were alone. Then they all three faced about, and stared hard in the direction of our house. Then they jabbered and disputed in their own language, and looked at each other like men in doubt. Then they all turned to their little English boy, as if they expected *him* to help them. And then the chief Indian, who spoke English, said to the boy, 'Hold out your hand.'

On hearing those dreadful words, my daughter Penelope said she didn't know what prevented her heart from flying straight out of her. I thought privately that it might have been her stays. All I said, however, was, 'You make my flesh creep.' (*Nota bene*: Women like these little compliments.)

Well, when the Indian said, 'Hold out your hand,' the boy shrunk back, and shook his head, and said he didn't like it. The Indian, thereupon, asked him (not at all unkindly), whether he would like to be sent back to London, and left where they had found him, sleeping in an empty basket in a market – a hungry, ragged, and forsaken little boy. This, it seems, ended the difficulty. The little chap unwillingly held out his hand. Upon that, the Indian took a bottle from his bosom, and poured out of it some black stuff, like ink, into the palm of the boy's hand. The Indian – first touching the boy's head, and making signs over it in the air – then said, 'Look.' The boy became quite stiff, and stood like a statue, looking into the ink in the hollow of his hand.

(So far, it seemed to me to be juggling, accompanied by a foolish waste of ink. I was beginning to feel sleepy again, when Penelope's next words stirred me up.)

The Indians looked up the road and down the road once more – and then the chief Indian said these words to the boy: 'See the English gentleman from foreign parts.'

The boy said, 'I see him.'

The Indian said, 'Is it on the road to this house, and on no other, that the English gentleman will travel to-day?'

The boy said, 'It is on the road to this house, and on no other, that the English gentleman will travel to-day.'

20

The Indian put a second question – after waiting a little first. He said: 'Has the English gentleman got It about him?'

The boy answered – also, after waiting a little first – 'Yes.'

The Indian put a third and last question: 'Will the English gentleman come here, as he has promised to come, at the close of day?'

The boy said, 'I can't tell.'

The Indian asked why.

The boy said, 'I am tired. The mist rises in my head, and puzzles me. I can see no more to-day.'

With that, the catechism ended. The chief Indian said something in his own language to the other two, pointing to the boy, and pointing towards the town, in which (as we afterwards discovered) they were lodged. He then, after making more signs on the boy's head, blew on his forehead, and so woke him up with a start. After that, they all went on their way towards the town, and the girls saw them no more.

Most things they say have a moral, if you only look for it. What was the moral of this?

The moral was, as I thought: First, that the chief juggler had heard Mr Franklin's arrival talked of among the servants out-of-doors, and saw his way to making a little money by it. Second, that he and his men and boy (with a view to making the said money) meant to hang about till they saw my lady drive home, and then to come back, and foretell Mr Franklin's arrival by magic. Third, that Penelope had heard them rehearsing their hocus-pocus, like actors rehearsing a play. Fourth, that I should do well to have an eye, that evening, on the plate-basket. Fifth, that Penelope would do well to cool down, and leave me, her father, to doze off again in the sun.

That appeared to me to be the sensible view. If you know anything of the ways of young women, you won't be surprised to hear that Penelope wouldn't take it. The moral of the thing was serious, according to my daughter. She particularly reminded me of the Indian's third question, Has the English gentleman got It about him? 'Oh, father!' says Penelope, clasping her hands, 'don't joke about this! What does "It" mean?'

'We'll ask Mr Franklin, my dear,' I said, 'if you can wait till Mr Franklin comes.' I winked to show I meant that in joke. Penelope took it quite seriously. My girl's earnestness tickled me. 'What on earth should Mr Franklin know about it?' I inquired. 'Ask him,' says Penelope. 'And see whether *he* thinks it a laughing matter, too.' With that parting shot, my daughter left me.

I settled it with myself, when she was gone, that I really would ask Mr Franklin – mainly to set Penelope's mind at rest. What was said between us, when I did ask him, later on that same day, you will find set out fully in its proper place. But as I don't wish to raise your expectations and then disappoint them, I will take leave to warn you here – before we go any further – that you won't find the ghost of a joke in our conversation on the subject of the jugglers. To my great surprise, Mr Franklin, like Penelope, took the thing seriously. How seriously, you will understand, when I tell you that, in his opinion, 'It' meant the Moonstone.

❧ FOUR ❧

I AM TRULY SORRY TO DETAIN you over me and my beehive chair. A sleepy old man, in a sunny back yard, is not an interesting object, I am well aware. But things must be put down in their places, as things actually happened – and you must please to jog on a little while longer with me, in expectation of Mr Franklin Blake's arrival later in the day.

Before I had time to doze off again, after my daughter Penelope had left me, I was disturbed by a rattling of plates and dishes in the servants' hall, which meant that dinner was ready. Taking my own meals in my own sitting-room, I had nothing to do with the servants' dinner, except to wish them a good stomach to it all round, previous to composing myself once more in my chair. I was just stretching my legs, when out bounced another woman on me. Not my daughter again; only Nancy, the kitchen-maid, this time. I was straight in her way out; and I observed, as she asked me to let her by, that she had a sulky face – a thing which, as head of the servants, I never allow, on principle, to pass me without inquiry.

'What are you turning your back on your dinner for?' I asked. 'What's wrong now, Nancy?'

Nancy tried to push by, without answering; upon which I rose up, and took her by the ear. She is a nice plump young lass, and it is customary with me to adopt that manner of showing that I personally approve of a girl.

'What's wrong now?' I said once more.

'Rosanna's late again for dinner,' says Nancy. 'And I'm sent to fetch her in. All the hard work falls on my shoulders in this house. Let me alone, Mr Betteredge!'

The person here mentioned as Rosanna was our second housemaid. Having a kind of pity for our second housemaid (why, you shall presently know), and seeing in Nancy's face that she would fetch her fellow-servant in with more hard words than might be needful under the circumstances, it struck me that I had nothing particular to do, and that I might as well fetch Rosanna myself; giving her a hint to be punctual in future, which I knew she would take kindly from *me*.

'Where is Rosanna?' I inquired.

'At the sands, of course!' says Nancy, with a toss of her head. 'She had another of her fainting fits this morning, and she asked to go out and get a breath of fresh air. I have no patience with her!'

'Go back to your dinner, my girl,' I said. 'I have patience with her, and I'll fetch her in.'

Nancy (who has a fine appetite) looked pleased. When she looks pleased, she looks nice. When she looks nice, I chuck her under the chin. It isn't immorality – it's only habit.

Well, I took my stick, and set off for the sands.

No! it won't do to set off yet. I am sorry again to detain you: but you really must hear the story of the sands, and the story of Rosanna – for this reason, that the matter of the Diamond touches them both nearly. How hard I try to get on with my statement without stopping by the way, and how badly I succeed! But, there! – Persons and Things do turn up so vexatiously in this life, and will in a manner insist on being noticed. Let us take it easy, and let us take it short; we shall be in the thick of the mystery soon, I promise you!

Rosanna (to put the Person before the Thing, which is but common politeness) was the only new servant in our house. About four months before the time I am writing of, my lady had been in London, and had gone over a Reformatory, intended to save forlorn women from drifting back into bad ways, after they had got released from prison. The matron, seeing my lady took an interest in the place, pointed out a girl to her, named Rosanna Spearman, and told her a most miserable story, which I haven't the heart to repeat here; for I don't like to be made wretched without any use, and no more do you. The upshot of it was, that Rosanna Spearman had been a thief, and not being of the sort that get up Companies in the City, and rob from thousands, instead of only robbing from one, the law laid hold of her, and the prison and the reformatory followed the lead of the law. The matron's opinion of Rosanna was (in spite of what she had done) that the girl was one in a thousand, and that she only wanted a chance to prove herself worthy of any Christian woman's interest in her. My lady (being a Christian woman, if ever there was one yet) said to the matron, upon that, 'Rosanna Spearman shall have her chance, in my service.' In a week afterwards, Rosanna Spearman entered this establishment as our second housemaid.

Not a soul was told the girl's story, excepting Miss Rachel and me. My lady, doing me the honour to consult me about most things, consulted me about Rosanna. Having fallen a good deal latterly into the late Sir John's way of always agreeing with my lady, I agreed with her heartily about Rosanna Spearman.

A fairer chance no girl could have had than was given to this poor girl of ours. None of the servants could cast her past life in her teeth, for none of the servants knew what it had been. She had her wages and her privileges, like the rest of them; and every now and then a friendly word from my lady, in private, to encourage her. In return, she showed herself, I am bound to say, well worthy of the kind treatment bestowed upon her. Though far from strong, and troubled occasionally with those fainting-fits already mentioned, she went about her work modestly and uncomplainingly, doing it carefully, and doing it well. But, somehow, she failed to make friends among the other women servants, excepting my daughter Penelope, who was always kind to Rosanna, though never intimate with her.

I hardly know what the girl did to offend them. There was certainly no beauty about her to make the others envious; she was the plainest woman in the house, with the additional misfortune of having one shoulder bigger than the other. What the servants chiefly resented, I think, was her silent tongue and her solitary ways. She read or worked in leisure hours when the rest gossiped. And when it came to her turn to go out, nine times out of ten she quietly put on her bonnet, and had her turn by herself. She never quarrelled, she never took offence; she only kept a certain distance, obstinately and civilly, between the rest of them and herself. Add to this that, plain as she was, there was just a dash of something that wasn't like a housemaid, and that *was* like a lady, about her. It might have been in her voice, or it might have been in her face. All I can say is, that the other women pounced on it like lightning the first day she came into the house, and said (which was most unjust) that Rosanna Spearman gave herself airs.

Having now told the story of Rosanna, I have only to notice one of the many queer ways of this strange girl to get on next to the story of the sands.

Our house is high up on the Yorkshire coast, and close by the sea. We have got beautiful walks all round us, in every direction but one. That one I acknowledge to be a horrid walk. It leads, for a quarter of a mile, through a melancholy plantation of firs, and brings you out between low cliffs on the loneliest and ugliest little bay on all our coast.

The sandhills here run down to the sea, and end in two spits of rock jutting out opposite each other, till you lose sight of them in the water. One is called the North Spit, and one the South. Between the two, shifting backwards and forwards at certain seasons of the year, lies the most horrible quicksand on the shores of Yorkshire. At the turn of the tide, something goes on in the unknown deeps below, which sets the whole face of the quicksand shivering and trembling in a manner most remarkable to see, and which has given to it, among the people in our parts, the name of The Shivering Sand. A great bank, half a mile out, nigh the mouth of the bay, breaks the force of the main ocean coming in from the offing. Winter and summer, when the tide flows over the quicksand, the sea seems to leave the waves behind it on the bank, and rolls its waters in smoothly with a heave, and covers the sand in silence. A lonesome and a horrid retreat, I can tell you! No boat ever ventures into this bay. No children from our fishing-village, called Cobb's Hole, ever come here to play. The very birds of the air, as it seems to me, give the Shivering Sand a wide berth. That a young woman, with dozens of nice walks to choose from, and company to go with her, if she only said 'Come!' should prefer this place, and should sit and work or read in it, all alone, when it's her turn out, I grant you, passes belief. It's true, nevertheless, account for it as you may, that this was Rosanna Spearman's favourite walk, except when she went once or twice to Cobb's Hole, to see the only friend she had in our neighbourhood, of whom more anon. It's also true that I was now setting out for this same place, to fetch the girl in to dinner, which brings us round happily to our former point, and starts us fair again on our way to the sands.

I saw no sign of the girl in the plantation. When I got out, through the sandhills, on to the beach, there she was, in her little straw bonnet, and her plain grey cloak that she always wore to hide her deformed shoulder as much as might be – there she was, all alone, looking out on the quicksand and the sea.

She started when I came up with her, and turned her head away from me. Not looking me in the face being another of the proceedings which, as head of the servants, I never allow, on principle, to pass without inquiry – I turned her round my way, and saw that she was crying. My bandanna handkerchief – one of six beauties given to me by me lady – was handy in my pocket. I took it out, and I said to Rosanna, 'Come and sit down, my dear, on the slope of the beach along with me. I'll dry your eyes for you first, and then I'll make so bold as to ask what you have been crying about.'

When you come to my age, you will find sitting down on the slope of a beach a much longer job than you think it now. By the time I was settled, Rosanna had dried her own eyes with a very inferior handkerchief to mine – cheap cambric. She looked very quiet, and very wretched; but she sat down by me like a good girl, when I told her. When you want to comfort a woman by the shortest way, take her on your knee. I thought of this golden rule. But there! Rosanna wasn't Nancy, and that's the truth of it!

'Now, tell me, my dear,' I said, 'what are you crying about?'

'About the years that are gone, Mr Betteredge,' says Rosanna quietly. 'My past life still comes back to me sometimes.'

'Come, come, my girl,' I said, 'your past life is all sponged out. Why can't you forget it?'

She took me by one of the lappets of my coat. I am a slovenly old man, and a good deal of my meat and drink gets splashed about on my clothes. Sometimes one of the women, and sometimes another, cleans me of my grease. The day before, Rosanna had taken out a spot for me on the lappet of my coat, with a new composition, warranted to remove anything. The grease was gone, but there was a little dull place left on the nap of the cloth where the grease had been. The girl pointed to that place, and shook her head.

'The stain is taken off,' she said. 'But the place shows, Mr Betteredge – the place shows!'

A remark which takes a man unawares by means of his own coat is not an easy remark to answer. Something in the girl herself, too, made me particularly sorry for her just then. She had nice brown eyes, plain as she was in other ways – and she looked at me with a sort of respect for my bappy old age and my good character, as things for ever out of her own reach, which made my heart heavy for our second housemaid. Not feeling myself able to comfort her, there was only one other thing to do. That thing was – to take her in to dinner.

'Help me up,' I said. 'You're late for dinner, Rosanna – and I have come to fetch you in.'

'You, Mr Betteredge!' says she.

'They told Nancy to fetch you,' I said. 'But I thought you might like your scolding better, my dear, if it came from me.'

Instead of helping me up, the poor thing stole her hand into mine, and gave it a little squeeze. She tried hard to keep from crying again, and succeeded – for which I respected her. 'You're very kind, Mr Betteredge,' she said. 'I don't want any dinner to-day – let me bide a little longer here.'

'What makes you like to be here?' I asked. 'What is it that brings you everlastingly to this miserable place?'

'Something draws me to it,' says the girl, making images with her finger in the sand. 'I try to keep away from it, and I can't. Sometimes,' says she in a low voice, as if she was frightened at her own fancy, 'sometimes, Mr Betteredge, I think that my grave is waiting for me here.'

'There's roast mutton and suet-pudding waiting for you!' says I. 'Go in to dinner directly. This is what comes, Rosanna, of thinking on an empty stomach!' I spoke severely, being naturally indignant (at my time of life) to hear a young woman of five-and-twenty talking about her latter end!

She didn't seem to hear me: she put her hand on my shoulder, and kept me where I was, sitting by her side.

'I think the place has laid a spell on me,' she said. 'I dream of it night after night; I think of it when I sit stitching at my work. You know I am grateful, Mr Betteredge – you know I try to deserve your kindness, and my lady's confidence in me. But I wonder sometimes whether the life here is too quiet and too good for such a woman as I am, after all I have gone through, Mr Betteredge – after all I have gone through. It's more lonely to me to be among the other servants, knowing I am not what they are, than it is to be here. My lady doesn't know, the matron at the reformatory doesn't know, what a dreadful reproach honest people are in themselves to a woman like me. Don't scold me, there's a dear good man. I do my work, don't I? Please not to tell my lady I am discontented – I am not. My mind's unquiet, sometimes, that's all.' She snatched her hand off my shoulder, and suddenly pointed down to the quicksand. 'Look!' she said. 'Isn't it wonderful? Isn't it terrible? I have seen it dozens of times, and it's always as new to me as if I had never seen it before!'

I looked where she pointed. The tide was on the turn, and the horrid sand began to shiver. The broad brown face of it heaved slowly, and then dimpled and quivered all over. 'Do you know what it looks like to *me*?' says Rosanna, catching me by the shoulder again. 'It looks as if it had hundreds of suffocating people under it – all struggling to get to the surface, and all sinking lower and lower in the dreadful deeps! Throw a stone in, Mr Betteredge! Throw a stone in, and let's see the sand suck it down!'

Here was unwholesome talk! Here was an empty stomach feeding on an unquiet mind! My answer – a pretty sharp one, in the poor girl's own interests, I promise you! – was at my tongue's end, when it was snapped short off on a sudden by a voice among the sand-hills shouting for me by my name. 'Betteredge!' cries the voice, 'where are you?' 'Here!' I shouted out in return, without a notion in my mind of who it was. Rosanna started to her feet, and stood looking towards the voice. I was just thinking of getting on my own legs next, when I was staggered by a sudden change in the girl's face.

Her complexion turned of a beautiful red, which I had never seen in it before; she brightened all over with a kind of speechless and breathless surprise. 'Who is it?' I asked. Rosanna gave me back my own question. 'Oh! who is it?' she said softly, more to herself than to me. I twisted round on the sand, and looked behind me. There, coming out on us from among the hills, was a bright-eyed young gentleman, dressed in a beautiful fawn-coloured suit, with gloves and hat to match, with a rose in his button-hole, and a smile on his face that might have set the Shivering Sand itself smiling at him in return. Before I could get on my legs, he plumped down on the sand by the side of me, put his arm round my neck, foreign fashion, and gave me a hug that fairly squeezed the breath out of my body. 'Dear old Betteredge!' says he. 'I owe you seven-and-sixpence. Now do you know who I am?'

Lord bless us and save us! Here – four good hours before we expected him – was Mr Franklin Blake!

Before I could say a word, I saw Mr Franklin, a little surprised to all appearance, look up from me to Rosanna. Following his lead, I looked at the girl too. She was blushing of a deeper red than ever, seemingly at having caught Mr Franklin's eye; and she turned and left us suddenly, in a confusion quite unaccountable to my mind, without either making her curtsey to the gentleman or saying a word to me. Very unlike her usual self: a civiller and better-behaved servant, in general, you never met with.

'That's an odd girl,' says Mr Franklin. 'I wonder what she sees in me to surprise her?'

'I suppose, sir,' I answered, drolling on our young gentleman's Continental education, 'it's the varnish from foreign parts.'

I set down here Mr Franklin's careless question, and my foolish answer, as a consolation and encouragement to all stupid people – it being, as I have remarked, a great satisfaction to our inferior fellow-creatures to find that their betters are, on occasions, no brighter than they are. Neither Mr Franklin, with his wonderful foreign training, nor I, with my age, experience, and natural mother-wit, had the ghost of an idea of what Rosanna Spearman's unaccountable behaviour really meant. She was out of our thoughts, poor soul, before we had seen the last flutter of her little grey cloak among the sandhills. And what of that? you will ask, naturally enough. Read on, good friend, as patiently as you can, and perhaps you will be as sorry for Rosanna Spearman as I was, when I found out the truth.

⬧ FIVE ⬦

THE FIRST THING I DID, after we were left together alone, was to make a third attempt to get up from my seat on the sand. Mr Franklin stopped me.

'There is one advantage about this horrid place,' he said; 'we have got it all to ourselves. Stay where you are, Betteredge; I have something to say to you.'

While he was speaking, I was looking at him, and trying to see something of the boy I remembered, in the man before me. The man put me out. Look as I might, I could see no more of his boy's rosy cheeks than of his boy's trim little jacket. His complexion had got pale: his face, at the lower part, was covered, to my great surprise and disappointment, with a curly brown beard and mustachios. He had a lively touch-and-go way with him, very pleasant and engaging, I admit; but nothing to compare with his free-and-easy manners of other times. To make matters worse, he had promised to be tall, and had not kept his promise. He was neat, and slim, and well made; but he wasn't by an inch or two up to the middle height. In short, he baffled me altogether. The years that had passed had left nothing of his old self, except the bright, straightforward look in his eyes. There I found our nice boy again, and there I concluded to stop in my investigation.

'Welcome back to the old place, Mr Franklin,' I said. 'All the more welcome, sir, that you have come some hours before we expected you.'

'I have a reason for coming before you expected me,' answered Mr Franklin. 'I suspect, Betteredge, that I have been followed and watched in London, for the last three or four days; and I have travelled by the morning instead of the afternoon train, because I wanted to give a certain dark-looking stranger the slip.'

Those words did more than surprise me. They brought back to my mind, in a flash, the three jugglers, and Penelope's notion that they meant some mischief to Mr Franklin Blake.

'Who's watching you, sir, – and why?' I inquired.

'Tell me about the three Indians you have had at the house to-day,' says Mr Franklin, without noticing my question. 'It's just possible, Betteredge, that my stranger and your three jugglers may turn out to be pieces of the same puzzle.'

'How do you come to know about the jugglers, sir?' I asked, putting one question on the top of another, which was bad manners, I own. But you don't expect much from poor human nature – so don't expect much from me.

'I saw Penelope at the house,' says Mr Franklin; 'and Penelope told me. Your daughter promised to be a pretty girl, Betteredge, and she has kept her promise. Penelope has got a small ear and a small foot. Did the late Mrs Betteredge possess those inestimable advantages?'

'The late Mrs Betteredge possessed a good many defects, sir,' says I. 'One of them (if you will pardon my mentioning it) was never keeping to the matter in hand. She was more like a fly than a woman: she couldn't settle on anything.'

'She would just have suited me,' says Mr Franklin. 'I never settle on anything either. Betteredge, your edge is better than ever. Your daughter said as much, when I asked for particulars about the jugglers. "Father will tell you, sir. He's a wonderful man for his age; and he expresses himself beautifully." Penelope's own words – blushing divinely. Not even my respect for you prevented me from – never mind; I knew her when she was a child, and she's none the worse for it. Let's be serious. What did the jugglers do?'

I was something dissatisfied with my daughter – not for letting Mr Franklin kiss her; Mr Franklin was welcome to *that* – but for forcing me to tell her foolish story at second hand. However, there was no help for it now but to mention the circumstances. Mr Franklin's merriment all died away as I went on. He sat knitting his eyebrows, and twisting his beard. When I had done, he repeated after me two of the questions which the chief juggler had put to the boy – seemingly for the purpose of fixing them well in his mind.

' "Is it on the road to this house, and on no other, that the English gentleman will travel to-day?" "Has the English gentleman got It about him?" I suspect,' says Mr Franklin, pulling a little sealed paper parcel out of his pocket, 'that "It" means *this*. And "this", Betteredge, means my uncle Herncastle's famous Diamond.'

'Good Lord, sir!' I broke out, 'how do you come to be in charge of the wicked Colonel's Diamond?'

'The wicked Colonel's will has left his Diamond as a birthday present to my cousin Rachel,' says Mr Franklin. 'And my father, as the wicked Colonel's executor, has given it in charge to me to bring down here.'

If the sea, then oozing in smoothly over the Shivering Sand, had been changed into dry land before my own eyes, I doubt if I could have been more surprised than I was when Mr Franklin spoke those words.

'The Colonel's Diamond left to Miss Rachel!' says I. 'And your father, sir, the Colonel's executor! Why, I would have laid any bet you like, Mr Franklin, that your father wouldn't have touched the Colonel with a pair of tongs!'

'Strong language, Betteredge! What was there against the Colonel? He belonged to your time, not to mine. Tell me what you know about him, and I'll tell you how my father came to be his executor, and more besides. I have made some discoveries in London about my uncle Herncastle and his Diamond, which have rather an ugly look to my eyes; and I want you to confirm them. You called him the "wicked Colonel" just now. Search your memory, my old friend, and tell me why.'

I saw he was in earnest, and I told him.

Here follows the substance of what I said, written out entirely for your benefit. Pay attention to it, or you will be all abroad, when we get deeper into the story. Clear your mind of the children, or the dinner, or the new bonnet, or what not. Try if you can't forget politics, horses, prices in the City, and grievances at the club. I hope you won't take this freedom on my part amiss; it's only a way I have of appealing to the gentle reader. Lord! haven't I seen you with the greatest authors in your hands, and don't know how ready your attention is to wander when it's a book that asks for it, instead of a person?

I spoke, a little way back, of my lady's father, the old lord with the short temper and the long tongue. He had five children in all. Two sons to begin with; then, after a long time, his wife broke out breeding again, and the three young ladies came briskly one after the other, as fast as the nature of things would permit; my mistress, as before mentioned, being the youngest and best of the three. Of the two sons, the eldest, Arthur, inherited the title and estates. The second, the Honourable John, got a fine fortune left him by a relative, and went into the army.

It's an ill bird, they say, that fouls its own nest. I look on the noble family of the Herncastles as being my nest; and I shall take it as a favour if I am not expected to enter into particulars on the subject of the Honourable John. He was, I honestly believe, one of the greatest blackguards that ever lived. I can hardly say more or less for him than that. He went into the army, beginning in the Guards. He had to leave the Guards before he was two-and-twenty – never mind why. They are very strict in the army, and they were too strict for the Honourable John. He went out to India to see whether they were equally strict there, and to try a little active service. In the matter of bravery (to give him his due), he was a mixture of bull-dog and game-cock, with a dash of the savage. He was at the taking of Seringapatam. Soon afterwards he changed into another regiment, and, in course of time, changed again into a third. In the third he got his last step as lieutenant-colonel, and, getting that, got also a sunstroke, and came home to England.

He came back with a character that closed the doors of all his family against him, my lady (then just married) taking the lead, and declaring (with Sir John's approval, of course) that her brother should never enter any house of hers. There was more than one slur on the Colonel that made people shy of him; but the blot of the Diamond is all I need mention here.

It was said he had got possession of his Indian jewel by means which, bold as he was, he didn't dare acknowledge. He never attempted to sell it – not being in need of money, and not (to give him his due again) making money an object. He never gave it away; he never even showed it to any living soul. Some said he was afraid of its getting him into a difficulty with the military authorities; others (very ignorant indeed of the real nature of the man) said he was afraid, if he showed it, of its costing him his life.

There was perhaps a grain of truth mixed up with this last report. It was false to say that he was afraid; but it was a fact that his life had been twice threatened in India; and it was firmly believed that the Moonstone was at the bottom of it. When he came back to England, and found himself avoided by everybody, the Moonstone was thought to be at the bottom of it again. The mystery of the Colonel's life got in the Colonel's way, and outlawed him, as you may say, among his own people. The men wouldn't let him into their clubs; the women – more than one – whom he wanted to marry, refused him; friends and relations got too near-sighted to see him in the street.

Some men in this mess would have tried to set themselves right with the world. But to give in, even when he was wrong, and had all society against him, was not the way of the Honourable John. He had kept the Diamond, in flat defiance of assassination, in India. He kept the Diamond, in flat defiance of public opinion, in England. There you have the portrait of the man before you, as in a picture: a character that braved everything; and a face, handsome as it was, that looked possessed by the devil.

We heard different rumours about him from time to time. Sometimes they said he was given up to smoking opium and collecting old books; sometimes he was reported to be trying strange things in chemistry; sometimes he was seen carousing and amusing himself among the lowest people in the lowest slums of London. Anyhow, a solitary, vicious, underground life was the life the Colonel led. Once, and once only, after his return to England, I myself saw him, face to face.

About two years before the time of which I am now writing, and about a year and a half before the time of his death, the Colonel came unexpectedly to my lady's house in London. It was the night of Miss Rachel's birthday, the twenty-first of June; and there was a party in honour of it, as usual. I received a message from the footman to say that a gentleman wanted to see me. Going up into the hall, there I found the Colonel, wasted, and worn, and old, and shabby, and as wild and as wicked as ever.

'Go up to my sister,' says he; 'and say that I have called to wish my niece many happy returns of the day.'

He had made attempts by letter, more than once already, to be reconciled with my lady, for no other purpose, I am firmly persuaded, than to annoy her. But this was the first time he had actually come to the house. I had it on the tip of my tongue to say that my mistress had a party that night. But the devilish look of him daunted me. I went upstairs with his message, and left him, by his own desire, waiting in the hall. The servants stood staring at him, at a distance, as if he was a walking engine of destruction, loaded with powder and shot, and likely to go off among them at a moment's notice.

My lady had a dash – no more – of the family temper. 'Tell Colonel Herncastle,' she said, when I gave her her brother's message, 'that Miss Verinder is engaged, and that I decline to see him.' I tried to plead for a civiller answer than that; knowing the Colonel's constitutional superiority to the restraints which govern gentlemen in general. Quite useless! The family temper flashed out at me directly. 'When I want your advice,' says my lady, 'you know that I always ask for it. I don't ask for it now.' I went down-stairs with the message, of which I took the liberty of presenting a new and amended edition of my own contriving, as follows: 'My lady and Miss Rachel regret that they are engaged, Colonel; and beg to be excused having the honour of seeing you.'

I expected him to break out, even at that polite way of putting it. To my surprise he did nothing of the sort; he alarmed me by taking the thing with an unnatural quiet. His eyes, of a glittering bright grey, just settled on me for a moment; and he laughed, not *out* of himself, like other people, but *into* himself, in a soft, chuckling, horridly mischievous way. 'Thank you, Betteredge,' he said. 'I shall remember my niece's birthday.' With that, he turned on his heel, and walked out of the house.

The next birthday came round, and we heard he was ill in bed. Six months afterwards – that is to say, six months before the time I am now writing of – there came a letter from a highly respectable clergyman to my lady. It communicated two wonderful things in the way of family news. First, that the Colonel had forgiven his sister on his death-bed. Second, that he had forgiven everybody else, and had made a most edifying end. I have myself (in spite of the bishops and the clergy) an unfeigned respect for the Church; but I am firmly persuaded, at the same time, that the devil remained in undisturbed possession of the Honourable John, and that the last abominable act in the life of that abominable man was (saving your presence) to take the clergyman in!

This was the sum-total of what I had to tell Mr Franklin. I remarked that he listened more and more eagerly the longer I went on. Also, that the story of the Colonel being sent away from his sister's door, on the occasion of his niece's birthday, seemed to strike Mr Franklin like a shot that had hit the mark. Though he didn't acknowledge it, I saw that I had made him uneasy, plainly enough, in his face.

'You have said your say, Betteredge,' he remarked. 'It's my turn now. Before, however, I tell you what discoveries I have made in London, and how I came to be mixed up in this matter of the Diamond, I want to know one thing. You look, my old friend, as if you didn't quite understand the object to be answered by this consultation of ours. Do your looks belie you?'

'No, sir,' I said. 'My looks, on this occasion at any rate, tell the truth.'

'In that case,' says Mr Franklin, 'suppose I put you up to my point of view, before we go any further. I see three very serious questions involved in the Colonel's birthday-gift to my cousin Rachel. Follow me carefully, Betteredge; and count me off on your fingers, if it will help you,' says Mr Franklin, with a certain pleasure in showing how clear-headed he could be, which reminded me wonderfully of old times when he was a boy. 'Question the first: Was the Colonel's Diamond the object of a conspiracy in India? Question the second: Has the conspiracy followed the Colonel's Diamond to England? Question the third: Did the Colonel know the conspiracy followed the Diamond; and has he purposely left a legacy of trouble and danger to his sister, through the innocent medium of his sister's child? *That* is what I am driving at, Betteredge. Don't let me frighten you.'

It was all very well to say that, but he *had* frightened me.

If he was right, here was our quiet English house suddenly invaded by a devilish Indian Diamond – bringing after it a conspiracy of living rogues, set loose on us by the vengeance of a dead man. There was our situation, as revealed to me in Mr Franklin's last words! Who ever heard the like of it – in the nineteenth century, mind; in an age of progress, and in a country which rejoices in the blessings of the British constitution? Nobody ever heard the like of it, and, consequently, nobody can be expected to believe it. I shall go on with my story, however, in spite of that.

When you get a sudden alarm, of the sort that I had got now, nine times out of ten the place you feel it in is your stomach. When you feel it in your stomach, your attention wanders, and you begin to fidget. I fidgeted silently in my place on the sand. Mr Franklin noticed me, contending with a perturbed stomach or mind – which you please; they mean the same thing – and, checking himself just as he was starting with his part of the story, said to me sharply, 'What do you want?'

What did I want? I didn't tell *him*; but I'll tell *you*, in confidence. I wanted a whiff of my pipe, and a turn at *Robinson Crusoe*.

⮞ SIX ⮜

KEEPING MY PRIVATE SENTIMENTS TO MYSELF, I respectfully requested Mr Franklin to go on. Mr Franklin replied, 'Don't fidget, Betteredge,' and went on.

Our young gentleman's first words informed me that his discoveries, concerning the wicked Colonel and the Diamond, had begun with a visit which he had paid (before he came to us) to the family lawyer, at Hampstead. A chance word dropped by Mr Franklin, when the two were alone, one day, after dinner, revealed that he had been charged by his father with a birthday present to be taken to Miss Rachel. One thing led to another; and it ended in the lawyer mentioning what the present really was, and how the friendly connection between the late Colonel and Mr Blake, Senior, had taken its rise. The facts here are really so extraordinary, that I doubt if I can trust my own language to do justice to them. I prefer trying to report Mr Franklin's discoveries, as nearly as may be, in Mr Franklin's own words.

'You remember the time, Betteredge,' he said, 'when my father was trying to prove his title to that unlucky Dukedom? Well! that was also the time when my uncle Herncastle returned from India. My father discovered that his brother-in-law was in possession of certain papers which were likely to be of service to him in his lawsuit. He called on the Colonel, on pretence of welcoming him back to England. The Colonel was not to be deluded in that way. 'You want something,' he said, 'or you would never have compromised your reputation by calling on *me*.' My father saw that the one chance for him was to show his hand: he admitted, at once, that he wanted the papers. The Colonel asked for a day to consider his answer. His answer came in the shape of a most extraordinary letter, which my friend the lawyer showed me. The Colonel began by saying that he wanted something of my father, and that he begged to propose an exchange of friendly services between them. The fortune of war (that was the expression he used) had placed him in possession of one of the largest Diamonds in the world; and he had reason to believe that neither he nor his precious jewel was safe in any house, in any quarter of the globe, which they occupied together. Under these alarming circumstances, he had determined to place his Diamond in the keeping of another person. That person was not expected to run

35

any risk. He might deposit the precious stone in any place especially guarded and set apart – like a banker's or jeweller's strong-room – for the safe custody of valuables of high price. His main personal responsibility in the matter was to be of the passive kind. He was to undertake – either by himself, or by a trustworthy representative – to receive at a prearranged address, on certain pre-arranged days in every year, a note from the Colonel, simply stating the fact that he was a living man at that date. In the event of the date passing over without the note being received, the Colonel's silence might be taken as a sure token of the Colonel's death by murder. In that case, and in no other, certain sealed instructions relating to the disposal of the Diamond, and deposited with it, were to be opened, and followed implicitly. If my father chose to accept this strange charge, the Colonel's papers were at his disposal in return. That was the letter.'

'What did your father do, sir?' I asked.

'Do?' says Mr Franklin. 'I'll tell you what he did. He brought the invaluable faculty, called common sense, to bear on the Colonel's letter. The whole thing, he declared, was simply absurd. Somewhere in his Indian wanderings, the Colonel had picked up with some wretched crystal which he took for a diamond. As for the danger of his being murdered, and the precautions devised to preserve his life and his piece of crystal, this was the nineteenth century, and any man in his senses had only to apply to the police. The Colonel had been a notorious opium-eater for years past; and, if the only way of getting at the valuable papers he possessed was by accepting a matter of opium as a matter of fact, my father was quite willing to take the ridiculous responsibility imposed on him – all the more readily that it involved no trouble to himself. The Diamond and the sealed instructions went into his banker's strong-room, and the Colonel's letters, periodically reporting him a living man, were received and opened by our family lawyer, Mr Bruff, as my father's representative. No sensible person, in a similar position, could have viewed the matter in any other way. Nothing in this world, Betteredge, is probable unless it appeals to our own trumpery experience; and we only believe in a romance when we see it in a newspaper.'

It was plain to me from this, that Mr Franklin thought his father's notion about the Colonel hasty and wrong.

'What is your own private opinion about the matter, sir?' I asked.

'Let's finish the story of the Colonel first,' says Mr Franklin. 'There is a curious want of system, Betteredge, in the English mind; and your question, my old friend, is an instance of it. When we are not occupied in making machinery, we are (mentally speaking) the most slovenly people in the universe.'

'So much,' I thought to myself, 'for a foreign education! He has learned that way of girding at us in France, I suppose.'

Mr Franklin took up the lost thread, and went on.

'My father,' he said, 'got the papers he wanted, and never saw his brother-in-law again from that time. Year after year, on the prearranged days, the prearranged letter came from the Colonel, and was opened by Mr Bruff. I have seen the letters, in a heap, all of them written in the same brief, business-like form of words: "Sir, – This is to certify that I am still a living man. Let the Diamond be. John Herncastle." That was all he ever wrote, and that came regularly to the day; until some six or eight months since, when the form of the letter varied for the first time. It ran now: – "Sir, – They tell me I am dying. Come to me, and help me to make my Will." Mr Bruff went, and found him, in the little suburban villa, surrounded by its own grounds, in which he had lived alone, ever since he had left India. He had dogs, cats, and birds to keep him company; but no human being near him, except the person who came daily to do the house-work, and the doctor at the bedside. The Will was a very simple matter. The Colonel had dissipated the greater part of his fortune in his chemical investigations. His Will began and ended in three clauses, which he dictated from his bed, in perfect possession of his faculties. The first clause provided for the safe keeping and support of his animals. The second founded a professorship of experimental chemistry at a northern university. The third bequeathed the Moonstone as a birthday present to his niece, on condition that my father would act as executor. My father at first refused to act. On second thoughts, however, he gave way, partly because he was assured that the executorship would involve him in no trouble; partly because Mr Bruff suggested, in Rachel's interest, that the Diamond might be worth something, after all.'

'Did the Colonel give any reason, sir,' I inquired, 'why he left the Diamond to Miss Rachel?'

'He not only gave the reason – he had the reason written in his Will,' said Mr Franklin. 'I have got an extract, which you shall see presently. Don't be slovenly-minded, Betteredge! One thing at a time. You have heard about the Colonel's Will; now you must hear what happened after the Colonel's death. It was formally necessary to have the Diamond valued, before the Will could be proved. All the jewellers consulted, at once confirmed the Colonel's assertion that he possessed one of the largest diamonds in the world. The question of accurately valuing it presented some serious difficulties. Its size made it a phenomenon in the diamond-market; its colour placed it in a category by itself; and, to add to these elements of uncertainty, there was a defect, in the shape of a flaw, in the very heart of the stone. Even with this last serious drawback, however, the lowest of the various estimates given was twenty thousand pounds. Conceive my father's astonishment! He had been within a hair's-breadth of refusing to act as executor, and of allowing this magnificent jewel to be lost to the family. The interest he took in the matter now, induced him to open the sealed instructions which had been deposited with the Diamond. Mr Bruff showed this document to me, with the other papers; and it suggests (to my mind) a clue to the nature of the conspiracy which threatened the Colonel's life.'

'Then you do believe, sir,' I said, 'that there was a conspiracy?'

'Not possessing my father's excellent common sense,' answered Mr Franklin, 'I believe the Colonel's life was threatened, exactly as the Colonel said. The sealed instructions, as I think, explain how it was that he died, after all, quietly in his bed. In the event of his death by violence (that is to say, in the absence of the regular letter from him at the appointed date), my father was then directed to send the Moonstone secretly to Amsterdam. It was to be deposited in that city with a famous diamond-cutter, and it was to be cut up into from four to six separate stones. The stones were then to be sold for what they would fetch, and the proceeds were to be applied to the founding of that professorship of experimental chemistry, which the Colonel has since endowed by his Will. Now, Betteredge, exert those sharp wits of yours, and observe the conclusion to which the Colonel's instructions point!'

I instantly exerted my wits. They were of the slovenly English sort; and they consequently muddled it all, until Mr Franklin took them in hand, and pointed out what they ought to see.

'Remark,' says Mr Franklin, 'that the integrity of the Diamond, as a whole stone, is here artfully made dependent on the preservation from violence of the Colonel's life. He is not satisfied with saying to the enemies he dreads, "Kill me – and you will be no nearer to the Diamond than you are now; it is where you can't get at it – in the guarded strong-room of a bank." He says instead, "Kill me – and the Diamond will be the Diamond no longer; its identity will be destroyed." What does that mean?'

Here I had (as I thought) a flash of the wonderful foreign brightness.

'I know,' I said. 'It means lowering the value of the stone and cheating the rogues in that way!'

'Nothing of the sort,' says Mr Franklin. 'I have inquired about that. The flawed Diamond, cut up, would actually fetch more than the Diamond as it now is; for this plain reason – that from four to six perfect brilliants might be cut from it, which would be, collectively, worth more money than the large – but imperfect – single stone. If robbery for the purpose of gain was at the bottom of the conspiracy, the Colonel's instructions absolutely made the Diamond better worth stealing. More money could have been got for it, and the disposal of it in the diamond-market would have been infinitely easier, if it had passed through the hands of the workmen of Amsterdam.'

'Lord bless us, sir!' I burst out. 'What was the plot, then?'

'A plot organized among the Indians who originally owned the jewel,' says Mr Franklin – 'a plot with some old Hindoo superstition at the bottom of it. That is my opinion, confirmed by a family paper which I have about me at this moment.'

I saw, now, why the appearance of the three Indian jugglers at our house had presented itself to Mr Franklin in the light of a circumstance worth noting.

'I don't want to force my opinion on you,' Mr Franklin went on. 'The idea of certain chosen servants of an old Hindoo superstition devoting themselves, through all difficulties and dangers, to watching the opportunity of recovering their sacred gem, appears to *me* to be perfectly consistent with everything that we know of the patience of Oriental races, and the influence of Oriental religions. But then I am an imaginative man; and the butcher, the baker, and the tax-gatherer, are not the only credible realities in existence to *my* mind. Let the guess I have made at the truth in this matter go for what it is worth, and let us get on to the only practical question that concerns us. Does the conspiracy against the Moonstone survive the Colonel's death? And did the Colonel know it, when he left the birthday gift to his niece?'

I began to see my lady and Miss Rachel at the end of it all, now. Not a word he said escaped me.

'I was not very willing, when I discovered the story of the Moonstone,' said Mr Franklin, 'to be the means of bringing it here. But Mr Bruff reminded me that somebody must put my cousin's legacy into my cousin's hands – and that I might as well do it as anybody else. After taking the Diamond out of the bank, I fancied I was followed in the streets by a shabby, dark-complexioned man. I went to my father's house to pick up my luggage, and found a letter there, which unexpectedly detained me in London. I went back to the bank with the Diamond, and thought I saw the shabby man again. Taking the Diamond once more out of the bank this morning, I saw the man for the third time, gave him the slip, and started (before he recovered the trace of me) by the morning instead of the afternoon train. Here I am, with the Diamond safe and sound – and what is the first news that meets me? I find that three strolling Indians have been at the house, and that my arrival from London, and something which I am expected to have about me, are two special objects of investigation to them when they believe themselves to be alone. I don't waste time and words on their pouring the ink into the boy's hand, and telling him to look in it for a man at a distance, and for something in that man's pocket. The thing (which I have often seen done in the

East) is "hocus-pocus" in my opinion, as it is in yours. The present question for us to decide is, whether I am wrongly attaching a meaning to a mere accident? or whether we really have evidence of the Indians being on the track of the Moonstone, the moment it is removed from the safe keeping of the bank?'

Neither he nor I seemed to fancy dealing with this part of the inquiry. We looked at each other, and then we looked at the tide, oozing in smoothly, higher and higher, over the Shivering Sand.

'What are you thinking of?' says Mr Franklin, suddenly.

'I was thinking, sir,' I answered, 'that I should like to shy the Diamond into the quicksand, and settle the question in *that* way.'

'If you have got the value of the stone in your pocket,' answered Mr Franklin, 'say so, Betteredge, and in it goes!'

It's curious to note, when your mind's anxious, how very far in the way of relief a very small joke will go. We found a fund of merriment, at the time, in the notion of making away with Miss Rachel's lawful property, and getting Mr Blake, as executor, into dreadful trouble – though where the merriment was, I am quite at a loss to discover now.

Mr Franklin was the first to bring the talk back to the talk's proper purpose. He took an envelope out of his pocket, opened it, and handed to me the paper inside.

'Betteredge,' he said, 'we must face the question of the Colonel's motive in leaving this legacy to his niece, for my aunt's sake. Bear in mind how Lady Verinder treated her brother from the time when he returned to England, to the time when he told you he should remember his niece's birthday. And read that.

He gave me the extract from the Colonel's Will. I have got it by me while I write these words; and I copy it, as follows, for your benefit:

'Thirdly, and lastly, I give and bequeath to my niece, Rachel Verinder, daughter and only child of my sister, Julia Verinder, widow – if her mother, the said Julia Verinder, shall be living on the said Rachel Verinder's next birthday after my death – the yellow Diamond belonging to me, and known in the East by the name of The Moonstone: subject to this condition, that her mother, the said Julia Verinder, shall be living at the time. And I hereby desire my executor to give my Diamond, either by his own hands or by the hands of some trustworthy representative whom he shall appoint, into the personal possession of my said niece Rachel, on her next birthday after my death, and in the presence, if possible, of my sister, the said Julia Verinder. And I desire that my said sister may be informed, by means of a true copy of this, the third and last clause of my Will, that I give the Diamond to her daughter Rachel, in token of my free forgiveness of the injury which her conduct towards me has been the means of inflicting on my reputation in my lifetime; and especially in proof that I pardon, as becomes a dying man, the insult offered to me as an officer and a gentleman, when her servant, by her orders, closed the door of her house against me, on the occasion of her daughter's birthday.'

More words followed these, providing, if my lady was dead, or if Miss Rachel was dead, at the time of the testator's decease, for the Diamond being sent to Holland, in accordance with the sealed instructions originally deposited with it. The proceeds of the sale were, in that case, to be added to the money already left by the Will for the professorship of chemistry at the university in the north.

I handed the paper back to Mr Franklin, sorely troubled what to say to him. Up to that moment, my own opinion had been (as you know) that the Colonel had died as wickedly as he had lived. I don't say the copy from his Will actually converted me from that opinion: I only say it staggered me.

'Well,' says Mr Franklin, 'now you have read the Colonel's own statement, what do you say? In bringing the Moonstone to my aunt's house, am I serving his vengeance blindfold, or am I vindicating him in the character of a penitent and Christian man?'

'It seems hard to say, sir,' I answered, 'that he died with a horrid revenge in his heart, and a horrid lie on his lips. God alone knows the truth. Don't ask *me*.'

Mr Franklin sat twisting and turning the extract from the Will in his fingers, as if he expected to squeeze the truth out of it in that manner. He altered quite remarkably, at the same time. From being brisk and bright, he now became, most unaccountably, a slow, solemn, and pondering young man.

'This question has two sides,' he said. 'An Objective side, and a Subjective side. Which are we to take?'

He had had a German education as well as a French. One of the two had been in undisturbed possession of him (as I supposed) up to this time. And now (as well as I could make out) the other was taking its place. It is one of my rules in life, never to notice what I don't understand. I steered a middle course between the Objective side and the Subjective side. In plain English I stared hard, and said nothing.

'Let's extract the inner meaning of this,' says Mr Franklin. 'Why did my uncle leave the Diamond to Rachel? Why didn't he leave it to my aunt?'

'That's not beyond guessing, sir, at any rate,' I said. 'Colonel Herncastle knew my lady well enough to know that she would have refused to accept any legacy that came to her from *him*.'

'How did he know that Rachel might not refuse to accept it, too?'

'Is there any young lady in existence, sir, who could resist the temptation of accepting such a birthday present as The Moonstone?'

'That's the Subjective view,' says Mr Franklin. 'It does you great credit, Betteredge, to be able to take the Subjective view. But there's another mystery about the Colonel's legacy which is not accounted for yet. How are we to explain his only giving Rachel her birthday present conditionally on her mother being alive?'

'I don't want to slander a dead man, sir,' I answered. 'But if he *has* purposely left a legacy of trouble and danger to his sister, by the means of her child, it must be a legacy made conditional on his sister's being alive to feel the vexation of it.'

'Oh! That's your interpretation of his motive, is it? The Subjective interpretation again! Have you ever been in Germany, Betteredge?'

'No, sir. What's your interpretation, if you please?'

'I can see,' says Mr Franklin, 'that the Colonel's object may, quite possibly, have been – not to benefit his niece, whom he had never even seen – but to prove to his sister that he had died forgiving her, and to prove it very prettily by means of a present made to her child. There is a totally different explanation from yours, Betteredge, taking its rise in a Subjective-Objective point of view. From all I can see, one interpretation is just as likely to be right as the other.'

Having brought matters to this pleasant and comforting issue, Mr Franklin appeared to think that he had completed all that was required of him. He laid down flat on his back on the sand, and asked what was to be done next.

He had been so clever, and clear-headed (before he began to talk the foreign gibberish), and had so completely taken the lead in the business up to the present time, that I was quite unprepared for such a sudden change as he now exhibited in this helpless leaning upon *me*. It was not till later that I learned – by assistance of Miss Rachel, who was the first to make the discovery – that these puzzling shifts and transformations in Mr Franklin were due to the effect on him of his foreign training. At the age when we are all of us most apt to take our colouring, in the form of a reflection from the colouring of other people, he had been sent abroad, and had been passed on from one nation to another, before there was time for any one colouring more than another to settle itself on him firmly. As a consequence of this, he had come back with so many different sides to his character, all more or less jarring with each other, that he seemed to pass his life in a state of perpetual contradiction with himself. He could be a busy man, and a lazy man; cloudy in the head, and clear in the head; a model of determination, and a spectacle of helplessness, all together. He had his French side, and his German side, and his Italian side – the original English foundation showing through, every now and then, as much as to say, 'Here I am, sorely transmogrified, as you see, but there's something of me left at the bottom of him still.' Miss Rachel used to remark that the Italian side of him was uppermost, on those occasions when he unexpectedly gave in, and asked you in his nice sweet-tempered way to take his own responsibilities on your shoulders. You will do him no injustice, I think, if you conclude that the Italian side of him was uppermost now.

'Isn't it your business, sir,' I asked, 'to know what to do next? Surely it can't be mine?'

Mr Franklin didn't appear to see the force of my question – not being in a position, at the time, to see anything but the sky over his head.

'I don't want to alarm my aunt without reason,' he said. 'And I don't want to leave her without what may be a needful warning. If you were in my place, Betteredge, tell me, in one word, what would you do?'

In one word, I told him: 'Wait.'

'With all my heart,' says Mr Franklin. 'How long?'

I proceeded to explain myself.

'As I understand it, sir,' I said, 'somebody is bound to put this plaguy Diamond into Miss Rachel's hands on her birthday – and you may as well do it as another. Very good. This is the twenty-fifth of May, and the birthday is on the twenty-first of June. We have got close on four weeks before us. Let's wait and see what happens in that time; and let's warn my lady or not, as the circumstances direct us.'

'Perfect, Betteredge, as far as it goes!' says Mr Franklin. 'But, between this and the birthday, what's to be done with the Diamond?'

'What your father did with it, to be sure, sir!' I answered. 'Your father put it in the safe keeping of a bank in London. You put it in the safe keeping of the bank at Frizinghall.' (Frizinghall was our nearest town, and the Bank of England wasn't safer than the bank there.) 'If I were you, sir,' I added, 'I would ride straight away with it to Frizinghall before the ladies come back.'

The prospect of doing something – and, what is more, of doing that something on a horse – brought Mr Franklin up like lightning from the flat of his back. He sprang to his feet, and pulled me up, without ceremony, on to mine. 'Betteredge, you are worth your weight in gold,' he said. 'Come along, and saddle the best horse in the stables directly!'

Here (God bless it!) was the original English foundation of him showing through all the foreign varnish at last! Here was the Master Franklin I remembered, coming out again in the good old way at the prospect of a ride, and reminding me of the good old times! Saddle a horse for him? I would have saddled a dozen horses, if he could only have ridden them all!

We went back to the house in a hurry; we had the fleetest horse in the stables saddled in a hurry; and Mr Franklin rattled off in a hurry, to lodge the cursed Diamond once more in the strong-room of a bank.

When I heard the last of his horse's hoofs on the drive, and when I turned about in the yard and found I was alone again, I felt half inclined to ask myself if I hadn't woke up from a dream.

❧ SEVEN ❧

WHILE I WAS IN THIS BEWILDERED frame of mind, sorely needing a little quiet time by myself to put me right again, my daughter Penelope got in my way (just as her late mother used to get in my way on the stairs), and instantly summoned me to tell her all that had passed at the conference between Mr Franklin and me. Under present circumstances, the one thing to be done was to clap the extinguisher upon Penelope's curiosity on the spot. I accordingly replied that Mr Franklin and I had both talked of foreign politics, till we could talk no longer, and had then mutually fallen asleep in the heat of the sun. Try that sort of answer when your wife or your daughter next worries you with an awkward question at an awkward time, and depend on the natural sweetness of women for kissing and making it up again at the next opportunity.

The afternoon wore on, and my lady and Miss Rachel came back.

Needless to say how astonished they were, when they heard that Mr Franklin Blake had arrived, and had gone off again on horseback. Needless also to say, that *they* asked awkward questions directly, and that the 'foreign politics' and the 'falling asleep in the sun' wouldn't serve a second time over with *them*. Being at the end of my invention, I said Mr Franklin's arrival by the early train was entirely attributable to one of Mr Franklin's freaks. Being asked, upon that, whether his galloping off again on horseback was another of Mr Franklin's freaks, I said, 'Yes, it was'; and slipped out of it – I think very cleverly – in that way.

Having got over my difficulties with the ladies, I found more difficulties waiting for me when I went back to my own room. In came Penelope – with the natural sweetness of women – to kiss and make it up again; and – with the natural curiosity of women – to ask another question. This time she only wanted me to tell her what was the matter with our second housemaid, Rosanna Spearman.

After leaving Mr Franklin and me at the Shivering Sand, Rosanna, it appeared, had returned to the house in a very unaccountable state of mind. She had turned (if Penelope was to be believed) all the colours of the rainbow. She had been merry without reason, and sad without reason. In one breath she asked hundreds of questions about Mr Franklin Blake, and in another breath she had been angry with Penelope for presuming to suppose that a strange gentleman could possess any interest for her. She had been surprised, smiling, and scribbling Mr Franklin's name inside her workbox. She had been surprised again, crying and looking at her deformed shoulder in the glass. Had she and Mr Franklin known anything of each other before to-day? Quite impossible! Had they heard anything of each other? Impossible again! I could speak to Mr Franklin's astonishment as genuine, when he saw how the girl stared at him. Penelope could speak to the girl's inquisitiveness as genuine, when she asked questions about Mr Franklin. The conference between us, conducted in this way, was tiresome enough, until my daughter suddenly ended it by bursting out with what I thought the most monstrous supposition I had ever heard in my life.

'Father!' says Penelope, quite seriously, 'there's only one explanation of it. Rosanna has fallen in love with Mr Franklin Blake at first sight!'

You have heard of beautiful young ladies falling in love at first sight, and have thought it natural enough. But a housemaid out of a reformatory, with a plain face and a deformed shoulder, falling in love, at first sight, with a gentleman who comes on a visit to her mistress's house, match me that, in the way of an absurdity, out of any story-book in Christendom, if you can! I laughed till the tears rolled down my cheeks. Penelope resented my merriment, in rather a strange way. 'I never knew you cruel before, father,' she said, very gently, and went out.

My girl's words fell upon me like a splash of cold water. I was savage with myself, for feeling uneasy in myself the moment she had spoken them – but so it was. We will change the subject, if you please. I am sorry I drifted into writing about it; and not without reason, as you will see when we have gone on together a little longer.

The evening came, and the dressing-bell for dinner rang, before Mr Franklin returned from Frizinghall. I took his hot water up to his room myself, expecting to hear, after this extraordinary delay, that something had happened. To my great disappointment (and no doubt to yours also), nothing had happened. He had not met with the Indians, either going or returning. He had deposited the Moonstone in the bank – describing it merely as a valuable of great price – and he had got the receipt for it safe in his pocket. I went down-stairs, feeling that this was rather a flat ending, after all our excitement about the Diamond earlier in the day.

How the meeting between Mr Franklin and his aunt and cousin went off, is more than I can tell you.

I would have given something to have waited at table that day. But, in my position in the household, waiting at dinner (except on high family festivals) was letting down my dignity in the eyes of the other servants – a thing which my lady considered me quite prone enough to do already, without seeking occasions for it. The news brought to me from the upper regions, that evening, came from Penelope and the footman. Penelope mentioned that she had never known Miss Rachel so particular about the dressing of her hair, and had never seen her look so bright and pretty as she did when she went down to meet Mr Franklin in the drawing-room. The footman's report was, that the preservation of a respectful composure in the presence of his betters, and the waiting on Mr Franklin Blake at dinner, were two of the hardest things to reconcile with each other that had ever tried his training in service. Later in the evening, we heard them singing and playing duets, Mr Franklin piping high, Miss Rachel piping higher, and my lady, on the piano, following them, as it were over hedge and ditch, and seeing them safe through it in a manner most wonderful and pleasant to hear through the open windows, on the terrace at night. Later still, I went to Mr Franklin in the smoking-room, with the soda-water and brandy, and found that Miss Rachel had put the Diamond clean out of his head. 'She's the most charming girl I have seen since I came back to England!' was all I could extract from him, when I endeavoured to lead the conversation to more serious things.

Towards midnight, I went round the house to lock up, accompanied by my second in command (Samuel, the footman), as usual. When all the doors were made fast, except the side door that opened on the terrace, I sent Samuel to bed, and stepped out for a breath of fresh air before I too went to bed in my turn.

The night was still and close, and the moon was at the full in the heavens. It was so silent out of doors, that I heard from time to time, very faint and low, the fall of the sea, as the ground-swell heaved it in on the sandbank near the mouth of our little bay. As the house stood, the terrace side was the dark side; but the broad moonlight showed fair on the gravel walk that ran along the next side to the terrace. Looking this way, after looking up at the sky, I saw the shadow of a person in the moonlight thrown forward from behind the corner of the house.

Being old and sly, I forbore to call out; but being also, unfortunately, old and heavy, my feet betrayed me on the gravel. Before I could steal suddenly round the corner, as I had proposed, I heard lighter feet than mine – and more than one pair of them as I thought – retreating in a hurry. By the time I had got to the corner, the trespassers, whoever they were, had run into the shrubbery at the off side of the walk, and were hidden from sight among the thick trees and bushes in that part of the grounds. From the shrubbery, they could easily make their way, over our fence, into the road. If I had been forty years younger, I might have had a chance of catching them before they got clear of our premises. As it was, I went back to set a-going a younger pair of legs than mine. Without disturbing anybody, Samuel and I got a couple of guns, and went all round the house and through the shrubbery. Having made sure that no persons were lurking about anywhere in our grounds, we turned back. Passing over the walk where I had seen the shadow, I now noticed, for the first time, a little bright object, lying on the clean gravel, under the light of the moon. Picking the object up, I discovered it was a small bottle, containing a thick sweet-smelling liquor, as black as ink.

I said nothing to Samuel. But, remembering what Penelope had told me about the jugglers, and the pouring of the little pool of ink into the palm of the boy's hand, I instantly suspected that I had disturbed the three Indians, lurking about the house, and bent, in their heathenish way, on discovering the whereabouts of the Diamond that night.

⊱ EIGHT ⊰

HERE, FOR ONE MOMENT, I find it necessary to call a halt.

On summoning up my own recollections – and on getting Penelope to help me, by consulting her journal – I find that we may pass pretty rapidly over the interval between Mr Franklin Blake's arrival and Miss Rachel's birthday. For the greater part of that time the days passed, and brought nothing with them worth recording. With your good leave, then, and with Penelope's help, I shall notice certain dates only in this place; reserving to myself to tell the story day by day, once more, as soon as we get to the time when the business of the Moonstone became the chief business of everybody in our house.

This said, we may now go on again – beginning, of course, with the bottle of sweet-smelling ink which I found on the gravel walk at night.

On the next morning (the morning of the twenty-sixth) I showed Mr Franklin this article of jugglery, and told him what I have already told you. His opinion was, not only that the Indians had been lurking about after the Diamond, but also that they were actually foolish enough to believe in their own magic— meaning thereby the making of signs on a boy's head, and the pouring of ink into a boy's hand, and then expecting him to see persons and things beyond the reach of human vision. In our country, as well as in the East, Mr Franklin informed me, there are people who practise this curious hocus-pocus (without the ink, however); and who call it by a French name, signifying something like brightness of sight. 'Depend upon it,' says Mr Franklin, 'the Indians took it for granted that we should keep the Diamond here; and they brought their clairvoyant boy to show them the way to it, if they succeeded in getting into the house last night.'

'Do you think they'll try again, sir?' I asked.

'It depends,' says Mr Franklin, 'on what the boy can really do. If he can see the Diamond through the iron-safe of the bank at Frizinghall, we shall be troubled with no more visits from the Indians for the present. If he can't, we shall have another chance of catching them in the shrubbery, before many more nights are over our heads.'

I waited pretty confidently for that latter chance; but, strange to relate, it never came.

Whether the jugglers heard, in the town, of Mr Franklin having been seen at the bank, and drew their conclusions accordingly; or whether the boy really did see the Diamond where the Diamond was now lodged (which I, for one, flatly disbelieve); or whether, after all, it was a mere effect of chance, this at any rate is the plain truth— not the ghost of an Indian came near the house again, through the weeks that passed before Miss Rachel's birthday. The jugglers remained in and about the town plying their trade; and Mr Franklin and I remained waiting to see what might happen, and resolute not to put the rogues on their guard by showing our suspicions of them too soon. With this report of the proceedings on either side, ends all that I have to say about the Indians for the present.

On the twenty-ninth of the month, Miss Rachel and Mr Franklin hit on a new method of working their way together through the time which might otherwise have hung heavy on their hands. There are reasons for taking particular notice here of the occupation that amused them. You will find it has a bearing on something that is still to come.

Gentlefolks in general have a very awkward rock ahead in life— the rock ahead of their own idleness. Their lives being, for the most part, passed in looking about them for something to do, it is curious to see— especially when their tastes are of what is called the intellectual sort— how often they drift blindfold into some nasty pursuit. Nine times out of ten they take to torturing something, or to spoiling something— and they firmly believe they are improving their minds, when the plain truth is, they are only making a mess in the house. I have seen them (ladies, I am sorry to say, as well as gentlemen) go out, day after day, for example, with empty pill-boxes, and catch newts, and beetles, and spiders, and frogs, and come home and stick pins through the miserable wretches, or cut them up, without a pang of remorse, into little pieces. You see my young master, or my young mistress, poring over one of their spiders' insides with a magnifying-glass; or you meet one of their frogs walking down-stairs without his head— and when you wonder what this cruel nastiness means, you are told that it means a taste in my young master or my young mistress for natural history. Sometimes, again, you see them occupied for hours together in spoiling a pretty flower with pointed instruments, out of a stupid curiosity to know what the flower is made of. Is its colour any prettier, or its scent any sweeter, when you *do* know? But there! the poor souls must get through the time, you see— they must get through the time. You dabbled in nasty mud, and made pies, when you were a child; and you dabble in nasty science, and dissect spiders, and spoil flowers, when you grow up. In the one case and in the other, the secret of it is, that you have got nothing to think of in your poor empty head, and nothing to do with your poor idle hands. And so it ends in your spoiling canvas with paints, and making a smell in the house; or in keeping tadpoles in a glass box full of dirty water, and turning everybody's stomach in the house; or in chipping off bits of stone here, there, and everywhere, and dropping grit into all the victuals in the house; or in staining your fingers in the pursuit of photography, and doing justice without mercy on everybody's face in the house. It often falls heavy enough, no doubt, on people who are really obliged to get their living, to be forced to work for the clothes that cover them, the roof that shelters them, and the food that keeps them going. But compare the hardest day's work you ever did with the idleness that splits flowers and pokes its way into spiders' stomachs, and thank your stars that your head has got something it *must* think of, and your hands something that they *must* do.

As for Mr Franklin and Miss Rachel, they tortured nothing, I am glad to say. They simply confined themselves to making a mess; and all they spoilt, to do them justice, was the panelling of a door.

Mr Franklin's universal genius, dabbling in everything, dabbled in what he called 'decorative painting.' He had invented, he informed us, a new mixture to moisten paint with, which he described as a 'vehicle.' What it was made of, I don't know. What it did, I can tell you in two words – it stank. Miss Rachel being wild to try her hand at the new process, Mr Franklin sent to London for the materials; mixed them up, with accompaniment of a smell which made the very dogs sneeze when they came into the room; put an apron and a bib over Miss Rachel's gown, and set her to work decorating her own little sitting-room – called, for want of English to name it in, her 'boudoir'. They began with the inside of the door. Mr Franklin scraped off all the nice varnish with pumice-stone, and made what he described as a surface to work on. Miss Rachel then covered the surface, under his directions and with his help, with patterns and devices – griffins, birds, flowers, cupids, and such like

– copied from designs made by a famous Italian painter, whose name escapes me: the one, I mean, who stocked the world with Virgin Maries, and had a sweetheart at the baker's. Viewed as work, this decoration was slow to do, and dirty to deal with. But our young lady and gentleman never seemed to tire of it. When they were not riding, or seeing company, or taking their meals, or piping their songs, there they were with their heads together, as busy as bees, spoiling the door. Who was the poet who said that Satan finds some mischief still for idle hands to do? If he had occupied my place in the family, and had seen Miss Rachel with her brush, and Mr Franklin with his vehicle, he could have written nothing truer of either of them than that.

The next date worthy of notice is Sunday the fourth of June.

On that evening we, in the servants' hall, debated a domestic question for the first time, which, like the decoration of the door, has its bearing on something that is still to come.

Seeing the pleasure which Mr Franklin and Miss Rachel took in each other's society, and noting what a pretty match they were in all personal respects, we naturally speculated on the chance of their putting their heads together with other objects in view besides the ornamenting of a door. Some of us said there would be a wedding in the house before the summer was over. Others (led by me) admitted it was likely enough Miss Rachel might be married; but we doubted (for reasons which will presently appear) whether her bride-groom would be Mr Franklin Blake.

That Mr Franklin was in love, on his side, nobody who saw and heard him could doubt. The difficulty was to fathom Miss Rachel. Let me do myself the honour of making you acquainted with her; after which, I will leave you to fathom her yourself – if you can.

My young lady's eighteenth birthday was the birthday now coming, on the twenty-first of June. If you happen to like dark women (who, I am informed, have gone out of fashion latterly in the gay world), and if you have no particular prejudice in favour of size, I answer for Miss Rachel as one of the prettiest girls your eyes ever looked on. She was small and slim, but all in fine proportion from top to toe. To see her sit down, to see her get up, and specially to see her walk, was enough to satisfy any man in his senses that the graces of her figure (if you will pardon me the expression) were in her flesh and not in her clothes. Her hair was the blackest I ever saw. Her eyes matched her hair. Her nose was not quite large enough, I admit. Her mouth and chin were (to quote Mr Franklin) morsels for the gods; and her complexion (on the same undeniable authority) was as warm as the sun itself, with this great advantage over the sun, that it was always in nice order to look at. Add to the foregoing that she carried her head as upright as a dart, in a dashing, spirited, thoroughbred way – that she had a clear voice, with a ring of the right metal in it, and a smile that began very prettily in her eyes before it got to her lips – and there behold the portrait of her, to the best of my painting, as large as life!

And what about her disposition next? Had this charming creature no faults? She had just as many faults as you have, ma'am – neither more nor less.

To put it seriously, my dear pretty Miss Rachel, possessing a host of graces and attractions, had one defect, which strict impartiality compels me to acknowledge. She was unlike most other girls of her age, in this – that she had ideas of her own, and was stiff-necked enough to set the fashions themselves at defiance, if the fashions didn't suit her views. In trifles, this independence of hers was all well enough; but in matters of importance, it carried her (as my lady thought, and as I thought) too far. She judged for herself, as few women of twice her age judge in general; never asked your advice; never told you beforehand what she was going to do; never came with secrets and confidences to anybody, from her mother downwards. In little things and great, with people she loved, and people she hated (and she did both with equal heartiness), Miss Rachel always went on a way of her own, sufficient for herself in the joys and sorrows of her life. Over and over again I have heard my lady say, 'Rachel's best friend and Rachel's worst enemy are, one and the other – Rachel herself.'

Add one thing more to this, and I have done.

With all her secrecy, and self-will, there was not so much as the shadow of anything false in her. I never remember her breaking her word; I never remember her saying No, and meaning Yes. I can call to mind, in her childhood, more than one occasion when the good little soul took the blame, and suffered the punishment, for some fault committed by a playfellow whom she loved. Nobody ever knew her to confess to it, when the thing was found out, and she was charged with it afterwards. But nobody ever knew her to lie about it, either. She looked you straight in the face, and shook her little saucy head, and said plainly, 'I won't tell you!' Punished again for this, she would own to being sorry for saying 'won't'; but, bread and water notwithstanding, she never told you. Self-willed – devilish self-willed sometimes – I grant; but the finest creature, nevertheless, that ever walked the ways of this lower world. Perhaps you think you see a certain contradiction here? In that case, a word in your ear. Study your wife closely, for the next four-and-twenty hours. If your good lady doesn't exhibit something in the shape of a contradiction in that time, Heaven help you! – you have married a monster.

I have now brought you acquainted with Miss Rachel, which you will find puts us face to face, next, with the question of that young lady's matrimonial views.

On June the twelfth, an invitation from my mistress was sent to a gentleman in London, to come and help to keep Miss Rachel's birthday. This was the fortunate individual on whom I believed her heart to be privately set! Like Mr Franklin, he was a cousin of hers. His name was Mr Godfrey Ablewhite.

My lady's second sister (don't be alarmed; we are not going very deep into family matters this time) – my lady's second sister, I say, had a disappointment in love; and taking a husband afterwards, on the neck or nothing principle, made what they call a misalliance. There was terrible work in the family when the Honourable Caroline insisted on marrying plain Mr Ablewhite, the banker at Frizinghall. He was very rich and very respectable, and he begot a prodigious large family – all in his favour, so far. But he had presumed to raise himself from a low station in the world – and that was against him. However, Time and the progress of modern enlightenment put things right; and the misalliance passed muster very well. We are all getting liberal now; and (provided you can scratch me, if I scratch you) what do I care, in or out of Parliament, whether you are a Dustman or a Duke? That's the modern way of looking at it – and I keep up with the modern way. The Ablewhites lived in a fine house and grounds, a little out of Frizinghall. Very worthy people, and greatly respected in the neighbourhood. We shall not be much troubled with them in these pages – excepting Mr Godfrey, who was Mr Ablewhite's second son, and who must take his proper place here, if you please, for Miss Rachel's sake.

With all his brightness and cleverness and general good qualities, Mr Franklin's chance of topping Mr Godfrey in our young lady's estimation was, in my opinion, a very poor chance indeed.

In the first place, Mr Godfrey was, in point of size, the finest man by far of the two. He stood over six feet high; he had a beautiful red and white colour; a smooth round face, shaved as bare as your hand; and a head of lovely long flaxen hair, falling negligently over the poll of his neck. But why do I try to give you this personal description of him? If you ever subscribed to a Ladies' Charity in London, you know Mr Godfrey Ablewhite as well as I do. He was a barrister by profession; a ladies' man by temperament; and a good Samaritan by choice. Female benevolence and female destitution could do nothing without him. Maternal societies for confining poor women; Magdalen societies for rescuing poor women; strong-minded societies for putting poor women into poor men's places, and leaving the men to shift for themselves; – he was vice-president, manager, referee to them all. Wherever there was a table with a committee of ladies sitting round it in council, there was Mr

Godfrey at the bottom of the board, keeping the temper of the committee, and leading the dear creatures along the thorny ways of business, hat in hand. I do suppose this was the most accomplished philanthropist (on a small independence) that England ever produced. As a speaker at charitable meetings the like of him for drawing your tears and your money was not easy to find. He was quite a public character. The last time I was in London, my mistress gave me two treats. She sent me to the theatre to see a dancing woman who was all the rage; and she sent me to Exeter Hall to hear Mr Godfrey. The lady did it, with a band of music. The gentleman did it, with a handkerchief and a glass of water. Crowds at the performance with the legs. Ditto at the performance with the tongue. And with all this, the sweetest-tempered person (I allude to Mr Godfrey) – the simplest and pleasantest and easiest to please – you ever met with. He loved everybody. And everybody loved *him*. What chance had Mr Franklin – what chance had anybody of average reputation and capacities – against such a man as this?

On the fourteenth, came Mr Godfrey's answer.

He accepted my mistress's invitation, from the Wednesday of the birthday to the evening of Friday – when his duties to the Ladies' Charities would oblige him to return to town. He also enclosed a copy of verses on what he elegantly called his cousin's 'natal day.' Miss Rachel, I was informed, joined Mr Franklin in making fun of the verses at dinner; and Penelope, who was all on Mr Franklin's side, asked me, in great triumph, what I thought of that. 'Miss Rachel has led *you* off on a false scent, my dear,' I replied; 'but my nose is not so easily mystified. Wait till Mr Ablewhite's verses are followed by Mr Ablewhite himself.'

My daughter replied, that Mr Franklin might strike in, and try his luck, before the verses were followed by the poet. In favour of this view, I must acknowledge that Mr Franklin left no chance untried of winning Miss Rachel's good graces.

Though one of the most inveterate smokers I ever met with, he gave up his cigar, because she said, one day, she hated the stale smell of it in his clothes. He slept so badly, after this effort of self-denial, for want of the composing effect of the tobacco to which he was used, and came down morning after morning looking so haggard and worn, that Miss Rachel herself begged him to take to his cigars again. No! he would take to nothing again that could cause her a moment's annoyance; he would fight it out resolutely, and get back his sleep, sooner or later, by main force of patience in waiting for it. Such devotion as this, you may say (as some of them said downstairs), could never fail of producing the right effect on Miss Rachel – backed up, too, as it was, by the decorating work every day on the door. All very well – but she had a photograph of Mr Godfrey in her bedroom; represented speaking at a public meeting, with all his hair blown out by the breath of his own eloquence, and his eyes, most lovely, charming the money out of your pockets. What do you say to that? Every morning – as Penelope herself owned to me – there was the man whom the women couldn't do without, looking on, in effigy, while Miss Rachel was having her hair combed. He would be looking on, in reality, before long – that was my opinion of it.

June the sixteenth brought an event which made Mr Franklin's chance look, to my mind, a worse chance than ever.

A strange gentleman, speaking English with a foreign accent, came that morning to the house, and asked to see Mr Franklin Blake on business. The business could not possibly have been connected with the Diamond, for these two reasons – first, that Mr Franklin told me nothing about it; secondly, that he communicated it (when the gentleman had gone, as I suppose) to my lady. She probably hinted something about it next to her daughter. At any rate, Miss Rachel was reported to have said some severe things to Mr Franklin, at the piano that evening, about the people he had lived among, and the principles he had adopted in foreign parts. The next day, for the first time, nothing was done towards the decoration of the door. I suspect some imprudence of Mr Franklin's on the Continent – with a woman or a debt at the bottom of it – had followed him to England. But that is all guesswork. In this case, not only Mr Franklin, but my lady too, for a wonder, left me in the dark.

On the seventeenth, to all appearance, the cloud passed away again. They returned to their decorating work on the door, and seemed to be as good friends as ever. If Penelope was to be believed, Mr Franklin had seized the opportunity of the reconciliation to make an offer to Miss Rachel, and had neither been accepted nor refused. My girl was sure (from signs and tokens which I need not trouble you with) that her young mistress had fought Mr Franklin off by declining to believe that he was in earnest, and had then secretly regretted treating him in that way afterwards. Though Penelope was admitted to more familiarity with her young mistress than maids generally are – for the two had been almost brought up together as children – still I knew Miss Rachel's reserved character too well to believe that she would show her mind to anybody in this way. What my daughter told me, on the present occasion, was, as I suspected, more what she wished than what she really knew.

On the nineteenth another event happened. We had the doctor in the house professionally. He was summoned to prescribe for a person whom

I have had occasion to present to you in these pages – our second housemaid, Rosanna Spearman.

This poor girl – who had puzzled me, as you know already, at the Shivering Sand – puzzled me more than once again, in the interval time of which I am now writing. Penelope's notion that her fellow-servant was in love with Mr Franklin (which my daughter, by my orders, kept strictly secret) seemed to me just as absurd as ever. But I must own that what I myself saw, and what my daughter saw also, of our second housemaid's conduct, began to look mysterious, to say the least of it.

For example, the girl constantly put herself in Mr Franklin's way – very slyly and quietly, but she did it. He took about as much notice of her as he took of the cat: it never seemed to occur to him to waste a look on Rosanna's plain face. The poor thing's appetite, never much, fell away dreadfully; and her eyes in the morning showed plain signs of waking and crying at night. One day Penelope made an awkward discovery, which we hushed up on the spot. She caught Rosanna at Mr Franklin's dressing-table, secretly removing a rose which Miss Rachel had given him to wear in his button-hole, and putting another rose like it, of her own picking, in its place. She was, after that, once or twice impudent to me, when I gave her a well-meant general hint to be careful in her conduct; and, worse still, she was not over-respectful now, on the few occasions when Miss Rachel accidentally spoke to her.

My lady noticed the change, and asked me what I thought about it. I tried to screen the girl by answering that I thought she was out of health; and it ended in the doctor being sent for, as already mentioned, on the nineteenth. He said it was her nerves, and doubted if she was fit for service. My lady offered to remove her for change of air to one of our farms, inland. She begged and prayed, with the tears in her eyes, to be let to stop; and, in an evil hour, I advised my lady to try her for a little longer. As the event proved, and as you will soon see, this was the worst advice I could have given. If I could only have looked a little way into the future, I would have taken Rosanna Spearman out of the house, then and there, with my own hand.

On the twentieth, there came a note from Mr Godfrey. He had arranged to stop at Frizinghall that night, having occasion to consult his father on business. On the afternoon of the next day, he and his two eldest sisters would ride over to us on horseback, in good time before dinner. An elegant little casket in China accompanied the note, presented to Miss Rachel, with her cousin's love and best wishes. Mr Franklin had only given her a plain locket not worth half the money. My daughter Penelope, nevertheless – such is the obstinacy of women – still backed him to win.

Thanks be to Heaven, we have arrived at the eve of the birthday at last! You will own, I think, that I have got you over the ground this time, without much loitering by the way. Cheer up! I'll ease you with another new chapter here – and, what is more, that chapter shall take you straight into the thick of the story.

❧ NINE ❧

JUNE TWENTY-FIRST, THE DAY OF THE BIRTHDAY, was cloudy and unsettled at sunrise, but towards noon it cleared up bravely.

We, in the servants' hall, began this happy anniversary, as usual, by offering our little presents to Miss Rachel, with the regular speech delivered annually by me as the chief. I follow the plan adopted by the Queen in opening Parliament – namely, the plan of saying much the same thing regularly every year. Before it is delivered, my speech (like the Queen's) is looked for as eagerly as if nothing of the kind had ever been heard before. When it is delivered, and turns out not to be the novelty anticipated, though they grumble a little, they look forward hopefully to something newer next year. An easy people to govern, in the Parliament and in the Kitchen – that's the moral of it.

After breakfast, Mr Franklin and I had a private conference on the subject of the Moonstone – the time having now come for removing it from the bank at Frizinghall, and placing it in Miss Rachel's own hands.

Whether he had been trying to make love to his cousin again, and had got a rebuff – or whether his broken rest, night after night, was aggravating the queer contradictions and uncertainties in his character – I don't know. But certain it is, that Mr Franklin failed to show himself at his best on the morning of the birthday. He was in twenty different minds about the Diamond in as many minutes. For my part, I stuck fast by the plain facts as we knew them. Nothing had happened to justify us in alarming my lady on the subject of the jewel; and nothing could alter the legal obligation that now lay on Mr Franklin to put it in his cousin's possession. That was my view of the matter; and, twist and turn it as he might, he was forced in the end to make it his view too. We arranged that he was to ride over, after lunch, to Frizinghall, and bring the Diamond back, with Mr Godfrey and the two young ladies, in all probability, to keep him company on the way home again.

This settled, our young gentleman went back to Miss Rachel.

They consumed the whole morning, and part of the afternoon, in the everlasting business of decorating the door, Penelope standing by to mix the colours, as directed; and my lady, as luncheon time drew near, going in and out of the room, with her handkerchief to her nose (for they used a deal of Mr Franklin's vehicle that day), and trying vainly to get the two artists away from their work. It was three o'clock before they took off their aprons, and released Penelope (much the worse for the vehicle), and cleaned themselves of their mess. But they had done what they wanted – they had finished the door on the birthday, and proud enough they were of it. The griffins, cupids, and so on, were, I must own, most beautiful to behold; though so many in number, so entangled in flowers and devices, and so topsy-turvy in their actions and attitudes, that you felt them unpleasantly in your head for hours after you had done with the pleasure of looking at them. If I add that Penelope ended her part of the morning's work by being sick in the back-kitchen, it is in no unfriendly spirit towards the vehicle. No! no! It left off stinking when it dried; and if Art requires these sort of sacrifices – though the girl is my own daughter – I say, let Art have them!

Mr Franklin snatched a morsel from the luncheon-table, and rode off to Frizinghall – to escort his cousins, as he told my lady. To fetch the Moonstone, as was privately known to himself and to me.

This being one of the high festivals on which I took my place at the sideboard, in command of the attendance at table, I had plenty to occupy my mind while Mr Franklin was away. Having seen to the wine, and reviewed my men and women who were to wait at dinner, I retired to collect myself before the company came. A whiff of – you know what, and a turn at a certain book which I have had occasion to mention in these pages, composed me, body and mind. I was aroused from what I am inclined to think must have been, not a nap, but a reverie, by the clatter of horses' hoofs outside; and, going to the door, received a caval-cade comprising Mr Franklin and his three cousins, escorted by one of old Mr Ablewhite's grooms.

Mr Godfrey struck me, strangely enough, as being like Mr Franklin in this respect – that he did not seem to be in his customary spirits. He kindly shook hands with me as usual, and was most politely glad to see his old friend Betteredge wearing so well. But there was a sort of cloud over him, which I couldn't at all account for; and when I asked how he had found his father in health, he answered rather shortly, 'Much as usual.' However, the two Miss Ablewhites were cheerful enough for twenty, which more than restored the balance. They were nearly as big as their brother; spanking, yellow-haired, rosy lasses, overflowing with superabundant flesh and blood; bursting from head to foot with health and spirits. The legs of the poor horses trembled with carrying them; and when they jumped from their saddles (without waiting to be helped), I declare they bounced on the ground as if they were made of india-rubber.

Everything the Miss Ablewhites said began with a large O; everything they did was done with a bang; and they giggled and screamed, in season and out of season, on the smallest provocation. Bouncers – that's what I call them.

Under cover of the noise made by the young ladies, I had an opportunity of saying a private word to Mr Franklin in the hall.

'Have you got the Diamond safe, sir?'

He nodded, and tapped the breast-pocket of his coat.

'Have you seen anything of the Indians?'

'Not a glimpse.' With that answer, he asked for my lady, and, hearing she was in the small drawing-room, went there straight. The bell rang, before he had been a minute in the room, and Penelope was sent to tell Miss Rachel that Mr Franklin Blake wanted to speak to her.

Crossing the hall, about half an hour afterwards, I was brought to a sudden standstill by an outbreak of screams from the small drawing-room. I can't say I was at all alarmed; for I recognized in the screams the favourite large O of the Miss Ablewhites. However, I went in (on pretence of asking for instructions about the dinner) to discover whether anything serious had really happened.

There stood Miss Rachel at the table, like a person fascinated, with the Colonel's unlucky Diamond in her hand. There, on either side of her, knelt the two Bouncers, devouring the jewel with their eyes, and screaming with ecstasy every time it flashed on them in a new light. There, at the opposite side of the table, stood Mr Godfrey, clapping his hands like a large child, and singing out softly, 'Exquisite! exquisite!' There sat Mr Franklin, in a chair by the bookcase, tugging at his beard, and looking anxiously towards the window. And there, at the window, stood the object he was contemplating – my lady, having the extract from the Colonel's Will in her hand, and keeping her back turned on the whole of the company.

She faced me, when I asked for my instructions; and I saw the family frown gathering over her eyes, and the family temper twitching at the corners of her mouth.

'Come to my room in half an hour,' she answered. 'I shall have something to say to you then.'

With those words, she went out. It was plain enough that she was posed by the same difficulty which had posed Mr Franklin and me in our conference at the Shiverirg Sand. Was the legacy of the Moonstone a proof that she had treated her brother with cruel injustice? or was it a proof that he was worse than the worst she had ever thought of him? Serious questions those for my lady to determine, while her daughter, innocent of all knowledge of the Colonel's character, stood there with the Colonel's birthday gift in her hand.

Before I could leave the room, in my turn, Miss Rachel, always considerate to the old servant who had been in the house when she was born, stopped me. 'Look, Gabriel!' she said, and flashed the jewel before my eyes in a ray of sunlight that poured through the window.

Lord bless us! it *was* a Diamond! As large, or nearly, as a plover's egg! The light that streamed from it was like the light of the harvest moon. When you looked down into the stone, you looked into a yellow deep that drew your eyes into it so that they saw nothing else. It seemed unfathomable; this jewel, that you could hold between your finger and thumb, seemed unfathomable as the heavens themselves. We set it in the sun, and then shut the light out of the room, and it shone awfully out of the depths of its own brightness, with a moony gleam, in the dark. No wonder Miss Rachel was fascinated: no wonder her cousins screamed. The Diamond laid such a hold on *me* that I burst out with as large an 'O' as the Bouncers themselves. The only one of us who kept his senses was Mr Godfrey. He put an arm round each of his sisters' waists, and, looking compassionately backwards and forwards between the Diamond and me, said, 'Carbon, Betteredge! mere carbon, my good friend, after all!'

His object, I suppose, was to instruct me. All he did, however, was to remind me of the dinner. I hobbled off to my army of waiters downstairs. As I went out, Mr Godfrey said, 'Dear old Betteredge, I have the truest regard for him!' He was embracing his sisters, and ogling Miss Rachel, while he honoured me with that testimony of affection. Something like a stock of love to draw on *there*! Mr Franklin was a perfect savage by comparison with him.

At the end of half an hour, I presented myself, as directed, in my lady's room.

What passed between my mistress and me, on this occasion, was, in the main, a repetition of what had passed between Mr Franklin and me at the Shivering Sand – with this difference, that I took care to keep my own counsel about the jugglers, seeing that nothing had happened to justify me in alarming my lady on this head. When I received my dismissal, I could see that she took the blackest view possible of the Colonel's motives, and that she was bent on getting the Moonstone out of her daughter's possession at the first opportunity.

On my way back to my own part of the house, I was encountered by Mr Franklin: He wanted to know if I had seen anything of his cousin Rachel. I had seen nothing of her. Could I tell him where his cousin Godfrey was? I didn't know; but I began to suspect that Cousin Godfrey might not be far away from Cousin Rachel. Mr Franklin's suspicions apparently took the same turn. He tugged hard at his beard, and went and shut himself up in the library, with a bang of the door that had a world of meaning in it.

I was interrupted no more in the business of preparing for the birthday dinner till it was time for me to smarten myself up for receiving the company. Just as I had got my white waistcoat on, Penelope presented herself at my toilet, on pretence of brushing what little hair I have got left, and improving the tie of my white cravat. My girl was in high spirits, and I saw she had something to say to me. She gave me a kiss on the top of my bald head, and whispered, 'News for you, father! Miss Rachel has refused him.'

'Who's "him?" ' I asked.

'The ladies' committee-man, father,' says Penelope. 'A nasty sly fellow! I hate him for trying to supplant Mr Franklin!'

If I had had breath enough, I should certainly have protested against this indecent way of speaking of an eminent philanthropic character. But my daughter happened to be improving the tie of my cravat at that moment, and the whole strength of her feelings found its way into her fingers. I never was more nearly strangled in my life.

'I saw him take her away alone into the rose-garden,' says Penelope. 'And I waited behind the holly to see how they came back. They had gone out arm-in-arm, both laughing. They came back, walking separate, as grave as grave could be, and looking straight away from each other in a manner which there was no mistaking. I never was more delighted, father, in my life! There's one woman in the world who can resist Mr Godfrey Ablewhite, at any rate; and, if I was a lady, I should be another!'

Here I should have protested again. But my daughter had got the hair-brush by this time, and the whole strength of her feelings had passed into *that*. If you are bald, you will understand how she scarified me. If you are not, skip this bit, and thank God you have got something in the way of a defence between your hair-brush and your head.

'Just on the other side of the holly,' Penelope went on, 'Mr Godfrey came to a standstill. "You prefer," says he, "that I should stop here as if nothing had happened?" Miss Rachel turned on him like lightning. "You have accepted my mother's invitation," she said; "and you are here to meet her guests. Unless you wish to make a scandal in the house, you will remain, of course!" She went on a few steps, and then seemed to relent a little. "Let us forget what has passed, Godfrey," she said, "and let us remain cousins still." She gave him her hand. He kissed it, which *I* should have considered taking a liberty, and then she left him. He waited a little by himself, with his head down, and his heel grinding a hole slowly in the gravel walk; you never saw a man look more put out in your life. "Awkward!" he said between his teeth, when he looked up, and went on to the house – "very awkward!" If that was his opinion of himself, he was quite right. Awkward enough, I'm sure. And the end of it is, father, what I told you all along,' cries Penelope, finishing me off with a last scarification, the hottest of all. 'Mr Franklin's the man!'

I got possession of the hair-brush, and opened my lips to administer the reproof which, you will own, my daughter's language and conduct richly deserved.

Before I could say a word, the crash of carriage-wheels outside struck in, and stopped me. The first of the dinner-company had come. Penelope instantly ran off. I put on my coat, and looked in the glass. My head was as red as a lobster; but, in other respects, I was as nicely dressed for the ceremonies of the evening as a man need be. I got into the hall just in time to announce the two first of the guests. You needn't feel particularly interested about them. Only the philanthropist's father and mother – Mr and Mrs Ablewhite.

◆ TEN ◆

ONE ON THE TOP OF THE OTHER, the rest of the company followed the Ablewhites, till we had the whole tale of them complete. Including the family, they were twenty-four in all. It was a noble sight to see, when they were settled in their places round the dinner-table, and the Rector of Frizinghall (with beautiful elocution) rose and said grace.

There is no need to worry you with a list of the guests. You will meet none of them a second time – in my part of the story, at any rate – with the exception of two.

Those two sat on either side of Miss Rachel, who, as queen of the day, was naturally the great attraction of the party. On this occasion, she was more particularly the centre-point towards which everybody's eyes were directed; for (to my lady's secret annoyance) she wore her wonderful birthday present, which eclipsed all the rest – the Moonstone. It was without any setting when it had been placed in her hands; but that universal genius, Mr Franklin, had contrived, with the help of his neat fingers and a little bit of silver wire, to fix it as a brooch in the bosom of her white dress. Everybody wondered at the prodigious size and beauty of the Diamond, as a matter of course. But the only two of the company who said anything out of the common way about it, were those two guests I have mentioned, who sat by Miss Rachel on her right hand and her left.

The guest on her left was Mr Candy, our doctor at Frizinghall.

This was a pleasant, companionable little man, with the drawback, however, I must own, of being too fond, in season and out of season, of his joke, and of his plunging in rather a headlong manner into talk with strangers, without waiting to feel his way first. In society he was constantly making mistakes, and setting people unintentionally by the ears together. In his medical practice he was a more prudent man; picking up his discretion (as his enemies said) by a kind of instinct, and proving to be generally right where more carefully conducted doctors turned out to be wrong. What *he* said about the Diamond to Miss Rachel was said, as usual, by way of a mystification or joke. He gravely entreated her (in the interests of science) to let him take it home and burn it. 'We will first heat it, Miss Rachel,' says the doctor, 'to such and such a degree; then we will expose it to a current of air; and, little by little – puff! – we evaporate the Diamond, and spare you a world of anxiety about the safe keeping of a valuable precious stone!' My lady, listening with rather a careworn expression on her face, seemed to wish that the doctor had been in earnest, and that he could have found Miss Rachel zealous enough in the cause of science to sacrifice her birthday gift.

The other guest, who sat on my young lady's right hand, was an eminent public character – being no other than the celebrated Indian traveller, Mr Murthwaite, who, at risk of his life, had penetrated in disguise where no European had ever set foot before.

This was a long, lean, wiry, brown, silent man. He had a weary look, and a very steady, attentive eye. It was rumoured that he was tired of the humdrum life among the people in our parts, and longing to go back and wander off on the tramp again in the wild places of the East. Except what he said to Miss Rachel about her jewel, I doubt if he spoke six words or drank so much as a single glass of wine, all through the dinner. The Moonstone was the only object that interested him in the smallest degree. The fame of it seemed to have reached him, in some of those perilous Indian places where his wanderings had lain. After looking at it silently for so long a time that Miss Rachel began to get confused, he said to her in his cool immovable way, 'If you ever go to India, Miss Verinder, don't take your uncle's birthday gift with you. A Hindoo diamond is sometimes part of a Hindoo religion. I know a certain city, and a certain temple in that city, where, dressed as you are now, your life would not be worth five minutes' purchase.' Miss Rachel, safe in England, was quite delighted to hear of her danger in India. The Bouncers were more delighted still; they dropped their knives and forks with a crash, and burst out together vehemently, 'O! how interesting!' My lady fidgeted in her chair, and changed the subject.

As the dinner got on, I became aware, little by little, that this festival was not prospering as other like festivals had prospered before it.

Looking back at the birthday now, by the light of what happened afterwards, I am half inclined to think that the cursed Diamond must have cast a blight on the whole company. I plied them well with wine; and being a privileged character, followed the unpopular dishes round the table, and whispered to the company confidentially, 'Please to change your mind and try it; for I know it will do you good.' Nine times out of ten they changed their minds – out of regard for their old original Betteredge, they were pleased to say – but all to no purpose. There were gaps of silence in the talk, as the dinner got on, that made me feel personally uncomfortable. When they did use their tongues again, they used them innocently, in the most unfortunate manner and to the worst possible purpose. Mr Candy, the doctor, for instance, said more unlucky things than I ever knew him to say before. Take one sample of the way in which he went on, and you will understand what I had to put up with at the sideboard, officiating as I was in the character of a man who had the prosperity of the festival at heart.

One of our ladies present at dinner was worthy Mrs Threadgall, widow of the late Professor of that name. Talking of her deceased husband perpetually, this good lady never mentioned to strangers that he *was* deceased. She thought, I suppose, that every able-bodied adult in England ought to know as much as that. In one of the gaps of silence, somebody mentioned the dry and rather nasty subject of human anatomy; whereupon good Mrs Threadgall straightway brought in her late husband as usual, without mentioning that he was dead. Anatomy she described as the Professor's favourite recreation in his leisure hours. As ill-luck would have it, Mr Candy, sitting opposite (who knew nothing of the deceased gentleman), heard her. Being the most polite of men, he seized the opportunity of assisting the Professor's anatomical amusements on the spot.

'They have got some remarkably fine skeletons lately at the College of Surgeons,' says Mr Candy, across the table, in a loud cheerful voice. 'I strongly recommend the Professor, ma'am, when he next has an hour to spare, to pay them a visit.'

You might have heard a pin fall. The company (out of respect to the Professor's memory) all sat speechless. I was behind Mrs Threadgall at the time, plying her confidentially with a glass of hock. She dropped her head, and said in a very low voice, 'My beloved husband is no more.'

Unlucky Mr Candy, hearing nothing, and miles away from suspecting the truth, went on across the table louder and politer than ever.

'The Professor may not be aware,' says he, 'that the card of a member of the College will admit him, on any day but Sunday, between the hours of ten and four.'

Mrs Threadgall dropped her head right into her tucker, and, in a lower voice still, repeated the solemn words, 'My beloved husband is no more.'

I winked hard at Mr Candy across the table. Miss Rachel touched his arm. My lady looked unutterable things at him. Quite useless! On he went, with a cordiality that there was no stopping anyhow. 'I shall be delighted,' says he, 'to send the Professor my card, if you will oblige me by mentioning his present address.'

'His present address, sir, *is the grave,*' says Mrs Threadgall, suddenly losing her temper, and speaking with an emphasis and fury that made the glasses ring again. 'The Professor has been dead these ten years!'

'Oh, good heavens!' says Mr Candy. Excepting the Bouncers, who burst out laughing, such a blank now fell on the company, that they might all have been going the way of the Professor, and hailing as he did from the direction of the grave.

So much for Mr Candy. The rest of them were nearly as provoking in their different ways as the doctor himself. When they ought to have spoken, they didn't speak; or when they did speak they were perpetually at cross purposes. Mr Godfrey, though so eloquent in public, declined to exert himself in private. Whether he was sulky, or whether he was bashful, after his discomfiture in the rose-garden, I can't say. He kept all his talk for the private ear of the lady (a member of our family) who sat next to him. She was one of his committee-women – a spiritually-minded person, with a fine show of collar-bone and a pretty taste in champagne; liked it dry, you understand, and plenty of it. Being close behind these two at the sideboard, I can testify, from what I heard pass between them, that the company lost a good deal of very improving conversation, which I caught up while drawing the corks, and carving the mutton, and so forth. What they said about their Charities I didn't hear. When I had time to listen to them, they had got a long way beyond their women to be confined, and their women to be rescued, and were disputing on serious subjects. Religion (I understand Mr Godfrey to say, between the corks and the carving) meant love. And love meant religion. And earth was heaven a little the worse for wear. And heaven was earth, done up again to look like new. Earth had some very objectionable people in it; but, to make amends for that, all the women in heaven would be members of a prodigious committee that never quarrelled, with all the men in attendance on them as ministering angels. Beautiful! beautiful! But why the mischief did Mr Godfrey keep it all to his lady and himself?

Mr Franklin again – surely, you will say, Mr Franklin stirred the company up into making a pleasant evening of it?

Nothing of the sort! He had quite recovered himself, and he was in wonderful force and spirits, Penelope having informed him, I suspect, of Mr Godfrey's reception in the rose-garden. But, talk as he might, nine times out of ten he pitched on the wrong subject, or he addressed himself to the wrong person; the end of it being that he offended some, and puzzled all of them. That foreign training of his – those French and German and Italian sides of him, to which I have already alluded – came out, at my lady's hospitable board, in a most bewildering manner.

What do you think, for instance, of his discussing the lengths to which a married woman might let her admiration go for a man who was not her husband, and putting it in his clear-headed witty French way to the maiden aunt of the Vicar of Frizinghall? What do you think, when he shifted to the German side, of his telling the lord of the manor, while that great authority on cattle was quoting his experience in the breeding of bulls, that experience, properly understood, counted for nothing, and that the proper way to breed bulls was to look deep into your own mind, evolve out of it the idea of a perfect bull, and produce him? What do you say, when our county member, growing hot, at cheese and salad time, about the spread of democracy in England, burst out as follows: 'If we once lose our ancient safeguards, Mr Blake, I beg to ask you, what have we got left?' – what do you say to Mr Franklin answering, from the Italian point of view: 'We have got three things left, sir – Love, Music, and Salad'? He not only terrified the company with such outbreaks as these, but, when the English side of him turned up in due course, he lost his foreign smoothness; and, getting on the subject of the medical profession, said such downright things in ridicule of doctors, that he actually put good-humoured little Mr Candy in a rage.

The dispute between them began in Mr Franklin being led – I forget how – to acknowledge that he had latterly slept very badly at night. Mr Candy thereupon told him that his nerves were all out of order, and that he ought to go through a course of medicine immediately. Mr Franklin replied that a course of medicine, and a course of groping in the dark, meant, in his estimation, one and the same thing. Mr Candy, hitting back smartly, said that Mr Franklin himself was, constitutionally speaking, groping in the dark after sleep, and that nothing but medicine could help him to find it. Mr Franklin, keeping the ball up on his side, said he had often heard of the blind leading the blind, and now, for the first time, he knew what it meant. In this way, they kept it going briskly, cut and thrust, till they both of them got hot – Mr Candy, in particular, so completely losing his self-control, in defence of his profession, that my lady was obliged to interfere, and forbid the dispute to go on. This necessary act of authority put the last extinguisher on the spirits of the company. The talk spurted up again here and there, for a minute or two at a time; but there was a miserable lack of life and sparkle in it. The

Devil (or the Diamond) possessed that dinner-party; and it was a relief to everybody when my mistress rose, and gave the ladies the signal to leave the gentlemen over their wine.

I had just ranged the decanters in a row before old Mr Ablewhite (who represented the master of the house), when there came a sound from the terrace which startled me out of my company manners on the instant. Mr Franklin and I looked at each other; it was the sound of the Indian drum. As I live by bread, here were the jugglers returning to us with the return of the Moonstone to the house!

As they rounded the corner of the terrace, and came in sight, I hobbled out to warm them off. But, as ill-luck would have it, the two Bouncers were beforehand with me. They whizzed out on to the terrace like a couple of skyrockets, wild to see the Indians exhibit their tricks. The other ladies followed; the gentlemen came out on their side. Before you could say, 'Lord bless us!' the rogues were making their salaams; and the Bouncers were kissing the pretty little boy.

Mr Franklin got on one side of Miss Rachel, and I put myself behind her. If our suspicions were right, there she stood, innocent of all knowledge of the truth, showing the Indians the Diamond in the bosom of her dress!

I can't tell you what tricks they performed, or how they did it. What with the vexation about the dinner, and what with the provocation of the rogues coming back just in the nick of time to see the jewel with their own eyes, I own I lost my head. The first thing that I remember noticing was the sudden appearance on the scene of the Indian traveller, Mr Murthwaite. Skirting the half-circle in which the gentlefolks stood or sat, he came quietly behind the jugglers, and spoke to them on a sudden in the language of their own country.

If he had pricked them with a bayonet, I doubt if the Indians could have started and turned on him with a more tigerish quickness than they did, on hearing the first words that passed his lips. The next moment, they were bowing and salaaming to him in their most polite and snaky way. After a few words in the unknown tongue had passed on either side, Mr Murthwaite withdrew as quietly as he had approached. The chief Indian, who acted as interpreter, thereupon wheeled about again towards the gentlefolks. I noticed that the fellow's coffee-coloured face had turned grey since Mr Murthwaite had spoken to him. He bowed to my lady, and informed her that the exhibition was over. The Bouncers, indescribably disappointed, burst out with a loud 'O!' directed against Mr Murthwaite for stopping the performance. The chief Indian laid his hand humbly on his breast, and said a second time that the juggling was over. The little boy went round with the hat. The ladies withdrew to the drawing-room; and the gentlemen (excepting Mr Franklin and Mr Murthwaite) returned to their wine. I and the footman followed the Indians, and saw them safe off the premises.

Going back by way of the shrubbery, I smelt tobacco, and found Mr Franklin and Mr Murthwaite (the latter smoking a cheroot) walking slowly up and down among the trees. Mr Franklin beckoned to me to join them.

'This,' says Mr Franklin, presenting me to the great traveller, 'is Gabriel Betteredge, the old servant and friend of our family of whom I spoke to you just now. Tell him, if you please, what you have just told me.'

Mr Murthwaite took his cheroot out of his mouth, and leaned, in his weary way, against the trunk of a tree.

'Mr Betteredge,' he began, 'those three Indians are no more jugglers than you and I are.'

Here was a new surprise! I naturally asked the traveller if he had ever met with the Indians before.

'Never,' says Mr Murthwaite; 'but I know what Indian juggling really is. All you have seen to-night is a very bad and clumsy imitation of it. Unless, after long experience, I am utterly mistaken, those men are high-caste Brahmins. I charged them with being disguised, and you saw how it told on them, clever as the Hindoo people are in concealing their feelings. There is a mystery about their conduct that I can't explain. They have doubly sacrificed their caste – first, in crossing the sea; secondly, in disguising themselves as jugglers. In the land they live in, that is a tremendous sacrifice to make. There must be some very serious motive at the bottom of it, and some justification of no ordinary kind to plead for them, in recovery of their caste, when they return to their own country.'

I was struck dumb. Mr Murthwaite went on with his cheroot. Mr Franklin, after what looked to me like a little private veering about between the different sides of his character, broke the silence as follows:

'I feel some hesitation, Mr Murthwaite, in troubling you with family matters, in which you can have no interest and which I am not very willing to speak of out of our own circle. But, after what you have said, I feel bound, in the interests of Lady Verinder and her daughter, to tell you something which may possibly put the clue into your hands. I speak to you in confidence; you will oblige me, I am sure, by not forgetting that?'

With this preface, he told the Indian traveller all that he had told me at the Shivering Sand. Even the immovable Mr Murthwaite was so interested in what he heard, that he let his cheroot go out.

'Now,' says Mr Franklin, when he had done, 'what does your experience say?'

'My experience,' answered the traveller, 'says that you have had more narrow escapes of your life, Mr Franklin Blake, than I have had of mine; and that is saying a great deal.'

It was Mr Franklin's turn to be astonished now.

'Is it really as serious as that?' he asked.

'In my opinion it is,' answered Mr Murthwaite. 'I can't doubt, after what you have told me, that the restoration of the Moonstone to its place on the forehead of the Indian idol, is the motive and the justification of that sacrifice of caste which I alluded to just now. Those men will wait their opportunity with the patience of cats, and will use it with the ferocity of tigers. How you have escaped them I can't imagine,' says the eminent traveller, lighting his cheroot again, and staring hard at Mr Franklin. 'You have been carrying the Diamond backwards and forwards, here and in London, and you are still a living man! Let us try and account for it. It was daylight, both times, I suppose, when you took the jewel out of the bank in London?'

'Broad daylight,' says Mr Franklin.

'And plenty of people in the streets?'

'Plenty.'

'You settled, of course, to arrive at Lady Verinder's house at a certain time? It's a lonely country between this and the station. Did you keep your appointment?'

'No. I arrived four hours earlier than my appointment.'

'I beg to congratulate you on that proceeding! When did you take the Diamond to the bank at the town here?'

'I took it an hour after I had brought it to this house – and three hours before anybody was prepared for seeing me in these parts.'

'I beg to congratulate you again! Did you bring it back here alone?'

'No. I happened to ride back with my cousins and the groom.'

'I beg to congratulate you for the third time! If you ever feel inclined to travel beyond the civilized limits, Mr Blake, let me know, and I will go with you. You are a lucky man.'

Here I struck in. This sort of thing didn't at all square with my English ideas.

'You don't really mean to say, sir,' I asked, 'that they would have taken Mr Franklin's life, to get their Diamond, if he had given them the chance?'

'Do you smoke, Mr Betteredge?' says the traveller.

'Yes, sir.'

'Do you care much for the ashes left in your pipe, when you empty it?'

'No, sir.'

'In the country those men came from, they care just as much about killing a man, as you care about emptying the ashes out of your pipe. If a thousand lives stood between them and the getting back of their

Diamond – and if they thought they could destroy those lives without discovery – they would take them all. The sacrifice of caste is a serious thing in India, if you like. The sacrifice of life is nothing at all.'

I expressed my opinion, upon this, that they were a set of murdering thieves. Mr Murthwaite expressed *his* opinion that they were a wonderful people. Mr Franklin, expressing no opinion at all, brought us back to the matter in hand.

'They have seen the Moonstone on Miss Verinder's dress,' he said. 'What is to be done?'

'What your uncle threatened to do,' answered Mr Murthwaite. 'Colonel Herncastle understood the people he had to deal with. Send the Diamond to-morrow (under guard of more than one man) to be cut up at Amsterdam. Make half a dozen diamonds of it, instead of one. There is an end of its sacred identity as The Moonstone – and there is an end of the conspiracy.'

Mr Franklin turned to me.

'There is no help for it,' he said. 'We must speak to Lady Verinder to-morrow.'

'What about to-night, sir?' I asked. 'Suppose the Indians come back?'

Mr Murthwaite answered me, before Mr Franklin could speak.

'The Indians won't risk coming back to-night,' he said. 'The direct way is hardly ever the way they take to anything – let alone a matter like this, in which the slightest mistake might be fatal to their reaching their end.'

'But suppose the rogues are bolder than you think, sir?' I persisted.

'In that case,' says Mr Murthwaite, 'let the dogs loose. Have you got any big dogs in the yard?'

'Two, sir. A mastiff and a bloodhound.'

'They will do. In the present emergency, Mr Betteredge, the mastiff and the bloodhound have one great merit – they are not likely to be troubled with your scruples about the sanctity of human life.'

The strumming of the piano reached us from the drawing-room, as he fired that shot at me. He threw away his cheroot, and took Mr Franklin's arm, to go back to the ladies. I noticed that the sky was clouding over fast, as I followed them to the house. Mr Murthwaite noticed it too. He looked round at me, in his dry, drolling way, and said:

'The Indians will want their umbrellas, Mr Betteredge, to-night!'

It was all very well for *him* to joke. But I was not an eminent traveller – and my way in this world had not led me into playing ducks and drakes with my own life, among thieves and murderers in the outlandish places of the earth. I went into my own little room, and sat down in my chair in a perspiration, and wondered helplessly what was to be done next. In this anxious frame of mind, other men might have ended by working themselves up into a fever; I ended in a different way. I lit my pipe, and took a turn at *Robinson Crusoe*.

Before I had been at it five minutes, I came to this amazing bit – page one hundred and sixty-one – as follows:

'Fear of Danger is ten thousand times more terrifying than Danger itself, when apparent to the Eyes; and we find the Burthen of Anxiety greater, by much, than the Evil which we are anxious about.'

The man who doesn't believe in *Robinson Crusoe*, after *that*, is a man with a screw loose in his understanding, or a man lost in the mist of his own self-conceit! Argument is thrown away upon him; and pity is better reserved for some person with a livelier faith.

I was far on with my second pipe, and still lost in admiration of that wonderful book, when Penelope (who had been handing round the tea) came in with her report from the drawing-room. She had left the Bouncers singing a duet – words beginning with a large 'O,' and music to correspond. She had observed that my lady made mistakes in her game of whist for the first time in our experience of her. She had seen the great traveller asleep in a corner. She had overheard Mr Franklin sharpening his wits on Mr Godfrey, at the expense of Ladies' Charities in general; and she had noticed that Mr Godfrey hit him back again rather more smartly than became a gentleman of his benevolent character. She had detected Miss Rachel, apparently engaged in appeasing Mrs Threadgall by showing her some photographs, and really occupied in stealing looks at Mr Franklin, which no intelligent lady's maid could misinterpret for a single instant. Finally, she had missed Mr Candy, the doctor, who had mysteriously disappeared from the drawing-room, and had then mysteriously returned, and entered into conversation with Mr Godfrey. Upon the whole, things were prospering better than the experience of the dinner gave us any right to expect. If we could only hold on for another hour, old Father Time would bring up their carriages, and relieve us of them altogether.

Everything wears off in this world; and even the comforting effect of *Robinson Crusoe* wore off, after Penelope left me. I got fidgety again, and resolved on making a survey of the grounds before the rain came. Instead of taking the footman, whose nose was human, and therefore useless in any emergency, I took the bloodhound with me. *His* nose for a stranger was to be depended on. We went all round the premises, and out into the road – and returned as wise as we went, having discovered no such thing as a lurking human creature anywhere.

The arrival of the carriages was the signal for the arrival of the rain. It poured as if it meant to pour all night. With the exception of the doctor, whose gig was waiting for him, the rest of the company went home snugly, under cover, in close carriages. I told Mr Candy that I was afraid he would get wet through. He told me, in return, that he wondered I had arrived at my time of life, without knowing that a doctor's skin was waterproof. So he drove away in the rain, laughing over his own little joke; and so we got rid of our dinner company.

The next thing to tell is the story of the night.

❧ ELEVEN ❦

WHEN THE LAST OF THE GUESTS had driven away, I went back into the inner hall, and found Samuel at the side-table, presiding over the brandy and soda-water. My lady and Miss Rachel came out of the drawing-room, followed by the two gentlemen. Mr Godfrey had some brandy and soda-water. Mr Franklin took nothing. He sat down, looking dead tired; the talking on this birthday occasion had, I suppose, been too much for him.

My lady, turning round to wish them good-night, looked hard at the wicked Colonel's legacy shining in her daughter's dress.

'Rachel,' she asked, 'where are you going to put your Diamond to-night?'

Miss Rachel was in high good spirits, just in that humour for talking nonsense, and perversely persisting in it as if it was sense, which you may sometimes have observed in young girls, when they are highly wrought up, at the end of an exciting day. First, she declared she didn't know where to put the Diamond. Then she said, 'On her dressing-table, of course, along with her other things. 'Then she remembered that the Diamond might take to shining of itself, with its awful moony light, in the dark – and that would terrify her in the dead of night. Then she bethought herself of an Indian cabinet which stood in her sitting-room; and instantly made up her mind to put the Indian diamond in the Indian cabinet, for the purpose of permitting two beautiful native productions to admire each other. Having let her little flow of nonsense run on as far as that point, her mother interposed and stopped her.

'My dear! your Indian cabinet has no lock to it,' says my lady.

'Good Heavens, mamma!' cried Miss Rachel, 'is this an hotel? Are there thieves in the house?'

Without taking notice of this fantastic way of talking, my lady wished the gentlemen good-night. She next turned to Miss Rachel, and kissed her. 'Why not let *me* keep the Diamond for you to-night?' she asked.

Miss Rachel received that proposal as she might, ten years since, have received a proposal to part her from a new doll. My lady saw there was no reasoning with her that night. 'Come into my room, Rachel, the first thing to-morrow morning,' she said. 'I shall have something to say to you.' With those last words she left us slowly; thinking her own thoughts, and, to all appearance, not best pleased with the way by which they were leading her.

Miss Rachel was the next to say good-night. She shook hands first with Mr Godfrey, who was standing at the other end of the hall, looking at a picture. Then she turned back to Mr Franklin, still sitting weary and silent in a corner.

What words passed between them I can't say. But standing near the old oak frame which holds our large looking-glass, I saw her reflected in it, slyly slipping the locket which Mr Franklin had given to her, out of the bosom of her dress, and showing it to him for a moment, with a smile which certainly meant something out of the common, before she tripped off to bed. This incident staggered me a little in the reliance I had previously felt on my own judgment. I began to think that Penelope might be right about the state of her young lady's affections, after all.

As soon as Miss Rachel left him eyes to see with, Mr Franklin noticed me. His variable humour, shifting about everything, had shifted about the Indians already.

'Betteredge,' he said, 'I'm half inclined to think I took Mr Murthwaite too seriously, when we had that talk in the shrubbery. I wonder whether he has been trying any of his traveller's tales on us? Do you really mean to let the dogs loose?'

'I'll relieve them of their collars, sir,' I answered, 'and leave them free to take a turn in the night, if they smell a reason for it.'

'All right,' says Mr Franklin. 'We'll see what is to be done to-morrow. I am not at all disposed to alarm my aunt, Betteredge, without a very pressing reason for it. Good-night.'

He looked so worn and pale as he nodded to me, and took his candle to go upstairs, that I ventured to advise his having a drop of brandy-and-water, by way of nightcap. Mr Godfrey, walking towards us from the other end of the hall, backed me. He pressed Mr Franklin, in the friendliest manner, to take something, before he went to bed.

I only note these trifling circumstances, because, after all I had seen and heard, that day, it pleased me to observe that our two gentlemen were on just as good terms as ever. Their warfare of words (heard by Penelope in the drawing-room), and their rivalry for the best place in Miss Rachel's good graces, seemed to have set no serious difference between them. But there! they were both good-tempered, and both men of the world. And there is certainly this merit in people of station, that they are not nearly so quarrelsome among each other as people of no station at all.

Mr Franklin declined the brandy-and-water, and went upstairs with Mr Godfrey, their rooms being next door to each other. On the landing, however, either his cousin persuaded him, or he veered about and changed his mind as usual . 'Perhaps I may want it in the night,' he called down to me. 'Send up some brandy-and-water into my room.'

I sent up Samuel with the brandy-and-water; and then went out, and unbuckled the dogs' collars. They both lost their heads with astonishment on being set loose at that time of night, and jumped upon me like a couple of puppies! However, the rain soon cooled them down again: they lapped a drop of water each, and crept back into their kennels. As I went into the house, I noticed signs in the sky which betokened a break in the weather for the better. For the present, it still poured heavily, and the ground was in a perfect sop.

Samuel and I went all over the house, and shut up as usual. I examined everything myself, and trusted nothing to my deputy on this occasion. All was safe and fast, when I rested my old bones in bed, between midnight and one in the morning.

The worries of the day had been a little too much for me, I suppose. At any rate, I had a touch of Mr Franklin's malady that night. It was sunrise, before I fell off at last into a sleep. All the time I lay awake, the house was as quiet as the grave. Not a sound stirred but the splash of the rain, and the sighing of the wind among the trees as a breeze sprang up with the morning.

About half-past seven I woke, and opened my window on a fine sunshiny day. The clock had struck eight, and I was just going out to chain up the dogs again, when I heard a sudden whisking of petticoats on the stairs behind me.

I turned about, and there was Penelope flying down after me like mad. 'Father!' she screamed, 'come upstairs, for God's sake! *The Diamond is gone!*'

'Are you out of your mind?' I asked her.

'Gone!' says Penelope. 'Gone, nobody knows how! Come up and see.'

She dragged me after her into our young lady's sitting-room, which opened into her bedroom. There, on the threshold of her bedroom door, stood Miss Rachel, almost as white in the face as the white dressing-gown that clothed her. There also stood the two doors of the Indian cabinet, wide open. One of the drawers inside was pulled out as far as it would go.

'Look!' says Penelope. 'I myself saw Miss Rachel put the Diamond into that drawer last night.'

I went to the cabinet. The drawer was empty.

'Is this true, miss?' I asked.

With a look that was not like herself, with a voice that was not like her own, Miss Rachel answered, as my daughter had answered: 'The Diamond is gone!'

Having said those words, she withdrew into her bedroom, and shut and locked the door.

Before we knew which way to turn next, my lady came in, hearing my voice in her daughter's sitting-room, and wondering what had happened. The news of the loss of the Diamond seemed to petrify her. She went straight to Miss Rachel's bedroom, and insisted on being admitted. Miss Rachel let her in.

The alarm, running through the house like fire, caught the two gentlemen next.

Mr Godfrey was the first to come out of his room. All he did when he heard what had happened was to hold up his hands in a state of bewilderment, which didn't say much for his natural strength of mind. Mr Franklin, whose clear head I had confidently counted on to advise us, seemed to be as helpless as his cousin when he heard the news in his turn. For a wonder, he had had a good night's rest at last; and the unaccustomed luxury of sleep had, as he said himself, apparently stupefied him. However, when he had swallowed his cup of coffee – which he always took, on the foreign plan, some hours before he ate any breakfast – his brains brightened; the clear-headed side of him turned up, and he took the matter in hand, resolutely and cleverly, much as follows:

He first sent for the servants, and told them to leave all the lower doors and windows (with the exception of the front door, which I had opened) exactly as they had been left when we locked up overnight. He next proposed to his cousin and to me to make quite sure, before we took any further steps, that the Diamond had not accidentally dropped somewhere out of sight – say at the back of the cabinet, or down behind the table on which the cabinet stood. Having searched in both places, and found nothing – having also questioned Penelope, and discovered from her no more than the little she had already told me – Mr Franklin suggested next extending our inquiries to Miss Rachel, and sent Penelope to knock at her bedroom door.

My lady answered the knock, and closed the door behind her. The moment after, we heard it locked inside by Miss Rachel. My mistress came out among us, looking sorely puzzled and distressed. 'The loss of the Diamond seems to have quite overwhelmed Rachel,' she said, in reply to Mr Franklin. 'She shrinks, in the strangest manner, from speaking of it, even to *me*. It is impossible you can see her for the present.'

Having added to our perplexities by this account of Miss Rachel, my lady, after a little effort, recovered her usual composure, and acted with her usual decision.

'I suppose there is no help for it?' she said, quietly. 'I suppose I have no alternative but to send for the police?'

'And the first thing for the police to do,' added Mr Franklin, catching her up, 'is to lay hands on the Indian jugglers who performed here last night'

My lady and Mr Godfrey (not knowing what Mr Franklin and I knew) both started, and both looked surprised.

'I can't stop to explain myself now,' Mr Franklin went on. 'I can only tell you that the Indians have certainly stolen the Diamond. Give me a letter of introduction,' says he, addressing my lady, 'to one of the magistrates at Frizinghall – merely telling him that I represent your interests and wishes, and let me ride off with it instantly. Our chance of catching the thieves may depend on our not wasting one unnecessary minute.' (*Nota bene*: Whether it was the French side or the English, the right side of Mr Franklin seemed to be uppermost now. The only question was, How long would it last?)

He put pen, ink, and paper before his aunt, who (as it appeared to me) wrote the letter he wanted a little unwillingly. If it had been possible to overlook such an event as the loss of a jewel worth twenty thousand pounds, I believe – with my lady's opinion of her late brother, and her distrust of his birthday-gift – it would have been privately a relief to her to let the thieves get off with the Moonstone scot free.

I went out with Mr Franklin to the stables, and took the opportunity of asking him how the Indians (whom I suspected, of course, as shrewdly as he did) could possibly have got into the house.

'One of them might have slipped into the hall, in the confusion, when the dinner company were going away,' says Mr Franklin. 'The fellow may have been under the sofa while my aunt and Rachel were talking about where the Diamond was to be put for the night. He would only have to wait till the house was quiet, and there it would be in the cabinet, to be had for the taking.' With those words, he called to the groom to open the gate, and galloped off.

This seemed certainly to be the only rational explanation. But how had the thief contrived to make his escape from the house? I had found the front door locked and bolted, as I had left it at night, when I went to open it, after getting up. As for the other doors and windows, there they were still, all safe and fast, to speak for themselves. The dogs, too? Suppose the thief had got away by dropping from one of the upper windows, how had he escaped the dogs? Had he come provided for them with drugged meat? As the doubt crossed my mind, the dogs

75

themselves came galloping at me round a corner, rolling each other over on the wet grass, in such lively health and spirits that it was with no small difficulty I brought them to reason, and chained them up again. The more I turned it over in my mind, the less satisfactory Mr Franklin's explanation appeared to be.

We had our breakfasts – whatever happens in a house, robbery or murder, it doesn't matter, you must have your breakfast. When we had done, my lady sent for me; and I found myself compelled to tell her all that I had hitherto concealed, relating to the Indians and their plot. Being a woman of a high courage, she soon got over the first startling effect of what I had to communicate. Her mind seemed to be far more perturbed about her daughter than about the heathen rogues and their conspiracy. 'You know how odd Rachel is, and how differently she behaves some-times from other girls,' my lady said to me. 'But I have never, in all my experience, seen her so strange and so reserved as she is now. The loss of her jewel seems almost to have turned her brain. Who would have thought that horrible Diamond could have laid such a hold on her in so short a time?'

It was certainly strange. Taking toys and trinkets in general, Miss Rachel was nothing like so mad after them as most young girls. Yet there she was, still locked up inconsolably in her bedroom. It is but fair to add that she was not the only one of us in the house who was thrown out of the regular groove. Mr Godfrey, for instance – though professionally a sort of consoler-general – seemed to be at a loss where to look for his own resources. Having no company to amuse him, and getting no chance of trying what his experience of women in distress could do towards comforting Miss Rachel, he wandered hither and thither about the house and gardens in an aimless uneasy way. He was in two different minds about what it became him to do, after the misfortune that had happened to us. Ought he to relieve the family, in their present situation, of the responsibility of him as a guest, or ought he to stay on the chance that even his humble services might be of some use? He decided ultimately that the last course was perhaps the most customary and considerate course to take, in such a very peculiar case of family distress as this was. Circumstances try the metal a man is really made of. Mr Godfrey, tried by circumstances, showed himself of weaker metal than I had thought him to be. As for the women-servants – excepting Rosanna Spearman, who kept by herself – they took to whispering together in corners, and staring at nothing suspiciously, as is the manner of that weaker half of the human family, when anything extraordinary happens in a house. I myself acknowledge to have been fidgety and ill-tempered. The cursed Moonstone had turned us all upside down.

A little before eleven, Mr Franklin came back. The resolute side of him had, to all appearance, given way, in the interval since his departure, under the stress that had been laid on it. He had left us at a gallop; he came back to us at a walk. When he went away, he was made of iron. When he returned, he was stuffed with cotton, as limp as limp could be.

'Well,' says my lady, 'are the police coming?'

'Yes,' says Mr Franklin; 'they said they would follow me in a fly. Superintendent Seegrave, of your local police force, and two of his men. A mere form! The case is hopeless.'

'What! have the Indians escaped, sir?' I asked.

'The poor ill-used Indians have been most unjustly put in prison,' says Mr Franklin. 'They are as innocent as the babe unborn. My idea that one of them was hidden in the house, has ended, like all the rest of my ideas, in smoke. It's been proved,' says Mr Franklin, dwelling with great relish on his own incapacity, 'to be simply impossible.'

After astonishing us by announcing this totally new turn in the matter of the Moonstone, our young gentleman, at his aunt's request, took a seat, and explained himself.

It appeared that the resolute side of him had held out as far as Frizing-hall. He had put the whole case plainly before the magistrate, and the magistrate had at once sent for the police. The first inquiries instituted about the Indians showed that they had not so much as attempted to leave the town. Further questions addressed to the police, proved that all three had been seen returning to Frizinghall with their boy, on the previous night between ten and eleven – which (regard being had to hours and distances) also proved that they had walked straight back, after performing on our terrace. Later still, at midnight, the police, having occasion to search the common lodging-house where they lived, had seen them all three again, and their little boy with them as usual. Soon after midnight I myself had safely shut up the house. Plainer evidence than this, in favour of the Indians, there could not well be. The magistrate said there was not even a case of suspicion against them so far. But, as it was just possible, when the police came to investigate the matter, that discoveries affecting the jugglers might be made, he would contrive, by committing them as rogues and vagabonds, to keep them at our disposal, under lock and key, for a week. They had ignorantly done something (I forget what) in the town, which barely brought them within the operation of the law. Every human institution (Justice included) will stretch a little, if you only pull it the right way. The worthy magistrate was an old friend of my lady's – and the Indians were 'committed' for a week, as soon as the court opened that morning.

Such was Mr Franklin's narrative of events at Frizinghall. The Indian clue to the mystery of the lost jewel was now, to all appearance, a clue that had broken in our hands. If the jugglers were innocent, who, in the name of wonder, had taken the Moonstone out of Miss Rachel's drawer?

Ten minutes later, to our infinite relief, Superintendent Seegrave arrived at the house. He reported passing Mr Franklin on the terrace, sitting in the sun (I suppose with the Italian side of him uppermost); and warning the police, as they went by, that the investigation was hopeless, before the investigation had begun.

For a family in our situation, the Superintendent of the Frizinghall police was the most comforting officer you could wish to see. Mr Seegrave was tall and portly, and military in his manners. He had a fine commanding voice, and a mighty resolute eye, and a grand frock-coat which buttoned beautifully up to his leather stock. 'I'm the man you want!' was written all over his face; and he ordered his two inferior policemen about with a severity which convinced us all that there was no trifling with *him*.

He began by going round the premises, outside and in; the result of that investigation proving to him that no thieves had broken in upon us from outside, and that the robbery, consequently, must have been committed by some person in the house. I leave you to imagine the state the servants were in when this official announcement first reached their ears. The Superintendent decided to begin by examining the boudoir; and, that done, to examine the servants next. At the same time, he posted one of his men on the staircase which led to the servants' bedrooms, with instructions to let nobody in the house pass him, till further orders.

At this latter proceeding, the weaker half of the human family went distracted on the spot. They bounced out of their corners; whisked upstairs in a body to Miss Rachel's room (Rosanna Spearman being carried away among them this time); burst in on Superintendent Seegrave; and all looking equally guilty, summoned him to say which of them he suspected, at once.

Mr Superintendent proved equal to the occasion – he looked at them with his resolute eye, and he cowed them with his military voice.

'Now, then, you women, go downstairs again, every one of you. I won't have you here. Look!' says Mr Superintendent, suddenly pointing to a little smear of the decorative painting on Miss Rachel's door – at the outer edge, just under the lock. 'Look what mischief the petticoats of some of you have done already. Clear out! clear out!' Rosanna Spearman, who was nearest to him, and nearest to the little smear on the door, set the example of obedience, and slipped off instantly to her work. The rest followed her out. The Superintendent finished his examination of the room; and, making nothing of it, asked me who had first discovered the robbery. My daughter had first discovered it. My daughter was sent for.

Mr Superintendent proved to be a little too sharp with Penelope at starting. 'Now, young woman, attend to me – and mind you speak the truth.' Penelope fired up instantly. 'I've never been taught to tell lies, Mr Policeman! – and if father can stand there and hear me accused of falsehood and thieving, and my own bedroom shut against me, and my character taken away, which is all a poor girl has left, he's not the good father I take him for!' A timely word from me put Justice and Penelope on a pleasanter footing together. The questions and answers went swimmingly; and ended in nothing worth mentioning. My daughter had seen Miss Rachel put the Diamond in the drawer of the cabinet, the last thing at night. She had gone in with Miss Rachel's cup of tea, at eight the next morning, and had found the drawer open and empty. Upon that, she had alarmed the house – and there was an end of Penelope's evidence.

Mr Superintendent next asked to see Miss Rachel herself. Penelope mentioned his request through the door. The answer reached us by the same road – 'I have nothing to tell the policeman – I can't see anybody.' Our experienced officer looked equally surprised and offended when he heard that reply. I told him my young lady was ill, and begged him to wait a little and see her later. We thereupon went downstairs again, and were met by Mr Godfrey and Mr Franklin, crossing the hall.

The two gentlemen, being inmates of the house, were summoned to say if they could throw any light on the matter. Neither of them knew anything about it. Had they heard any suspicious noises during the previous night? They had heard nothing but the pattering of the rain. Had I, lying awake longer than either of them, heard nothing either? Nothing! Released from examination, Mr Franklin (still sticking to the helpless view of our difficulty) whispered to me, – 'That man will be of no earthly use to us. Superintendent Seegrave is an ass.' Released in his turn, Mr Godfrey whispered to me, – 'Evidently a most competent person. Betteredge, I have the greatest faith in him!' Many men, many opinions, as one of the ancients said, before my time.

Mr Superintendent's next proceeding took him back to the 'boudoir' again, with my daughter and me at his heels. His object was to discover whether any of the furniture had been moved, during the night, out of its customary place – his previous investigation in the room having, apparently, not gone quite far enough to satisfy his mind on this point.

While we were still poking about among the chairs and tables, the door of the bedroom was suddenly opened. After having denied herself to everybody, Miss Rachel, to our astonishment, walked into the midst of us of her own accord. She took up her garden hat from a chair, and then went straight to Penelope with this question:—

'Mr Franklin Blake sent you with a message to me this morning?'

'Yes, miss.'

'He wished to speak to me, didn't he?'

'Yes, miss.'

'Where is he now?'

Hearing voices on the terrace below, I looked out of the window, and saw the two gentlemen walking up and down together. Answering for my daughter, I said, 'Mr Franklin is on the terrace, miss.'

Without another word, without heeding Mr Superintendent, who tried to speak to her; pale as death, and wrapped up strangely in her own thoughts, she left the room, and went down to her cousins on the terrace.

It showed a want of due respect, it showed a breach of good manners, on my part; but, for the life of me, I couldn't help looking out of the window when Miss Rachel met the gentlemen outside. She went up to Mr Franklin without appearing to notice Mr Godfrey, who thereupon drew back and left them by themselves. What she said to Mr Franklin appeared to be spoken vehemently. It lasted but for a short time; and (judging by what I saw of his face from the window) seemed to astonish him beyond all power of expression. While they were still together, my lady appeared on the terrace. Miss Rachel saw her – said a few last words to Mr Franklin – and suddenly went back into the house again, before her mother came up with her. My lady, surprised herself, and noticing Mr Franklin's surprise, spoke to him. Mr Godfrey joined them, and spoke also. Mr Franklin walked away a little, between the two, telling them what had happened, I suppose; for they both stopped short, after taking a few steps, like persons struck with amazement. I had just seen as much as this, when the door of the sitting-room was opened violently. Miss Rachel walked swiftly through to her bedroom, wild and angry, with fierce eyes and flaming cheeks. Mr Superintendent once more attempted to question her. She turned round on him at her bedroom door. '*I* have not sent for you!' she cried out, vehemently. '*I* don't want you. My Diamond is lost. Neither you nor anybody else will ever find it!' With those words she went in, and locked the door in our faces. Penelope, standing nearest to it, heard her burst out crying the moment she was alone again.

In a rage, one moment; in tears, the next! What did it mean?

I told the Superintendent it meant that Miss Rachel's temper was upset by the loss of her jewel. Being anxious for the honour of the family, it distressed me to see my young lady forget herself – even with a police-officer – and I made the best excuse I could, accordingly. In my own private mind, I was more puzzled by Miss Rachel's extraordinary language and conduct than words can tell. Taking what she had said at her bedroom door as a guide to guess by, I could only conclude that she was mortally offended by our sending for the police, and that Mr Franklin's astonishment on the terrace was caused by her having expressed herself to him (as the person chiefly instrumental in fetching the police) to that effect. If this guess was right, why – having lost her Diamond – should she object to the presence in the house of the very people whose business it was to recover it for her? And how, in Heaven's name, could *she* know that the Moonstone would never be found again?

As things stood, at present, no answer to those questions was to be hoped for from anybody in the house. Mr Franklin appeared to think it a point of honour to forbear repeating to a servant – even to so old a servant as I was – what Miss Rachel had said to him on the terrace. Mr Godfrey, who, as a gentleman and a relative, had been probably admitted into Mr Franklin's confidence, respected that confidence as he was bound to do. My lady, who was also in the secret no doubt, and who alone had access to Miss Rachel, owned openly that she could make nothing of her. 'You madden me when you talk of the Diamond!' All her mother's influence failed to extract from her a word more than that.

Here we were, then, at a deadlock about Miss Rachel – and at a deadlock about the Moonstone. In the first case, my lady was powerless to help us. In the second (as you shall presently judge), Mr Seegrave was fast approaching the condition of a superintendent at his wits' end.

Having ferreted about all over the 'boudoir', without making any discoveries among the furniture, our experienced officer applied to me to know, whether the servants in general were or were not acquainted with the place in which the Diamond had been put for the night.

'I knew where it was put, sir,' I said, 'to begin with. Samuel, the footman, knew also – for he was present in the hall, when they were talking about where the Diamond was to be kept that night. My daughter knew, as she has already told you. She or Samuel may have mentioned the thing to the other servants – or the other servants may have heard the talk for themselves, through the side-door of the hall, which might have been open to the back staircase. For all I can tell, everybody in the house may have known where the jewel was, last night.'

My answer presenting rather a wide field for Mr Superintendent's suspicions to range over, he tried to narrow it by asking about the servants' characters next.

I thought directly of Rosanna Spearman. But it was neither my place nor my wish to direct suspicion against a poor girl, whose honesty had been above all doubt as long as I had known her. The matron at the Reformatory had reported her to my lady as a sincerely penitent and thoroughly trustworthy girl. It was the Superintendent's business to discover reason for suspecting her first – and then, and not till then, it would be my duty to tell him how she came into my lady's service. 'All our people have excellent characters,' I said. 'And all have deserved the trust their mistress has placed in them.' After that, there was but one thing left for Mr Seegrave to do – namely, to set to work, and tackle the servants' characters himself.

One after another, they were examined. One after another, they proved to have nothing to say – and said it (so far as the women were concerned) at great length, and with a very angry sense of the embargo laid on their bedrooms. The rest of them being sent back to their places downstairs, Penelope was then summoned, and examined separately a second time.

My daughter's little outbreak of temper in the 'boudoir', and her readiness to think herself suspected, appeared to have produced an unfavourable impression on Superintendent Seegrave. It seemed also to dwell a little on his mind, that she had been the last person who saw the Diamond at night. When the second questioning was over, my girl came back to me in a frenzy. There was no doubt of it any longer – the police-officer had almost as good as told her she was the thief! I could scarcely believe him (taking Mr Franklin's view) to be quite such an ass as that. But, though he said nothing, the eye with which he looked at my daughter was not a very pleasant eye to see. I laughed it off with poor Penelope, as something too ridiculous to be treated seriously – which it certainly was. Secretly, I am afraid I was foolish enough to be angry too. It was a little trying – it was, indeed. My girl sat down in a corner, with her apron over her head, quite broken-hearted. Foolish of her, you will say: she might have waited till he openly accused her. Well, being a man of just and equal temper, I admit that. Still Mr Superintendent might have remembered – never mind what he might have remembered. The devil take him!

The next and last step in the investigation brought matters, as they say, to a crisis. The officer had an interview (at which I was present) with my lady. After informing her that the Diamond must have been taken by somebody in the house, he requested permission for himself and his men to search the servants' rooms and boxes on the spot. My good mistress, like the generous high-bred woman she was, refused to let us be treated like thieves. 'I will never consent to make such a return as that,' she said, 'or all I owe to the faithful servants who are employed in my house.'

Mr Superintendent made his bow, with a look in my direction, which said plainly, 'Why employ me, if you are to tie my hands in this way?' As head of the servants, I felt directly that we were bound, in justice to all parties, not to profit by our mistress's generosity. 'We gratefully thank your ladyship,' I said; 'but we ask permission to do what is right in this matter, by giving up our keys. When Gabriel Betteredge sets the example,' says I, stopping Superintendent Seegrave at the door, 'the rest of the servants will follow, I promise you. There are my keys, to begin with!' My lady took me by the hand, and thanked me with the tears in her eyes. Lord! what would I not have given, at that moment, for the privilege of knocking Superintendent Seegrave down!

As I had promised for them, the other servants followed my lead, sorely against the grain, of course, but all taking the view that I took. The women were a sight to see, while the police-officers were rummaging among their things. The cook looked as if she could grill Mr Superintendent alive on a furnace, and the other women looked as if they could eat him when he was done.

The search over, and no Diamond or sign of a Diamond being found, of course, anywhere, Superintendent Seegrave retired to my little room to consider with himself what he was to do next. He and his men had now been hours in the house, and had not advanced us one inch towards a discovery of how the Moonstone had been taken, or of whom we were to suspect as the thief.

While the police-officer was still pondering in solitude, I was sent for to see Mr Franklin in the library. To my unutterable astonishment, just as my hand was on the door, it was suddenly opened from the inside, and out walked Rosanna Spearman!

After the library had been swept and cleaned in the morning, neither first nor second housemaid had any business in that room at any later period of the day. I stopped Rosanna Spearman, and charged her with a breach of domestic discipline on the spot.

'What might you want in the library at this time of day?' I inquired.

'Mr Franklin Blake dropped one of his rings upstairs,' says Rosanna; 'and I have been into the library to give it to him.' The girl's face was all in a flush as she made me that answer; and she walked away with a toss of her head and a look of self-importance which I was quite at a loss to account for. The proceedings in the house had doubtless upset all the women-servants more or less; but none of them had gone clean out of their natural characters, as Rosanna, to all appearance, had now gone out of hers.

I found Mr Franklin writing at the library-table. He asked for a conveyance to the railway station the moment I entered the room. The first sound of his voice informed me that we now had the resolute side of him uppermost once more. The man made of cotton had disappeared; and the man made of iron sat before me again.

'Going to London, sir?' I asked.

'Going to telegraph to London,' says Mr Franklin. 'I have convinced my aunt that we must have a cleverer head than Superintendent Seegrave's to help us; and I have got her permission to despatch a telegram to my father. He knows the Chief Commissioner of Police, and the Commissioner can lay his hand on the right man to solve the mystery of the

Diamond. Talking of mysteries, by-the-by,' says Mr Franklin, dropping his voice, 'I have another word to say to you before you go to the stables. Don't breathe a word of it to anybody as yet; but either Rosanna Spearman's head is not quite right, or I am afraid she knows more about the Moonstone than she ought to know.'

I can hardly tell whether I was more startled or distressed at hearing him say that. If I had been younger, I might have confessed as much to Mr Franklin. But when you are old, you acquire one excellent habit. In cases where you don't see your way clearly, you hold your tongue.

'She came in here with a ring I dropped in my bedroom,' Mr Franklin went on. 'When I had thanked her, of course I expected her to go. Instead of that, she stood opposite to me at the table, looking at me in the oddest manner – half frightened, and half familiar – I couldn't make it out. "This is a strange thing about the Diamond, sir," she said, in a curiously sudden, headlong way. I said, "Yes, it was," and wondered what was coming next. Upon my honour, Betteredge, I think she must be wrong in the head! She said, "They will never find the Diamond, sir, will they? No! nor the person who took it – I'll answer for that." She actually nodded and smiled at me! Before I could ask her what she meant, we heard your step outside. I suppose she was afraid of your catching her here. At any rate, she changed colour, and left the room. What on earth does it mean?'

I could not bring myself to tell him the girl's story, even then. It would have been almost as good as telling him that she was the thief. Besides, even if I had made a clean breast of it, and even supposing she was the thief, the reason why she should let out her secret to Mr Franklin, of all the people in the world, would have been still as far to seek as ever.

'I can't bear the idea of getting the poor girl into a scrape, merely because she has a flighty way with her, and talks very strangely,' Mr Franklin went on. 'And yet if she had said to the Superintendent what she said to me, fool as he is, I'm afraid – ' He stopped there, and left the rest unspoken.

'The best way, sir,' I said, 'will be for me to say two words privately to my mistress about it at the first opportunity. My lady has a very friendly interest in Rosanna; and the girl may only have been forward and foolish, after all. When there's a mess of any kind in a house, sir, the women-servants like to look at the gloomy side – it gives the poor wretches a kind of importance in their own eyes. If there's anybody ill, trust the women for prophesying that the person will die. If it's a jewel lost, trust them for prophesying that it will never be found again.'

This view (which, I am bound to say, I thought a probable view myself, on reflection) seemed to relieve Mr Franklin mightily: he folded up his telegram, and dismissed the subject. On my way to the stables, to order the pony-chaise, I looked in at the servants' hall, where they were at dinner. Rosanna Spearman was not among them. On inquiry, I found that she had been suddenly taken ill, and had gone upstairs to her own room to lie down.

'Curious! She looked well enough when I saw her last,' I remarked.

Penelope followed me out. 'Don't talk in that way before the rest of them, father,' she said. 'You only make them harder on Rosanna than ever. The poor thing is breaking her heart about Mr Franklin Blake.'

Here was another view of the girl's conduct. If it was possible for Penelope to be right, the explanation of Rosanna's strange language and behaviour might have been all in this – that she didn't care what she said, so long as she could surprise Mr Franklin into speaking to her. Granting that to be the right reading of the riddle, it accounted, perhaps, for her flighty self-conceited manner when she passed me in the hall. Though he had only said three words, still she had carried her point, and Mr Franklin *had* spoken to her.

I saw the pony harnessed myself. In the infernal network of mysteries and uncertainties that now surrounded us, I declare it was a relief to observe how well the buckles and straps understood each other! When you had seen the pony backed into the shafts of the chaise, you had seen something there was no doubt about. And that, let me tell you, was becoming a treat of the rarest kind in our household.

Going round with the chaise to the front door, I found not only Mr Franklin, but Mr Godfrey and Superintendent Seegrave also waiting for me on the steps.

Mr Superintendent's reflections (after failing to find the Diamond in the servants' rooms or boxes) had led him, it appeared, to an entirely new conclusion. Still sticking to his first text, namely, that somebody in the house had stolen the jewel, our experienced officer was now of opinion that the thief (he was wise enough not to name poor Penelope, whatever he might privately think of her!) had been acting in concert with the Indians; and he accordingly proposed shifting his inquiries to the jugglers in the prison at Frizinghall. Hearing of this new move, Mr Franklin had volunteered to take the Superintendent back to the town, from which he could telegraph to London as easily as from our station. Mr Godfrey, still devoutly believing in Mr Seegrave, and greatly interested in witnessing the examination of the Indians, had begged leave to accompany the officer to Frizinghall. One of the two inferior policemen was to be left at the house, in case anything happened. The other was to go back with the Superintendent to the town. So the four places in the pony-chaise were just filled.

Before he took the reins to drive off, Mr Franklin walked me away a few steps out of hearing of the others.

'I will wait to telegraph to London,' he said, 'till I see what comes of our examination of the Indians. My own conviction is, that this muddle-headed local police-officer is as much in the dark as ever, and is simply trying to gain time. The idea of any of the servants being in league with the Indians is a preposterous absurdity, in my opinion. Keep about the house, Betteredge, till I come back, and try what you can make of Rosanna Spearman. I don't ask you to do anything degrading to your own self-respect, or anything cruel towards the girl. I only ask you to exercise your observation more carefully than usual. We will make as light of it as we can before my aunt – but this is a more important matter than you may suppose.'

'It's a matter of twenty thousand pounds, sir,' I said, thinking of the value of the Diamond.

'It's a matter of quieting Rachel's mind,' answered Mr Franklin gravely. 'I am very uneasy about her.'

He left me suddenly, as if he desired to cut short any further talk between us. I thought I understood why. Further talk might have let me into the secret of what Miss Rachel had said to him on the terrace.

So they drove away to Frizinghall. I was ready enough, in the girl's own interest, to have a little talk with Rosanna in private. But the needful opportunity failed to present itself. She only came downstairs again at tea-time. When she did appear, she was flighty and excited, had what they call an hysterical attack, took a dose of sal-volatile by my lady's order, and was sent back to her bed.

The day wore on to its end drearily and miserably enough, I can tell you. Miss Rachel still kept her room, declaring that she was too ill to come down to dinner that day. My lady was in such low spirits about her daughter, that I could not bring myself to make her additionally anxious, by reporting what Rosanna Spearman had said to Mr Franklin. Penelope persisted in believing that she was to be forthwith tried, sentenced, and transported for theft. The other women took to their Bibles and hymn-books, and looked as sour as verjuice over their reading – a result, which I have observed, in my sphere of life, to follow generally on the performance of acts of piety at unaccustomed periods of the day. As for me, I hadn't even heart enough to open my *Robinson Crusoe*. I went out into the yard, and, being hard up for a little cheerful society, set my chair by the kennels, and talked to the dogs.

Half an hour before dinner-time, the two gentlemen came back from Frizinghall, having arranged with Superintendent Seegrave that he was to return to us the next day. They had called on Mr Murthwaite, the Indian traveller, at his present residence, near the town. At Mr Franklin's request, he had kindly given them the benefit of his knowledge of the language, in dealing with those two, out of the three Indians, who knew nothing of English. The examination, conducted carefully, and at great length, had ended in nothing; not the shadow of a reason being discovered for suspecting the jugglers of having tampered with any of our servants. On reaching that conclusion, Mr Franklin had sent his telegraphic message to London, and there the matter now rested till tomorrow came.

So much for the history of the day that followed the birthday. Not a glimmer of light had broken in on us, so far. A day or two after, however, the darkness lifted a little. How, and with what result, you shall presently see.

◆ TWELVE ◆

THE THURSDAY NIGHT PASSED, and nothing happened. With the Friday morning came two pieces of news.

Item the first: the baker's man declared he had met Rosanna Spearman, on the previous afternoon, with a thick veil on, walking towards Frizinghall by the footpath way over the moor. It seemed strange that anybody should be mistaken about Rosanna, whose shoulder marked her out pretty plainly, poor thing – but mistaken the man must have been; for Rosanna, as you know, had been all the Thursday afternoon ill upstairs in her room.

Item the second came through the postman. Worthy Mr Candy had said one more of his many unlucky things, when he drove off in the rain on the birthday night, and told me that a doctor's skin was waterproof. In spite of his skin, the wet had got through him. He had caught a chill that night, and was now down with a fever. The last accounts, brought by the postman, represented him to be light-headed – talking nonsense as glibly, poor man, in his delirium as he often talked it in his sober senses. We were all sorry for the little doctor; but Mr Franklin appeared to regret his illness, chiefly on Miss Rachel's account. From what he said to my lady, while I was in the room at breakfast-time, he appeared to think that Miss Rachel – if the suspense about the Moonstone was not soon set at rest – might stand in urgent need of the best medical advice at our disposal.

Breakfast had not been over long, when a telegram from Mr Blake, the elder, arrived, in answer to his son. It informed us that he had laid hands (by help of his friend, the Commissioner) on the right man to help us.

The name of him was Sergeant Cuff; and the arrival of him from London might be expected by the morning train.

At reading the name of the new police-officer, Mr Franklin gave a start. It seems that he had heard some curious anecdotes about Sergeant Cuff, from his father's lawyer, during his stay in London. 'I begin to hope we are seeing the end of our anxieties already,' he said. 'If half the stories I have heard are true, when it comes to unravelling a mystery, there isn't the equal in England of Sergeant Cuff!'

We all got excited and impatient as the time drew near for the appearance of this renowned and capable character. Superintendent Seegrave, returning to us at his appointed time, and hearing that the Sergeant was expected, instantly shut himself up in a room, with pen, ink, and paper, to make notes of the Report which would be certainly expected from him. I should have liked to have gone to the station myself, to fetch the Sergeant. But my lady's carriage and horses were not to be thought of, even for the celebrated Cuff; and the pony-chaise was required later for Mr Godfrey. He deeply regretted being obliged to leave his aunt at such an anxious time; and he kindly put off the hour of his departure till as late as the last train, for the purpose of hearing what the clever London police officer thought of the case. But on Friday night he must be in town, having a Ladies' Charity, in difficulties, waiting to consult him on Saturday morning.

When the time came for the Sergeant's arrival, I went down to the gate to look out for him.

A fly from the railway drove up as I reached the lodge; and out got a grizzled, elderly man, so miserably lean that he looked as if he had not got an ounce of flesh on his bones in any part of him. He was dressed all in decent black, with a white cravat round his neck. His face was as sharp as a hatchet, and the skin of it was as yellow and dry and withered as an autumn leaf. His eyes, of a steely light grey, had a very disconcerting trick, when they encountered your eyes, of looking as if they expected something more from you than you were aware of yourself. His walk was soft; his voice was melancholy; his long lanky fingers were hooked like claws. He might have been a parson, or an undertaker – or anything else you like, except what he really was. A more complete opposite to Superintendent Seegrave than Sergeant Cuff, and a less comforting officer to look at, for a family in distress, I defy you to discover, search where you may.

'Is this Lady Verinder's?' he asked.

'Yes, sir.'

'I am Sergeant Cuff.'

'This way, sir, if you please.'

On our road to the house, I mentioned my name and position in the family, to satisfy him that he might speak to me about the business on which my lady was to employ him. Not a word did he say about the business, however, for all that. He admired the grounds, and remarked that he felt the sea air very brisk and refreshing. I privately wondered, on my side, how the celebrated Cuff had got his reputation. We reached the house, in the temper of two strange dogs, coupled up together for the first time in their lives by the same chain.

Asking for my lady, and hearing that she was in one of the conservatories, we went round to the gardens at the back, and sent a servant to seek her. While we were waiting, Sergeant Cuff looked through the evergreen arch on our left, spied out our rosery, and walked straight in, with the first appearance of anything like interest that he had shown yet. To the gardener's astonishment, and to my disgust, this celebrated policeman proved to be quite a mine of learning on the trumpery subject of rose-gardens.

'Ah, you've got the right exposure here to the south and sou'-west,' says the Sergeant, with a wag of his grizzled head, and a streak of pleasure in his melancholy voice. 'This is the shape for a rosery – nothing like a circle set in a square. Yes, yes; with walks between all the beds. But they oughtn't to be gravel walks like these. Grass, Mr Gardener – grass walks between your roses; gravel's too hard for them. That's a sweet pretty bed of white roses and blush roses. They always mix well together, don't they? Here's the white musk rose, Mr Betteredge – our old English rose holding up its head along with the best and the newest of them. Pretty dear!' says the Sergeant, fondling the Musk Rose with his lanky fingers, and speaking to it as if he was speaking to a child.

This was a nice sort of man to recover Miss Rachel's Diamond, and to find out the thief who stole it!

'You seem to be fond of roses, Sergeant?' I remarked.

'I haven't much time to be fond of anything,' says Sergeant Cuff. 'But when I have a moment's fondness to bestow, most times, Mr Betteredge, the roses get it. I began my life among them in my father's nursery garden, and I shall end my life among them, if I can. Yes. One of these days (please God) I shall retire from catching thieves, and try my hand at growing roses. There will be grass walks, Mr Gardener, between my beds,' says the Sergeant, on whose mind the gravel paths of our rosery seemed to dwell unpleasantly.

'It seems an odd taste, sir,' I ventured to say, 'for a man in your line of life.'

'If you will look about you (which most people won't do),' says Sergeant Cuff, 'you will see that the nature of a man's tastes is, most times, as opposite as possible to the nature of a man's business. Show me any two things more opposite one from the other than a rose and a thief; and I'll correct my tastes accordingly – if it isn't too late at any time of life. You find the damask rose a goodish stock for most of the tender sorts, don't you, Mr Gardener? Ah! I thought so. Here's a lady coming. Is it Lady Verinder?'

He had seen her before either I or the gardener had seen her – though we knew which way to look, and he didn't. I began to think him rather a quicker man than he appeared to be at first sight.

The Sergeant's appearance, or the Sergeant's errand – one or both – seemed to cause my lady some little embarrassment. She was, for the first time in all my experience of her, at a loss what to say at an interview with a stranger. Sergeant Cuff put her at ease directly. He asked if any other person had been employed about the robbery before we sent for him; and hearing that another person had been called in, and was now in the house, begged leave to speak to him before anything else was done.

My lady led the way back. Before he followed her, the Sergeant relieved his mind on the subject of the gravel walks by a parting word to the gardener. 'Get her ladyship to try grass,' he said, with a sour look at the paths. 'No gravel! no gravel!'

Why Superintendent Seegrave should have appeared to be several sizes smaller than life, on being presented to Sergeant Cuff, I can't undertake to explain. I can only state the fact. They retired together; and remained a weary long time shut up from all mortal intrusion. When they came out, Mr Superintendent was excited, and Mr Sergeant was yawning.

'The Sergeant wishes to see Miss Verinder's sitting-room,' says Mr Seegrave, addressing me with great pomp and eagerness. 'The Sergeant may have some questions to ask. Attend the Sergeant, if you please!'

While I was being ordered about in this way, I looked at the great Cuff. The great Cuff, on his side, looked at Superintendent Seegrave in that quietly expecting way which I have already noticed. I can't affirm that he was on the watch for his brother-officer's speedy appearance in the character of an Ass – I can only say that I strongly suspected it.

I led the way upstairs. The Sergeant went softly all over the Indian cabinet and all round the 'boudoir'; asking questions (occasionally only of Mr Superintendent, and continually of me), the drift of which I believe to have been equally unintelligible to both of us. In due time, his course brought him to the door, and put him face to face with the decorative painting that you know of. He laid one lean inquiring finger on the small smear, just under the lock, which Superintendent Seegrave had already noticed, when he reproved the women-servants for all crowding together into the room.

'That's a pity,' says Sergeant Cuff. 'How did it happen?'

He put the question to me. I answered that the women-servants had crowded into the room on the previous morning, and that some of their petticoats had done the mischief. 'Superintendent Seegrave ordered them out, sir,' I added, 'before they did any more harm.'

'Right!' says Mr Superintendent in his military way. 'I ordered them out. The petticoats did it, Sergeant – the petticoats did it.'

'Did you notice which petticoat did it?' asked Sergeant Cuff, still addressing himself, not to his brother-officer, but to me.

'No, sir.'

He turned to Superintendent Seegrave upon that, and said. 'You noticed, I suppose?'

Mr Superintendent looked a little taken aback; but he made the best of it. 'I can't charge my memory, Sergeant,' he said, 'a mere trifle – a mere trifle.'

Sergeant Cuff looked at Mr Seegrave as he had looked at the gravel walks in the rosery, and gave us, in his melancholy way, the first taste of his quality which we had had yet.

'I made a private inquiry last week, Mr Superintendent,' he said. 'At one end of the inquiry there was a murder, and at the other end there was a spot of ink on a tablecloth that nobody could account for. In all my experience along the dirtiest ways of this dirty little world, I have never met with such a thing as a trifle yet. Before we go a step further in this business we must see the petticoat that made the smear, and we must know for certain when that paint was wet.'

Mr Superintendent – taking his set-down rather sulkily – asked if he should summon the women. Sergeant Cuff, after considering a minute, sighed, and shook his head.

'No,' he said, 'we'll take the matter of the paint first. It's a question of Yes or No with the paint – which is short. It's a question of petticoats with the women – which is long. What o'clock was it when the servants were in this room yesterday morning? Eleven o'clock – eh? Is there anybody in the house who knows whether that paint was wet or dry, at eleven yesterday morning?

'Her ladyship's nephew, Mr Franklin Blake, knows,' I said.

'Is the gentleman in the house?'

Mr Franklin was as close at hand as could be – waiting for his first chance of being introduced to the great Cuff. In half a minute he was in the room, and was giving his evidence as follows:

'That door, Sergeant,' he said, 'has been painted by Miss Verinder, under my inspection, with my help, and in a vehicle of my own composition. The vehicle dries whatever colours may be used with it, in twelve hours.'

'Do you remember when the smeared bit was done, sir?' asked the Sergeant.

'Perfectly,' answered Mr Franklin. 'That was the last morsel of the door to be finished. We wanted to get it done, on Wednesday last – and I myself completed it by three in the afternoon, or soon after.'

'To-day is Friday,' said Sergeant Cuff, addressing himself to Superintendent Seegrave. 'Let us reckon back, sir. At three on the Wednesday afternoon, that bit of the painting was completed. The vehicle dried it in twelve hours – that is to say, dried it by three o'clock on Thursday morning. At eleven on Thursday morning you held your inquiry here. Take three from eleven, and eight remains. That paint had been *eight hours dry*, Mr Superintendent, when you supposed that the women-servants' petticoats smeared it.'

First knock-down blow for Mr Seegrave! If he had not suspected poor Penelope, I should have pitied him.

Having settled the question of the paint, Sergeant Cuff, from that moment, gave his brother-officer up as a bad job – and addressed himself to Mr Franklin, as the more promising assistant of the two.

'It's quite on the cards, sir,' he said, 'that you have put the clue into our hands.'

As the words passed his lips, the bedroom door opened, and Miss Rachel came out among us suddenly.

She addressed herself to the Sergeant, without appearing to notice (or to heed) that he was a perfect stranger to her.

'Did you say,' she asked, pointing to Mr Franklin, 'that *he* had put the clue into your hands?'

('This is Miss Verinder,' I whispered, behind the Sergeant.)

'That gentleman, miss,' says the Sergeant – with his steely-grey eyes carefully studying my young lady's face— 'has possibly put the clue into our hands.'

She turned for one moment, and tried to look at Mr Franklin. I say, tried, for she suddenly looked away again before their eyes met. There seemed to be some strange disturbance in her mind. She coloured up, and then she turned pale again. With the paleness, there came a new look into her face – a look which it startled me to see.

'Having answered your question, miss,' says the Sergeant, 'I beg leave to make an inquiry in my turn. There is a smear on the painting of your door, here. Do you happen to know when it was done? or who did it?'

Instead of making any reply, Miss Rachel went on with her questions, as if he had not spoken, or as if she had not heard him.

'Are you another police-officer?' she asked.

'I am Sergeant Cuff, miss, of the Detective Police.'

'Do you think a young lady's advice worth having?'

'I shall be glad to hear it, miss.'

'Do your duty by yourself – and don't allow Mr Franklin Blake to help you!'

She said those words so spitefully, so savagely, with such an extraordinary outbreak of ill-will towards Mr Franklin, in her voice and in her look, that – though I had known her from a baby, though I loved and honoured her next to my lady herself – I was ashamed of Miss Rachel for the first time in my life.

Sergeant Cuff's immovable eyes never stirred from off her face.

'Thank you, miss,' he said. 'Do you happen to know anything about the smear? Might you have done it by accident yourself?'

'I know nothing about the smear.'

With that answer, she turned away, and shut herself up again in her bedroom. This time, I heard her – as Penelope had heard her before – burst out crying as soon as she was alone again.

I couldn't bring myself to look at the Sergeant – I looked at Mr Franklin, who stood nearest to me. He seemed to be even more sorely distressed at what had passed than I was.

'I told you I was uneasy about her,' he said. 'And now you see why.'

'Miss Verinder appears to be a little out of temper about the loss of her Diamond,' remarked the Sergeant. 'It's a valuable jewel. Natural enough! natural enough!'

Here was the excuse that I had made for her (when she forgot herself before Superintendent Seegrave, on the previous day) being made for her over again, by a man who couldn't have had *my* interest in making it – for he was a perfect stranger! A kind of cold shudder ran through me, which I couldn't account for at the time. I know, now, that I must have got my first suspicion, at that moment, of a new light (and a horrid light) having suddenly fallen on the case, in the mind of Sergeant Cuff – purely and entirely in consequence of what he had seen in Miss Rachel, and heard from Miss Rachel, at that first interview between them.

'A young lady's tongue is a privileged member, sir,' says the Sergeant to Mr Franklin. 'Let us forget what has passed, and go straight on with this business. Thanks to you, we know when the paint was dry. The next thing to discover is when the paint was last seen without that smear. *You* have got a head on your shoulders – and you understand what I mean.'

Mr Franklin composed himself, and came back with an effort from Miss Rachel to the matter in hand.

'I think I do understand,' he said. 'The more we narrow the question of time, the more we also narrow the field of inquiry.'

'That's it, sir,' said the Sergeant. 'Did you notice your work here, on the Wednesday afternoon, after you had done it?'

Mr Franklin shook his head, and answered, 'I can't say I did.'

'Did *you*?' inquired Sergeant Cuff, turning to me.

'I can't say I did either, sir.'

'Who was the last person in the room, the last thing on Wednesday night?'

'Miss Rachel, I suppose, sir.'

Mr Franklin struck in there, 'Or possibly your daughter, Betteredge.' He turned to Sergeant Cuff, and explained that my daughter was Miss Verinder's maid.

'Mr Betteredge, ask your daughter to step up. Stop!' says the Sergeant, taking me away to the window, out of earshot. 'Your Superintendent here,' he went on, in a whisper, 'has made a pretty full report to me of the manner in which he has managed this case. Among other things, he has, by his own confession, set the servants' backs up. It's very important to smooth them down again. Tell your daughter, and tell the rest of them, these two things, with my compliments: First, that I have no evidence before me, yet, that the Diamond has been stolen; I only know that the Diamond has been lost. Second, that *my* business here with the servants is simply to ask them to lay their heads together and help me to find it.'

My experience of the women-servants, when Superintendent Seegrave laid his embargo on their rooms, came in handy here.

'May I make so bold, Sergeant, as to tell the women a third thing?' I asked. 'Are they free (with your compliments) to fidget up and down-stairs, and whisk in and out of their bedrooms, if the fit takes them?'

'Perfectly free,' says the Sergeant.

'*That* will smooth them down, sir,' I remarked, 'from the cook to the scullion.'

'Go, and do it at once, Mr Betteredge.'

I did it in less than five minutes. There was only one difficulty when I came to the bit about the bedrooms. It took a pretty stiff exertion of my authority, as chief, to prevent the whole of the female household from following me and Penelope upstairs, in the character of volunteer witnesses in a burning fever of anxiety to help Sergeant Cuff.

The Sergeant seemed to approve of Penelope. He became a trifle less dreary; and he looked much as he had looked when he noticed the white musk rose in the flower-garden. Here is my daughter's evidence, as drawn off from her by the Sergeant. She gave it, I think, very prettily – but, there! she is my child all over: nothing of her mother in her; Lord bless you, nothing of her mother in her!

Penelope examined: Took a lively interest in the painting on the door, having helped to mix the colours. Noticed the bit of work under the lock, because it was the last bit done. Had seen it, some hours afterwards, without a smear. Had left it, as late as twelve at night, without a smear. Had, at that hour, wished her young lady good-night in the bedroom;

had heard the clock strike in the 'boudoir'; had her hand at the time on the handle of the painted door; knew the paint was wet (having helped to mix the colours, as aforesaid); took particular pains not to touch it; could swear that she held up the skirts of her dress, and that there was no smear on the paint then; could *not* swear that her dress mightn't have touched it accidentally in going out; remembered the dress she had on, because it was new, a present from Miss Rachel; her father remembered, and could speak to it, too; could, and would, and did fetch it; dress recognized by her father as the dress she wore that night; skirts examined, a long job from the size of them; not the ghost of a paint-stain discovered anywhere. End of Penelope's evidence – and very pretty and convincing, too. Signed, Gabriel Betteredge.

The Sergeant's next proceeding was to question me about any large dogs in the house who might have got into the room, and done the mischief with a whisk of their tails. Hearing that this was impossible, he next sent for a magnifying-glass, and tried how the smear looked, seen that way. No skin-mark (as of a human hand) printed off on the paint. All the signs visible – signs which told that the paint had been smeared by some loose article of somebody's dress touching it in going by. That somebody (putting together Penelope's evidence and Mr Franklin's evidence) must have been in the room, and done the mischief, between midnight and three o'clock on the Thursday morning

Having brought his investigation to this point, Sergeant Cuff discovered that such a person as Superintendent Seegrave was still left in the room, upon which he summed up the proceedings for his brother-officer's benefit, as follows:

'This trifle of yours, Mr Superintendent,' says the Sergeant, pointing to the place on the door, 'has grown a little in importance since you noticed it last. At the present stage of the inquiry there are, as I take it, three discoveries to make, starting from that smear. Find out (first) whether there is any article of dress in this house with the smear of the paint on it. Find out (second) who that dress belongs to. Find out (third) how the person can account for having been in this room, and smeared the paint, between midnight and three in the morning. If the person can't satisfy you, you haven't far to look for the hand that has got the Diamond. I'll work this by myself, if you please, and detain you no longer from your regular business in the town. You have got one of your men here, I see. Leave him here at my disposal, in case I want him – and allow me to wish you good morning.'

Superintendent Seegrave's respect for the Sergeant was great; but his respect for himself was greater still. Hit hard by the celebrated Cuff, he hit back smartly, to the best of his ability, on leaving the room.

'I have abstained from expressing any opinion, so far,' says Mr

Superintendent, with his military voice still in good working order. 'I have now only one remark to offer, on leaving this case in your hands. There *is* such a thing, Sergeant, as making a mountain out of a molehill. Good morning.'

'There is also such a thing as making nothing out of a molehill, in consequence of your head being too high to see it.' Having returned his brother-officer's compliments in those terms, Sergeant Cuff wheeled about, and walked away to the window by himself.

Mr Franklin and I waited to see what was coming next. The Sergeant stood at the window with his hands in his pockets, looking out, and whistling the tune of 'The Last Rose of Summer' softly to himself. Later in the proceedings, I discovered that he only forgot his manners so far as to whistle, when his mind was hard at work, seeing its way inch by inch to its own private ends, on which occasions 'The Last Rose of Summer' evidently helped and encouraged him. I suppose it fitted in somehow with his character. It reminded him, you see, of his favourite roses, and, as *he* whistled it, it was the most melancholy tune going.

Turning from the window, after a minute or two, the Sergeant walked into the middle of the room, and stopped there, deep in thought, with his eyes on Miss Rachel's bedroom door. After a little he roused himself, nodded his head, as much as to say, 'That will do!' and, addressing me, asked for ten minutes' conversation with my mistress, at her ladyship's earliest convenience.

Leaving the room with this message, I heard Mr Franklin ask the Sergeant a question, and stopped to hear the answer also at the threshold of the door.

'Can you guess yet,' inquired Mr Franklin, 'who has stolen the Diamond?'

'*Nobody has stolen the Diamond*,' answered Sergeant Cuff.

We both started at that extraordinary view of the case, and both earnestly begged him to tell us what he meant.

'Wait a little,' said the Sergeant. 'The pieces of the puzzle are not all put together yet.'

THIRTEEN

I FOUND MY LADY IN HER own sitting-room. She started and looked annoyed when I mentioned that Sergeant Cuff wished to speak to her.

'*Must* I see him?' she asked. 'Can't you represent me, Gabriel?'

I felt at a loss to understand this, and showed it plainly, I suppose, in my face. My lady was so good as to explain herself.

'I am afraid my nerves are a little shaken,' she said. 'There is something in that police-officer from London which I recoil from – I don't know why. I have a presentiment that he is bringing trouble and misery with him into the house. Very foolish, and very unlike *me* – but so it is.'

I hardly knew what to say to this. The more *I* saw of Sergeant Cuff, the better I liked him. My lady rallied a little after having opened her heart to me – being, naturally, a woman of a high courage, as I have already told you.

'If I must see him, I must,' she said. 'But I can't prevail on myself to see him alone. Bring him in, Gabriel, and stay here as long as he stays.'

This was the first attack of the megrims that I remembered in my mistress since the time when she was a young girl. I went back to the 'boudoir'. Mr Franklin strolled out into the garden, and joined Mr Godfrey, whose time for departure was now drawing near. Sergeant Cuff and I went straight to my mistress's room.

I declare my lady turned a shade paler at the sight of him! She commanded herself, however, in other respects, and asked the Sergeant if he had any objection to my being present. She was so good as to add, that I was her trusted adviser, as well as her old servant, and that in anything which related to the household I was the person whom it might be most profitable to consult. The Sergeant politely answered that he would take my presence as a favour, having something to say about the servants in general, and having found my experience in that quarter already of some use to him. My lady pointed to two chairs, and we set in for our conference immediately.

'I have already formed an opinion on this case,' says Sergeant Cuff, 'which I beg your ladyship's permission to keep to myself for the present. My business now is to mention what I have discovered upstairs in Miss Verinder's sitting-room, and what I have decided (with your ladyship's leave) on doing next.'

He then went into the matter of the smear on the paint, and stated the conclusions he drew from it – just as he had stated them (only with greater respect of language) to Superintendent Seegrave. 'One thing,' he said, in conclusion, 'is certain. The Diamond is missing out of the drawer in the cabinet. Another thing is next to certain. The marks from the smear on the door must be on some article of dress belonging to somebody in this house. We must discover that article of dress before we go a step further.'

'And that discovery,' remarked my mistress, 'implies, I presume, the discovery of the thief?'

'I beg your ladyship's pardon – I don't say the Diamond is stolen. I only say, at present, that the Diamond is missing. The discovery of the stained dress may lead the way to finding it.'

Her ladyship looked at me. 'Do you understand this?' she said.

'Sergeant Cuff understands it, my lady,' I answered.

'How do you propose to discover the stained dress?' inquired my mistress, addressing herself once more to the Sergeant. 'My good servants, who have been with me for years, have, I am ashamed to say, had their boxes and rooms searched already by the other officer. I can't and won't permit them to be insulted in that way a second time!'

(There was a mistress to serve! There was a woman in ten thousand, if you like!)

'That is the very point I was about to put to your ladyship,' said the Sergeant. 'The other officer has done a world of harm to this inquiry, by letting the servants see that he suspected them. If I give them cause to think themselves suspected a second time, there's no knowing what obstacles they may not throw in my way – the women especially. At the same time, their boxes *must* be searched again – for this plain reason, that the first investigation only looked for the Diamond, and that the second investigation must look for the stained dress. I quite agree with you, my lady, that the servants' feelings ought to be consulted. But I am equally clear that the servants' wardrobes ought to be searched.'

This looked very like a deadlock. My lady said so, in choicer language than mine.

'I have got a plan to meet the difficulty,' said Sergeant Cuff, 'if your ladyship will consent to it. I propose explaining the case to the servants.'

'The women will think themselves suspected directly,' I said, interrupting him.

'The women won't, Mr Betteredge,' answered the Sergeant, 'if I can tell them I am going to examine the wardrobes of *every*body – from her ladyship downwards – who slept in the house on Wednesday night. It's a mere formality,' he added, with a sidelook at my mistress; 'but the servants will accept it as even dealing between them and their betters;

and, instead of hindering the investigation, they will make a point of honour of assisting it.'

I saw the truth of that. My lady, after her first surprise was over, saw the truth of it also.

'You are certain the investigation is necessary?' she said.

'It's the shortest way that I can see, my lady, to the end we have in view.'

My mistress rose to ring the bell for her maid. 'You shall speak to the servants,' she said, 'with the keys of my wardrobe in your hand.'

Sergeant Cuff stopped her by a very unexpected question.

'Hadn't we better make sure first,' he asked, 'that the other ladies and gentlemen in the house will consent, too?'

'The only other lady in the house is Miss Verinder,' answered my mistress, with a look of surprise. 'The only gentlemen are my nephews, Mr Blake and Mr Ablewhite. There is not the least fear of a refusal from any of the three.'

I reminded my lady here that Mr Godfrey was going away. As I said the words, Mr Godfrey himself knocked at the door to say good-bye, and was followed in by Mr Franklin, who was going with him to the station. My lady explained the difficulty. Mr Godfrey settled it directly. He called to Samuel, through the window, to take his portmanteau upstairs again, and he then put the key himself into Sergeant Cuff's hand. 'My luggage can follow me to London,' he said, 'when the inquiry is over.' The Sergeant received the key with a becoming apology. 'I am sorry to put you to any inconvenience, sir, for a mere formality; but the example of their betters will do wonders in reconciling the servants to this inquiry.' Mr Godfrey, after taking leave of my lady, in a most sympathizing manner, left a farewell message for Miss Rachel, the terms of which made it clear to my mind that he had not taken No for an answer, and that he meant to put the marriage question to her once more, at the next opportunity. Mr Franklin, on following his cousin out, informed the Sergeant that all his clothes were open to examination, and that nothing he possessed was kept under lock and key. Sergeant Cuff made his best acknowledgments. His views, you will observe, had been met with the utmost readiness by my lady, by Mr Godfrey, and by Mr Franklin. There was only Miss Rachel now wanting to follow their lead, before we called the servants together, and began the search for the stained dress.

My lady's unaccountable objection to the Sergeant seemed to make our conference more distasteful to her than ever, as soon as we were left alone again. 'If I send you down Miss Verinder's keys,' she said to him, 'I presume I shall have done all you want of me for the present?'

'I beg your ladyship's pardon,' said Sergeant Cuff. 'Before we begin, I should like, if convenient, to have the washing-book. The stained article of dress may be an article of linen. If the search leads to nothing, I want to be able to account next for all the linen in the house, and for all the linen sent to the wash. If there is an article missing, there will be at least a presumption that it has got the paint-stain on it, and that it has been purposely made away with, yesterday or to-day, by the person owning it. Superintendent Seegrave,' added the Sergeant, turning to me, 'pointed the attention of the women-servants to the smear, when they all crowded into the room on Thursday morning. That *may* turn out, Mr Betteredge, to have been one more of Superintendent Seegrave's many mistakes.'

My lady desired me to ring the bell, and order the washing-book. She remained with us until it was produced, in case Sergeant Cuff had any further request to make of her after looking at it.

The washing-book was brought in by Rosanna Spearman. The girl had come down to breakfast that morning miserably pale and haggard, but sufficiently recovered from her illness of the previous day to do her usual work. Sergeant Cuff looked attentively at our second housemaid – at her face, when she came in; at her crooked shoulder, when she went out.

'Have you anything more to say to me?' asked my lady, still as eager as ever to be out of the Sergeant's society.

The great Cuff opened the washing-book, understood it perfectly in half a minute, and shut it up again. 'I venture to trouble your ladyship with one last question,' he said. 'Has the young woman who brought us this book been in your employment as long as the other servants?'

'Why do you ask?' said my lady.

'The last time I saw her,' answered the Sergeant, 'she was in prison for theft.'

After that, there was no help for it, but to tell him the truth. My mistress dwelt strongly on Rosanna's good conduct in her service, and on the high opinion entertained of her by the matron at the reformatory. 'You don't suspect her, I hope?' my lady added, in conclusion, very earnestly.

'I have already told your ladyship that I don't suspect any person in the house of thieving – up to the present time.'

After that answer, my lady rose to go upstairs, and ask for Miss Rachel's keys. The Sergeant was beforehand with me in opening the door for her. He made a very low bow. My lady shuddered as she passed him.

We waited, and waited, and no keys appeared. Sergeant Cuff made no remark to me. He turned his melancholy face to the window; he put his lanky hands into his pockets; and he whistled 'The Last Rose of Summer' softly to himself.

At last, Samuel came in, not with the keys, but with a morsel of paper for me. I got at my spectacles, with some fumbling and difficulty, feeling the Sergeant's dismal eyes fixed on me all the time. There were two or three lines on the paper, written in pencil by my lady. They informed me that Miss Rachel flatly refused to have her wardrobe examined. Asked for her reasons, she had burst out crying. Asked again, she had said: 'I won't, because I won't. I must yield to force if you use it, but I will yield to nothing else.' I understood my lady's disinclination to face Sergeant Cuff with such an answer from her daughter as that. If I had not been too old for the amiable weaknesses of youth, I believe I should have blushed at the notion of facing him myself.

'Any news of Miss Verinder's keys?' asked the Sergeant.

'My young lady refuses to have her wardrobe examined.'

'Ah!' said the Sergeant.

His voice was not quite in such a perfect state of discipline as his face. When he said 'Ah!' he said it in the tone of a man who had heard something which he expected to hear. He half angered and half frightened me – why, I couldn't tell, but he did it.

'Must the search be given up?' I asked.

'Yes,' said the Sergeant, 'the search must be given up, because your young lady refuses to submit to it like the rest. We must examine all the wardrobes in the house or none. Send Mr Ablewhite's portmanteau to London by the next train, and return the washing-book, with my compliments and thanks, to the young woman who brought it in.'

He laid the washing-book on the table, and, taking out his penknife, began to trim his nails.

'You don't seem to be much disappointed,' I said.

'No,' said Sergeant Cuff; 'I am not much disappointed.'

I tried to make him explain himself.

'Why should Miss Rachel put an obstacle in your way?' I inquired. 'Isn't it her interest to help you?'

'Wait a little, Mr Betteredge – wait a little.'

Cleverer heads than mine might have seen his drift. Or a person less fond of Miss Rachel than I was, might have seen his drift. My lady's horror of him might (as I have since thought) have meant that *she* saw his drift (as the scripture says) 'in a glass darkly'. I didn't see it yet – that's all I know.

'What's to be done next?' I asked.

Sergeant Cuff finished the nail on which he was then at work, looked at it for a moment with a melancholy interest, and put up his penknife.

'Come out into the garden,' he said, 'and let's have a look at the roses.'

❧ FOURTEEN ❧

THE NEAREST WAY TO THE GARDEN, on going out of my lady's sitting-room, was by the shrubbery path, which you already know of. For the sake of your better understanding of what is now to come, I may add to this, that the shrubbery path was Mr Franklin's favourite walk. When he was out in the grounds, and when we failed to find him anywhere else, we generally found him here.

I am afraid I must own that I am rather an obstinate old man. The more firmly Sergeant Cuff kept his thoughts shut up from me, the more firmly I persisted in trying to look in at them. As we turned into the shrubbery path, I attempted to circumvent him in another way.

'As things are now,' I said, 'if I was in your place, I should be at my wits' end.'

'If you were in my place,' answered the Sergeant, 'you would have formed an opinion – and, as things are now, any doubt you might previously have felt about your own conclusions, would be completely set at rest. Never mind for the present what those conclusions are, Mr Betteredge. I haven't brought you out here to draw me like a badger; I have brought you out here to ask for some information. You might have given it to me no doubt, in the house, instead of out of it. But doors and listeners have a knack of getting together; and, in my line of life, we cultivate a healthy taste for the open air.'

Who was to circumvent *this* man? I gave in – and waited as patiently as I could to hear what was coming next.

'We won't enter into your young lady's motives,' the Sergeant went on; 'we will only say it's a pity she declines to assist me, because, by so doing, she makes this investigation more difficult than it might otherwise have been. We must now try to solve the mystery of the smear on the door – which, you may take my word for it, means the mystery of the Diamond also – in some other way. I have decided to see the servants, and to search their thoughts and actions, Mr Betteredge, instead of searching their wardrobes. Before I begin, however, I want to ask you a question or two. You are an observant man – did you notice anything strange in any of the servants (making due allowance, of course, for fright and fluster), after the loss of the Diamond was found out? Any particular quarrel among them? Any one of them not in his or her usual spirits? Unexpectedly out of temper, for instance? or unexpectedly taken ill?'

I had just time to think of Rosanna Spearman's sudden illness at yesterday's dinner – but not time to make any answer – when I saw Sergeant Cuff's eyes suddenly turn aside towards the shrubbery; and I heard him say softly to himself, 'Hullo!'

'What's the matter?' I asked.

'A touch of the rheumatics in my back,' said the Sergeant, in a loud voice, as if he wanted some third person to hear us. 'We shall have a change in the weather before long.'

A few steps further brought us to the corner of the house. Turning off sharp to the right, we entered on the terrace, and went down, by the steps in the middle, into the garden below. Sergeant Cuff stopped there, in the open space, where we could see round us on every side.

'About that young person, Rosanna Spearman?' he said. 'It isn't very likely, with her personal appearance, that she has got a lover. But, for the girl's own sake, I must ask you at once whether *she* has provided herself with a sweetheart, poor wretch, like the rest of them?'

What on earth did he mean, under present circumstances, by putting such a question to me as that? I stared at him, instead of answering him.

'I saw Rosanna Spearman hiding in the shrubbery as we went by,' said the Sergeant.

'When you said "Hullo"?'

'Yes – when I said "Hullo!" If there's a sweetheart in the case, the hiding doesn't much matter. If there isn't – as things are in this house – the hiding is a highly suspicious circumstance, and it will be my painful duty to act on it accordingly.'

What, in God's name, was I to say to him? I knew the shrubbery was Mr Franklin's favourite walk; I knew he would most likely turn that way when he came back from the station; I knew that Penelope had over and over again caught her fellow-servant hanging about there, and had always declared to me that Rosanna's object was to attract Mr Franklin's attention. If my daughter was right, she might well have been lying in wait for Mr Franklin's return when the Sergeant noticed her. I was put between the two difficulties of mentioning Penelope's fanciful notion as if it was mine, or of leaving an unfortunate creature to suffer the consequences, the very serious consequences, of exciting the suspicion of Sergeant Cuff. Out of pure pity for the girl – on my soul and my character, out of pure pity for the girl – I gave the Sergeant the necessary explanations, and told him that Rosanna had been mad enough to set her heart on Mr Franklin Blake.

Sergeant Cuff never laughed. On the few occasions when anything amused him, he curled up a little at the corners of the lips, nothing more. He curled up now.

'Hadn't you better say she's mad enough to be an ugly girl and only a servant?' he asked. 'The falling in love with a gentleman of Mr Franklin Blake's manners and appearance doesn't seem to me to be the maddest part of her conduct by any means. However, I'm glad the thing is cleared up: it relieves one's mind to have things cleared up. Yes, I'll keep it a secret, Mr Betteredge. I like to be tender to human infirmity – though I don't get many chances of exercising that virtue in my line of life. You think Mr Franklin Blake hasn't got a suspicion of the girl's fancy for him? Ah! he would have found it out fast enough if she had been nice-looking. The ugly women have a bad time of it in this world; let's hope it will be made up to them in another. You have got a nice garden here, and a well-kept lawn. See for yourself how much better the flowers look with grass about them instead of gravel. No, thank you. I won't take a rose. It goes to my heart to break them off the stem. Just as it goes to your heart, you know, when there's something wrong in the servants' hall. Did you notice anything you couldn't account for in any of the servants when the loss of the Diamond was first found out?'

I had got on very fairly well with Sergeant Cuff so far. But the slyness with which he slipped in that last question put me on my guard. In plain English, I didn't at all relish the notion of helping his inquiries, when those inquiries took him (in the capacity of snake in the grass) among my fellow-servants.

'I noticed nothing,' I said, 'except that we all lost our heads together, myself included.'

'Oh,' says the Sergeant, 'that's all you have to tell me, is it?'

I answered, with (as I flattered myself) an unmoved countenance, 'That is all.'

Sergeant Cuff's dismal eyes looked me hard in the face.

'Mr Betteredge,' he said, 'have you any objection to oblige me by shaking hands? I have taken an extraordinary liking to you.'

(Why he should have chosen the exact moment when I was deceiving him to give me that proof of his good opinion, is beyond all comprehension! I felt a little proud – I really did feel a little proud of having been one too many at last for the celebrated Cuff!)

We went back to the house; the Sergeant requesting that I would give him a room to himself, and then send in the servants (the indoor servants only), one after another, in the order of their rank, from first to last.

I showed Sergeant Cuff into my own room, and then called the servants together in the hall. Rosanna Spearman appeared among them, much as usual. She was as quick in her way as the Sergeant in his, and I suspect she had heard what he said to me about the servants in general, just before he discovered her. There she was, at any rate, looking as if she had never heard of such a place as the shrubbery in her life.

I sent them in, one by one, as desired. The cook was the first to enter the Court of Justice, otherwise my room. She remained but a short time. Report, on coming out: 'Sergeant Cuff is depressed in his spirits; but Sergeant Cuff is a perfect gentleman.' My lady's own maid followed. Remained much longer. Report, on coming out: 'If Sergeant Cuff doesn't believe a respectable woman, he might keep his opinion to himself, at any rate!' Penelope went next. Remained only a moment or two. Report, on coming out: 'Sergeant Cuff is much to be pitied. He must have been crossed in love, father, when he was a young man.' The first housemaid followed Penelope. Remained, like my lady's maid, a long time. Report, on coming out: 'I didn't enter her ladyship's service, Mr Betteredge, to be doubted to my face by a low police-officer!' Rosanna Spearman went next. Remained longer than any of them. No report on coming out – dead silence, and lips as pale as ashes. Samuel, the footman, followed Rosanna. Remained a minute or two. Report, on coming out: 'Whoever blacks Sergeant Cuff's boots ought to be ashamed of himself.' Nancy, the kitchenmaid, went last. Remained a minute or two. Report, on coming out: 'Sergeant Cuff has a heart; *he* doesn't cut jokes, Mr Betteredge, with a poor hard-working girl.'

Going into the Court of Justice, when it was all over, to hear if there were any further commands for me, I found the Sergeant at his old trick – looking out of window, and whistling 'The Last Rose of Summer' to himself.

'Any discoveries, sir?' I inquired.

'If Rosanna Spearman asks leave to go out,' said the Sergeant, 'let the poor thing go; but let me know first.'

I might as well have held my tongue about Rosanna and Mr Franklin! It was plain enough; the unfortunate girl had fallen under Sergeant Cuff's suspicions, in spite of all I could do to prevent it.

'I hope you don't think Rosanna is concerned in the loss of the Diamond?' I ventured to say.

The corners of the Sergeant's melancholy mouth curled up, and he looked hard in my face, just as he had looked in the garden.

'I think I had better not tell you, Mr Betteredge,' he said. 'You might lose your head, you know, for the second time.'

I began to doubt whether I had been one too many for the celebrated Cuff after all! It was rather a relief to me that we were interrupted here by a knock at the door, and a message from the cook. Rosanna Spearman *had* asked to go out, for the usual reason, that her head was bad, and she wanted a breath of fresh air. At a sign from the Sergeant, I said, Yes. 'Which is the servants' way out?' he asked, when the messenger had gone. I showed him the servants' way out. 'Lock the door of your room,' says the Sergeant; 'and if anybody asks for me, say I'm in there, composing my mind.' He curled up again at the corners of the lips, and disappeared.

Left alone, under those circumstances, a devouring curiosity pushed me on to make some discoveries for myself.

It was plain that Sergeant Cuff's suspicions of Rosanna had been roused by something that he had found out at his examination of the servants in my room. Now, the only two servants (excepting Rosanna herself) who had remained under examination for any length of time, were my lady's own maid and the first housemaid, those two being also the women who had taken the lead in persecuting their unfortunate fellow-servant from the first. Reaching these conclusions, I looked in on them, casually as it might be, in the servants' hall, and, finding tea going forward, instantly invited myself to that meal. (For, *nota bene*, a drop of tea is to a woman's tongue what a drop of oil is to a wasting lamp.)

My reliance on the tea-pot, as an ally, did not go unrewarded. In less than half an hour I knew as much as the Sergeant himself.

My lady's maid and the housemaid had, it appeared, neither of them believed in Rosanna's illness of the previous day. These two devils – I ask your pardon; but how else *can* you describe a couple of spiteful women? – had stolen upstairs, at intervals during the Thursday afternoon; had tried Rosanna's door and found it locked; had knocked, and not been answered; had listened, and not heard a sound inside. When the girl had come down to tea, and had been sent up, still out of sorts, to bed again, the two devils aforesaid had tried her door once more, and found it locked; had looked at the keyhole, and found it stopped up; had seen a light under the door at midnight, and had heard the crackling of a fire (a fire in a servant's bedroom in the month of June!) at four in the morning. All this they had told Sergeant Cuff, who, in return for their anxiety to enlighten him, had eyed them with sour and suspicious looks, and had shown them plainly that he didn't believe either one or the other. Hence, the unfavourable reports of him which these two women had brought out with them from the examination. Hence, also (without reckoning the influence of the tea-pot), their readiness to let their tongues run to any length on the subject of the Sergeant's ungracious behaviour to them.

Having had some experience of the great Cuff's roundabout ways, and having last seen him evidently bent on following Rosanna privately when she went out for her walk, it seemed clear to me that he had thought it unadvisable to let the lady's maid and the housemaid know how materially they had helped him. They were just the sort of women, if he had treated their evidence as trustworthy, to have been puffed up by it, and to have said or done something which would have put Rosanna Spearman on her guard.

I walked out in the fine summer afternoon, very sorry for the poor girl, and very uneasy in my mind at the turn things had taken. Drifting towards the shrubbery, some time later, there I met Mr Franklin. After returning from seeing his cousin off at the station, he had been with my lady, holding a long conversation with her. She had told him of Miss Rachel's unaccountable refusal to let her wardrobe be examined; and had put him in such low spirits about my young lady, that he seemed to shrink from speaking on the subject. The family temper appeared in his face that evening, for the first time in my experience of him.

'Well, Betteredge,' he said, 'how does the atmosphere of mystery and suspicion in which we are all living now, agree with you? Do you remember that morning when I first came here with the Moonstone? I wish to God we had thrown it into the quicksand!'

After breaking out in that way, he abstained from speaking again until he had composed himself. We walked silently, side by side, for a minute or two, and then he asked me what had become of Sergeant Cuff. It was impossible to put Mr Franklin off with the excuse of the Sergeant being in my room, composing his mind. I told him exactly what had happened, mentioning particularly what my lady's maid and the housemaid had said about Rosanna Spearman.

Mr Franklin's clear head saw the turn the Sergeant's suspicions had taken, in the twinkling of an eye.

'Didn't you tell me this morning,' he said, 'that one of the tradespeople declared he had met Rosanna yesterday, on the footway to Frizinghall, when we supposed her to be ill in her room?'

'Yes, sir.'

'If my aunt's maid and the other woman have spoken the truth, you may depend upon it the tradesman *did* meet her. The girl's attack of illness was a blind to deceive us. She had some guilty reason for going to the town secretly. The paint-stained dress is a dress of hers; and the fire heard crackling in her room at four in the morning was a fire lit to destroy it. Rosanna Spearman has stolen the Diamond. I'll go in directly, and tell my aunt the turn things have taken.'

'Not just yet, if you please, sir,' said a melancholy voice behind us.

We both turned about, and found ourselves face to face with Sergeant Cuff.

'Why not just yet?' asked Mr Franklin.

'Because, sir, if you tell her ladyship, her ladyship will tell Miss Verinder.'

'Suppose she does. What then?' Mr Franklin said those words with a sudden heat and vehemence, as if the Sergeant had mortally offended him.

'Do you think it's wise, sir,' said Sergeant Cuff, quietly, 'to put such a question as that to me – at such a time as this?'

There was a moment's silence between them: Mr Franklin walked close up to the Sergeant. The two looked each other straight in the face. Mr Franklin spoke first, dropping his voice as suddenly as he had raised it.

'I suppose you know, Mr Cuff,' he said, 'that you are treading on delicate ground?'

'It isn't the first time, by a good many hundreds, that I find myself treading on delicate ground,' answered the other, as immovable as ever.

'I am to understand that you forbid me to tell my aunt what has happened?'

'You are to understand, if you please, sir, that I throw up the case, if you tell Lady Verinder, or tell anybody, what has happened, until I give you leave.'

That settled it. Mr Franklin had no choice but to submit. He turned away in anger – and left us.

I had stood there listening to them, all in a tremble; not knowing whom to suspect, or what to think next. In the midst of my confusion, two things, however, were plain to me. First, that my young lady was, in some unaccountable manner, at the bottom of the sharp speeches that had passed between them. Second, that they thoroughly understood each other, without having previously exchanged a word of explanation on either side.

'Mr Betteredge,' says the Sergeant, 'you have done a very foolish thing in my absence. You have done a little detective business on your own account. For the future, perhaps you will be so obliging as to do your detective business along with me.'

He took me by the arm, and walked me away with him along the road by which he had come. I dare say I had deserved his reproof – but I was not going to help him to set traps for Rosanna Spearman, for all that. Thief or no thief, legal or not legal, I don't care – I pitied her.

'What do you want of me?' I asked, shaking him off, and stopping short.

'Only a little information about the country round here,' said the Sergeant.

I couldn't well object to improve Sergeant Cuff in his geography.

'Is there any path, in that direction, leading to the sea-beach from this house?' asked the Sergeant. He pointed, as he spoke, to the fir-plantation which led to the Shivering Sand.

'Yes,' I said, 'there is a path.'

'Show it to me.'

Side by side, in the grey of the summer evening, Sergeant Cuff and I set forth for the Shivering Sand.

❧ FIFTEEN ❧

THE SERGEANT REMAINED SILENT, thinking his own thoughts, till we entered the plantation of firs which led to the quicksand. There he roused himself, like a man whose mind was made up, and spoke to me again.

'Mr Betteredge,' he said, 'as you have honoured me by taking an oar in my boat, and as you may, I think, be of some assistance to me before the evening is out, I see no use in our mystifying one another any longer, and I propose to set you an example of plain speaking on my side. You are determined to give me no information to the prejudice of Rosanna Spearman, because she has been a good girl to *you*, and because you pity her heartily. Those humane considerations do you a world of credit, but they happen in this instance to be humane considerations clean thrown away. Rosanna Spearman is not in the slightest danger of getting into trouble – no, not if I fix her with being concerned in the disappearance of the Diamond, on evidence which is as plain as the nose on your face!'

'Do you mean that my lady won't prosecute?' I asked.

'I mean that your lady *can't* prosecute,' said the Sergeant. 'Rosanna Spearman is simply an instrument in the hands of another person, and Rosanna Spearman will be held harmless for that other person's sake.'

He spoke like a man in earnest – there was no denying that. Still, I felt something stirring uneasily against him in my mind. 'Can't you give that other person a name?' I said.

'Can't *you*, Mr Betteredge?

'No.'

Sergeant Cuff stood stock-still, and surveyed me with a look of melancholy interest.

'It's always a pleasure to me to be tender towards human infirmity,' he said. 'I feel particularly tender at the present moment, Mr Betteredge, towards you. And you, with the same excellent motive, feel particularly tender towards Rosanna Spearman, don't you? Do you happen to know whether she has had a new outfit of linen lately?'

What he meant by slipping in this extraordinary question unawares, I was at a total loss to imagine. Seeing no possible injury to Rosanna if I owned the truth, I answered that the girl had come to us rather sparely provided with linen, and that my lady, in recompense for her good conduct (I laid a stress on her good conduct), had given her a new outfit not a fortnight since.

'This is a miserable world,' says the Sergeant. 'Human life, Mr Betteredge, is a sort of target – misfortune is always firing at it, and always hitting the mark. But for that outfit, we should have discovered a new nightgown or petticoat among Rosanna's things, and have nailed her in that way. You're not at a loss to follow me, are you? You have examined the servants yourself, and you know what discoveries two of them made outside Rosanna's door. Surely you know what the girl was about yesterday, after she was taken ill? You can't guess? Oh dear me, it's as plain as that strip of light there, at the end of the trees. At eleven, on Thursday morning, Superintendent Seegrave (who is a mass of human infirmity) points out to all the women-servants the smear on the door. Rosanna has her own reasons for suspecting her own things; she takes the first opportunity of getting to her room, finds the paint-stain on her nightgown, or petticoat, or what not, shams ill and slips away to the town, gets the materials for making a new petticoat or nightgown, makes it alone in her room on the Thursday night, lights a fire (not to destroy it; two of her fellow-servants are prying outside her door, and she knows better than to make a smell of burning, and to have a lot of tinder to get rid of) – lights a fire, I say, to dry and iron the substitute dress after wringing it out, keeps the stained dress hidden (probably *on* her), and is at this moment occupied in making away with it, in some convenient place, on that lonely bit of beach ahead of us. I have traced her this evening to your fishing village, and to one particular cottage, which we may possibly have to visit, before we go back. She stopped in the cottage for some time, and she came out with (as I believe) something hidden under her cloak. A cloak (on a woman's back) is an emblem of charity – it covers a multitude of sins. I saw her set off northwards along the coast, after leaving the cottage. Is your sea-shore here considered a fine specimen of marine landscape, Mr Betteredge?'

I answered, 'Yes,' as shortly as might be.

'Tastes differ,' says Sergeant Cuff. 'Looking at it from my point of view, I never saw a marine landscape that I admired less. If you happen to be following another person along your sea-coast, and if that person happens to look round, there isn't a scrap of cover to hide you anywhere. I had to choose between taking Rosanna in custody on suspicion, or leaving her, for the time being, with her little game in her own hands. For reasons which I won't trouble you with, I decided on making any sacrifice rather than give the alarm as soon as to-night to a certain person who shall be nameless between us. I came back to the house to ask you to take me to the north-end of the beach by another way. Sand – in respect of its printing off people's footsteps – is one of the best detective officers I know. If we don't meet with Rosanna Spearman by coming round on her in this way, the sand may tell us what she has been at, if the light only lasts long enough. Here is the sand. If you will excuse my suggesting it – suppose you hold your tongue, and let me go first?'

If there is such a thing known at the doctor's shop as a *detective-fever*, that disease had now got fast hold of your humble servant. Sergeant Cuff went on between the hillocks of sand, down to the beach. I followed him (with my heart in my mouth); and waited at a little distance for what was to happen next.

As it turned out, I found myself standing nearly in the same place where Rosanna Spearman and I had been talking together when Mr Franklin suddenly appeared before us, on arriving at our house from London. While my eyes were watching the Sergeant, my mind wandered away in spite of me to what had passed, on that former occasion, between Rosanna and me. I declare I almost felt the poor thing slip her hand again into mine, and give it a little grateful squeeze to thank me for speaking kindly to her. I declare I almost heard her voice telling me again that the Shivering Sand seemed to draw her to it against her own will, whenever she went out – almost saw her face brighten again, as it brightened when she first set eyes upon Mr Franklin coming briskly out on us from among the hillocks. My spirits fell lower and lower as I thought of these things – and the view of the lonesome little bay, when I looked about to rouse myself, only served to make me feel more uneasy still.

The last of the evening light was fading away; and over all the desolate place there hung a still and awful calm. The heave of the main ocean on the great sandbank out in the bay, was a heave that made no sound. The inner sea lay lost and dim, without a breath of wind to stir it. Patches of nasty ooze floated, yellow-white, on the dead surface of the water. Scum and slime shone faintly in certain places, where the last of the light still caught them on the two great spits of rock jutting out, north and south, into the sea. It was now the time of the turn of the tide: and even as I stood there waiting, the broad brown face of the quicksand began to dimple and quiver – the only moving thing in all the horrid place.

I saw the Sergeant start as the shiver of the sand caught his eye. After looking at it for a minute or so, he turned and came back to me.

'A treacherous place, Mr Betteredge,' he said; 'and no signs of Rosanna Spearman anywhere on the beach, look where you may.'

He took me down lower on the shore, and I saw for myself that his footsteps and mine were the only footsteps printed off on the sand.

'How does the fishing village bear, standing where we are now?' asked Sergeant Cuff.

'Cobb's Hole,' I answered (that being the name of the place), 'bears as near as may be, due south.'

'I saw the girl this evening, walking northward along the shore, from Cobb's Hole,' said the Sergeant. 'Consequently, she must have been walking towards this place. Is Cobb's Hole on the other side of that point of land there? And can we get to it – now it's low water – by the beach?'

I answered, 'Yes,' to both those questions.

'If you'll excuse my suggesting it, we'll step out briskly,' said the Sergeant. 'I want to find the place where she left the shore, before it gets dark.'

We had walked, I should say, a couple of hundred yards towards Cobb's Hole, when Sergeant Cuff suddenly went down on his knees on the beach, to all appearance seized with a sudden frenzy for saying his prayers.

'There's something to be said for your marine landscape here, after all,' remarked the Sergeant. 'Here are a woman's footsteps, Mr Betteredge! Let us call them Rosanna's footsteps, until we find evidence to the contrary that we can't resist. Very confused footsteps, you will please to observe – purposely confused, I should say. Ah, poor soul, she understands the detective virtues of sand as well as I do! But hasn't she been in rather too great a hurry to tread out the marks thoroughly? I think she has. Here's one footstep going *from* Cobb's Hole; and here is another going back to it. Isn't that the toe of her shoe pointing straight to the water's edge? And don't I see two heel-marks further down the beach, close at the water's edge also? I don't want to hurt your feelings, but I'm afraid Rosanna is sly. It looks as if she had determined to get to that place you and I have just come from, without leaving any marks on the sand to trace her by. Shall we say that she walked through the water from this point till she got to that ledge of rocks behind us, and came back the same way, and then took to the beach again where those two heel-marks are still left. Yes, we'll say that. It seems to fit in with my notion that she had something under her cloak, when she left the cottage. No! not something to destroy – for, in that case, where would have been the need of all these precautions to prevent my tracing the place at which her walk ended? Something to hide is, I think, the better guess of the two. Perhaps, if we go on to the cottage, we may find out what that something is.'

At this proposal, my detective-fever suddenly cooled. 'You don't want me,' I said. 'What good can I do?'

'The longer I know you, Mr Betteredge,' said the Sergeant, 'the more virtues I discover. Modesty – oh dear me, how rare modesty is in this world! and how much of that rarity you possess! If I go alone to the cottage, the people's tongues will be tied at the first question I put to them. If I go with you, I go introduced by a justly respected neighbour, and a flow of conversation is the necessary result. It strikes me in that light; how does it strike you?'

Not having an answer of the needful smartness as ready as I could have wished, I tried to gain time by asking him what cottage he wanted to go to.

On the Sergeant describing the place, I recognized it as a cottage inhabited by a fisherman named Yolland, with his wife and two grown-up children, a son and a daughter. If you will look back, you will find that, in first presenting Rosanna Spearman to your notice, I have described her as occasionally varying her walk to the Shivering Sand, by a visit to some friends of hers at Cobb's Hole. Those friends were the Yollands – respectable, worthy people, a credit to the neighbourhood. Rosanna's acquaintance with them had begun by means of the daughter, who was afflicted with a misshapen foot, and who was known in our parts by the name of Limping Lucy. The two deformed girls had, I suppose, a kind of fellow-feeling for each other. Anyway, the Yollands and Rosanna always appeared to get on together, at the few chances they had of meeting, in a pleasant and friendly manner. The fact of Sergeant Cuff having traced the girl to *their* cottage, set the matter of my helping his inquiries in quite a new light. Rosanna had merely gone where she was in the habit of going; and to show that she had been in company with the fisherman and his family was as good as to prove that she had been innocently occupied, so far, at any rate. It would be doing the girl a service, therefore, instead of an injury, if I allowed myself to be convinced by Sergeant Cuff's logic. I professed myself convinced by it accordingly.

We went on to Cobb's Hole, seeing the footsteps on the sand, as long as the light lasted.

On reaching the cottage, the fisherman and his son proved to be out in the boat; and Limping Lucy, always weak and weary, was resting on her bed upstairs. Good Mrs Yolland received us alone in her kitchen. When she heard that Sergeant Cuff was a celebrated character in London, she clapped a bottle of Dutch gin and a couple of clean pipes on the table, and stared as if she could never see enough of him.

I sat quiet in a corner, waiting to hear how the Sergeant would find his way to the subject of Rosanna Spearman. His usual roundabout manner of going to work proved, on this occasion, to be more round-about than ever. How he managed it is more than I could tell at the time, and more than I can tell now. But this is certain, he began with the Royal Family, the Primitive Methodists, and the price of fish; and he got from that (in his dismal, underground way) to the loss of the Moonstone, the spitefulness of our first housemaid, and the hard behaviour of the women-servants generally towards Rosanna Spearman. Having reached his subject in this fashion, he described himself as making his inquiries about the lost Diamond, partly with a view to find it, and partly for the purpose of clearing Rosanna from the unjust suspicions of her enemies in the house. In about a quarter of an hour from the time when we entered the kitchen, good Mrs Yolland was persuaded that she was talking to Rosanna's best friend, and was pressing Sergeant Cuff to comfort his stomach and revive his spirits out of the Dutch bottle.

Being firmly persuaded that the Sergeant was wasting his breath to no purpose on Mrs Yolland, I sat enjoying the talk between them, much as I have sat, in my time, enjoying a stage play. The great Cuff showed a wonderful patience; trying his luck drearily this way and that way, and firing shot after shot, as it were, at random, on the chance of hitting the mark. Everything to Rosanna's credit, nothing to Rosanna's prejudice – that was how it ended, try as he might; with Mrs Yolland talking nineteen to the dozen, and placing the most entire confidence in him. His last effort was made, when we had looked at our watches, and had got on our legs previous to taking leave.

'I shall now wish you good-night, ma'am,' says the Sergeant. 'And I shall only say, at parting, that Rosanna Spearman has a sincere well-wisher in myself, your obedient servant. But, oh dear me! she will never get on in her present place; and my advice to her is – leave it.'

'Bless your heart alive! she is *going* to leave it!' cries Mrs Yolland. (*Nota bene* – I translate Mrs Yolland out of the Yorkshire language into the English language. When I tell you that the all-accomplished Cuff was every now and then puzzled to understand her until I helped him, you will draw your own conclusions as to what *your* state of mind would be if I reported her in her native tongue.)

Rosanna Spearman going to leave us! I pricked up my ears at that. It seemed strange, to say the least of it, that she should have given no warning, in the first place, to my lady or to me. A certain doubt came up in my mind whether Sergeant Cuff's last random shot might not have hit the mark. I began to question whether my share in the proceedings was quite as harmless a one as I had thought it. It might be all in the way of the Sergeant's business to mystify an honest woman by wrapping her round in a network of lies; but it was my duty to have remembered, as a good Protestant, that the father of lies is the Devil – and that mischief and the Devil are never far apart. Beginning to smell mischief in the air, I tried to take Sergeant Cuff out. He sat down again instantly, and asked for a little drop of comfort out of the Dutch bottle. Mrs Yolland sat down opposite to him, and gave him his nip. I went on to the door, excessively uncomfortable, and said I thought I must bid them good-night – and yet I didn't go.

'So she means to leave?' says the Sergeant. 'What is she to do when she does leave? Sad, sad! The poor creature has got no friends in the world, except you and me.'

'Ah, but she has though!' says Mrs Yolland. 'She came in here, as I told you, this evening; and, after sitting and talking a little with my girl Lucy and me, she asked to go upstairs by herself, into Lucy's room. It's the only room in our place where there's pen and ink. "I want to write a letter to a friend," she says, "and I can't do it for the prying and peeping of the servants up at the house." Who the letter was written to I can't tell you: it must have been a mortal long one, judging by the time she stopped upstairs over it. I offered her a postage-stamp when she came down. She hadn't got the letter in her hand, and she didn't accept the stamp. A little close, poor soul (as you know), about herself and her doings. But a friend she has got somewhere, I can tell you; and to that friend, you may depend upon it, she will go.'

'Soon?' asked the Sergeant.

'As soon as she can,' says Mrs Yolland.

Here I stepped in again from the door. As chief of my lady's establishment, I couldn't allow this sort of loose talk about a servant of ours going, or not going, to proceed any longer in my presence, without noticing it.

'You must be mistaken about Rosanna Spearman,' I said. 'If she had been going to leave her present situation, she would have mentioned it, in the first place, to *me*.'

'Mistaken?' cries Mrs Yolland. 'Why, only an hour ago she bought some things she wanted for travelling – of my own self, Mr Betteredge, in this very room. And that reminds me,' says the wearisome woman, suddenly beginning to feel in her pocket, 'of something I have got it on my mind to say about Rosanna and her money. Are you either of you likely to see her when you go back to the house?'

'I'll take a message to the poor thing, with the greatest pleasure,' answered Sergeant Cuff, before I could put in a word edgewise.

Mrs Yolland produced out of her pocket, a few shillings and sixpences, and counted them out with a most particular and exasperating carefulness in the palm of her hand. She offered the money to the Sergeant, looking mighty loth to part with it all the while.

'Might I ask you to give this back to Rosanna, with my love and respects?' says Mrs Yolland. 'She insisted on paying me for the one or two things she took a fancy to this evening – and money's welcome enough in our house, I don't deny it. Still, I'm not easy in my mind about taking the poor thing's little savings. And to tell you the truth, I don't think my man would like to hear that I had taken Rosanna Spearman's money, when he comes back to-morrow morning from his work. Please say she's heartily welcome to the things she bought of me – as a gift. And don't leave the money on the table,' says Mrs Yolland, putting it down suddenly before the Sergeant, as if it burnt her fingers – 'don't, there's a good man! For times are hard, and flesh is weak; and I *might* feel tempted to put it back in my pocket again.'

'Come along!' I said, 'I can't wait any longer: I must go back to the house.'

'I'll follow you directly,' says Sergeant Cuff.

For the second time, I went to the door; and, for the second time, try as I might, I couldn't cross the threshold.

'It's a delicate matter, ma'am,' I heard the Sergeant say, 'giving money back. You charged her cheap for the things, I'm sure?'

'Cheap!' says Mrs Yolland. 'Come and judge for yourself.'

She took up the candle and led the Sergeant to a corner of the kitchen. For the life of me, I couldn't help following them. Shaken down in the corner was a heap of odds and ends (mostly old metal), which the fisherman had picked up at different times from wrecked ships, and which he hadn't found a market for yet, to his own mind. Mrs Yolland dived into this rubbish, and brought up an old japanned tin case, with a cover to it, and a hasp to hang it up by – the sort of thing they use, on board ship, for keeping their maps and charts, and such-like, from the wet.

'There!' says she. 'When Rosanna came in this evening, she bought the fellow to that. "It will just do," she says, "to put my cuffs and collars in, and keep them from being crumpled in my box." One and ninepence, Mr Cuff. As I live by bread, not a halfpenny more!'

'Dirt cheap!' says the Sergeant, with a heavy sigh.

He weighed the case in his hand. I thought I heard a note or two of 'The Last Rose of Summer' as he looked at it. There was no doubt now! He had made another discovery to the prejudice of Rosanna Spearman, in the place of all others where I thought her character was safest, and all through me! I leave you to imagine what I felt, and how sincerely I repented having been the medium of introduction between Mrs Yolland and Sergeant Cuff.

'That will do,' I said. 'We really must go.'

Without paying the least attention to me, Mrs Yolland took another dive into the rubbish, and came up out of it, this time, with a dog-chain.

'Weigh it in your hand, sir,' she said to the Sergeant. 'We had three of these; and Rosanna has taken two of them. "What can you want, my dear, with a couple of dog-chains?" says I. "If I join them together they'll go round my box nicely," says she. "Rope's cheapest," says I. "Chain's surest," says she. "Who ever heard of a box corded with chain!" says I. "Oh, Mrs Yolland, don't make objections!" says she; "let me have my chains!" A strange girl, Mr Cuff – good as gold, and kinder than a sister to my Lucy – but always a little strange. There! I humoured her. Three and sixpence. On the word of an honest woman, three *and* sixpence, Mr Cuff!'

'Each?' says the Sergeant.

'Both together!' says Mrs Yolland. 'Three and sixpence for the two.'

'Given away, ma'am,' says the Sergeant, shaking his head. 'Clean given away!'

'There's the money,' says Mrs Yolland, getting back sideways to the little heap of silver on the table, as if it drew her in spite of herself. 'The tin case and the dog-chains were all she bought, and all she took away. One and ninepence and three and sixpence – total, five and three. With my love and respects – and I can't find it in my conscience to take a poor girl's savings, when she may want them herself.'

'I can't find it in *my* conscience, ma'am, to give the money back,' says Sergeant Cuff. 'You have as good as made her a present of the things – you have indeed.'

'Is that your sincere opinion, sir?' says Mrs Yolland brightening up wonderfully.

'There can't be a doubt about it,' answered the Sergeant. 'Ask Mr Betteredge.'

It was no use asking *me*. All they got out of *me* was, 'Goodnight.'

'Bother the money!' says Mrs Yolland. With those words, she appeared to lose all command over herself; and, making a sudden snatch at the heap of silver, put it back, holus-bolus, in her pocket. 'It upsets one's temper, it does, to see it lying there, and nobody taking it,' cries this unreasonable woman, sitting down with a thump, and looking at Sergeant Cuff, as much as to say, 'It's in my pocket again now – get it out if you can!'

This time, I not only went to the door, but went fairly out on the road back. Explain it how you may, I felt as if one or both of them had mortally offended me. Before I had taken three steps down the village, I heard the Sergeant behind me.

'Thank you for your introduction, Mr Betteredge,' he said. 'I am indebted to the fisherman's wife for an entirely new sensation. Mrs Yolland has puzzled me.'

It was on the tip of my tongue to have given him a sharp answer, for no better reason than this – that I was out of temper with him, because I was out of temper with myself. But when he owned to being puzzled, a comforting doubt crossed my mind whether any great harm had been done after all. I waited in discreet silence to hear more.

'Yes,' says the Sergeant, as if he was actually reading my thoughts in the dark. 'Instead of putting me on the scent, it may console you to know, Mr Betteredge (with your interest in Rosanna), that you have been the means of throwing me off. What the girl has done, to-night, is clear enough, of course. She has joined the two chains, and has fastened them to the hasp in the tin case. She has sunk the case, in the water or in the quicksand. She has made the loose end of the chain fast to some place under the rocks, known only to herself. And she will leave the case secure at its anchorage till the present proceedings have come to an end; after which she can privately pull it up again out of its hiding-place, at her own leisure and convenience. All perfectly plain, so far. But,' says the Sergeant, with the first tone of impatience in his voice that I had heard yet, 'the mystery is – what the devil has she hidden in the tin case?'

I thought to myself, 'The Moonstone!' But I only said to Sergeant Cuff, 'Can't you guess?'

'It's not the Diamond,' says the Sergeant. 'The whole experience of my life is at fault, if Rosanna Spearman has got the Diamond.'

On hearing those words, the infernal detective-fever began, I suppose, to burn in me again. At any rate, I forgot myself in the interest of guessing this new riddle. I said rashly, 'The stained dress!'

Sergeant Cuff stopped short in the dark, and laid his hand on my arm.

'Is anything thrown into that quicksand of yours, ever thrown up on the surface again?' he asked.

'Never,' I answered. 'Light or heavy, whatever goes into the Shivering Sand is sucked down, and seen no more.'

'Does Rosanna Spearman know that?'

'She knows it as well as I do.'

'Then,' says the Sergeant, 'what on earth has she got to do but to tie up a bit of stone in the stained dress, and throw it into the quicksand? There isn't the shadow of a reason why she should have hidden it – and yet she *must* have hidden it. Query,' says the Sergeant, walking on again, 'is the paint-stained dress a petticoat or a night-gown? or is it something else which there is a reason for preserving at any risk? Mr Betteredge, if nothing occurs to prevent it, I must go to Frizinghall to-morrow, and discover what she bought in the town, when she privately got the materials for making the substitute dress. It's a risk to leave the house, as things are now – but it's a worse risk still to stir another step in this matter in the dark. Excuse my being a little out of temper; I'm degraded in my own estimation – I have let Rosanna Spearman puzzle me.'

When we got back, the servants were at supper. The first person we saw in the outer yard was the policeman whom Superintendent Seegrave had left at the Sergeant's disposal. The Sergeant asked if Rosanna Spearman had returned. Yes. When? Nearly an hour since. What had she done? She had gone upstairs to take off her bonnet and cloak – and she was now at supper quietly with the rest.

Without making any remark, Sergeant Cuff walked on, sinking lower and lower in his own estimation, to the back of the house. Missing the entrance in the dark, he went on (in spite of my calling to him) till he was stopped by a wicket-gate which led into the garden. When I joined him to bring him back by the right way, I found that he was looking up attentively at one particular window, on the bedroom floor, at the back of the house.

Looking up, in my turn, I discovered that the object of his contemplation was the window of Miss Rachel's room, and that lights were passing backwards and forwards there as if something unusual was going on.

'Isn't that Miss Verinder's room?' asked Sergeant Cuff.

I replied that it was, and invited him to go in with me to supper. The Sergeant remained in his place, and said something about enjoying the smell of the garden at night. I left him to his enjoyment. Just as I was turning in at the door, I heard 'The Last Rose of Summer' at the wicket-gate. Sergeant Cuff had made another discovery! And my young lady's window was at the bottom of it this time!

The latter reflection took me back again to the Sergeant, with a polite intimation that I could not find it in my heart to leave him by himself. 'Is there anything you don't understand up there?' I added, pointing to Miss Rachel's window.

Judging by his voice, Sergeant Cuff had suddenly risen again to the right place in his own estimation. 'You are great people for betting in Yorkshire, are you not?' he asked.

'Well?' I said. 'Suppose we are?'

'If I was a Yorkshireman,' proceeded the Sergeant, taking my arm, 'I would lay you an even sovereign, Mr Betteredge, that your young lady has suddenly resolved to leave the house. If I won on that event, I should offer to lay another sovereign, that the idea has occurred to her within the last hour.'

The first of the Sergeant's guesses startled me. The second mixed itself up somehow in my head with the report we had heard from the policeman, that Rosanna Spearman had returned from the sands within the last hour. The two together had a curious effect on me as we went in to supper. I shook off Sergeant Cuff's arm, and, forgetting my manners, pushed by him through the door to make my own inquiries for myself.

Samuel, the footman, was the first person I met in the passage.

'Her ladyship is waiting to see you and Sergeant Cuff,' he said, before I could put any questions to him.

'How long has she been waiting?' asked the Sergeant's voice behind me.

'For the last hour, sir.'

There it was again! Rosanna had come back; Miss Rachel had taken some resolution out of the common; and my lady had been waiting to see the Sergeant – all within the last hour! It was not pleasant to find these very different persons and things linking themselves together in this way. I went on upstairs, without looking at Sergeant Cuff, or speaking to him. My hand took a sudden fit of trembling as I lifted it to knock at my mistress's door.

'I shouldn't be surprised,' whispered the Sergeant over my shoulder, 'If a scandal was to burst up in the house to-night. Don't be alarmed! I have put the muzzle on worse family difficulties than this, in my time.'

As he said the words, I heard my mistress's voice calling to us to come in.

❧ SIXTEEN ❧

WE FOUND MY LADY WITH NO light in the room but the reading-lamp. The shade was screwed down so as to overshadow her face. Instead of looking up at us in her usual straightforward way, she sat close at the table, and kept her eyes fixed obstinately on an open book.

'Officer,' she said, 'is it important to the inquiry you are conducting, to know beforehand if any person now in this house wishes to leave it?'

'Most important, my lady.'

'I have to tell you, then, that Miss Verinder proposes going to stay with her aunt, Mrs Ablewhite, of Frizinghall. She has arranged to leave us the first thing to-morrow morning.'

Sergeant Cuff looked at me. I made a step forward to speak to my mistress – and, feeling my heart fail me (if I must own it), took a step back again, and said nothing.

'May I ask your ladyship *when* Miss Verinder informed you that she was going to her aunt's?' inquired the Sergeant.

'About an hour since,' answered my mistress.

Sergeant Cuff looked at me once more. They say old people's hearts are not very easily moved. *My* heart couldn't have thumped much harder than it did now, if I had been five-and-twenty again!

'I have no claim, my lady,' says the Sergeant, 'to control Miss Verinder's actions. All I can ask you to do is to put off her departure, if possible, till later in the day. I must go to Frizinghall myself to-morrow morning – and I shall be back by two o'clock, if not before. If Miss Verinder can be kept here till that time, I should wish to say two words to her – unexpectedly – before she goes.'

My lady directed me to give the coachman her orders, that the carriage was not to come for Miss Rachel until two o'clock. 'Have you more to say?' she asked of the Sergeant, when this had been done.

'Only one thing, your ladyship. If Miss Verinder is surprised at this change in the arrangements, please not to mention me as being the cause of putting off her journey.'

My mistress lifted her head suddenly from her book as if she was going to say something – checked herself by a great effort – and, looking back again at the open page, dismissed us with a sign of her hand.

'That's a wonderful woman,' said Sergeant Cuff, when we were out in the hall again. 'But for her self-control, the mystery that puzzles you, Mr Betteredge, would have been at an end to-night.'

At those words, the truth rushed at last into my stupid old head. For the moment, I suppose I must have gone clean out of my senses. I seized the Sergeant by the collar of his coat, and pinned him against the wall.

'Damn you!' I cried out, 'there's something wrong about Miss Rachel – and you have been hiding it from me all this time!'

Sergeant Cuff looked up at me – flat against the wall – without stirring a hand, or moving a muscle of his melancholy face.

'Ah,' he said, 'you've guessed it at last.'

My hand dropped from his collar, and my head sunk on my breast. Please to remember, as some excuse for my breaking out as I did, that I had served the family for fifty years. Miss Rachel had climbed upon my knees, and pulled my whiskers, many and many a time when she was a child. Miss Rachel, with all her faults, had been, to my mind, the dearest and prettiest and best young mistress that ever an old servant waited on, and loved. I begged Sergeant Cuff's pardon, but I am afraid I did it with watery eyes, and not in a very becoming way.

'Don't distress yourself, Mr Betteredge,' says the Sergeant, with more kindness than I had any right to expect from him. 'In my line of life, if we were quick at taking offence, we shouldn't be worth salt to our porridge. If it's any comfort to you, collar me again. You don't in the least know how to do it; but I'll overlook your awkwardness in consideration of your feelings.'

He curled up at the corners of his lips, and, in his own dreary way, seemed to think he had delivered himself of a very good joke.

I led him into my own little sitting-room, and closed the door.

'Tell me the truth, Sergeant,' I said. 'What do you suspect? It's no kindness to hide it from me now.'

'I don't suspect,' said Sergeant Cuff. 'I know.'

My unlucky temper began to get the better of me again.

'Do you mean to tell me, in plain English,' I said, 'that Miss Rachel has stolen her own Diamond?'

'Yes,' says the Sergeant; 'that is what I mean to tell you, in so many words. Miss Verinder has been in secret possession of the Moonstone from first to last; and she has taken Rosanna Spearman into her confidence, because she has calculated on our suspecting Rosanna Spearman of the theft. There is the whole case in a nut-shell. Collar me again, Mr Betteredge. If it's any vent to your feelings, collar me again.'

God help me! my feelings were not to be relieved in that way. 'Give me your reasons!' That was all I could say to him.

'You shall hear my reasons to-morrow,' said the Sergeant. 'If Miss Verinder refuses to put off her visit to her aunt (which you will find Miss Verinder will do), I shall be obliged to lay the whole case before your mistress tomorrow. And, as I don't know what may come of it, I shall request you to be present, and to hear what passes on both sides. Let the matter rest for to-night. No, Mr Betteredge, you don't get a word more on the subject of the Moonstone out of me. There is your table spread for supper. That's one of the many human infirmities which I always treat tenderly. If you will ring the bell, I'll say grace. "For what we are going to receive—" '

'I wish you a good appetite to it, Sergeant,' I said. 'My appetite is gone. I'll wait and see you served, and then I'll ask you to excuse me, if I go away, and try to get the better of this by myself.'

I saw him served with the best of everything – and I shouldn't have been sorry if the best of everything had choked him. The head gardener (Mr Begbie) came in at the same time, with his weekly account. The Sergeant got on the subject of roses and the merits of grass walks and gravel walks immediately. I left the two together, and went out with a heavy heart. This was the first trouble I remember for many a long year which wasn't to be blown off by a whiff of tobacco, and which was even beyond the reach of *Robinson Crusoe*.

Being restless and miserable, and having no particular room to go to, I took a turn on the terrace, and thought it over in peace and quietness by myself. It doesn't much matter what my thoughts were. I felt wretchedly old, and worn out, and unfit for my place – and began to wonder, for the first time in my life, when it would please God to take me. With all this, I held firm, notwithstanding, to my belief in Miss Rachel. If Sergeant Cuff had been Solomon in all his glory, and had told me that my young lady had mixed herself up in a mean and guilty plot, I should have had but one answer for Solomon, wise as he was, 'You don't know her; and I do.'

My meditations were interrupted by Samuel. He brought me a written message from my mistress.

Going into the house to get a light to read it by, Samuel remarked that there seemed a change coming in the weather. My troubled mind had prevented me from noticing it before. But, now my attention was roused, I heard the dogs uneasy, and the wind moaning low. Looking up at the sky, I saw the rack of clouds getting blacker and blacker, and hurrying faster and faster over a watery moon. Wild weather coming – Samuel was right, wild weather coming.

The message from my lady informed me, that the magistrate at Frizinghall had written to remind her about the three Indians. Early in the coming week, the rogues must needs be released, and left free to follow their own devices. If we had any more questions to ask them, there was no time to lose. Having forgotten to mention this, when she had last seen Sergeant Cuff, my mistress now desired me to supply the omission. The Indians had gone clean out of my head (as they have, no doubt, gone clean out of yours). I didn't see much use in stirring that subject again. However, I obeyed my orders on the spot, as a matter of course.

I found Sergeant Cuff and the gardener, with a bottle of Scotch whisky between them, head over ears in an argument on the growing of roses. The Sergeant was so deeply interested that he held up his hand, and signed to me not to interrupt the discussion, when I came in. As far as I could understand it, the question between them was, whether the white moss-rose did, or did not, require to be budded on the dog-rose to make it grow well. Mr Begbie said, Yes; and Sergeant Cuff said, No. They appealed to me, as hotly as a couple of boys. Knowing nothing whatever about the growing of roses, I steered a middle course – just as her Majesty's judges do, when the scales of justice bother them by hanging even to a hair. 'Gentlemen,' I remarked, 'there is much to be said on both sides.' In the temporary lull produced by that impartial sentence, I laid my lady's written message on the table, under the eyes of Sergeant Cuff.

I had got by this time, as nearly as might be, to hate the Sergeant. But truth compels me to acknowledge that, in respect of readiness of mind, he was a wonderful man.

In half a minute after he had read the message, he had looked back into his memory for Superintendent Seegrave's report; had picked out that part of it in which the Indians were concerned; and was ready with his answer. A certain great traveller, who understood the Indians and their language, had figured in Mr Seegrave's report, hadn't he? Very well. Did I know the gentleman's name and address? Very well again. Would I write them on the back of my lady's message? Much obliged to me. Sergeant Cuff would look that gentleman up, when he went to Frizinghall in the morning.

'Do you expect anything to come of it?' I asked. 'Superintendent Seegrave found the Indians as innocent as the babe unborn.'

'Superintendent Seegrave has been proved wrong, up to this time, in all his conclusions,' answered the Sergeant. 'It may be worth while to find out to-morrow whether Superintendent Seegrave was wrong about the Indians as well.' With that he turned to Mr Begbie, and took up the argument again exactly at the place where it had left off. 'This question between us is a question of soils and seasons, and patience and pains, Mr Gardener. Now let me put it to you from another point of view. You take your white moss rose—'

By that time, I had closed the door on them, and was out of hearing of the rest of the dispute.

In the passage, I met Penelope hanging about, and asked what she was waiting for.

She was waiting for her young lady's bell, when her young lady chose to call her back to go on with the packing for the next day's journey. Further inquiry revealed to me, that Miss Rachel had given it as a reason for wanting to go to her aunt at Frizinghall, that the house was unendurable to her, and that she could bear the odious presence of a policeman under the same roof with herself no longer. On being informed, half an hour since, that her departure would be delayed till two in the afternoon, she had flown into a violent passion. My lady, present at the time, had severely rebuked her, and then (having apparently something to say, which was reserved for her daughter's private ear) had sent Penelope out of the room. My girl was in wretchedly low spirits about the changed state of things in the house. 'Nothing goes right, father; nothing is like what it used to be. I feel as if some dreadful misfortune was hanging over us all.'

That was my feeling too. But I put a good face on it, before my daughter. Miss Rachel's bell rang while we were talking. Penelope ran up the back stairs to go on with the packing. I went by the other way to the hall, to see what the glass said about the change in the weather.

Just as I approached the swing-door leading into the hall from the servants' offices, it was violently opened from the other side; and Rosanna•Spearman ran by me, with a miserable look of pain in her face, and one of her hands pressed hard over her heart, as if the pang was in that quarter. 'What's the matter, my girl?' I asked, stopping her. 'Are you ill?' 'For God's sake, don't speak to me,' she answered, and twisted herself out of my hands, and ran on towards the servants' staircase. I called to the cook (who was within hearing) to look after the poor girl. Two other persons proved to be within hearing, as well as the cook. Sergeant Cuff darted softly out of my room, and asked what was the matter. I answered 'Nothing.' Mr Franklin, on the other side, pulled open the swing-door, and beckoning me into the hall, inquired if I had seen anything of Rosanna Spearman.

'She has just passed me, sir, with a very disturbed face, and in a very odd manner.'

'I am afraid I am innocently the cause of that disturbance, Betteredge.'

'You, sir!'

'I can't explain it,' says Mr Franklin; 'but, if the girl *is* concerned in the loss of the Diamond, I do really believe she was on the point of confessing everything – to me, of all the people in the world – not two minutes since.'

Looking towards the swing-door, as he said those last words, I fancied I saw it opened a little way from the inner side.

Was there anybody listening? The door fell to, before I could get to it. Looking through, the moment after, I thought I saw the tails of Sergeant Cuff's respectable black coat disappearing round the corner of the passage. He knew, as well as I did, that he could expect no more help from me, now that I had discovered the turn which his investigations were really taking. Under those circumstances, it was quite in his character to help himself, and to do it by the underground way.

Not feeling sure that I had really seen the Sergeant – and not desiring to make needless mischief, where, Heaven knows, there was mischief enough going on already – I told Mr Franklin that I thought one of the dogs had got into the house – and then begged him to describe what had happened between Rosanna and himself.

'Were you passing through the hall, sir?' I asked. 'Did you meet her accidentally, when she spoke to you?'

Mr Franklin pointed to the billiard-table.

'I was knocking the balls about,' he said, 'and trying to get this miserable business of the Diamond out of my mind. I happened to look up – and there stood Rosanna Spearman at the side of me, like a ghost! Her stealing on me in that way was so strange, that I hardly knew what to do at first. Seeing a very anxious expression in her face, I asked her if she wished to speak to me. She answered, "Yes, if I dare." Knowing what suspicion attached to her, I could only put one construction on such language as that. I confess it made me uncomfortable. I had no wish to invite the girl's confidence. At the same time, in the difficulties that now beset us, I could hardly feel justified in refusing to listen to her, if she was really bent on speaking to me. It was an awkward position; and I dare say I got out of it awkwardly enough. I said to her, "I don't quite understand you. Is there anything you want me to do?" Mind, Betteredge, I didn't speak unkindly! The poor girl can't help being ugly – I felt that, at the time. The cue was still in my hand, and I went on knocking the balls about, to take off the awkwardness of the thing. As it turned out, I only made matters worse still. I'm afraid I mortified her without meaning it! She suddenly turned away. "He looks at the billiard balls," I heard her say. "Anything rather than look at *me*!" Before I could stop her, she had left the hall. I am not quite easy about it, Betteredge. Would you mind telling Rosanna that I meant no unkindness? I have been a little hard on her, perhaps, in my own thoughts – I have almost hoped that the loss of the Diamond might be traced to *her*. Not from any ill-will to the poor girl: but – ' He stopped there, and going back to the billiard-table, began to knock the balls about once more.

After what had passed between the Sergeant and me, I knew what it was that he had left unspoken as well as he knew it himself.

Nothing but the tracing of the Moonstone to our second housemaid could now raise Miss Rachel above the infamous suspicion that rested on her in the mind of Sergeant Cuff. It was no longer a question of quieting my young lady's nervous excitement; it was a question of proving her innocence. If Rosanna had done nothing to compromise herself, the hope which Mr Franklin confessed to having felt would have been hard enough on her in all conscience. But this was not the case. She had pretended to be ill, and had gone secretly to Frizinghall. She had been up all night, making something or destroying something, in private. And she had been at the Shivering Sand, that evening, under circumstances which were highly suspicious, to say the least of them. For all these reasons (sorry as I was for Rosanna) I could not but think that Mr Franklin's way of looking at the matter was neither unnatural nor unreasonable, in Mr Franklin's position. I said a word to him to that effect.

'Yes, yes!' he said in return. 'But there is just a chance – a very poor one, certainly – that Rosanna's conduct may admit of some explanation which we don't see at present. I hate hurting a woman's feelings, Betteredge! Tell the poor creature what I told you to tell her. And if she wants to speak to me – I don't care whether I get into a scrape or not – send her to me in the library.' With those kind words he laid down the cue and left me.

Inquiry at the servants' offices informed me that Rosanna had retired to her own room. She had declined all offers of assistance with thanks, and had only asked to be left to rest in quiet. Here, therefore, was an end of any confession on her part (supposing she really had a confession to make) for that night. I reported the result to Mr Franklin, who, thereupon, left the library, and went up to bed.

I was putting the lights out, and making the windows fast, when Samuel came in with news of the two guests whom I had left in my room.

The argument about the white moss rose had apparently come to an end at last. The gardener had gone home, and Sergeant Cuff was nowhere to be found in the lower regions of the house.

I looked into my room. Quite true – nothing was to be discovered there but a couple of empty tumblers and a strong smell of hot grog. Had the Sergeant gone of his own accord to the bed-chamber that was prepared for him? I went upstairs to see.

After reaching the second landing, I thought I heard a sound of quiet and regular breathing on my left-hand side. My left-hand side led to the corridor which communicated with Miss Rachel's room. I looked in, and there, coiled up on three chairs placed right across the passage – there, with a red handkerchief tied round his grizzled head, and his respectable black coat rolled up for a pillow, lay and slept Sergeant Cuff!

He woke, instantly and quietly, like a dog, the moment I approached him.

'Good-night, Mr Betteredge,' he said. 'And mind, if you ever take to growing roses, the white moss rose is all the better for *not* being budded on the dog-rose, whatever the gardener may say to the contrary!'

'What are you doing here?' I asked. 'Why are you not in your proper bed?'

'I am not in my proper bed,' answered the Sergeant, 'because I am one of the many people in this miserable world who can't earn their money honestly and easily at the same time. There was a coincidence, this evening, between the period of Rosanna Spearman's return from the Sands and the period when Miss Verinder stated her resolution to leave the house. Whatever Rosanna may have hidden, it's clear to my mind that your young lady couldn't go away until she knew that it *was* hidden. The two must have communicated privately once already to-night. If they try to communicate again, when the house is quiet, I want to be in the way, and stop it. Don't blame me for upsetting your sleeping arrangements, Mr Betteredge – blame the Diamond.'

'I wish to God the Diamond had never found its way into this house!' I broke out.

Sergeant Cuff looked with a rueful face at the three chairs on which he had condemned himself to pass the night.

'So do I,' he said, gravely.

❦ SEVENTEEN ❧

NOTHING HAPPENED IN THE NIGHT; and (I am happy to add) no attempt at communication between Miss Rachel and Rosanna rewarded the vigilance of Sergeant Cuff.

I had expected the Sergeant to set off for Frizinghall the first thing in the morning. He waited about, however, as if he had something else to do first. I left him to his own devices; and going into the grounds shortly after, met Mr Franklin on his favourite walk by the shrubbery side.

Before we had exchanged two words, the Sergeant unexpectedly joined us. He made up to Mr Franklin, who received him, I must own, haughtily enough. 'Have you anything to say to me?' was all the return he got for politely wishing Mr Franklin good morning.

'I have something to say to you, sir,' answered the Sergeant, 'on the subject of the inquiry I am conducting here. You detected the turn that inquiry was really taking, yesterday. Naturally enough, in your position, you are shocked and distressed. Naturally enough, also, you visit your own angry sense of your own family scandal upon me.'

'What do you want?' Mr Franklin broke in, sharply enough.

'I want to remind you, sir, that I have at any rate, thus far, not been *proved* to be wrong. Bearing that in mind, be pleased to remember, at the same time, that I am an officer of the law acting here under the sanction of the mistress of the house. Under these circumstances, is it, or is it not, your duty as a good citizen, to assist me with any special information which you may happen to possess?'

'I possess no special information,' says Mr Franklin.

Sergeant Cuff put that answer by him, as if no answer had been made.

'You may save my time, sir, from being wasted on an inquiry at a distance,' he went on, 'if you choose to understand me and speak out.'

'I don't understand you,' answered Mr Franklin; 'and I have nothing to say.'

'One of the female servants (I won't mention names) spoke to you privately, sir, last night.'

Once more Mr Franklin cut him short; once more Mr Franklin answered, 'I have nothing to say.'

Standing by in silence, I thought of the movement in the swing-door on the previous evening, and of the coat-tails which I had seen disappearing down the passage. Sergeant Cuff had, no doubt, just heard enough, before I interrupted him, to make him suspect that Rosanna had relieved her mind by confessing something to Mr Franklin Blake.

This notion had barely struck me – when who should appear at the end of the shrubbery walk but Rosanna Spearman in her own proper person! She was followed by Penelope, who was evidently trying to make her retrace her steps to the house. Seeing that Mr Franklin was not alone, Rosanna came to a standstill, evidently in great perplexity what to do next. Penelope waited behind her. Mr Franklin saw the girls as soon as I saw them. The Sergeant, with his devilish cunning, took on not to have noticed them at all. All this happened in an instant. Before either Mr Franklin or I could say a word, Sergeant Cuff struck in smoothly, with an appearance of continuing the previous conversation.

'You needn't be afraid of harming the girl, sir,' he said to Mr Franklin, speaking in a loud voice, so that Rosanna might hear him. 'On the contrary, I recommend you to honour me with your confidence, if you feel any interest in Rosanna Spearman.'

Mr Franklin instantly took on not to have noticed the girls either. He answered, speaking loudly on his side:

'I take no interest whatever in Rosanna Spearman.'

I looked towards the end of the walk. All I saw at the distance was that Rosanna suddenly turned round, the moment Mr Franklin had spoken. Instead of resisting Penelope, as she had done the moment before, she now let my daughter take her by the arm and lead her back to the house.

The breakfast-bell rang as the two girls disappeared – and even Sergeant Cuff was now obliged to give it up as a bad job! He said to me quietly, 'I shall go to Frizinghall, Mr Betteredge; and I shall be back before two.' He went his way without a word more – and for some few hours we were well rid of him.

'You must make it right with Rosanna,' Mr Franklin said to me, when we were alone. 'I seem to be fated to say or do something awkward, before that unlucky girl. You must have seen yourself that Sergeant Cuff laid a trap for both of us. If he could confuse *me*, or irritate *her* into breaking out, either she or I might have said something which would answer his purpose. On the spur of the moment, I saw no better way out of it than the way I took. It stopped the girl from saying anything, and it showed the Sergeant that I saw through him. He was evidently listening, Betteredge, when I was speaking to you last night.'

He had done worse than listen, as I privately thought to myself. He had remembered my telling him that the girl was in love with Mr Franklin; and he had calculated on *that*, when he appealed to Mr Franklin's interest in Rosanna – in Rosanna's hearing.

'As to listening, sir,' I remarked (keeping the other point to myself), 'we shall all be rowing in the same boat, if this sort of thing goes on much longer. Prying, and peeping, and listening are the natural occupations of people situated as we are. In another day or two, Mr Franklin, we shall all be struck dumb together – for this reason, that we shall all be listening to surprise each other's secrets, and all know it. Excuse my breaking out, sir. The horrid mystery hanging over us in this house gets into my head like liquor, and makes me wild. I won't forget what you have told me. I'll take the first opportunity of making it right with Rosanna Spearman.'

'You haven't said anything to her yet about last night, have you?' Mr Franklin asked.

'No, sir.'

'Then say nothing now. I had better not invite the girl's confidence, with the Sergeant on the look-out to surprise us together. My conduct is not very consistent, Betteredge – is it? I see no way out of this business, which isn't dreadful to think of, unless the Diamond is traced to Rosanna. And yet I can't, and won't, help Sergeant Cuff to find the girl out.'

Unreasonable enough, no doubt. But it was my state of mind as well. I thoroughly understood him. If you will, for once in your life, remember that you are mortal, perhaps you will thoroughly understand him too.

The state of things, indoors and out, while Sergeant Cuff was on his way to Frizinghall, was briefly this:

Miss Rachel waited for the time when the carriage was to take her to her aunt's, still obstinately shut up in her own room. My lady and Mr Franklin breakfasted together. After breakfast, Mr Franklin took one of his sudden resolutions, and went out precipitately to quiet his mind by a long walk. I was the only person who saw him go; and he told me he should be back before the Sergeant returned. The change in the weather, foreshadowed overnight, had come. Heavy rain had been followed, soon after dawn, by high wind. It was blowing fresh as the day got on. But though the clouds threatened more than once, the rain still held off. It was not a bad day for a walk, if you were young and strong, and could breast the great gusts of wind which came sweeping in from the sea.

I attended my lady after breakfast, and assisted her in the settlement of our household accounts. She only once alluded to the matter of the Moonstone, and that was in the way of forbidding any present mention of it between us. 'Wait till that man comes back,' she said, meaning the Sergeant. 'We *must* speak of it then: we are not obliged to speak of it now.'

After leaving my mistress, I found Penelope waiting for me in my room.

'I wish, father, you would come and speak to Rosanna,' she said. 'I am very uneasy about her.'

I suspected what was the matter readily enough. But it is a maxim of mine that men (being superior creatures) are bound to improve women – if they can. When a woman wants me to do anything (my daughter, or not, it doesn't matter), I always insist on knowing why. The oftener you make them rummage their own minds for a reason, the more manageable you will find them in all the relations of life. It isn't their fault (poor wretches!) that they act first, and think afterwards; it's the fault of the fools who humour them.

Penelope's reason why, on this occasion, may be given in her own words. 'I am afraid, father,' she said, 'Mr Franklin has hurt Rosanna cruelly, without intending it.'

'What took Rosanna into the shrubbery walk?' I asked.

'Her own madness,' says Penelope; 'I can call it nothing else. She was bent on speaking to Mr Franklin, this morning, come what might of it. I did my best to stop her; you saw that. If I could only have got her away before she heard those dreadful words—'

'There! there!' I said, 'don't lose your head. I can't call to mind that anything happened to alarm Rosanna.'

'Nothing to alarm her, father. But Mr Franklin said he took no interest whatever in her – and, oh, he said it in such a cruel voice!'

'He said it to stop the Sergeant's mouth,' I answered.

'I told her that,' says Penelope. 'But you see, father (though Mr Franklin isn't to blame), he's been mortifying and disappointing her for weeks and weeks past; and now this comes on the top of it all! She has no right, of course, to expect him to take any interest in her. It's quite monstrous that she should forget herself and her station in that way. But she seems to have lost pride, and proper feeling, and everything. She frightened me, father, when Mr Franklin said those words. They seemed to turn her into stone. A sudden quiet came over her, and she has gone about her work, ever since, like a woman in a dream.'

I began to feel a little uneasy. There was something in the way Penelope put it which silenced my superior sense. I called to mind, now my thoughts were directed that way, what had passed between Mr Franklin and Rosanna overnight. She looked cut to the heart on that occasion; and now, as ill-luck would have it, she had been unavoidably stung again, poor soul, on the tender place. Sad! sad! – all the more sad because the girl had no reason to justify her, and no right to feel it.

I had promised Mr Franklin to speak to Rosanna, and this seemed the fittest time for keeping my word.

We found the girl sweeping the corridor outside the bedrooms, pale and composed, and neat as ever in her modest print dress. I noticed a curious dimness and dullness in her eyes – not as if she had been crying, but as if she had been looking at something too long. Possibly, it was a misty something raised by her own thoughts. There was certainly no object about her to look at which she had not seen already hundreds on hundreds of times.

'Cheer up, Rosanna!' I said. 'You mustn't fret over your own fancies. I have got something to say to you from Mr Franklin.'

I thereupon put the matter in the right view before her, in the friendliest and most comforting words I could find. My principles, in regard to the other sex, are, as you may have noticed, very severe. But somehow or other, when I come face to face with the women, my practice (I own) is not conformable.

'Mr Franklin is very kind and considerate. Please to thank him.' That was all the answer she made me.

My daughter had already noticed that Rosanna went about her work like a woman in a dream. I now added to this observation, that she also listened and spoke like a woman in a dream. I doubted if her mind was in a fit condition to take in what I had said to her.

'Are you quite sure, Rosanna, that you understand me?' I asked.

'Quite sure.'

She echoed me, not like a living woman, but like a creature moved by machinery. She went on sweeping all the time. I took away the broom as gently and as kindly as I could.

'Come, come, my girl!' I said, 'this is not like yourself. You have got something on your mind. I'm your friend – and I'll stand your friend, even if you have done wrong. Make a clean breast of it, Rosanna – make a clean breast of it!'

The time had been, when my speaking to her in that way would have brought the tears into her eyes. I could see no change in them now.

'Yes,' she said, 'I'll make a clean breast of it.'

'To my lady?' I asked.

'No.'

'To Mr Franklin?'

'Yes; to Mr Franklin.'

I hardly knew what to say to that. She was in no condition to understand the caution against speaking to him in private, which Mr Franklin had directed me to give her. Feeling my way, little by little, I only told her Mr Franklin had gone out for a walk.

'It doesn't matter,' she answered. 'I shan't trouble Mr Franklin, to-day.'

'Why not speak to my lady?' I said. 'The way to relieve your mind is to speak to the merciful and Christian mistress who has always been kind to you.'

She looked at me for a moment with a grave and steady attention, as if she was fixing what I said in her mind. Then she took the broom out of my hands; and moved off with it slowly, a little way down the corridor.

'No,' she said, going on with her sweeping, and speaking to herself; 'I know a better way of relieving my mind than that.'

'What is it?'

'Please to let me go on with my work.'

Penelope followed her, and offered to help her.

She answered, 'No. I want to do my work. Thank you, Penelope.' She looked round at me. 'Thank you, Mr Betteredge.'

There was no moving her – there was nothing more to be said. I signed to Penelope to come away with me. We left her, as we had found her, sweeping the corridor, like a woman in a dream.

'This is a matter for the doctor to look into,' I said. 'It's beyond me.'

My daughter reminded me of Mr Candy's illness, owing (as you may remember) to the chill he had caught on the night of the dinner-party. His assistant – a certain Mr Ezra Jennings – was at our disposal, to be sure. But nobody knew much about him in our parts. He had been engaged by Mr Candy, under rather peculiar circumstances; and, right or wrong, we none of us liked him or trusted him. There were other doctors at Frizinghall. But they were strangers to our house; and Penelope doubted, in Rosanna's present state, whether strangers might not do her more harm than good.

I thought of speaking to my lady. But, remembering the heavy weight of anxiety which she already had on her mind, I hesitated to add to all the other vexations this new trouble. Still, there was a necessity for doing something. The girl's state was, to my thinking, downright alarming – and my mistress ought to be informed of it. Unwilling enough, I went to her sitting-room. No one was there. My lady was shut up with Miss Rachel. It was impossible for me to see her till she came out again.

I waited in vain till the clock on the front staircase struck the quarter to two. Five minutes afterwards, I heard my name called, from the drive outside the house. I knew the voice directly. Sergeant Cuff had returned from Frizinghall.

❧ EIGHTEEN ❧

GOING DOWN TO THE FRONT DOOR, I met the Sergeant on the steps.

It went against the grain with me, after what had passed between us, to show him that I felt any sort of interest in his proceedings. In spite of myself, however, I felt an interest that there was no resisting. My sense of dignity sank from under me, and out came the words: 'What news from Frizinghall?'

'I have seen the Indians,' answered Sergeant Cuff. 'And I have found out what Rosanna bought privately in the town, on Thursday last. The Indians will be set free on Wednesday in next week. There isn't a doubt on my mind, and there isn't a doubt on Mr Murthwaite's mind, that they came to this place to steal the Moonstone. Their calculations were all thrown out, of course, by what happened in the house on Wednesday night; and they have no more to do with the actual loss of the jewel than you have. But I can tell you one thing, Mr Betteredge – if *we* don't find the Moonstone, *they* will. You have not heard the last of the three jugglers yet.'

Mr Franklin came back from his walk as the Sergeant said those startling words. Governing his curiosity better than I had governed mine, he passed us without a word, and went on into the house.

As for me, having already dropped my dignity, I determined to have the whole benefit of the sacrifice. 'So much for the Indians,' I said. 'What about Rosanna next?'

Sergeant Cuff shook his head.

'The mystery in that quarter is thicker than ever,' he said. 'I have traced her to a shop at Frizinghall, kept by a linendraper named Maltby. She bought nothing whatever at any of the other drapers' shops, or at any milliners' or tailors' shops; and she bought nothing at Maltby's but a piece of long cloth. She was very particular in choosing a certain quality. As to quantity, she bought enough to make a nightgown.'

'Whose nightgown?' I asked.

'Her own, to be sure. Between twelve and three, on the Thursday morning, she must have slipped down to your young lady's room, to settle the hiding of the Moonstone while all the rest of you were in bed. In going back to her own room, her nightgown must have brushed the wet paint on the door. She couldn't wash out the stain; and she couldn't safely destroy the nightgown without first providing another like it, to make the inventory of her linen complete.'

'What proves that it was Rosanna's nightgown?' I objected.

'The material she bought for making the substitute dress,' answered the Sergeant. 'If it had been Miss Verinder's nightgown, she would have had to buy lace, and frilling, and Lord knows what besides; and she wouldn't have had time to make it in one night. Plain long cloth means a plain servant's nightgown. No, no, Mr Betteredge – all that is clear enough. The pinch of the question is – why, after having provided the substitute dress, does she hide the smeared nightgown, instead of destroying it? If the girl won't speak out, there is only one way of settling the difficulty. The hiding-place at the Shivering Sand must be searched – and the true state of the case will be discovered there.'

'How are you to find the place?' I inquired.

'I am sorry to disappoint you,' said the Sergeant – 'but that's a secret which I mean to keep to myself.'

(Not to irritate your curiosity, as he irritated mine, I may here inform you that he had come back from Frizinghall provided with a search-warrant. His experience in such matters told him that Rosanna was in all probability carrying about her a memorandum of the hiding-place, to guide her, in case she returned to it, under changed circumstances and after a lapse of time. Possessed of this memorandum, the Sergeant would be furnished with all that he could desire.)

'Now, Mr Betteredge,' he went on, 'suppose we drop speculation, and get to business. I told Joyce to have an eye on Rosanna. Where is Joyce?'

Joyce was the Frizinghall policeman, who had been left by Superintendent Seegrave at Sergeant Cuff's disposal. The clock struck two, as he put the question; and, punctual to the moment, the carriage came round to take Miss Rachel to her aunt's.

'One thing at a time,' said the Sergeant, stopping me as I was about to send in search of Joyce. 'I must attend to Miss Verinder first.'

As the rain was still threatening, it was the close carriage that had been appointed to take Miss Rachel to Frizinghall. Sergeant Cuff beckoned Samuel to come down to him from the rumble behind.

'You will see a friend of mine waiting among the trees, on this side of the lodge gate,' he said. 'My friend, without stopping the carriage, will get up into the rumble with you. You have nothing to do but to hold your tongue, and shut your eyes. Otherwise, you will get into trouble.'

With that advice, he sent the footman back to his place. What Samuel thought I don't know. It was plain, to my mind, that Miss Rachel was to be privately kept in view from the time when she left our house – if she did leave it. A watch set on my young lady! A spy behind her in the rumble of her mother's carriage! I could have cut my own tongue out for having forgotten myself so far as to speak to Sergeant Cuff.

The first person to come out of the house was my lady. She stood aside, on the top step, posting herself there to see what happened. Not a word did she say, either to the Sergeant or to me. With her lips closed, and her arms folded in the light garden cloak which she had wrapped round her on coming into the air, there she stood, as still as a statue, waiting for her daughter to appear.

In a minute more, Miss Rachel came downstairs – very nicely dressed in some soft yellow stuff, that set off her dark complexion, and clipped her tight (in the form of a jacket) round the waist. She had a smart little straw hat on her head, with a white veil twisted round it. She had primrose-coloured gloves that fitted her hands like a second skin. Her beautiful black hair looked as smooth as satin under her hat. Her little ears were like rosy shells – they had a pearl dangling from each of them. She came swiftly out to us, as straight as a lily on its stem, and as lithe and supple in every movement she made as a young cat. Nothing that I could discover was altered in her pretty face, but her eyes and her lips. Her eyes were brighter and fiercer than I liked to see; and her lips had so completely lost their colour and their smile that I hardly knew them again. She kissed her mother in a hasty and sudden manner on the cheek. She said, 'Try to forgive me, mamma' – and then pulled down her veil over her face so vehemently that she tore it. In another moment she had run down the steps, and had rushed into the carriage as if it was a hiding-place.

Sergeant Cuff was just as quick on his side. He put Samuel back, and stood before Miss Rachel, with the open carriage-door in his hand, at the instant when she settled herself in her place.

'What do you want?' says Miss Rachel, from behind her veil.

'I want to say one word to you, miss,' answered the Sergeant, 'before you go. I can't presume to stop your paying a visit to your aunt. I can only venture to say that your leaving us, as things are now, puts an obstacle in the way of my recovering your Diamond. Please to understand that; and now decide for yourself whether you go or stay.'

Miss Rachel never even answered him. 'Drive on, James!' she called out to the coachman.

Without another word, the Sergeant shut the carriage-door. Just as he closed it, Mr Franklin came running down the steps. 'Goodbye, Rachel,' he said, holding out his hand.

'Drive on!' cried Miss Rachel, louder than ever, and taking no more notice of Mr Franklin than she had taken of Sergeant Cuff.

Mr Franklin stepped back thunderstruck, as well he might be. The coachman, not knowing what to do, looked towards my lady, still standing immovable on the top step. My lady, with anger and sorrow and shame all struggling together in her face, made him a sign to start the horses, and then turned back hastily into the house. Mr Franklin, recovering the use of his speech, called after her, as the carriage drove off, 'Aunt! you were quite right. Accept my thanks for all your kindness – and let me go.'

My lady turned as though to speak to him. Then, as if distrusting herself, waved her hand kindly. 'Let me see you, before you leave us, Franklin,' she said, in a broken voice – and went on to her own room.

'Do me a last favour, Betteredge,' says Mr Franklin, turning to me, with the tears in his eyes. 'Get me away to the train as soon as you can!'

He too went his way into the house. For the moment, Miss Rachel had completely unmanned him. Judge from that, how fond he must have been of her!

Sergeant Cuff and I were left face to face, at the bottom of the steps. The Sergeant stood with his face set towards a gap in the trees, commanding a view of one of the windings of the drive which led from the house. He had his hands in his pockets, and he was softly whistling 'The Last Rose of Summer' to himself.

'There's a time for everything,' I said, savagely enough. 'This isn't a time for whistling.'

At that moment, the carriage appeared in the distance, through the gap, on its way to the lodge-gate. There was another man, besides Samuel, plainly visible in the rumble behind.

'All right!' said the Sergeant to himself. He turned round to me. 'It's no time for whistling, Mr Betteredge, as you say. It's time to take this business in hand, now, without sparing anybody. We'll begin with Rosanna Spearman. Where is Joyce?'

We both called for Joyce, and received no answer. I sent one of the stable-boys to look for him.

'You heard what I said to Miss Verinder?' remarked the Sergeant, while we were waiting.

'And you saw how she received it? I tell her plainly that her leaving us will be an obstacle in the way of my recovering her Diamond – and she leaves, in the face of that statement! Your young lady has got a travelling companion in her mother's carriage, Mr Betteredge – and the name of it is, the Moonstone.'

I said nothing. I only held on like death to my belief in Miss Rachel.

The stable-boy came back, followed – very unwillingly, as it appeared to me – by Joyce.

'Where is Rosanna Spearman?' asked Sergeant Cuff.

'I can't account for it, sir,' Joyce began; 'and I am very sorry. But somehow or other – '

'Before I went to Frizinghall,' said the Sergeant, cutting him short, 'I told you to keep your eyes on Rosanna Spearman, without allowing her to discover that she was being watched. Do you mean to tell me that you have let her give you the slip?'

'I am afraid, sir,' says Joyce, beginning to tremble, 'that I was perhaps a little *too* careful not to let her discover me. There are such a many passages in the lower parts of this house – '

'How long is it since you missed her?'

'Nigh on an hour since, sir.'

'You can go back to your regular business at Frizinghall,' said the Sergeant, speaking just as composedly as ever, in his usual quiet and dreary way. 'I don't think your talents are at all in our line, Mr Joyce. Your present form of employment is a trifle beyond you. Good morning.'

The man slunk off. I find it very difficult to describe how I was affected by the discovery that Rosanna Spearman was missing. I seemed to be in fifty different minds about it, all at the same time. In that state, I stood staring at Sergeant Cuff – and my powers of language quite failed me.

'No, Mr Betteredge,' said the Sergeant, as if he had discovered the uppermost thought in me, and was picking it out to be answered, before all the rest. 'Your young friend, Rosanna, won't slip through my fingers so easy as you think. As long as I know where Miss Verinder is, I have the means at my disposal of tracing Miss Verinder's accomplice. I prevented them from communicating last night. Very good. They will get together at Frizinghall, instead of getting together here. The present inquiry must be simply shifted (rather sooner than I had anticipated) from this house, to the house at which Miss Verinder is visiting. In the meantime, I'm afraid I must trouble you to call the servants together again.'

I went round with him to the servants' hall. It is very disgraceful, but it is not the less true, that I had another attack of the detective-fever, when he said those last words. I forgot that I hated Sergeant Cuff. I seized him confidentially by the arm. I said, 'For goodness' sake, tell us what you are going to do with the servants now?'

The great Cuff stood stockstill, and addressed himself in a kind of melancholy rapture to the empty air.

'If this man,' said the Sergeant (apparently meaning me), 'only understood the growing of roses, he would be the most completely perfect character on the face of creation!' After that strong expression of feeling, he sighed, and put his arm through mine. 'This is how it stands,' he said, dropping down again to business. 'Rosanna has done one of two things. She has either gone direct to Frizinghall (before I can get there), or she has gone first to visit her hiding-place at the Shivering Sand. The first thing to find out is, which of the servants saw the last of her before she left the house.'

On instituting this inquiry, it turned out that the last person who had set eyes on Rosanna was Nancy, the kitchenmaid.

Nancy had seen her slip out with a letter in her hand, and stop the butcher's man who had just been delivering some meat at the back door. Nancy had heard her ask the man to post the letter when he got back to Frizinghall. The man had looked at the address, and had said it was a round-about way of delivering a letter, directed to Cobb's Hole, to post it at Frizinghall – and that, moreover, on a Saturday, which would prevent the letter from getting to its destination until Monday morning. Rosanna had answered that the delivery of the letter being delayed till Monday was of no importance. The only thing she wished to be sure of was that the man would do what she told him. The man had promised to do it, and had driven away. Nancy had been called back to her work in the kitchen. And no other person had seen anything afterwards of Rosanna Spearman.

'Well?' I asked, when we were alone again.

'Well,' says the Sergeant. 'I must go to Frizinghall.'

'About the letter, sir?'

'Yes. The memorandum of the hiding-place is in that letter. I must see the address at the post-office. If it is the address I suspect, I shall pay our friend, Mrs Yolland, another visit on Monday next.'

I went with the Sergeant to order the pony-chaise. In the stable-yard we got a new light thrown on the missing girl.

◈ NINETEEN ◈

THE NEWS OF ROSANNA'S DISAPPEARANCE HAD, as it appeared, spread among the out-of-door servants. They too had made their inquiries; and they had just laid hands on a quick little imp, nicknamed 'Duffy' – who was occasionally employed in weeding the garden, and who had seen Rosanna Spearman as lately as half an hour since. Duffy was certain that the girl had passed him in the fir-plantation, not walking, but *running*, in the direction of the sea-shore.

'Does this boy know the coast hereabouts?' asked Sergeant Cuff.

'He has been born and bred on the coast,' I answered.

'Duffy!' says the Sergeant, 'do you want to earn a shilling? If you do, come along with me. Keep the pony-chaise ready, Mr Betteredge, till I come back.'

He started for the Shivering Sand, at a rate that my legs (though well enough preserved for my time of life) had no hope of matching. Little Duffy, as the way is with the young savages in our parts when they are in high spirits, gave a howl, and trotted off at the Sergeant's heels.

Here again, I find it impossible to give anything like a clear account of the state of my mind in the interval after Sergeant Cuff had left us. A curious and stupefying restlessness got possession of me. I did a dozen different needless things in and out of the house, not one of which I can now remember. I don't even know how long it was after the Sergeant had gone to the sands, when Duffy came running back with a message for me. Sergeant Cuff had given the boy a leaf torn out of his pocket-book, on which was written in pencil, 'Send me one of Rosanna Spearman's boots, and be quick about it.'

I despatched the first woman-servant I could find to Rosanna's room; and I sent the boy back to say that I myself would follow him with the boot.

This, I am well aware, was not the quickest way to take of obeying the directions which I had received. But I was resolved to see for myself what new mystification was going on, before I trusted Rosanna's boot in the Sergeant's hands. My old notion of screening the girl, if I could, seemed to have come back on me again, at the eleventh hour. This state of feeling (to say nothing of the detective-fever) hurried me off, as soon as I had got the boot, at the nearest approach to a run which a man turned seventy can reasonably hope to make.

As I got near the shore, the clouds gathered black, and the rain came down, drifting in great white sheets of water before the wind. I heard the thunder of the sea on the sand-bank at the mouth of the bay. A little further on, I passed the boy crouching for shelter under the lee of the sand-hills. Then I saw the raging sea, and the rollers tumbling in on the sand-bank, and the driven rain sweeping over the waters like a flying garment; and the yellow wilderness of the beach with one solitary black figure standing on it – the figure of Sergeant Cuff.

He waved his hand towards the north, when he first saw me. 'Keep on that side' he shouted. 'And come on down here to me!'

I went down to him, choking for breath, with my heart leaping as if it was like to leap out of me. I was past speaking. I had a hundred questions to put to him; and not one of them would pass my lips. His face frightened me. I saw a look in his eyes which was a look of horror. He snatched the boot out of my hand, and set it in a footmark on the sand, bearing south from us as we stood, and pointing straight towards the rocky ledge called the South Spit. The mark was not yet blurred out by the rain – and the girl's boot fitted it to a hair.

The Sergeant pointed to the boot in the footmark, without saying a word.

I caught at his arm, and tried to speak to him, and failed as I had failed when I tried before. He went on, following the footsteps down and down to where the rocks and the sand joined. The South Spit was just awash with the flowing tide; the waters heaved over the hidden face of the Shivering Sand. Now this way and now that, with an obstinate patience that was dreadful to see, Sergeant Cuff tried the boot in the footsteps, and always found it pointing the same way – straight *to* the rocks. Hunt as he might, no sign could he find anywhere of the footsteps walking *from* them.

He gave it up at last. Still keeping silence, he looked again at me; and then he looked out at the waters before us, heaving in deeper and deeper over the quicksand. I looked where he looked – and I saw his thought in his face. A dreadful dumb trembling crawled all over me on a sudden. I fell upon my knees on the beach.

'She has been back at the hiding-place,' I heard the Sergeant say to himself. 'Some fatal accident has happened to her on those rocks.'

The girl's altered looks, and words, and actions – the numbed, deadened way in which she listened to me, and spoke to me – when I had found her sweeping the corridor but a few hours since, rose up in my mind, and warned me, even as the Sergeant spoke, that his guess was wide of the dreadful truth. I tried to tell him of the fear that had frozen me up. I tried to say, 'The death she has died, Sergeant, was a death of her own seeking.' No! the words wouldn't come. The dumb trembling held me in its grip. I couldn't feel the driving rain. I couldn't see the rising tide. As in the vision of a dream, the poor lost creature came back before me. I saw her again as I had seen her in the past time – on the morning when I went to fetch her into the house. I heard her again, telling me that the Shivering Sand seemed to draw her to it against her will, and wondering whether her grave was waiting for her *there*. The horror of it struck at me, in some unfathomable way, through my own child. My girl was just her age. My girl, tried as Rosanna was tried, might have lived that miserable life, and died this dreadful death.

The Sergeant kindly lifted me up, and turned me away from the sight of the place where she had perished.

With that relief, I began to fetch my breath again, and to see things about me, as things really were. Looking towards the sand-hills, I saw the men-servants from out-of-doors, and the fisherman, named Yolland, all running down to us together; and all, having taken the alarm, calling out to know if the girl had been found. In the fewest words, the Sergeant showed them the evidence of the footmarks, and told them that a fatal accident must have happened to her. He then picked out the fisherman from the rest, and put a question to him, turning about again towards the sea: 'Tell me,' he said. 'Could a boat have taken her off, in such weather as this, from those rocks where her footmarks stop?'

The fisherman pointed to the rollers tumbling in on the sandbank, and to the great waves leaping up in clouds of foam against the headlands on either side of us.

'No boat that ever was built,' he answered, 'could have got to her through *that*.'

Sergeant Cuff looked for the last time at the footmarks on the sand, which the rain was now fast blurring out.

'There,' he said, 'is the evidence that she can't have left this place by land. And here,' he went on, looking at the fisherman, 'is the evidence that she can't have got away by sea.' He stopped, and considered for a minute. 'She was seen running towards this place, half an hour before I got here from the house,' he said to Yolland. 'Some time has passed since then. Call it, altogether, an hour ago. How high would the water be, at that time, on this side of the rocks?' He pointed to the south side – otherwise, the side which was not filled up by the quicksand.

'As the tide makes to-day,' said the fisherman, 'there wouldn't have been water enough to drown a kitten on that side of the Spit, an hour since.'

Sergeant Cuff turned about northward, towards the quicksand.

'How much on this side?' he asked.

'Less still,' answered Yolland. 'The Shivering Sand would have been just awash, and no more.'

The Sergeant turned to me, and said that the accident must have happened on the side of the quicksand. My tongue was loosened at that. 'No accident!' I told him. 'When she came to this place, she came, weary of her life, to end it here.'

He started back from me. 'How do you know?' he asked. The rest of them crowded round. The Sergeant recovered himself instantly. He put them back from me; he said I was an old man; he said the discovery had shaken me; he said, 'Let him alone a little.' Then he turned to Yolland, and asked, 'Is there any chance of finding her, when the tide ebbs again?' And Yolland answered, 'None. What the Sand gets, the Sand keeps for ever.' Having said that, the fisherman came a step nearer, and addressed himself to me.

'Mr Betteredge,' he said, 'I have a word to say to you about the young woman's death. Four foot out, broadwise, along the side of the Spit, there's a shelf of rock, about half a fathom down under the sand. My question is – why didn't she strike that? If she slipped, by accident, from off the Spit, she fell in where there's foothold at the bottom, at a depth that would barely cover her to the waist. She must have waded out, or jumped out, into the Deeps beyond – or she wouldn't be missing now. No accident, sir! The Deeps of the Quicksand have got her. And they have got her by her own act.'

After that testimony from a man whose knowledge was to be relied on, the Sergeant was silent. The rest of us, like him, held our peace. With one accord, we all turned back up the slope of the beach.

At the sandhillocks we were met by the under-groom, running to us from the house. The lad is a good lad, and has an honest respect for me. He handed me a little note, with a decent sorrow in his face. 'Penelope sent me with this, Mr Betteredge,' he said. 'She found it in Rosanna's room.'

It was her last farewell word to the old man who had done his best – thank God, always done his best – to befriend her.

'You have often forgiven me, Mr Betteredge, in past times. When you next see the Shivering Sand, try to forgive me once more. I have found my grave where my grave was waiting for me. I have lived, and died, sir, grateful for your kindness.'

There was no more than that. Little as it was, I hadn't manhood enough to hold up against it. Your tears come easy, when you're young, and beginning the world. Your tears come easy, when you're old, and leaving it. I burst out crying.

Sergeant Cuff took a step nearer to me – meaning kindly, I don't doubt. I shrank back from him. 'Don't touch me,' I said. 'It's the dread of you, that has driven her to it.'

'You are wrong, Mr Betteredge,' he answered, quietly. 'But there will be time enough to speak of it when we are indoors again.'

I followed the rest of them, with the help of the groom's arm. Through the driving rain we went back – to meet the trouble and the terror that were waiting for us at the house.

◈ TWENTY ◈

THOSE IN FRONT HAD SPREAD THE news before us. We found the servants in a state of panic. As we passed my lady's door, it was thrown open violently from the inner side. My mistress came out among us (with Mr

Franklin following, and trying vainly to compose her), quite beside herself with the horror of the thing.

'You are answerable for this!' she cried out, threatening the Sergeant wildly with her hand. 'Gabriel! give that wretch his money – and release me from the sight of him!'

The Sergeant was the only one among us who was fit to cope with her – being the only one among us who was in possession of himself.

'I am no more answerable for this distressing calamity, my lady, than you are,' he said. 'If, in half an hour from this, you still insist on my leaving the house, I will accept your ladyship's dismissal, but not your ladyship's money.'

It was spoken very respectfully, but very firmly at the same time – and it had its effect on my mistress as well as on me. She suffered Mr Franklin to lead her back into the room. As the door closed on the two, the Sergeant, looking about among the women-servants in his observant way, noticed that while all the rest were merely frightened, Penelope was in tears. 'When your father has changed his wet clothes,' he said to her, 'come and speak to us, in your father's room.'

Before the half-hour was out, I had got my dry clothes on, and had lent Sergeant Cuff such change of dress as he required. Penelope came in to us to hear what the Sergeant wanted with her. I don't think I ever felt what a good dutiful daughter I had, so strongly as I felt it at that moment. I took her and sat her on my knee – and I prayed God bless her. She hid her head on my bosom, and put her arms round my neck – and we waited a little while in silence. The poor dead girl must have been at the bottom of it, I think, with my daughter and with me. The Sergeant went to the window, and stood there looking out. I thought it right to thank him for considering us both in this way – and I did.

People in high life have all the luxuries to themselves – among others, the luxury of indulging their feelings. People in low life have no such privilege. Necessity, which spares our betters, has no pity on *us*. We learn to put our feelings back into ourselves, and to jog on with our duties as patiently as may be. I don't complain of this – I only notice it. Penelope and I were ready for the Sergeant, as soon as the Sergeant was ready on his side. Asked if she knew what had led her fellow-servant to destroy herself, my daughter answered (as you will foresee) that it was for love of Mr Franklin Blake. Asked next, if she had mentioned this notion of hers to any other person, Penelope answered, 'I have not mentioned it, for Rosanna's sake.' I felt it necessary to add a word to this. I said, 'And for Mr Franklin's sake, my dear, as well. If Rosanna *has* died for love of him, it is not with his knowledge or by his fault. Let him leave the house to-day, if he does leave it, without the useless pain of knowing the truth.' Sergeant Cuff said, 'Quite right,' and fell silent again;

comparing Penelope's notion (as it seemed to me) with some other notion of his own which he kept to himself.

At the end of the half-hour, my mistress's bell rang.

On my way to answer it, I met Mr Franklin coming out of his aunt's sitting-room. He mentioned that her ladyship was ready to see Sergeant Cuff – in my presence as before – and he added that he himself wanted to say two words to the Sergeant first. On our way back to my room, he stopped, and looked at the railway time-table in the hall.

'Are you really going to leave us, sir?' I asked. 'Miss Rachel will surely come right again, if you only give her time?'

'She will come right again,' answered Mr Franklin, 'when she hears that I have gone away, and that she will see me no more.'

I thought he spoke in resentment of my young lady's treatment of him. But it was not so. My mistress had noticed, from the time when the police first came into the house, that the bare mention of him was enough to set Miss Rachel's temper in a flame. He had been too fond of his cousin to like to confess this to himself, until the truth had been forced on him, when she drove off to her aunt's. His eyes once opened in that cruel way which you know of, Mr Franklin had taken his resolution – the one resolution which a man of any spirit *could* take – to leave the house.

What he had to say to the Sergeant was spoken in my presence. He described her ladyship as willing to acknowledge that she had spoken over-hastily. And he asked if Sergeant Cuff would consent – in that case – to accept his fee, and to leave the matter of the Diamond where the matter stood now. The Sergeant answered, 'No, sir. My fee is paid me for doing my duty. I decline to take it, until my duty is done.'

'I don't understand you,' says Mr Franklin.

'I'll explain myself, sir,' says the Sergeant. 'When I came here, I under-took to throw the necessary light on the matter of the missing Diamond. I am now ready, and waiting, to redeem my pledge. When I have stated the case to Lady Verinder as the case now stands, and when I have told her plainly what course of action to take for the recovery of the Moon-stone, the responsibility will be off my shoulders. Let her ladyship decide, after that, whether she does, or does not, allow me to go on. I shall then have done what I undertook to do – and I'll take my fee.'

In those words Sergeant Cuff reminded us that, even in the Detective Police, a man may have a reputation to lose.

The view he took was so plainly the right one, that there was no more to be said. As I rose to conduct him to my lady's room, he asked if Mr Franklin wished to be present. Mr Franklin answered, 'Not unless Lady Verinder desires it.' He added, in a whisper to me, as I was following the Sergeant out, 'I know what that man is going to say about Rachel;

and I am too fond of her to hear it, and keep my temper. Leave me by myself.'

I left him, miserable enough, leaning on the sill of my window, with his face hidden in his hands – and Penelope peeping through the door, longing to comfort him. In Mr Franklin's place, I should have called her in. When you are ill-used by one woman, there is great comfort in telling it to another – because, nine times out of ten, the other always takes your side. Perhaps, when my back was turned, he did call her in? In that case, it is only doing my daughter justice to declare that she would stick at nothing, in the way of comforting Mr Franklin Blake.

In the meantime, Sergeant Cuff and I proceeded to my lady's room.

At the last conference we had held with her, we had found her not over willing to lift her eyes from the book which she had on the table. On this occasion there was a change for the better. She met the Sergeant's eye with an eye that was as steady as his own. The family spirit showed itself in every line of her face; and I knew that Sergeant Cuff would meet his match, when a woman like my mistress was strung up to hear the worst he could say to her.

❧ TWENTY-ONE ❧

THE FIRST WORDS, WHEN WE had taken our seats, were spoken by my lady.

'Sergeant Cuff,' she said, 'there was perhaps some excuse for the inconsiderate manner in which I spoke to you half an hour since. I have no wish, however, to claim that excuse. I say, with perfect sincerity, that I regret it, if I wronged you.'

The grace of voice and manner with which she made him that atonement had its due effect on the Sergeant. He requested permission to justify himself – putting his justification as an act of respect to my mistress. It was impossible, he said, that he could be in any way responsible for the calamity which had shocked us all, for this sufficient reason, that his success in bringing his inquiry to its proper end depended on his neither saying nor doing anything that could alarm Rosanna Spearman. He appealed to me to testify whether he had, or had not, carried that object out. I could, and did, bear witness that he had. And there, as I thought, the matter might have been judiciously left to come to an end.

Sergeant Cuff, however, took it a step further, evidently (as you shall now judge) with the purpose of forcing the most painful of all possible explanations to take place between her ladyship and himself.

'I have heard a motive assigned for the young woman's suicide,' said the Sergeant, 'which may possibly be the right one. It is a motive quite unconnected with the case which I am conducting here. I am bound to add, however, that my own opinion points the other way. Some unbearable anxiety in connection with the missing Diamond, has, I believe, driven the poor creature to her own destruction. I don't pretend to know what that unbearable anxiety may have been. But I think (with your ladyship's permission) I can lay my hand on a person who is capable of deciding whether I am right or wrong.'

'Is the person now in the house?' my mistress asked, after waiting a little.

'The person has left the house, my lady.'

That answer pointed as straight to Miss Rachel as straight could be. A silence dropped on us which I thought would never come to an end. Lord! how the wind howled, and how the rain drove at the window, as I sat there waiting for one or other of them to speak again!

'Be so good as to express yourself plainly,' said my lady. 'Do you refer to my daughter?'

'I do,' said Sergeant Cuff, in so many words.

My mistress had her cheque-book on the table when we entered the room – no doubt to pay the Sergeant his fee. She now put it back in the drawer. It went to my heart to see how her poor hand trembled – the hand that had loaded her old servant with benefits; the hand that, I pray God, may take mine, when my time comes, and I leave my place for ever!

'I had hoped,' said my lady, very slowly and quietly, 'to have recompensed your services, and to have parted with you without Miss Verinder's name having been openly mentioned between us as it has been mentioned now. My nephew has probably said something of this, before you came into my room?'

'Mr Blake gave his message, my lady. And I gave Mr Blake a reason—'

'It is needless to tell me your reason. After what you have just said, you know as well as I do that you have gone too far to go back. I owe it to myself, and I owe it to my child, to insist on your remaining here, and to insist on your speaking out.'

The Sergeant looked at his watch.

'If there had been time, my lady,' he answered, 'I should have preferred writing my report, instead of communicating it by word of mouth. But, if this inquiry is to go on, time is of too much importance to be wasted in writing. I am ready to go into the matter at once. It is a very painful matter for me to speak of, and for you to hear—'

There my mistress stopped him once more.

'I may possibly make it less painful to you, and to my good servant and friend here,' she said, 'if I set the example of speaking boldly, on my side. You suspect Miss Verinder of deceiving us all, by secreting the Diamond for some purpose of her own? Is that true?'

'Quite true, my lady.'

'Very well. Now, before you begin, I have to tell you, as Miss Verinder's mother, that she is *absolutely incapable* of doing what you suppose her to have done. Your knowledge of her character dates from a day or two since. My knowledge of her character dates from the beginning of her life. State your suspicion of her as strongly as you please – it is impossible that you can offend me by doing so. I am sure, beforehand, that (with all your experience) the circumstances have fatally misled you in this case. Mind! I am in possession of no private information. I am as absolutely shut out of my daughter's confidence as you are. My one reason for speaking positively, is the reason you have heard already. I know my child.'

She turned to me, and gave me her hand. I kissed it in silence. 'You may go on,' she said, facing the Sergeant again as steadily as ever.

Sergeant Cuff bowed. My mistress had produced but one effect on him. His hatchetface softened for a moment, as if he was sorry for her. As to shaking him in his own conviction, it was plain to see that she had not moved him by a single inch. He settled himself in his chair; and he began his vile attack on Miss Rachel's character in these words:

'I must ask your ladyship,' he said, 'to look this matter in the face, from my point of view as well as from yours. Will you please to suppose yourself coming down here, in my place, and with my experience? and will you allow me to mention very briefly what that experience has been?'

My mistress signed to him that she would do this. The Sergeant went on:

'For the last twenty years,' he said, 'I have been largely employed in cases of family scandal, acting in the capacity of confidential man. The one result of my domestic practice which has any bearing on the matter now in hand, is a result which I may state in two words. It is well within my experience, that young ladies of rank and position do occasionally have private debts which they dare not acknowledge to their nearest relatives and friends. Sometimes, the milliner and the jeweller are at the bottom of it. Sometimes, the money is wanted for purposes which I don't suspect in this case, and which I won't shock you by mentioning. Bear in mind what I have said, my lady – and now let us see how events in this house have forced me back on my own experience, whether I liked it or not!'

He considered with himself for a moment, and went on – with a horrid clearness that obliged you to understand him; with an abominable justice that favoured nobody.

'My first information relating to the loss of the Moonstone,' said the Sergeant, 'came to me from Superintendent Seegrave. He proved to my complete satisfaction that he was perfectly incapable of managing the case. The one thing he said which struck me as worth listening to, was this – that Miss Verinder had declined to be questioned by him, and had spoken to him with a perfectly incomprehensible rudeness and contempt. I thought this curious – but I attributed it mainly to some clumsiness on the Superintendent's part which might have offended the young lady. After that, I put it by in my mind, and applied myself, single-handed, to the case. It ended, as you are aware, in the discovery of the smear on the door, and in Mr Franklin Blake's evidence satisfying me, that this same smear, and the loss of the Diamond, were pieces of the same puzzle. So far, if I suspected anything, I suspected that the Moonstone had been stolen, and that one of the servants might prove to be the thief. Very good. In this state of things, what happens? Miss Verinder suddenly comes out of her room, and speaks to me. I observe three suspicious appearances in that young lady. She is still violently agitated, though more than four-and-twenty hours have passed since the Diamond was lost. She treats me, as she has already treated Superintendent Seegrave. And she is mortally offended with Mr Franklin Blake. Very good again. Here (I say to myself) is a young lady who has lost a valuable jewel – a young lady, also, as my own eyes and ears inform me, who is of an impetuous temperament. Under these circumstances, and with that character, what does she do? She betrays an incomprehensible resentment against Mr Blake, Mr Superintendent, and myself – otherwise, the very three people who have all, in their different ways, been trying to help her to recover her lost jewel. Having brought my inquiry to that point – *then*, my lady, and not till then, I begin to look back into my own mind for my own experience. My own experience explains Miss Verinder's otherwise incomprehensible conduct. It associates her with those other young ladies that I know of. It tells me she has debts she daren't acknowledge, that must be paid. And it sets me asking myself, whether the loss of the Diamond may not mean – that the Diamond must be secretly pledged to pay them. That is the conclusion which my experience draws from plain facts. What does your ladyship's experience say against it?'

'What I have said already,' answered my mistress. 'The circumstances have misled you.'

I said nothing on my side. *Robinson Crusoe* – God knows how – had got into my muddled old head. If Sergeant Cuff had found himself, at that moment, transported to a desert island, without a man Friday to keep him company, or a ship to take him off – he would have found himself exactly where I wished him to be! (*Nota bene*: – I am an average good Christian, when you don't push my Christianity too far. And all the rest of you – which is a great comfort – are, in this respect, much the same as I am.)

Sergeant Cuff went on:

'Right or wrong, my lady,' he said, 'having drawn my conclusion, the next thing to do was to put it to the test. I suggested to your ladyship the examination of all the wardrobes in the house. It was a means of finding the article of dress which had, in all probability, made the smear; and it was a means of putting my conclusion to the test. How did it turn out? Your ladyship consented; Mr Blake consented; Mr Ablewhite consented. Miss Verinder alone stopped the whole proceeding by refusing point-blank. That result satisfied me that my view was the right one. If your ladyship and Mr Betteredge persist in not agreeing with me, you must be blind to what happened before you this very day. In your hearing, I told the young lady that her leaving the house (as things were then) would put an obstacle in the way of my recovering her jewel. You saw yourselves that she drove off in the face of that statement. You saw yourselves that, so far from forgiving Mr Blake for having done more than all the rest of you to put the clue into my hands, she publicly insulted Mr Blake, on the steps of her mother's house. What do these things mean? If Miss Verinder is not privy to the suppression of the Diamond, what do these things mean?'

This time he looked my way. It was downright frightful to hear him piling up proof after proof against Miss Rachel, and to know, while one was longing to defend her, that there was no disputing the truth of what he said. I am (thank God!) constitutionally superior to reason. This enabled me to hold firm to my lady's view, which was my view also. This roused my spirit, and made me put a bold face on it before Sergeant Cuff. Profit, good friends, I beseech you, by my example. It will save you from many troubles of the vexing sort. Cultivate a superiority to reason, and see how you pare the claws of all the sensible people when they try to scratch you for your own good!

Finding that I made no remark, and that my mistress made no remark, Sergeant Cuff proceeded. Lord! how it did enrage me to notice that he was not in the least put out by our silence!

'There is the case, my lady, as it stands against Miss Verinder alone,' he said. 'The next thing is to put the case as it stands against Miss Verinder and the deceased Rosanna Spearman, taken together. We will go back for a moment, if you please, to your daughter's refusal to let her wardrobe be examined. My mind being made up, after that circumstance, I had two questions to consider next. First, as to the right method of conducting my inquiry. Second, as to whether Miss Verinder had an accomplice among the female servants in the house. After carefully thinking it over, I determined to conduct the inquiry in, what we should call at our office, a highly irregular manner. For this reason: I had a family scandal to deal with, which it was my business to keep within the family limits. The less noise made, and the fewer strangers employed to help me, the better. As to the usual course of taking people in custody on suspicion, going before the magistrate, and all the rest of it – nothing of the sort was to be thought of, when your ladyship's daughter was (as I believed) at the bottom of the whole business. In this case, I felt that a person of Mr Betteredge's character and position in the house – knowing the servants as he did, and having the honour of the family at heart – would be safer to take as an assistant than any other person whom I could lay my hand on. I should have tried Mr Blake as well – but for one obstacle in the way. *He saw* the drift of my proceedings at a very early date; and, with his interest in Miss Verinder, any mutual understanding was impossible between him and me. I trouble your ladyship with these particulars to show you that I have kept the family secret within the family circle. I am the only outsider who knows it – and my professional existence depends on holding my tongue.'

Here I felt that my professional existence depended on not holding *my* tongue. To be held up before my mistress, in my old age, as a sort of deputy-policeman, was, once again, more than my Christianity was strong enough to bear.

'I beg to inform your ladyship,' I said, 'that I never, to my knowledge, helped this abominable detective business, in any way, from first to last; and I summon Sergeant Cuff to contradict me, if he dares!'

Having given vent in those words, I felt greatly relieved. Her ladyship honoured me by a little friendly pat on the shoulder. I looked with righteous indignation at the Sergeant to see what he thought of such a testimony as *that*. The Sergeant looked back like a lamb, and seemed to like me better than ever.

My lady informed him that he might continue his statement. 'I understand,' she said, 'that you have honestly done your best, in what you believe to be my interest. I am ready to hear what you have to say next.'

'What I have to say next,' answered Sergeant Cuff, 'relates to Rosanna Spearman. I recognized the young woman, as your ladyship may remember, when she brought the washing-book into this room. Up to that time I was inclined to doubt whether Miss Verinder had trusted her secret to any one. When I saw Rosanna, I altered my mind. I suspected her at once of being privy to the suppression of the Diamond. The poor creature has met her death by a dreadful end, and I don't want your ladyship to think, now she's gone, that I was unduly hard on her. If this had been a common case of thieving, I should have given Rosanna the benefit of the doubt just as freely as I should have given it to any of the other servants in the house. Our experience of the Reformatory women is, that when tried in service – and when kindly and judiciously treated – they prove themselves in the majority of cases to be honestly penitent, and honestly worthy of the pains taken with them. But this was not a common case of thieving. It was a case – in my mind – of a deeply planned fraud, with the owner of the Diamond at the bottom of it. Holding this view, the first consideration which naturally presented itself to me, in connection with Rosanna, was this. Would Miss Verinder be satisfied (begging your ladyship's pardon) with leading us all to think that the Moonstone was merely lost? Or would she go a step further, and delude us into believing that the Moonstone was stolen? In the latter event there was Rosanna Spearman – with the character of a thief – ready to her hand; the person of all others to lead your ladyship off, and to lead me off, on a false scent.'

Was it possible (I asked myself) that he could put his case against Miss Rachel and Rosanna in a more horrid point of view than this? It *was* possible, as you shall now see.

'I had another reason for suspecting the deceased woman,' he said, 'which appears to me to have been stronger still. Who would be the very person to help Miss Verinder in raising money privately on the Diamond? Rosanna Spearman. No young lady in Miss Verinder's position could manage such a risky matter as that by herself. A go-between she must have, and who so fit, I ask again, as Rosanna Spearman? Your ladyship's deceased housemaid was at the top of her profession when she was a thief. She had relations, to my certain knowledge, with one of the few men in London (in the money-lending line) who would advance a large sum on such a notable jewel as the Moonstone, without asking awkward questions, or insisting on awkward conditions. Bear this in mind, my lady; and now let me show you how my suspicions have been justified by Rosanna's own acts, and by the plain inferences to be drawn from them.'

He thereupon passed the whole of Rosanna's proceedings under review. You are already as well acquainted with those proceedings as I am; and you will understand how unanswerably this part of his report fixed the guilt of being concerned in the disappearance of the Moonstone on the memory of the poor dead girl. Even my mistress was daunted by what he said now. She made him no answer when he had done. It didn't seem to matter to the Sergeant whether he was answered or not. On he went (devil take him!), just as steady as ever.

'Having stated the whole case as I understand it,' he said, 'I have only to tell your ladyship, now, what I propose to do next. I see two ways of bringing this inquiry successfully to an end. One of those ways I look upon as a certainty. The other, I admit, is a bold experiment, and nothing more. Your ladyship shall decide. Shall we take the certainty first?'

My mistress made him a sign to take his own way, and choose for himself.

'Thank you,' said the Sergeant. 'We'll begin with the certainty, as your ladyship is so good as to leave it to me. Whether Miss Verinder remains at Frizinghall, or whether she returns here, I propose, in either case, to keep a careful watch on all her proceedings – on the people she sees, on the rides and walks she may take, and on the letters she may write and receive.'

'What next?' asked my mistress.

'I shall next,' answered the Sergeant, 'request your ladyship's leave to introduce into the house, as a servant in the place of Rosanna Spearman, a woman accustomed to private inquiries of this sort, for whose discretion I can answer.'

'What next?' repeated my mistress.

'Next,' proceeded the Sergeant, 'and last, I propose to send one of my brother-officers to make an arrangement with that money-lender in London, whom I mentioned just now as formerly acquainted with Rosanna Spearman – and whose name and address, your ladyship may rely on it, have been communicated by Rosanna to Miss Verinder. I don't deny that the course of action I am now suggesting will cost money, and consume time. But the result is certain. We run a line round the Moonstone, and we draw that line closer and closer till we find it in Miss Verinder's possession, supposing she decides to keep it. If her debts press, and she decides on sending it away, then we have our man ready, and we meet the Moonstone on its arrival in London.'

To hear her own daughter made the subject of such a proposal as this, stung my mistress into speaking angrily for the first time.

'Consider your proposal declined, in every particular,' she said. 'And go on to your other way of bringing the inquiry to an end.'

'My other way,' said the Sergeant, going on as easy as ever, 'is to try that bold experiment to which I have alluded. I think I have formed a pretty correct estimate of Miss Verinder's temperament. She is quite capable (according to my belief) of committing a daring fraud. But she is too hot and impetuous in temper, and too little accustomed to deceit as a habit, to act the hypocrite in small things, and to restrain herself under all provocations. Her feelings, in this case, have repeatedly got beyond her control, at the very time when it was plainly her interest to conceal them. It is on this peculiarity in her character that I now propose to act. I want to give her a great shock suddenly, under circumstances that will touch her to the quick. In plain English, I want to tell Miss

Verinder, without a word of warning, of Rosanna's death – on the chance that her own better feelings will hurry her into making a clean breast of it. Does your ladyship accept *that* alternative?'

My mistress astonished me beyond all power of expression. She answered him on the instant:

'Yes; I do.'

'The pony-chaise is ready,' said the Sergeant. 'I wish your ladyship good morning.'

My lady held up her hand, and stopped him at the door.

'My daughter's better feelings shall be appealed to, as you propose,' she said. 'But I claim the right, as her mother, of putting her to the test myself. You will remain here, if you please; and I will go to Frizinghall.'

For once in his life, the great Cuff stood speechless with amazement, like an ordinary man.

My mistress rang the bell, and ordered her waterproof things. It was still pouring with rain; and the close carriage had gone, as you know, with Miss Rachel to Frizinghall. I tried to dissuade her ladyship from facing the severity of the weather. Quite useless! I asked leave to go with her, and hold the umbrella. She wouldn't hear of it. The pony-chaise came round, with the groom in charge. 'You may rely on two things,' she said to Sergeant Cuff, in the hall. 'I will try the experiment on Miss Verinder as boldly as you could try it yourself. And I will inform you of the result, either personally or by letter, before the last train leaves for London to-night.'

With that, she stepped into the chaise, and, taking the reins herself, drove off to Frizinghall.

▬ TWENTY-TWO ▬

My mistress having left us, I had leisure to think of Sergeant Cuff. I found him sitting in a snug corner of the hall, consulting his memorandum book, and curling up viciously at the corners of the lips.

'Making notes of the case?' I asked.

'No,' said the Sergeant. 'Looking to see what my next professional engagement is.'

'Oh!' I said. 'You think it's all over then, here?'

'I think,' answered Sergeant Cuff, 'that Lady Verinder is one of the cleverest women in England. I also think a rose much better worth looking at than a diamond. Where is the gardener, Mr Betteredge?'

There was no getting a word more out of him on the matter of the Moonstone. He had lost all interest in his own inquiry; and he would persist in looking for the gardener. An hour afterwards, I heard them at high words in the conservatory, with the dog-rose once more at the bottom of the dispute.

In the meantime, it was my business to find out whether Mr Franklin persisted in his resolution to leave us by the afternoon train. After having been informed of the conference in my lady's room, and of how it had ended, he immediately decided on waiting to hear the news from Frizinghall. This very natural alteration in his plans – which, with ordinary people, would have led to nothing in particular – proved, in Mr Franklin's case, to have one objectionable result. It left him unsettled, with a legacy of idle time on his hands, and in so doing, it let out all the foreign sides of his character, one on the top of another, like rats out of a bag.

Now as an Italian-Englishman, now as a German-Englishman, and now as a French-Englishman, he drifted in and out of all the sitting-rooms in the house, with nothing to talk of but Miss Rachel's treatment of him; and with nobody to address himself to but me. I found him (for example) in the library, sitting under the map of Modern Italy, and quite unaware of any other method of meeting his troubles, except the method of talking about them. 'I have several worthy aspirations, Betteredge; but what am I to do with them now? I am full of dormant good qualities, if Rachel would only have helped me to bring them out!' He was so eloquent in drawing the picture of his own neglected merits, and so pathetic in lamenting over it when it was done, that I felt quite at my wits' end how to console him, when it suddenly occurred to me that here was a case for the wholesome application of a bit of *Robinson Crusoe*. I hobbled out to my own room, and hobbled back with that immortal book. Nobody in the library! The map of Modern Italy stared at *me*; and *I* stared at the map of Modern Italy.

I tried the drawing-room. There was his handkerchief on the floor, to prove that he had drifted in. And there was the empty room to prove that he had drifted out again.

I tried the dining-room, and discovered Samuel with a biscuit and a glass of sherry, silently investigating the empty air. A minute since, Mr Franklin had rung furiously for a little light refreshment. On its production, in a violent hurry, by Samuel, Mr Franklin had vanished before the bell downstairs had quite done ringing with the pull he had given to it.

I tried the morning-room, and found him at last. There he was at the window, drawing hieroglyphics with his finger in the damp on the glass.

'Your sherry is waiting for you, sir,' I said to him. I might as well have addressed myself to one of the four walls of the room; he was down in the bottomless deep of his own meditations, past all pulling up. 'How do *you* explain Rachel's conduct, Betteredge?' was the only answer I received. Not being ready with the needful reply, I produced *Robinson Crusoe*, in which I am firmly persuaded some explanation might have been found, if we had only searched long enough for it. Mr Franklin shut up *Robinson Crusoe*, and floundered into his German-English gibberish on the spot. 'Why not look into it?' he said, as if I had personally objected to looking into it. 'Why the devil lose your patience, Betteredge, when patience is all that's wanted to arrive at the truth? Don't interrupt me. Rachel's conduct is perfectly intelligible, if you will only do her the common justice to take the Objective view first, and the Subjective view next, and the Objective-Subjective view to wind up with. What do we know? We know that the loss of the Moonstone, on Thursday morning last, threw her into a state of nervous excitement, from which she has not recovered yet. Do you mean to deny the Objective view, so far? Very well, then – don't interrupt me. Now, being in a state of nervous excitement, how are we to expect that she should behave as she might otherwise have behaved to any of the people about her? Arguing in this way, from within-outwards, what do we reach? We reach the Subjective view. I defy you to controvert the Subjective view. Very well then – what follows? Good Heavens! the Objective-Subjective explanation follows, of course! Rachel, properly speaking, is *not* Rachel, but Somebody Else. Do I mind being cruelly treated by Somebody Else? You are unreasonable enough, Betteredge; but you can hardly accuse me of that. Then how does it end? It ends, in spite of your confounded English narrowness and prejudice, in my being perfectly happy and comfortable. Where's the sherry?'

My head was by this time in such a condition, that I was not quite sure whether it was my own head, or Mr Franklin's. In this deplorable state, I contrived to do, what I take to have been, three Objective things. I got Mr Franklin his sherry; I retired to my own room; and I solaced myself with the most composing pipe of tobacco I ever remember to have smoked in my life.

Don't suppose, however, that I was quit of Mr Franklin on such easy terms as these. Drifting again, out of the morning-room into the hall, he found his way to the offices next, smelt my pipe, and was instantly reminded that he had been simple enough to give up smoking for Miss Rachel's sake. In the twinkling of an eye, he burst in on me with his cigar-case, and came out strong on the one everlasting subject, in his neat, witty, unbelieving, French way. 'Give me a light, Betteredge. Is it conceivable that a man can have smoked as long as I have, without discovering that there is a complete system for the treatment of women at the bottom of his cigar-case? Follow me carefully, and I will prove it in two words. You choose a cigar, you try it, and it disappoints you. What do you do upon that? You throw it away and try another. Now observe the application! You choose a woman, you try her, and she breaks your heart. Fool! take a lesson from your cigar-case. Throw her away, and try another!'

I shook my head at that. Wonderfully clever, I dare say, but my own experience was dead against it. 'In the time of the late Mrs Betteredge,' I said, 'I felt pretty often inclined to try your philosophy, Mr Franklin. But the law insists on your smoking your cigar, sir, when you have once chosen it.' I pointed that observation with a wink. Mr Franklin burst out laughing – and we were as merry as crickets, until the next new side of his character turned up in due course. So things went on with my young master and me; and so, (while the Sergeant and the gardener were wrangling over the roses) we two spent the interval before the news came back from Frizinghall.

The pony-chaise returned a good half-hour before I had ventured to expect it. My lady had decided to remain for the present, at her sister's house. The groom brought two letters from his mistress; one addressed to Mr Franklin, and the other to me.

Mr Franklin's letter I sent to him in the library – into which refuge his driftings had now taken him for the second time. My own letter, I read in my own room. A cheque, which dropped out when I opened it, informed me (before I had mastered the contents) that Sergeant Cuff's dismissal from the inquiry after the Moonstone was now a settled thing.

I sent to the conservatory to say that I wished to speak to the Sergeant directly. He appeared, with his mind full of the gardener and the dog-rose, declaring that the equal of Mr Begbie for obstinacy never had existed yet, and never would exist again. I requested him to dismiss such wretched trifling as this from our conversation, and to give his best attention to a really serious matter. Upon that he exerted himself sufficiently to notice the letter in my hand. 'Ah!' he said in a weary way, 'you have heard from her ladyship. Have I anything to do with it, Mr Betteredge?'

'You shall judge for yourself, Sergeant.' I thereupon read him the letter (with my best emphasis and discretion), in the following words:

'My good Gabriel, – I request that you will inform Sergeant Cuff, that I have performed the promise I made to him; with this result, so far as Rosanna Spearman is concerned. Miss Verinder solemnly declares, that she has never spoken a word in private to Rosanna, since that unhappy woman first entered my house. They never met, even accidentally, on the night when the Diamond was lost; and no communication of any sort whatever took place between them, from the Thursday morning when the alarm was first raised in the house, to this present Saturday afternoon, when Miss Verinder left us. After telling my daughter suddenly, and in so many words, of Rosanna Spearman's suicide – this is what has come of it.'

Having reached that point, I looked up, and asked Sergeant Cuff what he thought of the letter, so far?

'I should only offend you if I expressed *my* opinion,' answered the Sergeant. 'Go on, Mr Betteredge,' he said, with the most exasperating resignation, 'go on.'

When I remembered that this man had had the audacity to complain of our gardener's obstinacy, my tongue itched to 'go on' in other words than my mistress's. This time, however, my Christianity held firm. I proceeded steadily with her ladyship's letter:

'Having appealed to Miss Verinder in the manner which the officer thought most desirable, I spoke to her next in the manner which I myself thought most likely to impress her. On two different occasions, before my daughter left my roof, I privately warned her that she was exposing herself to suspicion of the most unendurable and most degrading kind. I have now told her, in the plainest terms, that my apprehensions have been realized.

'Her answer to this, on her own solemn affirmation, is as plain as words can be. In the first place, she owes no money privately to any living creature. In the second place, the Diamond is not now, and never has been, in her possession, since she put it into her cabinet on Wednesday night.

'The confidence which my daughter has placed in me goes no further than this. She maintains an obstinate silence, when I ask her if she can explain the disappearance of the Diamond. She refuses, with tears, when I appeal to her to speak out for my sake. "The day will come when you will know why I am careless about being suspected, and why I am silent even to *you*. I have done much to make my mother pity me – nothing to make my mother blush for me." Those are my daughter's own words.

'After what has passed between the officer and me, I think – stranger as he is – that he should be made acquainted with what Miss Verinder has said, as well as you. Read my letter to him, and then place in his hands the cheque which I enclose. In resigning all further claim on his services, I have only to say that I am convinced of his honesty and his intelligence; but I am more firmly persuaded than ever, that the circumstances, in this case, have fatally misled him.'

There the letter ended. Before presenting the cheque, I asked Sergeant Cuff if he had any remark to make.

'It's no part of my duty, Mr Betteredge,' he answered, 'to make remarks on a case, when I have done with it.'

I tossed the cheque across the table to him. 'Do you believe in *that* part of her ladyship's letter?' I said, indignantly.

The Sergeant looked at the cheque, and lifted up his dismal eyebrows in acknowledgment of her ladyship's liberality.

'This is such a generous estimate of the value of my time,' he said, 'that I feel bound to make some return for it. I'll bear in mind the amount in this cheque, Mr Betteredge, when the occasion comes round for remembering it.'

'What do you mean?' I asked.

'Her ladyship has smoothed matters over for the present very cleverly,' said the Sergeant. 'But *this* family scandal is of the sort that bursts up again when you least expect it. We shall have more detective-business on our hands, sir, before the Moonstone is many months older.'

If those words meant anything, and if the manner in which he spoke them meant anything – it came to this. My mistress's letter had proved, to his mind, that Miss Rachel was hardened enough to resist the strongest appeal that could be addressed to her, and that she had deceived her own mother (good God, under what circumstances!) by a series of abominable lies. How other people, in my place, might have replied to the Sergeant, I don't know. I answered what he said in these plain terms:

'Sergeant Cuff, I consider your last observation as an insult to my lady and her daughter!'

'Mr Betteredge, consider it as a warning to yourself, and you will be nearer the mark.'

Hot and angry as I was, the infernal confidence with which he gave me that answer closed my lips.

I walked to the window to compose myself. The rain had given over; and, who should I see in the courtyard, but Mr Begbie, the gardener, waiting outside to continue the dog-rose controversy with Sergeant Cuff.

'My compliments to the Sergeant,' said Mr Begbie, the moment he set eyes on me. 'If he's minded to walk to the station, I'm agreeable to go with him.'

'What!' cries the Sergeant, behind me, 'are you not convinced yet?'

'The de'il a bit I'm convinced!' answered Mr Begbie.

'Then I'll walk to the station!' says the Sergeant.

'Then I'll meet you at the gate!' says Mr Begbie.

I was angry enough, as you know – but how was any man's anger to hold out against such an interruption as this? Sergeant Cuff noticed the change in me, and encouraged it by a word in season. 'Come! come!' he said, 'why not treat my view of the case as her ladyship treats it? Why not say, the circumstances have fatally misled me?'

To take anything as her ladyship took it, was a privilege worth enjoying – even with the disadvantage of its having been offered to me by Sergeant Cuff. I cooled slowly down to my customary level. I regarded any other opinion of Miss Rachel, than my lady's opinion or mine, with a lofty contempt. The only thing I could *not* do, was to keep off the subject of the Moonstone! My own good sense ought to have warned me, I know, to let the matter rest – but, there! the virtues which distinguish the present generation were not invented in my time. Sergeant Cuff had hit me on the raw, and, though I did look down upon him with contempt, the tender place still tingled for all that. The end of it was that I perversely led him back to the subject of her ladyship's letter. 'I am quite satisfied myself,' I said. 'But never mind that! Go on, as if I was still open to conviction. You think Miss Rachel is not to be believed on her word; and you say we shall hear of the Moonstone again. Back your opinion, Sergeant,' I concluded, in an airy way. 'Back your opinion.'

Instead of taking offence, Sergeant Cuff seized my hand, and shook it till my fingers ached again.

'I declare to heaven,' says this strange officer solemnly, 'I would take to domestic service to-morrow, Mr Betteredge, if I had a chance of being employed along with you! To say you are as transparent as a child, sir, is to pay the children a compliment which nine out of ten of them don't deserve. There! there! we won't begin to dispute again. You shall have it out of me on easier terms than that. I won't say a word more about her ladyship, or about Miss Verinder – I'll only turn prophet, for once in a way, and for your sake. I have warned you already that you haven't done with the Moonstone yet. Very well. Now I'll tell you, at parting, of three things which will happen in the future, and which, I believe, will force themselves on your attention, whether you like it or not.'

'Go on!' I said, quite unabashed, and just as airy as ever.

'First,' said the Sergeant, 'you will hear something from the Yollands – when the postman delivers Rosanna's letter at Cobb's Hole, on Monday next.'

If he had thrown a bucket of cold water over me, I doubt if I could have felt it much more unpleasantly than I felt those words. Miss Rachel's assertion of her innocence had left Rosanna's conduct – the making the new nightgown, the hiding the smeared nightgown, and all the rest of it – entirely without explanation. And this had never occurred to me, till Sergeant Cuff forced it on my mind all in a moment!

'In the second place,' proceeded the Sergeant, 'you will hear of the three Indians again. You will hear of them in the neighbourhood, if Miss Rachel remains in the neighbourhood. You will hear of them in London, if Miss Rachel goes to London.'

Having lost all interest in the three jugglers, and having thoroughly convinced myself of my young lady's innocence, I took this second prophecy easily enough. 'So much for two of the three things that are going to happen,' I said. 'Now for the third!'

'Third, and last,' said Sergeant Cuff, 'you will, sooner or later, hear something of that money-lender in London, whom I have twice taken the liberty of mentioning already. Give me your pocket-book, and I'll make a note for you of his name and address – so that there may be no mistake about it if the thing really happens.'

He wrote accordingly on a blank leaf: – 'Mr Septimus Luker, Middlesex Place, Lambeth, London.'

'There,' he said, pointing to the address, 'are the last words, on the subject of the Moonstone, which I shall trouble you with for the present. Time will show whether I am right or wrong. In the meanwhile, sir, I carry away with me a sincere personal liking for you, which I think does honour to both of us. If we don't meet again before my professional retirement takes place, I hope you will come and see me in a little house near London, which I have got my eye on. There will be grass walks, Mr Betteredge, I promise you, in *my* garden. And as for the white moss-rose—'

'The de'il a bit ye'll get the white moss-rose to grow, unless ye bud him on the doguerose first,' cried a voice at the window.

We both turned round. There was the everlasting Mr Begbie, too eager for the controversy to wait any longer at the gate. The Sergeant wrung my hand, and darted out into the courtyard, hotter still on his side. 'Ask him about the moss-rose, when he comes back, and see if I have left him a leg to stand on!' cried the Great Cuff, hailing me through the window in his turn. 'Gentlemen, both!' I answered, moderating them again as I had moderated them once already. 'In the matter of the moss-rose there is a great deal to be said on both sides!' I might as well (as the Irish say) have whistled jigs to a milestone. Away they went together, fighting the battle of the roses without asking or giving quarter on either side. The last I saw of them, Mr Begbie was shaking his obstinate head, and Sergeant Cuff had got him by the arm like a prisoner in charge. Ah, well! well! I own I couldn't help liking the Sergeant – though I hated him all the time.

Explain that state of mind, if you can. You will soon be rid, now, of me and my contradictions. When I have reported Mr Franklin's departure, the history of the Saturday's events will be finished at last. And when I have next described certain strange things that happened in the course of the new week, I shall have done my part of the Story, and shall hand over the pen to the person who is appointed to follow my lead. If you are as tired of reading this narrative as I am of writing it – Lord, how we shall enjoy ourselves on both sides a few pages further on!

⚬ TWENTY-THREE ⚭

I HAD KEPT THE PONY-CHAISE READY, in case Mr Franklin persisted in leaving us by the train that night. The appearance of the luggage, followed downstairs by Mr Franklin himself, informed me plainly enough that he had held firm to a resolution for once in his life.

'So you have really made up your mind, sir?' I said, as we met in the hall. 'Why not wait a day or two longer, and give Miss Rachel another chance?'

The foreign varnish appeared to have all worn off Mr Franklin, now that the time had come for saying good-bye. Instead of replying to me in words, he put the letter which her ladyship had addressed to him into my hand. The greater part of it said over again what had been said already in the other communication received by me. But there was a bit about Miss Rachel added at the end, which will account for the steadiness of Mr Franklin's determination, if it accounts for nothing else.

'You will wonder, I dare say' (her ladyship wrote), 'at my allowing my own daughter to keep me perfectly in the dark. A Diamond worth twenty thousand pounds has been lost – and I am left to infer that the mystery of its disappearance is no mystery to Rachel, and that some incomprehensible obligation of silence has been laid on her, by some person or persons utterly unknown to me, with some object in view at which I cannot even guess. Is it conceivable that I should allow myself to be trifled with in this way? It is quite conceivable, in Rachel's present state. She is in a condition of nervous agitation pitiable to see. I dare not approach the subject of the Moonstone again until time has done something to quiet her. To help this end, I have not hesitated to dismiss the police-officer. The mystery which baffles us, baffles him too. This is not a matter in which any stranger can help us. He adds to what I have to suffer; and he maddens Rachel if she only hears his name.

'My plans for the future are as well settled as they can be. My present

162

idea is to take Rachel to London – partly to relieve her mind by a complete change, partly to try what may be done by consulting the best medical advice. Can I ask you to meet us in town? My dear Franklin, you, in your way, must imitate my patience, and wait, as I do, for a fitter time. The valuable assistance which you rendered to the inquiry after the lost jewel is still an unpardoned offence, in the present dreadful state of Rachel's mind. Moving blindfold in this matter, you have added to the burden of anxiety which she has had to bear, by innocently threatening her secret with discovery, through your exertions. It is impossible for me to excuse the perversity that holds you responsible for consequences which neither you nor I could imagine or foresee. She is not to be reasoned with – she can only be pitied. I am grieved to have to say it, but, for the present, you and Rachel are better apart. The only advice I can offer you is, to give her time.'

I handed the letter back, sincerely sorry for Mr Franklin, for I knew how fond he was of my young lady; and I saw that her mother's account of her had cut him to the heart. 'You know the proverb, sir,' was all I said to him. 'When things are at the worst, they're sure to mend. Things can't be much worse, Mr Franklin, than they are now.'

Mr Franklin folded up his aunt's letter, without appearing to be much comforted by the remark which I had ventured on addressing to him.

'When I came here from London with that horrible Diamond,' he said, 'I don't believe there was a happier household in England than this. Look at the household now! Scattered, disunited – the very air of the place poisoned with mystery and suspicion! Do you remember that morning at the Shivering Sand, when we talked about my uncle Herncastle, and his birthday gift? The Moonstone has served the Colonel's vengeance, Betteredge, by means which the Colonel himself never dreamt of!'

With that he shook me by the hand, and went out to the pony-chaise. I followed him down the steps. It was very miserable to see him leaving the old place, where he had spent the happiest years of his life, in this way. Penelope (sadly upset by all that had happened in the house) came round crying, to bid him good-bye. Mr Franklin kissed her. I waved my hand as much as to say, 'You're heartily welcome, sir.' Some of the other female servants appeared, peeping after him round the corner. He was one of those men whom the women all like. At the last moment, I stopped the pony-chaise, and begged as a favour that he would let us hear from him by letter. He didn't seem to heed what I said – he was looking round from one thing to another, taking a sort of farewell of the old house and grounds. 'Tell us where you are going to, sir!' I said, holding on by the chaise, and trying to get at his future plans in that way. Mr Franklin pulled his hat down suddenly over his eyes. 'Going?' says he, echoing the word after me. 'I am going to the devil!' The pony started at the word, as if he had felt a Christian horror of it. 'God bless you, sir, go where you may!' was all I had time to say, before he was out of sight and hearing. A sweet and pleasant gentleman! With all his faults and follies, a sweet and pleasant gentleman! He left a sad gap behind him, when he left my lady's house.

It was dull and dreary enough, when the long summer evening closed in, on that Saturday night.

I kept my spirits from sinking by sticking fast to my pipe and my *Robinson Crusoe*. The women (excepting Penelope) beguiled the time by talking of Rosanna's suicide. They were all obstinately of opinion that the poor girl had stolen the Moonstone, and that she had destroyed herself in terror of being found out. My daughter, of course, privately held fast to what she had said all along. Her notion of the motive which was really at the bottom of the suicide failed, oddly enough, just where my young lady's assertion of her innocence failed also. It left Rosanna's secret journey to Frizinghall, and Rosanna's proceedings in the matter of the nightgown entirely unaccounted for. There was no use in pointing this out to Penelope; the objection made about as much impression on her as a shower of rain on a waterproof coat. The truth is, my daughter inherits my superiority to reason— and, in respect to that accomplishment, has got a long way ahead of her own father.

On the next day (Sunday), the close carriage, which had been kept at Mr Ablewhite's, came back to us empty. The coachman brought a message for me, and written instructions for my lady's own maid and for Penelope.

The message informed me that my mistress had determined to take Miss Rachel to her house in London, on the Monday. The written instructions informed the two maids of the clothing that was wanted, and directed them to meet their mistresses in town at a given hour. Most of the other servants were to follow. My lady had found Miss Rachel so unwilling to return to the house, after what had happened in it, that she had decided on going to London direct from Frizinghall. I was to remain in the country, until further orders, to look after things indoors and out. The servants left with me were to be put on board wages.

Being reminded, by all this, of what Mr Franklin had said about our being a scattered and disunited household, my mind was led naturally to Mr Franklin himself. The more I thought of him, the more uneasy I felt about his future proceedings. It ended in my writing, by the Sunday's post, to his father's valet, Mr Jeffco (whom I had known in former years) to beg he would let me know what Mr Franklin had settled to do, on arriving in London.

The Sunday evening was, if possible, duller even than the Saturday evening. We ended the day of rest, as hundreds of thousands of people end it regularly, once a week, in these islands— that is to say, we all anticipated bedtime, and fell asleep in our chairs.

How the Monday affected the rest of the household I don't know. The Monday gave *me* a good shake up. The first of Sergeant Cuff's prophecies of what was to happen— namely, that I should hear from the Yollands— came true on that day.

I had seen Penelope and my lady's maid off on the railway with the luggage for London, and was pottering about the grounds, when I heard my name called. Turning round, I found myself face to face with the fisherman's daughter, Limping Lucy. Bating her lame foot and her leanness (this last a horrid drawback to a woman, in my opinion), the girl had some pleasing qualities in the eye of a man. A dark, keen, clever face, and a nice clear voice, and a beautiful brown head of hair counted among her merits. A crutch appeared in the list of her misfortunes. And a temper reckoned high in the sum-total of her defects.

'Well, my dear,' I said, 'what do you want with me?'

'Where's the man you call Franklin Blake?' says the girl, fixing me with a fierce look, as she rested herself on her crutch.

'That's not a respectful way to speak of any gentleman,' I answered. 'If you wish to inquire for my lady's nephew, you will please to mention him as Mr Franklin Blake.'

She limped a step nearer to me, and looked as if she could have eaten me alive. '*Mr* Franklin Blake?' she repeated after me. 'Murderer Franklin Blake would be a fitter name for him.'

My practice with the late Mrs Betteredge came in handy here. Whenever a woman tries to put *you* out of temper, turn the tables, and put *her* out of temper instead. They are generally prepared for every effort you can make in your own defence, but that. One word does it as well as a hundred; and one word did it with Limping Lucy. I looked her pleasantly in the face; and I said— 'Pooh!'

The girl's temper flamed out directly. She poised herself on her sound foot, and she took her crutch, and beat it furiously three times on the ground. 'He's a murderer! he's a murderer! he's a murderer! He has been the death of Rosanna Spearman!' She screamed that answer out at the top of her voice. One or two of the people at work in the grounds near us looked up— saw it was Limping Lucy— knew what to expect from that quarter— and looked away again.

'He has been the death of Rosanna Spearman?' I repeated. 'What makes you say that, Lucy?'

'What do you care? What does any man care? Oh! if she had only thought of the men as I think, she might have been living now!'

'She always thought kindly of *me*, poor soul,' I said; 'and, to the best of my ability, I always tried to act kindly by *her*.'

I spoke those words in as comforting a manner as I could. The truth is, I hadn't the heart to irritate the girl by another of my smart replies. I had only noticed her temper at first. I noticed her wretchedness now—and wretchedness is not uncommonly insolent, you will find, in humble life. My answer melted Limping Lucy. She bent her head down, and laid it on the top of her crutch.

'I loved her,' the girl said softly. 'She had lived a miserable life, Mr Betteredge— vile people had ill-treated her and led her wrong— and it hadn't spoiled her sweet temper. She was an angel. She might have been happy with me. I had a plan for our going to London together like sisters, and living by our needles. That man came here, and spoilt it all. He bewitched her. Don't tell me he didn't mean it, and didn't know it. He ought to have known it. He ought to have taken pity on her. "I can't live without him— and, oh, Lucy, he never even looks at me." That's what she said. Cruel, cruel, cruel. I said, "No man is worth fretting for in that way." And she said, "There are men worth dying for, Lucy, and he is one of them." I had saved up a little money. I had settled things with father and mother. I meant to take her away from the mortification she was suffering here. We should have had a little lodging in London, and lived together like sisters. She had a good education, sir, as you know, and she wrote a good hand. She was quick at her needle. I have a good education, and I write a good hand. I am not as quick at my needle as she was— but I could have done. We might have got our living nicely. And, oh! what happens this morning? what happens this morning? Her letter comes and tells me that she has done with the burden of her life. Her letter comes, and bids me good-bye for ever. Where is he?' cries the girl, lifting her head from the crutch, and flaming out again through her tears. 'Where's this gentleman that I mustn't speak of, except with respect? Ha, Mr Betteredge, the day is not far off when the poor will rise against the rich. I pray Heaven they may begin with *him*. I pray Heaven they may begin with *him*.'

Here was another of your average good Christians, and here was the usual break-down, consequent on that same average Christianity being pushed too far! The parson himself (though I own this is saying a great deal) could hardly have lectured the girl in the state she was in now. All I ventured to do was to keep her to the point – in the hope of something turning up which might be worth hearing.

'What do you want with Mr Franklin Blake?' I asked.

'I want to see him.'

'For anything particular?'

'I have got a letter to give him.'

'From Rosanna Spearman?'

'Yes.'

'Sent to you in your own letter?'

'Yes.'

Was the darkness going to lift? Were all the discoveries that I was dying to make, coming and offering themselves to me of their own accord? I was obliged to wait a moment. Sergeant Cuff had left his infection behind him. Certain signs and tokens, personal to myself, warned me that the detective-fever was beginning to set in again.

'You can't see Mr Franklin,' I said.

'I must, and will, see him.'

'He went to London last night.'

Limping Lucy looked me hard in the face, and saw that I was speaking the truth. Without a word more, she turned about again instantly towards Cobb's Hole.

'Stop!' I said. 'I expect news of Mr Franklin Blake to-morrow. Give me your letter, and I'll send it on to him by the post.'

Limping Lucy steadied herself on her crutch and looked back at me over her shoulder.

'I am to give it from my hands into his hands,' she said. 'And I am to give it to him in no other way.'

'Shall I write, and tell him what you have said?'

'Tell him I hate him. And you will tell him the truth.'

'Yes, yes. But about the letter—?'

'If he wants the letter, he must come back here, and get it from Me.'

With those words she limped off on the way to Cobb's Hole. The detective-fever burnt up all my dignity on the spot. I followed her, and tried to make her talk. All in vain. It was my misfortune to be a man – and Limping Lucy enjoyed disappointing me. Later in the day, I tried my luck with her mother. Good Mrs Yolland could only cry, and recommend a drop of comfort out of the Dutch bottle. I found the fisherman on the beach. He said it was 'a bad job', and went on mending his net. Neither father nor mother knew more than I knew. The one way left to try was the chance, which might come with the morning, of writing to Mr Franklin Blake.

I leave you to imagine how I watched for the postman on Tuesday morning. He brought me two letters. One, from Penelope (which I had hardly patience enough to read), announced that my lady and Miss

Rachel were safely established in London. The other, from Mr Jeffco, informed me that his master's son had left England already.

On reaching the metropolis, Mr Franklin had, it appeared, gone straight to his father's residence. He arrived at an awkward time. Mr Blake, the elder, was up to his eyes in the business of the House of Commons, and was amusing himself at home that night with the favourite parliamentary plaything which they call 'a private bill'. Mr Jeffco himself showed Mr Franklin into his father's study. 'My dear Franklin! why do you surprise me in this way? Anything wrong?' 'Yes; something wrong with Rachel; I am dreadfully distressed about it.' 'Grieved to hear it. But I can't listen to you now.' 'When *can* you listen?' 'My dear boy! I won't deceive you. I can *listen* at the end of the session, not a moment before. Good-night.' 'Thank you, sir. Good-night.'

Such was the conversation, inside the study, as reported to me by Mr Jeffco. The conversation outside the study, was shorter still. 'Jeffco, see what time the tidal train starts to-morrow morning.' 'At six-forty, Mr Franklin.' 'Have me called at five.' 'Going abroad, sir?' 'Going, Jeffco, wherever the railway chooses to take me.' 'Shall I tell your father, sir?' 'Yes; tell him at the end of the session.'

The next morning Mr Franklin had started for foreign parts. To what particular place he was bound, nobody (himself included) could presume to guess. We might hear of him next in Europe, Asia, Africa, or America. The chances were as equally divided as possible, in Mr Jeffco's opinion, among the four quarters of the globe.

This news – by closing up all prospect of my bringing Limping Lucy and Mr Franklin together – at once stopped any further progress of mine on the way to discovery. Penelope's belief that her fellow-servant had destroyed herself through unrequited love for Mr Franklin Blake, was confirmed – and that was all. Whether the letter which Rosanna had left to be given to him after her death did, or did not, contain the confession which Mr Franklin had suspected her of trying to make to him in her life-time, it was impossible to say. It might be only a farewell word, telling nothing but the secret of her unhappy fancy for a person beyond her reach. Or it might own the whole truth about the strange proceedings in which Sergeant Cuff had detected her, from the time when the Moonstone was lost, to the time when she rushed to her own destruction at the Shivering Sand. A sealed letter it had been placed in Limping Lucy's hands, and a sealed letter it remained to me and to every one about the girl, her own parents included. We all suspected her of having been in the dead woman's confidence; we all tried to make her speak; we all failed. Now one, and now another, of the servants – still holding to the belief that Rosanna had stolen the Diamond and had hidden it – peered and poked about the rocks to which she had been traced, and peered and poked in vain. The tide ebbed, and the tide flowed; the summer went on, and the autumn came. And the Quicksand, which hid her body, hid her secret too.

The news of Mr Franklin's departure from England on the Sunday morning, and the news of my lady's arrival in London with Miss Rachel on the Monday afternoon, had reached me, as you are aware, by the Tuesday's post. The Wednesday came, and brought nothing. The Thursday produced a second budget of news from Penelope.

My girl's letter informed me that some great London doctor had been consulted about her young lady, and had earned a guinea by remarking that she had better be amused. Flower-shows, operas, balls – there was a whole round of gaieties in prospect; and Miss Rachel, to her mother's astonishment, eagerly took to it all. Mr Godfrey had called; evidently as sweet as ever on his cousin, in spite of the reception he had met with, when he tried his luck on the occasion of the birthday. To Penelope's great regret, he had been most graciously received, and had added Miss Rachel's name to one of his Ladies' Charities on the spot. My mistress was reported to be out of spirits, and to have held two long interviews with her lawyer. Certain speculations followed, referring to a poor relation of the family – one Miss Clack, whom I have mentioned in my account of the birthday dinner, as sitting next to Mr Godfrey, and having a pretty taste in champagne. Penelope was astonished to find that Miss Clack had not called yet. She would surely not be long before she fastened herself on my lady as usual – and so forth, and so forth, in the way women have of girding at each other, on and off paper. This would not have been worth mentioning, I admit, but for one reason. I hear you are likely to be turned over to Miss Clack, after parting with me. In that case, just do me the favour of not believing a word she says, if she speaks of your humble servant.

On Friday, nothing happened – except that one of the dogs showed signs of a breaking-out behind the ears. I gave him a dose of syrup of buck-thorn, and put him on a diet of pot-liquor and vegetables till further orders. Excuse my mentioning this. It has slipped in somehow. Pass it over please. I am fast coming to the end of my offences against your cultivated modern taste. Besides, the dog was a good creature, and deserved a good physicking; he did indeed.

Saturday, the last day of the week, is also the last day in my narrative.

The morning's post brought me a surprise in the shape of a London newspaper. The handwriting on the direction puzzled me. I compared it with the money-lender's name and address as recorded in my pocket-book, and identified it at once as the writing of Sergeant Cuff.

Looking through the paper eagerly enough, after this discovery, I found an ink-mark drawn round one of the police reports. Here it is, at your service. Read it as I read it, and you will set the right value on the Sergeant's polite attention in sending me the news of the day:

'Lambeth – Shortly before the closing of the court, Mr Septimus Luker, the well-known dealer in ancient gems, carvings, intagli, &c., &c., applied to the sitting magistrate for advice. The applicant stated that he had been annoyed, at intervals throughout the day, by the proceedings of some of those strolling Indians who infest the streets. The persons complained of were three in number. After having been sent away by the police, they had returned again and again, and had attempted to enter the house on pretence of asking for charity. Warned off in the front, they had been discovered again at the back of the premises. Besides the annoyance complained of, Mr Luker expressed himself as being under some apprehension that robbery might be contemplated. His collection contained many unique gems, both classical and Oriental, of the highest value. He had only the day before been compelled to dismiss a skilled workman in ivory carving from his employment (a native of India, as we understood), on suspicion of attempted theft; and he felt by no means sure that this man and the street-jugglers of whom he complained, might not be acting in concert. It might be their object to collect a crowd, and create a disturbance in the street, and, in the confusion thus caused, to obtain access to the house.

In reply to the magistrate, Mr Luker admitted that he had no evidence to produce of any attempt at robbery being in contemplation. He could speak positively to the annoyance and interruption caused by the Indians, but not to anything else. The magistrate remarked that, if the annoyance were repeated, the applicant could summon the Indians to that court, where they might easily be dealt with under the Act. As to the valuables in Mr Luker's possession, Mr Luker himself must take the best measures for their safe custody. He would do well perhaps to communicate with the police, and to adopt such additional precautions as their experience might suggest. The applicant thanked his worship, and withdrew.'

One of the wise ancients is reported (I forget on what occasion) as having recommended his fellow-creatures to 'look to the end'. Looking to the end of these pages of mine, and wondering for some days past how I should manage to write it, I find my plain statement of facts coming to a conclusion, most appropriately, of its own self. We have gone on, in this matter of the Moonstone, from one marvel to another; and here we end with the greatest marvel of all – namely, the accomplishment of

Sergeant Cuff's three predictions in less than a week from the time when he had made them.

After hearing from the Yollands on the Monday, I had now heard of the Indians, and heard of the money-lender, in the news from London – Miss Rachel herself, remember, being also in London at the time. You see, I put things at their worst, even when they tell dead against my own view. If you desert me, and side with the Sergeant, on the evidence before you – if the only rational explanation you can see is, that Miss Rachel and Mr Luker must have got together, and that the Moonstone must be now in pledge in the money-lender's house – I own I can't blame you for arriving at that conclusion. In the dark, I have brought you thus far. In the dark I am compelled to leave you, with my best respects.

Why compelled? it may be asked. Why not take the persons who have gone along with me, so far, up into those regions of superior enlightenment in which I sit myself?

In answer to this, I can only state that I am acting under orders, and that those orders have been given to me (as I understand) in the interests of truth. I am forbidden to tell more in this narrative than I knew myself at the time. Or, to put it plainer, I am to keep strictly within the limits of my own experience, and am not to inform you of what other persons told me – for the very sufficient reason that you are to have the information from those other persons themselves, at first hand. In this matter of the Moonstone the plan is, not to present reports, but to produce witnesses. I picture to myself a member of the family reading these pages fifty years hence. Lord! what a compliment he will feel it, to be asked to take nothing on hearsay, and to be treated in all respects like a Judge on the bench.

At this place, then, we part – for the present, at least – after long journeying together, with a companionable feeling, I hope, on both sides. The devil's dance of the Indian Diamond has threaded its way to London; and to London you must go after it, leaving me at the country-house. Please to excuse the faults of this composition – my talking so much of myself, and being too familiar, I am afraid, with you. I mean no harm; and I drink most respectfully (having just done dinner) to your health and prosperity, in a tankard of her ladyship's ale. May you find in these leaves of my writing, what Robinson Crusoe found in his experience on the desert island – namely, 'something to comfort yourselves from, and to set in the Description of Good and Evil, on the Credit Side of the Account.' – Farewell.

THE END OF THE FIRST PERIOD

The Discovery of the Truth

(1848–1849)

The Events related in several Narratives

First Narrative

Contributed by Miss Clack; *niece of the late* Sir John Verinder

✎ ONE ✎

I AM INDEBTED TO MY dear parents (both now in heaven) for having had habits of order and regularity instilled into me at a very early age.

In that happy bygone time, I was taught to keep my hair tidy at all hours of the day and night, and to fold up every article of my clothing carefully, in the same order, on the same chair, in the same place at the foot of the bed, before retiring to rest. An entry of the day's events in my little diary invariably preceded the folding up. The 'Evening Hymn' (repeated in bed) invariably followed the folding up. And the sweet sleep of childhood invariably followed the 'Evening Hymn'.

In later life (alas!) the Hymn has been succeeded by sad and bitter meditations; and the sweet sleep has been but ill exchanged for the broken slumbers which haunt the uneasy pillow of care. On the other hand, I have continued to fold my clothes, and to keep my little diary. The former habit links me to my happy childhood – before papa was ruined. The latter habit – hitherto mainly useful in helping me to discipline the fallen nature which we all inherit from Adam – has unexpectedly proved important to my humble interests in quite another way. It has enabled poor Me to serve the caprice of a wealthy member of the family into which my late uncle married. I am fortunate enough to be useful to Mr Franklin Blake.

I have been cut off from all news of my relatives by marriage for some time past. When we are isolated and poor, we are not infrequently forgotten. I am now living, for economy's sake, in a little town in Brittany, inhabited by a select circle of serious English friends, and possessed of the inestimable advantages of a Protestant clergyman and a cheap market.

In this retirement – a Patmos amid the howling ocean of popery that surrounds us – a letter from England has reached me at last. I find my insignificant existence suddenly remembered by Mr Franklin Blake. My wealthy relative – would that I could add my spiritually-wealthy relative!

– writes, without even an attempt at disguising that he wants something of me. The whim has seized him to stir up the deplorable scandal of the Moonstone: and I am to help him by writing the account of what I myself witnessed while visiting at Aunt Verinder's house in London. Pecuniary remuneration is offered to me – with the want of feeling peculiar to the rich. I am to re-open wounds that Time has barely closed; I am to recall the most intensely painful remembrances – and this done, I am to feel myself compensated by a new laceration, in the shape of Mr Blake's cheque. My nature is weak. It cost me a hard struggle, before Christian humility conquered sinful pride, and self-denial accepted the cheque.

Without my diary, I doubt – pray let me express it in the grossest terms! – if I could have honestly earned my money. With my diary, the poor labourer (who forgives Mr Blake for insulting her) is worthy of her hire. Nothing escaped me at the time I was visiting dear Aunt Verinder. Everything was entered (thanks to my early training) day by day as it happened; and everything down to the smallest particular, shall be told here. My sacred regard for truth is (thank God) far above my respect for persons. It will be easy for Mr Blake to suppress what may not prove to be sufficiently flattering in these pages to the person chiefly concerned in them. He has purchased my time; but not even *his* wealth can purchase my conscience too.*

My diary informs me, that I was accidentally passing Aunt Verinder's house in Montagu Square, on Monday, 3 July 1848.

Seeing the shutters opened, and the blinds drawn up, I felt that it would be an act of polite attention to knock, and make inquiries. The person who answered the door, informed me that my aunt and her daughter (I really cannot call her my cousin!) had arrived from the country a week since, and meditated making some stay in London. I sent up a message at once, declining to disturb them, and only begging to know whether I could be of any use.

The person who answered the door, took my message in insolent

* Note. *Added by Franklin Blake*. – Miss Clark may make her mind quite easy on this point. Nothing will be added, altered, or removed, in her manuscript, or in any of the other manuscripts which pass through my hands. Whatever opinions any of the writers may express, whatever peculiarities of treatment may mark, and perhaps in a literary sense, disfigure, the narratives which I am now collecting, not a line will be tampered with anywhere, from first to last. As genuine documents they are sent to me – and as genuine documents I shall preserve them; endorsed by the attestations of witnesses who can speak to the facts. It only remains to be added, that 'the person chiefly concerned' in Miss Clack's narrative, is happy enough at the present moment, not only to brave the smartest exercise of Miss Clack's pen, but even to recognize its unquestionable value as an instrument for the exhibition of Miss Clack's character.

silence, and left me standing in the hall. She is the daughter of a heathen old man named Betteredge – long, too long, tolerated in my aunt's family. I sat down in the hall to wait for my answer – and, having always a few tracts in my bag, I selected one which proved to be quite providentially applicable to the person who answered the door. The hall was dirty, and the chair was hard; but the blessed consciousness of returning good for evil raised me quite above any trifling considerations of that kind. The tract was one of a series addressed to young women on the sinfulness of dress. In style it was devoutly familiar. Its title was, 'A Word With You On Your Cap-Ribbons.'

'My lady is much obliged, and begs you will come and lunch to-morrow at two.'

I passed over the manner in which she gave her message, and the dreadful boldness of her look. I thanked this young castaway; and I said, in a tone of Christian interest, 'Will you favour me by accepting a tract?'

She looked at the title. 'Is it written by a man or a woman, Miss? If it's written by a woman, I had rather not read it on that account. If it's written by a man, I beg to inform him that he knows nothing about it.' She handed me back the tract, and opened the door. We must sow the good seed somehow. I waited till the door was shut on me, and slipped the tract into the letter-box. When I had dropped another tract through the area railings, I felt relieved, in some small degree, of a heavy responsibility towards others.

We had a meeting that evening of the Select Committee of the Mothers'-Small-Clothes-Conversion-Society. The object of this excellent Charity is – as all serious people know – to rescue unredeemed fathers' trousers from the pawnbroker, and to prevent their resumption, on the part of the irreclaimable parent, by abridging them immediately to suit the proportions of the innocent son. I was a member, at that time, of the select committee; and I mention the Society here, because my precious and admirable friend, Mr Godfrey Ablewhite, was associated with our work of moral and material usefulness. I had expected to see him in the board-room, on the Monday evening of which I am now writing, and had proposed to tell him, when we met, of dear Aunt Verinder's arrival in London. To my great disappointment he never appeared. On my express-ing a feeling of surprise at his absence, my sisters of the Committee all looked up together from their trousers (we had a great pressure of business that night), and asked in amazement, if I had not heard the news. I acknowledged my ignorance, and was then told, for the first time, of an event which forms, so to speak, the starting-point of this narrative. On the previous Friday, two gentlemen – occupying widely-different positions in society – had been the victims of an outrage which had startled all London. One of the gentlemen was Mr Septimus Luker, of Lambeth. The other was Mr Godfrey Ablewhite.

Living in my present isolation, I have no means of introducing the newspaper-account of the outrage into my narrative. I was also deprived, at the time, of the inestimable advantage of hearing the events related by the fervid eloquence of Mr Godfrey Ablewhite. All I can do is to state the facts as they were stated, on that Monday evening, to me; proceeding on the plan which I have been taught from infancy to adopt in folding up my clothes. Everything shall be put neatly, and everything shall be put in its place. These lines are written by a poor weak woman. From a poor weak woman who will be cruel enough to expect more?

The date – thanks to my dear parents, no dictionary that ever was written can be more particular than I am about dates – was Friday, 30 June 1848.

Early on that memorable day, our gifted Mr Godfrey happened to be cashing a cheque at a banking-house in Lombard Street. The name of the firm is accidentally blotted in my diary, and my sacred regard for truth forbids me to hazard a guess in a matter of this kind. Fortunately, the name of the firm doesn't matter. What does matter is a circumstance that occurred when Mr Godfrey had transacted his business. On gaining the door, he encountered a gentleman – a perfect stranger to him – who was accidentally leaving the office exactly at the same time as himself. A momentary contest of politeness ensued between them as to who should be the first to pass through the door of the bank. The stranger insisted on making Mr Godfrey precede him; Mr Godfrey said a few civil words; they bowed, and parted in the street.

Thoughtless and superficial people may say, Here is surely a very trumpery little incident related in an absurdly circumstantial manner. Oh, my young friends and fellow sinners! beware of presuming to exercise your poor carnal reason. Oh, be morally tidy! Let your faith be as your stockings, and your stockings as your faith. Both ever spotless, and both ready to put on at a moment's notice!

I beg a thousand pardons. I have fallen insensibly into my Sunday-school style. Most inappropriate in such a record as this. Let me try to be worldly – let me say that trifles, in this case as in many others, led to terrible results. Merely promising that the polite stranger was Mr Luker, of Lambeth, we will now follow Mr Godfrey home to his residence at Kilburn.

He found waiting for him, in the hall, a poorly clad but delicate and interesting-looking little boy. The boy handed him a letter, merely mentioning that he had been entrusted with it by an old lady whom he did not know, and who had given him no instructions to wait for an answer. Such incidents as these were not uncommon in Mr Godfrey's large experience as a promoter of public charities. He let the boy go, and opened the letter.

The handwriting was entirely unfamiliar to him. It requested his attendance, within an hour's time, at a house in Northumberland Street, Strand, which he had never had occasion to enter before. The object sought was to obtain from the worthy manager certain details on the subject of the Mothers'-Small-Clothes-Conversion-Society, and the information was wanted by an elderly lady who proposed adding largely to the resources of the charity, if her questions were met by satisfactory replies. She mentioned her name, and she added that the shortness of her stay in London prevented her from giving any longer notice to the eminent philanthropist whom she addressed.

Ordinary people might have hesitated before setting aside their own engagements to suit the convenience of a stranger. The Christian Hero never hesitates where good is to be done. Mr Godfrey instantly turned back, and proceeded to the house in Northumberland Street. A most respectable though somewhat corpulent man answered the door, and, on hearing Mr Godfrey's name, immediately conducted him into an empty apartment at the back, on the drawing-room floor. He noticed two unusual things on entering the room. One of them was a faint odour of musk and camphor. The other was an ancient Oriental manuscript, richly illuminated with Indian figures and devices, that lay open to inspection on a table.

He was looking at the book, the position of which caused him to stand with his back turned towards the closed folding doors communicating with the front room, when, without the slightest previous noise to warn him, he felt himself suddenly seized round the neck from behind. He had just time to notice that the arm round his neck was naked and of a tawny-brown colour, before his eyes were bandaged, his mouth was gagged, and he was thrown helpless on the floor by (as he judged) two men. A third rifled his pockets, and – if, as a lady, I may venture to use such an expression – searched him, without ceremony, through and through to his skin.

Here I should greatly enjoy saying a few cheering words on the devout confidence which could alone have sustained Mr Godfrey in an emergency so terrible as this. Perhaps, however, the position and appearance of my admirable friend at the culminating period of the outrage (as above described) are hardly within the proper limits of female discussion. Let me pass over the next few moments, and return to Mr Godfrey at the time when the odious search of his person had been completed. The outrage had been perpetrated throughout in dead silence. At the end of it some words were exchanged, among the invisible wretches, in a language which he did not understand, but in tones which were plainly expressive (to his cultivated ear) of disappointment and rage. He was suddenly lifted from the ground, placed in a chair, and bound there hand and foot. The next moment he felt the air flowing in from the open door, listened, and concluded that he was alone again in the room.

An interval elapsed, and he heard a sound below like the rustling sound of a woman's dress. It advanced up the stairs, and stopped. A female scream rent the atmosphere of guilt. A man's voice below exclaimed, 'Hullo!' A man's feet ascended the stairs. Mr Godfrey felt Christian fingers unfastening his bandage, and extracting his gag. He looked in amazement at two respectable strangers, and faintly articulated, 'What does it mean?' The two respectable strangers looked back, and said, 'Exactly the question we were going to ask *you*.'

The inevitable explanation followed. No! Let me be scrupulously particular. Sal-volatile and water followed, to compose dear Mr Godfrey's nerves. The explanation came next.

It appeared, from the statement of the landlord and landlady of the house (persons of good repute in the neighbourhood), that their first- and second-floor apartments had been engaged, on the previous day, for a week certain, by a most respectable-looking gentleman – the same who has been already described as answering the door to Mr Godfrey's knock. The gentleman had paid the week's rent and all the week's extras in advance, stating that the apartments were wanted for three Oriental noblemen, friends of his, who were visiting England for the first time. Early on the morning of the outrage, two of the Oriental strangers, accompanied by their respectable English friend, took possession of the apartments. The third was expected to join them shortly; and the luggage (reported as very bulky) was announced to follow when it had passed through the Custom-house, late in the afternoon. Not more than ten minutes previous to Mr Godfrey's visit, the third foreigner had arrived. Nothing out of the common had happened, to the knowledge of the landlord and landlady downstairs, until within the last five minutes – when they had seen the three foreigners, accompanied by their respectable English friend, all leave the house together, walking quietly in the direction of the Strand. Remembering that a visitor had called, and not having seen the visitor also leave the house, the landlady had thought it rather strange that the gentleman should be left by himself upstairs. After a short discussion with her husband, she had considered it advisable to ascertain whether anything was wrong. The result had followed, as I have already attempted to describe it; and there the explanation of the landlord and the landlady came to an end.

An investigation was next made in the room. Dear Mr Godfrey's property was found scattered in all directions. When the articles were collected, however, nothing was missing; his watch, chain, purse, keys, pocket-handkerchief, note-book, and all his loose papers had been closely examined, and had then been left unharmed to be resumed by the owner. In the same way, not the smallest morsel of property belonging to the proprietors of the house had been abstracted. The Oriental noblemen had removed their own illuminated manuscript, and had removed nothing else.

What did it mean? Taking the worldly point of view, it appeared to mean that Mr Godfrey had been the victim of some incomprehensible error, committed by certain unknown men. A dark conspiracy was on foot in the midst of us; and our beloved and innocent friend had been entangled in its meshes. When the Christian hero of a hundred charitable victories plunges into a pitfall that has been dug for him by mistake, oh, what a warning it is to the rest of us to be unceasingly on our guard! How soon may our own evil passions prove to be Oriental noblemen who pounce on us unawares!

I could write pages of affectionate warning on this one theme, but (alas!) I am not permitted to improve – I am condemned to narrate. My wealthy relative's cheque – henceforth, the incubus of my existence – warns me that I have not done with this record of violence yet. We must leave Mr Godfrey to recover in Northumberland Street, and must follow the proceedings of Mr Luker, at a later period of the day.

After leaving the bank, Mr Luker had visited various parts of London on business errands. Returning to his own residence, he found a letter waiting for him, which was described as having been left a short time previously by a boy. In this case, as in Mr Godfrey's case, the handwriting was strange; but the name mentioned was the name of one of Mr Luker's customers. His correspondent announced (writing in the third person – apparently by the hand of a deputy) that he had been unexpectedly summoned to London. He had just established himself in lodgings in Alfred Place, Tottenham Court Road; and he desired to see Mr Luker immediately, on the subject of a purchase which he contemplated making. The gentleman was an enthusiastic collector of oriental antiquities, and had been for many years a liberal patron of the establishment in Lambeth. Oh, when shall we wean ourselves from the worship of Mammon! Mr Luker called a cab, and drove off instantly to his liberal patron.

Exactly what had happened to Mr Godfrey in Northumberland Street now happened to Mr Luker in Alfred Place. Once more the respectable man answered the door, and showed the visitor upstairs into the back drawing-room. There, again, lay the illuminated manuscript on a table. Mr Luker's attention was absorbed, as Mr Godfrey's attention had been absorbed, by this beautiful work of Indian art. He too was aroused from his studies by a tawny naked arm round his throat, by a bandage over his eyes, and by a gag in his mouth. He too was thrown prostrate, and searched to the skin. A longer interval had then elapsed than had passed in the experience of Mr Godfrey; but it had ended as before, in the persons of the house suspecting something wrong, and going upstairs to see what had happened. Precisely the same explanation which the landlord in Northumberland Street had given to Mr Godfrey, the landlord in Alfred Place now gave to Mr Luker. Both had been imposed on in the same way by the plausible address and well-filled purse of the respectable stranger, who introduced himself as acting for his foreign friends. The one point of difference between the two cases occurred when the scattered contents of Mr Luker's pockets were being collected from the floor. His watch and purse were safe, but (less fortunate than Mr Godfrey) one of the loose papers that he carried about him had been taken away. The paper in question acknowledged the receipt of a valuable of great price which Mr Luker had that day left in the care of his bankers. This document would be useless for purposes of fraud, inasmuch as it provided that the valuable should only be given up on the personal application of the owner. As soon as he recovered himself, Mr Luker hurried to the bank, on the chance that the thieves who had robbed him might ignorantly present themselves with the receipt. Nothing had been seen of them when he arrived at the establishment, and nothing was seen of them afterwards. Their respectable English friend had (in the opinion of the bankers) looked the receipt over before they attempted to make use of it, and had given them the necessary warning in good time.

Information of both outrages was communicated to the police, and the needful investigations were pursued, I believe, with great energy. The authorities held that a robbery had been planned, on insufficient information received by the thieves. They had been plainly not sure whether Mr Luker had, or had not, trusted the transmission of his precious gem to another person; and poor polite Mr Godfrey had paid the penalty of having been seen accidentally speaking to him. Add to this, that Mr Godfrey's absence from our Monday evening meeting had been occasioned by a consultation of the authorities, at which he was requested to assist – and all the explanations required being now given, I may proceed with the simpler story of my own little personal experiences in Montagu Square.

I was punctual to the luncheon hour on Tuesday. Reference to my diary shows this to have been a chequered day – much in it to be devoutly regretted, much in it to be devoutly thankful for.

Dear Aunt Verinder received me with her usual grace and kindness. But I noticed, after a little while, that something was wrong. Certain anxious looks escaped my aunt, all of which took the direction of her daughter. I never see Rachel myself without wondering how it can be that so insignificant-looking a person should be the child of such distinguished parents as Sir John and Lady Verinder. On this occasion, however, she not only disappointed – she really shocked me. There was an absence of all lady-like restraint in her language and manner most painful to see. She was possessed by some feverish excitement which made her distressingly loud when she laughed, and sinfully wasteful and capricious in what she ate and drank at lunch. I felt deeply for her poor mother, even before the true state of the case had been confidentially made known to me.

Luncheon over, my aunt said: 'Remember what the doctor told you, Rachel, about quieting yourself with a book after taking your meals.'

'I'll go into the library, mamma,' she answered. 'But if Godfrey calls, mind I am told of it. I am dying for more news of him, after his adventure in Northumberland Street.' She kissed her mother on the forehead, and looked my way. 'Good-bye, Clack,' she said, carelessly. Her insolence roused no angry feeling in me. I only made a private memorandum to pray for her.

When we were left by ourselves, my aunt told me the whole horrible story of the Indian Diamond, which, I am happy to know, it is not necessary to repeat here. She did not conceal from me that she would have preferred keeping silence on the subject. But when her own servants all knew of the loss of the Moonstone, and when some of the circumstances had actually found their way into the newspapers – when strangers were speculating whether there was any connection between what had happened at Lady Verinder's country-house, and what had happened in Northumberland Street and Alfred Place – concealment was not to be thought of; and perfect frankness became a necessity as well as a virtue.

Some persons, hearing what I now heard, would have been probably overwhelmed with astonishment. For my own part, knowing Rachel's spirit to have been essentially unregenerate from her childhood upwards, I was prepared for whatever my aunt could tell me on the subject of her daughter. It might have gone on from bad to worse till it ended in Murder; and I should still have said to myself, The natural result! oh, dear, dear, the natural result! The one thing that *did* shock me was the course my aunt had taken under the circumstances. Here surely was a case for a clergyman, if ever there was one yet! Lady Verinder had thought it a case for a physician. All my poor aunt's early life had been passed in her father's godless household. The natural result again! Oh, dear, dear, the natural result again!

'The doctors recommend plenty of exercise and amusement for Rachel, and strongly urge me to keep her mind as much as possible from dwelling on the past,' said Lady Verinder.

'Oh, what heathen advice!' I thought to myself. 'In this Christian country, what heathen advice!'

My aunt went on, 'I do my best to carry out my instructions. But this strange adventure of Godfrey's happens at a most unfortunate time. Rachel has been incessantly restless and excited since she first heard of it. She left me no peace till I had written and asked my nephew Ablewhite to come here. She even feels an interest in the other person who was roughly used – Mr Luker, or some such name – though the man is, of course, a total stranger to her.'

'Your knowledge of the world, dear aunt, is superior to mine,' I suggested diffidently. 'But there must be a reason surely for this extraordinary conduct on Rachel's part. She is keeping a sinful secret from you and from everybody. May there not be something in these recent events which threatens her secret with discovery?'

'Discovery?' repeated my aunt. 'What can you possibly mean? Discovery through Mr Luker? Discovery through my nephew?'

As the word passed her lips, a special providence occurred. The servant opened the door, and announced Mr Godfrey Ablewhite.

❧ TWO ❧

MR GODFREY FOLLOWED THE ANNOUNCEMENT of his name – as Mr Godfrey does everything else – exactly at the right time. He was not so close on the servant's heels as to startle us. He was not so far behind as to cause us the double inconvenience of a pause and an open door. It is in the completeness of his daily life that the true Christian appears. This dear man was very complete.

'Go to Miss Verinder,' said my aunt, addressing the servant, 'and tell her Mr Ablewhite is here.'

We both inquired after his health. We both asked him together whether he felt like himself again, after his terrible adventure of the past week. With perfect tact, he contrived to answer us at the same moment. Lady Verinder had his reply in words. I had his charming smile.

'What,' he cried, with infinite tenderness, 'have I done to deserve all this sympathy? My dear aunt! my dear Miss Clack! I have merely been mistaken for somebody else. I have only been blindfolded; I have only been strangled; I have only been thrown flat on my back, on a very thin carpet, covering a particularly hard floor. Just think how much worse it might have been! I might have been murdered; I might have been robbed. What have I lost? Nothing but Nervous Force – which the law doesn't recognize as property; so that, strictly speaking, I have lost nothing at all. If I could have had my own way, I would have kept my adventure to myself – I shrink from all this fuss and publicity. But Mr Luker made *his* injuries public, and *my* injuries, as the necessary consequence, have been proclaimed in their turn. I have become the property of the newspapers, until the gentle reader gets sick of the subject. I am very sick indeed of it myself. May the gentle reader soon be like me! And how is dear Rachel? Still enjoying the gaieties of London? So glad to hear it! Miss Clack, I need all your indulgence. I am sadly behind-hand with my Committee Work and my dear Ladies. But I really do hope to look in at the Mothers'-Small-Clothes next week. Did you make cheering progress at Monday's Committee? Was the Board hopeful about future prospects? And are we nicely off for Trousers?'

The heavenly gentleness of his smile made his apologies irresistible. The richness of his deep voice added its own indescribable charm to the interesting business question which he had just addressed to me. In truth, we were almost *too* nicely off for Trousers; we were quite overwhelmed by them. I was just about to say so, when the door opened again, and an element of worldly disturbance entered the room, in the person of Miss Verinder.

She approached dear Mr Godfrey at a most unladylike rate of speed, with her hair shockingly untidy, and her face, what *I* should call, unbecomingly flushed.

'I am charmed to see you, Godfrey,' she said, addressing him, I grieve to add, in the off-hand manner of one young man talking to another. 'I wish you had brought Mr Luker with you. You and he (as long as our present excitement lasts) are the two most interesting men in all London. It's morbid to say this; it's unhealthy; it's all that a well-regulated mind like Miss Clack's most instinctively shudders at. Never mind that. Tell me the whole of the Northumberland Street story directly. I know the newspapers have left some of it out.'

Even dear Mr Godfrey partakes of the fallen nature which we all inherit from Adam – it is a very small share of our human legacy, but, alas! he has it. I confess it grieved me to see him take Rachel's hand in both of his own hands, and lay it softly on the left side of his waistcoat. It was a direct encouragement to her reckless way of talking, and her insolent reference to me.

'Dearest Rachel,' he said, in the same voice which had thrilled me when he spoke of our prospects and our trousers, 'the newspapers have told you everything – and they have told it much better than I can.'

'Godfrey thinks we all make too much of the matter,' my aunt remarked. 'He has just been saying that he doesn't care to speak of it.'

'Why?'

She put the question with a sudden flash in her eyes, and a sudden look up into Mr Godfrey's face. On his side, he looked down at her with an indulgence so injudicious and so ill-deserved, that I really felt called on to interfere.

'Rachel, darling!' I remonstrated, gently, 'true greatness and true courage are ever modest.'

'You are a very good fellow in your way, Godfrey,' she said – not taking the smallest notice, observe, of me, and still speaking to her cousin as if she was one young man addressing another. 'But I am quite sure you are not great; I don't believe you possess any extraordinary courage; and I am firmly persuaded – if you ever had any modesty – that your lady-worshippers relieved you of that virtue a good many years since. You have some private reason for not talking of your adventure in Northumberland Street; and I mean to know it.'

'My reason is the simplest imaginable, and the most easily acknowledged,' he answered, still bearing with her. 'I am tired of the subject.'

'You are tired of the subject? My dear Godfrey, I am going to make a remark.'

'What is it?'

'You live a great deal too much in the society of women. And you have contracted two very bad habits in consequence. You have learnt to talk nonsense seriously, and you have got into a way of telling fibs for the pleasure of telling them. You can't go straight with your lady-worshippers. I mean to make you go straight with *me*. Come, and sit down. I am brimful of downright questions; and I expect you to be brimful of downright answers.'

She actually dragged him across the room to a chair by the window, where the light would fall on his face. I deeply feel being obliged to report such language, and to describe such conduct. But, hemmed in as I am, between Mr Franklin Blake's cheque on one side and my own sacred regard for truth on the other, what am I to do? I looked at my aunt. She sat unmoved; apparently in no way disposed to interfere. I had never noticed this kind of torpor in her before. It was, perhaps, the reaction after the trying time she had had in the country. Not a pleasant symptom to remark, be it what it might, at dear Lady Verinder's age, and with dear Lady Verinder's autumnal exuberance of figure.

In the meantime, Rachel had settled herself at the window with our amiable and forbearing – our too forbearing – Mr Godfrey. She began the string of questions with which she had threatened him, taking no more notice of her mother, or of myself, than if we had not been in the room.

'Have the police done anything, Godfrey?'

'Nothing whatever.'

'It is certain, I suppose, that the three men who laid the trap for you were the same three men who afterwards laid the trap for Mr Luker?'

'Humanly speaking, my dear Rachel, there can be no doubt of it.'

'And not a trace of them has been discovered?'

'Not a trace.'

'It is thought – is it not? – that these three men are the three Indians who came to our house in the country.'

'Some people think so.'

'Do you think so?'

'My dear Rachel, they blindfolded me before I could see their faces. I know nothing whatever of the matter. How can I offer an opinion on it?'

Even the angelic gentleness of Mr Godfrey was, you see, beginning to give way at last under the persecution inflicted on him. Whether unbridled curiosity, or ungovernable dread, dictated Miss Verinder's questions I do not presume to inquire. I only report that, on Mr Godfrey's attempting to rise, after giving her the answer just described, she actually took him by the two shoulders, and pushed him back into his chair – Oh, don't say this was immodest! don't even hint that the recklessness of guilty terror could alone account for such conduct as I have described! We must not judge others. My Christian friends, indeed, indeed, indeed, we must not judge others!

She went on with her questions, unabashed. Earnest Biblical students will perhaps be reminded – as I was reminded – of the blinded children of the devil, who went on with their orgies, unabashed, in the time before the Flood.

'I want to know something about Mr Luker, Godfrey.'

'I am again unfortunate, Rachel. No man knows less of Mr Luker than I do.'

'You never saw him before you and he met accidentally at the bank?'

'Never.'

'You have seen him since?'

'Yes. We have been examined together, as well as separately, to assist the police.'

'Mr Luker was robbed of a receipt which he had got from his banker's – was he not? What was the receipt for?'

'For a valuable gem which he had placed in the safe keeping of the bank.'

'That's what the newspapers say. It may be enough for the general reader; but it is not enough for me. The banker's receipt must have mentioned what the gem was?'

'The banker's receipt, Rachel – as I have heard it described – mentioned nothing of the kind. A valuable gem, belonging to Mr Luker; deposited by Mr Luker; sealed with Mr Luker's seal; and only to be given up on Mr Luker's personal application. That was the form, and that is all I know about it.'

She waited a moment, after he had said that. She looked at her mother, and sighed. She looked back again at Mr Godfrey, and went on.

'Some of our private affairs, at home,' she said, 'seem to have got into the newspapers?'

'I grieve to say, it is so.'

'And some idle people, perfect strangers to us, are trying to trace a connection between what happened at our house in Yorkshire and what has happened since, here in London?'

'The public curiosity, in certain quarters, is, I fear, taking that turn.'

'The people who say that the three unknown men who ill-used you and Mr Luker are the three Indians, also say that the valuable gem – '

There she stopped. She had become gradually, within the last few moments, whiter and whiter in the face. The extraordinary blackness of her hair made this paleness, by contrast, so ghastly to look at, that we all thought she would faint, at the moment when she checked herself in the middle of her question. Dear Mr Godfrey made a second attempt to leave his chair. My aunt entreated her to say no more. I followed my aunt with a modest medicinal peace-offering, in the shape of a bottle of salts. We none of us produced the slightest effect on her. 'Godfrey, stay where you are. Mamma, there is not the least reason to be alarmed about me. Clack, you're dying to hear the end of it – I won't faint, expressly to oblige *you*.'

Those were the exact words she used – taken down in my diary the moment I got home. But, oh, don't let us judge! My Christian friends, don't let us judge!

She turned once more to Mr Godfrey. With an obstinacy dreadful to see, she went back again to the place where she had checked herself, and completed her question in these words:

'I spoke to you, a minute since, about what people were saying in certain quarters. Tell me plainly, Godfrey, do they any of them say that Mr Luker's valuable gem is – the Moonstone?'

As the name of the Indian Diamond passed her lips, I saw a change come over my admirable friend. His complexion deepened. He lost the genial suavity of manner which is one of his greatest charms. A noble indignation inspired his reply.

'They *do* say it,' he answered. 'There are people who don't hesitate to accuse Mr Luker of telling a falsehood to serve some private interests of his own. He has over and over again solemnly declared that, until this scandal assailed him, he had never even heard of the Moonstone. And these vile people reply, without a shadow of proof to justify them, He has his reasons for concealment; we decline to believe him on his oath. Shameful! shameful!'

Rachel looked at him very strangely – I can't well describe how – while he was speaking. When he had done, she said.

'Considering that Mr Luker is only a chance acquaintance of yours, you take up his cause, Godfrey, rather warmly.'

My gifted friend made her one of the most truly evangelical answers I ever heard in my life.

'I hope, Rachel, I take up the cause of all oppressed people rather warmly,' he said.

The tone in which those words were spoken might have melted a stone. But, oh dear, what is the hardness of stone? Nothing, compared to the hardness of the unregenerate human heart! She sneered. I blush to record it – she sneered at him to his face.

'Keep your noble sentiments for your Ladies' Committees, Godfrey. I am certain that the scandal which has assailed Mr Luker, has not spared You.'

Even my aunt's torpor was roused by those words.

'My dear Rachel,' she remonstrated. 'you have really no right to say that!'

'I mean no harm, mamma – I mean good. Have a moment's patience with me, and you will see.'

She looked back at Mr Godfrey, with what appeared to be a sudden pity for him. She went the length – the very unladylike length – of taking him by the hand.

'I am certain,' she said, 'that I have found out the true reason of your unwillingness to speak of this matter before my mother and before me. An unlucky accident has associated you in people's minds with Mr Luker. You have told me what scandal says of *him*. What does scandal say of *you*?'

Even at the eleventh hour, dear Mr Godfrey – always ready to return good for evil – tried to spare her.

'Don't ask me!' he said. 'It's better forgotten, Rachel – it is, indeed.'

'I *will* hear it!' she cried out, fiercely, at the top of her voice.

'Tell her, Godfrey!' entreated my aunt. 'Nothing can do her such harm as your silence is doing now!'

Mr Godfrey's fine eyes filled with tears. He cast one last appealing look at her – and then he spoke the fatal words:

'If you will have it, Rachel – scandal says that the Moonstone is in pledge to Mr Luker, and that I am the man who has pawned it.'

She started to her feet with a scream. She looked backwards and forwards from Mr Godfrey to my aunt, and from my aunt to Mr Godfrey, in such a frantic manner that I really thought she had gone mad.

'Don't speak to me! Don't touch me!' she exclaimed, shrinking back from all of us (I declare like some hunted animal!) into a corner of the room. 'This is my fault! I must set it right. I have sacrificed myself – I had a right to do that, if I liked. But to let an innocent man be ruined; to keep a secret which destroys his character for life – Oh, good God, it's too horrible! I can't bear it!'

My aunt half rose from her chair, then suddenly sat down again. She called to me faintly, and pointed to a little phial in her work-box.

'Quick!' she whispered. 'Six drops, in water. Don't let Rachel see.'

Under other circumstances, I should have thought this strange. There was no time now to think – there was only time to give the medicine. Dear Mr Godfrey unconsciously assisted me in concealing what I was about from Rachel, by speaking composing words to her at the other end of the room.

'Indeed, indeed, you exaggerate,' I heard him say. 'My reputation stands too high to be destroyed by a miserable passing scandal like this. It will be all forgotten in another week. Let us never speak of it again.' She was perfectly inaccessible, even to such generosity as this. She went on from bad to worse.

'I must, and will, stop it,' she said. 'Mamma! hear what I say, Miss Clack! hear what I say. I know the hand that took the Moonstone. I know—' she laid a strong emphasis on the words; she stamped her foot in the rage that possessed her – '*I know that Godfrey Ablewhite is innocent.* Take me to the magistrate, Godfrey! Take me to the magistrate, and I will swear it!'

My aunt caught me by the hand, and whispered, 'Stand between us for a minute or two. Don't let Rachel see me.' I noticed a bluish tinge in her face which alarmed me. She saw I was startled. 'The drops will put me right in a minute or two,' she said, and so closed her eyes, and waited a little.

While this was going on, I heard dear Mr Godfrey still gently remonstrating.

'You must not appear publicly in such a thing as this,' he said. '*Your* reputation, dearest Rachel, is something too pure and too sacred to be trifled with.'

'*My* reputation!' She burst out laughing. 'Why, I am accused, Godfrey, as well as you. The best detective-officer in England declares that I have stolen my own Diamond. Ask him what he thinks – and he will tell you that I have pledged the Moonstone to pay my private debts!' She stopped, ran across the room – and fell on her knees at her mother's feet. 'Oh, mamma! mamma! mamma! I must be mad – mustn't I? – not to own the truth *now*?' She was too vehement to notice her mother's condition – she was on her feet again, and back with Mr Godfrey, in an instant. 'I won't let you – I won't let any innocent Man – be accused and disgraced through my fault. If you won't take me before the magistrate, draw out a declaration of your innocence on paper, and I will sign it. Do as I tell you, Godfrey, or I'll write it to the newspapers – I'll go out, and cry it in the streets!'

We will not say this was the language of remorse – we will say it was the language of hysterics. Indulgent Mr Godfrey pacified her by taking a sheet of paper, and drawing out the declaration. She signed it in a feverish hurry. 'Show it everywhere – don't think of *me*,' she said, as she gave it to him. 'I am afraid, Godfrey, I have not done you justice, hitherto, in my thoughts. You are more unselfish – you are a better man than I believed you to be. Come here when you can, and I will try and repair the wrong I have done you.'

She gave him her hand. Alas, for our fallen nature! Alas, for Mr Godfrey! He not only forgot himself so far as to kiss her hand – he adopted a gentleness of tone in answering her which, in such a case, was little better than a compromise with sin. 'I will come, dearest,' he said, 'on condition that we don't speak of this hateful subject again.' Never had I seen and heard our Christian Hero to less advantage than on this occasion.

Before another word could be said by anybody, a thundering knock at the street door startled us all. I looked through the window, and saw the World, the Flesh, and the Devil waiting before the house – as typified in a carriage and horses, a powdered footman, and three of the most audaciously dressed women I ever beheld in my life.

Rachel started, and composed herself. She crossed the room to her mother.

'They have come to take me to the flower-show,' she said. 'One word, mamma, before I go. I have not distressed you, have I?'

(Is the bluntness of moral feeling which could ask such a question as that, after what had just happened, to be pitied or condemned? I like to lean towards mercy. Let us pity it.)

The drops had produced their effect. My poor aunt's complexion was like itself again. 'No, no, my dear,' she said. 'Go with our friends, and enjoy yourself.'

Her daughter stooped, and kissed her. I had left the window, and was near the door, when Rachel approached it to go out. Another change had come over her – she was in tears. I looked with interest at the momentary softening of that obdurate heart. I felt inclined to say a few earnest words. Alas! my well-meant sympathy only gave offence. 'What do you mean by pitying me?' she asked, in a bitter whisper, as she passed to the door. 'Don't you see how happy I am? I'm going to the flower-show, Clack; and I've got the prettiest bonnet in London.' She completed the hollow mockery of that address by blowing me a kiss – and so left the room.

I wish I could describe in words the compassion that I felt for this miserable and misguided girl. But I am almost as poorly provided with words as with money. Permit me to say – my heart bled for her.

Returning to my aunt's chair, I observed dear Mr Godfrey searching for something softly, here and there, in different parts of the room. Before I could offer to assist him, he had found what he wanted. He came back to my aunt and me, with his declaration of innocence in one hand, and with a box of matches in the other.

'Dear aunt, a little conspiracy!' he said, 'Dear Miss Clack, a pious fraud which even your high moral rectitude will excuse! Will you leave Rachel to suppose that I accept the generous self-sacrifice which has signed this paper? And will you kindly bear witness that I destroy it in your presence, before I leave the house?' He kindled a match, and, lighting the paper, laid it to burn in a plate on the table. 'Any trifling inconvenience that I may suffer is as nothing,' he remarked, 'compared with the importance of preserving that pure name from the contaminating contact of the world. There! We have reduced it to a little harmless heap of ashes; and our dear impulsive Rachel will never know what we have done! How do you feel? My precious friends, how do you feel? For my poor part, I am as light-hearted as a boy!'

He beamed on us with his beautiful smile; he held out a hand to my aunt, and a hand to me. I was too deeply affected by his noble conduct to speak. I closed my eyes; I put his hand, in a kind of spiritual self-forgetfulness, to my lips. He murmured a soft remonstrance. Oh, the ecstasy, the pure, unearthly ecstasy of that moment! I sat – I hardly know on what – quite lost in my own exalted feelings. When I opened my eyes again, it was like descending from heaven to earth. There was nobody but my aunt in the room. He had gone.

I should like to stop here – I should like to close my narrative with the record of Mr Godfrey's noble conduct. Unhappily, there is more, much more, which the unrelenting pecuniary pressure of Mr Blake's cheque obliges me to tell. The painful disclosures which were to reveal themselves in my presence, during that Tuesday's visit to Montagu Square, were not at an end yet.

Finding myself alone with Lady Verinder, I turned naturally to the subject of her health; touching delicately on the strange anxiety which she had shown to conceal her indisposition, and the remedy applied to it, from the observation of her daughter.

My aunt's reply greatly surprised me.

'Drusilla,' she said (if I have not already mentioned that my christian name is Drusilla, permit me to mention it now), 'you are touching – quite innocently, I know – on a very distressing subject.'

I rose immediately. Delicacy left me but one alternative – the alternative, after first making my apologies, of taking my leave. Lady Verinder stopped me, and insisted on my sitting down again.

'You have surprised a secret,' she said, 'which I had confided to my sister Mrs Ablewhite, and to my lawyer Mr Bruff, and to no one else. I can trust in their discretion; and I am sure, when I tell you the circumstances, I can trust in yours. Have you any pressing engagement, Drusilla? or is your time your own this afternoon?'

It is needless to say that my time was entirely at my aunt's disposal.

'Keep me company then,' she said, 'for another hour. I have something to tell you which I believe you will be sorry to hear. And I shall have a service to ask of you afterwards, if you don't object to assist me.'

It is again needless to say that, so far from objecting, I was all eagerness to assist her.

'You can wait here,' she went on, ''till Mr Bruff comes at five. And you can be one of the witnesses, Drusilla, when I sign my Will.'

Her Will! I thought of the drops which I had seen in her work-box. I thought of the bluish tinge which I had noticed in her complexion. A light which was not of this world – a light shining prophetically from an unmade grave – dawned on my mind. My aunt's secret was a secret no longer.

❧ THREE ❧

CONSIDERATION FOR POOR LADY VERINDER forbade me even to hint that I had guessed the melancholy truth, before she opened her lips. I waited her pleasure in silence; and, having privately arranged to say a few sustaining words at the first convenient opportunity, felt prepared for any duty that could claim me, no matter how painful it might be.

'I have been seriously ill, Drusilla, for some time past,' my aunt began. 'And, strange to say, without knowing it myself.'

I thought of the thousands and thousands of perishing human

creatures who were all at that moment spiritually ill, without knowing it themselves. And I greatly feared that my poor aunt might be one of the number. 'Yes, dear,' I said, sadly. 'Yes.'

'I brought Rachel to London, as you know, for medical advice,' she went on. 'I thought it right to consult two doctors.'

Two doctors! And, oh me (in Rachel's state), not one clergyman! 'Yes, dear?' I said once more. 'Yes?'

'One of the two medical men,' proceeded my aunt, 'was a stranger to me. The other had been an old friend of my husband's, and had always felt a sincere interest in me for my husband's sake. After prescribing for Rachel, he said he wished to speak to me privately in another room. I expected, of course, to receive some special directions for the management of my daughter's health. To my surprise, he took me gravely by the hand, and said, 'I have been looking at you, Lady Verinder, with a professional as well as a personal interest. You are, I am afraid, far more urgently in need of medical advice than your daughter.' He put some questions to me, which I was at first inclined to treat lightly enough, until I observed that my answers distressed him. It ended in his making an appointment to come and see me, accompanied by a medical friend, on the next day, at an hour when Rachel would not be at home. The result of that visit – most kindly and gently conveyed to me – satisfied both the physicians that there had been precious time lost, which could never be regained, and that my case had now passed beyond the reach of their art. For more than two years I have been suffering under an insidious form of heart disease, which, without any symptoms to alarm me, has, by little and little, fatally broken me down. I may live for some months, or I may die before another day has passed over my head – the doctors cannot, and dare not, speak more positively than this. It would be vain to say, my dear, that I have not had some miserable moments since my real situation has been made known to me. But I am more resigned than I was, and I am doing my best to set my worldly affairs in order. My one great anxiety is that Rachel should be kept in ignorance of the truth. If she knew it, she would at once attribute my broken health to anxiety about the Diamond, and would reproach herself bitterly, poor child, for what is in no sense her fault. Both the doctors agree that the mischief began two, if not three years since. I am sure you will keep my secret, Drusilla – for I am sure I see sincere sorrow and sympathy for me in your face.'

Sorrow and sympathy! Oh, what Pagan emotions to expect from a Christian English-woman anchored firmly on her faith!

Little did my poor aunt imagine what a gush of devout thankfulness thrilled through me as she approached the close of her melancholy story. Here was a career of usefulness opened before me! Here was a beloved relative and perishing fellow-creature, on the eve of the great change, utterly unprepared; and led, providentially led, to reveal her situation to Me! How can I describe the joy with which I now remembered that the precious clerical friends on whom I could rely, were to be counted, not by ones or twos, but by tens and twenties! I took my aunt in my arms – my overflowing tenderness was not to be satisfied, *now*, with anything less than an embrace. 'Oh!' I said to her, fervently, 'the indescribable interest with which you inspire me! Oh! the good I mean to do you, dear, before we part!' After another word or two of earnest prefatory warning, I gave her her choice of three precious friends, all plying the work of mercy from morning to night in her own neighbourhood; all equally inexhaustible in exhortation; all affectionately ready to exercise their gifts at a word from *me*. Alas! the result was far from encouraging. Poor Lady Verinder looked puzzled and frightened, and met everything I could say to her with the purely worldly objection that she was not strong enough to face strangers. I yielded – for the moment only, of course. My large experience (as Reader and Visitor, under not less, first and last, than fourteen beloved clerical friends) informed me that this was another case for preparation by books. I possessed a little library of works, all suitable to the present emergency, all calculated to arouse, convince, prepare, enlighten, and fortify my aunt. 'You will read, dear, won't you?' I said, in my most winning way. 'You will read, if I bring you my own precious books? Turned down at all the right places, aunt. And marked in pencil where you are to stop and ask yourself, ' "Does this apply to me?" ' Even that simple appeal – so absolutely heathenizing is the influence of the world – appeared to startle my aunt. She said, 'I will do what I can, Drusilla, to please you,' with a look of surprise, which was at once instructive and terrible to see. Not a moment was to be lost. The clock on the mantelpiece informed me that I had just time to hurry home; to provide myself with a first series of selected readings (say a dozen only); and to return in time to meet the lawyer, and witness Lady Verinder's Will. Promising faithfully to be back by five o'clock, I left the house on my errand of mercy.

When no interests but my own are involved, I am humbly content to get from place to place by the omnibus. Permit me to give an idea of my devotion to my aunt's interests by recording that, on this occasion, I committed the prodigality of taking a cab.

I drove home, selected and marked my first series of readings, and drove back to Montagu Square, with a dozen works in a carpet-bag, the like of which, I firmly believe, are not to be found in the literature of any other country in Europe. I paid the cabman exactly his fare. He received it with an oath; upon which I instantly gave him a tract. If I had presented a pistol at his head, this abandoned wretch could hardly have exhibited greater consternation. He jumped up on his box, and, with profane exclamations of dismay, drove off furiously. Quite useless, I am happy to say! I sowed the good seed, in spite of him, by throwing a second tract in at the window of the cab.

The servant who answered the door – not the person with the cap-ribbons, to my great relief, but the footman – informed me that the doctor had called, and was still shut up with Lady Verinder. Mr Bruff, the lawyer, had arrived a minute since and was waiting in the library. I was shown into the library to wait too.

Mr Bruff looked surprised to see me. He is the family solicitor, and we had met more than once, on previous occasions, under Lady Verinder's roof. A man, I grieve to say, grown old and grizzled in the service of the world. A man who, in his hours of business, was the chosen prophet of Law and Mammon; and who, in his hours of leisure, was equally capable of reading a novel and of tearing up a tract.

'Have you come to stay here, Miss Clack?' he asked, with a look at my carpet-bag.

To reveal the contents of my precious bag to such a person as this would have been simply to invite an outburst of profanity. I lowered myself to his own level, and mentioned my business in the house.

'My aunt has informed me that she is about to sign her Will,' I answered. 'She has been so good as to ask me to be one of the witnesses.'

'Aye? aye? Well, Miss Clack, you will do. You are over twenty-one, and you have not the slightest pecuniary interest in Lady Verinder's Will.'

Not the slightest pecuniary interest in Lady Verinder's Will. Oh, how thankful I felt when I heard that! If my aunt, possessed of thousands, had remembered poor Me, to whom five pounds is an object – if my name had appeared in the Will, with a little comforting legacy attached to it – my enemies might have doubted the motive which had loaded me with the choicest treasures of my library, and had drawn upon my failing resources for the prodigal expenses of a cab. Not the cruellest scoffer of them all could doubt now. Much better as it was! Oh, surely, surely, much better as it was!

I was aroused from these consoling reflections by the voice of Mr Bruff. My meditative silence appeared to weigh upon the spirits of this worldling, and to force him, as it were, into talking to me against his own will.

'Well, Miss Clack, what's the last news in the charitable circles? How is your friend Mr Godfrey Ablewhite, after the mauling he got from the rogues in Northumberland Street? Egad! they're telling a pretty story about that charitable gentleman at my club!'

I had passed over the manner in which this person had remarked that I was more than twenty-one, and that I had no pecuniary interest in my aunt's Will. But the tone in which he alluded to dear Mr Godfrey was too much for my forbearance. Feeling bound, after what had passed in my presence that afternoon, to assert the innocence of my admirable friend, whenever I found it called in question – I own to having also felt bound to include in the accomplishment of this righteous purpose, a stinging castigation in the case of Mr Bruff.

'I live very much out of the world,' I said; 'and I don't possess the advantage, sir, of belonging to a club. But I happen to know the story to which you allude; and I also know that a viler falsehood than that story never was told.'

'Yes, yes, Miss Clack – you believe in your friend. Natural enough. Mr Godfrey Ablewhite won't find the world in general quite so easy to convince as a committee of charitable ladies. Appearances are dead against him. He was in the house when the Diamond was lost. And he was the first person in the house to go to London afterwards. Those are ugly circumstances, ma'am, viewed by the light of later events.'

I ought, I know, to have set him right before he went any farther. I ought to have told him that he was speaking in ignorance of a testimony to Mr Godfrey's innocence, offered by the only person who was undeniably competent to speak from a positive knowledge of the subject. Alas! the temptation to lead the lawyer artfully on to his own discomfiture was too much for me. I asked what he meant by 'later events' – with an appearance of the utmost innocence.

'By later events, Miss Clack, I mean events in which the Indians are concerned,' proceeded Mr Bruff, getting more and more superior to poor Me, the longer he went on. 'What do the Indians do, the moment they are let out of the prison at Frizinghall? They go straight to London, and fix on Mr Luker. What follows? Mr Luker feels alarmed for the safety of "a valuable of great price", which he has got in the house. He lodges it privately (under a general description) in his bankers' strong-room. Wonderfully clever of him: but the Indians are just as clever on their side. They have their suspicions that the "valuable of great price" is being shifted from one place to another; and they hit on a singularly bold and complete way of clearing those suspicions up. Whom do they seize and search? Not Mr Luker only – which would be intelligible enough – but Mr Godfrey Ablewhite as well. Why? Mr Ablewhite's explanation is, that they acted on blind suspicion, after seeing him accidentally speaking to Mr Luker. Absurd! Half a dozen other people spoke to Mr Luker that morning. Why were they not followed home too, and decoyed into the trap? No! no! The plain inference is, that Mr Ablewhite had his private interest in the "valuable" as well as Mr Luker, and that the Indians were so uncertain as to which of the two had the disposal of it, that there was no alternative but to search them both. Public opinion says that, Miss Clack. And public opinion, on this occasion, is not easily refuted.'

He said those last words, looking so wonderfully wise in his own worldly conceit, that I really (to my shame be it spoken) could not resist leading him a little farther still, before I overwhelmed him with the truth.

'I don't presume to argue with a clever lawyer like you,' I said. 'But is it quite fair, sir, to Mr Ablewhite to pass over the opinion of the famous London police-officer who investigated this case? Not the shadow of a suspicion rested upon anybody but Miss Verinder, in the mind of Sergeant Cuff.'

'Do you mean to tell me, Miss Clack, that you agree with the Sergeant? 'I judge nobody, sir, and I offer no opinion.'

'And I commit both those enormities, ma'am. I judge the Sergeant to have been utterly wrong; and I offer the opinion that, if he had known Rachel's character as I know it, he would have suspected everybody in the house but *her*. I admit that she has her faults – she is secret, and self-willed; odd and wild, and unlike other girls of her age. But true as steel, and high-minded and generous to a fault. If the plainest evidence in the world pointed one way, and if nothing but Rachel's word of honour pointed the other, I would take her word before the evidence, lawyer as I am! Strong language, Miss Clack; but I mean it.'

'Would you object to illustrate your meaning, Mr Bruff, so that I may be sure I understand it? Suppose you found Miss Verinder quite unaccountably interested in what has happened to Mr Ablewhite and Mr Luker? Suppose she asked the strangest questions about this dreadful scandal, and displayed the most ungovernable agitation when she found out the turn it was taking?'

'Suppose anything you please, Miss Clack, it wouldn't shake my belief in Rachel Verinder by a hair's-breadth.'

'She is so absolutely to be relied on as that?'

'So absolutely to be relied on as that?'

'Then permit me to inform you, Mr Bruff, that Mr Godfrey Ablewhite was in this house not two hours since, and that his entire innocence of all concern in the disappearance of the Moonstone was proclaimed by Miss Verinder herself, in the strongest language I ever heard used by a young lady in my life.'

I enjoyed the triumph – the unholy triumph, I fear, I must admit – of seeing Mr Bruff utterly confounded and overthrown by a few plain words from Me. He started to his feet, and stared at me in silence. I kept my seat, undisturbed, and related the whole scene as it had occurred.

'And what do you say about Mr Ablewhite *now?*' I asked, with the utmost possible gentleness, as soon as I had done.

'If Rachel has testified to his innocence, Miss Clack, I don't scruple to say that I believe in his innocence as firmly as you do. I have been misled by appearances, like the rest of the world; and I will make the best atonement I can, by publicly contradicting the scandal which has assailed your friend wherever I meet with it. In the meantime, allow me to congratulate you on the masterly manner in which You have opened the full fire of your batteries on me at the moment when I least expected it. You would have done great things in my profession, ma'am, if you had happened to be a man.'

With those words he turned away from me, and began walking irritably up and down the room.

I could see plainly that the new light I had thrown on the subject had greatly surprised and disturbed him. Certain expressions dropped from his lips, as he became more and more absorbed in his own thoughts, which suggested to my mind the abominable view that he had hitherto taken of the mystery of the lost Moonstone. He had not scrupled to suspect dear Mr Godfrey of the infamy of stealing the Diamond, and to attribute Rachel's conduct to a generous resolution to conceal the crime. On Miss Verinder's own authority – a perfectly unassailable authority, as you are aware, in the estimation of Mr Bruff – that explanation of the circumstances was now shown to be utterly wrong. The perplexity into which I had plunged this high legal authority was so overwhelming that he was quite unable to conceal it from notice. 'What a case!' I heard him say to himself, stopping at the window in his walk, and drumming on the glass with his fingers. 'It not only defies explanation, it's even beyond conjecture.'

There was nothing in these words which made any reply at all needful, on my part – and yet, I answered them! It seems hardly credible that I should not have been able to let Mr Bruff alone, even now. It seems almost beyond mere mortal perversity that I should have discovered, in what he had just said, a new opportunity of making myself personally disagreeable to him. But – ah, my friends! nothing is beyond mortal perversity; and anything is credible when our fallen natures get the better of us!

'Pardon me for intruding on your reflections,' I said to the unsuspecting Mr Bruff. 'But surely there is a conjecture to make which has not occurred to us yet.'

'Maybe, Miss Clack. I own I don't know what it is.'

'Before I was so fortunate, sir, as to convince you of Mr Ablewhite's innocence, you mentioned it as one of the reasons for suspecting him, that he was in the house at the time when the Diamond was lost. Permit me to remind you that Mr Franklin Blake was also in the house at the time when the Diamond was lost.'

The old worldling left the window, took a chair exactly opposite to mine, and looked at me steadily, with a hard and vicious smile.

'You are not so good a lawyer, Miss Clack,' he remarked in a meditative manner, 'as I supposed. You don't know how to let well alone.'

'I am afraid I fail to follow you, Mr Bruff,' I said, modestly.

'It won't do, Miss Clack – it really won't do a second time. Franklin Blake is a prime favourite of mine, as you are well aware. But that doesn't matter. I'll adopt your view, on this occasion, before you have time to turn round on me. You're quite right, ma'am. I have suspected Mr Ablewhite, on grounds which abstractedly justify suspecting Mr Blake too. Very good – let's suspect them together. It's quite in his character, we will say, to be capable of stealing the Moonstone. The only question is, whether it was his interest to do so.'

'Mr Franklin Blake's debts,' I remarked, 'are matters of family notoriety.'

'And Mr Godfrey Ablewhite's debts have not arrived at that stage of development yet. Quite true. But there happen to be two difficulties in the way of your theory, Miss Clack. I manage Franklin Blake's affairs, and I beg to inform you that the vast majority of his creditors (knowing his father to be a rich man) are quite content to charge interest on their debts, and to wait for their money. There is the first difficulty – which is tough enough. You will find the second tougher still. I have it on the authority of Lady Verinder herself, that her daughter was ready to marry Franklin Blake, before that infernal Indian Diamond disappeared from the house. She had drawn him on and put him off again, with the coquetry of a young girl. But she had confessed to her mother that she loved cousin Franklin, and her mother had trusted cousin Franklin with the secret. So there he was, Miss Clack, with his creditors content to wait, and with the certain prospect before him of marrying an heiress. By all means consider him a scoundrel; but tell me, if you please, why he should steal the Moonstone?'

'The human heart is unsearchable,' I said gently. 'Who is to fathom it?'

'In other words, ma'am – though he hadn't the shadow of a reason for taking the Diamond – he might have taken it, nevertheless, through natural depravity. Very well. Say he did. Why the devil—'

'I beg your pardon, Mr Bruff. If I hear the devil referred to in that manner, I must leave the room.'

'I beg *your* pardon, Miss Clack – I'll be more careful in my choice of language for the future. All I meant to ask was this. Why – even supposing he did take the Diamond – should Franklin Blake make himself the most prominent person in the house, in trying to recover it? You may tell me he cunningly did that to divert suspicion from himself. I answer that he had no need to divert suspicion – because nobody suspected him. He first steals the Moonstone (without the slightest reason) through natural depravity; and he then acts a part, in relation to the loss of the jewel, which there is not the slightest necessity to act, and which leads to his mortally offending the young lady who would otherwise have married him. That is the monstrous proposition which you are driven to assert, if you attempt to associate the disappearance of the Moonstone with Franklin Blake. No, no, Miss Clack! After what has passed here to-day, between us two, the dead-lock, in this case, is complete. Rachel's own innocence is (as her mother knows, and as I know) beyond a doubt. Mr Ablewhite's innocence is equally certain – or Rachel would never have testified to it. And Franklin Blake's innocence, as you have just seen, unanswerably asserts itself. On the one hand, we are morally certain of all these things. And, on the other hand, we are equally sure that somebody has brought the Moonstone to London, and that Mr Luker, or his banker, is in private possession of it at this moment. What is the use of my experience, what is the use of any person's experience, in such a case as that? It baffles me; it baffles you; it baffles everybody.'

No – not everybody. It had not baffled Sergeant Cuff. I was about to mention this, with all possible mildness, and with every necessary protest against being supposed to cast a slur upon Rachel – when the servant came in to say that the doctor had gone, and that my aunt was waiting to receive us.

This stopped the discussion. Mr Bruff collected his papers, looking a little exhausted by the demands which our conversation had made on him. I took up my bag-full of precious publications, feeling as if I could have gone on talking for hours. We proceeded in silence to Lady Verinder's room.

Permit me to add here, before my narrative advances to other events, that I have not described what passed between the lawyer and me, without having a definite object in view. I am ordered to include in my contribution to the shocking story of the Moonstone a plain disclosure, not only of the turn which suspicion took, but even of the names of the persons on whom suspicion rested, at the time when the Indian Diamond was believed to be in London. A report of my conversation in the library with Mr Bruff appeared to me to be exactly what was wanted to answer this purpose – while, at the same time, it possessed the great moral advantage of rendering a sacrifice of sinful self-esteem essentially necessary on my part. I have been obliged to acknowledge that my fallen nature got the better of me. In making that humiliating confession, *I get* the better of my fallen nature. The moral balance is restored; the spiritual atmosphere feels clear once more. Dear friends, we may go on again.

⋐ FOUR ⋑

THE SIGNING OF THE WILL was a much shorter matter than I had anticipated. It was hurried over, to my thinking, in indecent haste. Samuel,
the footman, was sent for to act as second witness – and the pen was
put at once into my aunt's hand. I felt strongly urged to say a few
appropriate words on this solemn occasion. But Mr Bruff's manner convinced me that it was wisest to check the impulse while he was in the
room. In less than two minutes it was all over – and Samuel (unbenefited
by what I might have said) had gone downstairs again.

Mr Bruff folded up the Will, and then looked my way; apparently
wondering whether I did or did not mean to leave him alone with my
aunt. I had my mission of mercy to fulfil, and my bag of precious
publications ready on my lap. He might as well have expected to move
St Paul's Cathedral by looking at it, as to move Me. There was one merit
about him (due no doubt to his worldly training) which I have no wish
to deny. He was quick at seeing things. I appeared to produce almost
the same impression on him which I had produced on the cabman. *He*
too uttered a profane expression, and withdrew in a violent hurry, and
left me mistress of the field.

As soon as we were alone, my aunt reclined on the sofa, and then
alluded, with some appearance of confusion, to the subject of her Will.

'I hope you won't think yourself neglected, Drusilla,' she said. 'I mean
to *give* you your little legacy, my dear, with my own hand.'

Here was a golden opportunity! I seized it on the spot. In other words,
I instantly opened my bag, and took out the top publication. It proved
to be an early edition – only the twenty-fifth – of the famous anonymous
work (believed to be by precious Miss Bellows), entitled *The Serpent at
Home*. The design of the book – with which the worldly reader may not
be acquainted – is to show how the Evil One lies in wait for us in all the
most apparently innocent actions of our daily lives. The chapters best
adapted to female perusal are 'Satan in the Hair Brush'; 'Satan behind
the Looking Glass'; 'Satan under the Tea Table'; 'Satan out of the Window'
– and many others.

'Give your attention, dear aunt, to this precious book – and you will
give me all I ask.' With those words, I handed it to her open, at a marked

202

passage – one continuous burst of burning eloquence! Subject: Satan among the Sofa Cushions.

Poor Lady Verinder (reclining thoughtlessly on her own sofa cushions) glanced at the book, and handed it back to me looking more confused than ever.

'I'm afraid, Drusilla,' she said, 'I must wait till I am a little better, before I can read that. The doctor – '

The moment she mentioned the doctor's name, I knew what was coming. Over and over again in my past experience among my perishing fellow-creatures, the members of the notoriously infidel profession of Medicine had stepped between me and my mission of mercy – on the miserable pretence that the patient wanted quiet, and that the disturbing influence of all others which they most dreaded, was the influence of Miss Clack and her Books. Precisely the same blinded materialism (working treacherously behind my back) now sought to rob me of the only right of property that my property could claim – my right of spiritual property in my perishing aunt.

'The doctor tells me,' my poor misguided relative went on, 'that I am not so well to-day. He forbids me to see any strangers; and he orders me, if I read at all, only to read the lightest and the most amusing books. "Do nothing, Lady Verinder, to wear your head, or to quicken your pulse" – those were his last words, Drusilla, when he left me to-day.'

There was no help for it but to yield again – for the moment only, as before. Any open assertion of the infinitely superior importance of such a ministry as mine, compared with the ministry of the medical man, would only have provoked the doctor to practise on the human weakness of his patient, and to threaten to throw up the case. Happily, there are more ways than one of sowing the good seed, and few persons are better versed in those ways than myself.

'You might feel stronger, dear, in an hour or two,' I said. 'Or you might wake, to-morrow morning, with a sense of something wanting, and even this unpretending volume might be able to supply it. You will let me leave the book, aunt? The doctor can hardly object to that!'

I slipped it under the sofa cushions, half in, and half out, close by her handkerchief, and her smelling-bottle. Every time her hand searched for either of these, it would touch the book; and, sooner or later (who knows?) the book might touch *her*. After making this arrangement, I thought it wise to withdraw. 'Let me leave you to repose, dear aunt; I will call again to-morrow.' I looked accidentally towards the window as I said that. It was full of flowers, in boxes and pots. Lady Verinder was extravagantly fond of these perishable treasures, and had a habit of rising every now and then, and going to look at them and smell them. A new idea flashed across my mind. 'Oh! may I take a flower?' I said –

and got to the window unsuspected, in that way. Instead of taking away a flower, I added one, in the shape of another book from my bag, which I left, to surprise my aunt, among the geraniums and roses. The happy thought followed, 'Why not do the same for her, poor dear, in every other room that she enters?' I immediately said good-bye; and, crossing the hall, slipped into the library. Samuel, coming up to let me out, and supposing I had gone, went downstairs again. On the library table I noticed two of the 'amusing books' which the infidel doctor had recommended. I instantly covered them from sight with two of my own precious publications. In the breakfast-room I found my aunt's favourite canary singing in his cage. She was always in the habit of feeding the bird herself. Some groundsel was strewed on a table which stood immediately under the cage. I put a book among the groundsel. In the drawing-room I found more cheering opportunities of emptying my bag. My aunt's favourite musical pieces were on the piano. I slipped in two more books among the music. I disposed of another in the back drawing-room, under some unfinished embroidery, which I knew to be of Lady Verinder's working. A third little room opened out of the back drawing-room, from which it was shut off by curtains instead of a door. My aunt's plain old-fashioned fan was on the chimney-piece. I opened my ninth book at a very special passage, and put the fan in as a marker, to keep the place. The question then came, whether I should go higher still, and try the bedroom floor – at the risk, undoubtedly, of being insulted, if the person with the cap-ribbons happened to be in the upper regions of the house, and to find me out. But oh, what of that? It is a poor Christian that is afraid of being insulted. I went upstairs, prepared to bear anything. All was silent and solitary – it was the servants' tea-time, I suppose. My aunt's room was in front. The miniature of my late dear uncle, Sir John, hung on the wall opposite the bed. It seemed to smile at me; it seemed to say, 'Drusilla! deposit a book.' There were tables on either side of my aunt's bed. She was a bad sleeper, and wanted, or thought she wanted, many things at night. I put a book near the matches on one side, and a book under the box of chocolate drops on the other. Whether she wanted a light, or whether she wanted a drop, there was a precious publication to meet her eye, or to meet her hand, and to say with silent eloquence, in either case, 'Come, try me! try me!' But one book was now left at the bottom of my bag, and but one apartment was still unexplored – the bathroom, which opened out of the bedroom. I peeped in; and the holy inner voice that never deceives, whispered to me, 'You have met her, Drusilla, everywhere else; meet her at the bath, and the work is done.' I observed a dressing-gown thrown across a chair. It had a pocket in it, and in that pocket I put my last book. Can words express my exquisite sense of duty done, when I had slipped out of the house, unsuspected by any of them, and when I found myself in the street with my empty bag under my arm? Oh, my worldly friends, pursuing the phantom, Pleasure, through the guilty mazes of Dissipation, how easy it is to be happy, if you will only be good!

When I folded up my things that night – when I reflected on the *true* riches which I had scattered with such a lavish hand, from top to bottom of the house of my wealthy aunt – I declare I felt as free from all anxiety as if I had been a child again. I was so light-hearted that I sang a verse of the Evening Hymn. I was so light-hearted that I fell asleep before I could sing another. Quite like a child again! quite like a child again!

So I passed that blissful night. On rising the next morning, how young I felt! I might add, how young I looked, if I were capable of dwelling on the concerns of my own perishable body. But I am not capable – and I add nothing.

Towards luncheon time – not for the sake of the creature-comforts, but for the certainty of finding dear aunt – I put on my bonnet to go to Montagu Square. Just as I was ready, the maid at the lodgings in which I then lived looked in at the door, and said, 'Lady Verinder's servant, to see Miss Clack.'

I occupied the parlour-floor, at that period of my residence in London. The front parlour was my sitting-room. Very small, very low in the ceiling, very poorly furnished – but, oh, so neat! I looked into the passage to see which of Lady Verinder's servants had asked for me. It was the young footman, Samuel – a civil fresh-coloured person, with a teachable look and a very obliging manner. I had always felt a spiritual interest in Samuel, and a wish to try him with a few serious words. On this occasion, I invited him into my sitting-room.

He came in, with a large parcel under his arm. When he put the parcel down, it appeared to frighten him. 'My lady's love, Miss; and I was to say that you would find a letter inside.' Having given that message, the fresh-coloured young footman surprised me by looking as if he would have liked to run away.

I detained him to make a few kind inquiries. Could I see my aunt, if I called in Montagu Square? No; she had gone out for a drive. Miss Rachel had gone with her, and Mr Ablewhite had taken a seat in the carriage, too. Knowing how sadly dear Mr Godfrey's charitable work was in arrear, I thought it odd that he should be going out driving, like an idle man. I stopped Samuel at the door, and made a few more kind inquiries. Miss Rachel was going to a ball that night, and Mr Ablewhite had arranged to come to coffee, and go with her. There was a morning concert advertised for to-morrow, and Samuel was ordered to take places for a large party, including a place for Mr Ablewhite. 'All the tickets may be gone, Miss,' said this innocent youth, 'if I don't run and get them at once!' He ran as he said the words – and I found myself alone again, with some anxious thoughts to occupy me.

We had a special meeting of the Mothers' Small-Clothes-Conversion Society, that night, summoned expressly with a view to obtaining Mr Godfrey's advice and assistance. Instead of sustaining our sisterhood, under an overwhelming flow of Trousers which quite prostrated our little community, he had arranged to take coffee in Montagu Square, and to go to a ball afterwards! The afternoon of the next day had been selected for the Festival of the British-Ladies'-Servants'-Sunday-Sweet-heart-Supervision Society. Instead of being present, the life and soul of that struggling Institution, he had engaged to make one of a party of worldlings at a morning concert! I asked myself what did it mean? Alas! it meant that our Christian Hero was to reveal himself to me in a new character, and to become associated in my mind with one of the most awful back-slidings of modern times.

To return, however, to the history of the passing day. On finding myself alone in my room, I naturally turned my attention to the parcel which appeared to have so strangely intimidated the fresh-coloured young footman. Had my aunt sent me my promised legacy? and had it taken the form of cast-off clothes, or worn-out silver spoons, or unfashionable jewellery, or anything of that sort? Prepared to accept all, and to resent nothing, I opened the parcel – and what met my view? The twelve precious publications which I had scattered through the house, on the previous day; all returned to me by the doctor's orders! Well might the youthful Samuel shrink when he brought his parcel into my room! Well might he run when he had performed his miserable errand! As to my aunt's letter, it simply amounted, poor soul, to this – that she dare not disobey her medical man.

What was to be done now? With my training and my principles, I never had a moment's doubt.

Once self-supported by conscience, once embarked on a career of manifest usefulness, the true Christian never yields. Neither public nor private influences produce the slightest effect on us, when we have once got our mission. Taxation may be the consequence of a mission; riots may be the consequence of a mission; wars may be the consequence of a mission: we go on with our work, irrespective of every human consider-ation which moves the world outside us. We are above reason; we are beyond ridicule; we see with nobody's eyes, we hear with nobody's ears, we feel with nobody's hearts, but our own. Glorious, glorious privilege! And how is it earned? Ah, my friends, you may spare yourselves the useless inquiry! We are the only people who can earn it – for we are the only people who are always right.

In the case of my misguided aunt, the form which pious perseverance was next to take revealed itself to me plainly enough.

Preparation by clerical friends had failed, owing to Lady Verinder's own reluctance. Preparation by books had failed, owing to the doctor's infidel obstinacy. So be it! What was the next thing to try? The next thing to try was – Preparation by Little Notes. In other words, the books themselves having been sent back, select extracts from the books, copied by different hands, and all addressed as letters to my aunt, were, some to be sent by post, and some to be distributed about the house on the plan I had adopted on the previous day. As letters they would excite no suspicion; as letters they would be opened – and, once opened, might be read. Some of them I wrote myself. 'Dear aunt, may I ask your attention to a few lines?' &c. 'Dear aunt, I was reading last night, and I chanced on the following passage,' &c. Other letters were written for me by my valued fellow-workers, the sisterhood at the Mothers' Small-Clothes. 'Dear madam, pardon the interest taken in you by a true, though humble, friend.' 'Dear madam, may a serious person surprise you by saying a few cheering words?' Using these and other similar forms of courteous appeal, we reintroduced all my precious passages under a form which not even the doctor's watchful materialism could suspect. Before the shades of evening had closed around us, I had a dozen awakening letters for my aunt, instead of a dozen awakening books. Six I made immediate arrangements for sending through the post, and six I kept in my pocket for personal distribution in the house the next day.

Soon after two o'clock I was again on the field of pious conflict, addressing more kind inquiries to Samuel at Lady Verinder's door.

My aunt had had a bad night. She was again in the room in which I had witnessed her Will, resting on the sofa, and trying to get a little sleep.

I said I would wait in the library, on the chance of seeing her. In the fervour of my zeal to distribute the letters, it never occurred to me to inquire about Rachel. The house was quiet, and it was past the hour at which the musical performance began. I took it for granted that she and her party of pleasure-seekers (Mr Godfrey, alas! included) were all at the concert, and eagerly devoted myself to my good work, while time and opportunity were still at my own disposal.

My aunt's correspondence of the morning – including the six awakening letters which I had posted overnight – was lying unopened on the library table. She had evidently not felt herself equal to dealing with a large mass of letters – and she might be daunted by the number of them, if she entered the library later in the day. I put one of my second set of six letters on the chimney-piece by itself; leaving it to attract her curiosity, by means of its solitary position, apart from the rest. A second letter I put purposely on the floor in the breakfast-room. The first servant who went in after me would conclude that my aunt had dropped it, and would be specially careful to restore it to her. The field thus sown on the basement story, I ran lightly upstairs to scatter my mercies next over the drawing-room floor.

Just as I entered the front room, I heard a double-knock at the street-door – a soft, fluttering, considerate little knock. Before I could think of slipping back to the library (in which I was supposed to be waiting), the active young footman was in the hall, answering the door. It mattered little, as I thought. In my aunt's state of health, visitors in general were not admitted. To my horror and amazement, the performer of the soft little knock proved to be an exception to general rules. Samuel's voice below me (after apparently answering some questions which I did not hear) said, unmistakably, 'Upstairs, if you please, sir.' The next moment I heard footsteps – a man's footsteps – approaching the drawing-room floor. Who could this favoured male, visitor possibly be? Almost as soon as I asked myself the question, the answer occurred to me. Who *could* it be but the doctor?

In the case of any other visitor, I should have allowed myself to be discovered in the drawing-room. There would have been nothing out of the common in my having got tired of the library, and having gone upstairs for a change. But my own self-respect stood in the way of my meeting the person who had insulted me by sending me back my books. I slipped into the little third room, which I have mentioned as communicating with the back drawing-room, and dropped the curtains which closed the open doorway. If I only waited there for a minute or two, the usual result in such cases would take place. That is to say, the doctor would be conducted to his patient's room.

I waited a minute or two, and more than a minute or two. I heard the visitor walking restlessly backwards and forwards. I also heard him talking to himself. I even thought I recognized the voice. Had I made a mistake? Was it not the doctor, but somebody else? Mr Bruff, for instance? No! an unerring instinct told me it was not Mr Bruff. Whoever he was, he was still talking to himself. I parted the heavy curtains the least little morsel in the world, and listened.

The words I heard were, 'I'll do it to-day!' And the voice that spoke them was Mr Godfrey Ablewhite's.

∾ FIVE ∾

MY HAND DROPPED FROM THE curtain. But don't suppose – oh, don't suppose – that the dreadful embarrassment of my situation was the uppermost idea in my mind! So fervent still was the sisterly interest I felt in Mr Godfrey, that I never stopped to ask myself why he was not at the concert. No! I thought only of the words – the startling words – which had just fallen from his lips. He would do it to-day. He had said, in a tone of terrible resolution, he would do it to-day. What, oh what, would he do! Something even more deplorably unworthy of him than what he had done already? Would he apostatize from the faith? Would he abandon us at the Mothers' Small-Clothes? Had we seen the last of his angelic smile in the committee-room? Had we heard the last of his unrivalled eloquence at Exeter Hall? I was so wrought up by the bare idea of such awful eventualities as these in connection with such a man, that I believe I should have rushed from my place of concealment, and implored him in the name of all the Ladies' Committees in London to explain himself – when I suddenly heard another voice in the room. It penetrated through the curtains; it was loud, it was bold, it was wanting in every female charm. The voice of Rachel Verinder!

'Why have you come up here, Godfrey?' she asked. 'Why didn't you go into the library?'

He laughed softly, and answered, 'Miss Clack is in the library.'

'Clack in the library!' She instantly seated herself on the ottoman in the back drawing-room. 'You are quite right, Godfrey. We had much better stop here.'

I had been in a burning fever, a moment since, and in some doubt what to do next. I became extremely cold now, and felt no doubt whatever. To show myself, after what I had heard, was impossible. To retreat – except into the fireplace – was equally out of the question. A martyrdom was before me. In justice to myself, I noiselessly arranged the curtains so that I could both see and hear. And then I met my martyrdom, with the spirit of a primitive Christian.

'Don't sit on the ottoman,' the young lady proceeded. 'Bring a chair, Godfrey. I like people to be opposite to me when I talk to them.'

He took the nearest seat. It was a low chair. He was very tall, and many sizes too large for it. I never saw his legs to such disadvantage before.

'Well?' she went on. 'What did you say to them?'

'Just what you said, dear Rachel, to me.'

'That mamma was not at all well to-day? And that I didn't quite like leaving her to go to the concert?'

'Those were the words. They were grieved to lose you at the concert, but they quite understood. All sent their love; and all expressed a cheering belief that Lady Verinder's indisposition would soon pass away.'

'*You* don't think it's serious, do you, Godfrey?'

'Far from it! In a few days, I feel quite sure, all will be well again.'

'I think so, too. I was a little frightened at first, but I think so too. It was very kind to go and make my excuses for me to people who are almost strangers to you. But why not have gone with them to the concert? It seems very hard that you should miss the music too.'

'Don't say that, Rachel! If you only knew how much happier I am – here, with you!'

He clasped his hands, and looked at her. In the position which he occupied, when he did that, he turned my way. Can words describe how I sickened when I noticed exactly the same pathetic expression on his face, which had charmed me when he was pleading for destitute millions of his fellow-creatures on the platform at Exeter Hall!

'It's hard to get over one's bad habits, Godfrey. But do try to get over the habit of paying compliments – do, to please me.'

'I never paid *you* a compliment, Rachel, in my life. Successful love may sometimes use the language of flattery, I admit. But hopeless love, dearest, always speaks the truth.'

He drew his chair close, and took her hand, when he said 'hopeless love'. There was a momentary silence. He, who thrilled everybody, had doubtless thrilled *her*. I thought I now understood the words which had dropped from him when he was alone in the drawing-room, 'I'll do it to-day.' Alas! the most rigid propriety could hardly have failed to discover that he was doing it now.

'Have you forgotten what we agreed on, Godfrey, when you spoke to me in the country? We agreed that we were to be cousins, and nothing more.'

'I break the agreement, Rachel, every time I see you.'

'Then don't see me.'

'Quite useless! I break the agreement every time I think of you. Oh, Rachel! how kindly you told me, only the other day, that my place in your estimation was a higher place than it had ever been yet! Am I mad to build the hopes I do on those dear words? Am I mad to dream of some future day when your heart may soften to me? Don't tell me so, if

I am! Leave me my delusion, dearest! I must have *that* to cherish, and to comfort me, if I have nothing else!'

His voice trembled, and he put his white handkerchief to his eyes. Exeter Hall again! Nothing wanting to complete the parallel but the audience, the cheers, and the glass of water.

Even *her* obdurate nature was touched. I saw her lean a little nearer to him. I heard a new tone of interest in her next words.

'Are you really sure, Godfrey, that you are so fond of me as that?'

'Sure! You know what I was, Rachel. Let me tell you what I am. I have lost every interest in life, but my interest in you. A transformation has come over me which I can't account for, myself. Would you believe it? My charitable business is an unendurable nuisance to me; and when I see a Ladies' Committee now, I wish myself at the uttermost ends of the earth!'

If the annals of apostasy offer anything comparable to such a declaration as that, I can only say that the case in point is not producible from the stores of *my* reading. I thought of the Mothers' Small-Clothes. I thought of the Sunday-Sweetheart-Supervision. I thought of the other Societies, too numerous to mention, all built up on this man as on a tower of strength. I thought of the struggling Female Boards, who, so to speak, drew the breath of their business-life through the nostrils of Mr Godfrey – of that same Mr Godfrey who had just reviled our good work as a 'nuisance' – and just declared that he wished he was at the uttermost ends of the earth when he found himself in our company! My young female friends will feel encouraged to persevere, when I mention that it tried even My discipline before I could devour my own righteous indignation in silence. At the same time, it is only justice to myself to add, that I didn't lose a syllable of the conversation. Rachel was the next to speak.

'You have made your confession,' she said. 'I wonder whether it would cure you of your unhappy attachment to me, if I made mine?'

He started. I confess I started too. He thought, and I thought, that she was about to divulge the mystery of the Moonstone.

'Would you think, to look at me,' she went on, 'that I am the wretchedest girl living? It's true, Godfrey. What greater wretchedness can there be than to live degraded in your own estimation? That is my life now.'

'My dear Rachel! it's impossible you can have any reason to speak of yourself in that way!'

'How do you know I have no reason?'

'Can you ask me the question! I know it, because I know *you*. Your silence, dearest, has never lowered you in the estimation of your true friends. The disappearance of your precious birthday gift may seem

strange; your unexplained connection with that event may seem stranger
still—'

'Are you speaking of the Moonstone, Godfrey?'

'I certainly thought that you referred—'

'I referred to nothing of the sort. I can hear of the loss of the Moonstone,
let who will speak of it, without feeling degraded in my own estimation.
If the story of the Diamond ever comes to light, it will be known that I
accepted a dreadful responsibility; it will be known that I involved myself
in the keeping of a miserable secret – but it will be as clear as the sun at
noonday that I did nothing mean! You have misunderstood me, Godfrey.
It's my fault for not speaking more plainly. Cost me what it may, I will
be plainer now. Suppose you were not in love with me? Suppose you
were in love with some other woman?'

'Yes?'

'Suppose you discovered that woman to be utterly unworthy of you?
Suppose you were quite convinced that it was a disgrace to you to waste
another thought on her? Suppose the bare idea of ever marrying such a
person made your face burn, only with thinking of it?'

'Yes?'

'And, suppose, in spite of all that – you couldn't tear her from your
heart? Suppose the feeling she had roused in you (in the time when you
believed in her) was not a feeling to be hidden? Suppose the love this
wretch had inspired in you – ? Oh, how can I find words to say it in!
How can I make a *man* understand that a feeling which horrifies me at
myself, can be a feeling that fascinates me at the same time? It's the
breath of my life, Godfrey, and it's the poison that kills me – both in one!
Go away! I must be out of my mind to talk as I am talking now. No!
you mustn't leave me – you mustn't carry away a wrong impression. I
must say, what is to be said in my own defence. Mind this! *He* doesn't
know – he never will know, what I have told *you*. I will never see him –
I don't care what happens – I will never, never, never see him again!
Don't ask me his name! Don't ask me any more! Let's change the subject.
Are you doctor enough, Godfrey, to tell me why I feel as if I was stifling
for want of breath? Is there a form of hysterics that bursts into words
instead of tears? I dare say! What does it matter? You will get over any
trouble I have caused you, easily enough now. I have dropped to my
right place in your estimation, haven't I? Don't notice me! Don't pity
me! For God's sake, go away!'

She turned round on a sudden, and beat her hands wildly on the back
of the ottoman. Her head dropped on the cushions; and she burst out
crying. Before I had time to feel shocked at this, I was horror-struck by
an entirely unexpected proceeding on the part of Mr Godfrey. Will it be
credited that he fell on his knees at her feet? – on *both* knees, I solemnly

declare! May modesty mention that he put his arms round her next? And may reluctant admiration acknowledge that he electrified her with two words?

'Noble creature!'

No more than that! But he did it with one of the bursts which have made his fame as a public speaker. She sat, either quite thunderstruck, or quite fascinated – I don't know which – without even making an effort to put his arms back where his arms ought to have been. As for me, my sense of propriety was completely bewildered. I was so painfully uncertain whether it was my first duty to close my eyes, or to stop my ears, that I did neither. I attribute my being still able to hold the curtain in the right position for looking and listening, entirely to suppressed hysterics. In suppressed hysterics, it is admitted, even by the doctors, that one must hold something.

'Yes,' he said, with all the fascination of his evangelical voice and manner, 'you are a noble creature! A woman who can speak the truth, for the truth's own sake – a woman who will sacrifice her pride, rather than sacrifice an honest man who loves her – is the most priceless of all treasures. When such a woman marries, if her husband only wins her esteem and regard, he wins enough to ennoble his whole life. You have spoken, dearest, of your place in my estimation. Judge what that place is – when I implore you on my knees, to let the cure of your poor wounded heart be my care. Rachel! will you honour me, will you bless me, by being my wife?'

By this time I should certainly have decided on stopping my ears, if Rachel had not encouraged me to keep them open, by answering him in the first sensible words I had ever heard fall from her lips.

'Godfrey!' she said, 'you must be mad!'

'I never spoke more reasonably, dearest – in your interests, as well as in mine. Look for a moment to the future. Is your happiness to be sacrificed to a man who has never known how you feel towards him, and whom you are resolved never to see again? Is it not your duty to yourself to forget this ill-fated attachment? and is forgetfulness to be found in the life you are leading now? You have tried that life, and you are wearying of it already. Surround yourself with nobler interests than the wretched interests of the world. A heart that loves and honours you; a home whose peaceful claims and happy duties win gently on you day by day – try the consolation, Rachel, which is to be found *there*! I don't ask for your love – I will be content with your affection and regard. Let the rest be left, confidently left, to your husband's devotion, and to Time that heals even wounds as deep as yours.'

She began to yield already. Oh, what a bringing-up she must have had! Oh, how differently I should have acted in her place!

'Don't tempt me, Godfrey,' she said; 'I am wretched enough and reckless enough as it is. Don't tempt me to be more wretched and more reckless still!'

'One question, Rachel. Have you any personal objection to me?'

'I! I always liked you. After what you have just said to me, I should be insensible indeed if I didn't respect and admire you as well.'

'Do you know many wives, my dear Rachel, who respect and admire their husbands? And yet they and their husbands get on very well. How many brides go to the altar with hearts that would bear inspection by the men who take them there? And yet it doesn't end unhappily – somehow or other the nuptial establishment jogs on. The truth is, that women try marriage as a Refuge, far more numerously than they are willing to admit; and, what is more, they find that marriage has justified their confidence in it. Look at your own case once again. At your age, and with your attractions, is it possible for you to sentence yourself to a single life? Trust my knowledge of the world – nothing is less possible. It is merely a question of time. You may marry some other man, some years hence. Or you may marry the man, dearest, who is now at your feet, and who prizes your respect and admiration above the love of any other woman on the face of the earth.'

'Gently, Godfrey! you are putting something into my head which I never thought of before. You are tempting me with a new prospect, when all my other prospects are closed before me. I tell you again, I am miserable enough and desperate enough, if you say another word, to marry you on your own terms. Take the warning, and go!'

'I won't even rise from my knees, till you have said yes!'

'If I say yes you will repent, and I shall repent, when it is too late!'

'We shall both bless the day, darling, when I pressed, and when you yielded.'

'Do you feel as confidently as you speak?'

'You shall judge for yourself. I speak from what I have seen in my own family. Tell me what you think of our household at Frizinghall. Do my father and mother live unhappily together?'

'Far from it – so far as I can see.'

'When my mother was a girl, Rachel (it is no secret in the family), she had loved as you love – she had given her heart to a man who was unworthy of her. She married my father, respecting him, admiring him, but nothing more. Your own eyes have seen the result. Is there no encouragement in it for you and for me?'*

'You won't hurry me, Godfrey?'

'My time shall be yours.'

* See Betteredge's Narrative, chapter viii.

'You won't ask me for more than I can give?'

'My angel! I only ask you to give me yourself.'

'Take me!'

In those two words she accepted him!

He had another burst – a burst of unholy rapture this time. He drew her nearer and nearer to him till her face touched his; and then – No! I really cannot prevail upon myself to carry this shocking disclosure any farther. Let me only say, that I tried to close my eyes before it happened, and that I was just one moment too late. I had calculated, you see, on her resisting. She submitted. To every right-feeling person of my own sex, volumes could say no more.

Even my innocence in such matters began to see its way to the end of the interview now. They understood each other so thoroughly by this time, that I fully expected to see them walk off together, arm in arm, to be married. There appeared, however, judging by Mr Godfrey's next words, to be one more trifling formality which it was necessary to observe. He seated himself – unforbidden this time – on the ottoman by her side. 'Shall I speak to your dear mother?'

She asked. 'Or will you?'

She declined both alternatives.

'Let my mother hear nothing from either of us, until she is better. I wish it to be kept a secret for the present, Godfrey. Go now, and come back this evening. We have been here alone together quite long enough.'

She rose, and, in rising, looked for the first time towards the little room in which my martyrdom was going on.

'Who has drawn those curtains?' she exclaimed. 'The room is close enough, as it is, without keeping the air out of it in that way.'

She advanced to the curtains. At the moment when she laid her hand on them – at the moment when the discovery of me appeared to be quite inevitable – the voice of the fresh-coloured young footman, on the stairs, suddenly suspended any further proceedings on her side or on mine. It was unmistakably the voice of a man in great alarm.

'Miss Rachel!' he called out, 'where are you, Miss Rachel?'

She sprang back from the curtains, and ran to the door.

The footman came just inside the room. His ruddy colour was all gone. He said, 'Please to come downstairs, Miss! My lady has fainted, and we can't bring her to again.'

In a moment more I was alone, and free to go downstairs in my turn, quite unobserved.

Mr Godfrey passed me in the hall, hurrying out, to fetch the doctor. 'Go in, and help them!' he said, pointing to the room. I found Rachel on her knees by the sofa, with her mother's head on her bosom. One look at my aunt's face (knowing what I knew) was enough to warn me of the dreadful truth. I kept my thoughts to myself till the doctor came in. It was not long before he arrived. He began by sending Rachel out of the room – and then he told the rest of us that Lady Verinder was no more. Serious persons, in search of proofs of hardened scepticism, may be interested in hearing that he showed no signs of remorse when he looked at Me.

At a later hour I peeped into the breakfast-room, and the library. My aunt had died without opening one of the letters which I had addressed to her. I was so shocked at this, that it never occurred to me, until some days afterwards, that she had also died without giving me my little legacy.

◉ SIX ◉

(1) 'MISS CLACK PRESENTS HER COMPLIMENTS TO Mr Franklin Blake; and, in sending him the fifth chapter of her humble narrative, begs to say that she feels quite unequal to enlarge as she could wish on an event so awful, under the circumstances, as Lady Verinder's death. She has, there-fore, attached to her own manuscript, copious Extracts from precious publications in her possession, all bearing on this terrible subject. And may those Extracts (Miss Clack fervently hopes) sound as the blast of a trumpet in the ears of her respected kinsman, Mr Franklin Blake.'

(2) 'Mr Franklin Blake presents his compliments to Miss Clack, and begs to thank her for the fifth chapter of her narrative. In returning the extracts sent with it, he will refrain from mentioning any personal objec-tion which he may entertain to this species of literature, and will merely say that the proposed additions to the manuscript are not necessary to the fulfilment of the purpose that he has in view.'

(3) 'Miss Clack begs to acknowledge the return of her Extracts. She affectionately reminds Mr Franklin Blake that she is a Christian, and that it is, therefore, quite impossible for him to offend her. Miss C. persists in feeling the deepest interest in Mr Blake, and pledges herself, on the first occasion when sickness may lay him low, to offer him the use of her Extracts for the second time. In the meanwhile she would be glad to know, before beginning the final chapters of her narrative, whether she may be permitted to make her humble contribution complete, by availing herself of the light which later discoveries have thrown on the mystery of the Moonstone.'

(4) 'Mr Franklin Blake is sorry to disappoint Miss Clack. He can only repeat the instructions which he had the honour of giving her when she began her narrative. She is requested to limit herself to her own individual experience of persons and events, as recorded in her diary. Later discoveries she will be good enough to leave to the pens of those persons who can write in the capacity of actual witnesses.'

(5) 'Miss Clack is extremely sorry to trouble Mr Franklin Blake with another letter. Her Extracts have been returned, and the expression of her matured views on the subject of the Moonstone has been forbidden. Miss Clack is painfully conscious that she ought (in the worldly phrase) to feel herself put down. But, no – Miss C. has learnt Perseverance in the School of Adversity. Her object in writing is to know whether Mr Blake (who prohibits everything else) prohibits the appearance of the present correspondence in Miss Clack's narrative? Some explanation of the position in which Mr Blake's interference has placed her as an authoress, seems due on the ground of common justice. And Miss Clack, on her side, is most anxious that her letters should be produced to speak for themselves.'

(6) 'Mr Franklin Blake agrees to Miss Clack's proposal, on the understanding that she will kindly consider this intimation of his consent as closing the correspondence between them.'

(7) 'Miss Clack feels it an act of Christian duty (before the correspondence closes) to inform Mr Franklin Blake that his last letter – evidently intended to offend her – has not succeeded in accomplishing the object of the writer. She affectionately requests Mr Blake to retire to the privacy of his own room, and to consider with himself whether the training which can thus elevate a poor weak woman above the reach of insult, be not worthy of greater admiration than he is now disposed to feel for it. On being favoured with an intimation to that effect, Miss C. solemnly pledges herself to send back the complete series of her Extracts to Mr Franklin Blake.'

[To this letter no answer was received. Comment is needless.

(Signed) Drusilla Clack.]

❧ SEVEN ❧

THE FOREGOING CORRESPONDENCE WILL SUFFICIENTLY EXPLAIN why no choice is left to me but to pass over Lady Verinder's death with the simple announcement of the fact which ends my fifth chapter.

Keeping myself for the future strictly within the limits of my own personal experience, I have next to relate that a month elapsed from the time of my aunt's decease before Rachel Verinder and I met again. That meeting was the occasion of my spending a few days under the same roof with her. In the course of my visit, something happened, relating to her marriage-engagement with Mr Godfrey Ablewhite, which is important enough to require special notice in these pages. When this last of many painful family circumstances has been disclosed, my task will be completed; for I shall then have told all that I know, as an actual (and most unwilling) witness of events.

My aunt's remains were removed from London, and were buried in the little cemetery attached to the church in her own park. I was invited to the funeral with the rest of the family. But it was impossible (with my religious views) to rouse myself in a few days only from the shock which this death had caused me. I was informed, moreover, that the rector of Frizinghall was to read the service. Having myself in past times seen this clerical castaway making one of the players at Lady Verinder's whist-table, I doubt, even if I had been fit to travel, whether I should have felt justified in attending the ceremony.

Lady Verinder's death left her daughter under the care of her brother-in-law, Mr Ablewhite the elder. He was appointed guardian by the will, until his niece married, or came of age. Under these circumstances, Mr Godfrey informed his father, I suppose, of the new relation in which he stood towards Rachel. At any rate, in ten days from my aunt's death, the secret of the marriage engagement was no secret at all within the circle of the family, and the grand question for Mr Ablewhite senior – another confirmed castaway! – was how to make himself and his authority most agreeable to the wealthy young lady who was going to marry his son.

Rachel gave him some trouble at the outset, about the choice of a place in which she could be prevailed upon to reside. The house in Montagu Square was associated with the calamity of her mother's death. The house in Yorkshire was associated with the scandalous affair of the lost Moonstone. Her guardian's own residence at Frizinghall was open to neither of these objections. But Rachel's presence in it, after her recent bereavement, operated as a check on the gaieties of her cousins, the Miss Ablewhites – and she herself requested that her visit might be deferred to a more favourable opportunity. It ended in a proposal, emanating from old Mr Ablewhite, to try a furnished house at Brighton. His wife, an invalid daughter, and Rachel were to inhabit it together, and were to expect him to join them later in the season. They would see no society but a few old friends, and they would have his son Godfrey, travelling backwards and forwards by the London train, always at their disposal.

I describe this aimless flitting about from one place of residence to another – this insatiate restlessness of body and appalling stagnation of soul – merely with the view to arriving at results. The event which (under Providence) proved to be the means of bringing Rachel Verinder and myself together again, was no other than the hiring of the house at Brighton.

My Aunt Ablewhite is a large, silent, fair-complexioned woman, with one noteworthy point in her character. From the hour of her birth she has never been known to do anything for herself. She has gone through life, accepting everybody's help, and adopting everybody's opinions. A more hopeless person, in a spiritual point of view, I have never met with – there is absolutely, in this perplexing case, no obstructive material to work upon. Aunt Ablewhite would listen to the Grand Lama of Thibet exactly as she listens to Me, and would reflect his views quite as readily as she reflects mine. She found the furnished house at Brighton by stopping at an hotel in London, composing herself on a sofa, and sending for her son. She discovered the necessary servants by breakfasting in bed one morning (still at the hotel), and giving her maid a holiday on condition that the girl 'would begin enjoying herself by fetching Miss Clack'. I found her placidly fanning herself in her dressing-gown at eleven o'clock. 'Drusilla, dear, I want some servants. You are so clever – please get them for me.' I looked round the untidy room. The church-bells were going for a week-day service; they suggested a word of affectionate remonstrance on my part. 'Oh, aunt!' I said sadly. 'Is *this* worthy of a Christian Englishwoman? Is the passage from time to eternity to be made in *this* manner?' My aunt answered, 'I'll put on my gown, Drusilla, if you will be kind enough to help me.' What was to be said after that? I have done wonders with murderesses – I have never advanced an inch with Aunt Ablewhite. 'Where is the list,' I asked, 'of the servants whom you require?' My aunt shook her head; she hadn't even energy enough to keep the list. 'Rachel has got it, dear,' she said, 'in the next room.' I went into the next room, and so saw Rachel again, for the first time since we had parted in Montagu Square.

She looked pitiably small and thin in her deep mourning. If I attached any serious importance to such a perishable trifle as personal appearance, I might be inclined to add that hers was one of those unfortunate complexions which always suffers when not relieved by a border of white next the skin. But what are our complexions and our looks? Hindrances and pitfalls, dear girls, which beset us on our way to higher things! Greatly to my surprise, Rachel rose when I entered the room, and came forward to meet me with outstretched hand.

'I am glad to see you,' she said. 'Drusilla, I have been in the habit of speaking very foolishly and very rudely to you, on former occasions. I beg your pardon. I hope you will forgive me.'

My face, I suppose, betrayed the astonishment I felt at this. She coloured up for a moment, and then proceeded to explain herself.

'In my poor mother's lifetime,' she went on, 'her friends were not always my friends, too. Now I have lost her, my heart turns for comfort to the people she liked. She liked you. Try to be friends with me, Drusilla, if you can.'

To any rightly-constituted mind, the motive thus acknowledged was simply shocking. Here in Christian England was a young woman in a state of bereavement, with so little idea of where to look for true comfort, that she actually expected to find it among her mother's friends! Here was a relative of mine, awakened to a sense of her shortcomings towards others, under the influence, not of conviction and duty, but of sentiment and impulse! Most deplorable to think of – but, still, suggestive of something hopeful, to a person of my experience in plying the good work. There could be no harm, I thought, in ascertaining the extent of the change which the loss of her mother had wrought in Rachel's character. I decided, as a useful test, to probe her on the subject of her marriage engagement to Mr Godfrey Ablewhite.

Having first met her advances with all possible cordiality, I sat by her on the sofa, at her own request. We discussed family affairs and future plans – always excepting that one future plan which was to end in her marriage. Try as I might to turn the conversation that way, she resolutely declined to take the hint. Any open reference to the question, on my part, would have been premature at this early stage of our reconciliation. Besides, I had discovered all I wanted to know. She was no longer the reckless, defiant creature whom I had heard and seen, on the occasion of my martyrdom in Montagu Square. This was, of itself, enough to encourage me to take her future conversion in hand – beginning with a few words of earnest warning directed against the hasty formation of the marriage tie, and so getting on to higher things. Looking at her, now, with this new interest – and calling to mind the headlong suddenness with which she had met Mr Godfrey's matrimonial views – I felt the solemn duty of interfering, with a fervour which assured me that I should achieve no common results. Rapidity of proceeding was, as I believed, of importance in this case. I went back at once to the question of the servants wanted for the furnished house.

'Where is the list, dear?'

Rachel produced it.

'Cook, kitchen-maid, housemaid, and footman,' I read. 'My dear Rachel, these servants are only wanted for a term – the term during which your guardian has taken the house. We shall have great difficulty in finding persons of character and capacity to accept a temporary engagement of that sort, if we try in London. Has the house in Brighton been found yet?'

'Yes. Godfrey has taken it; and persons in the house wanted him to hire them as servants. He thought they would hardly do for us, and came back having settled nothing.'

'And you have no experience yourself in these matters, Rachel?'

'None whatever.'

'And Aunt Ablewhite won't exert herself?'

'No, poor dear. Don't blame her, Drusilla. I think she is the only really happy woman I have ever met with.'

'There are degrees in happiness, darling. We must have a little talk, some day, on that subject. In the meantime I will undertake to meet the difficulty about the servants. Your aunt will write a letter to the people of the house—'

'She will sign a letter, if I write it for her, which comes to the same thing.'

'Quite the same thing. I shall get the letter, and I will go to Brighton to-morrow.'

'How extremely kind of you! We will join you as soon as you are ready for us. And you will stay, I hope, as *my* guest. Brighton is so lively; you are sure to enjoy it.'

In those words the invitation was given, and the glorious prospect of interference was opened before me.

It was then the middle of the week. By Saturday afternoon the house was ready for them. In that short interval I had sifted, not the characters only, but the religious views as well, of all the disengaged servants who applied to me, and had succeeded in making a selection which my conscience approved. I also discovered, and called on, two serious friends of mine, residents in the town, to whom I knew I could confide the pious object which had brought me to Brighton. One of them – a clerical friend – kindly helped me to take sittings for our little party in the church in which he himself ministered. The other – a single lady, like myself – placed the resources of her library (composed throughout of precious publications) entirely at my disposal. I borrowed half a dozen works, all carefully chosen with a view to Rachel. When these had been judiciously distributed in the various rooms she would be likely to occupy, I considered that my preparations were complete. Sound doctrine in the servants who waited on her; sound doctrine in the minister who preached to her; sound doctrine in the books that lay on her table – such was the treble welcome which my zeal had prepared for the motherless girl! A heavenly composure filled my mind, on that Saturday afternoon, as I sat at the window waiting the arrival of my relatives. The giddy throng passed and repassed before my eyes. Alas! how many of them felt my exquisite sense of duty done? An awful question. Let us not pursue it.

Between six and seven the travellers arrived. To my indescribable surprise, they were escorted, not by Mr Godfrey (as I had anticipated) but by the lawyer, Mr Bruff.

'How do you do, Miss Clack?' he said. 'I mean to stay this time.'

That reference to the occasion on which I had obliged him to postpone his business to mine, when we were both visiting in Montagu Square, satisfied me that the old worldling had come to Brighton with some object of his own in view. I had prepared quite a little Paradise for my beloved Rachel – and here was the Serpent already!

'Godfrey was very much vexed, Drusilla, not to be able to come with us,' said my Aunt Ablewhite. 'There was something in the way which kept him in town. Mr Bruff volunteered to take his place, and make a holiday of it till Monday morning. By-the-by, Mr Bruff, I'm ordered to take exercise, and I don't like it. That,' added Aunt Ablewhite, pointing out of window to an invalid going by in a chair on wheels, drawn by a man, 'is my idea of exercise. If it's air you want, you get it in your chair. And if it's fatigue you want, I am sure it's fatiguing enough to look at the man.'

Rachel stood silent, at a window by herself, with her eyes fixed on the sea.

'Tired, love?' I inquired.

'No. Only a little out of spirits,' she answered. 'I have often seen the sea, on our Yorkshire coast, with that light on it. And I was thinking, Drusilla, of the days that can never come again.'

Mr Bruff remained to dinner, and stayed through the evening. The more I saw of him, the more certain I felt that he had some private end to serve in coming to Brighton. I watched him carefully. He maintained the same appearance of ease, and talked the same godless gossip, hour after hour, until it was time to take leave. As he shook hands with Rachel, I caught his hard and cunning eye resting on her for a moment with a peculiar interest and attention. She was plainly concerned in the object that he had in view. He said nothing out of the common to her or to any one on leaving. He invited himself to luncheon the next day, and then he went away to his hotel.

It was impossible the next morning to get my Aunt Ablewhite out of her dressing-gown in time for church. Her invalid daughter (suffering from nothing, in my opinion, but incurable laziness, inherited from her mother) announced that she meant to remain in bed for the day. Rachel and I went alone together to church. A magnificent sermon was preached by my gifted friend on the heathen indifference of the world to the sinfulness of little sins. For more than an hour his eloquence (assisted by his glorious voice) thundered through the sacred edifice. I said to Rachel, when we came out, 'Has it found its way to your heart, dear?' And she answered, 'No; it has only made my head ache.' This might have been discouraging to some people; but, once embarked on a career of manifest usefulness, nothing discourages Me.

We found Aunt Ablewhite and Mr Bruff at luncheon. When Rachel declined eating anything, and gave as a reason for it that she was suffering from a headache, the lawyer's cunning instantly saw, and seized, the chance that she had given him.

'There is only one remedy for a headache,' said this horrible old man. 'A walk, Miss Rachel, is the thing to cure you. I am entirely at your service, if you will honour me by accepting my arm.'

'With the greatest pleasure. A walk is the very thing I was longing for.'

'It's past two,' I gently suggested. 'And the afternoon service, Rachel, begins at three.'

'How can you expect me to go to church again,' she asked, petulantly, 'with such a headache as mine?'

Mr Bruff officiously opened the door for her. In another minute more they were both out of the house. I don't know when I have felt the solemn duty of interfering so strongly as I felt it at that moment. But what was to be done? Nothing was to be done but to interfere at the first opportunity, later in the day.

On my return from the afternoon service I found that they had just got back. One look at them told me that the lawyer had said what he wanted to say. I had never before seen Rachel so silent and so thoughtful. I had never before seen Mr Bruff pay her such devoted attention, and look at her with such marked respect. He had (or pretended that he had) an engagement to dinner that day – and he took an early leave of us all; intending to go back to London by the first train the next morning.

'Are you sure of your own resolution?' he said to Rachel at the door.

'Quite sure,' she answered – and so they parted.

The moment his back was turned, Rachel withdrew to her own room. She never appeared at dinner. Her maid (the person with the cap-ribbons) was sent downstairs to announce that her headache had returned. I ran up to her and made all sorts of sisterly offers through the door. It was locked, and she kept it locked. Plenty of obstructive material to work on here! I felt greatly cheered and stimulated by her locking the door.

When her cup of tea went up to her the next morning, I followed it in. I sat by her bedside and said a few earnest words. She listened with languid civility. I noticed my serious friend's precious publications huddled together on a table in a corner. Had she chanced to look into them? – I asked. Yes – and they had not interested her. Would she allow me to read a few passages of the deepest interest, which had probably escaped her eye? No, not now – she had other things to think of. She gave these answers, with her attention apparently absorbed in folding and refolding the frilling of her night-gown. It was plainly necessary to rouse her by some reference to those worldly interests which she still had at heart.

'Do you know, love,' I said, 'I had an odd fancy, yesterday, about Mr Bruff? I thought, when I saw you after your walk with him, that he had been telling you some bad news.'

Her fingers dropped from the frilling of her night-gown, and her fierce black eyes flashed at me.

'Quite the contrary!' she said. 'It was news I was interested in hearing – and I am deeply indebted to Mr Bruff for telling me of it.'

'Yes?' I said, in a tone of gentle interest.

Her fingers went back to the frilling, and she turned her head sullenly away from me. I had been met in this manner, in the course of plying the good work, hundreds of times. She merely stimulated me to try again. In my dauntless zeal for her welfare, I ran the great risk, and openly alluded to her marriage engagement.

'News you were interested in hearing?' I repeated. 'I suppose, my dear Rachel, that must be news of Mr Godfrey Ablewhite?'

She started up in the bed, and turned deadly pale. It was evidently on the tip of her tongue to retort on me with the unbridled insolence of former times. She checked herself – laid her head back on the pillow – considered a minute – and then answered in these remarkable words:

'*I shall never marry Mr Godfrey Ablewhite.*'

It was my turn to start at that.

'What can you possibly mean?' I exclaimed. 'The marriage is considered by the whole family as a settled thing!'

'Mr Godfrey Ablewhite is expected here to-day,' she said, doggedly. 'Wait till he comes – and you will see.'

'But my dear Rachel – '

She rang the bell at the head of her bed. The person with the cap-ribbons appeared.

'Penelope! my bath.'

Let me give her her due. In the state of my feelings at that moment, I do sincerely believe that she had hit on the only possible way of forcing me to leave the room.

By the mere worldly mind my position towards Rachel might have been viewed as presenting difficulties of no ordinary kind. I had reckoned on leading her to higher things by means of a little earnest exhortation on the subject of her marriage. And now, if she was to be believed, no such event as her marriage was to take place at all. But ah, my friends! a working Christian of my experience (with an evangelizing prospect before her) takes broader views than these. Supposing Rachel really broke off the marriage, on which the Ablewhites, father and son, counted as a settled thing, what would be the result? It could only end, if she held firm, in an exchanging of hard words and bitter accusations on both sides. And what would be the effect on Rachel when the stormy interview was over? A salutary moral depression would be the effect. Her pride would be exhausted, her stubbornness would be exhausted, by the resolute resistance which it was in her character to make under the circumstances. She would turn for sympathy to the nearest person who had sympathy to offer. And I was that nearest person – brimful of comfort, charged to over-flowing with seasonable and reviving words. Never had the evangelizing prospect looked brighter, to *my* eyes, than it looked now.

She came down to breakfast, but she ate nothing, and hardly uttered a word.

After breakfast she wandered listlessly from room to room – then suddenly roused herself, and opened the piano. The music she selected to play was of the most scandalously profane sort, associated with performances on the stage which it curdles one's blood to think of. It would have been premature to interfere with her at such a time as this. I privately ascertained the hour at which Mr Godfrey Ablewhite was expected, and then I escaped the music by leaving the house.

Being out alone, I took the opportunity of calling upon my two resident friends. It was an indescribable luxury to find myself indulging in earnest conversation with serious persons. Infinitely encouraged and refreshed, I turned my steps back again to the house, in excellent time to await the arrival of our expected visitor. I entered the dining-room, always empty at that hour of the day, and found myself face to face with Mr Godfrey Ablewhite!

He made no attempt to fly the place. Quite the contrary. He advanced to meet me with the utmost eagerness.

'Dear Miss Clack, I have been only waiting to see *you*! Chance set me free of my London engagements to-day sooner than I had expected, and I have got here, in consequence, earlier than my appointed time.'

Not the slightest embarrassment encumbered his explanation, though this was his first meeting with me after the scene in Montagu Square. He was not aware, it is true, of my having been a witness of that scene. But he knew, on the other hand, that my attendances at the Mothers' Small-Clothes, and my relations with friends attached to other charities, must have informed me of his shameless neglect of his Ladies and of his Poor. And yet there he was before me, in full possession of his charming voice and his irresistible smile!

'Have you seen Rachel yet?' I asked.

He sighed gently, and took me by the hand. I should certainly have snatched my hand away, if the manner in which he gave his answer had not paralysed me with astonishment.

'I have seen Rachel,' he said with perfect tranquillity. 'You are aware, dear friend, that she was engaged to me? Well, she has taken a sudden resolution to break the engagement. Reflection has convinced her that she will best consult her welfare and mine by retracting a rash promise, and leaving me free to make some happier choice elsewhere. That is the only reason she will give, and the only answer she will make to every question that I can ask of her.'

'What have you done on your side?' I inquired. 'Have you submitted?'

'Yes,' he said with the most unruffled composure, 'I have submitted.'

His conduct, under the circumstances, was so utterly inconceivable, that I stood bewildered with my hand in his. It is a piece of rudeness to stare at anybody, and it is an act of indelicacy to stare at a gentleman. I committed both those improprieties. And I said, as if in a dream. 'What does it mean?'

'Permit me to tell you,' he replied. 'And suppose we sit down?'

He led me to a chair. I have an indistinct remembrance that he was very affectionate. I don't think he put his arm round my waist to support me – but I am not sure. I was quite helpless, and his ways with ladies were very endearing. At any rate, we sat down. I can answer for that, if I can answer for nothing more.

❧ EIGHT ❧

'I HAVE LOST A BEAUTIFUL GIRL, an excellent social position, and a handsome income,' Mr Godfrey began; 'and I have submitted to it without a struggle. What can be the motive for such extraordinary conduct as that? My precious friend, there is no motive.'

'No motive?' I repeated.

'Let me appeal, my dear Miss Clack, to your experience of children,' he went on. 'A child pursues a certain course of conduct. You are greatly struck by it, and you attempt to get at the motive. The dear little thing is incapable of telling you its motive. You might as well ask the grass why it grows, or the birds why they sing. Well! in this matter, I am like the dear little thing – like the grass – like the birds. I don't know why I made a proposal of marriage to Miss Verinder. I don't know why I have shamefully neglected my dear Ladies. I don't know why I have apostatized from the Mothers'-Small-Clothes. You say to the child, Why have you been naughty? And the little angel puts its finger into its mouth, and doesn't know. My case exactly, Miss Clack! I couldn't confess it to anybody else. I feel impelled to confess it to *you!*'

I began to recover myself. A mental problem was involved here. I am deeply interested in mental problems – and I am not, it is thought, without some skill in solving them.

'Best of friends, exert your intellect, and help me,' he proceeded. 'Tell me – why does a time come when these matrimonial proceedings of mine begin to look like something done in a dream? Why does it suddenly occur to me that my true happiness is in helping my dear Ladies, in going my modest round of useful work, in saying my few earnest words when called on by my Chairman? What do I want with a position? I have got a position. What do I want with an income? I can pay for my bread and cheese, and my nice little lodging, and my two coats a year. What do I want with Miss Verinder? She has told me with her own lips (this, dear lady, is between ourselves) that she loves another man, and that her only idea in marrying me is to try and put that other man out of her head. What a horrid union is this! Oh, dear me, what a horrid union is this! Such are my reflections, Miss Clack, on my way to Brighton. I approach Rachel with the feeling of a criminal who is going to receive his sentence. When I find that she has changed her mind too – when I hear her propose to break the engagement – I experience (there is no sort of doubt about it) a most overpowering sense of relief. A month ago I was pressing her rapturously to my bosom. An hour ago, the happiness of knowing that I shall never press her again, intoxicates me like strong liquor. The thing seems impossible – the thing can't be. And yet there are the facts, as I had the honour of stating them when we first sat down together in these two chairs. I have lost a beautiful girl, an excellent social position, and a handsome income; and I have submitted to it without a struggle. Can *you* account for it, dear friend? It's quite beyond *me*.'

His magnificent head sank on his breast, and he gave up his own mental problem in despair.

I was deeply touched. The case (if I may speak as a spiritual physician) was now quite plain to me. It is no uncommon event, in the experience of us all, to see the possessors of exalted ability occasionally humbled to the level of the most poorly-gifted people about them. The object, no doubt, in the wise economy of Providence, is to remind greatness that it is mortal, and that the power which has conferred, it can also take it away. It was now – to my mind – easy to discern one of these salutary humiliations in the deplorable proceedings on dear Mr Godfrey's part, of which I had been the unseen witness. And it was equally easy to recognize the welcome reappearance of his own finer nature in the horror with which he recoiled from the idea of a marriage with Rachel, and in the charming eagerness which he showed to return to his Ladies and his Poor.

I put this view before him in a few simple and sisterly words. His joy was beautiful to see. He compared himself, as I went on, to a lost man emerging from the darkness into the light. When I answered for a loving reception of him at the Mothers' Small-Clothes, the grateful heart of our Christian Hero overflowed. He pressed my hands alternately to his lips. Overwhelmed by the exquisite triumph of having got him back among us, I let him do what he liked with my hands. I closed my eyes. I felt my head, in an ecstasy of spiritual self-forgetfulness, sinking on his shoulder. In a moment more I should certainly have swooned away in his arms, but for an interruption from the outer world, which brought me to myself again. A horrid rattling of knives and forks sounded outside the door, and the footman came in to lay the table for luncheon.

Mr Godfrey started up, and looked at the clock on the mantelpiece.

'How time flies with *you*!' he exclaimed. 'I shall barely catch the train.'

I ventured on asking why he was in such a hurry to get back to town. His answer reminded me of family difficulties that were still to be reconciled, and of family disagreements that were yet to come.

'I have heard from my father,' he said. 'Business obliges him to leave

Frizinghall for London to-day, and he proposes coming on here, either this evening or to-morrow. I must tell him what has happened between Rachel and me. His heart is set on our marriage – there will be great difficulty, I fear, in reconciling him to the breaking-off of the engagement. I must stop him, for all our sakes, from coming here till he is reconciled. Best and dearest of friends, we shall meet again!'

With those words he hurried out. In equal haste on my side, I ran upstairs to compose myself in my own room before meeting Aunt Able-white and Rachel at the luncheon-table.

I am well aware – to dwell for a moment yet on the subject of Mr Godfrey – that the all-profaning opinion of the world has charged him with having his own private reasons for releasing Rachel from her engagement, at the first opportunity she gave him. It has also reached my ears, that his anxiety to recover his place in my estimation has been attributed, in certain quarters, to a mercenary eagerness to make his peace (through me) with a venerable committee-woman at the Mothers' Small-Clothes, abundantly blessed with the goods of this world, and a beloved and intimate friend of my own. I only notice these odious slanders for the sake of declaring that they never had a moment's influence on my mind. In obedience to my instructions, I have exhibited the fluctuations in my opinion of our Christian Hero, exactly as I find them recorded in my diary. In justice to myself, let me here add that, once reinstated in his place in my estimation, my gifted friend never lost that place again. I write with the tears in my eyes, burning to say more. But no – I am cruelly limited to my actual experience of persons and things. In less than a month from the time of which I am now writing, events in the money-market (which diminished even *my* miserable little income) forced me into foreign exile, and left me with nothing but a loving remembrance of Mr Godfrey which the slander of the world has assailed, and assailed in vain.

Let me dry my eyes, and return to my narrative.

I went downstairs to luncheon, naturally anxious to see how Rachel was affected by her release from her marriage engagement.

It appeared to me – but I own I am a poor authority in such matters – that the recovery of her freedom had set her thinking again of that other man whom she loved, and that she was furious with herself for not being able to control a revulsion of feeling of which she was secretly ashamed. Who was the man? I had my suspicions – but it was needless to waste time in idle speculation. When I had converted her, she would, as a matter of course, have no concealments from Me. I should hear all about the man; I should hear all about the Moonstone. If I had had no higher object in stirring her up to a sense of spiritual things, the motive of relieving her mind of its guilty secrets would have been enough of itself to encourage me to go on.

Aunt Ablewhite took her exercise in the afternoon in an invalid chair. Rachel accompanied her. 'I wish I could drag the chair,' she broke out, recklessly. 'I wish I could fatigue myself till I was ready to drop.'

She was in the same humour in the evening. I discovered in one of my friend's precious publications – the Life, Letters, and Labours of Miss Jane Ann Stamper, forty-fourth edition – passages which bore with a marvellous appropriateness on Rachel's present position. Upon my proposing to read them, she went to the piano. Conceive how little she must have known of serious people, if she supposed that my patience was to be exhausted in that way! I kept Miss Jane Ann Stamper by me, and waited for events with the most unfaltering trust in the future.

Old Mr Ablewhite never made his appearance that night. But I knew the importance which his worldly greed attached to his son's marriage with Miss Verinder – and I felt a positive conviction (do what Mr Godfrey might to prevent it) that we should see him the next day. With his interference in the matter, the storm on which I had counted would certainly come, and the salutary exhaustion of Rachel's resisting powers would as certainly follow. I am not ignorant that old Mr Ablewhite has the reputation generally (especially among his inferiors) of being a remarkably good-natured man. According to my observation of him, he deserves his reputation as long as he has his own way, and not a moment longer.

The next day, exactly as I had foreseen, Aunt Ablewhite was as near to being astonished as her nature would permit, by the sudden appearance of her husband. He had barely been a minute in the house, before he was followed, to *my* astonishment this time, by an unexpected complication, in the shape of Mr Bruff.

I never remember feeling the presence of the lawyer to be more unwelcome than I felt it at that moment. He looked ready for anything in the way of an obstructive proceeding – capable even of keeping the peace, with Rachel for one of the combatants!

'This is a pleasant surprise, sir,' said Mr Ablewhite, addressing himself with his deceptive cordiality to Mr Bruff. 'When I left your office yesterday, I didn't expect to have the honour of seeing you at Brighton to-day.'

'I turned over our conversation in my mind, after you had gone,' replied Mr Bruff. 'And it occurred to me that I might perhaps be of some use on this occasion. I was just in time to catch the train, and I had no opportunity of discovering the carriage in which you were travelling.'

Having given that explanation, he seated himself by Rachel. I retired modestly to a corner – with Miss Jane Ann Stamper on my lap, in case of emergency. My aunt sat at the window; placidly fanning herself as usual. Mr Ablewhite stood up in the middle of the room, with his bald head much pinker than I had ever seen it yet, and addressed himself in the most affectionate manner to his niece.

'Rachel, my dear,' he said, 'I have heard some very extraordinary news from Godfrey. And I am here to inquire about it. You have a sitting-room of your own in this house. Will you honour me by showing me the way to it?'

Rachel never moved. Whether she was determined to bring matters to a crisis, or whether she was prompted by some private sign from Mr Bruff, is more than I can tell. She declined doing old Mr Ablewhite the honour of conducting him into her sitting-room.

'Whatever you wish to say to me,' she answered, 'can be said here – in the presence of my relatives, and in the presence' (she looked at Mr Bruff) 'of my mother's trusted old friend.'

'Just as you please, my dear,' said the amiable Mr Ablewhite. He took a chair. The rest of them looked at his face – as if they expected it, after seventy years of worldly training, to speak the truth. *I* looked at the top of his bald head; having noticed on other occasions that the temper which was really in him had a habit of registering itself *there*.

'Some weeks ago,' pursued the old gentleman, 'my son informed me that Miss Verinder had done him the honour to engage herself to marry him. Is it possible, Rachel, that he can have misinterpreted – or presumed upon – what you really said to him?'

'Certainly not,' she replied. 'I did engage myself to marry him.'

'Very frankly answered!' said Mr Ablewhite. 'And most satisfactory, my dear, so far. In respect to what happened some weeks since, Godfrey has made no mistake. The error is evidently in what he told me yesterday. I begin to see it now. You and he have had a lovers' quarrel – and my foolish son has interpreted it seriously. Ah! I should have known better than that at his age.'

The fallen nature in Rachel – the mother Eve, so to speak – began to chafe at this.

'Pray let us understand each other, Mr Ablewhite,' she said. 'Nothing in the least like a quarrel took place yesterday between your son and me. If he told you that I proposed breaking off our marriage engagement, and that he agreed on his side – he told you the truth.'

The self-registering thermometer at the top of Mr Ablewhite's bald head, began to indicate a rise of temper. His face was more amiable than ever – but *there* was the pink at the top of his face, a shade deeper already!

'Come, come, my dear!' he said, in his most soothing manner, 'now don't be angry, and don't be hard on poor Godfrey! He has evidently said some unfortunate thing. He was always clumsy from a child – but he means well, Rachel, he means well!'

'Mr Ablewhite, I have either expressed myself very badly, or you are purposely mistaking me. Once for all, it is a settled thing between your son and myself that we remain, for the rest of our lives, cousins and nothing more. Is that plain enough?'

The tone in which she said those words made it impossible, even for old Mr Ablewhite, to mistake her any longer. His thermometer went up another degree, and his voice when he next spoke, ceased to be the voice which is appropriate to a notoriously good-natured man.

'I am to understand, then,' he said, 'that your marriage engagement is broken off?'

'You are to understand that, Mr Ablewhite, if you please.'

'I am also to take it as a matter of fact that the proposal to withdraw from the engagement came, in the first instance, from *you*?'

'It came, in the first instance, from me. And it met, as I have told you, with your son's consent and approval.'

The thermometer went up to the top of the register. I mean, the pink changed suddenly to scarlet.

'My son is a mean-sprited hound!' cried this furious old worldling. 'In justice to myself as his father – not in justice to *him* – I beg to ask you, Miss Verinder, what complaint you have to make of Mr Godfrey Ablewhite?

Here Mr Bruff interfered for the first time.

'You are not bound to answer that question,' he said to Rachel.

Old Mr Ablewhite fastened on him instantly.

'Don't forget, sir,' he said, 'that you are a self-invited guest here. Your interference would have come with a better grace if you had waited until it was asked for.'

Mr Bruff took no notice. The smooth varnish on *his* wicked old face never cracked. Rachel thanked him for the advice he had given to her, and then turned to old Mr Ablewhite – preserving her composure in a manner which (having regard to her age and her sex) was simply awful to see.

'Your son put the same question to me which you have just asked,' she said. 'I had only one answer for him, and I have only one answer for you. I proposed that we should release each other, because reflection had convinced me that I should best consult his welfare and mine by retracting a rash promise, and leaving him free to make his choice elsewhere.'

'What has my son done?' persisted Mr Ablewhite. 'I have a right to know that. What has my son done?'

She persisted just as obstinately on her side.

'You have had the only explanation which I think it necessary to give to you, or to him,' she answered.

'In plain English, it's your sovereign will and pleasure, Miss Verinder, to jilt my son?'

Rachel was silent for a moment. Sitting close behind her, I heard her sigh. Mr Bruff took her hand, and gave it a little squeeze. She recovered herself, and answered Mr Ablewhite as boldly as ever.

'I have exposed myself to worse misconstruction than that,' she said. 'And I have borne it patiently. The time has gone by, when you could mortify me by calling me a jilt.'

She spoke with a bitterness of tone which satisfied me that the scandal of the Moonstone had been in some way recalled to her mind. 'I have no more to say,' she added, wearily, not addressing the words to any one in particular, and looking away from us all, out of the window that was nearest to her.

Mr Ablewhite got upon his feet, and pushed away his chair so violently that it toppled over and fell on the floor.

'I have something more to say on my side,' he announced, bringing down the flat of his hand on the table with a bang. 'I have to say that if my son doesn't feel this insult, I do!'

Rachel started, and looked at him in sudden surprise.

'Insult?' she repeated. 'What do you mean?'

'Insult!' reiterated Mr Ablewhite. 'I know your motive, Miss Verinder, for breaking your promise to my son! I know it as certainly as if you had confessed it in so many words. Your cursed family pride is insulting Godfrey, as it insulted *me* when I married your aunt. Her family – her beggarly family – turned their backs on her for marrying an honest man, who had made his own place and won his own fortune. I had no ancestors. I wasn't descended from a set of cut-throat scoundrels who lived by robbery and murder. I couldn't point to the time when the Ablewhites hadn't a shirt to their backs, and couldn't sign their own names. Ha! ha! I wasn't good enough for the Herncastles, when *I* married. And, now it comes to the pinch, my son isn't good enough for *you*. I suspected it, all along. You have got the Herncastle blood in you, my young lady! I suspected it all along.'

'A very unworthy suspicion,' remarked Mr Bruff. 'I am astonished that you have the courage to acknowledge it.'

Before Mr Ablewhite could find words to answer in, Rachel spoke in a tone of the most exasperating contempt.

'Surely,' she said to the lawyer, 'this is beneath notice. If he can think in *that* way, let us leave him to think as he pleases.'

From scarlet, Mr Ablewhite was now becoming purple. He gasped for breath; he looked backwards and forwards from Rachel to Mr Bruff in such a frenzy of rage with both of them that he didn't know which to attack first. His wife, who had sat impenetrably fanning herself up to this time, began to be alarmed, and attempted, quite uselessly, to quiet him. I had, throughout this distressing interview, felt more than one inward call to interfere with a few earnest words, and had controlled myself under a dread of the possible results, very unworthy of a Christian Englishwoman who looks, not to what is meanly prudent, but to what is morally right. At the point at which matters had now arrived, I rose superior to all considerations of mere expediency. If I had contemplated interposing any remonstrance of my own humble devising, I might possibly have still hesitated. But the distressing domestic emergency which now confronted me, was most marvellously and beautifully provided for in the Correspondence of Miss Jane Ann Stamper – Letter one thousand and one, on 'Peace in Families'. I rose in my modest corner, and I opened my precious book.

'Dear Mr Ablewhite,' I said, 'one word!'

When I first attracted the attention of the company by rising, I could see that he was on the point of saying something rude to me. My sisterly form of address checked him. He stared at me in heathen astonishment.

'As an affectionate well-wisher and friend,' I proceeded, 'and as one long accustomed to arouse, convince, prepare, enlighten, and fortify others, permit me to take the most pardonable of all liberties – the liberty of composing your mind.'

He began to recover himself; he was on the point of breaking out – he *would* have broken out, with anybody else. But my voice (habitually gentle) possesses a high note or so, in emergencies. In this emergency, I felt imperatively called upon to have the highest voice of the two.

I held up my precious book before him; I rapped the open page impressively with my forefinger. 'Not my words!' I exclaimed, in a burst of fervent interruption. 'Oh, don't suppose that I claim attention for My humble words! Manna in the wilderness, Mr Ablewhite! Dew on the parched earth! Words of comfort, words of wisdom, words of love – the blessed, blessed, blessed words of Miss Jane Ann Stamper!'

I was stopped there by a momentary impediment of the breath. Before I could recover myself, this monster in human form shouted out furiously, –

'Miss Jane Ann Stamper be – !'

It is impossible for me to write the awful word, which is here represented by a blank. I shrieked as it passed his lips; I flew to my little bag on the side-table; I shook out all my tracts; I seized the one particular tract on profane swearing, entitled, 'Hush, for Heaven's Sake!'; I handed it to him with an expression of agonized entreaty. He tore it in two, and threw it back at me across the table. The rest of them rose in alarm, not knowing what might happen next. I instantly sat down again in my corner. There had once been an occasion, under somewhat similar circumstances, when Miss Jane Ann Stamper had been taken by the two shoulders and turned out of a room. I waited, inspired by *her* spirit, for a repetition of *her* martyrdom.

But no – it was not to be. His wife was the next person whom he addressed. 'Who – who – who,' he said, stammering with rage, 'asked this impudent fanatic into the house? Did you?'

Before Aunt Ablewhite could say a word, Rachel answered for her.

'Miss Clack is here,' she said, 'as my guest.'

Those words had a singular effect on Mr Ablewhite. They suddenly changed him from a man in a state of red-hot anger to a man in a state of icy-cold contempt. It was plain to everybody that Rachel had said something – short and plain as her answer had been – which gave him the upper hand of her at last.

'Oh?' he said. 'Miss Clack is here as *your* guest – in *my* house?'

It was Rachel's turn to lose her temper at that. Her colour rose, and her eyes brightened fiercely. She turned to the lawyer, and, pointing to Mr Ablewhite, asked haughtily, 'What does he mean?'

Mr Bruff interfered for the third time.

'You appear to forget,' he said, addressing Mr Ablewhite, 'that you took this house as Miss Verinder's guardian, for Miss Verinder's use.'

'Not quite so fast,' interposed Mr Ablewhite. 'I have a last word to say, which I should have said some time since, if this – ' he looked my way, pondering what abominable name he should call me – 'if this Rampant Spinster had not interrupted us. I beg to inform you, sir, that, if my son is not good enough to be Miss Verinder's husband, I cannot presume to consider his father good enough to be Miss Verinder's guardian. Understand, if you please, that I refuse to accept the position which is offered to me by Lady Verinder's will. In your legal phrase, I decline to act. This house has necessarily been hired in my name. I take the entire responsibility of it on my shoulders. It is my house. I can keep it, or let it, just as I please. I have no wish to hurry Miss Verinder. On the contrary, I beg her to remove her guest and her luggage, at her own entire convenience.' He made a low bow, and walked out of the room.

That was Mr Ablewhite's revenge on Rachel, for refusing to marry his son!

The instant the door closed, Aunt Ablewhite exhibited a phenomenon which silenced us all. She became endowed with energy enough to cross the room!

'My dear,' she said, taking Rachel by the hand, 'I should be ashamed of my husband, if I didn't know that it is his temper which I has spoken to you, and not himself. You,' continued Aunt Ablewhite, turning on me in my corner with another endownment of energy, in her looks this time instead of her limbs – 'you are the mischievous person who irritated him. I hope I shall never see you or your tracts again.' She went back to Rachel and kissed her. 'I beg your pardon, my dear,' she said, 'in my husband's name. What can I do for you?'

Consistently perverse in everything – capricious and unreasonable in all the actions of her life – Rachel melted into tears at those commonplace words, and returned her aunt's kiss in silence.

'If I may be permitted to answer for Miss Verinder,' said Mr Bruff, 'might I ask you, Mrs Ablewhite, to send Penelope down with her mistress's bonnet and shawl. Leave us ten minutes together,' he added, in a lower tone, 'and you may rely on my setting matters right, to your satisfaction as well as to Rachel's.'

The trust of the family in this man was something wonderful to see. Without a word more, on her side, Aunt Ablewhite left the room.

'Ah!' said Mr Bruff, looking after her. 'The Herncastle blood has its drawbacks, I admit. But there *is* something in good breeding after all!'

Having made that purely worldly remark, he looked hard at my corner, as if he expected me to go. My interest in Rachel – an infinitely higher interest than his – riveted me to my chair.

Mr Bruff gave it up, exactly as he had given it up at Aunt Verinder's, in Montagu Square. He led Rachel to a chair by the window, and spoke to her there.

'My dear young lady,' he said, 'Mr Ablewhite's conduct has naturally shocked you, and taken you by surprise. If it was worth while to contest the question with such a man, we might soon show him that he is not to have things all his own way. But it isn't worth while. You were quite right in what you said just now; he is beneath our notice.'

He stopped, and looked round at my corner. I sat there quite immovable, with my tracts at my elbow, and with Miss Jane Ann Stamper on my lap.

'You know,' he resumed, turning back again to Rachel, 'that it was part of your poor mother's fine nature always to see the best of the people about her, and never the worst. She named her brother-in-law your guardian because she believed in him, and because she thought it would please her sister. I had never liked Mr Ablewhite myself, and I induced your mother to let me insert a clause in the will, empowering her executors, in certain events, to consult with me about the appointment of a new guardian. One of those events has happened to-day; and I find myself in a position to end all these dry business details, I hope agreeably, with a message from my wife. Will you honour Mrs Bruff by becoming her guest? And will you remain under my roof, and be one of my family, until we wise people have laid our heads together, and have settled what is to be done next?'

At those words, I rose to interfere. Mr Bruff had done exactly what I had dreaded he would do, when he asked Mrs Ablewhite for Rachel's bonnet and shawl.

Before I could interpose a word, Rachel had accepted his invitation in the warmest terms. If I suffered the arrangement thus made between them to be carried out – if she once passed the threshold of Mr Bruff's door – farewell to the fondest hope of my life, the hope of bringing my lost sheep back to the fold! The bare idea of such a calamity as this quite overwhelmed me. I cast the miserable trammels of worldly discretion to the winds, and spoke with the fervour that filled me, in the words that came first.

'Stop!' I said – 'Stop! I must be heard. Mr Bruff! you are not related to her, and I am. *I* invite her – I summon the executors to appoint *me* guardian. Rachel, dearest Rachel, I offer you my modest home; come to London by the next train, love, and share it with me!'

Mr Bruff said nothing. Rachel looked at me with a cruel astonishment which she made no effort to conceal.

'You are very kind, Drusilla,' she said. 'I shall hope to visit you whenever I happen to be in London. But I have accepted Mr Bruff's invitation, and I think it will be best, for the present, if I remain under Mr Bruff's care.'

'Oh, don't say so!' I pleaded. 'I can't part with you, Rachel, – I can't part with you!'

I tried to fold her in my arms. But she drew back. My fervour did not communicate itself; it only alarmed her.

'Surely,' she said, 'this is a very unnecessary display of agitation? I don't understand it.'

'No more do I,' said Mr Bruff.

Their hardness – their hideous, worldly hardness – revolted me.

'Oh, Rachel! Rachel!' I burst out. 'Haven't you seen *yet*, that my heart yearns to make a Christian of you? Has no inner voice told you that I am trying to do for *you*, what I was trying to do for your dear mother when death snatched her out of my hands?'

Rachel advanced a step nearer, and looked at me very strangely.

'I don't understand your reference to my mother,' she said. 'Miss Clack, will you have the goodness to explain yourself?'

Before I could answer, Mr Bruff came forward, and offering his arm to Rachel, tried to lead her out of the room.

'You had better not pursue the subject, my dear,' he said. 'And Miss Clack had better not explain herself.'

If I had been a stock or a stone, such an interference as this must have roused me into testifying to the truth. I put Mr Bruff aside indignantly with my own hand, and, in solemn and suitable language, I stated the view with which sound doctrine does not scruple to regard the awful calamity of dying unprepared.

Rachel started back from me – I blush to write it – with a scream of horror.

'Come away!' she said to Mr Bruff. 'Come away, for God's sake, before that woman can say any more! Oh, think of my poor mother's harmless, useful, beautiful life! You were at the funeral, Mr Bruff; you saw how everybody loved her; you saw the poor helpless people crying at her grave over the loss of their best friend. And that wretch stands there, and tries to make me doubt that my mother, who was an angel on earth, is an angel in heaven now! Don't stop to talk about it! Come away! It stifles me to breathe the same air with her! It frightens me to feel that we are in the same room together!'

Deaf to all remonstrance, she ran to the door.

At the same moment, her maid entered with her bonnet and shawl. She huddled them on anyhow. 'Pack my things,' she said, 'and bring them to Mr Bruff's.' I attempted to approach her – I was shocked and grieved, but, it is needless to say, not offended. I only wished to say to her, 'May your hard heart be softened! I freely forgive you!' She pulled down her veil, and tore her shawl away from my hand, and, hurrying out, shut the door in my face. I bore the insult with my customary fortitude. I remember it now with my customary superiority to all feeling of offence.

Mr Bruff had his parting word of mockery for me, before he too hurried out, in his turn.

'You had better not have explained yourself, Miss Clack,' he said, and bowed, and left the room.

The person with the cap-ribbons followed.

'It's easy to see who has set them all by the ears together,' she said. 'I'm only a poor servant – but I declare I'm ashamed of you!' She too went out, and banged the door after her.

I was left alone in the room. Reviled by them all, deserted by them all, I was left alone in the room.

Is there more to be added to this plain statement of facts – to this touching picture of a Christian persecuted by the world? No! my diary reminds me that one more of the many chequered chapters in my life, ends here. From that day forth, I never saw Rachel Verinder again. She had my forgiveness at the time when she insulted me. She has had my prayerful good wishes ever since. And when I die – to complete the return on my part of good for evil – she will have the *Life, Letters, and Labours of Miss Jane Ann Stamper* left her as a legacy by my will.

Second Narrative

Contributed by Mathew Bruff, *Solicitor, of Gray's Inn Square.*

✎ ONE ✎

MY FAIR FRIEND, MISS CLACK, having laid down the pen, there are two reasons for my taking it up next, in my turn.

In the first place, I am in a position to throw the necessary light on certain points of interest which have thus far been left in the dark. Miss Verinder had her own private reason for breaking her marriage engagement – and I was at the bottom of it. Mr Godfrey Ablewhite had his own private reason for withdrawing all claim to the hand of his charming cousin – and I discovered what it was.

In the second place, it was my good or ill fortune, I hardly know which, to find myself personally involved – at the period of which I am now writing – in the mystery of the Indian Diamond. I had the honour of an interview, at my own office, with an Oriental stranger of distinguished manners, who was no other, unquestionably, than the chief of the three Indians. Add to this, that I met with the celebrated traveller, Mr Murthwaite, the day afterwards, and that I held a conversation with him on the subject of the Moonstone, which has a very important bearing on later events. And there you have the statement of my claims to fill the position which I occupy in these pages.

The true story of the broken marriage engagement comes first in point of time and must therefore take the first place in the present narrative. Tracing my way back along the chain of events, from one end to the other, I find it necessary to open the scene, oddly enough as you will think, at the bedside of my excellent client and friend, the late Sir John Verinder.

Sir John had his share – perhaps rather a large share – of the more harmless and amiable of the weaknesses incidental to humanity. Among these, I may mention as applicable to the matter in hand, an invincible reluctance – so long as he enjoyed his usual good health – to face the responsibility of making his will. Lady Verinder exerted her influence to rouse him to a sense of duty in this matter; and I exerted my influence. He admitted the justice of our views – but he went no further than that, until he found himself afflicted with the illness which ultimately brought him to his grave. Then, I was sent for at last, to take my client's instructions on the subject of his will. They proved to be the simplest instructions I had ever received in the whole of my professional career.

Sir John was dozing, when I entered the room. He roused himself at the sight of me.

'How do you do, Mr Bruff?' he said, 'I shan't be very long about this. And then I'll go to sleep again.' He looked on with great interest while, I collected pens, ink, and paper. 'Are you ready?' he asked. I bowed, and took a dip of ink, and waited for my instructions.

'I leave everything to my wife,' said Sir John. 'That's all.' He turned round on his pillow, and composed himself to sleep again.

I was obliged to disturb him.

'Am I to understand,' I asked, 'that you leave the whole of the property, of every sort and description, of which you die possessed, absolutely to Lady Verinder?'

'Yes,' said Sir John. 'Only, I put it shorter. Why can't you put it shorter, and let me go to sleep again? Everything to my wife. That's my Will.'

His property was entirely at his own disposal, and was of two kinds. Property in land (I purposely abstain from using technical language), and property in money. In the majority of cases, I am afraid I should have felt it my duty to my client to ask him to reconsider his Will. In the case of Sir John, I knew Lady Verinder to be, not only worthy of the unreserved trust which her husband had placed in her (all good wives are worthy of that) – but to be also capable of properly administering a trust (which, in my experience of the fair sex, not one in a thousand of them is competent to do). In ten minutes, Sir John's Will was drawn, and executed, and Sir John himself, good man, was finishing his interrupted nap.

Lady Verinder amply justified the confidence which her husband had placed in her. In the first days of her widowhood, she sent for me, and made her Will. The view she took of her position was so thoroughly sound and sensible, that I was relieved of all necessity for advising her. My responsibility began and ended with shaping her instructions into the proper legal form. Before Sir John had been a fortnight in his grave, the future of his daughter had been most wisely and most affectionately provided for.

The Will remained in its fireproof box at my office, through more years than I like to reckon up. It was not till the summer of eighteen hundred and forty-eight that I found occasion to look at it again under very melancholy circumstances.

At the date I have mentioned, the doctors pronounced the sentence on poor Lady Verinder, which was literally a sentence of death. I was the first person whom she informed of her situation; and I found her anxious to go over her Will again with me.

It was impossible to improve the provisions relating to her daughter. But, in the lapse of time, her wishes in regard to certain minor legacies, left to different relatives, had undergone some modification; and it became necessary to add three or four Codicils to the original document. Having done this at once, for fear of accidents, I obtained her ladyship's permission to embody her recent instructions in a second Will. My object was to avoid certain inevitable confusions and repetitions which now disfigured the original document, and which, to own the truth, grated sadly on my professional sense of the fitness of things.

The execution of this second Will has been described by Miss Clack, who was so obliging as to witness it. So far as regarded Rachel Verinder's pecuniary interests, it was, word for word, the exact counterpart of the first Will. The only changes introduced related to the appointment of a guardian, and to certain provisions concerning that appointment, which were made under my advice. On Lady Verinder's death, the Will was placed in the hands of my proctor to be 'proved' (as the phrase is) in the usual way.

In about three weeks from that time – as well as I can remember – the first warning reached me of something unusual going on under the surface. I happened to be looking in at my friend the proctor's office, and I observed that he received me with an appearance of greater interest than usual.

'I have some news for you,' he said. 'What do you think I heard at Doctors' Commons this morning? Lady Verinder's Will has been asked for, and examined, already!'

This was news indeed! There was absolutely nothing which could be contested in the Will; and there was nobody I could think of who had the slightest interest in examining it. (I shall perhaps do well if I explain in this place, for the benefit of the few people who don't know it already, that the law allows all Wills to be examined at Doctors' Commons by anybody who applies, on the payment of a shilling fee.)

'Did you hear who asked for the Will?' I asked.

'Yes; the clerk had no hesitation in telling *me*. Mr Smalley, of the firm of Skipp and Smalley, asked for it. The Will has not been copied yet into the great Folio Registers. So there was no alternative but to depart from the usual course, and to let him see the original document. He looked it over carefully, and made a note in his pocket-book. Have you any idea of what he wanted with it?'

I shook my head. 'I shall find out,' I answered, 'before I am a day older.' With that I went back at once to my own office.

If any other firm of solicitors had been concerned in this unaccountable examination of my deceased client's Will, I might have found some difficulty in making the necessary discovery. But I had a hold over Skipp and Smalley which made my course in this matter a comparatively easy one. My common-law clerk (a most competent and excellent man) was a brother of Mr Smalley's; and, owing to this sort of indirect connection with me, Skipp and Smalley had, for some years past, picked up the crumbs that fell from my table, in the shape of cases brought to my office, which, for various reasons, I did not think it worth while to undertake. My professional patronage was, in this way, of some importance to the firm. I intended, if necessary, to remind them of that patronage, on the present occasion.

The moment I got back I spoke to my clerk; and, after telling him what had happened, I sent him to his brother's office, 'with Mr Bruff's compliments, and he would be glad to know why Messrs Skipp and Smalley had found it necessary to examine Lady Verinder's Will.'

This message brought Mr Smalley back to my office, in company with his brother. He acknowledged that he had acted under instructions received from a client. And then he put it to me, whether it would not be a breach of professional confidence on his part to say more.

We had a smart discussion upon that. He was right, no doubt; and I was wrong. The truth is, I was angry and suspicious – and I insisted on knowing more. Worse still, I declined to consider any additional information offered me, as a secret placed in my keeping: I claimed perfect freedom to use my own discretion. Worse even than that, I took an unwarrantable advantage of my position. 'Choose, sir,' I said to Mr Smalley, 'between the risk of losing your client's business and the risk of losing Mine.' Quite indefensible, I admit – an act of tyranny, and nothing less. Like other tyrants, I carried my point. Mr Smalley chose his alternative, without a moment's hesitation. He smiled resignedly, and gave up the name of his client:

Mr Godfrey Ablewhite.

That was enough for me – I wanted to know no more.

Having reached this point in my narrative, it now becomes necessary to place the reader of these lines – so far as Lady Verinder's Will is concerned – on a footing of perfect equality, in respect of information, with myself.

Let me state, then, in the fewest possible words, that Rachel Verinder had nothing but a life-interest in the property. Her mother's excellent sense, and my long experience, had combined to relieve her of all responsibility, and to guard her from all danger of becoming the victim in the future of some needy and unscrupulous man. Neither she, nor her husband (if she married), could raise sixpence, either on the property in land, or on the property in money. They would have the houses in London and in Yorkshire to live in, and they would have the handsome income – and that was all.

When I came to think over what I had discovered, I was sorely perplexed what to do next.

Hardly a week had passed since I had heard (to my surprise and distress) of Miss Verinder's proposed marriage. I had the sincerest admiration and affection for her; and I had been inexpressibly grieved when I heard that she was about to throw herself away on Mr Godfrey Ablewhite. And now, here was the man – whom I had always believed to be a smooth-tongued impostor – justifying the very worst that I had thought of him, and plainly revealing the mercenary object of the marriage, on his side! And what of that? – you may reply – the thing is done every day. Granted, my dear sir. But would you think of it quite as lightly as you do, if the thing was done (let us say) with your own sister?

The first consideration which now naturally occurred to me was this. Would Mr Godfrey Ablewhite hold to his engagement, after what his lawyer had discovered for him?

It depended entirely on his pecuniary position, of which I knew nothing. If that position was not a desperate one, it would be well worth his while to marry Miss Verinder for her income alone. If, on the other hand, he stood in urgent need of realizing a large sum by a given time, then Lady Verinder's Will would exactly meet the case, and would preserve her daughter from falling into a scoundrel's hands.

In the latter event, there would be no need for me to distress Miss Rachel, in the first days of her mourning for her mother, by an immediate revelation of the truth. In the former event, if I remained silent, I should be conniving at a marriage which would make her miserable for life.

My doubts ended in my calling at the hotel in London, at which I knew Mrs Ablewhite and Miss Verinder to be staying. They informed me that they were going to Brighton the next day, and that an unexpected obstacle prevented Mr Godfrey Ablewhite from accompanying them. I at once proposed to take his place. While I was only thinking of Rachel Verinder, it was possible to hesitate. When I actually saw her, my mind was made up directly, come what might of it, to tell her the truth.

I found my opportunity, when I was out walking with her, on the day after my arrival.

'May I speak to you,' I asked, 'about your marriage engagement?'

'Yes,' she said, indifferently, 'if you have nothing more interesting to talk about.'

'Will you forgive an old friend and servant of your family, Miss Rachel, if I venture on asking whether your heart is set on this marriage?'

'I am marrying in despair, Mr Bruff – on the chance of dropping into some sort of stagnant happiness which may reconcile me to my life.'

Strong language! and suggestive of something below the surface, in the shape of a romance. But I had my own object in view, and I declined (as we lawyers say) to pursue the question into its side-issues.

'Mr Godfrey Ablewhite can hardly be of your way of thinking,' I said. '*His* heart must be set on the marriage at any rate?'

'He says so, and I suppose I ought to believe him. He would hardly marry me, after what I have owned to him, unless he was fond of me.'

Poor thing! the bare idea of a man marrying her for his own selfish and mercenary ends had never entered her head. The task I had set myself began to look like a harder task than I had bargained for.

'It sounds strangely,' I went on, 'in my old-fashioned ears—'

'What sounds strangely?' she asked.

'To hear you speak of your future husband as if you were not quite sure of the sincerity of his attachment. Are you conscious of any reason in your own mind for doubting him?'

Her astonishing quickness of perception detected a change in my voice, or my manner, when I put that question, which warned her that I had been speaking all along with some ulterior object in view. She stopped, and taking her arm out of mine, looked me searchingly in the face.

'Mr Bruff,' she said, 'you have something to tell me about Godfrey Ablewhite. Tell it.'

I knew her well enough to take her at her word. I told it.

She put her arm again into mine, and walked on with me slowly. I felt her hand tightening its grasp mechanically on my arm, and I saw her getting paler and paler as I went on – but, not a word passed her lips while I was speaking. When I had done, she still kept silence. Her head drooped a little, and she walked by my side, unconscious of my presence, unconscious of everything about her; lost – buried, I might almost say – in her own thoughts.

I made no attempt to disturb her. My experience of her disposition warned me, on this, as on former occasions, to give her time.

The first instinct of girls in general, on being told of anything which interests them, is to ask a multitude of questions, and then to run off, and talk it all over with some favourite friend. Rachel Verinder's first instinct, under similar circumstances, was to shut herself up in her own mind, and to think it over by herself. This absolute self-dependence is a great virtue in a man. In a woman it has the serious drawback of morally separating her from the mass of her sex, and so exposing her to misconstruction by the general opinion. I strongly suspect myself of thinking as

the rest of the world think in this matter – except in the case of Rachel
Verinder. The self-dependence in *her* character, was one of its virtues in
my estimation; partly, no doubt, because I sincerely admired and liked
her; partly, because the view I took of her connection with the loss of
the Moonstone was based on my own special knowledge of her disposition. Badly as appearances might look, in the matter of the Diamond –
shocking as it undoubtedly was to know that she was associated in any
way with the mystery of an undiscovered theft – I was satisfied nevertheless that she had done nothing unworthy of her, because I was also
satisfied that she had not stirred a step in the business, without shutting
herself up in her own mind, and thinking it over first.

We had walked on, for nearly a mile I should say, before Rachel roused
herself. She suddenly looked up at me with a faint reflection of her smile
of happier times – the most irresistible smile I have ever seen on a
woman's face.

'I owe much already to your kindness,' she said. 'And I feel more
deeply indebted to it now than ever. If you hear any rumours of my
marriage when you get back to London, contradict them at once, on
my authority.'

'Have you resolved to break your engagement?' I asked.

'Can you doubt it?' she returned proudly, 'after what you have told
me!'

'My dear Miss Rachel, you are very young – and you may find more
difficulty in withdrawing from your present position than you anticipate.
Have you no one – I mean a lady, of course – whom you could consult?'

'No one,' she answered.

It distressed me, it did indeed distress me, to hear her say that. She
was so young and so lonely – and she bore it so well! The impulse to
help her got the better of any sense of my own unfitness which I might
have felt under the circumstances; and I stated such ideas on the subject
as occurred to me on the spur of the moment, to the best of my ability.
I have advised a prodigious number of clients, and have dealt with some
exceedingly awkward difficulties, in my time. But this was the first
occasion on which I had ever found myself advising a young lady how
to obtain her release from a marriage engagement. The suggestion I
offered amounted briefly to this. I recommended her to tell Mr Godfrey
Ablewhite at a private interview, of course – that he had, to her certain
knowledge, betrayed the mercenary nature of the motive on his side. She
was then to add that their marriage, after what she had discovered, was
a simple impossibility – and she was to put it to him, whether he thought
it wisest to secure her silence by falling in with her views, or to force
her, by opposing them, to make the motive under which she was acting

generally known. If he attempted to defend himself, or to deny the facts, she was, in that event, to refer him to *me*.

Miss Verinder listened attentively till I had done. She then thanked me very prettily for my advice, but informed me at the same time that it was impossible for her to follow it.

'May I ask,' I said, 'what objection you see to following it?'

She hesitated – and then met me with a question on her side.

'Suppose you were asked to express your opinion of Mr Godfrey Ablewhite's conduct?' she began.

'Yes?'

'What would you call it?'

'I should call it the conduct of a meanly deceitful man.'

'Mr Bruff! I have believed in that man. I have promised to marry that man. How can I tell him he is mean, how can I tell him he has deceived me, how can I disgrace him in the eyes of the world after that? I have degraded myself by ever thinking of him as my husband. If I say what you tell me to say to him – I am owning that I have degraded myself to his face. I can't do that. After what has passed between us, I can't do that! The shame of it would be nothing to *him*. But the shame of it would be unendurable to *me*.'

Here was another of the marked peculiarities in her character disclosing itself to me without reserve. Here was her sensitive horror of the bare contact with anything mean, blinding her to every consideration of what she owed to herself, hurrying her into a false position which might compromise her in the estimation of all her friends! Up to this time, I had been a little diffident about the propriety of the advice I had given to her. But, after what she had just said, I had no sort of doubt that it was the best advice that could have been offered; and I felt no sort of hesitation in pressing it on her again.

She only shook her head, and repeated her objection in other words.

'He has been intimate enough with me to ask me to be his wife. He has stood high enough in my estimation to obtain my consent. I can't tell him to his face that he is the most contemptible of living creatures, after that!'

'But, my dear Miss Rachel,' I remonstrated, 'it's equally impossible for you to tell him that you withdraw from your engagement without giving some reason for it.'

'I shall say that I have thought it over, and that I am satisfied it will be best for both of us if we part.'

'No more than that?'

'No more.'

'Have you thought of what he may say, on his side?'

'He may say what he pleases.'

It was impossible not to admire her delicacy and her resolution, and it was equally impossible not to feel that she was putting herself in the wrong. I entreated her to consider her own position. I reminded her that she would be exposing herself to the most odious misconstruction of her motives. 'You can't brave public opinion,' I said, 'at the command of private feeling.'

'I can,' she answered. 'I have done it already.'

'What do you mean?'

'You have forgotten the Moonstone, Mr Bruff. Have I not braved public opinion, *there*, with my own private reasons for it?'

Her answer silenced me for the moment. It set me trying to trace the explanation of her conduct, at the time of the loss of the Moonstone, out of the strange avowal which had just escaped her. I might perhaps have done it when I was younger. I certainly couldn't do it now.

I tried a last remonstrance before we returned to the house. She was just as immovable as ever. My mind was in a strange conflict of feelings about her when I left her that day. She was obstinate; she was wrong. She was interesting; she was admirable; she was deeply to be pitied. I made her promise to write to me the moment she had any news to send. And I went back to my business in London, with a mind exceedingly ill at ease.

On the evening of my return, before it was possible for me to receive my promised letter, I was surprised by a visit from Mr Ablewhite the elder, and was informed that Mr Godfrey had got his dismissal – *and had accepted it* – that very day.

With the view I already took of the case, the bare fact stated in the words that I have underlined, revealed Mr Godfrey Ablewhite's motive for submission as plainly as if he had acknowledged it himself. He needed a large sum of money; and he needed it by a given time. Rachel's income, which would have helped him to anything else, would not help him here; and Rachel had accordingly released herself, without encountering a moment's serious opposition on his part. If I am told that this is a mere speculation, I ask, in my turn, What other theory will account for his giving up a marriage which would have maintained him in splendour for the rest of his life?

Any exultation I might otherwise have felt at the lucky turn which things had now taken, was effectually checked by what passed at my interview with old Mr Ablewhite.

He came, of course, to know whether I could give him any explanation of Miss Verinder's extraordinary conduct. It is needless to say that I was quite unable to afford him the information he wanted. The annoyance which I thus inflicted, following on the irritation produced by a recent interview with his son, threw Mr Ablewhite off his guard. Both his looks and his language convinced me that Miss Verinder would find him a merciless man to deal with, when he joined the ladies at Brighton the next day.

I had a restless night, considering what I ought to do next. How my reflections ended, and how thoroughly well founded my distrust of Mr Ablewhite proved to be, are items of information which (as I am told) have already been put tidily in their proper places, by that exemplary person, Miss Clack. I have only to add – in completion of her narrative – that Miss Verinder found the quiet and repose which she sadly needed, poor thing, in my house at Hampstead. She honoured us by making a long stay. My wife and daughters were charmed with her; and, when the executors decided on the appointment of a new guardian, I feel sincere pride and pleasure in recording that my guest and my family parted like old friends, on either side.

❧ TWO ❧

THE NEXT THING I HAVE TO DO, is to present such additional information as I possess on the subject of the Moonstone, or, to speak more correctly, on the subject of the Indian plot to steal the Diamond. The little that I have to tell is (as I think I have already said) of some importance, nevertheless, in respect of its bearing very remarkably on events which are still to come.

About a week or ten days after Miss Verinder had left us, one of my clerks entered the private room at my office, with a card in his hand, and informed me that a gentleman was below, who wanted to speak to me.

I looked at the card. There was a foreign name written on it, which has escaped my memory, it was followed by a line written in English at the bottom of the card, which I remember perfectly well:

'Recommended by Mr Septimus Luker.'

The audacity of a person in Mr Luker's position presuming to recommend anybody to *me*, took me so completely by surprise, that I sat silent for the moment, wondering whether my own eyes had not deceived me. The clerk, observing my bewilderment, favoured me with the result of his own observation of the stranger who was waiting downstairs.

'He is rather a remarkable-looking man, sir. So dark in the complexion

that we all set him down in the office for an Indian, or something of that
sort.'

Associating the clerk's idea with the line inscribed on the card in my
hand, I thought it possible that the Moonstone might be at the bottom
of Mr Luker's recommendation, and of the stranger's visit at my office.
To the astonishment of my clerk, I at once decided on granting an
interview to the gentleman below.

In justification of the highly unprofessional sacrifice to mere curiosity
which I thus made, permit me to remind anybody who may read these
lines, that no living person (in England, at any rate) can claim to have
had such an intimate connection with the romance of the Indian Diamond
as mine has been. I was trusted with the secret of Colonel Herncastle's
plan for escaping assassination. I received the Colonel's letters, periodically reporting himself a living man. I drew his Will, leaving the Moonstone to Miss Verinder. I persuaded his executor to act, on the chance
that the jewel might prove to be a valuable acquisition to the family.
And, lastly, I combatted Mr Franklin Blake's scruples, and induced him
to be the means of transporting the Diamond to Lady Verinder's house.
If anyone can claim a prescriptive right of interest in the Moonstone, and
in everything connected with it, I think it is hardly to be denied that I
am the man.

The moment my mysterious client was shown in, I felt an inner conviction that I was in the presence of one of the three Indians – probably of
the chief. He was carefully dressed in European costume. But his swarthy
complexion, his long lithe figure, and his grave and graceful politeness
of manner were enough to betray his Oriental origin to any intelligent
eyes that looked at him.

I pointed to a chair, and begged to be informed of the nature of his
business with me.

After first apologizing – in an excellent selection of English words –
for the liberty which he had taken in disturbing me, the Indian produced
a small parcel the outer covering of which was of cloth of gold. Removing
this and a second wrapping of some silken fabric, he placed a little box,
or casket, on my table, most beautifully and richly inlaid in jewels, on
an ebony ground.

'I have come, sir,' he said, 'to ask you to lend me some money. And I
leave this as an assurance to you that my debt will be paid back.'

I pointed to his card. 'And you apply to me,' I rejoined, 'at Mr Luker's
recommendation?'

The Indian bowed.

'May I ask how it is that Mr Luker himself did not advance the money
that you require?'

'Mr Luker informed me, sir, that he had no money to lend.'

'And so he recommended you to come to me?'

The Indian, in his turn, pointed to the card. 'It is written there,' he said.

Briefly answered, and thoroughly to the purpose! If the Moonstone had been in my possession, this Oriental gentleman would have murdered me, I am well aware, without a moment's hesitation. At the same time, and barring that slight drawback, I am bound to testify that he was the perfect model of a client. He might not have respected my life. But he did what none of my own countrymen had ever done, in all my experience of them – he respected my time.

'I am sorry,' I said, 'that you should have had the trouble of coming to me. Mr Luker is quite mistaken in sending you here. I am trusted, like other men in my profession, with money to lend. But I never lend it to strangers, and I never lend it on such a security as you have produced.'

Far from attempting, as other people would have done, to induce me to relax my own rules, the Indian only made me another bow, and wrapped up his box in its two coverings without a word of protest. He rose – this admirable assassin rose to go, the moment I had answered him!

'Will your condescension towards a stranger, excuse my asking one question,' he said, 'before I take my leave?'

I bowed on my side. Only one question at parting! The average in my experience was fifty.

'Supposing, sir, it had been possible (and customary) for *you* to lend me the money,' he said, 'in what space of time would it have been possible (and customary) for *me* to pay it back?'

'According to the usual course pursued in this country,' I answered, 'you would have been entitled to pay the money back (if you liked) in one year's time from the date at which it was first advanced to you.'

The Indian made me a last bow, the lowest of all – and suddenly and softly walked out of the room.

It was done in a moment, in a noiseless, supple, cat-like way, which a little startled me, I own. As soon as I was composed enough to think, I arrived at one distinct conclusion in reference to the otherwise incomprehensible visitor who had favoured me with a call.

His face, voice, and manner – while I was in his company – were under such perfect control that they set all scrutiny at defiance. But he had given me one chance of looking under the smooth outer surface of him, for all that. He had not shown the slightest sign of attempting to fix anything that I had said to him in his mind, until I mentioned the time at which it was customary to permit the earliest repayment, on the part of a debtor, of money that had been advanced as a loan. When

I gave him that piece of information, he looked me straight in the face, while I was speaking, for the first time. The inference I drew from this was – that he had a special purpose in asking me his last question, and a special interest in hearing my answer to it. The more carefully I reflected on what had passed between us, the more shrewdly I suspected the production of the casket, and the application for the loan, of having been mere formalities, designed to pave the way for the parting inquiry addressed to me.

I had satisfied myself of the correctness of this conclusion – and was trying to get on a step further, and penetrate the Indian's motives next – when a letter was brought to me, which proved to be from no less a person than Mr Septimus Luker himself. He asked my pardon in terms of sickening servility, and assured me that he could explain matters to my satisfaction, if I would honour him by consenting to a personal interview.

I made another unprofessional sacrifice to mere curiosity. I honoured him by making an appointment at my office, for the next day.

Mr Luker was, in every respect, such an inferior creature to the Indian – he was so vulgar, so ugly, so cringing, and so prosy – that he is quite unworthy of being reported, at any length, in these pages. The substance of what he had to tell me may be fairly stated as follows:

The day before I had received the visit of the Indian, Mr Luker had been favoured with a call from that accomplished gentleman. In spite of his European disguise, Mr Luker had instantly identified his visitor with the chief of the three Indians, who had formerly annoyed him by loitering about his house, and who had left him no alternative but to consult a magistrate. From this startling discovery he had rushed to the conclusion (naturally enough I own) that he must certainly be in the company of one of the three men who had blindfolded him, gagged him, and robbed him of his banker's receipt. The result was that he became quite paralysed with terror, and that he firmly believed his last hour had come.

On his side, the Indian preserved the character of a perfect stranger. He produced the little casket, and made exactly the same application which he had afterwards made to me. As the speediest way of getting rid of him, Mr Luker had at once declared that he had no money. The Indian had thereupon asked to be informed of the best and safest person to apply to for the loan he wanted. Mr Luker had answered that the best and safest person, in such cases, was usually a respectable solicitor. Asked to name some individual of that character and profession, Mr Luker had mentioned me – for the one simple reason that, in the extremity of his terror, mine was the first name which occurred to him. 'The perspiration was pouring off me like rain, sir,' the wretched creature concluded. 'I didn't know what I was talking about. And I hope you'll look over it, Mr Bruff, sir, in consideration of my having been really and truly frightened out of my wits.'

I excused the fellow graciously enough. It was the readiest way of releasing myself from the sight of him. Before he left me, I detained him to make one inquiry. Had the Indian said anything noticeable, at the moment of quitting Mr Luker's house?

Yes! The Indian had put precisely the same question to Mr Luker, at parting, which he had put to me; receiving, of course, the same answer as the answer which I had given him.

What did it mean? Mr Luker's explanation gave me no assistance towards solving the problem. My own unaided ingenuity, consulted next, proved quite unequal to grapple with the difficulty. I had a dinner engagement that evening; and I went upstairs, in no very genial frame of mind, little suspecting that the way to my dressing-room and the way to discovery, meant, on this particular occasion, one and the same thing.

⊛   THREE   ⊛

THE PROMINENT PERSONAGE AMONG THE guests at the dinner-party I found to be Mr Murthwaite.

On his appearance in England, after his wanderings, society had been greatly interested in the traveller, as a man who had passed through many dangerous adventures, and who had escaped to tell the tale. He had now announced his intention of returning to the scene of his exploits, and of penetrating into regions left still unexplored. This magnificent indifference to placing his safety in peril for the second time, revived the flagging interest of the worshippers in the hero. The law of chances was clearly against his escaping on this occasion. It is not every day that we can meet an eminent person at dinner, and feel that there is a reasonable prospect of the news of his murder being the news that we hear of him next.

When the gentlemen were left by themselves in the dining-room, I found myself sitting next to Mr Murthwaite. The guests present being all English, it is needless to say that, as soon as the wholesome check exercised by the presence of the ladies was removed, the conversation turned on politics as a necessary result.

In respect to this all-absorbing national topic, I happen to be one of the most un-English Englishmen living. As a general rule, political talk appears to me to be of all talk the most dreary and the most profitless. Glancing at Mr Murthwaite, when the bottles had made their first round of the table, I found that he was apparently of my way of thinking. He was doing it very dexterously – with all possible consideration for the feelings of his host – but it is not the less certain that he was composing himself for a nap. It struck me as an experiment worth attempting, to try whether a judicious allusion to the subject of the Moonstone would keep him awake, and, if it did, to see what *he* thought of the last new complication in the Indian conspiracy, as revealed in the prosaic precincts of my office.

'If I am not mistaken, Mr Murthwaite,' I began, 'you were acquainted with the late Lady Verinder, and you took some interest in the strange succession of events which ended in the loss of the Moonstone?'

The eminent traveller did me the honour of waking up in an instant, and asking me who I was.

I informed him of my professional connection with the Herncastle family, not forgetting the curious position which I had occupied towards the Colonel and his Diamond in the bygone time.

Mr Murthwaite shifted round in his chair, so as to put the rest of the company behind him (Conservatives and Liberals alike), and concentrated his whole attention on plain Mr Bruff, of Gray's Inn Square.

'Have you heard anything, lately, of the Indians?' he asked.

'I have every reason to believe,' I answered, 'that one of them had an interview with me, in my office, yesterday.'

Mr Murthwaite was not an easy man to astonish; but that last answer of mine completely staggered him. I described what had happened to Mr Luker, and what had happened to myself, exactly as I have described it here. 'It is clear that the Indian's parting inquiry had an object,' I added. 'Why should he be so anxious to know the time at which a borrower of money is usually privileged to pay the money back?'

'Is it possible that you don't see his motive, Mr Bruff?'

'I am ashamed of my stupidity, Mr Murthwaite – but I certainly don't see it.'

The great traveller became quite interested in sounding the immense vacuity of my dullness to its lowest depths.

'Let me ask you one question,' he said. 'In what position does the conspiracy to seize the Moonstone now stand?'

'I can't say,' I answered. 'The Indian plot is a mystery to me.'

'The Indian plot, Mr Bruff, can only be a mystery to you, because you have never seriously examined it. Shall we run it over together, from the time when you drew Colonel Herncastle's Will, to the time when the Indian called at your office? In your position, it may be of very serious importance to the interests of Miss Verinder, that you should be able to take a clear view of this matter in case of need. Tell me, bearing that in mind, whether you will penetrate the Indian's motive for yourself? or whether you wish me to save you the trouble of making any inquiry into it?'

It is needless to say that I thoroughly appreciated the practical purpose which I now saw that he had in view, and that the first of the two alternatives was the alternative I chose.

'Very good,' said Mr Murthwaite. 'We will take the question of the ages of the three Indians first. I can testify that they all look much about the same age – and you can decide for yourself, whether the man whom you saw was, or was not, in the prime of life. Not forty, you think? My idea too. We will say not forty. Now look back to the time when Colonel Herncastle came to England, and when you were concerned in the plan he adopted to preserve his life. I don't want you to count the years. I will only say, it is clear that these present Indians, at their age, must be the successors of three other Indians (high caste Brahmins all of them, Mr Bruff, when they left their native country!) who followed the Colonel to these shores. Very well. These present men of ours have succeeded to the men who were here before them. If they had only done that, the matter would not have been worth inquiring into. But they have done more. They have succeeded to the organization which their predecessors established in this country. Don't start! The organization is a very trumpery affair, according to our ideas, I have no doubt. I should reckon it up as including the command of money; the services, when needed, of that shady sort of Englishman, who lives in the byways of foreign life in London; and, lastly, the secret sympathy of such few men of their own country, and (formerly, at least) of their own religion, as happen to be employed in ministering to some of the multitudinous wants of this great city. Nothing very formidable, as you see! But worth notice at starting, because we *may* find occasion to refer to this modest little Indian organization as we go on. Having now cleared the ground, I am going to ask you a question; and I expect your experience to answer it. What was the event which gave the Indians their first chance of seizing the Diamond?'

I understood the allusion to my experience.

'The first chance they got.' I replied, 'was clearly offered to them by Colonel Herncastle's death. They would be aware of his death. I suppose, as a matter of course?'

'As a matter of course. And his death, as you say, gave them their first chance. Up to that time the Moonstone was safe in the strong-room of the bank. You drew the Colonel's Will leaving his jewel to his niece; and the Will was proved in the usual way. As a lawyer, you can be at no loss to know what course the Indians would take (under English advice) after *that*.'

'They would provide themselves with a copy of the Will from Doctors' Commons,' I said.

'Exactly. One or other of those shady Englishmen to whom I have alluded. would get them the copy you have described. That copy would inform them that the Moonstone was bequeathed to the daughter of Lady Verinder, and that Mr Blake the elder, or some person appointed by him, was to place it in her hands. You will agree with me that the necessary information about persons in the position of Lady Verinder and Mr Blake, would be perfectly easy information to obtain. The one difficulty for the Indians would be to decide, whether they should make their attempt on the Diamond when it was in course of removal from the keeping of the bank, or whether they should wait until it was taken down to Yorkshire to Lady Verinder's house. The second way would be manifestly the safest way – and there you have the explanation of the appearance of the Indians at Frizinghall, disguised as jugglers, and waiting their time. In London, it is needless to say, they had their organization at their disposal to keep them informed of events. Two men would do it. One to follow anybody who went from Mr Blake's house to the bank. And one to treat the lower men servants with beer, and to hear the news of the house. These commonplace precautions would readily inform them that Mr Franklin Blake had been to the bank, and that Mr Franklin Blake was the only person in the house who was going to visit Lady Verinder. What actually followed upon that discovery, you remember, no doubt, quite as correctly as I do.'

I remembered that Franklin Blake had detected one of the spies, in the street – that he had, in consequence, advanced the time of his arrival in Yorkshire by some hours – and that (thanks to old Betteredge's excellent advice) he had lodged the Diamond in the bank at Frizinghall, before the Indians were so much as prepared to see him in the neighbourhood. All perfectly clear so far. But, the Indians being ignorant of the precaution thus taken, how was it that they had made no attempt on Lady Verinder's house (in which they must have supposed the Diamond to be) through the whole of the interval that elapsed before Rachel's birthday?

In putting this difficulty to Mr Murthwaite, I thought it right to add that I had heard of the little boy, and the drop of ink, and the rest of it, and that any explanation based on the theory of clairvoyance was an explanation which would carry no conviction whatever with it, to *my* mind.

'Nor to mine either,' said Mr Murthwaite. 'The clairvoyance in this case is simply a development of the romantic side of the Indian character. It would be a refreshment and an encouragement to those men – quite inconceivable, I grant you, to the English mind – to surround their wearisome and perilous errand in this country with a certain halo of the marvellous and the supernatural. Their boy is unquestionably a sensitive subject to the mesmeric influence – and, under that influence, he has no doubt reflected what was already in the mind of the person mesmerizing him. I have tested the theory of clairvoyance – and I have never found the manifestations get beyond that point. The Indians don't investigate the matter in this way; the Indians look upon their boy as a Seer of things invisible to their eyes – and, I repeat, in that marvel they find the source of a new interest in the purpose that unites them. I only notice this as offering a curious view of human character, which must be quite new to you. We have nothing whatever to do with clairvoyance, or with mesmerism, or with anything else that is hard of belief to a practical man, in the inquiry that we are now pursuing. My object in following the Indian plot, step by step, is to trace results back, by rational means, to natural causes. Have I succeeded to your satisfaction so far?'

'Not a doubt – of it, Mr Murthwaite! I am waiting, however, with some anxiety, to hear the rational explanation of the difficulty which I have just had the honour of submitting to you.'

Mr Murthwaite smiled. 'It's the easiest difficulty to deal with of all.' he said. 'Permit me to begin by admitting your statement of the case as a perfectly correct one. The Indians were undoubtedly not aware of what Mr Franklin Blake had done with the Diamond – for we find them making their first mistake, on the first night of Mr Blake's arrival at his aunt's house.'

'Their first mistake?' I repeated.

'Certainly! The mistake of allowing themselves to be surprised, lurking about the terrace at night, by Gabriel Betteredge. However, they had the merit of seeing for themselves that they had taken a false step – for, as you say, again, with plenty of time at their disposal, they never came near the house for weeks afterwards.'

'Why, Mr Murthwaite? That's what I want to know! Why?'

'Because no Indian, Mr Bruff, ever runs an unnecessary risk. The clause you drew in Colonel Herncastle's Will, informed them (didn't it?) that the Moonstone was to pass absolutely into Miss Verinder's possession on her birthday. Very well. Tell me which was the safest course for men in their position? To make their attempt on the Diamond while it was under the control of Mr Franklin Blake, who had shown already that he could suspect and outwit them? Or to wait till the Diamond was at the disposal of a young girl, who would innocently delight in wearing the magnificent jewel at every possible opportunity? Perhaps you want a proof that my theory is correct? Take the conduct of the Indians themselves as the proof. They appeared at the house, after waiting all those weeks, on Miss Verinder's birthday; and they were rewarded for the patient accuracy of their calculations by seeing the Moonstone in the

bosom of her dress! When I heard the story of the Colonel and
the Diamond, later in the evening, I felt so sure about the risk Mr Franklin
Blake had run (they would have certainly attacked him, if he had not
happened to ride back to Lady Verinder's in the company of other
people); and I was so strongly convinced of the worse risks still, in store
for Miss Verinder, that I recommended following the Colonel's plan, and
destroying the identity of the gem by having it cut into separate stones.
How its extraordinary disappearance, that night, made my advice useless, and utterly defeated the Hindoo plot – and how all further action on
the part of the Indians was paralyzed the next day by their confinement in
prison as rogues and vagabonds – you know as well as I do. The first
act in the conspiracy closes there. Before we go on to the second, may I
ask whether I have met your difficulty, with an explanation which is
satisfactory to the mind of a practical man?'

It was impossible to deny that he had met my difficulty fairly; thanks
to his superior knowledge of the Indian character – and thanks to his
not having had hundreds of other Wills to think of since Colonel Herncastle's time!

'So far, so good,' resumed Mr Murthwaite. 'The first chance the Indians
had of seizing the Diamond was a chance lost, on the day when they
were committed to the prison at Frizinghall. When did the second chance
offer itself? The second chance offered itself – as I am in a condition to
prove – while they were still in confinement.'

He took out his pocket-book, and opened it at a particular leaf, before
he went on.

'I was staying,' he resumed, 'with some friends at Frizinghall, at the
time. A day or two before the Indians were set free (on a Monday, I
think), the governor of the prison came to me with a letter. It had been
left for the Indians by one Mrs Macann, of whom they had hired the
lodging in which they lived; and it had been delivered at Mrs Macann's
door, in ordinary course of post, on the previous morning. The prison
authorities had noticed that the post-mark was 'Lambeth', and that the
address on the outside, though expressed in correct English, was, in
form, oddly at variance with the customary method of directing a letter.
On opening it, they had found the contents to be written in a foreign
language, which they rightly guessed at as Hindustani. Their object in
coming to me was, of course, to have the letter translated to them. I took
a copy in my pocket-book of the original, and of my translation – and
there they are at your service.'

He handed me the open pocket-book. The address on the letter was
the first thing copied. It was all written in one paragraph, without any
attempt at punctuation, thus: 'To the three Indian men living with the
lady called Macann at Frizinghall in Yorkshire.' The Hindoo characters

followed; and the English translation appeared at the end, expressed in these mysterious words:

'In the name of the Regent of the Night, whose seat is on the Antelope, whose arms embrace the four corners of the earth.

'Brothers, turn your faces to the south, and come to me in the street of many noises, which leads down to the muddy river.

'The reason is this.

'My own eyes have seen it.'

There the letter ended, without either date or signature. I handed it back to Mr Murthwaite, and owned that this curious specimen of Hindoo correspondence rather puzzled me.

'I can explain the first sentence to you,' he said; 'and the conduct of the Indians themselves will explain the rest. The god of the moon is represented, in the Hindoo mythology, as a four-armed deity, seated on an antelope; and one of his titles is the regent of the night. Here, then, to begin with, is something which looks suspiciously like an indirect reference to the Moonstone. Now, let us see what the Indians did, after the prison authorities had allowed them to receive their letter. On the very day when they were set free they went at once to the railway station, and took their places in the first train that started for London. We all thought it a pity at Frizinghall that their proceedings were not privately watched. But, after Lady Verinder had dismissed the police officer, and had stopped all further inquiry into the loss of the Diamond, no one else could presume to stir in the matter. The Indians were free to go to London, and to London they went. What was the next news we heard of them, Mr Bruff?'

'They were annoying Mr Luker,' I answered, 'by loitering about the house at Lambeth.'

'Did you read the report of Mr Luker's application to the magistrate?'

'Yes.'

'In the course of his statement he referred, if you remember, to a foreign workman in his employment, whom he had just dismissed on suspicion of attempted theft, and whom he also distrusted as possibly acting in collusion with the Indians who had annoyed him. The inference is pretty plain, Mr Bruff, as to who wrote that letter which puzzled you just now, and as to which of Mr Luker's Oriental treasures the workman had attempted to steal.'

The inference (as I hastened to acknowledge) was too plain to need being pointed out. I had never doubted that the Moonstone had found its way into Mr Luker's hands, at the time Mr Murthwaite alluded to. My only question had been, How had the Indians discovered the circumstance? This question (the most difficult to deal with of all, as I had thought) had now received its answer, like the rest. Lawyer as I was,

I began to feel that I might trust Mr Murthwaite to lead me blindfold through the last windings of the labyrinth, along which he had guided me thus far. I paid him the compliment of telling him this, and found my little concession very graciously received.

'You shall give me a piece of information in your turn before we go on,' he said. 'Somebody must have taken the Moonstone from Yorkshire to London. And somebody must have raised money on it, or it would never have been in Mr Luker's possession. Has there been any discovery made of who that person was?'

'None that I know of.'

'There was a story (was there not?) about Mr Godfrey Ablewhite. I am told he is an eminent philanthropist – which is decidedly against him, to begin with.'

I heartily agreed in this with Mr Murthwaite. At the same time, I felt bound to inform him (without, it is needless to say, mentioning Miss Verinder's name) that Mr Godfrey Ablewhite had been cleared of all suspicion, on evidence which I could answer for as entirely beyond dispute.

'Very well,' said Mr Murthwaite, quietly, 'let us leave it to time to clear the matter up. In the meanwhile, Mr Bruff, we must get back again to the Indians, on your account. Their journey to London simply ended in their becoming the victims of another defeat. The loss of their second chance of seizing the Diamond is mainly attributable, as I think, to the cunning and foresight of Mr Luker – who doesn't stand at the top of the prosperous and ancient profession of usury for nothing! By the prompt dismissal of the man in his employment, he deprived the Indians of the assistance which their confederate would have rendered them in getting into the house. By the prompt transport of the Moonstone to his banker's, he took the conspirators by surprise before they were prepared with a new plan for robbing him. How the Indians, in this latter case, suspected what he had done, and how they contrived to possess them-selves of his banker's receipt, are events too recent to need dwelling on. Let it be enough to say that they know the Moonstone to be once more out of their reach; deposited (under the general description of 'a valuable of great price') in a banker's strong-room. Now, Mr Bruff, what is their third chance of seizing the Diamond? and when will it come?'

As the question passed his lips, I penetrated the motive of the Indian's visit to my office at last!

'I see it!' I exclaimed. 'The Indians take it for granted, as we do, that the Moonstone has been pledged; and they want to be certainly informed of the earliest period at which the pledge can be redeemed – because that will be the earliest period at which the Diamond can be removed from the safe keeping of the bank!'

'I told you you would find it out for yourself, Mr Bruff, if I only gave you a fair chance. In a year from the time when the Moonstone was pledged, the Indians will be on the watch for their third chance. Mr Luker's own lips have told them how long they will have to wait, and your respectable authority has satisfied them that Mr Luker has spoken the truth. When do we suppose, at a rough guess, that the Diamond found its way into the money-lender's hands?'

'Towards the end of last June.' I answered, 'as well as I can reckon it.'

'And we are now in the year 'forty-eight. Very good. If the unknown person who has pledged the Moonstone can redeem it in a year, the jewel will be in that person's possession again at the end of June, 'forty-nine. I shall be thousands of miles away from England and English news at that date. But it may be worth your while to take a note of it, and to arrange to be in London at the time.'

'You think something serious will happen?' I said.

'I think I shall be safer,' he answered, 'among the fiercest fanatics of Central Asia than I should be if I crossed the door of the bank with the Moonstone in my pocket. The Indians have been defeated twice running, Mr Bruff. It's my firm belief that they won't be defeated a third time.'

Those were the last words he said on the subject. The coffee came in; the guests rose, and dispersed themselves about the room; and we joined the ladies of the dinner-party upstairs.

I made a note of the date, and it may not be amiss if I close my narrative by repeating that note here

June, 'forty-nine. Expect news of the Indians, towards the end of the month.

And that done, I hand the pen, which I have now no further claim to use, to the writer who follows me next.

Third Narrative

contributed by Franklin Blake

&ed; ONE &eb;

IN THE SPRING OF THE YEAR eighteen hundred and forty-nine I was wandering in the East, and had then recently altered the travelling plans which I had laid out some months before, and which I had communicated to my lawyer and my banker in London.

This change made it necessary for me to send one of my servants to obtain my letters and remittances from the English consul in a certain city, which was no longer included as one of my resting-places in my new travelling scheme. The man was to join me again at an appointed place and time. An accident, for which he was not responsible, delayed him on his errand. For a week I and my people waited, encamped on the borders of a desert. At the end of that time the missing man made his appearance, with the money and the letters, at the entrance of my tent.

'I am afraid I bring you bad news, sir,' he said, and pointed to one of the letters, which had a mourning border round it, and the address on which was in the handwriting of Mr Bruff.

I know nothing, in a case of this kind, so unendurable as suspense. The letter with the mourning border was the letter that I opened first.

It informed me that my father was dead, and that I was heir to his great fortune. The wealth which had thus fallen into my hands brought its responsibilities with it; and Mr Bruff entreated me to lose no time in returning to England.

By daybreak the next morning I was on my way back to my own country.

The picture presented of me, by my old friend Betteredge, at the time of my departure from England, is (as I think) a little overdrawn. He has, in his own quaint way, interpreted seriously one of his young mistress's many satirical references to my foreign education; and has persuaded himself that he actually saw those French, German, and Italian sides to

261

my character, which my lively cousin only professed to discover in jest, and which never had any real existence, except in our good Betteredge's own brain. But, barring this drawback, I am bound to own that he has stated no more than the truth in representing me as wounded to the heart by Rachel's treatment, and as leaving England in the first keenness of suffering caused by the bitterest disappointment of my life.

I went abroad, resolved – if change and absence could help me – to forget her. It is, I am persuaded, no true view of human nature which denies that change and absence *do* help a man under these circumstances: they force his attention away from the exclusive contemplation of his own sorrow. I never forgot her; but the pang of remembrance lost its worst bitterness, little by little, as time, distance, and novelty interposed themselves more and more effectually between Rachel and me.

On the other hand, it is no less certain that, with the act of turning homeward, the remedy which had gained its ground so steadily, began now, just as steadily, to drop back. The nearer I drew to the country which she inhabited, and to the prospect of seeing her again, the more irresistibly her influence began to recover its hold on me. On leaving England, she was the last person in the world, whose name I would have suffered to pass my lips. On returning to England, she was the first person I inquired after, when Mr Bruff and I met again.

I was informed, of course, of all that had happened in my absence: in other words of all that has been related here in continuation of Betteredge's narrative – one circumstance only being excepted. Mr Bruff did not, at that time, feel himself at liberty to inform me of the motives which had privately influenced Rachel and Godfrey Ablewhite in recalling the marriage promise, on either side. I troubled him with no embarrassing questions on this delicate subject. It was relief enough to me, after the jealous disappointment caused by hearing that she had ever contemplated being Godfrey's wife, to know that reflection had convinced her of acting rashly, and that she had effected her own release from her marriage engagement.

Having heard the story of the past, my next inquiries (still inquiries after Rachel!) advanced naturally to the present time. Under whose care had she been placed after leaving Mr Bruff's house? and where was she living now?

She was living under the care of a widowed sister of the late Sir John Verinder – one Mrs Merridew – whom her mother's executors had requested to act as guardian, and who had accepted the proposal. They were reported to me, as getting on together admirably well, and as being now established, for the season, in Mrs Merridew's house in Portland Place.

Half an hour after receiving this information, I was on my way to Portland Place – without having had the courage to own it to Mr Bruff!

The man who answered the door was not sure whether Miss Verinder was at home or not. I sent him upstairs with my card, as the speediest way of setting the question at rest. The man came down again with an impenetrable face, and informed me that Miss Verinder was out.

I might have suspected other people of purposely denying themselves to me. But it was impossible to suspect Rachel. I left word that I would call again at six o'clock that evening.

At six o'clock I was informed for the second time that Miss Verinder was not at home. Had any message been left for me? No message had been left for me. Had Miss Verinder not received My card? The servant begged my pardon – Miss Verinder *had* received it.

The inference was too plain to be resisted. Rachel declined to see me.

On my side, I declined to be treated in this way, without making an attempt, at least, to discover a reason for it. I sent up my name to Mrs Merridew, and requested her to favour me with a personal interview at any hour which it might be most convenient to her to name.

Mrs Merridew made no difficulty about receiving me at once. I was shown into a comfortable little sitting-room, and found myself in the presence of a comfortable little elderly lady. She was so good as to feel great regret and much surprise, entirely on my account. She was at the same time, however, not in a position to offer me any explanation, or to press Rachel on a matter which appeared to relate to a question of private feeling alone. This was said over and over again, with a polite patience that nothing could tire; and this was all I gained by applying to Mrs Merridew.

My last chance was to write to Rachel. My servant took a letter to her the next day, with strict instructions to wait for an answer.

The answer came back, literally in one sentence.

'Miss Verinder begs to decline entering into any correspondence with Mr Franklin Blake.'

Fond as I was of her, I felt indignantly the insult offered to me in that reply. Mr Bruff came in to speak to me on business, before I had recovered possession of myself. I dismissed the business on the spot, and laid the whole case before him. He proved to be as incapable of enlightening me as Mrs Merridew herself. I asked him if any slander had been spoken of me in Rachel's hearing. Mr Bruff was not aware of any slander of which I was the object. Had she referred to me in any way, while she was staying under Mr Bruff's roof? Never. Had she not so much as asked, during all my long absence, whether I was living or dead? No such question had ever passed her lips. I took out of my pocket-book the letter which poor Lady Verinder had written to me from Frizinghall, on the day when I left her house in Yorkshire. And I pointed Mr Bruff's attention to these two sentences in it:

'The valuable assistance which you rendered to the inquiry after the lost jewel is still an unpardoned offence, in the present dreadful state of Rachel's mind. Moving blindfold in this matter, you have added to the burden of anxiety which she has had to bear, by innocently threatening her secret with discovery through your exertions.'

'Is it possible,' I asked, 'that the feeling towards me which is there described, is as bitter as ever against me now?'

Mr Bruff looked unaffectedly distressed.

'If you insist on an answer,' he said, 'I own I can place no other interpretation on her conduct than that.'

I rang the bell, and directed my servant to pack my portmanteau, and to send out for a railway guide. Mr Bruff asked, in astonishment, what I was going to do.

'I am going to Yorkshire,' I answered, 'by the next train.'

'May I ask for what purpose?'

'Mr Bruff, the assistance I innocently rendered to the inquiry after the Diamond was an unpardoned offence, in Rachel's mind, nearly a year since; and it remains an unpardoned offence still. I won't accept that position! I am determined to find out the secret of her silence towards her mother, and her enmity towards *me*. If time, pains, and money can do it, I will lay my hand on the thief who took the Moonstone!'

The worthy old gentleman attempted to remonstrate – to induce me to listen to reason – to do his duty towards me, in short. I was deaf to everything that he could urge. No earthly consideration would, at that moment, have shaken the resolution that was in me.

'I shall take up the inquiry again,' I went on, 'at the point where I dropped it; and I shall follow it onwards, step by step, till I come to the present time. There are missing links in the evidence, as *I* left it, which Gabriel Betteredge can supply, and to Gabriel Betteredge I go!'

Towards sunset, that evening, I stood again on the well-remembered terrace, and looked once more at the peaceful old country house. The gardener was the first person whom I saw in the deserted grounds. He had left Betteredge, an hour since, sunning himself in the customary corner of the back yard. I knew it well; and I said I would go and seek him myself.

I walked round by the familiar paths and passages, and looked in at the open gate of the yard.

There he was – the dear old friend of the happy days that were never to come again – there he was in the old corner, on the old beehive chair, with his pipe in his mouth, and his *Robinson Crusoe* on his lap, and his two friends, the dogs, dozing on either side of him! In the position in which I stood, my shadow was projected in front of me by the last slanting rays of the sun. Either the dogs saw it, or their keen scent informed them of my approach: they started up with a growl. Starting in his turn, the old man quieted them by a word, and then shaded his failing eyes with his hand, and looked inquiringly at the figure at the gate.

My own eyes were full of tears. I was obliged to wait for a moment before I could trust myself to speak to him.

❧ TWO ❧

'BETTEREDGE!' I SAID, POINTING TO THE well-remembered book on his knee, 'has *Robinson Crusoe* informed you, this evening, that you might expect to see Franklin Blake?'

'By the lord Harry, Mr Franklin!' cried the old man, 'that's exactly what *Robinson Crusoe* has done!'

He struggled to his feet with my assistance, and stood for a moment, looking backwards and forwards between *Robinson Crusoe* and me, apparently at a loss to discover which of us had surprised him most. The verdict ended in favour of the book. Holding it open before him in both hands, he surveyed the wonderful volume with a stare of unutterable anticipation – as if he expected to see Robinson Crusoe himself walk out of the pages, and favour us with a personal interview.

'Here's the bit, Mr Franklin!' he said, as soon as he had recovered the use of his speech. 'As I live by bread, sir, here's the bit I was reading, the moment before you came in! Page one hundred and fifty-six as follows – "I stood like one Thunderstruck, or as if I had seen an Apparition." If that isn't as much as to say: "Expect the sudden appearance of Mr Franklin Blake" – there's no meaning in the English language!' said Betteredge, closing the book with a bang, and getting one of his hands free at last to take the hand which I offered him.

I had expected him, naturally enough under the circumstances, to overwhelm me with questions. But no – the hospitable impulse was the uppermost impulse in the old servant's mind, when a member of the family appeared (no matter how!) as a visitor at the house.

'Walk in, Mr Franklin,' he said, opening the door behind him, with his quaint old-fashioned bow. 'I'll ask what brings you here afterwards – I must make you comfortable first. There have been sad changes, since you went away. The house is shut up, and the servants are gone. Never mind that! I'll cook your dinner; and the gardener's wife will make your bed – and if there's a bottle of our famous Latour claret left in the cellar, down your throat, Mr Franklin, that bottle shall go. I bid you welcome, sir! I bid you heartily welcome!' said the poor old fellow, fighting manfully against the gloom of the deserted house, and receiving me with the sociable and courteous attention of the bygone time.

It vexed me to disappoint him. But the house was Rachel's house, now. Could I eat in it, or sleep in it, after what had happened in London? The commonest sense of self-respect forbade me – properly forbade me – to cross the threshold.

I took Betteredge by the arm, and led him out into the garden. There was no help for it. I was obliged to tell him the truth. Between his attachment to Rachel, and his attachment to me, he was sorely puzzled and distressed at the turn things had taken. His opinion, when he expressed it, was given in his usual downright manner, and was agreeably redolent of the most positive philosophy I know – the philosophy of the Betteredge school.

'Miss Rachel has her faults – I've never denied it,' he began. 'And riding the high horse, now and then, is one of them. She has been trying to ride over *you* – and you have put up with it. Lord, Mr Franklin, don't you know women by this time better than that? You have heard me talk of the late Mrs Betteredge?'

I had heard him talk of the late Mrs Betteredge pretty often – invariably producing her as his one undeniable example of the inbred frailty and perversity of the other sex. In that capacity he exhibited her now.

'Very well, Mr Franklin. Now listen to me. Different women have different ways of riding the high horse. The late Mrs Betteredge took her exercise on that favourite female animal whenever I happened to deny her anything that she had set her heart on. So sure as I came home from my work on these occasions, so sure was my wife to call to me up the kitchen stairs, and to say that, after my brutal treatment of her, she hadn't the heart to cook me my dinner. I put up with it for some time – just as you are putting up with it now from Miss Rachel. At last my patience wore out. I went downstairs, and I took Mrs Betteredge – affectionately, you understand – up in my arms, and carried her, holus-bolus, into the best parlour, where she received her company. I said, 'That's the right place for you, my dear,' and so went back to the kitchen. I locked myself in, and took off my coat, and turned up my shirt-sleeves, and cooked my own dinner. When it was done, I served it up in my best manner, and enjoyed it most heartily. I had my pipe and my drop of grog afterwards; and then I cleared the table, and washed the crockery, and cleaned the knives and forks, and put the things away, and swept up the hearth.

When things were as bright and clean again, as bright and clean could be, I opened the door, and let Mrs Betteredge in. 'I've had my dinner, my dear,' I said; 'and I hope you will find that I have left the kitchen all that your fondest wishes can desire.' For the rest of that woman's life, Mr Franklin, I never had to cook my dinner again! Moral: You have put up with Miss Rachel in London; don't put up with her in Yorkshire. Come back to the house.'

Quite unanswerable! could only assure my good friend that even *his* powers of persuasion were, in this case, thrown away on me.

'It's a lovely evening,' I said. 'I shall walk to Frizinghall, and stay at the hotel, and you must come to-morrow morning and breakfast with me. I have something to say to you.'

Betteredge shook his head gravely.

'I'm heartily sorry for this,' he said. 'I had hoped, Mr Franklin, to hear that things were all smooth and pleasant again between you and Miss Rachel. If you must have your own way, sir,' he continued, after a moment's reflection, 'there is no need to go to Frizinghall to-night for a bed. It's to be had nearer than that. There's Hotherstone's Farm, barely two miles from here. You can hardly object to *that* on Miss Rachel's account,' the old man added slily. 'Hotherstone lives, Mr Franklin, on his own freehold.'

I remembered the place the moment Betteredge mentioned it. The farm-house stood in a sheltered inland valley, on the banks of the prettiest stream in that part of Yorkshire: and the farmer had a spare bedroom and parlour, which he was accustomed to let to artists, anglers, and tourists in general. A more agreeable place of abode, during my stay in the neighbourhood, I could not have wished to find.

'Are the rooms to let?' I inquired.

'Mrs Hotherstone herself, sir, asked for my good word to recommend the rooms, yesterday.'

'I'll take them, Betteredge, with the greatest pleasure.'

We went back to the yard, in which I had left my travelling-bag. After putting a stick through the handle, and swinging the bag over his shoulder, Betteredge appeared to relapse into the bewilderment which my sudden appearance had caused, when I surprised him in the beehive chair. He looked incredulously at the house, and then he wheeled about, and looked more incredulously still at me.

'I've lived a goodish long time in the world,' said this best and dearest of all old servants – 'but the like of this, I never did expect to see. There stands the house, and here stands Mr Franklin Blake – and, Damme, if one of them isn't turning his back on the other, and going to sleep in a lodging!'

He led the way out, wagging his head and growling ominously.

'There's only one more miracle that *can* happen,' he said to me, over his shoulder. 'The next thing you'll do, Mr Franklin, will be to pay me back that seven-and-sixpence you borrowed of me when you were a boy.'

This stroke of sarcasm put him in a better humour with himself and with me. We left the house, and passed through the lodge gates. Once clear of the grounds, the duties of hospitality (in Betteredge's code of morals) ceased, and the privileges of curiosity began.

He dropped back, so as to let me get on a level with him. 'Fine evening for a walk, Mr Franklin,' he said, as if we had just accidentally encountered each other at that moment. 'Supposing you had gone to the hotel at Frizinghall, sir?'

'Yes?'

'I should have had the honour of breakfasting with you, to-morrow morning.'

'Come and breakfast with me at Hotherstone's Farm, instead.'

'Much obliged to you for your kindness, Mr Franklin. But it wasn't exactly breakfast that I was driving at. I think you mentioned that you had something to say to me? If it's no secret, sir,' said Betteredge, suddenly abandoning the crooked way, and taking the straight one, 'I'm burning to know what's brought you down here, if you please, in this sudden way.'

'What brought me here before?' I asked.

'The Moonstone, Mr Franklin. But what brings you now, sir?'

'The Moonstone again, Betteredge.'

The old man suddenly stood still, and looked at me in the grey twilight as if he suspected his own ears of deceiving him.

'If that's a joke, sir,' he said, 'I'm afraid I'm getting a little dull in my old age. I don't take it.'

'It's no joke,' I answered. 'I have come here to take up the inquiry which was dropped when I left England. I have come here to do what nobody has done yet – to find out who took the Diamond.'

'Let the Diamond be, Mr Franklin! Take my advice, and let the Diamond be! That cursed Indian jewel has misguided everybody who has come near it. Don't waste your money and your temper – in the fine springtime of your life, sir – by meddling with the Moonstone. How can *you* hope to succeed (saving your presence), when Sergeant Cuff himself made a mess of it? Sergeant Cuff!' repeated Betteredge, shaking his forefinger at me sternly. 'The greatest policeman in England!'

'My mind is made up, my old friend. Even Sergeant Cuff doesn't daunt me. By-the-by, I may want to speak to him, sooner or later. Have you heard anything of him lately?'

'The Sergeant won't help you,' Mr Franklin.

'Why not?'

'There has been an event, sir, in the police-circles, since you went away. The great Cuff has retired from business. He has got a little cottage at Dorking; and he's up to his eyes in the growing of roses. I have it in his own handwriting, Mr Franklin. He has grown the white moss-rose, without budding it on the dog-rose first. And Mr Begbie the gardener is to go to Dorking, and own that the Sergeant has beaten him at last.'

'It doesn't much matter,' I said. 'I must do without Sergeant Cuff's help. And I must trust to you, at starting.'

It is likely enough that I spoke rather carelessly. At any rate, Betteredge seemed to be piqued by something in the reply which I had just made to him. 'You might trust to worse than me, Mr Franklin – I can tell you that,' he said a little sharply.

The tone in which he retorted, and a certain disturbance, after he had spoken, which I detected in his manner, suggested to me that he was possessed of some information which he hesitated to communicate.

'I expect you to help me,' I said, 'in picking up the fragments of evidence which Sergeant Cuff has left behind him. I know you can do that. Can you do no more?'

'What more can you expect from me, sir?' asked Betteredge, with an appearance of the utmost humility.

'I expect more – from what you said just now.'

'Mere boasting, Mr Franklin,' returned the old man obstinately. 'Some people are born boasters, and they never get over it to their dying day. I'm one of them.'

There was only one way to take with him. I appealed to his interest in Rachel, and his interest in me.

'Betteredge, would you be glad to hear that Rachel and I were good friends again?'

'I have served your family, sir, to mighty little purpose, if you doubt it!'

'Do you remember how Rachel treated me, before I left England?'

'As well as if it was yesterday! My lady herself wrote you a letter about it; and you were so good as to show the letter to me. It said that Miss Rachel was mortally offended with you, for the part you had taken in trying to recover her jewel. And neither my lady, nor you, nor anybody else could guess why.'

'Quite true, Betteredge! And I come back from my travels, and find her mortally offended with me still. I knew that the Diamond was at the bottom of it, last year, and I know that the Diamond is at the bottom of it now. I have tried to speak to her, and she won't see me. I have tried to write to her, and she won't answer me. How, in Heaven's name, am I to clear the matter up? The chance of searching into the loss of the Moonstone, is the one chance of inquiry that Rachel herself has left me!'

Those words evidently put the case before him, as he had not seen it yet. He asked a question which satisfied me that I had shaken him.

'There is no ill-feeling in this, Mr Franklin, on your side – is there?'

'There was some anger,' I answered, 'when I left London. But that is all worn out now. I want to make Rachel come to an understanding with me – and I want nothing more.'

'You don't feel any fear, sir – supposing you make any discoveries – in regard to what you may find out about Miss Rachel?'

I understood the jealous belief in his young mistress which prompted those words.

'I am as certain of her as you are,' I answered. 'The fullest disclosure of her secret will reveal nothing that can alter her place in your estimation, or in mine.'

Betteredge's last-left scruples vanished at that.

'If I am doing wrong to help you, Mr Franklin,' he exclaimed, 'all I can say is – I am as innocent of seeing it as the babe unborn! I can put you on the road to discovery, if you can only go on by yourself. You remember that poor girl of ours – Rosanna Spearman?'

'Of course!'

'You always thought she had some sort of confession, in regard to this matter of the Moonstone, which she wanted to make to you?'

'I certainly couldn't account for her strange conduct in any other way.'

'You may set that doubt at rest, Mr Franklin, whenever you please.'

It was my turn to come to a standstill now. I tried vainly, in the gathering darkness, to see his face. In the surprise of the moment, I asked a little impatiently what he meant.

'Steady, sir!' proceeded Betteredge. 'I mean what I say. Rosanna Spearman left a sealed letter behind her – a letter addressed to *you.*'

'Where is it?'

'In the possession of a friend of hers, at Cobb's Hole. You must have heard tell, when you were here last, sir, of Limping Lucy – a lame girl with a crutch.'

'The fisherman's daughter?'

'The same, Mr Franklin.'

'Why wasn't the letter forwarded to me?'

'Limping Lucy has a will of her own, sir. She wouldn't give it into any hands but yours. And you had left England before I could write to you.'

'Let's go back, Betteredge, and get it at once!'

'Too late, sir, to-night. They're great savers of candles along our coast; and they go to bed early at Cobb's Hole.'

'Nonsense! We might get there in half an hour.'

'*You* might, sir. And when you did get there, you would find the door locked.' He pointed to a light, glimmering below us; and, at the same moment, I heard through the stillness of the evening the bubbling of a stream. 'There's the Farm, Mr Franklin! Make yourself comfortable for to-night, and come to me to-morrow morning – if you'll be so kind?'

'You will go with me to the fisherman's cottage?'

'Yes, sir.'

'Early?'

'As early, Mr Franklin, as you like.'

We descended the path that led to the Farm.

❧   THREE   ❧

I HAVE ONLY THE MOST INDISTINCT recollection of what happened at Hotherstone's Farm.

I remember a hearty welcome; a prodigious supper, which would have fed a whole village in the East; a delightfully clean bedroom, with nothing in it to regret but that detestable product of the folly of our forefathers – a feather-bed; a restless night, with much kindling of matches, and many lightings of one little candle; and an immense sensation of relief when the sun rose, and there was a prospect of getting up.

It had been arranged over-night with Betteredge, that I was to call for him, on our way to Cobb's Hole, as early as I liked – which, interpreted by my impatience to get possession of the letter, meant as early as I could. Without waiting for breakfast at the Farm, I took a crust of bread in my hand, and set forth, in some doubt whether I should not surprise the excellent Betteredge in his bed. To my great relief he proved to be quite as excited about the coming event as I was. I found him ready, and waiting for me, with his stick in his hand.

'How are you this morning, Betteredge?'

'Very poorly, sir.'

'Sorry to hear it. What do you complain of?'

'I complain of a new disease, Mr Franklin, of my own inventing. I don't want to alarm you, but you're certain to catch it before the morning is out.'

'The devil I am!'

'Do you feel an uncomfortable heat at the pit of your stomach, sir? and a nasty thumping at the top of your head? Ah! not yet? It will lay hold of you at Cobb's Hole, Mr Franklin. I call it the detective-fever; and I first caught it in the company of Sergeant Cuff.'

'Aye! aye! and the cure in this instance is to open Rosanna Spearman's letter, I suppose? Come along, and let's get it.'

Early as it was, we found the fisherman's wife astir in her kitchen. On my presentation by Betteredge, good Mrs Yolland performed a social ceremony, strictly reserved (as I afterwards learnt) for strangers of distinction. She put a bottle of Dutch gin and a couple of clean pipes on the table, and opened the conversation by saying, 'What news from London, sir?'

Before I could find an answer to this immensely comprehensive question, an apparition advanced towards me, out of a dark corner of the kitchen. A wan, wild, haggard girl, with remarkably beautiful hair, and with a fierce keenness in her eyes, came limping up on a crutch to the table at which I was sitting, and looked at me as if I was an object of mingled interest and horror, which it quite fascinated her to see.

'Mr Betteredge,' she said, without taking her eyes off me, 'mention his name again, if you please.'

'This gentleman's name,' answered Betteredge (with a strong emphasis on *gentleman*), 'is Mr Franklin Blake.'

The girl turned her back on me, and suddenly left the room. Good Mrs Yolland – as I believe – made some apologies for her daughter's odd behaviour, and Betteredge (probably) translated them into polite English. I speak of this in complete uncertainty. My attention was absorbed in following the sound of the girl's crutch. Thump-thump, up the wooden stairs; thump-thump across the room above our heads; thump-thump down the stairs again – and there stood the apparition at the open door, with a letter in its hand, beckoning me out!

I left more apologies in course of delivery behind me, and followed this strange creature – limping on before me, faster and faster – down the slope of the beach. She led me behind some boats, out of sight and hearing of the few people in the fishing-village, and then stopped, and faced me for the first time.

'Stand there,' she said, 'I want to look at you.'

There was no mistaking the expression on her face. I inspired her with the strongest emotions of abhorrence and disgust. Let me not be vain enough to say that no woman had ever looked at me in this manner before. I will only venture on the more modest assertion that no woman had ever let me perceive it yet. There is a limit to the length of the inspection which a man can endure, under certain circumstances. I attempted to direct Limping Lucy's attention to some less revolting object than my face.

'I think you have got a letter to give me,' I began. 'Is it the letter there, in your hand?'

'Say that again,' was the only answer I received.

I repeated the words, like a good child learning its lesson.

'No,' said the girl, speaking to herself, but keeping her eyes still mercilessly fixed on me. 'I can't find out what she saw in his face. I can't guess what she heard in his voice.' She suddenly looked away from me, and rested her head wearily on the top of her crutch. 'Oh, my poor dear!' she said, in the first soft tones which had fallen from her, in my hearing. 'Oh, my lost darling! what could you see in this man?' She lifted her head again fiercely, and looked at me once more. 'Can you eat and drink?' she asked.

I did my best to preserve my gravity, and answered, 'Yes.'

'Can you sleep?'

'Yes.'

'When you see a poor girl in service, do you feel no remorse?'

'Certainly not. Why should I?'

She abruptly thrust the letter (as the phrase is) into my face.

'Take it!' she exclaimed furiously. 'I never set eyes on you before. God Almighty forbid I should ever set eyes on you again.'

With those parting words she limped away from me at the top of her speed. The one interpretation that I could put on her conduct has, no doubt, been anticipated by everybody. I could only suppose that she was mad.

Having reached that inevitable conclusion, I turned to the more interesting object of investigation which was presented to me by Rosanna Spearman's letter. The address was written as follows: – 'For Franklin Blake, Esq. To be given into his own hands (and not to be trusted to any one else), by Lucy Yolland.'

I broke the seal. The envelope contained a letter: and this, in its turn, contained a slip of paper. I read the letter first: –

'Sir – If you are curious to know the meaning of my behaviour to you, whilst you were staying in the house of my mistress, Lady Verinder, do what you are told to do in the memorandum enclosed with this – and do it without any person being present to overlook you. Your humble servant,

Rosanna Spearman.'

I turned to the slip of paper next. Here is the literal copy of it, word for word:

'Memorandum: – To go to the Shivering Sand at the turn of the tide. To walk out on the South Spit, until I get the South Spit Beacon, and the flagstaff at the Coast-guard station above Cobb's Hole in a line together. To lay down on the rocks, a stick, or any straight thing to guide my hand, exactly in the line of the beacon and the flagstaff. To take care, in doing this, that one end of the stick shall be at the edge of the rocks, on the side of them which overlooks the quicksand. To feel along the stick, among the seaweed (beginning from the end of the stick which points towards the beacon), for the Chain. To run my hand along the Chain, when found, until I come to the part of it which stretches over the edge of the rocks, down into the quicksand. *And then, to pull the chain.*'

Just as I had read the last words – underlined in the original – I heard the voice of Betteredge behind me. The inventor of the detective-fever had completely succumbed to that irresistible malady. 'I can't stand it any longer, Mr Franklin. What does her letter say? For mercy's sake, sir, tell us, what does her letter say?'

I handed him the letter, and the memorandum. He read the first without appearing to be much interested in it. But the second – the memorandum – produced a strong impression on him.

'The Sergeant said it!' cried Betteredge. 'From first to last, sir, the Sergeant said she had got a memorandum of the hiding-place. And here it is! Lord save us, Mr Franklin, here is the secret that puzzled everybody, from the great Cuff downwards, ready and waiting, as one may say, to show itself to *you*! It's the ebb now, sir, as anybody may see for themselves. How long will it be till the turn of the tide?' He looked up, and observed a lad at work, at some little distance from us, mending a net. 'Tammie Bright!' he shouted, at the top of his voice.

'I hear you!' Tammie shouted back.

'When's the turn of the tide?'

'In an hour's time.'

We both looked at our watches.

'We can go round by the coast, Mr Franklin,' said Betteredge; 'and get to the quicksand in that way, with plenty of time to spare. What do you say, sir?'

'Come along?'

On our way to the Shivering Sand, I applied to Betteredge to revive my memory of events (as affecting Rosanna Spearman) at the period of Sergeant Cuff's inquiry. With my old friend's help, I soon had the succession of circumstances clearly registered in my mind. Rosanna's journey to Frizinghall, when the whole household believed her to be ill in her own room – Rosanna's mysterious employment of the night-time, with her door locked, and her candle burning till the morning – Rosanna's suspicious purchase of the japanned tin case, and the two dog-chains from Mrs Yolland – the Sergeant's positive conviction that Rosanna had hidden something at the Shivering Sand, and the Sergeant's absolute ignorance as to what that something might be – all these strange results of the abortive inquiry into the loss of the Moonstone, were clearly present to me again, when we reached the quicksand, and walked out together on the low ledge of rocks called the South Spit.

With Betteredge's help, I soon stood in the right position to see the Beacon and the Coast-guard flagstaff in a line together. Following the memorandum as our guide, we next laid my stick in the necessary direction, as neatly as we could, on the uneven surface of the rocks. And then we looked at our watches once more.

It wanted nearly twenty minutes yet of the turn of the tide. I suggested waiting through this interval on the beach, instead of on the wet and slippery surface of the rocks. Having reached the dry sand, I prepared to sit down; and, greatly to my surprise, Betteredge prepared to leave me.

'What are you going away for?' I asked.

'Look at the letter again, sir, and you will see.'

A glance at the letter reminded me that I was charged, when I made my discovery, to make it alone.

'It's hard enough for me to leave you, at such a time as this,' said Betteredge. 'But she died a dreadful death, poor soul – and I feel a kind of call on me, Mr Franklin, to humour that fancy of hers. Besides,' he added, confidentially, 'there's nothing in the letter against your letting out the secret afterwards. I'll hang about in the fir plantation, and wait till you pick me up. Don't be longer than you can help, sir. The detective-fever isn't an easy disease to deal with, under *these* circumstances.'

With that parting caution, he left me.

The interval of expectation, short as it was when reckoned by the measure of time, assumed formidable proportions when reckoned by the measure of suspense. This was one of the occasions on which the invaluable habit of smoking becomes especially precious and consolatory. I lit a cigar, and sat down on the slope of the beach.

The sunlight poured its unclouded beauty on every object that I could see. The exquisite freshness of the air made the mere act of living and breathing a luxury. Even the lonely little bay welcomed the morning with a show of cheerfulness; and the bared wet surface of the quicksand itself, glittering with a golden brightness, hid the horror of its false brown face under a passing smile. It was the finest day I had seen since my return to England.

The turn of the tide came, before my cigar was finished. I saw the preliminary heaving of the Sand, and then the awful shiver that crept over its surface – as if some spirit of terror lived and moved and shuddered in the fathomless deeps beneath. I threw away my cigar, and went back again to the rocks.

My directions in the memorandum instructed me to feel along the line traced by the stick, beginning with the end which was nearest to the beacon.

I advanced, in this manner, more than half-way along the stick, without encountering anything but the edges of the rocks. An inch or two further on, however, my patience was rewarded. In a narrow little fissure, just within reach of my forefinger, I felt the chain. Attempting, next, to follow it, by touch, in the direction of the quicksand, I found my progress stopped by a thick growth of seaweed – which had fastened itself into the fissure, no doubt, in the time that had elapsed since Rosanna Spearman had chosen her hiding-place.

It was equally impossible to pull up the seaweed, or to force my hand through it. After marking the spot indicated by the end of the stick which was placed nearest to the quicksand, I determined to pursue the search for the chain on a plan of my own. My idea was to 'sound' immediately under the rocks, on the chance of recovering the lost trace of the chain at the point at which it entered the sand. I took up the stick, and knelt down on the brink of the South Spit.

In this position, my face was within a few feet of the surface of the quicksand. The sight of it so near me, still disturbed at intervals by its hideous shivering fit, shook my nerves for the moment. A horrible fancy that the dead woman might appear on the scene of her suicide, to assist my search – an unutterable dread of seeing her rise through the heaving surface of the sand, and point to the place – forced itself into my mind, and turned me cold in the warm sunlight. I own I closed my eyes at the moment when the point of the stick first entered the quicksand.

The instant afterwards, before the stick could have been submerged more than a few inches, I was free from the hold of my own superstitious terror, and was throbbing with excitement, from head to foot. Sounding blindfold, at my first attempt – at that first attempt I had sounded right! The stick struck the chain.

Taking a firm hold of the roots of the seaweed with my left hand, I laid myself down over the brink, and felt with my right hand under the overhanging edges of the rock. My right hand found the chain.

I drew it up without the slightest difficulty. And there was the japanned tin case fastened to the end of it.

The action of the water had so rusted the chain, that it was impossible for me to unfasten it from the hasp which attached it to the case. Putting the case between my knees, and exerting my utmost strength, I contrived to draw off the cover. Some white substance filled the whole interior when I looked in. I put in my hand, and found it to be linen.

In drawing out the linen, I also drew out a letter crumpled up with it. After looking at the direction, and discovering that it bore my name, I put the letter in my pocket, and completely removed the linen. It came out in a thick roll, moulded, of course, to the shape of the case in which it had been so long confined, and perfectly preserved from any injury by the sea.

I carried the linen to the dry sand of the beach, and there unrolled and smoothed it out. There was no mistaking it as an article of dress. It was a nightgown.

The uppermost side, when I spread it out, presented to view innumerable folds and creases, and nothing more. I tried the undermost side, next – and instantly discovered the smear of the paint from the door of Rachel's boudoir!

My eyes remained riveted on the stain, and my mind took me back at a leap from present to past. The very words of Sergeant Cuff recurred to me, as if the man himself was at my side again, pointing to the unanswerable inference which he drew from the smear on the door.

'Find out whether there is any article of dress in this house with the stain of paint on it. Find out who that dress belongs to. Find out how the person can account for having been in the room, and smeared the paint, between midnight and three in the morning. If the person can't satisfy you, you haven't far to look for the hand that took the Diamond.'

One after another those words travelled over my memory, repeating themselves again and again with a wearisome, mechanical reiteration. I was roused from what felt like a trance of many hours – from what was really, no doubt, the pause of a few moments only – by a voice calling to me. I looked up, and saw that Betteredge's patience had failed him at last. He was just visible between the sand hills, returning to the beach.

The old man's appearance recalled me, the moment I perceived it, to my sense of present things, and reminded me that the inquiry which I had pursued thus far, still remained incomplete. I had discovered the smear on the nightgown. To whom did the nightgown belong?

My first impulse was to consult the letter in my pocket – the letter which I had found in the case.

As I raised my hand to take it out, I remembered that there was a shorter way to discovery than this. The nightgown itself would reveal the truth; for, in all probability, the nightgown was marked with its owner's name.

I took it up from the sand, and looked for the mark.

I found the mark, and read –

MY OWN NAME.

There were the familiar letters which told me that the nightgown was mine. I looked up from them. There was the sun; there were the glittering waters of the bay; there was old Betteredge, advancing nearer and nearer to me. I looked back again at the letters. My own name. Plainly confronting me – my own name.

'If time, pains, and money can do it, I will lay my hand on the thief who took the Moonstone.' – I had left London, with those words on my lips. I had penetrated the secret which the quicksand had kept from every other living creature. And, on the unanswerable evidence of the paint-stain, I had discovered Myself as the Thief.

❧ FOUR ❧

I HAVE NOT A WORD TO say about my own sensations.

My impression is, that the shock inflicted on me completely suspended my thinking and feeling power. I certainly could not have known what I was about, when Betteredge joined me – for I have it on his authority that I laughed, when he asked what was the matter, and, putting the nightgown into his hands, told him to read the riddle for himself.

Of what was said between us on the beach, I have not the faintest recollection. The first place in which I can now see myself again plainly is the plantation of firs. Betteredge and I are walking back together to the house; and Betteredge is telling me that I shall be able to face it, and he will be able to face it, when we have had a glass of grog.

The scene shifts from the plantation, to Betteredge's little sitting-room. My resolution not to enter Rachel's house is forgotten. I feel gratefully the coolness and shadiness and quiet of the room. I drink the grog (a perfectly new luxury to me, at that time of day), which my good old friend mixes with icy-cold water from the well. Under any other circumstances, the drink would simply stupify me. As things are, it strings up my nerves. I begin to 'face it', as Betteredge has predicted. And Betteredge, on his side, begins to 'face it', too.

The picture which I am now presenting of myself, will, I suspect, be thought a very strange one, to say the least of it. Placed in a situation which may, I think, be described as entirely without parallel, what is the first proceeding to which I resort? Do I seclude myself from all human society? Do I set my mind to analyse the abominable impossibility which, nevertheless, confronts me as an undeniable fact? Do I hurry back to London by the first train to consult the highest authorities, and to set a searching inquiry on foot immediately? No. I accept the shelter of a house which I had resolved never to degrade myself by entering again; and I sit, tippling spirits and water in the company of an old servant, at ten o'clock in the morning. Is this the conduct that might have been expected from a man placed in my horrible position? I can only answer that the sight of old Betteredge's familiar face was an inexpressible comfort to me, and that the drinking of old Betteredge's grog helped me, as I believe nothing else would have helped me, in the state of complete bodily and mental prostration into which I had fallen. I can only offer this excuse for myself; and I can only admire that invariable preservation of dignity, and that strictly logical consistency of conduct which distinguish every man and woman who may read these lines, in every emergency of their lives from the cradle to the grave.

'Now, Mr Franklin, there's one thing certain, at any rate,' said Betteredge, throwing the nightgown down on the table between us, and pointing to it as if it was a living creature that could hear him. '*He's* a liar, to begin with.'

This comforting view of the matter was not the view that presented itself to my mind.

'I am as innocent of all knowledge of having taken the Diamond as you are,' I said. 'But there is the witness against me! The paint on the nightgown, and the name on the nightgown, are facts.'

Betteredge lifted my glass, and put it persuasively into my hand.

'Facts?' he repeated.' Take a drop more grog, Mr Franklin, and you'll get over the weakness of believing in facts! Foul play, sir!' he continued, dropping his voice confidentially. 'That is how I read the riddle. Foul play somewhere – and you and I must find it out. Was there nothing else in the tin case, when you put your hand into it?'

The question instantly reminded me of the letter in my pocket. I took it out, and opened it. It was a letter of many pages, closely written. I looked impatiently for the signature at the end. 'Rosanna Spearman.'

As I read the name, a sudden remembrance illuminated my mind, and a sudden suspicion rose out of the new light.

'Stop!' I exclaimed. 'Rosanna Spearman came to my aunt out of a Reformatory? Rosanna Spearman had once been a thief?'

'There's no denying that, Mr Franklin. What of it now, if you please?'

'What of it now? How do we know she may not have stolen the Diamond after all? How do we know she may not have smeared my nightgown purposely with the paint – ?'

Betteredge laid his hand on my arm, and stopped me before I could say any more.

'You will be cleared of this, Mr Franklin, beyond all doubt. But I hope you won't be cleared in *that* way. See what the letter says, sir. In justice to the girl's memory, see what it says.'

I felt the earnestness with which he spoke – felt it as a friendly rebuke to me. 'You shall form your own judgment on her letter,' I said, 'I will read it out.'

I began – and read these lines:

'Sir – I have something to own to you. A confession which means much misery, may sometimes be made in very few words. This confession can be made in three words. I love you.'

The letter dropped from my hand. I looked at Betteredge. 'In the name of Heaven,' I said, 'what does it mean?'

He seemed to shrink from answering the question.

'You and Limping Lucy were alone together this morning, sir,' he said. 'Did she say nothing about Rosanna Spearman?'

'She never even mentioned Rosanna Spearman's name.'

'Please to go back to the letter, Mr Franklin. I tell you plainly, I can't find it in my heart to distress you, after what you have had to bear already. Let her speak for herself, sir. And get on with your grog. For your own sake, get on with your grog.'

I resumed the reading of the letter.

'It would be very disgraceful to me to tell you this, if I was a living woman when you read it. I shall be dead and gone, sir, when you find my letter. It is that which makes me bold. Not even my grave will be left to tell of me. I may own the truth – with the quicksand waiting to hide me when the words are written.

'Besides, you will find your nightgown in my hiding-place, with the smear of the paint on it; and you will want to know how it came to be hidden by me? and why I said nothing to you about it in my life-time? I have only one reason to give. I did these strange things, because I loved you.

'I won't trouble you with much about myself, or my life, before you came to my lady's house. Lady Verinder took me out of a reformatory. I had gone to the reformatory from the prison. I was put in the prison, because I was a thief. I was a thief, because my mother went on the streets when I was quite a little girl. My mother went on the streets, because the gentleman who was my father deserted her. There is no need to tell such a common story as this, at any length. It is told quite often enough in the newspapers.

'Lady Verinder was very kind to me, and Mr Betteredge was very kind to me. Those two, and the matron at the reformatory are the only good people I have ever met with in all my life. I might have got on in my place – not happily – but I might have got on, if you had not come visiting. I don't blame you, sir. It's my fault – all my fault.

'Do you remember when you came out on us from among the sand hills, that morning, looking for Mr Betteredge? You were like a prince in a fairy-story. You were like a lover in a dream. You were the most adorable human creature I had ever seen. Something that felt like the happy life I had never led yet, leapt up in me at the instant I set eyes on you. Don't laugh at this if you can help it. Oh, if I could only make you feel how serious it is to *me!*

'I went back to the house, and wrote your name and mine in my work-box, and drew a true lovers' knot under them. Then, some devil – no, I ought to say some good angel – whispered to me, "Go and look in the glass." The glass told me – never mind what. I was too foolish to take the warning. I went on getting fonder and fonder of you, just as if I was a lady in your own rank of life, and the most beautiful creature your eyes ever rested on. I tried – oh, dear, how I tried – to get you to look at me. If you had known how I used to cry at night with the misery and the mortification of your never taking any notice of me, you would have pitied me perhaps, and have given me a look now and then to live on.

'It would have been no very kind look, perhaps, if you had known how I hated Miss Rachel. I believe I found out you were in love with her, before you knew it yourself. She used to give you roses to wear in your button-hole. Ah, Mr Franklin, you wore *my* roses oftener than either you or she thought! The only comfort I had at that time, was putting my rose secretly in your glass of water, in place of hers – and then throwing her rose away.

'If she had been really as pretty as you thought her, I might have borne it better. No; I believe I should have been more spiteful against her still. Suppose you put Miss Rachel into a servant's dress, and took her ornaments off? I don't know what is the use of my writing in this way. It can't be denied that she had a bad figure; she was too thin. But who can tell what the men like? And young ladies may behave in a manner which would cost a servant her place. It's no business of mine. I can't expect you to read my letter, if I write it in this way. But it does stir one up to hear Miss Rachel called pretty, when one knows all the time that it's her dress does it, and her confidence in herself.

'Try not to lose patience with me, sir. I will get on as fast as I can to the time which is sure to interest you – the time when the Diamond was lost.

'But there is one thing which I have got it on my mind to tell you first.

'My life was not a very hard life to bear, while I was a thief. It was only when they had taught me at the reformatory to feel my own degradation, and to try for better things, that the days grew long and weary. Thoughts of the future forced themselves on me now. I felt the dreadful reproach that honest people – even the kindest of honest people – were to me in themselves. A heart-breaking sensation of loneliness kept with me, go where I might, and do what I might, and see what persons I might. It was my duty, I know, to try and get on with my fellow-servants in my new place. Somehow, I couldn't make friends with them. They looked (or I thought they looked) as if they suspected what I had been. I don't regret, far from it, having been roused to make the effort to be a reformed woman – but, indeed, indeed it was a weary life. You had come across it like a beam of sunshine at first – and then you too failed me. I was mad enough to love you; and I couldn't even attract your notice. There was great misery – there really was great misery in that.

'Now I am coming to what I wanted to tell you. In those days of bitterness, I went two or three times, when it was my turn to go out, to my favourite place – the beach above the Shivering Sand. And I said to myself, "I think it will end here. When I can bear it no longer, I think it will end here." You will understand, sir, that the place had laid a kind of spell on me before you came. I had always had a notion that something would happen to me at the quicksand. But I had never looked at it, with the thought of its being the means of my making away with myself, till the time came of which I am now writing. Then I did think that here was a place which would end all my troubles for me in a moment or two – and hide me for ever afterwards.

'This is all I have to say about myself, reckoning from the morning when I first saw you, to the morning when the alarm was raised in the house that the Diamond was lost.

'I was so aggravated by the foolish talk among the women servants, all wondering who was to be suspected first; and I was so angry with you (knowing no better at that time) for the pains you took in hunting for the jewel, and sending for the police, that I kept as much as possible away by myself, until later in the day, when the officer from Frizinghall came to the house.

'Mr Seegrave began, as you may remember, by setting a guard on the women's bedrooms; and the women all followed him upstairs in a rage, to know what he meant by the insult he had put on them. I went with the rest, because if I had done anything different from the rest, Mr Seegrave was the sort of man who would have suspected me directly. We found him in Miss Rachel's room. He told us he wouldn't have a lot of women there; and he pointed to the smear on the painted door, and said some of our petticoats had done the mischief, and sent us all downstairs again.

'After leaving Miss Rachel's room, I stopped a moment on one of the landings, by myself, to see if I had got the paint-stain by any chance on *my* gown. Penelope Betteredge (the only one of the women with whom I was on friendly terms) passed, and noticed what I was about.

' "You needn't trouble yourself, Rosanna," she said. "The paint on

Miss Rachel's door has been dry for hours. If Mr Seegrave hadn't set a watch on our bedrooms, I might have told him as much. I don't know what *you* think – I was never so insulted before in my life!" '

'Penelope was a hot-tempered girl. I quieted her, and brought her back to what she had said about the paint on the door having been dry for hours.

' "How do you know that?" I asked.

' "I was with Miss Rachel, and Mr Franklin, all yesterday morning," Penelope said, "mixing the colours, while they finished the door. I heard Miss Rachel ask whether the door would be dry that evening, in time for the birthday company to see it. And Mr Franklin shook his head, and said it wouldn't be dry in less than twelve hours. It was long past luncheon-time – it was three o'clock before they had done. What does your arithmetic say, Rosanna? Mine says the door was dry by three this morning."

' "Did some of the ladies go upstairs yesterday evening to see it?" I asked. "I thought I heard Miss Rachel warning them to keep clear of the door."

' "None of the ladies made the smear," Penelope answered. "I left Miss Rachel in bed at twelve last night. And I noticed the door, and there was nothing wrong with it then."

' "Oughtn't you to mention this to Mr Seegrave, Penelope?"

' "I wouldn't say a word to help Mr Seegrave for anything that could be offered to me!"

'She went to her work, and I went to mine.

'My work, sir, was to make your bed, and to put your room tidy. It was the happiest hour I had in the whole day. I used to kiss the pillow on which your head had rested all night. No matter who has done it since, you have never had your clothes folded as nicely as I folded them for you. Of all the little knick-knacks in your dressing-case, there wasn't one that had so much as a speck on it. You never noticed it, any more than you noticed me. I beg your pardon; I am forgetting myself. I will make haste, and go on again.

'Well, I went in that morning to do my work in your room. There was your nightgown tossed across the bed, just as you had thrown it off. I took it up to fold it – and I saw the stain of the paint from Miss Rachel's door!

'I was so startled by the discovery that I ran out, with the nightgown in my hand, and made for the back stairs, and locked myself into my own room, to look at it in a place where nobody could intrude and interrupt me.

'As soon as I got my breath again, I called to mind my talk with

Penelope, and I said to myself, "Here's the proof that he was in Miss Rachel's sitting-room between twelve last night, and three this morning!"

'I shall not tell you in plain words what was the first suspicion that crossed my mind, when I had made that discovery. You would only be angry – and, if you were angry, you might tear my letter up and read no more of it.

'Let it be enough, if you please, to say only this. After thinking it over to the best of my ability, I made it out that the thing wasn't likely, for a reason that I will tell you. If you had been in Miss Rachel's sitting-room, at that time of night, with Miss Rachel's knowledge (and if you had been foolish enough to forget to take care of the wet door) *she* would have reminded you – *she* would never have let you carry away such a witness against her, as the witness I was looking at now! At the same time, I own I was not completely certain in my own mind that I had proved my own suspicion to be wrong. You will not have forgotten that I have owned to hating Miss Rachel. Try to think, if you can, that there was a little of that hatred in all this. It ended in my determining to keep the nightgown, and to wait, and watch, and see what use I might make of it. At that time, please to remember, not the ghost of an idea entered my head that *you* had stolen the Diamond.'

There, I broke off in the reading of the letter for the second time.

I had read those portions of the miserable woman's confession which related to myself, with unaffected surprise, and, I can honestly add, with sincere distress. I had regretted, truly regretted, the aspersion which I had thoughtlessly cast on her memory, before I had seen a line of her letter. But when I had advanced as far as the passage which is quoted above, I own I felt my mind growing bitterer and bitterer against Rosanna Spearman as I went on. 'Read the rest for yourself,' I said, handing the letter to Betteredge across the table. 'If there is anything in it that I *must* look at, you can tell me as you go on.'

'I understand you, Mr Franklin,' he answered. 'It's natural, sir, in *you*. And, God help us all!' he added, in a lower tone, 'it's no less natural in *her*.'

I proceed to copy the continuation of the letter from the original, in my own possession: –

'Having determined to keep the nightgown, and to see what use my love, or my revenge (I hardly know which) could turn it to in the future, the next thing to discover was how to keep it without the risk of being found out.

'There was only one way – to make another nightgown exactly like it, before Saturday came, and brought the laundry-woman and her inventory to the house.

'I was afraid to put it off till next day (the Friday); being in doubt lest some accident might happen in the interval. I determined to make the new nightgown on that same day (the Thursday), while I could count, if I played my cards properly, on having my time to myself. The first thing to do (after locking up your nightgown in my drawer) was to go back to your bedroom – not so much to put it to rights (Penelope would have done that for me, if I had asked her) as to find out whether you had smeared off any of the paintstain from your nightgown, on the bed, or on any piece of furniture in the room.

'I examined everything narrowly, and at last, I found a few faint streaks of the paint on the inside of your dressing-gown – not the linen dressing-gown you usually wore in that summer season, but a flannel dressing-gown which you had with you also. I suppose you felt chilly after walking to and fro in nothing but your night-dress, and put on the warmest thing you could find. At any rate, there were the stains, just visible, on the inside of the dressing-gown. I easily got rid of these by scraping away the stuff of the flannel. This done, the only proof left against you was the proof locked up in my drawer.

'I had just finished your room when I was sent for to be questioned by Mr Seegrave, along with the rest of the servants. Next came the examination of all our boxes. And then followed the most extraordinary event of the day – to *me* – since I had found the paint on your nightgown. This event came out of the second questioning of Penelope Betteredge by Superintendent Seegrave.

'Penelope returned to us quite beside herself with rage at the manner in which Mr Seegrave had treated her. He had hinted, beyond the possibility of mistaking him, that he suspected her of being the thief. We were all equally astonished at hearing this, and we all asked, Why?

' "Because the Diamond was in Miss Rachel's sitting-room," Penelope answered. "And because I was the last person in the sitting-room at night!"

'Almost before the words had left her lips, I remembered that another person had been in the sitting-room later than Penelope. That person was yourself. My head whirled round, and my thoughts were in dreadful confusion. In the midst of it all, something in my mind whispered to me that the smear on your nightgown might have a meaning entirely different to the meaning which I had given to it up to that time. "If the last person who was in the room is the person to be suspected," I thought to myself, "the thief is not Penelope, but Mr Franklin Blake!"

'In the case of any other gentleman, I believe I should have been ashamed of suspecting him of theft, almost as soon as the suspicion had passed through my mind.

'But the bare thought that you had let yourself down to my level, and that I, in possessing myself of your nightgown, had also possessed myself of the means of shielding you from being discovered, and disgraced for life – I say, sir, the bare thought of this seemed to open such a chance before me of winning your good will, that I passed blindfold, as one may say, from suspecting to believing. I made up my mind, on the spot, that you had shown yourself the busiest of anybody in fetching the police, as a blind to deceive us all; and that the hand which had taken Miss Rachel's jewel could by no possibility be any other hand than yours.

'The excitement of this new discovery of mine must I think, have turned my head for a while. I felt such a devouring eagerness to see you – to try you with a word or two about the Diamond and to *make* you look at me, and speak to me, in that way – that I put my hair tidy, and made myself as nice as I could, and went to you boldly in the library where I knew you were writing.

'You had left one of your rings upstairs, which made as good an excuse for my intrusion as I could have desired. But, oh, sir! if you have ever loved, you will understand how it was that all my courage cooled, when I walked into the room, and found myself in your presence. And then, you looked up at me so coldly, and you thanked me for finding your ring in such an indifferent manner, that my knees trembled under me, and I felt as if I should drop on the floor at your feet. When you had thanked me, you looked back, if you remember, at your writing. I was so mortified at being treated in this way, that I plucked up spirit enough to speak. I said, "This is a strange thing about the Diamond, sir." And you looked up again, and said, "Yes, it is!" You spoke civilly (I can't deny that); but still you kept a distance – a cruel distance between us. Believing, as I did, that you had got the lost Diamond hidden about you, while you were speaking, your coolness so provoked me that I got bold enough, in the heat of the moment, to give you a hint. I said, "They will never find the Diamond, sir, will they? No! nor the person who took it – I'll answer for that." I nodded, and smiled at you, as much as to say, "I know!" *This* time, you looked up at me with something like interest in your eyes; and I felt that a few more words on your side and mine might bring out the truth. Just at that moment, Mr Betteredge spoilt it all by coming to the door. I knew his footstep, and I also knew that it was against his rules for me to be in the library at that time of day – let alone being there along with you. I had only just time to get out of my own accord, before he could come in and tell me to go. I was angry and disappointed; but I was not entirely without hope for all that. The ice, you see, was broken between us – and I thought I would take care, on the next occasion, that Mr Betteredge was out of the way.

'When I got back to the servants' hall, the bell was going for our dinner. Afternoon already! and the materials for making the new nightgown were still to be got! There was but one chance of getting them. I shammed ill at dinner; and so secured the whole of the interval from then till tea-time to my own use.

'What I was about, while the household believed me to be lying down in my own room; and how I spent the night, after shamming ill again at tea-time, and having been sent up to bed, there is no need to tell you. Sergeant Cuff discovered that much, if he discovered nothing more. And I can guess how. I was detected (though I kept my veil down) in the draper's shop at Frizinghall. There was a glass in front of me, at the counter where I was buying the longcloth; and – in that glass – I saw one of the shopmen point to my shoulder and whisper to another. At night again, when I was secretly at work, locked into my room, I heard the breathing of the women servants who suspected me, outside my door.

'It didn't matter then; it doesn't matter now. On the Friday morning, hours before Sergeant Cuff entered the house, there was the new nightgown – to make up your number in place of the nightgown that I had got – made, wrung out, dried, ironed, marked, and folded as the laundry woman folded all the others, safe in your drawer. There was no fear (if the linen in the house was examined) of the newness of the nightgown betraying me. All your underclothing had been renewed, when you came to our house – I suppose on your return home from foreign parts.

'The next thing was the arrival of Sergeant Cuff; and the next great surprise was the announcement of what he thought about the smear on the door.

'I had believed you to be guilty (as I have owned) more because I wanted you to be guilty than for any other reason. And now, the Sergeant had come round by a totally different way to the same conclusion (respecting the nightgown) as mine! And I had got the dress that was the only proof against you! And not a living creature knew it – yourself included! I am afraid to tell you how I felt when I called these things to mind – you would hate my memory for ever afterwards.'

At that place, Betteredge looked up from the letter.

'Not a glimmer of light so far, Mr Franklin,' said the old man, taking off his heavy tortoiseshell spectacles, and pushing Rosanna Spearman's confession a little away from him. 'Have you come to any conclusion, sir, in your own mind, while I have been reading?'

'Finish the letter first, Betteredge; there may be something to lighten us at the end of it. I shall have a word or two to say to you after that.'

'Very good, sir. I'll just rest my eyes, and then I'll go on again. In the meantime, Mr Franklin – I don't want to hurry you – but would you mind telling me, in one word, whether you see your way out of this dreadful mess yet?'

'I see my way back to London,' I said, 'to consult Mr Bruff. If he can't help me – '

'Yes, sir?'

'And if the Sergeant won't leave his retirement at Dorking – '

'He won't, Mr Franklin!'

'Then, Betteredge – as far as I can see now – I am at the end of my resources. After Mr Bruff and the Sergeant, I don't know of a living creature who can be of the slightest use to me.'

As the words passed my lips, some person outside knocked at the door of the room.

Betteredge looked surprised as well as annoyed by the interruption.

'Come in,' he called out, irritably, 'whoever you are!'

The door opened, and there entered to us, quietly, the most remarkable-looking man that I had ever seen. Judging him by his figure and his movements, he was still young. Judging him by his face, and comparing him with Betteredge, he looked the elder of the two. His complexion was of a gipsy darkness; his fleshless cheeks had fallen into deep hollows, over which the bone projected like a pent-house. His nose presented the fine shape and modelling so often found among the ancient people of the East, so seldom visible among the newer races of the West. His forehead rose high and straight from the brow. His marks and wrinkles were innumerable. From this strange face, eyes, stranger still, of the softest brown – eyes dreamy and mournful, and deeply sunk in their orbits – looked out at you, and (in my case, at least) took your attention captive at their will. Add to this a quantity of thick closely-curling hair, which, by some freak of Nature, had lost its colour in the most startlingly partial and capricious manner. Over the top of his head it was still of the deep black which was its natural colour. Round the sides of his head – without the slightest gradation of grey to break the force of the extraordinary contrast – it had turned completely white. The line between the two colours preserved no sort of regularity. At one place, the white hair ran up into the black; at another, the black hair ran down into the white. I looked at the man with a curiosity which, I am ashamed to say, I found it quite impossible to control. His soft brown eyes looked back at me gently; and he met my involuntary rudeness in staring at him, with an apology which I was conscious that I had not deserved.

'I beg your pardon,' he said. 'I had no idea that Mr Betteredge was engaged.' He took a slip of paper from his pocket, and handed it to Betteredge. 'The list for next week,' he said. His eyes just rested on me again – and he left the room as quietly as he had entered it.

'Who is that?' I asked.

'Mr Candy's assistant,' said Betteredge. 'By-the-by, Mr Franklin, you will be sorry to hear that the little doctor has never recovered from that illness he caught, going home from the birthday dinner. He's pretty well in health; but he lost his memory in the fever, and he has never recovered more than the wreck of it since. The work all falls on his assistant. Not much of it now, except among the poor. *They* can't help themselves, you know. *They* must put up with the man with the piebald hair, and the gipsy complexion – or they would get no doctoring at all.'

'You don't seem to like him, Betteredge?'

'Nobody likes him, sir.'

'Why is he so unpopular?'

'Well, Mr Franklin, his appearance is against him, to begin with. And then there's a story that Mr Candy took him with a very doubtful character. Nobody knows who he is – and he hasn't a friend in the place. How can you expect one to like him, after that?'

'Quite impossible, of course! May I ask what he wanted with you, when he gave you that bit of paper?'

'Only to bring me the weekly list of the sick people about here, sir, who stand in need of a little wine. My lady always had a regular distribution of good sound port and sherry among the infirm poor; and Miss Rachel wishes the custom to be kept up. Times have changed! times have changed! I remember when Mr Candy himself brought the list to my mistress. Now it's Mr Candy's assistant who brings the list to me. I'll go on with the letter, if you will allow me, sir,' said Betteredge, drawing Rosanna Spearman's confession back to him. 'It isn't lively reading, I grant you. But, there! it keeps me from getting sour with thinking of the past.' He put on his spectacles, and wagged his head gloomily. 'There's a bottom of good sense, Mr Franklin, in our conduct to our mothers, when they first start us on the journey of life. We are all of us more or less unwilling to be brought into the world. And we are all of us right.'

Mr Candy's assistant had produced too strong an impression on me to be immediately dismissed from my thoughts. I passed over the last unanswerable utterance of the Betteredge philosophy; and returned to the subject of the man with the piebald hair.

'What is his name?' I asked.

'As ugly a name as need be,' Betteredge answered, gruffly. 'Ezra Jennings.'

⊷ FIVE ⊷

HAVING TOLD ME THE NAME OF Mr Candy's assistant, Betteredge appeared to think that we had wasted enough of our time on an insignificant subject. He resumed the perusal of Rosanna Spearman's letter.

On my side, I sat at the window, waiting until he had done. Little by little, the impression produced on me by Ezra Jennings – it seemed perfectly unaccountable, in such a situation as mine, that any human being should have produced an impression on me at all! – faded from my mind. My thoughts flowed back into their former channel. Once more, I forced myself to look my own incredible position resolutely in the face. Once more, I reviewed in my own mind the course which I had at last summoned composure enough to plan out for the future.

To go back to London that day; to put the whole case before Mr Bruff; and, last and most important, to obtain (no matter by what means or at what sacrifice) a personal interview with Rachel – this was my plan of action, so far as I was capable of forming it at the time. There was more than an hour still to spare before the train started. And there was the bare chance that Betteredge might discover something in the unread portion of Rosanna Spearman's letter, which it might be useful for me to know before I left the house in which the Diamond had been lost. For that chance I was now waiting.

The letter ended in these terms:

'You have no need to be angry, Mr Franklin, even if I did feel some little triumph at knowing that I held all your prospects in life in my own hands. Anxieties and fears soon came back to me. With the view Sergeant Cuff took of the loss of the Diamond, he would be sure to end in examining our linen and our dresses. There was no place in my room – there was no place in the house – which I could feel satisfied would be safe from him. How to hide the nightgown so that not even the Sergeant could find it? and how to do that without losing one moment of precious time? – these were not easy questions to answer. My uncertainties ended in my taking a way that may make you laugh. I undressed, and put the nightgown on me. You had worn it – and I had another little moment of pleasure in wearing it after you.

'The next news that reached us in the servants' hall showed that I had not made sure of the nightgown a moment too soon. Sergeant Cuff wanted to see the washing-book.

'I found it, and took it to him in my lady's sitting-room. The Sergeant and I had come across each other more than once in former days. I was certain he would know me again – and I was *not* certain of what he might do when he found me employed as servant in a house in which a valuable jewel had been lost. In this suspense, I felt it would be a relief to me to get the meeting between us over, and to know the worst of it at once.

'He looked at me as if I was a stranger, when I handed him the washing-book; and he was very specially polite in thanking me for bringing it. I thought those were both bad signs. There was no knowing what he might say of me behind my back; there was no knowing how soon I might not find myself taken in custody on suspicion, and searched. It was then time for your return from seeing Mr Godfrey Ablewhite off by the railway; and I went to your favourite walk in the shrubbery, to try for another chance of speaking to you – the last chance, for all I knew to the contrary, that I might have.

'You never appeared; and, what was worse still, Mr Betteredge and Sergeant Cuff passed by the place where I was hiding – and the Sergeant saw me.

'I had no choice, after that, but to return to my proper place and my proper work, before more disasters happened to me. Just as I was going to step across the path, you came back from the railway. You were making straight for the shrubbery, when you saw me – I am certain, sir, you saw me – and you turned away as if I had got the plague, and went into the house.*

'I made the best of my way indoors again, returning by the servants' entrance. There was nobody in the laundry-room at that time; and I sat down there alone. I have told you already of the thoughts which the Shivering Sand put into my head. Those thoughts came back to me now. I wondered in myself which it would be hardest to do, if things went on in this manner – to bear Mr Franklin Blake's indifference to me, or to jump into the quicksand and end it for ever in that way?

'It's useless to ask me to account for my own conduct, at this time. I try – and I can't understand it myself.

'Why didn't I stop you, when you avoided me in that cruel manner? Why didn't I call out, "Mr Franklin, I have got something to say to you;

---

*Note. by Franklin Blake. – The writer is entirely mistaken, poor creature. I never noticed her. My intention was certainly to have taken a turn in the shrubbery. But, remembering at the same moment that my aunt might wish to see me, after my return from the railway, I altered my mind, and went into the house.

it concerns yourself, and you must, and shall, hear it?" You were at my mercy – I had got the whip-hand of you, as they say. And better than that, I had the means (if I could only make you trust me) of being useful to you in the future. Of course, I never supposed that you – a gentleman – had stolen the Diamond for the mere pleasure of stealing it. No. Penelope had heard Miss Rachel, and I had heard Mr Betteredge, talk about your extravagance and your debts. It was plain enough to me that you had taken the Diamond to sell it, or pledge it, and so to get the money of which you stood in need. Well! I could have told you of a man in London who would have advanced a good large sum on the jewel, and who would have asked no awkward questions about it either.

'Why didn't I speak to you! why didn't I speak to you!

'I wonder whether the risks and difficulties of keeping the nightgown were as much as I could manage, without having other risks and difficulties added to them? This might have been the case with some women – but how could it be the case with me? In the days when I was a thief, I had run fifty times greater risks, and found my way out of difficulties to which *this* difficulty was mere child's play. I had been apprenticed, as you may say, to frauds and deceptions – some of them on such a grand scale, and managed so cleverly, that they became famous, and appeared in the newspapers. Was such a little thing as the keeping of the nightgown likely to weigh on my spirits, and to set my heart sinking within me, at the time when I ought to have spoken to you? What nonsense to ask the question! The thing couldn't be.

'Where is the use of my dwelling in this way on my own folly? The plain truth is plain enough, surely? Behind your back, I loved you with all my heart and soul. Before your face – there's no denying it – I was frightened of you; frightened of making you angry with me; frightened of what you might say to me (though you *had* taken the Diamond) if I presumed to tell you that I had found it out. I had gone as near to it as I dared when I spoke to you in the library. You had not turned your back on me then. You had not started away from me as if I had got the plague. I tried to provoke myself into feeling angry with you, and to rouse up my courage in that way. No! I couldn't feel anything but the misery and the mortification of it. "You're a plain girl; you have got a crooked shoulder; you're only a housemaid – what do you mean by attempting to speak to Me?" You never uttered a word of that, Mr Franklin; but you said it all to me, nevertheless! Is such madness as this to be accounted for? No. There is nothing to be done but to confess it, and let it be.

'I ask your pardon, once more, for this wandering of my pen. There is no fear of its happening again. I am close at the end now.

'The first person who disturbed me by coming into the empty room was Penelope. She had found out my secret long since, and she had done her best to bring me to my senses – and done it kindly too.

' "Ah!" she said, "I know why you're sitting here, and fretting, all by yourself. The best thing that can happen for your advantage, Rosanna, will be for Mr Franklin's visit here to come to an end. It's my belief that he won't be long now before he leaves the house." '

'In all my thoughts of you I had never thought of your going away. I couldn't speak to Penelope. I could only look at her.

' "I've just left Miss Rachel," Penelope went on. "And a hard matter I have had of it to put up with her temper. She says the house is unbearable to her with the police in it; and she's determined to speak to my lady this evening, and to go to her Aunt Ablewhite to-morrow. If she does that, Mr Franklin will be the next to find a reason for going away, you may depend on it!"

'I recovered the use of my tongue at that. "Do you mean to say Mr Franklin will go with her?" I asked.

' "Only too gladly, if she would let him; but she won't. *He* has been made to feel her temper; *he* is in her black books too – and that after having done all he can to help her, poor fellow! No! no! If they don't make it up before to-morrow, you will see Miss Rachel go one way, and Mr Franklin another. Where he may betake himself to I can't say. But he will never stay here, Rosanna, after Miss Rachel has left us."

'I managed to master the despair I felt at the prospect of your going away. To own the truth, I saw a little glimpse of hope for myself if there was really a serious disagreement between Miss Rachel and you. "Do you know," I asked, "what the quarrel is between them?"

' "It is all on Miss Rachel's side," Penelope said. "And, for anything I know to the contrary, it's all Miss Rachel's temper, and nothing else. I am loth to distress you, Rosanna; but don't run away with the notion that Mr Franklin is ever likely to quarrel with *her*. He's a great deal too fond of her for that!"

'She had only just spoken those cruel words when there came a call to us from Mr Betteredge. All the indoor servants were to assemble in the hall. And then we were to go in, one by one, and be questioned in Mr Betteredge's room by Sergeant Cuff.

'It came to my turn to go in, after her ladyship's maid and the upper housemaid had been questioned first. Sergeant Cuff's inquiries – though he wrapped them up very cunningly – soon showed me that those two women (the bitterest enemies I had in the house) had made their discoveries outside my door, on the Tuesday afternoon, and again on the Thursday night. They had told the Sergeant enough to open his eyes to some part of the truth. He rightly believed me to have made a new nightgown secretly, but he wrongly believed the paint-stained nightgown to be mine. I felt satisfied of another thing, from what he said, which it puzzled me to understand. He suspected me, of course, of being concerned in the disappearance of the Diamond. But, at the same time, he let me see – purposely, as I thought – that he did not consider me as the person chiefly answerable for the loss of the jewel. He appeared to think that I had been acting under the direction of somebody else. Who that person might be, I couldn't guess then, and can't guess now.

'In this uncertainty, one thing was plain – that Sergeant Cuff was miles away from knowing the whole truth. You were safe as long as the nightgown was safe – and not a moment longer.

'I quite despair of making you understand the distress and terror which pressed upon me now. It was impossible for me to risk wearing your nightgown any longer. I might find myself taken off, at a moment's notice, to the police court at Frizinghall, to be charged on suspicion, and searched accordingly. While Sergeant Cuff still left me free, I had to choose – and at once – between destroying the nightgown, or hiding it in some safe place, at some safe distance from the house.

'If I had only been a little less fond of you, I think I should have destroyed it. But oh! how could I destroy the only thing I had which proved that I had saved you from discovery? If we did come to an explanation together, and if you suspected me of having some bad motive, and denied it all, how could I win upon you to trust me, unless I had the nightgown to produce? Was it wronging you to believe, as I did, and do still, that you might hesitate to let a poor girl like me be the sharer of your secret, and your accomplice in the theft which your money-troubles had tempted you to commit? Think of your cold behaviour to me, sir, and you will hardly wonder at my unwillingness to destroy the only claim on your confidence and your gratitude which it was my fortune to possess.

'I determined to hide it; and the place I fixed on was the place I knew best – the Shivering Sand.

'As soon as the questioning was over, I made the first excuse that came into my head, and got leave to go out for a breath of fresh air. I went straight to Cobb's Hole, to Mr Yolland's cottage. His wife and daughter were the best friends I had. Don't suppose I trusted them with your secret – I have trusted nobody. All I wanted was to write this letter to you, and to have a safe opportunity of taking the nightgown off me. Suspected as I was, I could do neither of those things, with any sort of security, up at the house.

'And now I have nearly got through my long letter, writing it alone in Lucy Yolland's bedroom. When it is done, I shall go downstairs with the nightgown rolled up, and hidden under my cloak. I shall find the means I want for keeping it safe and dry in its hiding-place, among the litter of old things in Mrs Yolland's kitchen. And then I shall go to the Shivering Sand – don't be afraid of my letting my footmarks betray me! – and hide the nightgown down in the sand, where no living creature can find it without being first let into the secret by myself.

'And, when that's done, what then?

'Then, Mr Franklin, I shall have two reasons for making another attempt to say the words to you which I have not said yet. If you leave the house, as Penelope believes you will leave it, and if I haven't spoken to you before that, I shall lose my opportunity forever. That is one reason. Then, again, there is the comforting knowledge – if my speaking does make you angry – that I have got the nightgown ready to plead my cause for me as nothing else can. That is my other reason. If these two together don't harden my heart against the coldness which has hitherto frozen it up (I mean the coldness of your treatment of me), there will be the end of my efforts – and the end of my life.

'Yes. If I miss my next opportunity – if you are as cruel as ever, and if I feel it again as I have felt it already – goodbye to the world which has grudged me the happiness that it gives to others. Goodbye to life, which nothing but a little kindness from *you* can ever make pleasurable to me again. Don't blame yourself, sir, if it ends in this way. But try – do try – to feel some forgiving sorrow for me! I shall take care that you find out what I have done for you, when I am past telling you of it myself. Will you say something kind of me then – in the same gentle way that you have when you speak to Miss Rachel? If you do that, and if there are such things as ghosts, I believe my ghost will hear it, and tremble with the pleasure of it.

'It's time I left off. I am making myself cry. How am I to see my way to the hiding-place if I let these useless tears come and blind me?

'Besides, why should I look at the gloomy side? Why not believe, while I can, that it will end well after all? I may find you in a good humour to-night – or, if not, I may succeed better to-morrow morning. I shan't improve my plain face by fretting – shall I? Who knows but I may have filled all these weary long pages of paper for nothing? They will go, for safety's sake (never mind now for what other reason) into the hiding-place along with the nightgown. It has been hard, hard work writing my letter. Oh! if we only end in understanding each other, how I shall enjoy tearing it up!

'I beg to remain, sir, your true lover and humble servant,

Rosanna Spearman.'

The reading of the letter was completed by Betteredge in silence. After carefully putting it back in the envelope, he sat thinking, with his head bowed down, and his eyes on the ground.

'Betteredge,' I said, 'is there any hint to guide me at the end of the letter?'

He looked up slowly, with a heavy sigh.

'There is nothing to guide you, Mr Franklin,' he answered. 'If you take my advice you will keep the letter in the cover till these present anxieties of yours have come to an end. It will sorely distress you, whenever you read it. Don't read it now.'

I put the letter away in my pocket-book.

A glance back at the sixteenth and seventeenth chapters of Betteredge's Narrative will show that there really was a reason for my thus sparing myself, at a time when my fortitude had been already cruelly tried. Twice over, the unhappy woman had made her last attempt to speak to me. And twice over, it had been my misfortune (God knows how innocently!) to repel the advances she had made to me. On the Friday night, as Betteredge truly describes it, she had found me alone at the billiard-table. Her manner and language suggested to me – and would have suggested to any man, under the circumstances – that she was about to confess a guilty knowledge of the disappearance of the Diamond. For her own sake, I had purposely shown no special interest in what was coming; for her own sake, I had purposely looked at the billiard balls, instead of looking at *her* – and what had been the result? I had sent her away from me, wounded to the heart! On the Saturday again – on the day when she must have foreseen, after what Penelope had told her, that my departure was close at hand – the same fatality still pursued us. She had once more attempted to meet me in the shrubbery walk, and she had found me there in company with Betteredge and Sergeant Cuff. In her hearing, the Sergeant, with his own underhand object in view, had appealed to my interest in Rosanna Spearman. Again for the poor creature's own sake, I had met the police-officer with a flat denial, and had declared – loudly declared, so that she might hear me too – that I felt 'no interest whatever in Rosanna Spearman'. At those words, solely designed to warn her against attempting to gain my private ear, she had turned away and left the place: cautioned of her danger, as I then believed; self-doomed to destruction, as I know now. From that point, I have already traced the succession of events which led me to the astounding discovery at the quicksand. The retrospect is now complete. I may leave the miserable story of Rosanna Spearman – to which, even at this distance of time, I cannot revert without a pang of distress – to suggest for itself all that is here purposely left unsaid. I may pass from the suicide at the Shivering Sand, with its strange and terrible influence on my present position and future prospects, to interests which concern the living people of this narrative, and to events which were already paving my way for the slow and toilsome journey from the darkness to the light.

�ङ SIX ⋚

I WALKED TO THE RAILWAY STATION accompanied, it is needless to say, by Gabriel Betteredge. I had the letter in my pocket, and the nightgown safely packed in a little bag – both to be submitted, before I slept that night, to the investigation of Mr Bruff.

We left the house in silence. For the first time in my experience of him, I found old Betteredge in my company without a word to say to me. Having something to say on my side, I opened the conversation as soon as we were clear of the lodge gates.

'Before I go to London,' I began, 'I have two questions to ask you. They relate to myself, and I believe they will rather surprise you.'

'If they will put that poor creature's letter out of my head, Mr Franklin, they may do anything else they like with me. Please to begin surprising me, sir, as soon as you can.'

'My first question, Betteredge, is this. Was I drunk on the night of Rachel's Birthday?'

'*You* drunk!' exclaimed the old man. 'Why it's the great defect of your character, Mr Franklin, that you only drink with your dinner, and never touch a drop of liquor afterwards!'

'But the birthday was a special occasion. I might have abandoned my regular habits, on that night of all others.'

Betteredge considered for a moment.

'You did go out of your habits, sir,' he said. 'And I'll tell you how. You looked wretchedly ill – and we persuaded you to have a drop of brandy and water to cheer you up a little.'

'I am not used to brandy and water. It is quite possible – '

'Wait a bit, Mr Franklin. I knew you were not used, too. I poured you out half a wineglass-full of our fifty-year-old Cognac; and (more shame for me!) I drowned that noble liquor in nigh on a tumbler-full of cold water. A child couldn't have got drunk on it – let alone a grown man!'

I knew I could depend on his memory, in a matter of this kind. It was plainly impossible that I could have been intoxicated. I passed on to the second question.

'Before I was sent abroad, Betteredge, you saw a great deal of me when I was a boy? Now tell me plainly, do you remember anything strange of me, after I had gone to bed at night? Did you ever discover me walking in my sleep?'

Betteredge stopped, looked at me for a moment, nodded his head, and walked on again.

'I see your drift now, Mr Franklin!' he said. 'You're trying to account for how you got the paint on your nightgown, without knowing it yourself. It won't do, sir. You're miles away still from getting at the truth. Walk in your sleep? You never did such a thing in your life!'

Here again, I felt that Betteredge must be right. Neither at home nor abroad had my life ever been of the solitary sort. If I had been a sleepwalker, there were hundreds on hundreds of people who must have discovered me, and who, in the interest of my own safety, would have warned me of the habit, and have taken precautions to restrain it.

Still, admitting all this, I clung – with an obstinacy which was surely natural and excusable, under the circumstances – to one or other of the only two explanations that I could see which accounted for the unendurable position in which I then stood. Observing that I was not yet satisfied, Betteredge shrewdly adverted to certain later events in the history of the Moonstone; and scattered both my theories to the wind at once and for ever.

'Let's try it another way, sir,' he said. 'Keep your own opinion, and see how far it will take you towards finding out the truth. If we are to believe the nightgown which I don't for one – you not only smeared off the paint from the door, without knowing it, but you also took the Diamond without knowing it. Is that right, so far?'

'Quite right. Go on.'

'Very good, sir. We'll say you were drunk, or walking in your sleep, when you took the jewel. That accounts for the night and morning, after the birthday. But how does it account for what has happened since that time? The Diamond has been taken to London, since that time. The Diamond has been pledged to Mr Luker, since that time. Did you do those two things, without knowing it, too? Were you drunk when I saw you off in the pony-chaise on that Saturday evening? And did you walk in your sleep to Mr Luker's, when the train had brought you to your journey's end? Excuse me for saying it, Mr Franklin, but this business has so upset you, that you're not fit yet to judge for yourself. The sooner you lay your head alongside of Mr Bruff's head, the sooner you will see your way out of the deadlock that has got you now.'

We reached the station, with only a minute or two to spare.

I hurriedly gave Betteredge my address in London, so that he might write to me, if necessary; promising, on my side, to inform him of any news which I might have to communicate. This done, and just as I was bidding him farewell, I happened to glance towards the book-and-newspaper stall. There was Mr Candy's remarkable-looking assistant again, speaking to the keeper of the stall! Our eyes met at the same moment. Ezra Jennings took off his hat to me. I returned the salute, and got into a carriage just as the train started. It was a relief to my mind, I suppose, to dwell on any subject which appeared to be, personally, of no sort of importance to me. At all events, I began the momentous journey back which was to take me to Mr Bruff, wondering – absurdly enough, I admit – that I should have seen the man with the piebald hair twice in one day!

The hour at which I arrived in London precluded all hope of my finding Mr Bruff at his place of business. I drove from the railway to his private residence at Hampstead, and disturbed the old lawyer dozing alone in his dining-room, with his favourite pug-dog on his lap, and his bottle of wine at his elbow.

I shall best describe the effect which my story produced on the mind of Mr Bruff by relating his proceedings when he had heard it to the end. He ordered lights, and strong tea, to be taken into his study; and he sent a message to the ladies of his family, forbidding them to disturb us on any pretence whatever. These preliminaries disposed of, he first examined the nightgown, and then devoted himself to the reading of Rosanna Spearman's letter.

The reading completed, Mr Bruff addressed me for the first time since we had been shut up together in the seclusion of his own room.

'Franklin Blake,' said the old gentleman, 'this is a very serious matter, in more respects than one. In my opinion, it concerns Rachel quite as nearly as it concerns you. Her extraordinary conduct is no mystery *now*. She believes you have stolen the Diamond.'

I had shrunk from reasoning my own way fairly to that revolting conclusion. But it had forced itself on me, nevertheless. My resolution to obtain a personal interview with Rachel, rested really and truly on the ground just stated by Mr Bruff.

'The first step to take in this investigation,' the lawyer proceeded, 'is to appeal to Rachel. She has been silent all this time, from motives which I (who know her character) can readily understand. It is impossible, after what has happened, to submit to that silence any longer. She must be persuaded to tell us, or she must be forced to tell us, on what grounds she bases her belief that you took the Moonstone. The chances are, that the whole of this case, serious as it seems now, will tumble to pieces, if we can only break through Rachel's inveterate reserve, and prevail upon her to speak out.'

'That is a very comforting opinion for *me*,' I said. 'I own I should like to know – '

'You would like to know how I can justify it,' interposed Mr Bruff. 'I can tell you in two minutes. Understand, in the first place, that I look at this matter from a lawyer's point of view. It's a question of evidence, with me. Very well. The evidence breaks down, at the outset, on one important point.'

'On what point?'

'You shall hear. I admit that the mark of the name proves the nightgown to be yours. I admit that the mark of the paint proves the nightgown to have made the smear on Rachel's door. But what evidence is there to prove that you are the person who wore it, on the night when the Diamond was lost?'

The objection struck me, all the more forcibly that it reflected an objection which I had felt myself.

'As to this,' pursued the lawyer, taking up Rosanna Spearman's confession, 'I can understand that the letter is a distressing one to *you*. I can understand that you may hesitate to analyse it from a purely impartial point of view. But *I* am not in your position. I can bring my professional experience to bear on this document, just as I should bring it to bear on any other. Without alluding to the woman's career as a thief, I will merely remark that her letter proves her to have been an adept at deception, on her own showing; and I argue from that, that I am justified in suspecting her of not having told the whole truth. I won't start any theory, at present, as to what she may or may not have done. I will only say that, if Rachel has suspected you *on the evidence of the nightgown only*, the chances are ninety-nine to a hundred that Rosanna Spearman was the person who showed it to her. In that case, there is the woman's letter, confessing that she was jealous of Rachel, confessing that she changed the roses, confessing that she saw a glimpse of hope for herself, in the prospect of a quarrel between Rachel and you. I don't stop to ask who took the Moonstone (as a means to her end, Rosanna Spearman would have taken fifty Moonstones) – I only say that the disappearance of the jewel gave this reclaimed thief who was in love with you, an opportunity of setting you and Rachel at variance for the rest of your lives. She had not decided on destroying herself, *then*, remember; and, having the opportunity, I distinctly assert that it was in her character, and in her position at the time, to take it. What do you say to that?'

'Some such suspicion,' I answered, 'crossed my own mind, as soon as I opened the letter.'

'Exactly! And when you had read the letter, you pitied the poor creature, and couldn't find it in your heart to suspect her. Does you credit, my dear sir – does you credit!'

'But suppose it turns out that I did wear the nightgown? What then?'

'I don't see how that fact is to be proved,' said Mr Bruff. 'But assuming the proof to be possible, the vindication of your innocence would be no easy matter. We won't go into that, now. Let us wait and see whether Rachel hasn't suspected you on the evidence of the nightgown only.'

'Good God, how coolly you talk of Rachel suspecting me!' I broke out. 'What right has she to suspect Me, on any evidence, of being a thief?'

'A very sensible question, my dear sir. Rather hotly put – but well worth considering for all that. What puzzles you, puzzles me too. Search your memory, and tell me this. Did anything happen while you were staying at the house – not, of course, to shake Rachel's belief in your honour – but, let us say, to shake her belief (no matter with how little reason) in your principles generally?'

I started, in ungovernable agitation, to my feet. The lawyer's question reminded me, for the first time since I had left England, that something *had* happened.

In the eighth chapter of Betteredge's Narrative, an allusion will be found to the arrival of a foreigner and a stranger at my aunt's house, who came to see me on business. The nature of his business was this.

I had been foolish enough (being, as usual, straitened for money at the time) to accept a loan from the keeper of a small restaurant in Paris, to whom I was well known as a customer. A time was settled between us for paying the money back; and when the time came, I found it (as thousands of other honest men have found it) impossible to keep my engagement. I sent the man a bill. My name was unfortunately too well known on such documents: he failed to negotiate it. His affairs had fallen into disorder, in the interval since I had borrowed of him; bankruptcy stared him in the face; and a relative of his, a French lawyer, came to England to find me, and to insist upon the payment of my debt. He was a man of violent temper; and he took the wrong way with me. High words passed on both sides; and my aunt and Rachel were unfortunately in the next room, and heard us. Lady Verinder came in, and insisted on knowing what was the matter. The Frenchman produced his credentials, and declared me to be responsible for the ruin of a poor man, who had trusted in my honour. My aunt instantly paid him the money, and sent him off. She knew me better of course than to take the Frenchman's view of the transaction. But she was shocked at my carelessness, and justly angry with me for placing myself in a position, which, but for her interference, might have become a very disgraceful one. Either her mother told her, or Rachel heard what passed – I can't say which. She took her own romantic, high-flown view of the matter. I was 'heartless'; I was 'dishonourable'; I had 'no principle'; there was 'no knowing what I might do next' – in short, she said some of the severest things to me which I had ever heard from a young lady's lips. The breach between us lasted for the whole of the next day. The day after, I succeeded in making my peace, and thought no more of it. Had Rachel reverted to this unlucky accident, at the critical moment when my place in her estimation was again, and far more seriously, assailed? Mr Bruff, when I had mentioned the circumstances to him, answered the question at once in the affirmative.

'It would have its effect on her mind,' he said gravely. 'And I wish, for your sake, the thing had not happened. However, we have discovered that there *was* a predisposing influence against you – and there is one uncertainty cleared out of our way, at any rate. I see nothing more that we can do now. Our next step in this inquiry must be the step that takes us to Rachel.'

He rose, and began walking thoughtfully up and down the room. Twice, I was on the point of telling him that I had determined on seeing Rachel personally; and twice, having regard to his age and his character, I hesitated to take him by surprise at an unfavourable moment.

'The grand difficulty is,' he resumed, 'how to make her show her whole mind in this matter, without reserve. Have you any suggestions to offer?'

'I have made up my mind, Mr Bruff, to speak to Rachel myself.'

'You!' He suddenly stopped in his walk, and looked at me as if he thought I had taken leave of my senses. 'You, of all the people in the world!' He abruptly checked himself, and took another turn in the room. 'Wait a little,' he said. 'In cases of this extraordinary kind, the rash way is sometimes the best way.' He considered the question for a moment or two, under that new light, and ended boldly by a decision in my favour. 'Nothing venture, nothing have,' the old gentleman resumed. 'You have a chance in your favour which I don't possess – and you shall be the first to try the experiment.'

'A chance in my favour?' I repeated, in the greatest surprise.

Mr Bruff's face softened, for the first time, into a smile.

'This is how it stands,' he said. 'I tell you fairly, I don't trust your discretion, and I don't trust your temper. But I do trust in Rachel's still preserving, in some remote little corner of her heart, a certain perverse weakness for *you*. Touch that – and trust to the consequences for the fullest disclosures that can flow from a woman's lips! The question is – how are you to see her?'

'She has been a guest of yours at this house,' I answered. 'May I venture to suggest – if nothing was said about me beforehand – that I might see her here?'

'Cool!' said Mr Bruff. With that one word of comment on the reply that I had made to him, he took another turn up and down the room.

'In plain English,' he said, 'my house is to be turned into a trap to catch Rachel; with a bait to tempt her, in the shape of an invitation from my wife and daughters. If you were anybody else but Franklin Blake, and if this matter was one atom less serious than it really is, I should refuse point-blank. As things are, I firmly believe Rachel will live to thank me for turning traitor to her in my old age. Consider me your accomplice. Rachel shall be asked to spend the day here; and you shall receive due notice of it.'

'When? To-morrow?'

'To-morrow won't give us time enough to get her answer. Say the day after.'

'How shall I hear from you?'

'Stay at home all the morning and expect me to call on you.'

I thanked him for the inestimable assistance which he was rendering to me, with the gratitude that I really felt; and, declining a hospitable invitation to sleep that night at Hampstead, returned to my lodgings in London.

Of the day that followed, I have only to say that it was the longest day of my life. Innocent as I knew myself to be, certain as I was that the abominable imputation which rested on me must sooner or later be cleared off, there was nevertheless a sense of self-abasement in my mind which instinctively disinclined me to see any of my friends. We often hear (almost invariably, however, from superficial observers) that guilt can look like innocence. I believe it to be infinitely the truer axiom of the two that innocence can look like guilt. I caused myself to be denied all day, to every visitor who called; and I only ventured out under cover of the night.

The next morning, Mr Bruff surprised me at the breakfast-table. He handed me a large key, and announced that he felt ashamed of himself for the first time in his life.

'Is she coming?'

'She is coming to-day, to lunch and spend the afternoon with my wife and my girls.'

'Are Mrs Bruff, and your daughters, in the secret?'

'Inevitably. But women, as you may have observed, have no principles. My family don't feel my pangs of conscience. The end being to bring you and Rachel together again, my wife and daughters pass over the means employed to gain it, as composedly as if they were Jesuits.'

'I am infinitely obliged to them. What is this key?'

'The key of the gate in my back-garden wall. Be there at three this afternoon. Let yourself into the garden, and make your way in by the conservatory door. Cross the small drawing-room, and open the door in front of you which leads into the music-room. There, you will find Rachel – and find her, alone.'

'How can I thank you!'

'I will tell you how. Don't blame *me* for what happens afterwards.'

With those words, he went out.

I had many weary hours still to wait through. To while away the time, I looked at my letters. Among them was a letter from Betteredge.

I opened it eagerly. To my surprise and disappointment, it began with an apology warning me to expect no news of any importance. In the next sentence the everlasting Ezra Jennings appeared again! He had stopped Betteredge on the way out of the station, and had asked who I was. Informed on this point, he had mentioned having seen me to his master, Mr Candy. Mr Candy hearing of this, had himself driven over to Betteredge, to express his regret at our having missed each other. He had a reason for wishing particularly to speak to me; and when I was next in the neighbourhood of Frizinghall, he begged I would let him know. Apart from a few characteristic utterances of the Betteredge philosophy, this was the sum and substance of my correspondent's letter. The warm-hearted, faithful old man acknowledged that he had written 'mainly for the pleasure of writing to me'.

I crumpled up the letter in my pocket, and forgot it the moment after, in the all-absorbing interest of my coming interview with Rachel.

As the clock of Hampstead church struck three, I put Mr Bruff's key into the lock of the door in the wall. When I first stepped into the garden, and while I was securing the door again on the inner side, I own to having felt a certain guilty doubtfulness about what might happen next. I looked furtively on either side of me, suspicious of the presence of some unexpected witness in some unknown corner of the garden. Nothing appeared, to justify my apprehensions. The walks were, one and all, solitudes; and the birds and the bees were the only witnesses.

I passed through the garden; entered the conservatory; and crossed the small drawingroom. As I laid my hand on the door opposite, I heard a few plaintive chords struck on the piano in the room within. She had often idled over the instrument in this way, when I was staying at her mother's house. I was obliged to wait a little, to steady myself. The past and present rose side by side, at that supreme moment – and the contrast shook me.

After the lapse of a minute, I roused my manhood, and opened the door.

❧ SEVEN ❧

AT THE MOMENT WHEN I SHOWED myself in the doorway, Rachel rose from the piano.

I closed the door behind me. We confronted each other in silence, with the full length of the room between us. The movement she had made in rising appeared to be the one exertion of which she was capable. All use of every other faculty, bodily or mental, seemed to be merged in the mere act of looking at me.

A fear crossed my mind that I had shown myself too suddenly. I advanced a few steps towards her. I said gently, 'Rachel!'

The sound of my voice brought the life back to her limbs, and the colour to her face. She advanced, on her side, still without speaking. Slowly, as if acting under some influence independent of her own will, she came nearer and nearer to me; the warm dusky colour flushing her cheeks, the light of reviving intelligence brightening every instant in her eyes. I forgot the object that had brought me into her presence; I forgot the vile suspicion that rested on my good name; I forgot every consideration, past, present, and future, which I was bound to remember. I saw nothing but the woman I loved coming nearer and nearer to me. She trembled; she stood irresolute. I could resist it no longer – I caught her in my arms, and covered her face with kisses.

There was a moment when I thought the kisses were returned; a moment when it seemed as if she, too, might have forgotten. Almost before the idea could shape itself in my mind, her first voluntary action made me feel that she remembered. With a cry which was like a cry of horror – with a strength which I doubt if I could have resisted if I had tried – she thrust me back from her. I saw merciless anger in her eyes; I saw merciless contempt on her lips. She looked me over, from head to foot, as she might have looked at a stranger who had insulted her.

'You coward!' she said. 'You mean, miserable, heartless coward!'

Those were her first words! The most unendurable reproach that a woman can address to a man, was the reproach that she picked out to address to Me.

'I remember the time, Rachel,' I said, 'when you could have told me that I had offended you, in a worthier way than that. I beg your pardon.'

Something of the bitterness that I felt may have communicated itself to my voice. At the first words of my reply, her eyes, which had been turned away the moment before, looked back at me unwillingly. She answered in a low tone, with a sullen submission of manner which was quite new in my experience of her.

'Perhaps there is some excuse for me,' she said. 'After what you have done, is it a manly action, on your part, to find your way to me as you have found it to-day? It seems a cowardly experiment, to try an experiment on my weakness for you. It seems a cowardly surprise, to surprise me into letting you kiss me. But that is only a woman's view. I ought to have known it couldn't be your view. I should have done better if I had controlled myself, and said nothing.'

The apology was more unendurable than the insult. The most degraded man living would have felt humiliated by it.

'If my honour was not in your hands,' I said, 'I would leave you this instant, and never see you again. You have spoken of what I have done. What have I done?'

'What have you done! *You* ask that question of *me*?'

'I ask it.'

'I have kept your infamy a secret,' she answered. 'And I have suffered the consequences of concealing it. Have I no claim to be spared the insult of your asking me what you have done? Is *all* sense of gratitude dead in you? You were once a gentleman. You were once dear to my mother, and dearer still to me – '

Her voice failed her. She dropped into a chair, and turned her back on me, and covered her face with her hands.

I waited a little before I trusted myself to say any more. In that moment of silence, I hardly know which I felt most keenly – the sting which her contempt had planted in me, or the proud resolution which shut me out from all community with her distress.

'If you will not speak first,' I said, 'I must. I have come here with something serious to say to you. Will you do me the common justice of listening while I say it?'

She neither moved, nor answered. I made no second appeal to her; I never advanced an inch nearer to her chair. With a pride which was as obstinate as her pride, I told her of my discovery at the Shivering Sand, and of all that had led to it. The narrative, of necessity, occupied some little time. From beginning to end, she never looked round at me, and she never uttered a word.

I kept my temper. My whole future depended, in all probability, on my not losing possession of myself at that moment. The time had come to put Mr Bruff's theory to the test. In the breathless interest of trying that experiment, I moved round so as to place myself in front of her.

'I have a question to ask you,' I said. 'It obliges me to refer again to a painful subject. Did Rosanna Spearman show you the nightgown? Yes, or No?'

She started to her feet; and walked close up to me of her own accord. Her eyes looked me searchingly in the face, as if to read something there which they had never read yet.

'Are you mad?' she asked.

I still restrained myself. I said quietly, 'Rachel, will you answer my question?'

She went on, without heeding me.

'Have you some object to gain which I don't understand? Some mean fear about the future, in which I am concerned? They say your father's death has made you a rich man. Have you come here to compensate me for the loss of my Diamond? And have you heart enough left to feel ashamed of your errand? Is *that* the secret of your pretence of innocence, and your story about Rosanna Spearman? Is there a motive of shame at the bottom of all the falsehood, this time?'

I stopped her there. I could control myself no longer.

'You have done me an infamous wrong!' I broke out hotly. 'You suspect me of stealing your Diamond. I have a right to know, and I *will* know, the reason why!'

'Suspect you!' she exclaimed, her anger rising with mine. '*You villain, I saw you take the Diamond with my own eyes!*'

The revelation which burst upon me in those words, the overthrow which they instantly accomplished of the whole view of the case on which Mr Bruff had relied, struck me helpless. Innocent as I was, I stood before her in silence. To her eyes, to any eyes, I must have looked like a man overwhelmed by the discovery of his own guilt.

She drew back from the spectacle of my humiliation, and of her triumph. The sudden silence that had fallen upon me seemed to frighten her. 'I spared you, at the time,' she said. 'I would have spared you now, if you had not forced me to speak.' She moved away as if to leave the room – and hesitated before she got to the door. 'Why did you come here to humiliate yourself?' she asked. 'Why did you come here to humiliate me?' She went on a few steps, and paused once more. 'For God's sake, say something!' she exclaimed, passionately. 'If you have any mercy left, don't let me degrade myself in this way! Say something – and drive me out of the room!'

I advanced towards her, hardly conscious of what I was doing. I had possibly some confused idea of detaining her until she had told me more. From the moment when I knew that the evidence on which I stood condemned in Rachel's mind, was the evidence of her own eyes, nothing – not even my conviction of my own innocence – was clear to my mind.

I took her by the hand; I tried to speak firmly and to the purpose. All I could say was, 'Rachel, you once loved me.'

She shuddered, and looked away from me. Her hand lay powerless and trembling in mine. 'Let go of it,' she said faintly.

My touch seemed to have the same effect on her which the sound of my voice had produced when I first entered the room. After she had said the word which called me a coward, after she had made the avowal which branded me as a thief – while her hand lay in mine I was her master still!

I drew her gently back into the middle of the room. I seated her by the side of me. 'Rachel,' I said, 'I can't explain the contradiction in what I am going to tell you. I can only speak the truth as you have spoken it. You saw me – with your own eyes, you saw me take the Diamond. Before God who hears us, I declare that I now know I took it for the first time! Do you doubt me still?'

She had neither heeded nor heard me. 'Let go of my hand,' she repeated faintly. That was her only answer. Her head sank on my shoulder; and her hand unconsciously closed on mine, at the moment when she asked me to release it.

I refrained from pressing the question. But there my forbearance stopped. My chance of ever holding up my head again among honest men depended on my chance of inducing her to make her disclosure complete. The one hope left for me was the hope that she might have overlooked something in the chain of evidence – some mere trifle, perhaps, which might nevertheless, under careful investigation, be made the means of vindicating my innocence in the end. I own I kept possession of her hand. I own I spoke to her with all that I could summon back of the sympathy and confidence of the bygone time.

'I want to ask you something,' I said. 'I want you to tell me everything that happened, from the time when we wished each other good night, to the time when you saw me take the Diamond.'

She lifted her head from my shoulder, and made an effort to release her hand. 'Oh, why go back to it!' she said. 'Why go back to it!'

'I will tell you why, Rachel. You are the victim, and I am the victim, of some monstrous delusion which has worn the mask of truth. If we look at what happened on the night of your birthday, together, we may end in understanding each other yet.'

Her head dropped back on my shoulder. The tears gathered in her eyes, and fell slowly over her cheeks. 'Oh!' she said, 'have I never had that hope? Have I not tried to see it, as you are trying now?'

'You have tried by yourself,' I answered. 'You have not tried with me to help you.'

Those words seemed to awaken in her something of the hope which I felt myself when I uttered them. She replied to my questions with more than docility – she exerted her intelligence; she willingly opened her whole mind to me.

'Let us begin,' I said, 'with what happened after we had wished each other good night. Did you go to bed? or did you sit up?'

'I went to bed.'

'Did you notice the time? Was it late?'

'Not very. About twelve o'clock, I think.'

'Did you fall asleep?'

'No. I couldn't sleep that night.'

'You were restless?'

'I was thinking of you.'

The answer almost unmanned me. Something in the tone, even more than in the words, went straight to my heart. It was only after pausing a little first that I was able to go on.

'Had you any light in your room?' I asked.

'None – until I got up again, and lit my candle.'

'How long was that, after you had gone to bed?'

'About an hour after, I think. About one o'clock.'

'Did you leave your bedroom?'

'I was going to leave it. I had put on my dressing-gown; and I was going into my sitting-room to get a book – '

'Had you opened your bedroom door?'

'I had just opened it.'

'But you had not gone into the sitting-room?'

'No – I was stopped from going into it.'

'What stopped you?'

'I saw a light, under the door; and I heard footsteps approaching it.'

'Were you frightened?'

'Not then. I knew my poor mother was a bad sleeper; and I remembered that she had tried hard, that evening, to persuade me to let her take charge of my Diamond. She was unreasonably anxious about it, as I thought; and I fancied she was coming to me to see if I was in bed, and to speak to me about the Diamond again, if she found that I was up.'

'What did you do?'

'I blew out my candle, so that she might think I was in bed. I was unreasonable, on my side – I was determined to keep my Diamond in the place of my own choosing.'

'After blowing the candle out, did you go back to bed?'

'I had no time to go back. At the moment when I blew the candle out, the sitting-room door opened, and I saw – '

'You saw?'

'You.'

'Dressed as usual?'

'No.'

'In my nightgown?'

'In your nightgown – with your bedroom candle in your hand.'

'Alone?'

'Alone.'

'Could you see my face?'

'Yes.'

'Plainly?'

'Quite plainly. The candle in your hand showed it to me.'

'Were my eyes open?'

'Yes.'

'Did you notice anything strange in them? Anything like a fixed, vacant expression?'

'Nothing of the sort. Your eyes were bright – brighter than usual. You looked about in the room, as if you knew you were where you ought not to be, and as if you were afraid of being found out.'

'Did you observe one thing when I came into the roor – did you observe how I walked?'

'You walked as you always do. You came in as far as the middle of the room – and then you stopped and looked about you.'

'What did you do, on first seeing me?'

'I could do nothing. I was petrified. I couldn't speak, I couldn't call out, I couldn't even move to shut my door.'

'Could I see you, where you stood?'

'You might certainly have seen me. But you never looked towards me. It's useless to ask the question. I am sure you never saw me.'

'How are you sure?'

'Would you have taken the Diamond? would you have acted as you did afterwards? would you be here now – if you had seen that I was awake and looking at you? Don't make me talk of that part of it! I want to answer you quietly. Help me to keep as calm as I can. Go on to something else.'

She was right – in every way, right. I went on to other things.

'What did I do, after I had got to the middle of the room, and had stopped there?'

'You turned away, and went straight to the corner near the window – where my Indian cabinet stands.'

'When I was at the cabinet, my back must have been turned towards you. How did you see what I was doing?'

'When you moved, I moved.'

'So as to see what I was about with my hands?'

'There are three glasses in my sitting-room. As you stood there, I saw all that you did, reflected in one of them.'

'What did you see?'

'You put your candle on the top of the cabinet. You opened, and shut, one drawer after another, until you came to the drawer in which I had put my Diamond. You looked at the open drawer for a moment. And then you put your hand in, and took the Diamond out.'

'How do you know I took the Diamond out?'

'I saw your hand go into the drawer. And I saw the gleam of the stone between your finger and thumb, when you took your hand out.'

'Did my hand approach the drawer again – to close it, for instance?'

'No. You had the Diamond in your right hand; and you took the candle from the top of the cabinet with your left hand.'

'Did I look about me again, after that?'

'No.'

'Did I leave the room immediately?'

'No. You stood quite still, for what seemed a long time. I saw your face sideways in the glass. You looked like a man thinking, and dissatisfied with his own thoughts.'

'What happened next?'

'You roused yourself on a sudden, and you went straight out of the room.'

'Did I close the door after me?'

'No. You passed out quickly into the passage, and left the door open.'

'And then?'

'Then, your light disappeared, and the sound of your steps died away, and I was left alone in the dark.'

'Did nothing happen – from that time, to the time when the whole house knew that the Diamond was lost?'

'Nothing.'

'Are you sure of that? Might you not have been asleep a part of the time?'

'I never slept. I never went back to my bed. Nothing happened until Penelope came in, at the usual time in the morning.'

I dropped her hand, and rose, and took a turn in the room. Every question that I could put had been answered. Every detail that I could desire to know had been placed before me. I had even reverted to the idea of sleep-walking, and the idea of intoxication; and, again, the worthlessness of the one theory and the other had been proved – on the authority, this time, of the witness who had seen me. What was to be said next? what was to be done next? There rose the horrible fact of the Theft – the one visible, tangible object that confronted me, in the midst of the impenetrable darkness which enveloped all besides! Not a glimpse of light to guide me, when I had possessed myself of Rosanna Spearman's secret at the Shivering Sand. And not a glimpse of light now, when I had appealed to Rachel herself, and had heard the hateful story of the night from her own lips.

She was the first, this time, to break the silence.

'Well?' she said, 'you have asked, and I have answered. You have made me hope something from all this, because *you* hoped something from it. What have you to say now?'

The tone in which she spoke warned me that my influence over her was a lost influence once more.

'We were to look at what happened on my birthday night, together,' she went on; 'and we were then to understand each other. Have we done that?'

She waited pitilessly for my reply. In answering her I committed a fatal error – I let the exasperating helplessness of my situation get the better of my self-control. Rashly and uselessly, I reproached her for the silence which had kept me until that moment in ignorance of the truth.

'If you had spoken when you ought to have spoken,' I began: 'if you had done me the common justice to explain yourself – '

She broke in on me with a cry of fury. The few words I had said seemed to have lashed her on the instant into a frenzy of rage.

'Explain myself!' she repeated. 'Oh! is there another man like this in the world? I spare him, when my heart is breaking; I screen him when my own character is at stake; and he – of all human beings, he – turns on me now, and tells me that I ought to have explained myself! After believing in him as I did, after loving him as I did, after thinking of him by day, and dreaming of him by night – he wonders I didn't charge him with his disgrace the first time we met: "My heart's darling, you are a Thief! My hero whom I love and honour, you have crept into my room under cover of the night, and stolen my Diamond!" That is what I ought to have said. You villain, you mean, mean, mean villain, I would have lost fifty Diamonds, rather than see your face lying to me, as I see it lying now!'

I took up my hat. In mercy to *her* – yes! I can honestly say it – in mercy to *her*, I turned away without a word, and opened the door by which I had entered the room.

She followed, and snatched the door out of my hand; she closed it, and pointed back to the place that I had left.

'No!' she said. 'Not yet! It seems that *I* owe a justification of my conduct to *you*. You shall stay and hear it. Or you shall stoop to the lowest infamy of all, and force your way out.'

It wrung my heart to see her; it wrung my heart to hear her. I answered by a sign – it was all I could do – that I submitted myself to her will.

The crimson flush of anger began to fade out of her face, as I went back, and took my chair in silence. She waited a little, and steadied herself. When she went on, but one sign of feeling was discernible in her. She spoke without looking at me. Her hands were fast clasped in her lap, and her eyes were fixed on the ground.

'I ought to have done you the common justice to explain myself,' she said, repeating my own words. 'You shall see whether I did try to do you justice, or not. I told you just now that I never slept, and never returned to my bed, after you had left my sitting-room. It's useless to trouble you by dwelling on what I thought – you would not understand my thoughts – I will only tell you what I did, when time enough had passed to help me to recover myself. I refrained from alarming the house, and telling everybody what had happened – as I ought to have done. In spite of what I had seen, I was fond enough of you to believe – no matter what! – any impossibility, rather than admit it to my own mind that you were deliberately a thief. I thought and thought – and I ended in writing to you.'

'I never received the letter.'

'I know you never received it. Wait a little, and you shall hear why. My letter would have told you nothing openly. It would not have ruined you for life, if it had fallen into some other person's hands. It would only have said – in a manner which you yourself could not possibly have mistaken – that I had reason to know you were in debt, and that it was in my experience and in my mother's experience of you, that you were not very discreet, or very scrupulous about how you got money when you wanted it. You would have remembered the visit of the French lawyer, and you would have known what I referred to. If you had read on with some interest after that, you would have come to an offer I had to make to you – the offer, privately (not a word, mind, to be said openly about it between us!), of the loan of as large a sum of money as I could get. – And I would have got it!' she exclaimed, her colour beginning to rise again, and her eyes looking up at me once more. 'I would have pledged the Diamond myself, if I could have got the money in no other way! In those words I wrote to you. Wait! I did more than that. I arranged with Penelope to give you the letter when nobody was near. I planned to shut myself into my bedroom, and to have the sitting-room left open and empty all the morning. And I hoped – with all my heart and soul I hoped! – that you would take the opportunity, and put the Diamond back secretly in the drawer.'

I attempted to speak. She lifted her hand impatiently, and stopped me.

In the rapid alternations of her temper, her anger was beginning to rise again. She got up from her chair, and approached me.

'I know what you are going to say,' she went on. 'You are going to remind me again that you never received my letter. I can tell you why. I tore it up.'

'For what reason?' I asked.

'For the best of reasons. I preferred tearing it up to throwing it away upon such a man as you! What was the first news that reached me in the morning? Just as my little plan was complete, what did I hear? I heard that you – you!!! – were the foremost person in the house in fetching the police. You were the active man; you were the leader; you were working harder than any of them to recover the jewel! You even carried your audacity far enough to ask to speak to *me* about the loss of the Diamond – the Diamond which you yourself had stolen; the Diamond which was all the time in your own hands! After that proof of your horrible falseness and cunning, I tore up my letter. But even then – even when I was maddened by the searching and questioning of the police-man, whom *you* had sent in – even then, there was some infatuation in my mind which wouldn't let me give you up. I said to myself, "He has played his vile farce before everybody else in the house. Let me try if he can play it before me." Somebody told me you were on the terrace. I went down to the terrace. I forced myself to look at you; I forced myself to speak to you. Have you forgotten what I said?'

I might have answered that I remembered every word of it. But what purpose, at that moment, would the answer have served?

How could I tell her that what she had said had astonished me, had distressed me, had suggested to me that she was in a state of dangerous nervous excitement, had even roused a moment's doubt in my mind whether the loss of the jewel was as much a mystery to her as to the rest of us – but had never once given so much as a glimpse at the truth? Without the shadow of a proof to produce in vindication of my innocence, how could I persuade her that I knew no more than the veriest stranger could have known of what was really in her thoughts when she spoke to me on the terrace?

'It may suit your convenience to forget; it suits my convenience to remember,' she went on. 'I know what I said – for I considered it with myself, before I said it. I gave you one opportunity after another of owning the truth. I left nothing unsaid that I *could* say – short of actually telling you that I knew you had committed the theft. And all the return you made, was to look at me with your vile pretence of astonishment, and your false face of innocence – just as you have looked at me to-day; just as you are looking at me now! I left you, that morning, knowing you at last for what you were – for what you are – as base a wretch as ever walked the earth!'

'If you had spoken out at the time, you might have left me, Rachel, knowing that you had cruelly wronged an innocent man.'

'If I had spoken out before other people,' she retorted, with another burst of indignation, 'you would have been disgraced for life! If I had spoken out to no ears but yours, you would have denied it, as you are denying it now! Do you think I should have believed you? Would a man hesitate at a lie, who had done what I saw *you* do – who had behaved about it afterwards, as I saw *you* behave? I tell you again, I shrank from the horror of hearing you lie, after the horror of seeing you thieve. You talk as if this was a misunderstanding which a few words might have set right! Well! the misunderstanding is at an end. Is the thing set right? No! the thing is just where it was. I don't believe you *now*! I don't believe you found the nightgown, I don't believe in Rosanna Spearman's letter, I don't believe a word you have said. You stole it – I saw you! You affected to help the police – I saw you! You pledged the Diamond to the money-lender in London – I am sure of it! You cast the suspicion of your disgrace (thanks to my base silence!) on an innocent man! You fled to the Continent with your plunder the next morning! After all that vileness, there was but one thing more you *could* do. You could come here with a last falsehood on your lips – you could come here, and tell me that I have wronged you!'

If I had stayed a moment more, I know not what words might have escaped me which I should have remembered with vain repentance and regret. I passed by her, and opened the door for the second time. For the second time – with the frantic perversity of a roused woman – she caught me by the arm, and barred my way out.

'Let me go, Rachel,' I said. 'It will be better for both of us. Let me go.'

The hysterical passion swelled in her bosom – her quickened convulsive breathing almost beat on my face, as she held me back at the door.

'Why did you come here?' she persisted, desperately. 'I ask you again – why did you come here? Are you afraid I shall expose you? Now you are a rich man, now you have got a place in the world, now you may marry the best lady in the land – are you afraid I shall say the words which I have never said yet to anybody but you? I can't say the words! I can't expose you! I am worse, if worse can be, than you are yourself.' Sobs and tears burst from her. She struggled with them fiercely; she held me more and more firmly. 'I can't tear you out of my heart,' she said, 'even now! You may trust in the shameful, shameful weakness which can only struggle against you in this way!' She suddenly let go of me – she threw up her hands, and wrung them frantically in the air. 'Any other woman living would shrink from the disgrace of touching him!'

she exclaimed. 'Oh, God! I despise myself even more heartily than I despise *him*!'

The tears were forcing their way into my eyes in spite of me – the horror of it was to be endured no longer.

'You shall know that you have wronged me, yet,' I said. 'Or you shall never see me again!'

With those words, I left her. She started up from the chair on which she had dropped the moment before: she started up – the noble creature! – and followed me across the outer room, with a last merciful word at parting.

'Franklin!' she said, 'I forgive you! Oh, Franklin, Franklin! we shall never meet again. Say you forgive *me*!'

I turned, so as to let my face show her that I was past speaking – I turned, and waved my hand, and saw her dimly, as in a vision, through the tears that had conquered me at last.

The next moment, the worst bitterness of it was over. I was out in the garden again. I saw her, and heard her, no more.

＆ EIGHT ＆

LATE THAT EVENING, I WAS surprised at my lodgings by a visit from Mr Bruff.

There was a noticeable change in the lawyer's manner. It had lost its usual confidence and spirit. He shook hands with me, for the first time in his life, in silence.

'Are you going back to Hampstead?' I asked, by way of saying something.

'I have just left Hampstead,' he answered. 'I know, Mr Franklin, that you have got at the truth at last. But, I tell you plainly, if I could have foreseen the price that was to be paid for it, I should have preferred leaving you in the dark.'

'You have seen Rachel?'

'I have come here after taking her back to Portland Place; it was impossible to let her return in the carriage by herself. I can hardly hold you responsible – considering that you saw her in my house and by my permission – for the shock that this unlucky interview has inflicted on her. All I can do is to provide against a repetition of the mischief. She is young – she has a resolute spirit – she will get over this, with time and rest to help her. I want to be assured that you will do nothing to hinder her recovery. May I depend on your making no second attempt to see her – except with my sanction and approval?'

'After what she has suffered, and after what I have suffered,' I said, 'you may rely on me.'

'I have your promise?'

'You have my promise.'

Mr Bruff looked relieved. He put down his hat, and drew his chair nearer to mine.

'That's settled!' he said. 'Now, about the future – *your* future, I mean. To my mind, the result of the extraordinary turn which the matter has now taken is briefly this. In the first place, we are sure that Rachel has told you the whole truth, as plainly as words can tell it. In the second place – though we know that there must be some dreadful mistake somewhere – we can hardly blame her for believing you to be guilty, on the evidence of her own senses; backed, as that evidence has been, by circumstances which appear, on the face of them, to tell dead against you.'

There I interposed. 'I don't blame Rachel,' I said. 'I only regret that she could not prevail on herself to speak more plainly to me at the time.'

'You might as well regret that Rachel is not somebody else,' rejoined Mr Bruff. 'And even then, I doubt if a girl of any delicacy, whose heart had been set on marrying you, could have brought herself to charge you to your face with being a thief. Anyhow, it was not in Rachel's nature to do it. In a very different matter to this matter of yours – which placed her, however, in a position not altogether unlike her position towards you – I happen to know that she was influenced by a similar motive to the motive which actuated her conduct in your case. Besides, as she told me herself, on our way to town this evening, if she *had* spoken plainly, she would no more have believed your denial then than she believes it now. What answer can you make to that? There is no answer to be made to it. Come, come, Mr Franklin! my view of the case has been proved to be all wrong, I admit – but, as things are now, my advice may be worth having for all that. I tell you plainly, we shall be wasting our time, and cudgelling our brains to no purpose, if we attempt to try back, and unravel this frightful complication from the beginning. Let us close our minds resolutely to all that happened last year at Lady Verinder's country house; and let us look to what we *can* discover in the future, instead of to what we can *not* discover in the past.'

'Surely you forget,' I said, 'that the whole thing is essentially a matter of the past – so far as I am concerned?'

'Answer me this,' retorted Mr Bruff. 'Is the Moonstone at the bottom of all the mischief – or is it not?'

'It is – of course.'

'Very good. What do we believe was done with the Moonstone, when it was taken to London?'

'It was pledged to Mr Luker.'

'We know that you are not the person who pledged it. Do we know who did?'

'No.'

'Where do we believe the Moonstone to be now?'

'Deposited in the keeping of Mr Luker's bankers.'

'Exactly. Now observe. We are already in the month of June. Towards the end of the month (I can't be particular to a day) a year will have elapsed from the time when we believe the jewel to have been pledged. There is a chance – to say the least – that the year's time has expired. If he redeems it, Mr Luker must himself – according to the terms of his own arrangement – take the Diamond out of his bankers' hands. Under these circumstances, I propose setting a watch at the bank, as the present month draws to an end, and discovering who the person is to whom Mr Luker restores the Moonstone. Do you see it now?'

I admitted (a little unwillingly) that the idea was a new one, at any rate.

'It's Mr Murthwaite's idea quite as much as mine,' said Mr Bruff. 'It might have never entered my head, but for a conversation we had together some time since. If Mr Murthwaite is right, the Indians are likely to be on the look-out at the bank, towards the end of the month too – and something serious may come of it. What comes of it doesn't matter to you and me – except as it may help us to lay our hands on the mysterious Somebody who pawned the Diamond. That person, you may rely on it, is responsible (I don't pretend to know how) for the position in which you stand at this moment; and that person alone can set you right in Rachel's estimation.'

'I can't deny,' I said, 'that the plan you propose meets the difficulty in a way that is very daring, and very ingenious, and very new. But—'

'But you have an objection to make?'

'Yes. My objection is, that your proposal obliges us to wait.'

'Granted. As I reckon the time, it requires you to wait about a fortnight – more or less. Is that so very long?'

'It's a lifetime, Mr Bruff, in such a situation as mine. My existence will be simply unendurable to me, unless I do something towards clearing my character at once.'

'Well, well, I understand that. Have you thought yet of what you can do?'

'I have thought of consulting Sergeant Cuff.'

'He has retired from the police. It's useless to expect the Sergeant to help you.'

'I know where to find him; and I can but try.'

'Try,' said Mr Bruff, after a moment's consideration. 'The case has assumed such an extraordinary aspect since Sergeant Cuff's time, that you *may* revive his interest in the inquiry. Try, and let me hear the result. In the meanwhile,' he continued, rising, 'if you make no discoveries between this, and the end of the month, am I free to try, on my side, what can be done by keeping a look-out at the bank?'

'Certainly,' I answered – 'unless I relieve you of any necessity for trying the experiment in the interval.'

Mr Bruff smiled, and took up his hat.

'Tell Sergeant Cuff,' he rejoined, 'that *I* say the discovery of the truth depends on the discovery of the person who pawned the Diamond. And let me hear what the Sergeant's experience says to that.'

So we parted.

Early the next morning, I set forth for the little town of Dorking – the place of Sergeant Cuff's retirement, as indicated to me by Betteredge.

Inquiring at the hotel, I received the necessary directions for finding the Sergeant's cottage. It was approached by a quiet by-road, a little way out of the town, and it stood snugly in the middle of its own plot of garden ground, protected by a good brick wall at the back and the sides, and by a high quickset hedge in front. The gate, ornamented at the upper part by smartly-painted trellis-work, was locked. After ringing at the bell, I peered through the trellis-work, and saw the great Cuff's favourite flower everywhere; blooming in his garden, clustering over his door, looking in at his windows. Far from the crimes and the mysteries of the great city, the illustrious thief-taker was placidly living out the last Sybarite years of his life, smothered in roses!

A decent elderly woman opened the gate to me, and at once annihilated all the hopes I had built on securing the assistance of Sergeant Cuff. He had started, only the day before, on a journey to Ireland.

'Has he gone there on business?' I asked.

The woman smiled. 'He has only one business now, sir,' she said; 'and that's roses. Some great man's gardener in Ireland has found out something new in the growing of roses – and Mr Cuff's away to inquire into it.'

'Do you know when he will be back?'

'It's quite uncertain, sir. Mr Cuff said he should come back directly, or be away some time, just according as he found the new discovery worth nothing, or worth looking into. If you have any message to leave for him, I'll take care, sir, that he gets it.'

'I gave her my card, having first written on it in pencil: 'I have something to say about the Moonstone. Let me hear from you as soon as you get back.' That done, there was nothing left but to submit to circumstances, and return to London.

In the irritable condition of my mind, at the time of which I am now writing, the abortive result of my journey to the Sergeant's cottage simply aggravated the restless impulse in me to be doing something. On the day of my return from Dorking, I determined that the next morning should find me bent on a new effort at forcing my way, through all obstacles, from the darkness to the light.

What form was my next experiment to take?

If the excellent Betteredge had been present while I was considering that question, and if he had been let into the secret of my thoughts, he would, no doubt, have declared that the German side of me was, on this occasion, my uppermost side. To speak seriously, it is perhaps possible that my German training was in some degree responsible for the labyrinth of useless speculations in which I now involved myself. For the greater part of the night, I sat smoking, and building up theories, one more profoundly improbable than another. When I did get to sleep, my waking fancies pursued me in dreams. I rose the next morning, with Objective-Subjective and Subjective-Objective inextricably entangled together in my mind; and I began the day which was to witness my next effort at practical action of some kind, by doubting whether I had any sort of right (on purely philosophical grounds) to consider any sort of thing (the Diamond included) as existing at all.

How long I might have remained lost in the mist of my own metaphysics, if I had been left to extricate myself, it is impossible for me to say. As the event proved, accident came to my rescue, and happily delivered me. I happened to wear, that morning, the same coat which I had worn on the day of my interview with Rachel. Searching for something else in one of the pockets, I came upon a crumpled piece of paper, and, taking it out, found Betteredge's forgotten letter in my hand.

It seemed hard on my good old friend to leave him without a reply. I went to my writing-table, and read his letter again.

A letter which has nothing of the slightest importance in it, is not always an easy letter to answer. Betteredge's present effort at corresponding with me came within this category. Mr Candy's assistant, otherwise Ezra Jennings, had told his master that he had seen me; and Mr Candy, in his turn, wanted to see me and say something to me, when I was next in the neighbourbood of Frizinghall. What was to be said in answer to that, which would be worth the paper it was written on? I sat idly drawing likenesses from memory of Mr Candy's remarkable-looking assistant, on the sheet of paper which I had vowed to dedicate to Betteredge – until it suddenly occurred to me that here was the irrepressible Ezra Jennings getting in my way again! I threw a dozen portraits, at least, of the man with the piebald hair (the hair in every case, remarkably like), into the waste-paper basket – and then and there, wrote my answer to Betteredge. It was a perfectly commonplace letter – but it had one excellent effect on me. The effort of writing a few sentences, in plain English, completely cleared my mind of the cloudy nonsense which had filled it since the previous day.

Devoting myself once more to the elucidation of the impenetrable puzzle which my own position presented to me, I now tried to meet the difficulty by investigating it from a plainly practical point of view. The events of the memorable night being still unintelligible to me, I looked a little farther back, and searched my memory of the earlier hours of the birthday for any incident which might prove of some assistance to me in finding the clue.

Had anything happened while Rachel and I were finishing the painted door? or, later, when I rode over to Frizinghall? or afterwards, when I went back with Godfrey Ablewhite and his sisters? or, later again, when I put the Moonstone into Rachel's hands? or, later still, when the company came, and we all assembled round the dinner-table? My memory disposed of that string of questions readily enough, until I came to the last. Looking back at the social events of the birthday dinner, I found myself brought to a standstill at the outset of the inquiry. I was not even capable of accurately remembering the number of the guests who had sat at the same table with me.

To feel myself completely at fault here, and to conclude, thereupon, that the incidents of the dinner might especially repay the trouble of investigating them, formed parts of the same mental process, in my case. I believe other people, in a similar situation, would have reasoned as I did. When the pursuit of our own interests causes us to become objects of inquiry to ourselves, we are naturally suspicious of what we don't know. Once in possession of the names of the persons who had been present at the dinner, I resolved – as a means of enriching the deficient resources of my own memory – to appeal to the memory of the rest of the guests; to write down all that they could recollect of the social events of the birthday; and to test the result, thus obtained, by the light of what had happened afterwards, when the company had left the house.

This last and newest of my many contemplated experiments in the art of inquiry – which Betteredge would probably have attributed to the clear-headed, or French, side of me being uppermost for the moment – may fairly claim record here, on its own merits. Unlikely as it may seem, I had now actually groped my way to the root of the matter at last. All I wanted was a hint to guide me in the right direction at starting. Before another day had passed over my head, that hint was given me by one of the company who had been present at the birthday feast!

With the plan of proceeding which I now had in view, it was first necessary to possess the complete list of the guests. This I could easily obtain from Gabriel Betteredge. I determined to go back to Yorkshire on that day, and to begin my contemplated investigation the next morning.

It was just too late to start by the train which left London before noon. There was no alternative but to wait, nearly three hours, for the departure of the next train. Was there anything I could do in London, which might usefully occupy this interval of time?

My thoughts went back again obstinately to the birthday dinner.

Though I had forgotten the numbers, and, in many cases, the names of the guests, I remembered readily enough that by far the larger proportion of them came from Frizinghall, or from its neighbourhood. But the larger proportion was not all. Some few of us were not regular residents in the county. I myself was one of the few. Mr Murthwaite was another. Godfrey Ablewhite was a third. Mr Bruff – no: I called to mind that business had prevented Mr Bruff from making one of the party. Had any ladies been present, whose usual residence was in London? I could only remember Miss Clack as coming within this latter category. However, here were three of the guests, at any rate, whom it was clearly advisable for me to see before I left town. I drove off at once to Mr Bruff's office; not knowing the addresses of the persons of whom I was in search, and thinking it probable that he might put me in the way of finding them.

Mr Bruff proved to be too busy to give me more than a minute of his valuable time. In that minute, however, he contrived to dispose – in the most discouraging manner – of all the questions I had to put to him.

In the first place, he considered my newly-discovered method of finding a clue to the mystery as something too purely fanciful to be seriously discussed. In the second, third, and fourth places, Mr Murthwaite was now on his way back to the scene of his past adventures; Miss Clack had suffered losses, and had settled, from motives of economy, in France; Mr Godfrey Ablewhite might, or might not, be discoverable somewhere in London. Suppose I inquired at his club? And suppose I excused Mr Bruff, if he went back to his business and wished me good morning?

The field of inquiry in London, being now so narrowed as only to include the one necessity of discovering Godfrey's address, I took the lawyer's hint, and drove to his club.

In the hall, I met with one of the members, who was an old friend of my cousin's, and who was also an acquaintance of my own. This gentleman, after enlightening me on the subject of Godfrey's address, told me of two recent events in his life, which were of some importance in themselves, and which had not previously reached my ears.

It appeared that Godfrey, far from being discouraged by Rachel's withdrawal from her engagement to him, had made matrimonial advances soon afterwards to another young lady, reputed to be a great heiress. His suit had prospered, and his marriage had been considered as a settled and certain thing. But, here again, the engagement had been suddenly and unexpectedly broken off – owing, it was said, on this occasion, to a serious difference of opinion between the bridegroom and the lady's father, on the question of settlements.

As some compensation for this second matrimonial disaster, Godfrey had soon afterwards found himself the object of fond pecuniary remembrance, on the part of one of his many admirers. A rich old lady – highly respected at the Mothers' Small-Clothes-Conversion-Society, and a great friend of Miss Clack's (to whom she had left nothing but a mourning ring) – had bequeathed to the admirable and meritorious Godfrey a legacy of five thousand pounds. After receiving this handsome addition to his own modest pecuniary resources, he had been heard to say that he felt the necessity of getting a little respite from his charitable labours, and that his doctor prescribed 'a run on the Continent, as likely to be productive of much future benefit to his health'. If I wanted to see him, it would be advisable to lose no time in paying my contemplated visit.

I went, then and there, to pay my visit.

The same fatality which had made me just one day too late in calling on Sergeant Cuff, made me again one day too late in calling on Godfrey. He had left London, on the previous morning, by the tidal train, for Dover. He was to cross to Ostend; and his servant believed he was going on to Brussels. The time of his return was rather uncertain; but I might be sure he would be away at least three months.

I went back to my lodgings a little depressed in spirits. Three of the guests at the birthday dinner – and those three all exceptionally intelligent people – were out of my reach, at the very time when it was most important to be able to communicate with them. My last hopes now rested on Betteredge, and on the friends of the late Lady Verinder whom I might still find living in the neighbourhood of Rachel's country house.

On this occasion, I travelled straight to Frizinghall – the town being now the central point in my field of inquiry. I arrived too late in the evening to be able to communicate with Betteredge. The next morning, I sent a messenger with a letter, requesting him to join me at the hotel, at his earliest convenience.

Having taken the precaution – partly to save time, partly to accommodate Betteredge – of sending my messenger in a fly, I had a reasonable prospect, if no delays occurred, of seeing the old man within less than two hours from the time when I had sent for him. During this interval, I arranged to employ myself in opening my contemplated inquiry, among the guests present at the birthday dinner who were personally known to me, and who were easily within my reach. These were my relatives, the Ablewhites, and Mr Candy. The doctor had expressed a special wish to see me, and the doctor lived in the next street. So to Mr Candy I went first.

After what Betteredge had told me, I naturally anticipated finding traces in the doctor's face of the severe illness from which he had suffered. But I was utterly unprepared for such a change as I saw in him when he entered the room and shook hands with me. His eyes were dim; his hair had turned completely grey; his face was wizen; his figure had shrunk. I looked at the once lively, rattlepated, humorous little doctor – associated in my remembrance with the perpetration of incorrigible social indiscretions and innumerable boyish jokes – and I saw nothing left of his former self, but the old tendency to vulgar smartness in his dress. The man was a wreck; but his clothes and his jewellery – in cruel mockery of the change in him – were as gay and as gaudy as ever.

'I have often thought of you, Mr Blake,' he said; 'and I am heartily glad to see you again at last. If there is anything I can do for you, pray command my services, sir – pray command my services!'

He said those few commonplace words with needless hurry and eagerness, and with a curiosity to know what had brought me to Yorkshire, which he was perfectly – I might say childishly – incapable of concealing from notice.

With the object that I had in view, I had of course foreseen the necessity of entering into some sort of personal explanation, before I could hope to interest people, mostly strangers to me, in doing their best to assist my inquiry. On the journey to Frizinghall I had arranged what my explanation was to be – and I seized the opportunity now offered to me of trying the effect of it on Mr Candy.

'I was in Yorkshire, the other day, and I am in Yorkshire again now, on rather a romantic errand,' I said. 'It is a matter, Mr Candy, in which the late Lady Verinder's friends all took some interest. You remember the mysterious loss of the Indian Diamond, now nearly a year since? Circumstances have lately happened which lead to the hope that it may yet be found – and I am interesting myself, as one of the family, in recovering it. Among the obstacles in my way, there is the necessity of collecting again all the evidence which was discovered at the time, and more if possible. There are peculiarities in this case which make it desirable to revive my recollection of everything that happened in the house, on the evening of Miss Verinder's birthday. And I venture to appeal to her late mother's friends who were present on that occasion, to lend me the assistance of their memories—'

I had got as far as that in rehearsing my explanatory phrases, when I was suddenly checked by seeing plainly in Mr Candy's face that my experiment on him was a total failure.

The little doctor sat restlessly picking at the points of his fingers all the time I was speaking. His dim watery eyes were fixed on my face with an expression of vacant and wistful inquiry very painful to see. What he was thinking of, it was impossible to divine. The one thing clearly visible was that I had failed, after the first two or three words, in fixing his attention. The only chance of recalling him to himself appeared to lie in changing the subject. I tried a new topic immediately.

'So much,' I said, gaily, 'for what brings me to Frizinghall! Now, Mr Candy, it's your turn. You sent me a message by Gabriel Betteredge—'

He left off picking at his fingers, and suddenly brightened up.

'Yes! yes! yes!' he exclaimed eagerly. 'That's it! I sent you a message!'

'And Betteredge duly communicated it by letter,' I went on. 'You had something to say to me, the next time I was in your neighbourhood. Well, Mr Candy, here I am!'

'Here you are!' echoed the doctor. 'And Betteredge was quite right. I had something to say to you. That was my message. Betteredge is a wonderful man. What a memory! At his age, what a memory!'

He dropped back into silence, and began picking at his fingers again. Recollecting what I had heard from Betteredge about the effect of the fever on his memory, I went on with the conversation, in the hope that I might help him at starting.

'It's a long time since we met,' I said. 'We last saw each other at the last birthday dinner my poor aunt was ever to give.'

'That's it!' cried Mr Candy. 'The birthday dinner!' He started impulsively to his feet, and looked at me. A deep flush suddenly overspread his faded face, and he abruptly sat down again, as if conscious of having betrayed a weakness which he would fain have concealed. It was plain, pitiably plain, that he was aware of his own defect of memory, and that he was bent on hiding it from the observation of his friends.

Thus far, he had appealed to my compassion only. But the words he had just said – few as they were – roused my curiosity instantly to the highest pitch. The birthday dinner had already become the one event in the past, at which I looked back with strangely mixed feelings of hope and distrust. And here was the birthday dinner unmistakably proclaiming itself as the subject on which Mr Candy had something important to say to me!

I attempted to help him out once more. But, this time, my own interests were at the bottom of my compassionate motive, and they hurried me on a little too abruptly to the end I had in view.

'It's nearly a year now,' I said, 'since we sat at that pleasant table. Have you made any memorandum – in your diary, or otherwise – of what you wanted to say to me?'

Mr Candy understood the suggestion, and showed me that he understood it, as an insult.

'I require no memorandums, Mr Blake,' he said, stiffly enough. 'I am not such a very old man, yet – and my memory (thank God) is to be thoroughly depended on!'

It is needless to say that I declined to understand that he was offended with me.

'I wish I could say the same of *my* memory,' I answered. 'When *I try* to think of matters that are a year old, I seldom find my remembrance as vivid as I could wish it to be. Take the dinner at Lady Verinder's, for instance—'

Mr Candy brightened up again, the moment the allusion passed my lips.

'Ah! the dinner, the dinner at Lady Verinder's!' he exclaimed, more eagerly than ever. 'I have got something to say to you about that.'

His eyes looked at me again with the painful expression of inquiry, so wistful, so vacant, so miserably helpless to see. He was evidently trying hard, and trying in vain, to recover the lost recollection. 'It was a very pleasant dinner,' he burst out suddenly, with an air of saying exactly what he wanted to say. 'A very pleasant dinner, Mr Blake, wasn't it?' He nodded and smiled, and appeared to think, poor fellow, that he had succeeded in concealing the total failure of his memory, by a well-timed exertion of his own presence of mind.

It was so distressing that I at once shifted the talk – deeply as I was interested in his recovering the lost remembrance – to topics of local interest.

Here, he got on glibly enough. Trumpery little scandals and quarrels in the town, some of them as much as a month old, appeared to recur to his memory readily. He chattered on, with something of the smooth gossiping fluency of former times. But there were moments, even in the full flow of his talkativeness, when he suddenly hesitated – looked at me for a moment with the vacant inquiry once more in his eyes – controlled himself – and went on again. I submitted patiently to my martyrdom (it is surely nothing less than martyrdom to a man of cosmopolitan sympathies, to absorb in silent resignation the news of a country town?) until the clock on the chimney-piece told me that my visit had been prolonged beyond half an hour. Having now some right to consider the sacrifice as complete, I rose to take leave. As we shook hands, Mr Candy reverted to the birthday festival of his own accord.

'I am so glad we have met again,' he said. 'I had it on my mind – I really had it on my mind, Mr Blake, to speak to you. About the dinner at Lady Verinder's, you know! A pleasant dinner – really a pleasant dinner now, wasn't it?'

On repeating the phrase, he seemed to feel hardly as certain of having prevented me from suspecting his lapse of memory, as he had felt on the frrst occasion. The wistful look clouded his face again; and, after apparently designing to accompany me to the street door, he suddenly changed his mind, rang the bell for the servant, and remained in the drawing-room.

I went slowly down the doctor's stairs, feeling the disheartening conviction that he really had something to say which it was vitally important to me to hear, and that he was morally incapable of saying it. The effort of remembering that he wanted to speak to me was, but too evidently, the only effort that his enfeebled memory was now able to achieve.

Just as I had reached the bottom of the stairs, and had turned a corner on my way to the outer hall, a door opened softly somewhere on the ground floor of the house, and a gentle voice said behind me:

'I am afraid, sir, you find Mr Candy sadly changed?'

I turned round, and found myself face to face with Ezra Jennings.

◆ NINE ◆

THE DOCTOR'S PRETTY HOUSEMAID STOOD waiting for me, with the street-door open in her hand. Pouring brightly into the hall, the morning light fell full on the face of Mr Candy's assistant when I turned, and looked at him.

It was impossible to dispute Betteredge's assertion that the appearance of Ezra Jennings, speaking from the popular point of view, was against him. His gipsy-complexion, his fleshless cheeks, his gaunt facial bones, his dreamy eyes, his extraordinary parti-coloured hair, the puzzling contradiction between his face and figure which made him look old and young both together – were all more or less calculated to produce an unfavourable impression of him on a stranger's mind. And yet – feeling this as I certainly did – it is not to be denied that Ezra Jennings made some inscrutable appeal to my sympathies, which I found it impossible to resist. While my knowledge of the world warned me to answer the question which he had put, acknowledging that I did indeed find Mr Candy sadly changed, and then to proceed on my way out of the house – my interest in Ezra Jennings held me rooted to the place, and gave him the opportunity of speaking to me in private about his employer, for which he had been evidently on the watch.

'Are you walking my way, Mr Jennings?' I said, observing that he held his hat in his hand. 'I am going to call on my aunt, Mrs Ablewhite.'

Ezra Jennings replied that he had a patient to see, and that he was walking my way.

We left the house together. I observed that the pretty servant girl – who was all smiles and amiability, when I wished her good morning on my way out – received a modest little message from Ezra Jennings, relating to the time at which he might be expected to return, with pursed-up lips, and with eyes which ostentatiously looked anywhere rather than look in his face. The poor wretch was evidently no favourite in the house. Out of the house, I had Betteredge's word for it that he was unpopular everywhere. 'What a life!' I thought to myself, as we descended the doctor's doorsteps.

Having already referred to Mr Candy's illness on his side. Ezra Jennings now appeared determined to leave it to me to resume the subject. His silence said significantly, 'It's your turn now.' I, too, had my reasons for referring to the doctor's illness; and I readily accepted the responsibility of speaking first.

'Judging by the change I see in him,' I began, 'Mr Candy's illness must have been far more serious than I had supposed.'

'It is almost a miracle,' said Ezra Jennings, 'that he lived through it.'

'Is his memory never any better than I have found it to-day? He has been trying to speak to me—'

'Of something which happened before he was taken ill?' asked the assistant, observing that I hesitated.

'Yes.'

'His memory of events, at that past time, is hopelessly enfeebled,' said Ezra Jennings. 'It is almost to be deplored, poor fellow, that even the wreck of it remains. While he remembers dimly plans that he formed – things, here and there, that he had to say or do, before his illness – he is perfectly incapable of recalling what the plans were, or what the thing was that he had to say or do. He is painfully conscious of his own deficiency, and painfully anxious, as you must have seen, to hide it from observation. If he could only have recovered in a complete state of oblivion as to the past, he would have been a happier man. Perhaps we should all be happier,' he added, with a sad smile, 'if we could but completely forget!'

'There are some events surely in all men's lives,' I replied, 'the memory of which they would be unwilling entirely to lose?'

'That is, I hope, to be said of most men, Mr Blake. I am afraid it cannot truly be said of *all*. Have you any reason to suppose that the lost remembrance which Mr Candy tried to recover – while you were speaking to him just now – was a remembrance which it was important to *you* that he should recall?'

In saying those words, he had touched, of his own accord, on the very point upon which I was anxious to consult him. The interest I felt in this strange man had impelled me, in the first instance, to give him the opportunity of speaking to me; reserving what I might have to say, on my side, in relation to his employer, until I was first satisfied that he was a person in whose delicacy and discretion I could trust. The little that he had said, thus far, had been sufficient to convince me that I was speaking to a gentleman. He had what I may venture to describe as the *unsought self-possession*, which is a sure sign of good breeding, not in England only, but everywhere else in the civilized world. Whatever the object which he had in view, in putting the question that he had just addressed to me, I felt no doubt that I was justified – so far – in answering him without reserve.

'I believe, I have a strong interest,' I said, 'in tracing the lost remembrance which Mr Candy was unable to recall. May I ask whether you can suggest to me any method by which I might assist his memory?'

Ezra Jennings looked at me, with a sudden flash of interest in his dreamy brown eyes.

'Mr Candy's memory is beyond the reach of assistance,' he said. 'I have tried to help it often enough, since his recovery, to be able to speak positively on that point.'

This disappointed me; and I owned it.

'I confess you led me to hope for a less discouraging answer than that,' I said.

Ezra Jennings smiled. 'It may not, perhaps, be a final answer, Mr Blake. It may be possible to trace Mr Candy's lost recollection, without the necessity of appealing to Mr Candy himself.'

'Indeed? Is it an indiscretion, on my part, to ask: how?'

'By no means. My only difficulty in answering your question, is the difficulty of explaining myself. May I trust to your patience, if I refer once more to Mr Candy's illness: and if I speak of it this time, without sparing you certain professional details?'

'Pray go on! You have interested me already in hearing the details.'

My eagerness seemed to amuse – perhaps, I might rather say, to please him. He smiled again. We had by this time left the last houses in the town behind us. Ezra Jennings stopped for a moment, and picked some wild flowers from the hedge by the roadside. 'How beautiful they are!' he said, simply, showing his little nose-gay to me. 'And how few people in England seem to admire them as they deserve!'

'You have not always been in England?' I said.

'No. I was born, and partly brought up, in one of our colonies. My father was an Englishman; but my mother – We are straying away from our subject, Mr Blake; and it is my fault. The truth is, I have associations with these modest little hedgeside flowers – It doesn't matter; we were speaking of Mr Candy. To Mr Candy let us return.'

Connecting the few words about himself which thus reluctantly escaped him, with the melancholy view of life which led him to place the conditions of human happiness in complete oblivion of the past, I felt satisfied that the story which I had read in his face was, in two particulars at least, the story that it really told. He had suffered as few men suffer; and there was the mixture of some foreign race in his English blood.

'You have heard, I dare say, of the original cause of Mr Candy's illness?' be resumed. 'The night of Lady Verinder's dinner-party was a night of heavy rain. My employer drove home through it in his gig, and reached the house, wetted to the skin. He found an urgent message from a patient, waiting for him; and he most unfortunately went at once to visit the sick person, without stopping to change his clothes. I was myself professionally detained, that night, by a case at some distance from Frizinghall. When I got back the next morning, I found Mr Candy's groom waiting in great alarm to take me to his master's room. By that time the mischief was done; the illness had set in.'

'The illness has only been described to me, in general terms, as a fever,' I said.

'I can add nothing which will make the description more accurate,' answered Ezra Jennings. 'From first to last the fever assumed no specific form. I sent at once to two of Mr Candy's medical friends in the town, both physicians, to come and give me their opinion of the case. They agreed with me that it looked serious; but they both strongly dissented from the view I took of the treatment. We differed entirely in the conclusions which we drew from the patient's pulse. The two doctors, arguing from the rapidity of the beat, declared that a lowering treatment was the only treatment to be adopted. On my side, I admitted the rapidity of the pulse, but I also pointed to its alarming feebleness as indicating an exhausted condition of the system, and as showing a plain necessity for the administration of stimulants. The two doctors were for keeping him on gruel, lemonade, barley-water, and so on. I was for giving him champagne, or brandy, ammonia, and quinine. A serious difference of opinion, as you see! – a difference between two physicians of established local repute, and a stranger who was only an assistant in the house. For the first few days, I had no choice but to give way to my elders and betters; the patient steadily sinking all the time. I made a second attempt to appeal to the plain, undeniably plain, evidence of the pulse. Its rapidity was unchecked, and its feebleness had increased. The two doctors took offence at my obstinacy. They said, "Mr Jennings, either we manage this case, or you manage it. Which is it to be?" I said, "Gentlemen, give me five minutes to consider, and that plain question shall have a plain reply." When the time expired, I was ready with my answer. I said. "You positively refuse to try the stimulant treatment?" They refused in so many words. "I mean to try it at once, gentlemen." – "Try it, Mr Jennings; and we withdraw from the case." I sent down to the cellar for a bottle of champagne; and I administered half a tumbler-full of it to the patient with my own hand. The two physicians took up their hats in silence, and left the house.'

'You had assumed a serious responsibility,' I said. 'In your place, I am afraid I should have shrunk from it.'

'In my place, Mr Blake, you would have remembered that Mr Candy had taken you into his employment, under circumstances which made you his debtor for life. In my place, you would have seen him sinking, hour by hour; and you would have risked anything, rather than let the one man on earth who had befriended you, die before your eyes. Don't suppose that I had no sense of the terrible position in which I had placed myself! There were moments when I felt all the misery of my friendlessness, all the peril of my dreadful responsibility. If I had been a happy man, if I had led a prosperous life, I believe I should have sunk under the task I had imposed on myself. But I had no happy time to look back at, no past peace of mind to force itself into contrast with my present anxiety and suspense – and I held firm to my resolution through it all. I took an interval in the middle of the day, when my patient's condition was at its best, for the repose I needed. For the rest of the four-and-twenty hours, as long as his life was in danger, I never left his bedside. Towards sunset, as usual in such cases, the delirium incidental to the fever came on. It lasted more or less through the night; and then intermitted, at that terrible time in the early morning – from two o'clock to five – when the vital energies even of the healthiest of us are at their lowest. It is then that Death gathers in his human harvest most abundantly. It was then that Death and I fought our fight over the bed, which should have the man who lay on it. I never hesitated in pursuing the treatment on which I had staked everything. When wine failed, I tried brandy. When the other stimulants lost their influence, I doubled the dose. After an interval of suspense – the like of which I hope to God I shall never feel again – there came a day when the rapidity of the pulse slightly, but appreciably, diminished; and, better still, there came also a change in the beat – an unmistakable change to steadiness and strength. *Then*, I knew that I had saved him; and then I own I broke down. I laid the poor fellow's wasted hand back on the bed, and burst out crying. An hysterical relief, Mr Blake – nothing more! Physiology says, and says truly, that some men are born with female constitutions – and I am one of them!'

He made that bitterly professional apology for his tears, speaking quietly and unaffectedly, as he had spoken throughout. His tone and manner, from beginning to end, showed him to be especially, almost morbidly, anxious not to set himself up as an object of interest to me.

'You may well ask why I have wearied you with all these details,' he went on. 'It is the only way I can see, Mr Blake, of properly introducing to you what I have to say next. Now you know exactly what my position was, at the time of Mr Candy's illness, you will the more readily understand the sore need I had of lightening the burden on my mind by giving it, at intervals, some sort of relief. I have had the presumption to occupy my leisure, for some years past, in writing a book, addressed to the members of my profession – a book on the intricate and delicate subject of the brain and the nervous system. My work will probably never be finished; and it will certainly never be published. It has none the less been the friend of many lonely hours; and it helped me to while away the anxious time – the time of waiting, and nothing else – at Mr Candy's bedside. I told you he was delirious, I think? And I mentioned the time at which his delirium came on?'

'Yes.'

'Well, I had reached a section of my book, at that time, which touched on this same question of delirium. I won't trouble you at any length with my theory on the subject – I will confine myself to telling you only what it is your present interest to know. It has often occurred to me in the course of my medical practice, to doubt whether we can justifiably infer – in cases of delirium – that the loss of the faculty of speaking connectedly, implies of necessity the loss of the faculty of thinking connectedly as well. Poor Mr Candy's illness gave me an opportunity of putting this doubt to the test. I understand the art of writing in shorthand; and I was able to take down the patient's "wanderings", exactly as they fell from his lips. – Do you see, Mr Blake, what I am coming to at last?'

I saw it clearly, and waited with breathless interest to hear more.

'At odds and ends of time,' Ezra Jennings went on, 'I reproduced my shorthand notes, in the ordinary form of writing – leaving large spaces between the broken phrases, and even the single words, as they had fallen disconnectedly from Mr Candy's lips. I then treated the result thus obtained, on something like the principle which one adopts in putting together a child's "puzzle". It is all confusion to begin with; but it may be all brought into order and shape, if you can only find the right way. Acting on this plan, I filled in each blank space on the paper, with what the words or phrases on either side of it suggested to me as the speaker's meaning; altering over and over again, until my additions followed naturally on the spoken words which came before them, and fitted naturally into the spoken words which came after them. The result was, that I not only occupied in this way many vacant and anxious hours, but that I arrived at something which was (as it seemed to me) a confirmation of the theory that I held. In plainer words, after putting the broken sentences together I found the superior faculty of thinking going on, more or less connectedly, in my patient's mind, while the inferior faculty of expression was in a state of almost complete incapacity and confusion.'

'One word!' I interposed, eagerly. 'Did my name occur in any of his wanderings?'

'You shall hear, Mr Blake. Among my written proofs of the assertion which I have just advanced – or, I ought to say, among the written experiments, tending to put my assertion to the proof – there *is* one, in which your name occurs. For nearly the whole of one night, Mr Candy's mind was occupied with *something* between himself and you. I have got the broken words, as they dropped from his lips, on one sheet of paper. And I have got the links of my own discovering which connect those words together, on another sheet of paper. The product (as the arithmeticians would say) is an intelligible statement – first, of something actually done in the past; secondly, of something which Mr Candy contemplated doing in the future, if his illness had not got in the way, and stopped him. The question is whether this does, or does not, represent the lost recollection which he vainly attempted to find when you called on him this morning?'

'Not a doubt of it!' I answered. 'Let us go back directly, and look at the papers!'

'Quite impossible, Mr Blake.'

'Why?'

'Put yourself in my position for a moment,' said Ezra Jennings. 'Would *you* disclose to another person what had dropped unconsciously from the lips of your suffering patient and your helpless friend, without first knowing that there was a necessity to justify you in opening your lips?

I felt that he was unanswerable, here; but I tried to argue the question, nevertheless.

'My conduct in such a delicate matter as you describe,' I replied, 'would depend greatly on whether the disclosure was of a nature to compromise my friend, or not.'

'I have disposed of all necessity for considering that side of the question, long since,' said Ezra Jennings. 'Wherever my notes included anything which Mr Candy might have wished to keep secret, those notes have been destroyed. My manuscript-experiments at my friend's bedside, include nothing, now, which he would have hesitated to communicate to others, if he had recovered the use of his memory. In your case, I have every reason to suppose that my notes contain something which he actually wished to say to you—'

'And yet, you hesitate?'

'And yet, I hesitate. Remember the circumstances, under which I obtained the information which I possess! Harmless as it is, I cannot prevail upon myself to give it up to you, unless you first satisfy me that there is a reason for doing so. He was so miserably ill, Mr Blake! and he was so helplessly dependent upon Me! Is it too much to ask, if I request you only to hint to me what your interest is in the lost recollection – or what you believe that lost recollection to be?'

To have answered him with the frankness which his language and his manner both claimed from me, would have been to commit myself to openly acknowledging that I was suspected of the theft of the Diamond. Strongly as Ezra Jennings had intensified the first impulsive interest which I had felt in him, he had not overcome my unconquerable reluctance to disclose the degrading position in which I stood. I took refuge once more in the explanatory phrases with which I had prepared myself to meet the curiosity of strangers.

This time, I had no reason to complain of a want of attention on the part of the person to whom I addressed myself. Ezra Jennings listened patiently, even anxiously, until I had done.

'I am sorry to have raised your expectations, Mr Blake, only to disappoint them,' he said. 'Throughout the whole period of Mr Candy's illness, from first to last, not one word about the Diamond escaped his lips. The matter with which I heard him connect your name has, I can assure you, no discoverable relation whatever with the loss or the recovery of Miss Verinder's jewel.'

We arrived, as he said those words, at a place where the highway along which we had been walking, branched off into two roads. One led to Mr Ablewhite's house; and the other to a moorland village some two or three miles off. Ezra Jennings stopped at the road which led to the village.

'My way lies in this direction,' he said. 'I am really and truly sorry, Mr Blake, that I can be of no use to you.'

His voice told me that he spoke sincerely. His soft brown eyes rested on me for a moment with a look of melancholy interest. He bowed, and went, without another word, on his way to the village.

For a minute or more, I stood and watched him, walking farther and farther away from me; carrying farther and farther away with him what I now firmly believed to be the clue of which I was in search. He turned, after walking on a little way, and looked back. Seeing me still standing at the place where we had parted, he stopped, as if doubting whether I might not wish to speak to him again. There was no time for me to reason out my own situation – to remind myself that I was losing my opportunity, at what might be the turning-point of my life, and all to flatter nothing more important than my own self-esteem! There was only time to call him back first, and to think afterwards. I suspect I am one of the rashest of existing men. I called him back – and then I said to myself, 'Now there is no help for it. I must tell him the truth!'

He retraced his steps directly. I advanced along the road to meet him.

'Mr Jennings,' I said, 'I have not treated you quite fairly. My interest in tracing Mr Candy's lost recollection, is not the interest of recovering the Moonstone. A serious personal matter is at the bottom of my visit to Yorkshire. I have but one excuse for not having dealt frankly with you in this matter. It is more painful to me than I can say, to mention to anybody what my position really is.'

Ezra Jennings looked at me with the first appearance of embarrassment which I had seen in him yet.

'I have no right, Mr Blake, and no wish,' he said, 'to intrude myself into your private affairs. Allow me to ask your pardon, on my side, for having (most innocently) put you to a painful test.'

'You have a perfect right,' I rejoined, 'to fix the terms on which you feel justified in revealing what you heard at Mr Candy's bedside. I understand, and respect, the delicacy which influences you in this matter. How can I expect to be taken into your confidence, if I decline to admit you into mine? You ought to know, and you shall know, why I am interested in discovering what Mr Candy wanted to say to me. If I turn out to be mistaken in my anticipations, and if you prove unable to help me when you are really aware of what I want, I shall trust to your honour to keep my secret – and something tells me that I shall not trust in vain.'

'Stop, Mr Blake. I have a word to say, which must be said before you go any farther.' I looked at him in astonishment. The grip of some terrible emotion seemed to have seized him, and shaken him to the soul. His gipsy complexion had altered to a livid greyish paleness; his eyes had suddenly become wild and glittering; his voice had dropped to a tone – low, stern, and resolute – which I now heard for the first time. The latent resources in the man, for good or for evil – it was hard, at that moment, to say which – leapt up in him and showed themselves to me, with the suddenness of a flash of light.

'Before you place any confidence in me,' he went on, 'you ought to know, and you *must* know, under what circumstances I have been received into Mr Candy's house. It won't take long. I don't profess, sir, to tell my story (as the phrase is) to any man. My story will die with me. All I ask, is to be permitted to tell you, what I have told Mr Candy. If you are still in the mind, when you have heard that, to say what you have proposed to say, you will command my attention, and command my services. Shall we walk on?'

The suppressed misery in his face silenced me. I answered his question by a sign. We walked on.

After advancing a few hundred yards, Ezra Jennings stopped at a gap in the rough stone wall which shut off the moor from the road, at this part of it.

'Do you mind resting a little, Mr Blake?' he asked. 'I am not what I was – and some things shake me.'

I agreed of course. He led the way through the gap to a patch of turf on the heathy ground, screened by bushes and dwarf trees on the side nearest to the road, and commanding in the opposite direction a grandly desolate view over the broad brown wilderness of the moor. The clouds had gathered, within the last half-hour. The light was dull; the distance was dim. The lovely face of Nature met us, soft and still and colourless – met us without a smile.

We sat down in silence. Ezra Jennings laid aside his hat, and passed his hand wearily over his forehead, wearily through his startling white and black hair. He tossed his little nosegay of wild flowers away from him, as if the remembrances which it recalled were remembrances which hurt him now.

'Mr Blake!' he said, suddenly. 'You are in bad company. The cloud of a horrible accusation has rested on me for years. I tell you the worst at once. I am a man whose life is a wreck, and whose character is gone.'

I attempted to speak. He stopped me.

'No,' he said. 'Pardon me; not yet. Don't commit yourself to expressions of sympathy which you may afterwards wish to recall. I have mentioned an accusation which has rested on me for years. There are circumstances in connexion with it that tell against me. I cannot bring myself to acknowledge what the accusation is. And I am incapable, perfectly incapable, of proving my innocence. I can only assert my innocence. I assert it, sir, on my oath, as a Christian. It is useless to appeal to my honour as a man.'

He paused again. I looked round at him. He never looked at me in return. His whole being seemed to be absorbed in the agony of recollecting, and in the effort to speak.

'There is much that I might say,' he went on, 'about the merciless treatment of me by my own family, and the merciless enmity to which I have fallen a victim. But the harm is done; the wrong is beyond all remedy. I decline to weary or distress you, sir, if I can help it. At the outset of my career in this country, the vile slander to which I have referred struck me down at once and for ever. I resigned my aspirations in my profession – obscurity was the only hope left for me. I parted with the woman I loved – how could I condemn her to share my disgrace? A medical assistant's place offered itself, in a remote corner of England. I got the place. It promised me peace; it promised me obscurity, as I thought. I was wrong. Evil report, with time and chance to help it, travels patiently, and travels far. The accusation from which I had fled, followed me. I got warning of its approach. I was able to leave my situation voluntarily, with the testimonials that I had earned. They got me another situation in another remote district. Time passed again; and again the slander that was death to my character found me out. On this occasion I had no warning. My employer said, "Mr Jennings, I have no complaint to make against you; but you must set yourself right, or leave me." I had but one choice – I left him. It's useless to dwell on what I suffered after that. I am only forty years old now. Look at my face, and let it tell for me the story of some miserable years. It ended in my drifting to this place, and meeting with Mr Candy. He wanted an assistant. I referred him, on the question of capacity, to my last employer. The question of character remained. I told him what I have told you – and more. I warned him that there were difficulties in the way, even if he believed me. "Here, as elsewhere," I said, "I scorn the guilty evasion of living under an assumed name: I am no safer at Frizinghall than at other places from the cloud that follows me, go where I may." He answered, "I don't do things by halves – I believe you, and I pity you. If *you* will risk what may happen, *I* will risk it too." God Almighty bless him! He has given me shelter, he has given me employment, he has given me rest of mind – and I have the certain conviction (I have had it for some months past) that nothing will happen now to make him regret it.'

'The slander has died out?' I said.

'The slander is as active as ever. But when it follows me here, it will come too late.'

'You will have left the place?'

'No, Mr Blake – I shall be dead. For ten years past, I have suffered from an incurable internal complaint. I don't disguise from you that I should have let the agony of it kill me long since but for one last interest in life, which makes my existence of some importance to me still. I want to provide for a person – very dear to me – whom I shall never see again. My own little patrimony is hardly sufficient to make her independent of the world. The hope, if I could only live long enough, of increasing it to a certain sum, has impelled me to resist the disease by such palliative means as I could devise. The one effectual palliative in my case, is – opium. To that all-potent and all-merciful drug, I am indebted for a respite of many years from my sentence of death. But even the virtues of opium have their limit. The progress of the disease has gradually forced me from the use of opium, to the abuse of it. I am feeling the penalty at last. My nervous system is shattered; my nights are nights of horror. The end is not far off now. Let it come – I have not lived and worked in vain. The little sum is nearly made up; and I have the means of completing it, if my last reserves of life fail me sooner than I expect. I hardly know how I have wandered into telling you this. I don't think I am mean enough to appeal to your pity. Perhaps, I fancy you may be all the readier to believe me, if you know that what I have said to you, I have said with the certain knowledge in me that I am a dying man. There is no disguising, Mr Blake, that you interest me. I have attempted to make my poor friend's loss of memory the means of bettering my acquaintance with you. I have speculated on the chance of your feeling a passing curiosity about what he wanted to say, and of my being able to satisfy it. Is there no excuse for my intruding myself on you? Perhaps there is some excuse. A man who has lived as I have lived has his bitter moments when he ponders over human destiny. You have youth, health, riches, a place in the world, a prospect before you. You, and such as you, show me the sunny side of human life, and reconcile me with the world that I am leaving, before I go. However this talk between us may end, I shall not forget that you have done me a kindness in doing that. It rests with you, sir, to say what you proposed saying, or to wish me good morning.'

I had but one answer to make to that appeal. Without a moment's hesitation, I told him the truth, as unreservedly as I have told it in these pages.

He started to his feet, and looked at me with breathless eagerness as I approached the leading incident of my story.

'It is certain that I went into the room,' I said; 'it is certain that I took the Diamond. I can only meet those two plain facts by declaring that, do what I might, I did it without my own knowledge—'

Ezra Jennings caught me excitedly by the arm.

'Stop!' he said. 'You have suggested more to me than you suppose. Have *you* ever been accustomed to the use of opium?'

'I never tasted it in my life.'

'Were your nerves out of order, at this time last year? Were you unusually restless and irritable?'

'Yes.'

'Did you sleep badly?'

338

'Wretchedly. Many nights I never slept at all.'

'Was the birthday night an exception? Try, and remember. Did you sleep well on that one occasion?'

'I do remember! I slept soundly.'

He dropped my arm as suddenly as he had taken it – and looked at me with the air of a man whose mind was relieved of the last doubt that rested on it.

'This is a marked day in your life, and in mine,' he said, gravely. 'I am absolutely certain, Mr Blake, of one thing – I have got what Mr Candy wanted to say to you this morning, in the notes that I took at my patient's bedside. Wait! that is not all. I am firmly persuaded that I can prove you to have been unconscious of what you were about, when you entered the room and took the Diamond. Give me time to think, and time to question you. I believe the vindication of your innocence is in my hands!'

'Explain yourself, for God's sake! What do you mean?'

In the excitement of our colloquy, we had walked on a few steps, beyond the clump of dwarf trees which had hitherto screened us from view. Before Ezra Jennings could answer me, he was hailed from the high-road by a man, in great agitation, who had been evidently on the look-out for him.

'I am coming,' he called back; 'I am coming as fast as I can!' He turned to me. 'There is an urgent case waiting for me at the village yonder; I ought to have been there half an hour since – I must attend to it at once. Give me two hours from this time, and call at Mr Candy's again – and I will engage to be ready for you.'

'How am I to wait!' I exclaimed, impatiently. 'Can't you quiet my mind by a word of explanation before we part?'

'This is far too serious a matter to be explained in a hurry, Mr Blake. I am not wilfully trying your patience – I should only be adding to your suspense, if I attempted to relieve it as things are now. At Frizinghall, sir, in two hours' time!'

The man on the high-road hailed him again. He hurried away, and left me.

∂ TEN ∾

HOW THE INTERVAL OF SUSPENSE to which I was now condemned might have affected other men in my position, I cannot pretend to say. The influence of the two hours' probation upon *my* temperament, was simply this. I felt physically incapable of remaining still in any one place, and morally incapable of speaking to any one human being, until I had first heard all that Ezra Jennings had to say to me.

In this frame of mind, I not only abandoned my contemplated visit to Mrs Ablewhite – I even shrank from encountering Gabriel Betteredge himself.

Returning to Frizinghall, I left a note for Betteredge, telling him that I had been unexpectedly called away, for a few hours, but that he might certainly expect me to return towards 15.00 in the afternoon. I requested him, in the interval, to order his dinner at the usual hour, and to amuse himself as he pleased. He had, as I well knew, hosts of friends in Frizinghall; and he would be at no loss how to fill up his time until I returned to the hotel.

This done, I made the best of my way out of the town again, and roamed the lonely moorland country which surrounds Frizinghall, until my watch told me that it was time, at last, to return to Mr Candy's house.

I found Ezra Jennings, ready and waiting for me.

He was sitting alone in a bare little room, which communicated by a glazed door with a surgery. Hideous coloured diagrams of the ravages of hideous diseases, decorated the barren buff-coloured walls. A bookcase filled with dingy medical works, and ornamented at the top with a skull, in place of the customary bust; a large deal table copiously splashed with ink; wooden chairs of the sort that are seen in kitchens and cottages; a threadbare drugget in the middle of the floor; a sink of water, with a basin and waste-pipe roughly let into the wall, horribly suggestive of its connection with surgical operations – comprised the entire furniture of the room. The bees were humming among a few flowers placed in pots outside the window; the birds were singing in the garden, and the faint intermittent jingle of a tuneless piano in some neighbouring house, forced itself now and again, on the ear. In any other place, these everyday sounds might have spoken pleasantly of the everyday world outside.

Here, they came in as intruders on a silence which nothing but human suffering had the privilege to disturb. I looked at the mahogany instrument case, and at the huge roll of lint, occupying places of their own on the bookshelves, and shuddered inwardly as I thought of the sounds, familiar and appropriate to the everyday use of Ezra Jennings' room.

'I make no apology, Mr Blake, for the place in which I am receiving you,' he said. 'It is the only room in the house, at this hour of the day, in which we can feel quite sure of being left undisturbed. Here are my papers ready for you; and here are two books to which we may have occasion to refer, before we have done. Bring your chair to the table, and we shall be able to consult them together.'

I drew up to the table; and Ezra Jennings handed me his manuscript notes. They consisted of two large folio leaves of paper. One leaf contained writing which only covered the surface at intervals. The other presented writing, in red and black ink, which completely filled the page from top to bottom. In the irritated state of my curiosity, at that moment, I laid aside the second sheet of paper in despair.

'Have some mercy on me!' I said. 'Tell me what I am to expect, before I attempt to read this.'

'Willingly, Mr Blake! Do you mind my asking you one or two more questions?'

'Ask me anything you like!'

He looked at me with the sad smile on his lips, and the kindly interest in his soft brown eyes.

'You have already told me,' he said, 'that you have never – to your knowledge – tasted opium in your life.'

'To my knowledge,' I repeated.

'You will understand directly, why I speak with that reservation. Let us go on. You are not aware of ever having taken opium. At this time, last year, you were suffering from nervous irritation, and you slept wretchedly at night. On the night of the birthday, however, there was an exception to the rule – you slept soundly. Am I right, so far?'

'Quite right.'

'Can you assign any cause for the nervous suffering, and your want of sleep?'

'I can assign no cause. Old Betteredge made a guess at the cause, I remember. But that is hardly worth mentioning.'

'Pardon me. Anything is worth mentioning in such a case as this. Betteredge attributed your sleeplessness to something. To what?'

'To my leaving off smoking.'

'Had you been an habitual smoker?'

'Yes.'

'Did you leave off the habit suddenly?'

'Yes.'

'Betteredge was perfectly right, Mr Blake. When smoking is a habit, a man must have no common constitution who can leave it off suddenly without some temporary damage to his nervous system. Your sleepless nights are accounted for, to my mind. My next question refers to Mr Candy. Do you remember having entered into anything like a dispute with him – at the birthday dinner, or afterwards – on the subject of his profession?'

The question instantly awakened one of my dormant remembrances, in connection with the birthday festival. The foolish wrangle which took place, on that occasion, between Mr Candy and myself, will be found, described at much greater length than it deserves, in the tenth chapter of Betteredge's Narrative. The details there presented of the dispute – so little had I thought of it afterwards – entirely failed to recur to my memory. All that I could now recall, and all that I could tell Ezra Jennings was, that I had attacked the art of medicine at the dinner-table, with sufficient rashness and sufficient pertinacity to put even Mr Candy out of temper for the moment. I also remembered that Lady Verinder had interfered to stop the dispute, and that the little doctor and I had 'made it up again', as the children say, and had become as good friends as ever, before we shook hands that night.

'There is one thing more,' said Ezra Jennings, 'which it is very important I should know. Had you any reason for feeling any special anxiety about the Diamond, at this time last year?'

'I had the strongest reasons for feeling anxiety about the Diamond. I knew it to be the object of a conspiracy; and I was warned to take measures for Miss Verinder's protection, as the possessor of the stone.'

'Was the safety of the Diamond the subject of conversation between you and any other person, immediately before you retired to rest on the birthday night?'

'It was the subject of a conversation, between Lady Verinder and her daughter—'

'Which took place in your hearing?'

'Yes.'

Ezra Jennings took up his notes from the table, and placed them in my hands.

'Mr Blake,' he said, 'if you read those notes now, by the light which my questions and your answers have thrown on them, you will make two astounding discoveries, concerning yourself. You will find: – First, that, you entered Miss Verinder's sitting-room and took the Diamond, in a state of trance, produced by opium. Secondly, that the opium was given to you by Mr Candy – without your own knowledge – as a practical refutation of the opinions which you had expressed to him at the birthday dinner.'

I sat, with the papers in my hand, completely stupefied.

'Try, and forgive poor Mr Candy,' said the assistant gently. 'He has done dreadful mischief, I own; but he has done it innocently. If you will look at the notes, you will see that – but for his illness – he would have returned to Lady Verinder's the morning after the party, and would have acknowledged the trick that he had played you. Miss Verinder would have heard of it, and Miss Verinder would have questioned him – and the truth which has laid hidden for a year, would have been discovered in a day.'

I began to regain my self-possession. 'Mr Candy is beyond the reach of my resentment,' I said angrily. 'But the trick that he played me is not the less an act of treachery, for all that. I may forgive, but I shall not forget it.'

'Every medical man commits that act of treachery, Mr Blake, in the course of his practice. The ignorant distrust of opium (in England) is by no means confined to the lower and less cultivated classes. Every doctor in large practice finds himself, every now and then, obliged to deceive his patients, as Mr Candy deceived you. I don't defend the folly of playing you a trick under the circumstances. I only plead with you for a more accurate and more merciful construction of motives.'

'How was it done?' I asked. 'Who gave me the laudanum, without my knowing it myself?'

'I am not able to tell you. Nothing relating to that part of the matter dropped from Mr Candy's lips, all through his illness. Perhaps, your own memory may point to the person to be suspected?'

'No.'

'It is useless, in that case, to pursue the inquiry. The laudanum was secretly given to you in some way. Let us leave it there, and go on to matters of more immediate importance. Read my notes, if you can. Familiarize your mind with what has happened in the past. I have something very bold and very startling to propose to you, which relates to the future.'

Those last words roused me.

I looked at the papers, in the order in which Ezra Jennings had placed them in my hands. The paper which contained the smaller quantity of writing was the uppermost of the two. On this, the disconnected words, and fragments of sentences, which had dropped from Mr Candy in his delirium, appeared as follows:

' . . . Mr Franklin Blake . . . and agreeable . . . down a peg . . . medicine . . . confesses . . . sleep at night . . . tell him . . . out of order . . . medicine . . . he tells me . . . and groping in the dark mean one and the same thing . . . all the company at the dinner-table . . . I say . . . groping after sleep . . . nothing but medicine . . . he says . . . leading the blind . . . know what it means . . . witty . . . a night's rest in spite of his teeth . . . wants sleep . . . Lady Verinder's medicine chest . . . five-and-twenty minims . . . without his knowing it . . . to-morrow morning . . . Well, Mr Blake . . . medicine to-day . . . never . . . without it . . . out, Mr Candy . . . excellent . . . without it . . . down on him truth . . . something besides . . . excellent . . . dose of laudanum, sir . . . bed . . . what . . . medicine now.'

There, the first of the two sheets of paper came to an end. I handed it back to Ezra Jennings.

'That is what you heard at his bedside?' I said.

'Literally and exactly what I heard,' he answered – 'except that the repetitions are not transferred here from my short-hand notes. He reiterated certain words and phrases a dozen times over, fifty times over, just as he attached more or less importance to the idea which they represented. The repetitions, in this sense, were of some assistance to me in putting together those fragments. Don't suppose,' he added, pointing to the second sheet of paper, 'that I claim to have reproduced the expressions which Mr Candy himself would have used if he had been capable of speaking connectedly. I only say that I have penetrated through the obstacle of the disconnected expression, to the thought which was underlying it connectedly all the time. Judge for yourself.'

I turned to the second sheet of paper, which I now knew to be the key to the first.

Once more, Mr Candy's wanderings appeared, copied in black ink; the intervals between the phrases being filled up by Ezra Jennings in red ink. I reproduce the result here, in one plain form; the original language and the interpretation of it coming close enough together in these pages to be easily compared and verified.

' . . . Mr Franklin Blake is clever and agreeable, but he wants taking down a peg when he talks of medicine. He confesses that he has been suffering from want of sleep at night. I tell him that his nerves are out of order, and that he ought to take medicine. He tells me that taking medicine and groping in the dark mean one and the same thing. This before all the company at the dinner-table. I say to him, you are groping after sleep, and nothing but medicine can help you to find it. He says to me, I have heard of the blind leading the blind, and now I know what it means. Witty – but I can give him a night's rest in spite of his teeth. He really wants sleep; and Lady Verinder's medicine chest is at my disposal. Give him five-and-twenty minims of laudanum to-night, without his knowing it; and then call to-morrow morning. "Well, Mr Blake, will you try a little medicine to-day? You will never sleep without it." – "There you are out, Mr Candy: I have had an excellent night's rest without it." Then, come down on him with the truth! "You have had something besides an excellent night's rest; you had a dose of laudanum, sir, before you went to bed. What do you say to the art of medicine, now?" '

Admiration of the ingenuity which had woven this smooth and finished texture out of the ravelled skein, was naturally the first impression that I felt, on handing the manuscript back to Ezra Jennings. He modestly interrupted the first few words in which my sense of surprise expressed itself, by asking me if the conclusion which he had drawn from his notes was also the conclusion at which my own mind had arrived.

'Do you believe as I believe,' he said, 'that you were acting under the influence of the laudanum in doing all that you did, on the night of Miss Verinder's birthday, in Lady Verinder's house?'

'I am too ignorant of the influence of laudanum to have an opinion of my own,' I answered. 'I can only follow your opinion, and feel convinced that you are right.'

'Very well. The next question is this. You are convinced; and I am convinced – how are we to carry our conviction to the minds of other people?'

I pointed to the two manuscripts, lying on the table between us. Ezra Jennings shook his head.

'Useless, Mr Blake! Quite useless, as they stand now, for three unanswerable reasons. In the first place, those notes have been taken, under circumstances entirely out of the experience of the mass of mankind. Against them, to begin with! In the second place, those notes represent a medical and metaphysical theory. Against them, once more! In the third place, those notes are of *my* making; there is nothing but *my* assertion to the contrary, to guarantee that they are not fabrications. Remember what I told you on the moor – and ask yourself what my assertion is worth. No! my notes have but one value, looking to the verdict of the world outside. Your innocence is to be vindicated; and they show how it can be done. We must put our conviction to the proof – and You are the man to prove it?'

'How?' I asked.

He leaned eagerly nearer to me across the table that divided us. 'Are you willing to try a bold experiment?'

'I will do anything to clear myself of the suspicion that rests on me now.'

'Will you submit to some personal inconvenience for a time?'

'To any inconvenience, no matter what it may be.'

'Will you be guided implicitly by my advice? It may expose you to the ridicule of fools; it may subject you to the remonstrances of friends whose opinions you are bound to respect—'

'Tell me what to do!' I broke out impatiently. 'And, come what may, I'll do it.'

'You shall do this, Mr Blake,' he answered. 'You shall steal the Diamond, unconsciously, for the second time, in the presence of witnesses whose testimony is beyond dispute!'

I started to my feet. I tried to speak. I could only look at him. 'I believe it *can* be done,' he went on. 'And it *shall* be done – if you will only help me. Try to compose yourself – sit down, and hear what I have to say to you. You have resumed the habit of smoking; I have seen that for myself. How long have you resumed it?'

'For nearly a year.'

'Do you smoke more, or less, than you did?'

'More.'

'Will you give up the habit again? Suddenly, mind! – as you gave it up before.'

I began dimly to see his drift. 'I will give it up, from this moment,' I answered.

'If the same consequences follow, which followed last June,' said Ezra Jennings – 'if you suffer once more as you suffered then, from sleepless nights, we shall have gained our first step. We shall have put you back again into something assimilating to your nervous condition on the birthday night. If we can next revive, or nearly revive, the domestic circumstances which surrounded you; and if we can occupy your mind again with the various questions concerning the Diamond which formerly agitated it, we shall have replaced you, as nearly as possible, in the same position, physically and morally, in which the opium found you last year. In that case we may fairly hope that a repetition of the dose will lead, in a greater or lesser degree, to a repetition of the result. There is my proposal, expressed in a few hasty words. You shall now see what reasons I have to justify me in making it.'

He turned to one of the books at his side, and opened it at a place marked by a small slip of paper.

'Don't suppose that I am going to weary you with a lecture on physiology,' he said. 'I think myself bound to prove, in justice to both of us, that I am not asking you to try this experiment in deference to any theory of my own devising. Admitted principles, and recognized authorities, justify me in the view that I take. Give me five minutes of your attention; and I will undertake to show you that Science sanctions my proposal, fanciful as it may seem. Here, in the first place, is the physiological principle on which I am acting, stated by no less a person than Dr Carpenter. Read it for yourself.'

He handed me the slip of paper which had marked the place in the book. It contained a few lines of writing, as follows: –

'There seems much ground for the belief, that *every* sensory impression which has once been recognized by the perceptive consciousness, is registered (so to speak) in the brain, and may be reproduced at some subsequent time, although there may be no consciousness of its existence in the mind during the whole intermediate period.' 'Is that plain, so far?' asked Ezra Jennings.

'Perfectly plain.'

He pushed the open book across the table to me, and pointed to a passage, marked by pencil lines.

'Now,' he said, 'read that account of a case, which has – as I believe – a direct bearing on your own position, and on the experiment which I am tempting you to try. Observe, Mr Blake, before you begin, that I am now referring you to one of the greatest of English physiologists. The book in your hand is Doctor Elliotson's *Human Physiology*; and the case which the doctor cites, rests on the well-known authority of Mr Combe.'

The passage pointed out to me, was expressed in these terms: –

'Dr Abel informed me,' says Mr Combe, 'of an Irish porter to a warehouse, who forgot, when sober, what he had done when drunk; but, being drunk, again recollected the transactions of his former state of intoxication. On one occasion, being drunk, he had lost a parcel of some value, and in his sober moments could give no account of it. Next time he was intoxicated, he recollected that he had left the parcel at a certain house, and there being no address on it, it had remained there safely, and was got on his calling for it.'

'Plain again?' asked Ezra Jennings.

'As plain as need be.'

He put back the slip of paper in its place, and closed the book.

'Are you satisfied that I have not spoken without good authority to support me?' he asked. 'If not, I have only to go to those bookshelves, and you have only to read the passages which I can point out to you.'

'I am quite satisfied,' I said, 'without reading a word more.'

'In that case, we may return to your own personal interest in this matter. I am bound to tell you that there is something to be said against the experiment as well as for it. If we could, this year, exactly reproduce, in your case, the conditions as they existed last year, it is physiologically certain that we should arrive at exactly the same result. But this – there is no denying it – is simply impossible. We can only hope to approximate to the conditions; and if we don't succeed in getting you nearly enough back to what you were, this venture of ours will fail. If we do succeed – and I am myself hopeful of success – you may at least so far repeat your proceedings on the birthday night, as to satisfy any reasonable person that you are guiltless, morally speaking, of the theft of the Diamond. I believe, Mr Blake, I have now stated the question, on both sides of it, as fairly as I can, within the limits that I have imposed on myself. If there is anything that I have not made clear to you, tell me what it is – and if I can enlighten you, I will.'

'All that you have explained to me,' I said, 'I understand perfectly. But I own I am puzzled on one point, which you have not made clear to me yet.'

'What is the point?'

'I don't understand the effect of the laudanum on me. I don't understand my walking downstairs, and along corridors, and my opening and shutting the drawers of a cabinet, and my going back again to my own room. All these are active proceedings. I thought the influence of opium was first to stupefy you, and then to send you to sleep.'

'The common error about opium, Mr Blake! I am, at this moment, exerting my intelligence (such as it is) in your service, under the influence of a dose of laudanum, some ten times larger than the dose Mr Candy administered to you. But don't trust to my authority – even on a question which comes within my own personal experience. I anticipated the objection you have just made: and I have again provided myself with independent testimony, which will carry its due weight with it in your own mind, and in the minds of your friends.'

He handed me the second of the two books which he had by him on the table.

'There,' he said, 'are the far-famed *Confessions of an English Opium Eater*! Take the book away with you, and read it. At the passage which I have marked, you will find that when De Quincey had committed what he calls "a debauch of opium", he either went to the gallery at the Opera to enjoy the music, or he wandered about the London markets on Saturday night, and interested himself in observing all the little shifts and bargainings of the poor in providing their Sunday's dinner. So much for the capacity of a man to occupy himself actively, and to move about from place to place under the influence of opium.'

'I am answered so far,' I said; 'but I am not answered yet as to the effect produced by the opium on myself.'

'I will try to answer you in a few words,' said Ezra Jennings. 'The action of opium is comprised, in the majority of cases, in two influences – a stimulating influence first, and a sedative influence afterwards. Under the stimulating influence, the latest and most vivid impressions left on your mind – namely, the impressions relating to the Diamond – would be likely, in your morbidly sensitive nervous condition, to become intensified in your brain, and would subordinate to themselves your judgment and your will – exactly as an ordinary dream subordinates to itself your judgment and your will. Little by little, under this action, any apprehensions about the safety of the Diamond which you might have felt during the day, would be liable to develop themselves from the state of doubt to the state of certainty – would impel you into practical action to preserve the jewel – would direct your steps, with that motive in view, into the room which you entered – and would guide your hand to the drawers of the cabinet, until you had found the drawer which held the stone. In the spiritualized intoxication of opium, you would do all that. Later, as the sedative action began to gain on the stimulant action, you would slowly become inert and stupefied. Later still you would fall into a deep sleep. When the morning came, and the effect of the opium had been all slept off, you would wake as absolutely ignorant of what you had done in the night as if you had been living at the Antipodes. – Have I made it tolerably clear to you, so far?'

'You have made it so clear,' I said, 'that I want you to go farther. You have shown me how I entered the room, and how I came to take the Diamond. But Miss Verinder saw me leave the room again, with the jewel in my hand. Can you trace my proceedings from that moment? Can you guess what I did next?'

'That is the very point I was coming to,' he rejoined. 'It is a question with me whether the experiment which I propose as a means of vindicating your innocence, may not also be made a means of recovering the lost Diamond as well. When you left Miss Verinder's sitting-room, with the jewel in your hand, you went back in all probability to your own room—'

'Yes! – and what then?'

'It is possible, Mr Blake – I dare not say more – that your idea of preserving the Diamond led, by a natural sequence, to the idea of hiding the Diamond, and that the place in which you hid it was somewhere in your bedroom. In that event, the case of the Irish porter may be your case. You may remember, under the influence of the second dose of opium, the place in which you hid the Diamond under the influence of the first.'

It was my turn, now, to enlighten Ezra Jennings. I stopped him, before he could say any more.

'You are speculating,' I said, 'on a result which cannot possibly take place. The Diamond is, at this moment, in London.'

He started, and looked at me in great surprise.

'In London?' he repeated. 'How did it get to London from Lady Verinder's house?'

'Nobody knows.'

'You removed it with your own hand from Miss Verinder's room. How was it taken out of your keeping?'

'I have no idea how it was taken out of my keeping.'

'Did you see it, when you woke in the morning?'

'No.'

'Has Miss Verinder recovered possession of it?'

'No.'

'Mr Blake! there seems to be something here which wants clearing up. May I ask how you know that the Diamond is, at this moment, in London?'

I had put precisely the same question to Mr Bruff, when I made my first inquiries about the Moonstone, on my return to England. In answering Ezra Jennings, I accordingly repeated what I had myself heard from the lawyer's own lips – and what is already familiar to the readers of these pages.

He showed plainly that he was not satisfied with my reply.

'With all deference to you,' he said, 'and with all deference to your legal adviser, I maintain the opinion which I expressed just now. It rests, I am well aware, on a mere assumption. Pardon me for reminding you, that your opinion also rests on a mere assumption as well.'

The view he took of the matter was entirely new to me. I waited anxiously to hear how he would defend it.

'*I* assume,' pursued Ezra Jennings, 'that the influence of the opium – after impelling you to possess yourself of the Diamond, with the purpose of securing its safety – might also impel you, acting under the same influence and the same motive, to hide it somewhere in your own room. *You* assume that the Hindoo conspirators could by no possibility commit a mistake. The Indians went to Mr Luker's house after the Diamond – and, therefore, in Mr Luker's possession the Diamond must be! Have you any evidence to prove that the Moonstone was taken to London at all? You can't even guess how, or by whom, it was removed from Lady Verinder's house! Have you any evidence that the jewel was pledged to Mr Luker? He declares that he never heard of the Moonstone; and his bankers' receipt acknowledges nothing but the deposit of a valuable of great price. The Indians assume that Mr Luker is lying – and you assume again that the Indians are right. All I say, in differing with you, is – that my view is possible. What more, Mr Blake, either logically or legally, can be said for yours?'

It was put strongly; but there was no denying that it was put truly as well.

'I confess you stagger me,' I replied. 'Do you object to my writing to Mr Bruff, and telling him what you have said?'

'On the contrary, I shall be glad if you will write to Mr Bruff. If we consult his experience, we may see the matter under a new light. For the present, let us return to our experiment with the opium. We have decided that you leave off the habit of smoking, from this moment?'

'From this moment.'

'That is the first step. The next step is to reproduce, as nearly as we can, the domestic circumstances which surrounded you last year.'

How was this to be done? Lady Verinder was dead. Rachel and I, so long as the suspicion of theft rested on me, were parted irrevocably. Godfrey Ablewhite was away, travelling on the Continent. It was simply impossible to reassemble the people who had inhabited the house, when I had slept in it last. The statement of this objection did not appear to embarrass Ezra Jennings. He attached very little importance he said to reassembling the same people – seeing that it would be vain to expect them to reassume the various positions which they had occupied towards me in the past times. On the other hand, he considered it essential to the success of the experiment, that I should see the same objects about me which had surrounded me when I was last in the house.

'Above all things,' he said, 'you must sleep in the room which you slept in, on the birthday night, and it must be furnished in the same way. The stairs, the corridors, and Miss Verinder's sitting-room, must also be restored to what they were when you saw them last. It is absolutely necessary, Mr Blake, to replace every article of furniture in that part of the house which may now be put away. The sacrifice of your cigars will be useless, unless we can get Miss Verinder's permission to do that.'

'Who is to apply to her for permission?' I asked.

'Is it not possible for *you* to apply?'

'Quite out of the question. After what has passed between us, on the subject of the lost Diamond, I can neither see her, nor write to her, as things are now.'

Ezra Jennings paused, and considered for a moment.

'May I ask you a delicate question?' he said.

I signed to him to go on.

'Am I right, Mr Blake, in fancying (from one or two things which have dropped from you) that you felt no common interest in Miss Verinder, in former times?'

'Quite right.'

'Was the feeling returned?'

'It was.'

'Do you think Miss Verinder would be likely to feel a strong interest in the attempt to prove your innocence?'

'I am certain of it.'

'In that case, *I* will write to Miss Verinder – if you will give me leave.'

'Telling her of the proposal that you have made to me?'

'Telling her of everything that has passed between us to-day.'

It is needless to say that I eagerly accepted the service which he had offered to me.

'I shall have time to write by to-day's post,' he said, looking at his watch. 'Don't forget to lock up your cigars, when you get back to the hotel! I will call to-morrow morning and hear how you have passed the night.'

I rose to take leave of him; and attempted to express the grateful sense of his kindness which I really felt.

He pressed my hand gently. 'Remember what I told you on the moor,' he answered. 'If I can do you this little service, Mr Blake, I shall feel it like a last gleam of sunshine, falling on the evening of a long and clouded day.'

We parted. It was then the fifteenth of June. The events of the next ten days – every one of them more or less directly connected with the experiment of which I was the passive object – are all placed on record, exactly as they happened, in the Journal habitually kept by Mr Candy's assistant. In the pages of Ezra Jennings, nothing is concealed, and nothing is forgotten. Let Ezra Jennings tell how the venture with the opium was tried, and how it ended.

Fourth Narrative

Extracted from the Journal of Ezra Jennings

1849. – 15 June. . . . With some interruption from patients, and some interruption from pain, I finished my letter to Miss Verinder in time for to-day's post. I failed to make it as short a letter as I could have wished. But I think I have made it plain. It leaves her entirely mistress of her own decision. If she consents to assist the experiment, she consents of her own free will, and not as a favour to Mr Franklin Blake or to me.

* * * * *

16 June. – Rose late, after a dreadful night; the vengeance of yesterday's opium pursuing me through a series of frightful dreams. At one time, I was whirling through empty space with the phantoms of the dead, friends and enemies together. At another, the one beloved face which I shall never see again, rose at my bedside, hideously phosphorescent in the black darkness, and glared and grinned at me. A slight return of the old pain, at the usual time in the early morning, was welcome as a change. It dispelled the visions – and it was bearable because it did that.

My bad night made it late in the morning, before I could get to Mr Franklin Blake. I found him stretched on the sofa, breakfasting on brandy and soda-water, and a dry biscuit.

'I am beginning, as well as you could possibly wish,' he said. 'A miserable, restless night; and a total failure of appetite this morning. Exactly what happened last year, when I gave up my cigars. The sooner I am ready for my second dose of laudanum, the better I shall be pleased.'

'You shall have it on the earliest possible day,' I answered. 'In the meantime, we must be as careful of your health as we can. If we allow you to become exhausted, we shall fail in that way. You must get an appetite for your dinner. In other words, you must get a ride or a walk this morning, in the fresh air.'

'I will ride, if they can find me a horse here. By-the-by, I wrote to Mr Bruff, yesterday. Have you written to Miss Verinder?

'Yes – by last night's post.'

'Very good. We shall have some news worth hearing, to tell each other to-morrow. Don't go yet! I have a word to say to you. You appeared to think, yesterday, that our experiment with the opium was not likely to be viewed very favourably by some of my friends. You were quite right. I call old Gabriel Betteredge one of my friends; and you will be amused

353

to hear that he protested strongly when I saw him yesterday. "You have done a wonderful number of foolish things in the course of your life, Mr Franklin; but this tops them all!" There is Betteredge's opinion! You will make allowance for his prejudices, I am sure, if you and he happen to meet?'

I left Mr Blake, to go my rounds among my patients; feeling the better and the happier even for the short interview that I had had with him.

What is the secret of the attraction that there is for me in this man? Does it only mean that I feel the contrast between the frankly kind manner in which he has allowed me to become acquainted with him, and the merciless dislike and distrust with which I am met by other people? Or is there really something in him which answers to the yearning that I have for a little human sympathy – the yearning, which has survived the solitude and persecution of many years; which seems to grow keener and keener, as the time comes nearer and nearer when I shall endure and feel no more? How useless to ask these questions! Mr Blake has given me a new interest in life. Let that be enough, without seeking to know what the new interest is.

* * * * *

17 June. – Before breakfast, this morning, Mr Candy informed me that he was going away for a fortnight, on a visit to a friend in the south of England. He gave me as many special directions, poor fellow, about the patients, as if he still had the large practice which he possessed before he was taken ill. The practice is worth little enough now! Other doctors have superseded *him*; and nobody who can help it will employ *me*.

It is perhaps fortunate that he is to be away just at this time. He would have been mortified if I had not informed him of the experiment which I am going to try with Mr Blake. And I hardly know what undesirable results might not have happened, if I had taken him into my confidence. Better as it is. Unquestionably, better as it is.

The post brought me Miss Verinder's answer, after Mr Candy had left the house.

A charming letter! It gives me the highest opinion of her. There is no attempt to conceal the interest that she feels in our proceedings. She tells me, in the prettiest manner, that my letter has satisfied her of Mr Blake's innocence, without the slightest need (so far as she is concerned) of putting my assertion to the proof. She even upbraids herself – most undeservedly, poor thing! – for not having divined at the time what the true solution of the mystery might really be. The motive underlying all this, proceeds evidently from something more than a generous eagerness to make atonement for a wrong which she has innocently inflicted on another person. It is plain that she has loved him, throughout the estrangement between them. In more than one place the rapture of discovering that he has deserved to be loved, breaks its way innocently through the stoutest formalities of pen and ink, and even defies the stronger restraint still of writing to a stranger. Is it possible (I ask myself, in reading this delightful letter) that I, of all men in the world, am chosen to be the means of bringing these two young people together again? My own happiness has been trampled under foot; my own love has been torn from me. Shall I live to see a happiness of others, which is of my making – a love renewed, which is of my bringing back? O merciful Death! let me see it before your arms enfold me, before your voice whispers to me, 'Rest at last!'

There are two requests contained in the letter. One of them prevents me from showing it to Mr Franklin Blake. I am authorized to tell him that Miss Verinder willingly consents to place her house at our disposal; and, that said, I am desired to add no more.

So far, it is easy to comply with her wishes. But the second request embarrasses me seriously.

Not content with having written to Mr Betteredge, instructing him to carry out whatever directions I may have to give, Miss Verinder asks leave to assist me, by personally superintending the restoration of her own sitting-room. She only waits a word of reply from me, to make the journey to Yorkshire, and to be present as one of the witnesses on the night when the opium is tried for the second time.

Here, again, there is a motive under the surface; and, here again, I fancy that I can find it out.

What she has forbidden me to tell Mr Franklin Blake, she is (as I interpret it) eager to tell him with her own lips, *before* he is put to the test which is to vindicate his character in the eyes of other people. I understand and admire this generous anxiety to acquit him, without waiting until his innocence may, or may not, be proved. It is the atonement that she is longing to make, poor girl, after having innocently and inevitably wronged him. But the thing cannot be done. I have no sort of doubt that the agitation which a meeting between them would produce on both sides – reviving dormant feelings, appealing to old memories, awakening new hopes – would, in their effect on the mind of Mr Blake, be almost certainly fatal to the success of our experiment. It is hard enough, as things are, to reproduce in him the conditions as they existed, or nearly as they existed, last year. With new interests and new emotions to agitate him, the attempt would be simply useless.

And yet, knowing this, I cannot find it in my heart to disappoint her. I must try if I can discover some new arrangement, before post-time, which will allow me to say Yes to Miss Verinder, without damage to the service which I have bound myself to tender to Mr Franklin Blake.

Two o'clock. – I have just returned from my round of medical visits; having begun, of course, by calling at the hotel.

Mr Blake's report of the night is the same as before. He has had some intervals of broken sleep, and no more. But he feels it less to-day, having slept after yesterday's dinner. This after-dinner sleep is the result, no doubt, of the ride which I advised him to take. I fear I shall have to curtail his restorative exercise in the fresh air. He must not be too well; he must not be too ill. It is a case (as a sailor would say) of very fine steering.

He has not heard yet from Mr Bruff. I found him eager to know if I had received any answer from Miss Verinder.

I told him exactly what I was permitted to tell, and no more. It was quite needless to invent excuses for not showing him the letter. He told me bitterly enough, poor fellow, that he understood the delicacy which disinclined me to produce it. 'She consents, of course, as a matter of common courtesy and common justice,' he said. 'But she keeps her own opinion of me, and waits to see the result.' I was sorely tempted to hint that he was now wronging her as she had wronged him. On reflection, I shrank from forestalling her in the double luxury of surprising and forgiving him.

My visit was a very short one. After the experience of the other night, I have been compelled once more to give up my dose of opium. As a necessary result, the agony of the disease that is in me has got the upper hand again. I felt the attack coming on, and left abruptly, so as not to alarm or distress him. It only lasted a quarter of an hour this time, and it left me strength enough to go on with my work.

Five o'clock – I have written my reply to Miss Verinder.

The arrangement I have proposed reconciles the interests on both sides, if she will only consent to it. After first stating the objections that there are to a meeting between Mr Blake and herself, before the experiment is tried, I have suggested that she should so time her journey as to arrive at the house privately, on the evening when we make the attempt. Travelling by the afternoon train from London, she would delay her arrival until nine o'clock. At that hour, I have undertaken to see Mr Blake safely into his bedchamber; and so to leave Miss Verinder free to occupy her own rooms until the time comes for administering the laudanum. When that has been done, there can be no objection to her watching the result, with the rest of us. On the next morning, she shall show Mr Blake (if she likes) her correspondence with me, and shall satisfy him in that way that he was acquitted in her estimation, before the question of his innocence was put to the proof.

In that sense, I have written to her. This is all that I can do to-day.

To-morrow I must see Mr Betteredge, and give the necessary directions for re-opening the house.

* * * * *

18 June. – Late again, in calling on Mr Franklin Blake. More of that horrible pain in the early morning; followed, this time, by complete prostration, for some hours. I foresee, in spite of the penalties which it exacts from me, that I shall have to return to the opium for the hundredth time. If I had only myself to think of, I should prefer the sharp pains to the frightful dreams. But the physical suffering exhausts me. If I let myself sink, it may end in my becoming useless to Mr Blake at the time when he wants me most.

It was nearly one o'clock before I could get to the hotel to-day. The visit, even in my shattered condition, proved to be a most amusing one – thanks entirely to the presence on the scene of Gabriel Betteredge.

I found him in the room, when I went in. He withdrew to the window and looked out, while I put my first customary question to my patient. Mr Blake had slept badly again, and he felt the loss of rest this morning more than he had felt it yet.

I asked next if he had heard from Mr Bruff.

A letter had reached him that morning. Mr Bruff expressed the strongest disapproval of the course which his friend and client was taking under my advice. It was mischievous – for it excited hopes that might never be realized. It was quite unintelligible to *his* mind, except that it looked like a piece of trickery, akin to the trickery of mesmerism, clairvoyance, and the like. It unsettled Miss Verinder's house, and it would end in unsettling Miss Verinder herself. He had put the case (without mentioning names) to an eminent physician; and the eminent physician had smiled, had shaken his head, and had said – nothing. On these grounds, Mr Bruff entered his protest, and left it there.

My next inquiry related to the subject of the Diamond. Had the lawyer produced any evidence to prove that the jewel was in London?

No, the lawyer had simply declined to discuss the question. He was himself satisfied that the Moonstone had been pledged to Mr Luker. His eminent absent friend, Mr Murthwaite (whose consummate knowledge of the Indian character no one could deny), was satisfied also. Under these circumstances, and with the many demands already made on him, he must decline entering into any disputes on the subject of evidence. Time would show; and Mr Bruff was willing to wait for time.

It was quite plain – even if Mr Blake had not made it plainer still by reporting the substance of the letter, instead of reading what was actually written – that distrust of *me* was at the bottom of all this. Having myself foreseen that result, I was neither mortified nor surprised. I asked Mr

Blake if his friend's protest had shaken him. He answered emphatically, that it had not produced the slightest effect on his mind. I was free after that to dismiss Mr Bruff from consideration – and I did dismiss him accordingly.

A pause in the talk between us, followed – and Gabriel Betteredge came out from his retirement at the window.

'Can you favour me with your attention, sir?' he inquired, addressing himself to me.

'I am quite at your service,' I answered.

Betteredge took a chair and seated himself at the table. He produced a huge old-fashioned leather pocket-book, with a pencil of dimensions to match. Having put on his spectacles, he opened the pocket-book, at a blank page, and addressed himself to me once more.

'I have lived,' said Betteredge, looking at me sternly, 'nigh on fifty years in the service of my late lady. I was page-boy before that, in the service of the old lord, her father. I am now somewhere between seventy and eighty years of age – never mind exactly where! I am reckoned to have got as pretty a knowledge and experience of the world as most men. And what does it all end in? It ends, Mr Ezra Jennings, in a conjuring trick being performed on Mr Franklin Blake, by a doctor's assistant with a bottle of laudanum – and by the living jingo, I'm appointed, in my old age, to be conjuror's boy!'

Mr Blake burst out laughing. I attempted to speak. Betteredge held up his hand, in token that he had not done yet.

'Not a word, Mr Jennings!' he said. 'It don't want a word, sir, from you. I have got my principles, thank God. If an order comes to me, which is own brother to an order come from Bedlam, it don't matter. So long as I get it from my master or mistress, as the case may be, I obey it. I may have my own opinion, which is also, you will please to remember, the opinion of Mr Bruff – the Great Mr Bruff!' said Betteredge, raising his voice, and shaking his head at me solemnly. 'It don't matter; I withdraw my opinion, for all that. My young lady says, "Do it." And I say, "Miss, it shall be done." Here I am, with my book and my pencil – the latter not pointed so well as I could wish, but when Christians take leave of their senses, who is to expect that pencils will keep their points? Give me your orders, Mr Jennings. I'll have them in writing, sir. I'm determined not to be behind 'em, or before 'em, by so much as a hair's-breadth. I'm a blind agent – that's what I am. A blind agent!' repeated Betteredge, with infinite relish of his own description of himself.

'I am very sorry,' I began, 'that you and I don't agree—'

'Don't bring *me* into it!' interposed Betteredge. 'This is not a matter of agreement, it's a matter of obedience. Issue your directions, sir – issue your directions!'

Mr Blake made me a sign to take him at his word. I 'issued my directions' as plainly and as gravely as I could.

'I wish certain parts of the house to be re-opened,' I said, 'and to be furnished, exactly as they were furnished at this time last year.'

Betteredge gave his imperfectly-pointed pencil a preliminary lick with his tongue. 'Name the parts, Mr Jennings!' he said loftily.

'First, the inner hall, leading to the chief staircase.'

' "First, the inner hall," ' Betteredge wrote. 'Impossible to furnish that, sir, as it was furnished last year – to begin with.'

'Why?'

'Because there was a stuffed buzzard, Mr Jennings, in the hall last year. When the family left, the buzzard was put away with the other things. When the buzzard was put away – he burst.'

'We will except the buzzard then.'

Betteredge took a note of the exception. ' "The inner hall to be furnished again, as furnished last year. A burst buzzard alone excepted." Please to go on, Mr Jennings.'

'The carpet to be laid down on the stairs, as before.'

' "The carpet to be laid down on the stairs, as before." Sorry to disappoint you, sir. But that can't be done either.'

'Why not?'

'Because the man who laid that carpet down, is dead, Mr Jennings – and the like of him for reconciling together a carpet and a corner, is not to be found in all England, look where you may.'

'Very well. We must try the next best man in England.'

Betteredge took another note; and I went on issuing my directions.

'Miss Verinder's sitting-room to be restored exactly to what it was last year. Also, the corridor leading from the sitting-room to the first landing. Also, the second corridor, leading from the second landing to the best bedrooms. Also, the bedroom occupied last June by Mr Franklin Blake.'

Betteredge's blunt pencil followed me conscientiously, word by word. 'Go on, sir,' he said, with sardonic gravity. 'There's a deal of writing left in the point of this pencil yet.'

I told him that I had no more directions to give. 'Sir,' said Betteredge, 'in that case, I have a point or two to put on my own behalf.' He opened the pocket-book at a new page, and gave the inexhaustible pencil another preliminary lick.

'I wish to know,' he began, 'whether I may, or may not, wash my hands—'

'You may decidedly,' said Mr Blake. 'I'll ring for the waiter.'

'—of certain responsibilities,' pursued Betteredge, impenetrably declining to see anybody in the room but himself and me.

'As to Miss Verinder's sitting-room, to begin with. When we took up the carpet last year, Mr Jennings, we found a surprising quantity of pins. Am I responsible for putting back the pins?

'Certainly not.'

Betteredge made a note of that concession, on the spot.

'As to the first corridor next,' he resumed. 'When we moved the ornaments in that part, we moved a statue of a fat naked child – profanely described in the catalogue of the house as "Cupid, god of Love". He had two wings last year, in the fleshy part of his shoulders. My eye being off him, for the moment, he lost one of them. Am I responsible for Cupid's wing?'

I made another concession, and Betteredge made another note.

'As to the second corridor,' he went on. 'There having been nothing in it, last year, but the doors of the rooms (to every one of which I can swear, if necessary), my mind is easy, I admit, respecting that part of the house only. But, as to Mr Franklin's bedroom (if *that* is to be put back to what it was before), I want to know who is responsible for keeping it in a perpetual state of litter, no matter how often it may be set right – his trousers here, his towels there, and his French novels everywhere. I say, who is responsible for untidying the tidiness of Mr Franklin's room, him or me?'

Mr Blake declared that he would assume the whole responsibility with the greatest pleasure. Betteredge obstinately declined to listen to any solution of the difficulty, without first referring it to my sanction and approval. I accepted Mr Blake's proposal; and Betteredge made a last entry in the pocket-book to that effect.

'Look in when you like, Mr Jennings, beginning from to-morrow,' he said, getting on his legs. 'You will find me at work, with the necessary persons to assist me. I respectfully beg to thank you, sir, for overlooking the case of the stuffed buzzard, and the other case of the Cupid's wing – as also for permitting me to wash my hands of all responsibility in respect of the pins on the carpet, and the litter in Mr Franklin's room. Speaking as a servant, I am deeply indebted to you. Speaking as a man, I consider you to be a person whose head is full of maggots, and I take up my testimony against your experiment as a delusion and a snare. Don't be afraid, on that account, of my feelings as a man getting in the way of my duty as a servant! You shall be obeyed. The maggots notwithstanding, sir, you shall be obeyed. If it ends in your setting the house on fire, Damme if I send for the engines, unless you ring the bell and order them first!'

With that farewell assurance, he made me a bow, and walked out of the room.

'Do you think we can depend on him?' I asked.

'Implicitly,' answered Mr Blake. 'When we go to the house, we shall find nothing neglected, and nothing forgotten.'

* * * * *

19 June. – Another protest against our contemplated proceedings! From a lady this time.

The morning's post brought me two letters. One, from Miss Verinder, consenting, in the kindest manner, to the arrangement that I have proposed. The other from the lady under whose care she is living – one Mrs Merridew.

Mrs Merridew presents her compliments, and does not pretend to understand the subject on which I have been corresponding with Miss Verinder, in its scientific bearings. Viewed in its social bearings, however, she feels free to pronounce an opinion. I am probably, Mrs Merridew thinks, not aware that Miss Verinder is barely nineteen years of age. To allow a young lady, at her time of life, to be present (without a 'chaperone') in a house full of men among whom a medical experiment is being carried on, is an outrage on propriety which Mrs Merridew cannot possibly permit. If the matter is allowed to proceed, she will feel it to be her duty – at a serious sacrifice of her own personal convenience – to accompany Miss Verinder to Yorkshire. Under these circumstances, she ventures to request that I will kindly reconsider the subject; seeing that Miss Verinder declines to be guided by any opinion but mine. Her presence cannot possibly be necessary; and a word from me, to that effect, would relieve both Mrs Merridew and myself of a very unpleasant responsibility.

Translated from polite commonplace, into plain English, the meaning of this is, as I take it, that Mrs Merridew stands in mortal fear of the opinion of the world. She has unfortunately appealed to the very last man in existence who has any reason to regard that opinion with respect. I won't disappoint Miss Verinder; and I won't delay a reconciliation between two young people who love each other, and who have been parted too long already. Translated from plain English into polite commonplace, this means that Mr Jennings presents his compliments to Mrs Merridew, and regrets that he cannot feel justified in interfering any farther in the matter.

Mr Blake's report of himself, this morning, was the same as before. We determined not to disturb Betteredge by overlooking him at the house to-day. To-morrow will be time enough for our first visit of inspection.

* * * * *

20 June. – Mr Blake is beginning to feel his continued restlessness at night. The sooner the rooms are refurnished, now, the better.

On our way to the house, this morning, he consulted me, with some nervous impatience and irresolution, about a letter (forwarded to him from London) which he had received from Sergeant Cuff.

The Sergeant writes from Ireland. He acknowledges the receipt (through his house-keeper) of a card and message which Mr Blake left at his residence near Dorking, and announces his return to England as likely to take place in a week or less. In the meantime, he requests to be favoured with Mr Blake's reasons for wishing to speak to him (as stated in the message) on the subject of the Moonstone. If Mr Blake can convict him of having made any serious mistake, in the course of his last year's inquiry concerning the Diamond, he will consider it a duty (after the liberal manner in which he was treated by the late Lady Verinder) to place himself at that gentleman's disposal. If not, he begs permission to remain in his retirement, surrounded by the peaceful floricultural attractions of a country life.

After reading the letter, I had no hesitation in advising Mr Blake to inform Sergeant Cuff, in reply, of all that had happened since the inquiry was suspended last year, and to leave him to draw his own conclusions from the plain facts.

On second thoughts, I also suggested inviting the Sergeant to be present at the experiment, in the event of his returning to England in time to join us. He would be a valuable witness to have, in any case; and, if I proved to be wrong in believing the Diamond to be hidden in Mr Blake's room his advice might be of great importance, at a future stage of the proceedings over which I could exercise no control. This last consideration appeared to decide Mr Blake. He promised to follow my advice.

The sound of the hammer informed us that the work of refurnishing was in full progress, as we entered the drive that led to the house.

Betteredge, attired for the occasion in a fisherman's red cap, and an apron of green baize, met us in the outer hall. The moment he saw me, he pulled out the pocket-book and pencil, and obstinately insisted on taking notes of everything that I said to him. Look where we might, we found, as Mr Blake had foretold, that the work was advancing as rapidly and as intelligently as it was possible to desire. But there was still much to be done in the inner hall, and in Miss Verinder's room. It seemed doubtful whether the house would be ready for us before the end of the week.

Having congratulated Betteredge on the progress that he had made (he persisted in taking notes every time I opened my lips; declining, at the same time, to pay the slightest attention to anything said by Mr Blake); and having promised to return for a second visit of inspection in a day or two, we prepared to leave the house, going out by the back way. Before we were clear of the passages downstairs, I was stopped by Betteredge, just as I was passing the door which led into his own room.

'Could I say two words to you in private?' he asked, in a mysterious whisper.

I consented of course. Mr Blake walked on to wait for me in the garden, while I accompanied Betteredge into his room. I fully anticipated a demand for certain new concessions, following the precedent already established in the cases of the stuffed buzzard, and the Cupid's wing. To my great surprise, Betteredge laid his hand confidentially on my arm, and put this extraordinary question to me:

'Mr Jennings, do you happen to be acquainted with *Robinson Crusoe*?'

I answered that I had read *Robinson Crusoe* when I was a child.

'Not since then?' inquired Betteredge.

'Not since then.'

He fell back a few steps, and looked at me with an expression of compassionate curiosity, tempered by superstitious awe.

'He has not read *Robinson Crusoe* since he was a child,' said Betteredge, speaking to himself – not to me. 'Let's try how *Robinson Crusoe* strikes him now!'

He unlocked a cupboard in a corner, and produced a dirty and dog's-eared book, which exhaled a strong odour of stale tobacco as he turned over the leaves. Having found a passage of which he was apparently in search, he requested me to join him in the corner; still mysteriously confidential, and still speaking under his breath.

'In respect to this hocus-pocus of yours, sir, with the laudanum and Mr Franklin Blake,' he began. 'While the workpeople are in the house, my duty as a servant gets the better of my feelings as a man. When the workpeople are gone, my feelings as a man get the better of my duty as a servant. Very good. Last night, Mr Jennings, it was borne in powerfully on my mind that this new medical enterprise of yours would end badly. If I had yielded to that secret Dictate, I should have put all the furniture away again with my own hand, and have warned the workmen off the premises when they came the next morning.'

'I am glad to find, from what I have seen upstairs,' I said, 'that you resisted the secret Dictate.'

'Resisted isn't the word,' answered Betteredge. 'Wrostled is the word. I wrostled, sir, between the silent orders in my bosom pulling me one way, and the written orders in my pocket-book pushing me the other, until (saving your presence) I was in a cold sweat. In that dreadful perturbation of mind and laxity of body, to what remedy did I apply? To the remedy, sir, which has never failed me yet for the last thirty years and more – to This Book!'

He hit the book a sounding blow with his open hand, and struck out of it a stronger smell of stale tobacco than ever.

'What did I find here,' pursued Betteredge, 'at the first page I opened? This awful bit, sir, page one hundred and seventy-eight, as follows: – "Upon these, and many like Reflections, I afterwards made it a certain rule with me, That whenever I found those secret Hints or Pressings of my Mind, to doing, or not doing any Thing that presented; or to going this Way, or that Way, I never failed to obey the secret Dictate." – As I live by bread, Mr Jennings, those were the first words that met my eye, exactly at the time when I myself was setting the secret Dictate at defiance! You don't see anything at all out of the common in that, do you, sir?'

'I see a coincidence – nothing more.'

'You don't feel at all shaken, Mr Jennings, in respect to this medical enterprise of yours?'

'Not the least in the world.'

Betteredge stared hard at me, in dead silence. He closed the book with great deliberation; he locked it up again in the cupboard with extraordinary care; he wheeled round, and stared hard at me once more. Then he spoke.

'Sir,' he said gravely, 'there are great allowances to be made for a man who has not read *Robinson Crusoe*, since he was a child. I wish you good morning.'

He opened his door with a low bow, and left me at liberty to find my own way into the garden. I met Mr Blake returning to the house.

'You needn't tell me what has happened,' he said. 'Betteredge has played his last card: he has made another prophetic discovery in *Robinson Crusoe*. Have you humoured his favourite delusion? No? You have let him see that you don't believe in *Robinson Crusoe*? Mr Jennings! you have fallen to the lowest possible place in Betteredge's estimation. Say what you like, and do what you like, for the future. You will find that he won't waste another word on you now.'

* * * * *

21 June. – A short entry must suffice in my journal to-day.

Mr Blake has had the worst night that he has passed yet. I have been obliged, greatly against my will, to prescribe for him. Men of his sensitive organization are fortunately quick in feeling the effect of remedial measures. Otherwise, I should be inclined to fear that he will be totally unfit for the experiment when the time comes to try it.

As for myself, after some little remission of my pains for the last two days, I had an attack this morning, of which I shall say nothing but that it has decided me to return to the opium. I shall close this book, and take my full dose – five hundred drops.

* * * * *

22 June. – Our prospects look better to-day. Mr Blake's nervous suffering is greatly allayed. He slept a little last night. *My* night, thanks to the opium, was the night of a man who is stunned. I can't say that I woke this morning; the fitter expression would be, that I recovered my senses.

We drove to the house to see if the refurnishing was done. It will be completed to-morrow – Saturday. As Mr Blake foretold, Betteredge raised no further obstacles. From first to last, he was ominously polite, and ominously silent.

My medical enterprise (as Betteredge calls it) must now, inevitably, be delayed until Monday next. To-morrow evening, the workmen will be late in the house. On the next day, the established Sunday tyranny which is one of the institutions of this free country, so times the trains as to make it impossible to ask anybody to travel to us from London. Until Monday comes, there is nothing to be done but to watch Mr Blake carefully, and to keep him, if possible, in the same state in which I find him to-day.

In the meanwhile, I have prevailed on him to write to Mr Bruff, making a point of it that he shall be present as one of the witnesses. I especially choose the lawyer, because he is strongly prejudiced against us. If we convince *him*, we place our victory beyond the possibility of dispute.

Mr Blake has also written to Sergeant Cuff; and I have sent a line to Miss Verinder. With these, and with old Betteredge (who is really a person of importance in the family) we shall have witnesses enough for the purpose – without including Mrs Merridew, if Mrs Merridew persists in sacrificing herself to the opinion of the world.

* * * * *

23 June. – The vengeance of the opium overtook me again last night. No matter; I must go on with it now till Monday is past and gone.

Mr Blake is not so well again to-day. At two this morning, he confesses that he opened the drawer in which his cigars are put away. He only succeeded in locking it up again by a violent effort. His next proceeding, in case of temptation, was to throw the key out of window. The waiter brought it in this morning, discovered at the bottom of an empty cistern – such is Fate! I have taken possession of the key, until Tuesday next.

* * * * *

24 June. – Mr Blake and I took a long drive in an open carriage. We both felt beneficially the blessed influence of the soft summer air. I dined with him at the hotel. To my great relief – for I found him in an over-wrought,

over-excited state, this morning – he had two hours' sound sleep on the sofa after dinner. If he has another bad night, now – I am not afraid of the consequences.

* * * * *

25 June, Monday. – The day of the experiment! It is five o'clock in the afternoon. We have just arrived at the house.

The first and foremost question, is the question of Mr Blake's health.

So far as it is possible for me to judge, he promises (physically speaking) to be quite as susceptible to the action of the opium to-night, as he was at this time last year. He is, this afternoon, in a state of nervous sensitiveness which just stops short of nervous irritation. He changes colour readily; his hand is not quite steady; and he starts at chance noises, and at unexpected appearances of persons and things.

These results have all been produced by deprivation of sleep, which is in its turn the nervous consequence of a sudden cessation in the habit of smoking, after that habit has been carried to an extreme. Here are the same causes at work again, which operated last year; and here are, apparently, the same effects. Will the parallel still hold good, when the final test has been tried? The events of the night must decide.

While I write these lines, Mr Blake is amusing himself at the billiard table in the inner hall, practising different strokes in the game, as he was accustomed to practise them when he was a guest in this house in June last. I have brought my journal here, partly with a view to occupying the idle hours which I am sure to have on my hands between this and to-morrow morning; partly in the hope that something may happen which it may be worth my while to place on record at the time.

Have I omitted anything, thus far? A glance at yesterday's entry shows me that I have forgotten to note the arrival of the morning's post. Let me set this right, before I close these leaves for the present, and join Mr Blake.

I received a few lines then, yesterday, from Miss Verinder. She has arranged to travel by the afternoon train, as I recommended. Mrs Merridew has insisted on accompanying her. The note hints that the old lady's generally excellent temper is a little ruffled, and requests all due indulgence for her, in consideration of her age and her habits. I will endeavour, in my relations with Mrs Merridew, to emulate the moderation which Betteredge displays in his relations with me. He received us to-day, portentously arrayed in his best black suit, and his stiffest white cravat. Whenever he looks my way, he remembers that I have not read *Robinson Crusoe* since I was a child, and he respectfully pities me.

Yesterday, also, Mr Blake had the lawyer's answer. Mr Bruff accepts the invitation – under protest. It is, he thinks, clearly necessary that a gentleman possessed of the average allowance of common sense, should accompany Miss Verinder to the scene of, what he will venture to call, the proposed exhibition. For want of a better escort, Mr Bruff himself will be that gentleman. – So here is poor Miss Verinder provided with two 'chaperons'. It is a relief to think that the opinion of the world must surely be satisfied with this!

Nothing has been heard of Sergeant Cuff. He is no doubt still in Ireland. We must not expect to see him to-night.

Betteredge has just come in, to say that Mr Blake has asked for me. I must lay down my pen for the present.

* * * * *

Seven o'clock. – We have been all over the refurnished rooms and stair-cases again; and we have had a pleasant stroll in the shrubbery which was Mr Blake's favourite walk when he was here last. In this way, I hope to revive the old impressions of places and things as vividly as possible in his mind.

We are now going to dine, exactly at the hour at which the birthday dinner was given last year. My object, of course, is a purely medical one in this case. The laudanum must find the process of digestion, as nearly as may be, where the laudanum found it last year.

At a reasonable time after dinner, I propose to lead the conversation back again – as inartificially as I can – to the subject of the Diamond, and of the Indian conspiracy to steal it. When I have filled his mind with these topics, I shall have done all that it is in my power to do, before the time comes for giving him the second dose.

* * * * *

Half-past eight. – I have only this moment found an opportunity of attending to the most important duty of all; the duty of looking in the family medicine chest, for the laudanum which Mr Candy used last year.

Ten minutes since, I caught Betteredge at an unoccupied moment, and told him what I wanted. Without a word of objection, without so much as an attempt to produce his pocket-book, he led the way (making allowances for me at every step) to the store-room in which the medicine chest is kept.

I discovered the bottle, carefully guarded by a glass stopper tied over with leather. The preparation which it contained was, as I had anticipated, the common Tincture of Opium. Finding the bottle still well filled, I have resolved to use it, in preference to employing either of the two prep-arations with which I had taken care to provide myself, in case of emergency.

The question of the quantity which I am to administer, presents certain difficulties. I have thought it over, and have decided on increasing the dose.

My notes inform me that Mr Candy only administered twenty-five minims. This is a small dose to have produced the results which followed – even in the case of a person so sensitive as Mr Blake. I think it highly probable that Mr Candy gave more than he supposed himself to have given – knowing, as I do, that he has a keen relish of the pleasures of the table, and that he measured out the laudanum on the birthday, after dinner. In any case, I shall run the risk of enlarging the dose to forty minims. On this occasion, Mr Blake knows beforehand that he is going to take the laudanum – which is equivalent, physiologically speaking, to his having (unconsciously to himself) a certain capacity in him to resist the effects. If my view is right, a larger quantity is therefore imperatively required, this time, to repeat the results which the smaller quantity produced, last year.

* * * * *

Ten o'clock. – The witnesses, or the company (which shall I call them?) reached the house an hour since.

A little before nine o'clock, I prevailed on Mr Blake to accompany me to his bedroom; stating, as a reason, that I wished him to look round it, for the last time, in order to make quite sure that nothing had been forgotten in the refurnishing of the room. I had previously arranged with Betteredge, that the bedchamber prepared for Mr Bruff should be the next room to Mr Blake's, and that I should be informed of the lawyer's arrival by a knock at the door. Five minutes after the clock in the hall had struck nine, I heard the knock; and, going out immediately, met Mr Bruff in the corridor.

My personal appearance (as usual) told against me. Mr Bruff's distrust looked at me plainly enough out of Mr Bruff's eyes. Being well used to producing this effect on strangers, I did not hesitate a moment in saying what I wanted to say, before the lawyer found his way into Mr Blake's room.

'You have travelled here, I believe, in company with Mrs Merridew and Miss Verinder?' I said.

'Yes,' answered Mr Bruff, as drily as might be.

'Miss Verinder has probably told you, that I wish her presence in the house (and Mrs Merridew's presence of course), to be kept a secret from Mr Blake, until my experiment on him has been tried first?'

'I know that I am to hold my tongue, sir!' said Mr Bruff, impatiently. 'Being habitually silent on the subject of human folly, I am all the readier to keep my lips closed on this occasion. Does that satisfy you?'

I bowed, and left Betteredge to show him to his room. Betteredge gave me one look at parting, which said, as if in so many words, 'You have caught a Tartar, Mr Jennings – and the name of him is Bruff.'

It was next necessary to get the meeting over with the two ladies. I descended the stairs – a little nervously, I confess – on my way to Miss Verinder's sitting-room.

The gardener's wife (charged with looking after the accommodation of the ladies) met me in the first-floor corridor. This excellent woman treats me with an excessive civility which is plainly the offspring of downright terror. She stares, trembles, and curtseys, whenever I speak to her. On my asking for Miss Verinder, she stared, trembled, and would no doubt have curtseyed next, if Miss Verinder herself had not cut that ceremony short, by suddenly opening her sitting-room door.

'Is that Mr Jennings?' she asked.

Before I could answer, she came out eagerly to speak to me in the corridor. We met under the light of a lamp on a bracket. At the first sight of me, Miss Verinder stopped, and hesitated. She recovered herself instantly, coloured for a moment – and then, with a charming frankness, offered me her hand.

'I can't treat you like a stranger, Mr Jennings,' she said. 'Oh, if you only knew how happy your letters have made me!'

She looked at my ugly wrinkled face, with a bright gratitude so new to me in my experience of my fellow-creatures, that I was at a loss how to answer her. Nothing had prepared me for her kindness and her beauty. The misery of many years has not hardened my heart, thank God. I was as awkward and as shy with her, as if I had been a lad in my teens.

'Where is he now?' she asked, giving free expression to her one dominant interest – the interest in Mr Blake. 'What is he doing? Has he spoken of me? Is he in good spirits? How does he bear the sight of the house, after what happened in it last year? When are you going to give him the laudanum? May I see you pour it out? I am so interested; I am so excited – I have ten thousand things to say to you, and they all crowd together so that I don't know what to say first. Do you wonder at the interest I take in this?'

'No,' I said. 'Venture to think that I thoroughly understand it.'

She was far above the paltry affectation of being confused. She answered me as she might have answered a brother or a father.

'You have relieved me of indescribable wretchedness; you have given me a new life. How can I be ungrateful enough to have any concealments from *you*? I love him,' she said simply, 'I have loved him from first to last – even when I was wronging him in my own thoughts; even when I was saying the hardest and the cruellest words to him. Is there any excuse for me, in that? I hope there is – I am afraid it is the only excuse

I have. When to-morrow comes, and he knows that I am in the house, do you think – ?'

She stopped again, and looked at me very earnestly.

'When to-morrow comes,' I said, 'I think you have only to tell him what you have just told me.'

Her face brightened; she came a step nearer to me. Her fingers trifled nervously with a flower which I had picked in the garden, and which I had put into the button-hole of my coat.

'You have seen a great deal of him lately,' she said. 'Have you, really and truly, seen *that*?'

'Really and truly,' I answered. 'I am quite certain of what will happen to-morrow. I wish I could feel as certain of what will happen to-night.'

At that point in the conversation, we were interrupted by the appearance of Betteredge, with the tea-tray. He gave me another significant look as he passed on into the sitting-room. 'Aye! aye! make your hay while the sun shines. The Tartar's upstairs, Mr Jennings – the Tartar's upstairs!'

We followed him into the room. A little old lady, in a corner, very nicely dressed, and very deeply absorbed over a smart piece of embroidery, dropped her work in her lap, and uttered a faint little scream at the first sight of my gipsy complexion and my piebald hair.

'Mrs Merridew,' said Miss Verinder, 'this is Mr Jennings.'

'I beg Mr Jennings' pardon,' said the old lady, looking at Miss Verinder, and speaking at *me*. 'Railway travelling always makes me nervous. I am endeavouring to quiet my mind by occupying myself as usual. I don't know whether my embroidery is out of place, on this extraordinary occasion. If it interferes with Mr Jennings' medical views, I shall be happy to put it away of course.'

I hastened to sanction the presence of the embroidery, exactly as I had sanctioned the absence of the burst buzzard and the Cupid's wing. Mrs Merridew made an effort – a grateful effort – to look at my hair. No! it was not to be done. Mrs Merridew looked back again at Miss Verinder.

'If Mr Jennings will permit me,' pursued the old lady, 'I should like to ask a favour. Mr Jennings is about to try a scientific experiment to-night. I used to attend scientific experiments when I was a girl at school. They invariably ended in an explosion. If Mr Jennings will be so very kind, I should like to be warned of the explosion this time. With a view to getting it over, if possible, before I go to bed.'

I attempted to assure Mrs Merridew that an explosion was not included in the programme on this occasion.

'No,' said the old lady. 'I am much obliged to Mr Jennings – I am aware that he is only deceiving me for my own good. I prefer plain dealing. I am quite resigned to the explosion – but I *do* want to get it over, if possible, before I go to bed.'

Here the door opened, and Mrs Merridew uttered another little scream. The advent of the explosion? No: only the advent of Betteredge.

'I beg your pardon, Mr Jennings,' said Betteredge, in his most elaborately confidential manner. 'Mr Franklin wishes to know where you are. Being under your orders to deceive him, in respect to the presence of my young lady in the house, I have said I don't know. That, you will please to observe, was a lie. Having one foot already in the grave, sir, the fewer lies you expect me to tell, the more I shall be indebted to you, when my conscience pricks me and my time comes.'

There was not a moment to be wasted on the purely speculative question of Betteredge's conscience. Mr Blake might make his appearance in search of me, unless I went to him at once in his own room. Miss Verinder followed me out into the corridor.

'They seem to be in a conspiracy to persecute you,' she said. 'What does it mean?'

'Only the protest of the world, Miss Verinder – on a very small scale – against anything that is new.'

'What are we to do with Mrs Merridew?'

'Tell her the explosion will take place at nine to-morrow morning.'

'So as to send her to bed?'

'Yes – so as to send her to bed.'

Miss Verinder went back to the sitting-room, and I went upstairs to Mr Blake.

To my surprise, I found him alone; restlessly pacing his room, and a little irritated at being left by himself.

'Where is Mr Bruff?' I asked.

He pointed to the closed door of communication between the two rooms. Mr Bruff had looked in on him, for a moment; had attempted to renew his protest against our proceedings; and had once more failed to produce the smallest impression on Mr Blake. Upon this, the lawyer had taken refuge in a black leather bag, filled to bursting with professional papers. 'The serious business of life,' he admitted, 'was sadly out of place on such an occasion as the present. But the serious business of life must be carried on, for all that. Mr Blake would perhaps kindly make allowance for the old-fashioned habits of a practical man. Time was money – and, as for Mr Jennings, he might depend on it that Mr Bruff would be forthcoming when called upon.' With that apology, the lawyer had gone back to his own room, and had immersed himself obstinately in his black bag.

I thought of Mrs Merridew and her embroidery, and of Betteredge and his conscience. There is a wonderful sameness in the solid side of the English character – just as there is a wonderful sameness in the solid expression of the English face.

'When are you going to give me the laudanum?' asked Mr Blake impatiently.

'You must wait a little longer,' I said. 'I will stay and keep you company till the time comes.'

It was then not ten o'clock. Inquiries which I had made, at various times, of Betteredge and Mr Blake, had led me to the conclusion that the dose of laudanum given by Mr Candy could not possibly have been administered before eleven. I had accordingly determined not to try the second dose until that time.

We talked a little; but both our minds were preoccupied by the coming ordeal. The conversation soon flagged – then dropped altogether. Mr Blake idly turned over the books on his bedroom table. I had taken the precaution of looking at them, when we first entered the room. *The Guardian*; *The Tatler*; Richardson's *Pamela*; Mackenzie's *Man of Feeling*; Roscoe's *Lorenzo de' Medici*; and Robertson's *Charles the Fifth* – all classical works; all (of course) immeasurably superior to anything produced in later times; and all (from my present point of view) possessing the one great merit of enchaining nobody's interest, and exciting nobody's brain. I left Mr Blake to the composing influence of Standard Literature, and occupied myself in making this entry in my journal.

My watch informs me that it is close on eleven o'clock. I must shut up these leaves once more.

* * * * *

Two o'clock – The experiment has been tried. With what result, I am now to describe.

At eleven o'clock, I rang the bell for Betteredge, and told Mr Blake that he might at last prepare himself for bed.

I looked out of window at the night. It was mild and rainy resembling, in this respect, the night of the birthday – the twenty-first of June, last year. Without professing to believe in omens, it was at least encouraging to find no direct nervous influences – no stormy or electric perturbations – in the atmosphere. Betteredge joined me at the window, and mysteriously put a little slip of paper into my hand. It contained these lines:

'Mrs Merridew has gone to bed, on the distinct understanding that the explosion is to take place at nine to-morrow morning, and that I am not to stir out of this part of the house until she comes and sets me free. She has no idea that the chief scene of the experiment is my sitting-room – or she would have remained in it for the whole night! I am alone, and very anxious. Pray let me see you measure out the laudanum; I want to have something to do with it, even in the unimportant character of a mere looker-on. – R. V.'

I followed Betteredge out of the room, and told him to remove the medicine-chest into Miss Verinder's sitting-room.

The order appeared to take him completely by surprise. He looked as if he suspected me of some occult medical design on Miss Verinder! 'Might I presume to ask,' he said, 'what my young lady and the medicine-chest have got to do with each other?'

'Stay in the sitting-room, and you will see.'

Betteredge appeared to doubt his own unaided capacity to superintend me effectually, on an occasion when a medicine-chest was included in the proceedings.

'Is there any objection, sir,' he asked, 'to taking Mr Bruff into this part of the business?'

'Quite the contrary! I am now going to ask Mr Bruff to accompany me downstairs.'

Betteredge withdrew to fetch the medicine-chest, without another word. I went back into Mr Blake's room, and knocked at the door of communication. Mr Bruff opened it, with his papers in his hand – immersed in Law; impenetrable to Medicine.

'I am sorry to disturb you,' I said. 'But I am going to prepare the laudanum for Mr Blake; and I must request you to be present, and to see what I do.'

'Yes?' said Mr Bruff, with nine-tenths of his attention riveted on his papers, and with one-tenth unwillingly accorded to me. 'Anything else?'

'I must trouble you to return here with me, and to see me administer the dose.'

'Anything else?'

'One thing more. I must put you to the inconvenience of remaining in Mr Blake's room, and of waiting to see what happens.'

'Oh, very good!' said Mr Bruff. 'My room, or Mr Blake's room – it doesn't matter which; I can go on with my papers anywhere. Unless you object, Mr Jennings, to my importing *that* amount of common sense into the proceedings?'

Before I could answer, Mr Blake addressed himself to the lawyer, speaking from his bed.

'Do you really mean to say that you don't feel any interest in what we are going to do?' he asked. 'Mr Bruff, you have no more imagination than a cow!'

'A cow is a very useful animal, Mr Blake,' said the lawyer. With that reply, he followed me out of the room, still keeping his papers in his hand.

We found Miss Verinder, pale and agitated, restlessly pacing her sitting-room from end to end. At a table in a corner, stood Betteredge, on guard over the medicine-chest. Mr Bruff sat down on the first chair that he could find, and (emulating the usefulness of the cow) plunged back again into his papers on the spot.

Miss Verinder drew me aside, and reverted instantly to her one all-absorbing interest – her interest in Mr Blake.

'How is he now?' she asked. 'Is he nervous? Is he out of temper? Do you think it will succeed? Are you sure it will do no harm?'

'Quite sure. Come, and see me measure it out.'

'One moment! It is past eleven now. How long will it be before anything happens?'

'It is not easy to say. An hour perhaps.'

'I suppose the room must be dark, as it was last year?'

'Certainly.'

'I shall wait in my bedroom – just as I did before. I shall keep the door a little way open. It was a little way open last year. I will watch the sitting-room door; and the moment it moves, I will blow out my light. It all happened in that way, on my birthday night. And it must all happen again in the same way, mustn't it?'

'Are you sure you can control yourself, Miss Verinder?'

'In *his* interests, I can do anything!' she answered fervently.

One look at her face told me that I could trust her. I addressed myself again to Mr Bruff.

'I must trouble you to put your papers aside for a moment,' I said.

'Oh, certainly!' He got up with a start – as if I had disturbed him at a particularly interesting place – and followed me to the medicine-chest. There, deprived of the breathless excitement incidental to the practice of his profession, he looked at Betteredge – and yawned wearily.

Miss Verinder joined me with a glass jug of cold water, which she had taken from a side-table. 'Let me pour out the water,' she whispered. 'I must have a hand in it!'

I measured out the forty minims from the bottle, and poured the laudanum into a medicine glass. 'Fill it till it is three parts full,' I said, and handed the glass to Miss Verinder. I then directed Betteredge to lock up the medicine-chest; informing him that I had done with it now. A look of unutterable relief overspread the old servant's countenance. He had evidently suspected me of a medical design on his young lady!

After adding the water as I had directed, Miss Verinder seized a moment – while Betteredge was locking the chest, and while Mr Bruff was looking back at his papers – and slyly kissed the rim of the medicine glass. 'When you give it to him,' said the charming girl, 'give it to him on that side!'

I took the piece of crystal which was to represent the Diamond from my pocket, and gave it to her.

'You must have a hand in this, too,' I said. 'You must put it where you put the Moonstone last year.'

She led the way to the Indian cabinet, and put the mock Diamond into the drawer which the real Diamond had occupied on the birthday night. Mr Bruff witnessed this proceeding, under protest, as he had witnessed everything else. But the strong dramatic interest which the experiment was now assuming, proved (to my great amusement) to be too much for Betteredge's capacity of self-restraint. His hand trembled as he held the candle, and he whispered anxiously, 'Are you sure, miss, it's the right drawer?'

I led the way out again, with the laudanum and water in my hand. At the door, I stopped to address a last word to Miss Verinder.

'Don't be long in putting out the lights,' I said.

'I will put them out at once,' she answered. 'And I will wait in my bedroom, with only one candle alight.'

She closed the sitting-room door behind us. Followed by Mr Bruff and Betteredge, I went back to Mr Blake's room.

We found him moving restlessly from side to side of the bed, and wondering irritably whether he was to have the laudanum that night. In the presence of the two witnesses, I gave him the dose, and shook up his pillows, and told him to lie down again quietly and wait.

His bed, provided with light chintz curtains, was placed, with the head against the wall of the room, so as to leave a good open space on either side of it. On one side, I drew the curtains completely – and in the part of the room thus screened from his view, I placed Mr Bruff and Betteredge, to wait for the result. At the bottom of the bed, I half drew the curtains – and placed my own chair at a little distance, so that I might let him see me or not see me, speak to me or not speak to me, just as the circumstances might direct. Having already been informed that he always slept with a light in the room, I placed one of the two lighted candles on a little table at the head of the bed, where the glare of the light would not strike on his eyes. The other candle I gave to Mr Bruff; the light, in this instance, being subdued by the screen of the chintz curtains. The window was open at the top, so as to ventilate the room. The rain fell softly, the house was quiet. It was twenty minutes past eleven, by my watch, when the preparations were completed, and I took my place on the chair set apart at the bottom of the bed.

Mr Bruff resumed his papers, with every appearance of being as deeply interested in them as ever. But looking towards him now, I saw certain signs and tokens which told me that the Law was beginning to lose its hold on him at last. The suspended interest of the situation in which we were now placed, was slowly asserting its influence even on *his* unimaginative mind. As for Betteredge, consistency of principle and dignity of conduct had become, in his case, mere empty words. He forgot that I was performing a conjuring trick on Mr Franklin Blake; he forgot that I had upset the house from top to bottom; he forgot that I had not read *Robinson Crusoe* since I was a child. 'For the Lord's sake, sir,' he whispered to me, 'tell us when it will begin to work.'

'Not before midnight,' I whispered back. 'Say nothing, and sit still.'

Betteredge dropped to the lowest depth of familiarity with me, without a struggle to save himself. He answered by a wink!

Looking next towards Mr Blake, I found him as restless as ever in his bed; fretfully wondering why the influence of the laudanum had not begun to assert itself yet. To tell him, in his present humour, that the more he fidgeted and wondered, the longer he would delay the result for which we were now waiting, would have been simply useless. The wiser course to take was to dismiss the idea of the opium from his mind, by leading him insensibly to think of something else.

With this view, I encouraged him to talk to me; contriving so to direct the conversation, on my side, as to lead it back again to the subject which had engaged us earlier in the evening – the subject of the Diamond. I took care to revert to those portions of the story of the Moonstone, which related to the transport of it from London to Yorkshire; to the risk which Mr Blake had run in removing it from the bank at Frizinghall; and to the unexpected appearance of the Indians at the house, on the evening of the birthday. And I purposely assumed, in referring to these events, to have misunderstood much of what Mr Blake himself had told me a few hours since. In this way, I set him talking on the subject with which it was now vitally important to fill his mind – without allowing him to suspect that I was making him talk for a purpose. Little by little, he became so interested in putting me right that he forgot to fidget in the bed. His mind was far away from the question of the opium, at the all-important time when his eyes first told me that the opium was beginning to lay its hold on his brain.

I looked at my watch. It wanted five minutes to twelve, when the premonitory symptoms of the working of the laudanum first showed themselves to me.

At this time, no unpractised eyes would have detected any change in him. But, as the minutes of the new morning wore away, the swiftly-subtle progress of the influence began to show itself more plainly. The sublime intoxication of opium gleamed in his eyes; the dew of a stealthy perspiration began to glisten on his face. In five minutes more, the talk which he still kept up with me, failed in coherence. He held steadily to the subject of the Diamond; but he ceased to complete his sentences. A little later, the sentences dropped to single words. Then, there was an interval of silence. Then, he sat up in bed. Then, still busy with the subject of the Diamond, he began to talk again – not to me, but to himself. That change told me that the first stage in the experiment was reached. The stimulant influence of the opium had got him.

The time, now, was twenty-three minutes past twelve. The next half-hour, at most, would decide the question of whether he would, or would not, get up from his bed, and leave the room.

In the breathless interest of watching him – in the unutterable triumph of seeing the first result of the experiment declare itself in the manner, and nearly at the time, which I had anticipated – I had utterly forgotten the two companions of my night vigil. Looking towards them now, I saw the Law (as represented by Mr Bruff's papers) lying unheeded on the floor. Mr Bruff himself was looking eagerly through a crevice left in the imperfectly drawn curtains of the bed. And Betteredge, oblivious of all respect for social distinctions, was peeping over Mr Bruff's shoulder.

They both started back, on finding that I was looking at them, like two boys caught out by their schoolmaster in a fault. I signed to them to take off their boots quietly, as I was taking off mine. If Mr Blake gave us the chance of following him, it was vitally necessary to follow him without noise.

Ten minutes passed – and nothing happened. Then, he suddenly threw the bed-clothes off him. He put one leg out of bed. He waited.

'I wish I had never taken it out of the bank,' he said to himself. 'It was safe in the bank.'

My heart throbbed fast; the pulses at my temples beat furiously. The doubt about the safety of the Diamond was, once more, the dominant impression in his brain! On that one pivot, the whole success of the experiment turned. The prospect thus suddenly opened before me, was too much for my shattered nerves. I was obliged to look away from him – or I should have lost my self-control.

There was another interval of silence.

When I could trust myself to look back at him, he was out of his bed, standing erect at the side of it. The pupils of his eyes were now contracted; his eyeballs gleamed in the light of the candle as he moved his head slowly to and fro. He was thinking; he was doubting – he spoke again.

'How do I know?' he said. 'The Indians may be hidden in the house?'

He stopped, and walked slowly to the other end of the room. He turned – waited – came back to the bed.

'It's not even locked up,' he went on. 'It's in the drawer of her cabinet. And the drawer doesn't lock.'

He sat down on the side of the bed. 'Anybody might take it,' he said. He rose again restlessly, and reiterated his first words.

'How do I know? The Indians may be hidden in the house.'

He waited again. I drew back behind the half-curtain of the bed. He looked about the room, with a vacant glitter in his eyes. It was a breath-less moment. There was a pause of some sort. A pause in the action of the opium? A pause in the action of the brain? Who could tell? Everything depended, now, on what he did next.

He laid himself down again on the bed!

A horrible doubt crossed my mind. Was it possible that the sedative action of the opium was making itself felt already? It was not in my experience that it should do this. But what is experience, where opium is concerned? There are probably no two men in existence on whom the drug acts in exactly the same manner. Was some constitutional peculiarity in him, feeling the influence in some new way? Were we to fail, on the very brink of success?

No! He got up again abruptly. 'How the devil am I to sleep,' he said, 'with *this* on my mind?'

He looked at the light, burning on the table at the head of his bed. After a moment, he took the candle in his hand.

I blew out the second candle, burning behind the closed curtains. I drew back, with Mr Bruff and Betteredge, into the farthest corner by the bed. I signed to them to be silent, as if their lives had depended on it.

We waited – seeing and hearing nothing. We waited, hidden from him by the curtains.

The light which he was holding on the other side of us, moved sud-denly. The next moment, he passed us, swift and noiseless, with the candle in his hand.

He opened the bedroom door, and went out.

We followed him along the corridor. We followed him down the stairs. We followed him along the second corridor. He never looked back; he never hesitated.

He opened the sitting-room door, and went in, leaving it open behind him.

The door was hung (like all the other doors in the house) on large old-fashioned hinges. When it was opened, a crevice was opened between the door and the post. I signed to my two companions to look through this, so as to keep them from showing themselves. I placed myself – outside the door also – on the opposite side. A recess in the wall was at my left hand, in which I could instantly hide myself, if he showed any signs of looking back into the corridor.

He advanced to the middle of the room, with the candle still in his hand: he looked about him – but he never looked back.

I saw the door of Miss Verinder's bedroom, standing ajar. She had put out her light. She controlled herself nobly. The dim white outline of her summer dress was all that I could see. Nobody who had not known it beforehand, would have suspected that there was a living creature in the room. She kept back, in the dark: not a word, not a movement escaped her.

It was now ten minutes past one. I heard, through the dead silence, the soft drip of the rain and the tremulous passage of the night air through the trees.

After waiting irresolute, for a minute or more, in the middle of the room, he moved to the corner near the window, where the Indian cabinet stood.

He put his candle on the top of the cabinet. He opened, and shut, one drawer after another, until he came to the drawer in which the mock Diamond was put. He looked into the drawer for a moment. Then, he took the mock Diamond out with his right hand. With the other hand, he took the candle from the top of the cabinet.

He walked back a few steps towards the middle of the room, and stood still again.

Thus far, he had exactly repeated what he had done on the birthday night. Would his next proceeding be the same as the proceeding of last year? Would he leave the room? Would he go back now, as I believed he had gone back then, to his bedchamber? Would he show us what he had done with the Diamond, when he had returned to his own room?

His first action, when he moved once more, proved to be an action which he had *not* performed, when he was under the influence of the opium for the first time. He put the candle down on a table, and wandered on a little towards the farther end of the room. There was a sofa here. He leaned heavily on the back of it, with his left hand – then roused himself, and returned to the middle of the room. I could now see his eyes. They were getting dull and heavy; the glitter in them was fast dying out.

The suspense of the moment proved too much for Miss Verinder's self-control. She advanced a few steps – then stopped again. Mr Bruff and Betteredge looked across the open doorway at me for the first time. The prevision of a coming disappointment was impressing itself on their minds as well as on mine.

Still, so long as he stood where he was, there was hope. We waited, in unutterable expectation, to see what would happen next.

The next event was decisive. He let the mock Diamond drop out of his hand.

It fell on the floor, before the doorway – plainly visible to him, and to every one. He made no effort to pick it up: he looked down at it vacantly, and, as he looked, his head sank on his breast. He staggered – roused himself for an instant – walked back unsteadily to the sofa – and sat down on it. He made a last effort; he tried to rise, and sank back. His head fell on the sofa cushions. It was then twenty-five minutes past one o'clock. Before I had put my watch back in my pocket, he was asleep.

It was all over now. The sedative influence had got him; the experiment was at an end.

I entered the room, telling Mr Bruff and Betteredge that they might follow me. There was no fear of disturbing him. We were free to move and speak.

'The first thing to settle,' I said, 'is the question of what we are to do with him. He will probably sleep for the next six or seven hours, at least. It is some distance to carry him back to his own room. When I was younger, I could have done it alone. But my health and strength are not what they were – I am afraid I must ask you to help me.'

Before they could answer, Miss Verinder called to me softly. She met me at the door of her room, with a light shawl, and with the counterpane from her own bed.

'Do you mean to watch him, while he sleeps?' she asked.

'Yes. I am not sure enough of the action of the opium, in his case, to be willing to leave him alone.'

She handed me the shawl and the counterpane.

'Why should you disturb him?' she whispered. 'Make his bed on the sofa. I can shut my door, and keep in my room.'

It was infinitely the simplest and the safest way of disposing of him for the night. I mentioned the suggestion to Mr Bruff and Betteredge – who both approved of my adopting it. In five minutes, I had laid him comfortably on the sofa, and had covered him lightly with the counterpane and the shawl. Miss Verinder wished us good night, and closed the door. At my request, we three then drew round the table in the middle of the room, on which the candle was still burning, and on which writing materials were placed.

'Before we separate,' I began, 'I have a word to say about the experiment which has been tried to-night. Two distinct objects were to be gained by it. The first of these objects was to prove, that Mr Blake entered this room, and took the Diamond, last year, acting unconsciously and irresponsibly, under the influence of opium. After what you have both seen, are you both satisfied, so far?'

They answered me in the affirmative, without a moment's hesitation.

'The second object,' I went on, 'was to discover what he did with the Diamond, after he was seen by Miss Verinder to leave her sitting-room with the jewel in his hand, on the birthday night. The gaining of this object depended, of course, on his still continuing exactly to repeat his proceedings of last year. He has failed to do that; and the purpose of the experiment is defeated accordingly. I can't assert that I am not disappointed at the result – but I can honestly say that I am not surprised by it. I told Mr Blake from the first, that our complete success in this matter, depended on our completely reproducing in him the physical and moral conditions of last year – and I warned him that this was the next thing to a downright impossibility. We have only partially reproduced the conditions, and the experiment has been only partially successful in consequence. It is also possible that I may have administered too large a dose of laudanum. But I myself look upon the first reason that I have given, as the true reason why we have to lament a failure, as well as to rejoice over a success.'

After saying those words, I put the writing materials before Mr Bruff, and asked him if he had any objection – before we separated for the night – to draw out, and sign, a plain statement of what he had seen. He at once took the pen, and produced the statement with the fluent readiness of a practised hand.

'I owe you this,' he said, signing the paper, 'as some atonement for what passed between us earlier in the evening. I beg your pardon, Mr Jennings, for having doubted you. You have done Franklin Blake an inestimable service. In our legal phrase, you have proved your case.'

Betteredge's apology was characteristic of the man.

'Mr Jennings,' he said, 'when you read *Robinson Crusoe* again (which I strongly recommend you to do), you will find that he never scruples to acknowledge it, when he turns out to have been in the wrong. Please to consider me, sir, as doing what Robinson Crusoe did, on the present occasion.' With those words he signed the paper in his turn.

Mr Bruff took me aside, as we rose from the table.

'One word about the Diamond,' he said. 'Your theory is that Franklin Blake hid the Moonstone in his room. My theory is, that the Moonstone is in the possession of Mr Luker's bankers in London. We won't dispute which of us is right. We will only ask, which of us is in a position to put his theory to the test?'

'The test, in my case,' I answered, 'has been tried to-night, and has failed.'

'The test, in my case,' rejoined Mr Bruff, 'is still in process of trial. For the last two days, I have had a watch set for Mr Luker at the bank; and I shall cause that watch to be continued until the last day of the month. I know that he must take the Diamond himself out of his bankers' hands – and I am acting on the chance that the person who has pledged the Diamond may force him to do this, by redeeming the pledge. In that case, I may be able to lay my hand on the person. If I succeed, I clear up the mystery, exactly at the point where the mystery baffles us now! Do you admit that, so far?'

I admitted it readily.

'I am going back to town by the morning train,' pursued the lawyer. 'I may hear, when I return, that a discovery has been made – and it may be of the greatest importance that I should have Franklin Blake at hand to appeal to, if necessary. I intend to tell him, as soon as he wakes, that he must return with me to London. After all that has happened, may I trust to your influence to back me?'

'Certainly!' I said.

Mr Bruff shook hands with me, and left the room. Betteredge followed him out.

I went to the sofa to look at Mr Blake. He had not moved since I had laid him down and made his bed – he lay locked in a deep and quiet sleep.

While I was still looking at him, I heard the bedroom door softly opened. Once more, Miss Verinder appeared on the threshold, in her pretty summer dress.

'Do me a last favour,' she whispered. 'Let me watch him with you.'

I hesitated – not in the interests of propriety; only in the interests of her night's rest. She came close to me, and took my hand.

'I can't sleep; I can't even sit still, in my own room,' she said. 'Oh, Mr Jennings, if you were me, only think how you would long to sit and look at him. Say, yes! Do!'

Is it necessary to mention that I gave way? Surely not!

She drew a chair to the foot of the sofa. She looked at him, in a silent ecstasy of happiness, till the tears rose in her eyes. She dried her eyes, and said she would fetch her work. She fetched her work, and never did a single stitch of it. It lay in her lap – she was not even able to look away from him long enough to thread her needle. I thought of my own youth; I thought of the gentle eyes which had once looked love at *me*. In the heaviness of my heart, I turned to my journal for relief, and wrote in it what is written here.

So we kept our watch together in silence. One of us absorbed in his writing; the other absorbed in her love.

Hour after hour, he lay in his deep sleep. The light of the new day grew and grew in the room, and still he never moved.

Towards six o'clock, I felt the warning which told me that my pains were coming back. I was obliged to leave her alone with him for a little while. I said I would go upstairs, and fetch another pillow for him out of his room. It was not a long attack, this time. In a little while, I was able to venture back, and let her see me again.

I found her at the head of the sofa, when I returned. She was just touching his forehead with her lips. I shook my head as soberly as I could, and pointed to her chair. She looked back at me with a bright smile, and a charming colour in her face. 'You would have done it,' she whispered, 'in my place!'

It is just eight o'clock. He is beginning to move for the first time.

Miss Verinder is kneeling by the side of the sofa. She has so placed herself that when his eyes first open, they must open on her face.

Shall I leave them together?

Yes!

* * * * *

Eleven o'clock. – The house is empty again. They have arranged it among themselves; they have all gone to London by the ten o'clock train. My brief dream of happiness is over. I have awakened again to the realities of my friendless and lonely life.

I dare not trust myself to write down the kind words that have been said to me – especially by Miss Verinder and Mr Blake. Besides, it is needless. Those words will come back to me in my solitary hours, and will help me through what is left of the end of my life. Mr Blake is to write, and tell me what happens in London. Miss Verinder is to return to Yorkshire in the autumn (for her marriage, no doubt); and I am to take a holiday, and be a guest in the house. Oh me, how I felt it, as the grateful happiness looked at me out of her eyes, and the warm pressure of her hand said, 'This is your doing!'

My poor patients are waiting for me. Back again, this morning, to the old routine! Back again, to-night, to the dreadful alternative between the opium and the pain!

God be praised for his mercy! I have seen a little sunshine – I have had a happy time.

Fifth Narrative

The Story resumed by Franklin Blake

❧ ONE ❧

BUT FEW WORDS ARE NEEDED, ON my part, to complete the narrative that has been presented in the Journal of Ezra Jennings.

Of myself, I have only to say that I awoke on the morning of the twenty-sixth, perfectly ignorant of all that I had said and done under the influence of the opium – from the time when the drug first laid its hold on me, to the time when I opened my eyes, in Rachel's sitting-room.

Of what happened after my waking, I do not feel called upon to render an account in detail. Confining myself merely to results, I have to report that Rachel and I thoroughly understood each other, before a single word of explanation had passed on either side. I decline to account, and Rachel declines to account, for the extraordinary rapidity of our reconciliation. Sir and Madam, look back at the time when you were passionately attached to each other – and you will know what happened, after Ezra Jennings had shut the door of the sitting-room, as well as I know it myself.

I have, however, no objection to add, that we should have been certainly discovered by Mrs Merridew, but for Rachel's presence of mind. She heard the sound of the old lady's dress in the corridor; and instantly ran out to meet her. I heard Mrs Merridew say, 'What is the matter?' and I heard Rachel answer, 'The explosion!' Mrs Merridew instantly permitted herself to be taken by the arm, and led into the garden, out of the way of the impending shock. On her return to the house, she met me in the hall, and expressed herself as greatly struck by the vast improvement in Science, since the time when she was a girl at school. 'Explosions, Mr Blake, are infinitely milder than they were. I assure you, I barely heard Mr Jennings's explosion from the garden. And no smell afterwards, that I can detect, now we have come back to the house! I must really apologize to your medical friend. It is only due to him to say, that he has managed it beautifully!'

So, after vanquishing Betteredge and Mr Bruff, Ezra Jennings vanquished Mrs Merridew herself. There is a great deal of undeveloped liberal feeling in the world, after all!

At breakfast, Mr Bruff made no secret of his reasons for wishing that I should accompany him to London by the morning train. The watch kept at the bank, and the result which might yet come of it, appealed so irresistibly to Rachel's curiosity, that she at once decided (if Mrs Merridew had no objection) on accompanying us back to town – so as to be within reach of the earliest news of our proceedings.

Mrs Merridew proved to be all pliability and indulgence, after the truly considerate manner in which the explosion had conducted itself; and Betteredge was accordingly informed that we were all four to travel back together by the morning train. I fully expected that he would have asked leave to accompany us. But Rachel had wisely provided her faithful old servant with an occupation that interested him. He was charged with completing the refurnishing of the house, and was too full of his domestic responsibilities to feel the 'detective-fever' as he might have felt it under other circumstances.

Our one subject of regret, in going to London, was the necessity of parting, more abruptly than we could have wished, with Ezra Jennings. It was impossible to persuade him to accompany us. I could only promise to write to him – and Rachel could only insist on his coming to see her when she returned to Yorkshire. There was every prospect of our meeting again in a few months – and yet there was something very sad in seeing our best and dearest friend left standing alone on the platform, as the train moved out of the station.

On our arrival in London, Mr Bruff was accosted at the terminus by a small boy, dressed in a jacket and trousers of threadbare black cloth, and personally remarkable in virtue of the extraordinary prominence of his eyes. They projected so far, and they rolled about so loosely, that you wondered uneasily why they remained in their sockets. After listening to the boy, Mr Bruff asked the ladies whether they would excuse our accompanying them back to Portland Place. I had barely time to promise Rachel that I would return, and tell her everything that had happened, before Mr Bruff seized me by the arm, and hurried me into a cab. The boy with the ill-secured eyes, took his place on the box by the driver, and the driver was directed to go to Lombard Street.

'News from the bank?' I asked, as we started.

'News of Mr Luker,' said Mr Bruff. 'An hour ago, he was seen to leave his house at Lambeth, in a cab, accompanied by two men, who were recognized by *my* men as police officers in plain clothes. If Mr Luker's dread of the Indians is at the bottom of this precaution, the inference is plain enough. He is going to take the Diamond out of the bank.'

'And we are going to the bank to see what comes of it?'

'Yes – or to hear what has come of it, if it is all over by this time. Did you notice my boy – on the box, there?'

'I noticed his eyes.'

Mr Bruff laughed. 'They call the poor little wretch "Gooseberry", at the office,' he said. 'I employ him to go on errands – and I only wish my clerks who have nicknamed him, were as thoroughly to be depended on as he is. Gooseberry is one of the sharpest boys in London, Mr Blake, in spite of his eyes.'

It was twenty minutes to five, when we drew up before the bank in Lombard Street. Gooseberry looked longingly at his master as he opened the cab door.

'Do you want to come in too?' asked Mr Bruff kindly.

'Come in then, and keep at my heels till further orders. He's as quick as lightning,' pursued Mr Bruff, addressing me in a whisper.

'Two words will do with Gooseberry, where twenty would be wanted with another boy.'

We entered the bank. The outer office – with the long counter, behind which the cashiers sat – was crowded with people; all waiting their turn to take money out, or to pay money in, before the bank closed at five o'clock.

Two men among the crowd approached Mr Bruff, as soon as he showed himself.

'Well?' asked the lawyer. 'Have you seen him?'

'He passed us here half an hour since, sir, and went on into the inner office.'

'Has he not come out again yet?'

'No, sir.'

Mr Bruff turned to me. 'Let us wait,' he said.

I looked round among the people about me for the three Indians. Not a sign of them was to be seen anywhere. The only person present with a noticeably dark complexion was a tall man in a pilot coat, and a round hat, who looked like a sailor. Could this be one of them in disguise? Impossible! The man was taller than any of the Indians; and his face, where it was not hidden by a bushy black beard, was at least twice the breadth of any of their faces.

'They must have their spy somewhere,' said Mr Bruff, looking at the dark sailor in his turn. 'And he may be the man.'

Before he could say more, his coat-tail was respectfully pulled by his attendant sprite with the gooseberry eyes. Mr Bruff looked where the boy was looking. 'Hush!' he said. 'Here is Mr Luker!'

The money-lender came out from the inner regions of the bank, followed by his two guardian policemen in plain clothes.

'Keep your eye on him,' whispered Mr Bruff. 'If he passes the Diamond to anybody, he will pass it here.'

Without noticing either of us, Mr Luker slowly made his way to the door – now in the thickest, now in the thinnest part of the crowd. I distinctly saw his hand move, as he passed a short, stout man, respectably dressed in a suit of sober grey. The man started a little, and looked after him. Mr Luker moved on slowly through the crowd. At the door, his guard placed themselves on either side of him. They were all three followed by one of Mr Bruff's men – and I saw them no more.

I looked round at the lawyer, and then looked significantly towards the man in the suit of sober grey. 'Yes!' whispered Mr Bruff, 'I saw it too!' He turned about, in search of his second man. The second man was nowhere to be seen. He looked behind him for his attendant sprite. Gooseberry had disappeared.

'What the devil does it mean?' said Mr Bruff angrily. 'They have both left us at the very time when we want them most.'

It came to the turn of the man in the grey suit to transact his business at the counter. He paid in a cheque – received a receipt for it – and turned to go out.

'What is to be done?' asked Mr Bruff. '*We* can't degrade ourselves by following him.'

'*I* can!' I said. 'I wouldn't lose sight of that man for ten thousand pounds!'

'In that case,' rejoined Mr Bruff, 'I wouldn't lose sight of *you*, for twice the money. A nice occupation for a man in my position,' he muttered to himself, as we followed the stranger out of the bank. 'For Heaven's sake don't mention it. I should be ruined if it was known.'

The man in the grey suit got into an omnibus, going westward. We got in after him. There were latent reserves of youth still left in Mr Bruff. I assert it positively – when he took his seat in the omnibus, he blushed!

The man with the grey suit stopped the omnibus, and got out in Oxford Street. We followed him again. He went into a chemist's shop.

Mr Bruff started. 'My chemist!' he exclaimed. 'I am afraid we have made a mistake.'

We entered the shop. Mr Bruff and the proprietor exchanged a few words in private. The lawyer joined me again, with a very crestfallen face.

'It's greatly to our credit,' he said, as he took my arm, and led me out— 'that's one comfort!'

'What is to our credit?' I asked.

'Mr Blake! you and I are the two worst amateur detectives that ever tried their hands at the trade. The man in the grey suit has been thirty years in the chemist's service. He was sent to the bank to pay money to his master's account – and he knows no more of the Moonstone than the babe unborn.'

I asked what was to be done next.

'Come back to my office,' said Mr Bruff. 'Gooseberry, and my second man, have evidently followed somebody else. Let us hope that *they* had their eyes about them at any rate!'

When we reached Gray's Inn Square, the second man had arrived there before us. He had been waiting for more than a quarter of an hour.

'Well?' asked Mr Bruff. 'What's your news?'

'I am sorry to say, sir,' replied the man, 'that I have made a mistake. I could have taken my oath that I saw Mr Luker pass something to an elderly gentleman, in a light-coloured paletot. The elderly gentleman turns out, sir, to be a most respectable master ironmonger in Eastcheap.'

'Where is Gooseberry?' asked Mr Bruff resignedly.

The man stared. 'I don't know, sir. I have seen nothing of him since I left the bank.'

Mr Bruff dismissed the man. 'One of two things,' he said to me. 'Either Gooseberry has run away, or he is hunting on his own account. What do you say to dining here, on the chance that the boy may come back in an hour or two? I have got some good wine in the cellar, and we can get a chop from the coffee-house.'

We dined at Mr Bruff's chambers. Before the cloth was removed, 'a person' was announced as wanting to speak to the lawyer. Was the person, Gooseberry? No: only the man who had been employed to follow Mr Luker when he left the bank.

The report, in this case, presented no feature of the slightest interest. Mr Luker had gone back to his own house, and had there dismissed his guard. He had not gone out again afterwards. Towards dusk, the shutters had been put up, and the doors had been bolted. The street before the house, and the alley behind the house, had been carefully watched. No signs of the Indians had been visible. No person whatever had been seen loitering about the premises. Having stated these facts, the man waited to know whether there were any further orders. Mr Bruff dismissed him for the night.

'Do you think Mr Luker has taken the Moonstone home with him?' I asked.

'Not he,' said Mr Bruff. 'He would never have dismissed his two policemen, if he had run the risk of keeping the Diamond in his own house again.'

We waited another half-hour for the boy, and waited in vain. It was then time for Mr Bruff to go to Hampstead, and for me to return to Rachel in Portland Place. I left my card, in charge of the porter at the chambers, with a line written on it to say that I should be at my lodgings at half-past ten, that night. The card was to be given to the boy, if the boy came back.

Some men have a knack of keeping appointments; and other men have a knack of missing them. I am one of the other men. Add to this, that I passed the evening at Portland Place, on the same seat with Rachel, in a room forty feet long, with Mrs Merridew at the further end of it. Does anybody wonder that I got home at half-past twelve instead of half-past ten? How thoroughly heartless that person must be! And how earnestly I hope I may never make that person's acquaintance!

My servant handed me a morsel of paper when he let me in.

I read, in a neat legal handwriting, these words: – 'If you please, sir, I am getting sleepy. I will come back to-morrow morning, between nine and ten.' Inquiry proved that a boy, with very extraordinary-looking eyes, had called, had presented my card and message, had waited an hour, had done nothing but fall asleep and wake up again, had written a line for me, and had gone home – after gravely informing the servant that 'he was fit for nothing unless he got his night's rest'.

At nine, the next morning, I was ready for my visitor. At half-past nine, I heard steps outside my door. 'Come in, Gooseberry!' I called out. 'Thank you, sir,' answered a grave and melancholy voice. The door opened. I started to my feet, and confronted – Sergeant Cuff!

'I thought I would look in here, Mr Blake, on the chance of your being in town, before I wrote to Yorkshire,' said the Sergeant.

He was as dreary and as lean as ever. His eyes had not lost their old trick (so subtly noticed in Betteredge's Narrative) of 'looking as if they expected something more from you than you were aware of yourself'. But, so far as dress can alter a man, the great Cuff was changed beyond all recognition. He wore a broad-brimmed white hat, a light shooting jacket, white trousers, and drab gaiters. He carried a stout oak stick. His whole aim and object seemed to be, to look as if he had lived in the country all his life. When I complimented him on his Metamorphosis, he declined to take it as a joke. He complained, quite gravely, of the noises and the smells of London. I declare I am far from sure that he did not speak with a slightly rustic accent! I offered him breakfast. The innocent countryman was quite shocked. *His* breakfast hour was half-past six – and *he* went to bed with the cocks and hens!

'I only got back from Ireland last night,' said the Sergeant, coming round to the practical object of his visit, in his own impenetrable manner. 'Before I went to bed, I read your letter, telling me what has happened since my inquiry after the Diamond was suspended last year. There's only one thing to be said about the matter, on my side. I completely mistook my case. How any man living was to have seen things in their true light, in such a situation as mine was at the time, I don't profess to know. But that doesn't alter the facts as they stand. I own that I made a mess of it. Not the first mess, Mr Blake, which has distinguished my professional career! It's only in books that the officers of the detective force are superior to the weakness of making a mistake.'

'You have come in the nick of time to recover your reputation,' I said.

'I beg your pardon, Mr Blake,' rejoined the Sergeant. 'Now I have retired from business, I don't care a straw about my reputation. I have done with my reputation, thank God! I am here, sir, in grateful remembrance of the late Lady Verinder's liberality to me. I will go back to my old work – if you want me, and if you will trust me – on that consideration, and on no other. Not a farthing of money is to pass, if you please, from you to me. This is on honour. Now tell me, Mr Blake, how the case stands since you wrote to me last.'

I told him of the experiment with the opium, and of what had occurred afterwards at the bank in Lombard Street. He was greatly struck by the experiment – it was something entirely new in his experience. And he was particularly interested in the theory of Ezra Jennings, relating to what I had done with the Diamond, after I had left Rachel's sitting-room, on the birthday night.

'I don't hold with Mr Jennings that you hid the Moonstone,' said Sergeant Cuff. 'But I agree with him, that you must certainly have taken it back to your own room.'

'Well?' I asked. 'And what happened then?'

'Have you no suspicion yourself of what happened, sir?'

'None whatever.'

'Has Mr Bruff no suspicion?'

'No more than I have.'

Sergeant Cuff rose, and went to my writing-table. He came back with a sealed envelope. It was marked 'Private'; it was addressed to me; and it had the Sergeant's signature in the corner.

'I suspected the wrong person, last year,' he said: 'and I may be suspecting the wrong person now. Wait to open the envelope, Mr Blake, till you have got at the truth. And then compare the name of the guilty person, with the name that I have written in that sealed letter.'

I put the letter into my pocket – and then asked for the Sergeant's opinion of the measures which we had taken at the bank.

'Very well intended, sir,' he answered, 'and quite the right thing to do. But there was another person who ought to have been looked after besides Mr Luker.'

'The person named in the letter you have just given to me?'

'Yes, Mr Blake, the person named in the letter. It can't be helped now. I shall have something to propose to you and Mr Bruff, sir, when the time comes. Let's wait, first, and see if the boy has anything to tell us that is worth hearing.'

It was close on ten o'clock, and the boy had not made his appearance. Sergeant Cuff talked of other matters. He asked after his old friend Betteredge, and his old enemy the gardener. In a minute more, he would no doubt have got from this, to the subject of his favourite roses, if my servant had not interrupted us by announcing that the boy was below.

On being brought into the room, Gooseberry stopped at the threshold of the door, and looked distrustfully at the stranger who was in my company. I told the boy to come to me.

'You may speak before this gentleman,' I said. 'He is here to assist me; and he knows all that has happened. Sergeant Cuff,' I added, 'this is the boy from Mr Bruff's office.'

In our modern system of civilization, celebrity (no matter of what kind) is the lever that will move anything. The fame of the great Cuff had even reached the ears of the small Gooseberry. The boy's ill-fixed eyes rolled, when I mentioned the illustrious name, till I thought they really must have dropped on the carpet.

'Come here, my lad,' said the Sergeant, 'and let's hear what you have got to tell us.'

The notice of the great man – the hero of many a famous story in every lawyer's office in London – appeared to fascinate the boy. He placed himself in front of Sergeant Cuff, and put his hands behind him, after the approved fashion of a neophyte who is examined in his catechism.

'What is your name?' said the Sergeant, beginning with the first question in the catechism.

'Octavius Guy,' answered the boy. 'They call me Gooseberry at the office because of my eyes.'

'Octavius Guy, otherwise Gooseberry,' pursued the Sergeant, with the utmost gravity, 'you were missed at the bank yesterday. What were you about?'

'If you please, sir, I was following a man.'

'Who was he?'

'A tall man, sir, with a big black beard, dressed like a sailor.'

'I remember the man!' I broke in. 'Mr Bruff and I thought he was a spy, employed by the Indians.'

Sergeant Cuff did not appear to be much impressed by what Mr Bruff and I had thought. He went on catechizing Gooseberry.

'Well?' he said – 'and why did you follow the sailor?'

'If you please, sir, Mr Bruff wanted to know whether Mr Luker passed anything to anybody on his way out of the bank. I saw Mr Luker pass something to the sailor with the black beard.'

'Why didn't you tell Mr Bruff what you saw?'

'I hadn't time to tell anybody, sir, the sailor went out in such a hurry.'

'And you ran out after him – eh?'

'Yes, sir.'

'Gooseberry,' said the Sergeant, patting his head, 'you have got something in that small skull of yours – and it isn't cotton-wool. I am greatly pleased with you, so far.'

The boy blushed with pleasure. Sergeant Cuff went on:

'Well? and what did the sailor do, when he got into the street?'

'He called a cab, sir.'

'And what did you do?'

'Held on behind, and run after it.'

Before the Sergeant could put his next question, another visitor was announced – the head clerk from Mr Bruff's office.

Feeling the importance of not interrupting Sergeant Cuff's examination of the boy, I received the clerk in another room. He came with bad news of his employer. The agitation and excitement of the last two days had proved too much for Mr Bruff. He had awoke that morning with an attack of gout; he was confined to his room at Hampstead; and, in the present critical condition of our affairs, he was very uneasy at being compelled to leave me without the advice and assistance of an experienced person. The chief clerk had received orders to hold himself at my disposal, and was willing to do his best to replace Mr Bruff.

I wrote at once to quiet the old gentleman's mind, by telling him of Sergeant Cuff's visit: adding that Gooseberry was at that moment under examination; and promising to inform Mr Bruff, either personally or by letter, of whatever might occur later in the day. Having despatched the clerk to Hampstead with my note, I returned to the room which I had left, and found Sergeant Cuff at the fireplace, in the act of ringing the bell.

'I beg your pardon, Mr Blake,' said the Sergeant. 'I was just going to send word by your servant that I wanted to speak to you. There isn't a doubt on my mind that this boy – this most meritorious boy,' added the Sergeant, patting Gooseberry on the head, 'has followed the right man. Precious time has been lost, sir, through your unfortunately not being at home at half-past ten last night. The only thing to do, now, is to send for a cab immediately.'

In five minutes more, Sergeant Cuff and I (with Gooseberry on the box to guide the driver) were on our way eastward, towards the City.

'One of these days,' said the Sergeant, pointing through the front window of the cab, 'that boy will do great things in my late profession. He is the brightest and cleverest little chap I have met with, for many a long year past. You shall hear the substance, Mr Blake, of what he told me while you were out of the room. You were present, I think, when he mentioned that he held on behind the cab, and ran after it?'

'Yes.'

'Well, sir, the cab went from Lombard Street to the Tower Wharf. The sailor with the black beard got out, and spoke to the steward of the Rotterdam steamboat, which was to start next morning. He asked if he could be allowed to go on board at once, and sleep in his berth overnight. The steward said, No. The cabins, and berths, and bedding were all to have a thorough cleaning that evening, and no passenger could be allowed to come on board, before the morning. The sailor turned round, and left the wharf. When he got into the street again, the boy noticed for the first time, a man dressed like a respectable mechanic, walking on the opposite side of the road, and apparently keeping the sailor in view. The sailor stopped at an eating-house in the neighbourhood, and went in. The boy – not being able to make up his mind, at the moment – hung about among some other boys, staring at the good things in the eating-house window. He noticed the mechanic waiting, as he himself was waiting – but still on the opposite side of the street. After a minute, a cab came by slowly, and stopped where the mechanic was standing. The boy could only see plainly one person in the cab, who leaned forward at the window to speak to the mechanic. He described that person, Mr Blake, without any prompting from me, as having a dark face, like the face of an Indian.'

It was plain, by this time, that Mr Bruff and I had made another mistake. The sailor with the black beard was clearly not a spy in the service of the Indian conspiracy. Was he, by any possibility, the man who had got the Diamond?

'After a little,' pursued the Sergeant, 'the cab moved on slowly down the street. The mechanic crossed the road, and went into the eating-house. The boy waited outside till he was hungry and tired – and then went into the eating-house, in his turn. He had a shilling in his pocket; and he dined sumptuously, he tells me, on a black-pudding, an eel-pie, and a bottle of ginger-beer. What can a boy *not* digest? The substance in question has never been found yet.'

'What did he see in the eating-house?' I asked.

'Well, Mr Blake, he saw the sailor reading the newspaper at one table, and the mechanic reading the newspaper at another. It was dusk before the sailor got up, and left the place. He looked about him suspiciously when he got out into the street. The boy – *being* a boy – passed unnoticed. The mechanic had not come out yet. The sailor walked on, looking about him, and apparently not very certain of where he was going next. The mechanic appeared once more, on the opposite side of the road. The sailor went on, till he got to Shore Lane, leading into Lower Thames Street.

393

There he stopped before a public-house, under the sign of "The Wheel of Fortune", and, after examining the place outside, went in. Gooseberry went in too. There were a great many people, mostly of the decent sort, at the bar. "The Wheel of Fortune" is a very respectable house, Mr Blake; famous for its porter and pork-pies.'

The Sergeant's digressions irritated me. He saw it; and confined himself more strictly to Gooseberry's evidence when he went on.

'The sailor,' he resumed, 'asked if he could have a bed. The landlord said "No; they were full." The barmaid corrected him, and said "Number Ten was empty." A waiter was sent for to show the sailor to Number Ten. Just before that, Gooseberry had noticed the mechanic among the people at the bar. Before the waiter had answered the call, the mechanic had vanished. The sailor was taken off to his room. Not knowing what to do next, Gooseberry had the wisdom to wait and see if anything happened. Something did happen. The landlord was called for. Angry voices were heard upstairs. The mechanic suddenly made his appearance again, collared by the landlord, and exhibiting, to Gooseberry's great surprise, all the signs and tokens of being drunk. The landlord thrust him out at the door, and threatened him with the police if he came back. From the altercation between them, while this was going on, it appeared that the man had been discovered in Number Ten, and had declared with drunken obstinacy, that he had taken the room. Gooseberry was so struck by this sudden intoxication of a previously sober person, that he couldn't resist running out after the mechanic into the street. As long as he was in sight of the public-house, the man reeled about in the most disgraceful manner. The moment he turned the corner of the street, he recovered his balance instantly, and became as sober a member of society as you could wish to see. Gooseberry went back to "The Wheel of Fortune", in a very bewildered state of mind. He waited about again, on the chance of something happening. Nothing happened; and nothing more was to be heard, or seen, of the sailor. Gooseberry decided on going back to the office. Just as he came to this conclusion, who should appear, on the opposite side of the street as usual, but the mechanic again! He looked up at one particular window at the top of the public-house, which was the only one that had a light in it. The light seemed to relieve his mind. He left the place directly. The boy made his way back to Gray's Inn – got your card and message – called – and failed to find you. There you have the state of the case, Mr Blake, as it stands at the present time.'

'What is your own opinion of the case, Sergeant?'

'I think it's serious, sir. Judging by what the boy saw, the Indians are in it, to begin with.'

'Yes. And the sailor is evidently the person to whom Mr Luker passed the Diamond. It seems odd that Mr Bruff, and I, and the man in Mr

Bruff's employment, should all have been mistaken about who the person was.'

'Not at all, Mr Blake. Considering the risk that person ran, it's likely enough that Mr Luker purposely misled you, by previous arrangement between them.'

'Do you understand the proceedings at the public-house?' I asked. 'The man dressed like a mechanic, was acting of course in the employment of the Indians. But I am as much puzzled to account for his sudden assumption of drunkenness as Gooseberry himself.'

'I think I can give a guess at what it means, sir,' said the Sergeant. 'If you will reflect, you will see that the man must have had some pretty strict instructions from the Indians. They were far too noticeable themselves to risk being seen at the bank, or in the public-house – they were obliged to trust everything to their deputy. Very good. Their deputy hears a certain number named, in the public-house, as the number of the room which the sailor is to have for the night – that being also the room (unless our notion is all wrong) which the Diamond is to have for the night, too. Under those circumstances, the Indians, you may rely on it, would insist on having a description of the room – of its position in the house, of its capability of being approached from the outside, and so on. What was the man to do, with such orders as these? Just what he did! He ran upstairs to get a look at the room, before the sailor was taken into it. He was found there, making his observations – and he shammed drunk, as the easiest way of getting out of the difficulty. That's how I read the riddle. After he was turned out of the public-house, he probably went with his report to the place where his employers were waiting for him. And his employers, no doubt, sent him back to make sure that the sailor was really settled at the public-house till the next morning. As for what happened at "The Wheel of Fortune", after the boy left – we ought to have discovered that last night. It's eleven in the morning, now. We must hope for the best, and find out what we can.'

In a quarter of an hour more, the cab stopped in Shore Lane, and Gooseberry opened the door for us to get out.

'All right?' asked the Sergeant.

'All right,' answered the boy.

The moment we entered 'The Wheel of Fortune', it was plain even to my inexperienced eyes that there was something wrong in the house.

The only person behind the counter at which the liquors were served, was a bewildered servant girl, perfectly ignorant of the business. One or two customers, waiting for their morning drink, were tapping impatiently on the counter with their money. The barmaid appeared from the inner regions of the parlour, excited and preoccupied. She answered

Sergeant Cuff's inquiry for the landlord, by telling him sharply that her master was upstairs, and was not to be bothered by anybody.

'Come along with me, sir,' said Sergeant Cuff, coolly leading the way upstairs, and beckoning to the boy to follow him.

The barmaid called to her master, and warned him that strangers were intruding themselves into the house. On the first floor we were encountered by the landlord, hurrying down, in a highly irritated state, to see what was the matter.

'Who the devil are you? and what do you want here?' he asked.

'Keep your temper,' said the Sergeant, quietly. 'I'll tell you who I am to begin with. I am Sergeant Cuff.'

The illustrious name instantly produced its effect. The angry landlord threw open the door of a sitting-room, and asked the Sergeant's pardon.

'I am annoyed and out of sorts, sir – that's the truth,' he said. 'Something unpleasant has happened in the house this morning. A man in my way of business has a deal to upset his temper, Sergeant Cuff.'

'Not a doubt of it,' said the Sergeant. 'I'll come at once, if you will allow me, to what brings us here. This gentleman and I want to trouble you with a few inquiries, on a matter of some interest to both of us.'

'Relating to what, sir?' asked the landlord.

'Relating to a dark man, dressed like a sailor, who slept here last night.'

'Good God! that's the man who is upsetting the whole house at this moment!' exclaimed the landlord. 'Do you, or does this gentleman know anything about him?'

'We can't be certain till we see him,' answered the Sergeant.

'See him?' echoed the landlord. 'That's the one thing that nobody has been able to do since seven o'clock this morning. That was the time when he left word, last night, that he was to be called. He *was* called – and there was no getting an answer from him, and no opening his door to see what was the matter. They tried again at eight, and they tried again at nine. No use! There was the door still locked – and not a sound to be heard in the room! I have been out this morning – and I only got back a quarter of an hour ago. I have hammered at the door myself – and all to no purpose. The potboy has gone to fetch a carpenter. If you can wait a few minutes, gentlemen, we will have the door opened, and see what it means.'

'Was the man drunk last night?' asked Sergeant Cuff.

'Perfectly sober, sir – or I would never have let him sleep in my house.'

'Did he pay for his bed beforehand?'

'No.'

'Could he leave the room in any way, without going out by the door?'

'The room is a garret,' said the landlord. 'But there's a trap-door in the ceiling, leading out on to the roof – and a little lower down the street, there's an empty house under repair. Do you think, Sergeant, the blackguard has got off in that way, without paying?'

'A sailor,' said Sergeant Cuff, 'might have done it – early in the morning, before the street was astir. He would be used to climbing, and his head wouldn't fail him on the roofs of the houses.'

As he spoke, the arrival of the carpenter was announced. We all went upstairs, at once, to the top story. I noticed that the Sergeant was unusually grave, even for *him*. It also struck me as odd that he told the boy (after having previously encouraged him to follow us), to wait in the room below till we came down again.

The carpenter's hammer and chisel disposed of the resistance of the door in a few minutes. But some article of furniture had been placed against it inside, as a barricade. By pushing at the door, we thrust this obstacle aside, and so got admission to the room. The landlord entered first; the Sergeant second; and I third. The other persons present followed us.

We all looked towards the bed, and all started.

The man had not left the room. He lay, dressed, on the bed – with a white pillow over his face, which completely hid it from view.

'What does that mean?' said the landlord pointing to the pillow.

Sergeant Cuff led the way to the bed, without answering, and removed the pillow.

The man's swarthy face was placid and still; his black hair and beard were slightly, very slightly, discomposed. His eyes stared wide-open, glassy and vacant, at the ceiling. The filmy look and the fixed expression of them horrified me. I turned away, and went to the open window. The rest of them remained, where Sergeant Cuff remained, at the bed.

'He's in a fit!' I heard the landlord say.

'He's dead,' the Sergeant answered. 'Send for the nearest doctor, and send for the police.'

The waiter was despatched on both errands. Some strange fascination seemed to hold Sergeant Cuff to the bed. Some strange curiosity seemed to keep the rest of them waiting, to see what the Sergeant would do next.

I turned again to the window. The moment afterwards, I felt a soft pull at my coat-tails, and a small voice whispered, 'Look here, sir!'

Gooseberry had followed us into the room. His loose eyes rolled frightfully – not in terror, but in exultation. He had made a detective-discovery on his own account. 'Look here, sir,' he repeated – and led me to a table in the corner of the room.

On the table stood a little wooden box, open, and empty. On one side of the box lay some jewellers' cotton. On the other side, was a torn sheet of white paper, with a seal on it, partly destroyed, and with an inscription in writing, which was still perfectly legible. The inscription was in these words:

'Deposited with Messrs Bushe, Lysaught, and Bushe, by Mr Septimus Luker, of Middlesex Place, Lambeth, a small wooden box, sealed up in this envelope, and containing a valuable of great price. The box, when claimed, to be only given up by Messrs Bushe and Co. on the personal application of Mr Luker.'

Those lines removed all further doubt, on one point at least. The sailor had been in possession of the Moonstone, when he had left the bank on the previous day.

I felt another pull at my coat-tails. Gooseberry had not done with me yet.

'Robbery!' whispered the boy, pointing, in high delight, to the empty box.

'You were told to wait downstairs,' I said. 'Go away!'

'And Murder!' added Gooseberry, pointing, with a keener relish still, to the man on the bed.

There was something so hideous in the boy's enjoyment of the horror of the scene, that I took him by the two shoulders and put him out of the room.

At the moment when I crossed the threshold of the door, I heard Sergeant Cuff's voice, asking where I was. He met me, as I returned into the room, and forced me to go back with him to the bedside.

'Mr Blake!' he said. 'Look at the man's face. It is a face disguised – and here's a proof of it!'

He traced with his finger a thin line of livid white, running backward from the dead man's forehead, between the swarthy complexion, and the slightly-disturbed black hair. 'Let's see what is under this,' said the Sergeant, suddenly seizing the black hair, with a firm grip of his hand.

My nerves were not strong enough to bear it. I turned away again from the bed.

The first sight that met my eyes, at the other end of the room, was the irrepressible Gooseberry, perched on a chair, and looking with breathless interest, over the heads of his elders, at the Sergeant's proceedings.

'He's pulling off his wig!' whispered Gooseberry, compassionating my position, as the only person in the room who could see nothing.

There was a pause – and then a cry of astonishment among the people round the bed.

'He's pulled off his beard!' cried Gooseberry.

There was another pause – Sergeant Cuff asked for something. The landlord went to the washhand-stand, and returned to the bed with a basin of water and a towel.

Gooseberry danced with excitement on the chair. 'Come up here, along with me, sir! He's washing off his complexion now!'

The Sergeant suddenly burst his way through the people about him, and came, with horror in his face, straight to the place where I was standing.

'Come back to the bed, sir!' he began. He looked at me closer, and checked himself, 'No!' he resumed. 'Open the sealed letter first – the letter I gave you this morning.'

I opened the letter.

'Read the name, Mr Blake, that I have written inside.'

I read the name that he had written. It was – *Godfrey Ablewhite*.

'Now,' said the Sergeant, 'come with me, and look at the man on the bed.'

I went with him, and looked at the man on the bed.

Godfrey Ablewhite!

Sixth Narrative

Contributed by Sergeant Cuff

I

Dorking, Surrey, 30 July 1849. To Franklin Blake, Esq. Sir, – I beg to apologize for the delay that has occurred in the production of the Report, with which I engaged to furnish you. I have waited to make it a complete Report; and I have been met, here and there, by obstacles which it was only possible to remove by some little expenditure of patience and time.

The object which I proposed to myself has now, I hope, been attained. You will find, in these pages, answers to the greater part – if not all – of the questions, concerning the late Mr Godfrey Ablewhite, which occurred to your mind when I last had the honour of seeing you.

I propose to tell you – in the first place – what is known of the manner in which your cousin met his death; appending to the statement such inferences and conclusions as we are justified (according to my opinion) in drawing from the facts.

I shall then endeavour – in the second place – to put you in possession of such discoveries as I have made, respecting the proceedings of Mr Godfrey Ablewhite, before, during, and after the time, when you and he met as guests at the late Lady Verinder's country-house.

II

As to your cousin's death, then, first.

It appears to me to be established, beyond any reasonable doubt, that he was killed (while he was asleep, or immediately on his waking) by being smothered with a pillow from his bed – that the persons guilty of murdering him are the three Indians – and that the object contemplated (and achieved) by the crime, was to obtain possession of the diamond, called the Moonstone.

The facts from which this conclusion is drawn, are derived partly from an examination of the room at the tavern; and partly from the evidence obtained at the Coroner's Inquest.

On forcing the door of the room, the deceased gentleman was discovered, dead, with the pillow of the bed over his face. The medical man who examined him, being informed of this circumstance, considered the post-mortem appearances as being perfectly compatible with murder by smothering – that is to say, with murder committed by some person, or persons, pressing the pillow over the nose and mouth of the deceased, until death resulted from congestion of the lungs.

Next, as to the motive for the crime.

A small box, with a sealed paper torn off from it (the paper containing an inscription) was found open, and empty, on a table in the room. Mr Luker has himself personally identified the box, the seal, and the inscription. He has declared that the box did actually contain the diamond, called the Moonstone; and he has admitted having given the box (thus sealed up) to Mr Godfrey Ablewhite (then concealed under a disguise), on the afternoon of the twenty-sixth of June last. The fair inference from all this is, that the stealing of the Moonstone was the motive of the crime.

Next, as to the manner in which the crime was committed.

On examination of the room (which is only seven feet high), a trap-door in the ceiling, leading out on to the roof of the house, was discovered open. The short ladder, used for obtaining access to the trap-door (and kept under the bed), was found placed at the opening, so as to enable any person or persons, in the room, to leave it again easily. In the trap-door itself was found a square aperture cut in the wood, apparently with some exceedingly sharp instrument, just behind the bolt which fastened the door on the inner side. In this way, any person from the outside could have drawn back the bolt, and opened the door, and have dropped (or have been noiselessly lowered by an accomplice) into the room – its height, as already observed, being only seven feet. That some person, or persons, must have got admission in this way, appears evident from the fact of the aperture being there. As to the manner in which he (or they) obtained access to the roof of the tavern, it is to be remarked that the third house, lower down in the street, was empty, and under repair – that a long ladder was left by the workmen, leading from the pavement to the top of the house – and that, on returning to their work, on the morning of the 27th, the men found the plank which they had tied to the ladder, to prevent any one from using it in their absence, removed, and lying on the ground. As to the possibility of ascending by this ladder, passing over the roofs of the houses, passing back, and descending again, unobserved – it is discovered, on the evidence of the night policeman, that he only passes through Shore Lane twice in an hour, when out on his beat. The testimony of the inhabitants also declares, that Shore Lane, after midnight, is one of the quietest and loneliest streets in London. Here again, therefore, it seems fair to infer that – with ordinary caution, and presence of mind – any man, or men, might have ascended by the ladder, and might have descended again, unobserved. Once on the roof of the tavern, it has been proved, by experiment, that a man might cut through the trap-door, while lying down on it, and that in such a position, the parapet in front of the house would conceal him from the view of any one passing in the street.

Lastly, as to the person, or persons, by whom the crime was committed.

It is known (1) that the Indians had an interest in possessing themselves of the Diamond. (2) It is at least probable that the man looking like an Indian, whom Octavius Guy saw at the window of the cab, speaking to the man dressed like a mechanic, was one of the three Hindoo conspirators. (3) It is certain that this same man dressed like a mechanic, was seen keeping Mr Godfrey Ablewhite in view, all through the evening of the 26th, and was found in the bedroom (before Mr Ablewhite was shown into it) under circumstances which lead to the suspicion that he was examining the room. (4) A morsel of torn gold thread was picked up in the bedroom, which persons expert in such matters, declare to be of Indian manufacture, and to be a species of gold thread not known in England. (5) On the morning of the 27th, three men, answering to the description of the three Indians, were observed in Lower Thames Street, were traced to the Tower Wharf, and were seen to leave London by the steamer bound for Rotterdam.

There is here, moral, if not legal, evidence, that the murder was committed by the Indians.

Whether the man personating a mechanic was, or was not, an accomplice in the crime, it is impossible to say. That he could have committed the murder alone, seems beyond the limits of probability. Acting by himself, he could hardly have smothered Mr Ablewhite – who was the taller and stronger man of the two – without a struggle taking place, or a cry being heard. A servant girl, sleeping in the next room, heard nothing. The landlord, sleeping in the room below, heard nothing. The whole evidence points to the inference that more than one man was concerned in this crime – and the circumstances, I repeat, morally justify the conclusion that the Indians committed it.

I have only to add, that the verdict at the Coroner's Inquest was Wilful Murder against some person, or persons, unknown. Mr Ablewhite's family have offered a reward, and no effort has been left untried to discover the guilty persons. The man dressed like a mechanic has eluded all inquiries. The Indians have been traced. As to the prospect of ultimately capturing these last, I shall have a word to say to you on that head, when I reach the end of the present Report.

In the meanwhile, having now written all that is needful on the subject of Mr Godfrey Ablewhite's death, I may pass next to the narrative of his proceedings before, during, and after the time, when you and he met at the late Lady Verinder's house.

III

With regard to the subject now in hand, I may state, at the outset, that Mr Godfrey Ablewhite's life had two sides to it.

The side turned up to the public view, presented the spectacle of a gentleman, possessed of considerable reputation as a speaker at charitable meetings, and endowed with administrative abilities, which he placed at the disposal of various Benevolent Societies, mostly of the female sort. The side kept hidden from the general notice, exhibited this same gentleman in the totally different character of a man of pleasure, with a villa in the suburbs which was not taken in his own name, and with a lady in the villa, who was not taken in his own name, either.

My investigations in the villa have shown me several fine pictures and statues; furniture tastefully selected, and admirably made; and a conservatory of the rarest flowers, the match of which it would not be easy to find in all London. My investigation of the lady has resulted in the discovery of jewels which are worthy to take rank with the flowers, and of carriages and horses which have (deservedly) produced a sensation in the Park, among persons well qualified to judge of the build of the one, and the breed of the others.

All this is, so far, common enough. The villa and the lady are such familiar objects in London life, that I ought to apologize for introducing them to notice. But what is not common and not familiar (in my experience), is that all these fine things were not only ordered, but paid for. The pictures, the statues, the flowers, the jewels, the carriages and the horses – inquiry proved, to my indescribable astonishment, that not a sixpence of debt was owing on any of them. As to the villa, it had been bought, out and out, and settled on the lady.

I might have tried to find the right reading of this riddle, and tried in vain – but for Mr Godfrey Ablewhite's death, which caused an inquiry to be made into the state of his affairs.

The inquiry elicited these facts:—

That Mr Godfrey Ablewhite was entrusted with the care of a sum of twenty thousand pounds – as one of two Trustees for a young gentleman, who was still a minor in the year eighteen hundred and forty-eight. That the Trust was to lapse, and that the young gentleman was to receive the twenty thousand pounds on the day when he came of age, in the month of February, eighteen hundred and fifty. That, pending the arrival of this period, an income of six hundred pounds was to be paid to him by his two Trustees, half-yearly – at Christmas and Midsummer Day. That this income was regularly paid by the active Trustee, Mr Godfrey Ablewhite. That the twenty thousand pounds (from which the income was supposed to be derived) had, every farthing of it, been sold out of the Funds, at different periods, ending with the end of the year eighteen hundred and forty-seven. That the power of attorney, authorizing the bankers to sell out the stock, and the various written orders telling them what amounts to sell out, were formally signed by both the Trustees. That the signature of the second Trustee (a retired army officer, living in the country) was a signature forged, in every case, by the active Trustee – otherwise Mr Godfrey Ablewhite.

In these facts, lies the explanation of Mr Godfrey's honourable conduct, in paying the debts incurred for the lady and the villa – and (as you will presently see) of more besides.

We may now advance to the date of Miss Verinder's birthday (in the year eighteen hundred and forty-eight) – the twenty-first of June.

On the day before, Mr Godfrey Ablewhite arrived at his father's house, and asked (as I know from Mr Ablewhite, senior, himself) for a loan of three hundred pounds. Mark the sum; and remember at the same time, that the half-yearly payment to the young gentleman was due on the twenty-fourth of the month. Also, that the whole of the young gentleman's fortune had been spent by his Trustee, by the end of the year 'forty-seven.

Mr Ablewhite, senior, refused to lend his son a farthing.

The next day Mr Godfrey Ablewhite rode over, with you, to Lady Verinder's house. A few hours afterwards, Mr Godfrey (as you yourself have told me) made a proposal of marriage to Miss Verinder. Here, he saw his way no doubt – if accepted – to the end of all his money anxieties, present and future. But, as events actually turned out, what happened? Miss Verinder refused him.

On the night of the birthday, therefore, Mr Godfrey Ablewhite's pecuniary position was this. He had three hundred pounds to find on the twenty-fourth of the month, and twenty thousand pounds to find in February eighteen hundred and fifty. Failing to raise these sums, at these times, he was a ruined man.

Under those circumstances, what takes place next?

You exasperate Mr Candy, the doctor, on the sore subject of his profession; and he plays you a practical joke, in return, with a dose of laudanum. He trusts the administration of the dose, prepared in a little phial, to Mr Godfrey Ablewhite – who has himself confessed the share he had in the matter, under circumstances which shall presently be related to you. Mr Godfrey is all the readier to enter into the conspiracy, having himself suffered from your sharp tongue in the course of the evening. He joins Betteredge in persuading you to drink a little brandy and water before you go to bed. He privately drops the dose of laudanum into your cold grog. And you drink the mixture.

Let us now shift the scene, if you please, to Mr Luker's house at

Lambeth. And allow me to remark, by way of preface, that Mr Bruff and I, together, have found a means of forcing the money-lender to make a clean breast of it. We have carefully sifted the statement he has addressed to us; and here it is at your service.

IV

Late on the evening of Friday, the twenty-third of June ('forty-eight), Mr Luker was surprised by a visit from Mr Godfrey Ablewhite. He was more than surprised, when Mr Godfrey produced the Moonstone. No such Diamond (according to Mr Luker's experience) was in the possession of any private person in Europe.

Mr Godfrey Ablewhite had two modest proposals to make, in relation to this magnificent gem. First, would Mr Luker be so good as to buy it? Secondly, would Mr Luker (in default of seeing his way to the purchase) undertake to sell it on commission, and to pay a sum down, on the anticipated result?

Mr Luker tested the Diamond, weighed the Diamond, and estimated the value of the Diamond, before he answered a word. *His* estimate (allowing for the flaw in the stone) was thirty thousand pounds.

Having reached that result, Mr Luker opened his lips, and put a question: 'How did you come by this?' Only six words! But what volumes of meaning in them!

Mr Godfrey Ablewhite began a story. Mr Luker opened his lips again and only said three words, this time. 'That won't do!'

Mr Godfrey Ablewhite began another story. Mr Luker wasted no more words on him. He got up, and rang the bell for the servant, to show the gentleman out.

Upon this compulsion, Mr Godfrey made an effort, and came out with a new and amended version of the affair, to the following effect.

After privately slipping the laudanum into your brandy and water, he wished you good-night, and went into his own room. It was the next room to yours; and the two had a door of communication between them. On entering his own room Mr Godfrey (as he supposed) closed this door. His money-troubles kept him awake. He sat, in his dressing-gown and slippers, for nearly an hour, thinking over his position. Just as he was preparing to get into bed, he heard you, talking to yourself, in your own room, and going to the door of communication, found that he had not shut it as he supposed.

He looked into your room to see what was the matter. He discovered you with the candle in your hand, just leaving your bedchamber. He heard you say to yourself, in a voice quite unlike your own voice, 'How do I know? The Indians may be hidden in the house.'

Up to that time, he had simply supposed himself (in giving you the laudanum) to be helping to make you the victim of a harmless practical joke. It now occurred to him, that the laudanum had taken some effect on you, which had not been foreseen by the doctor, any more than by himself. In the fear of an accident happening, he followed you softly to see what you would do.

He followed you to Miss Verinder's sitting-room, and saw you go in. You left the door open. He looked through the crevice thus produced, between the door and the post, before he ventured into the room himself.

In that position, he not only detected you in taking the Diamond out of the drawer – he also detected Miss Verinder, silently watching you from her bedroom, through her open door. His own eyes satisfied him that *she* saw you take the Diamond, too.

Before you left the sitting-room again, you hesitated a little. Mr Godfrey took advantage of this hesitation to get back again to his bedroom before you came out, and discovered him. He had barely got back, before you got back too. You saw him (as he supposed) just as he was passing through the door of communication. At any rate, you called to him in a strange, drowsy voice.

He came back to you. You looked at him in a dull sleepy way. You put the Diamond into his hand. You said to him, 'Take it back, Godfrey, to your father's bank. It's safe there – it's not safe here.' You turned away unsteadily, and put on your dressing-gown. You sat down in the large arm-chair in your room. You said, '*I* can't take it back to the bank. My head's like lead – and I can't feel my feet under me.' Your head sank on the back of the chair – you heaved a heavy sigh – and you fell asleep.

Mr Godfrey Ablewhite went back, with the Diamond, into his own room. His statement is, that he came to no conclusion, at that time – except that he would wait, and see what happened in the morning.

When the morning came, your language and conduct showed that you were absolutely ignorant of what you had said and done overnight. At the same time, Miss Verinder's language and conduct showed that she was resolved to say nothing (in mercy to you) on her side. If Mr Godfrey Ablewhite chose to keep the Diamond, he might do so with perfect impunity. The Moonstone stood between him and ruin. He put the Moonstone into his pocket.

V

This was the story told by your cousin (under pressure of necessity) to Mr Luker.

Mr Luker believed the story to be, as to all main essentials true – on this ground, that Mr Godfrey Ablewhite was too great a fool to have invented it. Mr Bruff and I agree with Mr Luker, in considering this test of the truth of the story to be a perfectly reliable one.

The next question, was the question of what Mr Luker would do in the matter of the Moonstone. He proposed the following terms, as the only terms on which he would consent to mix himself up with what was (even in his line of business) a doubtful and dangerous transaction.

Mr Luker would consent to lend Mr Godfrey Ablewhite the sum of two thousand pounds, on condition that the Moonstone was to be deposited with him as a pledge. If, at the expiration of one year from that date, Mr Godfrey Ablewhite paid three thousand pounds to Mr Luker, he was to receive back the Diamond, as a pledge redeemed. If he failed to produce the money at the expiration of the year, the pledge (otherwise the Moonstone) was to be considered as forfeited to Mr Luker – who would, in this latter case, generously make Mr Godfrey a present of certain promissory notes of his (relating to former dealings) which were then in the money-lender's possession.

It is needless to say, that Mr Godfrey indignantly refused to listen to these monstrous terms. Mr Luker thereupon, handed him back the Diamond, and wished him good night.

Your cousin went to the door, and came back again. How was he to be sure that the conversation of that evening, would be kept strictly secret between his friend and himself?

Mr Luker didn't profess to know how. If Mr Godfrey had accepted his terms, Mr Godfrey would have made him an accomplice, and might have counted on his silence as on a certainty. As things were, Mr Luker must be guided by his own interests. If awkward inquiries were made, how could he be expected to compromise himself, for the sake of a man who had declined to deal with him?

Receiving this reply, Mr Godfrey Ablewhite did, what all animals (human and otherwise) do, when they find themselves caught in a trap. He looked about him in a state of helpless despair. The day of the month, recorded on a neat little card in a box on the money-lender's chimney-piece, happened to attract his eye. It was the twenty-third of June. On the twenty-fourth, he had three hundred pounds to pay to the young gentleman for whom he was trustee, and no chance of raising the money, except the chance that Mr Luker had offered to him. But for this miserable obstacle, he might have taken the Diamond to Amsterdam, and have made a marketable commodity of it, by having it cut up into separate stones. As matters stood, he had no choice but to accept Mr Luker's terms. After all, he had a year at his disposal, in which to raise the three thousand pounds – and a year is a long time.

Mr Luker drew out the necessary documents on the spot. When they were signed, he gave Mr Godfrey Ablewhite two cheques. One, dated

23 June, for three hundred pounds. Another, dated a week on, for the remaining balance – seventeen hundred pounds.

How the Moonstone was trusted to the keeping of Mr Luker's bankers, and how the Indians treated Mr Luker and Mr Godfrey (after that had been done) you know already.

The next event in your cousin's life, refers again to Miss Verinder. He proposed marriage to her for the second time – and (after having been accepted) he consented, at her request, to consider the marriage as broken off. One of his reasons for making this concession has been penetrated by Mr Bruff. Miss Verinder had only a life interest in her mother's property – and there was no raising the twenty thousand pounds on *that*.

But you will say, he might have saved the three thousand pounds, to redeem the pledged Diamond, if he had married. He might have done so certainly – supposing neither his wife, nor her guardians and trustees, objected to his anticipating more than half of the income at his disposal, for some unknown purpose, in the first year of his marriage. But even if he got over this obstacle, there was another waiting for him in the background. The lady at the Villa had heard of his contemplated marriage. A superb woman, Mr Blake, of the sort that are not to be trifled with – the sort with the light complexion and the Roman nose. She felt the utmost contempt for Mr Godfrey Ablewhite. It would be silent contempt, if he made a handsome provision for her. Otherwise, it would be contempt with a tongue to it. Miss Verinder's life interest allowed him no more hope of raising the 'provision' than of raising the twenty thousand pounds. He couldn't marry – he really couldn't marry, under all the circumstances.

How he tried his luck again with another lady, and how *that* marriage also broke down on the question of money, you know already. You also know of the legacy of five thousand pounds, left to him shortly afterwards, by one of those many admirers among the soft sex whose good graces this fascinating man had contrived to win. That legacy (as the event has proved) led him to his death.

I have ascertained that when he went abroad, on getting his five thousand pounds, he went to Amsterdam. There, he made all the necessary arrangements for having the Diamond cut into separate stones. He came back (in disguise), and redeemed the Moonstone, on the appointed day. A few days were allowed to elapse (as a precaution agreed to by both parties) before the jewel was actually taken out of the bank. If he had got safe with it to Amsterdam, there would have been just time between July 'forty-nine and February 'fifty (when the young gentleman came of age) to cut the Diamond, and to make a marketable commodity (polished or unpolished) of the separate stones. Judge from this, what motives he had to run the risk which he actually ran. It was 'neck or nothing' with him – if ever it was 'neck or nothing' with a man yet.

I have only to remind you, before closing this Report, that there is a chance of laying hands on the Indians, and of recovering the Moonstone yet. They are now (there is every reason to believe) on their passage to Bombay, in an East Indiaman. The ship (barring accidents) will touch at no other port on her way out; and the authorities at Bombay (already communicated with by letter, overland) will be prepared to board the vessel, the moment she enters the harbour.

I have the honour to remain, dear sir, your obedient servant, Richard Cuff (late sergeant in the Detective Force, Scotland Yard, London).*

* Note. – Wherever the Report touches on the events of the birthday, or of the three days that followed it, compare with Betteredge's Narrative, chapters viii to xiii.

Seventh Narrative

In a letter from Mr Candy

FRIZINGHALL, WEDNESDAY, 26 SEPTEMBER 1849. – Dear Mr Franklin Blake, you will anticipate the sad news I have to tell you, on finding your letter to Ezra Jennings returned to you, unopened, in this enclosure. He died in my arms, at sunrise, on Wednesday last.

I am not to blame for having failed to warn you that his end was at hand. He expressly forbade me to write to you. 'I am indebted to Mr Franklin Blake,' he said, 'for having seen some happy days. Don't distress him, Mr Candy – don't distress him.'

His sufferings, up to the last six hours of his life, were terrible to see. In the intervals of remission, when his mind was clear, I entreated him to tell me of any relatives of his to whom I might write. He asked to be forgiven for refusing anything to *me*. And then he said – not bitterly – that he would die as he had lived, forgotten and unknown. He maintained that resolution to the last. There is no hope now of making any discoveries concerning him. His story is a blank.

The day before he died, he told me where to find all his papers. I brought them to him on his bed. There was a little bundle of old letters which he put aside. There was his unfinished book. There was his Diary – in many locked volumes. He opened the volume for this year, and tore out, one by one, the pages relating to the time when you and he were together. 'Give those,' he said, 'to Mr Franklin Blake. In years to come, he may feel an interest in looking back at what is written there.' Then he clasped his hands, and prayed God fervently to bless you, and those dear to you. He said he should like to see you again. But the next moment, he altered his mind. 'No,' he answered, when I offered to write. 'I won't distress him! I won't distress him!'

At his request, I next collected the other papers – that is to say, the bundle of letters, the unfinished book, and the volumes of the Diary – and enclosed them all in one wrapper, sealed with my own seal. 'Promise,' he said, 'that you will put this into my coffin with your own hand; and that you will see that no other hand touches it afterwards.'

I gave him my promise. And the promise has been performed.

He asked me to do one other thing for him – which it cost me a hard struggle to comply with. He said, 'Let my grave be forgotten. Give me your word of honour that you will allow no monument of any sort – not even the commonest tombstone – to mark the place of my burial. Let me sleep, nameless. Let me rest, unknown.' When I tried to plead with him to alter his resolution, he became for the first, and only time, violently agitated. I could not bear to see it; and I gave way. Nothing but a little grass mound, marks the place of his rest. In time, the tombstones will rise round it. And the people who come after us will look, and wonder, at the nameless grave.

As I have told you, for six hours before his death his sufferings ceased. He dozed a little. I think he dreamed. Once or twice, he smiled. A woman's name, as I suppose – the name of 'Ella' – was often on his lips at this time. A few minutes before the end came, he asked me to lift him on his pillow, to see the sun rise through the window. He was very weak. His head fell on my shoulder. He whispered, 'It's coming!' Then he said, 'Kiss me!' I kissed his forehead. On a sudden, he lifted his head. The sunlight touched his face. A beautiful expression, an angelic expression, came over it. He cried out three times, 'Peace! peace! peace!' His head sank back again on my shoulder, and the long trouble of his life was at an end.

So he has gone from us. This was, as I think, a great man – though the world never knew him. He bore a hard life bravely. He had the sweetest temper I have ever met with. The loss of him makes me feel very lonely. Perhaps I have never been quite myself again since my illness. Sometimes, I think of giving up my practice, and going away, and trying what some of the foreign baths and waters will do for me.

It is reported here, that you and Miss Verinder are to be married next month. Please to accept my best congratulations.

The pages of my poor friend's Journal are waiting for you at my house – sealed up, with your name on the wrapper. I was afraid to trust them to the post.

My best respects and good wishes attend Miss Verinder. I remain, dear Mr Franklin Blake, truly yours, Thomas Candy.

Eighth Narrative

Contributed by Gabriel Betteredge

I AM THE PERSON (AS YOU REMEMBER, NO DOUBT) who led the way in these pages, and opened the story. I am also the person who is left behind, as it were, to close the story up.

Let nobody suppose that I have any last words to say here, concerning the Indian Diamond. I hold that unlucky jewel in abhorrence – and I refer you to other authority than mine, for such news of the Moonstone as you may, at the present time, be expected to receive. My purpose, in this place, is to state a fact in the history of the family, which has been passed over by everybody, and which I won't allow to be disrespectfully smothered up in that way. The fact to which I allude is – the marriage of Miss Rachel and Mr Franklin Blake. This interesting event took place at our house in Yorkshire, on Tuesday, October ninth, eighteen hundred and forty-nine. I had a new suit of clothes on the occasion. And the married couple went to spend the honeymoon in Scotland.

Family festivals having been rare enough at our house, since my poor mistress's death, I own – on this occasion of the wedding – to having (towards the latter part of the day) taken a drop too much on the strength of it.

If you have ever done the same sort of thing yourself, you will understand and feel for me. If you have not, you will very likely say, 'Disgusting old man! why does he tell us this?' The reason why is now to come.

Having, then, taken my drop (bless you! you have got your favourite vice, too; only your vice isn't mine, and mine isn't yours), I next applied the one infallible remedy – that remedy being, as you know, *Robinson Crusoe*. Where I opened that unrivalled book, I can't say. Where the lines of print at last left off running into each other, I know, however, perfectly well. It was at page three hundred and eighteen – a domestic bit concerning Robinson Crusoe's marriage, as follows:

'With those Thoughts, I considered my new Engagement, that I had a Wife' – (Observe! so had Mr Franklin!) – 'one Child bore' – (Observe again! that might yet be Mr Franklin's case, too!) – 'and my Wife then' – What Robinson Crusoe's wife did, or did not do, 'then,' I felt no desire to discover. I scored the bit about the Child with my pencil, and put a morsel of paper for a mark to keep the place: 'Lie you there,' I said, 'till

412

the marriage of Mr Franklin and Miss Rachel is some months older – and then we'll see!'

The months passed (more than I had bargained for), and no occasion presented itself for disturbing that mark in the book. It was not till this present month of November, eighteen hundred and fifty, that Mr Franklin came into my room, in high good spirits, and said, 'Betteredge! I have got some news for you! Something is going to happen in the house, before we are many months older.'

'Does it concern the, family, sir?' I asked.

'It decidedly concerns the family,' says Mr Franklin.

'Has your good lady anything to do with it, if you please, sir?'

'She has a great deal to do with it,' says Mr Franklin, beginning to look a little surprised.

'You needn't say a word more, sir,' I answered. 'God bless you both! I'm heartily glad to hear it.'

Mr Franklin stared like a person thunderstruck. 'May I venture to inquire where you got your information?' he asked.

'I only got mine (imparted in the strictest secrecy) five minutes since.'

Here was an opportunity of producing *Robinson Crusoe*! Here was a chance of reading that domestic bit about the child which I had marked on the day of Mr Franklin's marriage! I read those miraculous words with an emphasis which did them justice, and then I looked him severely in the face. '*Now*, sir, do you believe in *Robinson Crusoe*?' I asked, with a solemnity suitable to the occasion.

'Betteredge!' says Mr Franklin, with equal solemnity, 'I'm convinced at last.' He shook hands with me – and I felt that I had converted him.

With the relation of this extraordinary circumstance, my reappearance in these pages comes to an end. Let nobody laugh at the unique anecdote here related. You are welcome to be as merry as you please over everything else I have written. But when I write of *Robinson Crusoe*, by the Lord it's serious – and I request you to take it accordingly!

When this is said, all is said. Ladies and gentlemen, I make my bow, and shut up the story.

The Finding of the Diamond

I

THE STATEMENT OF SERGEANT CUFF'S MAN (1849)

On the twenty-seventh of June last, I received instructions from Sergeant Cuff to follow three men; suspected of murder, and described as Indians. They had been seen on the Tower Wharf that morning, embarking on board the steamer bound for Rotterdam.

I left London by a steamer belonging to another company, which sailed on the morning of Thursday the twenty-eighth. Arriving at Rotterdam, I succeeded in finding the commander of the Wednesday's steamer. He informed me that the Indians had certainly been passengers on board his vessel – but as far as Gravesend only. Off that place, one of the three had inquired at what time they would reach Calais. On being informed that the steamer was bound to Rotterdam, the spokesman of the party expressed the greatest surprise and distress at the mistake which he and his two friends had made. They were all willing (he said) to sacrifice their passage money, if the commander of the steamer would only put them ashore. Commiserating their position, as foreigners in a strange land, and knowing no reason for detaining them, the commander signalled for a shore boat, and the three men left the vessel.

This proceeding of the Indians having been plainly resolved on beforehand, as a means of preventing their being traced, I lost no time in returning to England. I left the steamer at Gravesend, and discovered that the Indians had gone from that place to London. Thence, I again traced them as having left for Plymouth. Inquiries made at Plymouth, proved that they had sailed, forty-eight hours previously, in the *Bewley Castle*, East Indiaman, bound direct to Bombay.

On receiving this intelligence, Sergeant Cuff caused the authorities at Bombay to be communicated with, overland – so that the vessel might be boarded by the police immediately on her entering the port. This step having been taken, my connection with the matter came to an end. I have heard nothing more of it since that time.

STATEMENT OF THE CAPTAIN (1849)

I am requested by Sergeant Cuff to set in writing certain facts, concerning three men (believed to be Hindoos) who were passengers, last summer, in the ship *Bewley Castle*, bound for Bombay direct, under my command.

The Hindoos joined us at Plymouth. On the passage out, I heard no complaint of their conduct. They were berthed in the forward part of the vessel. I had but few occasions myself of personally noticing them.

In the latter part of the voyage, we had the misfortune to be becalmed for three days and nights, off the coast of India. I have not got the ship's journal to refer to, and I cannot now call to mind the latitude and longitude. As to our position, therefore, I am only able to state generally that the currents drifted us in towards the land, and that when the wind found us again, we reached our port in twenty-four hours afterwards.

The discipline of a ship (as all seafaring persons know) becomes relaxed in a long calm. The discipline of my ship became relaxed. Certain gentlemen among the passengers got some of the smaller boats lowered, and amused themselves by rowing about, and swimming, when the sun at evening time was cool enough to let them divert themselves in that way. The boats when done with, ought to have been slung up again in their places. Instead of this they were left moored to the ship's side. What with the heat, and what with the vexation of the weather, neither officers nor men seemed to be in heart for their duty while the calm lasted.

On the third night, nothing unusual was heard or seen by the watch on deck. When the morning came, the smallest of the boats was missing – and the three Hindoos were next reported to be missing too.

If these men had stolen the boat shortly after dark (which I have no doubt they did), we were near enough to the land to make it vain to send in pursuit of them, when the discovery was made in the morning. I have no doubt they got ashore, in that calm weather (making all due allowance for fatigue and clumsy rowing), before day-break.

On reaching our port, I there learnt, for the first time, the reason these passengers had for seizing their opportunity of escaping from the ship. I could only make the same statement to the authorities which I have made here. They considered me to blame for allowing the discipline of the vessel to be relaxed. I have expressed my regret on this score to them, and to my owners. Since that time, nothing has been heard to my knowledge of the three Hindoos. I have no more to add to what is here written.

THE STATEMENT OF MR MURTHWAITE (1850)

(In a letter to Mr Bruff)

Have any recollection, my dear sir, of a semi-savage person whom you met out at dinner, in London, in the autumn of 'forty-eight? Permit me to remind you that the person's name was Murthwaite, and that you and he had a long conversation together after dinner. The talk related to an Indian Diamond, called the Moonstone, and to a conspiracy then in existence to get possession of the gem.

Since that time, I have been wandering in Central Asia. Thence I have drifted back to the scene of some of my past adventures in the north and north-west of India. About a fortnight since, I found myself in a certain district or province (but little known to Europeans) called Kattiawar.

Here an adventure befell me, in which (incredible as it may appear) you are personally interested.

In the wild regions of Kattiawar (and how wild they are, you will understand, when I tell you that even the husbandmen plough the land, armed to the teeth), the population is fanatically devoted to the old Hindoo religion – to the ancient worship of Bramah and Vishnu. The few Mahometan families, thinly scattered about the villages in the interior, are afraid to taste meat of any kind. A Mahometan even suspected of killing that sacred animal, the cow, is, as a matter of course, put to death without mercy in these parts by the pious Hindoo neighbours who surround him. To strengthen the religious enthusiasm of the people, two of the most famous shrines of Hindoo pilgrimage are contained within the boundaries of Kattiawar. One of them is Dwarka, the birthplace of the god Krishna. The other is the sacred city of Somnauth – sacked, and destroyed, as long since as the eleventh century, by the Mahometan conqueror, Mahmoud of Ghizni.

Finding myself, for the second time, in these romantic regions, I resolved not to leave Kattiawar, without looking once more on the magnificent desolation of Somnauth. At the place where I planned to do this, I was (as nearly as I could calculate it) some three days distant, journeying on foot, from the sacred city.

I had not been long on the road, before I noticed that other people – by twos and threes – appeared to be travelling in the same direction as myself.

To such of these as spoke to me, I gave myself out as a Hindoo-Boodhist, from a distant province, bound on a pilgrimage. It is needless to say that my dress was of the sort to carry out this description. Add,

419

that I know the language as well as I know my own, and that I am lean enough and brown enough to make it no easy matter to detect my European origin – and you will understand that I passed muster with the people readily: not as one of themselves, but as a stranger from a distant part of their own country.

On the second day, the number of Hindoos travelling in my direction, had increased to fifties and hundreds. On the third day, the throng had swollen to thousands; all slowly converging to one point – the city of Somnauth.

A trifling service which I was able to render to one of my fellow-pilgrims, during the third day's journey, proved the means of introducing me to certain Hindoos of the higher caste. From these men I learnt that the multitude was on its way to a great religious ceremony, which was to take place on a hill at a little distance from Somnauth. The ceremony was in honour of the god of the Moon; and it was to be held at night.

The crowd detained us as we drew near to the place of celebration. By the time we reached the hill, the moon was high in the heaven. My Hindoo friends possessed some special privileges which enabled them to gain access to the shrine. They kindly allowed me to accompany them. When we arrived at the place, we found the shrine hidden from our view by a curtain hung between two magnificent trees. Beneath the trees, a flat projection of rock jutted out, and formed a species of natural platform. Below this, I stood, in company with my Hindoo friends.

Looking back down the hill, the view presented the grandest spectacle of Nature and Man, in combination, that I have ever seen. The lower slopes of the eminence melted imperceptibly into a grassy plain, the place of the meeting of three rivers. On one side, the graceful winding of the waters stretched away, now visible, now hidden by trees, as far as the eye could see. On the other, the waveless ocean slept in the calm of the night. People this lovely scene with tens of thousands of human creatures, all dressed in white, stretching down the sides of the hill, overflowing into the plain, and fringing the nearer banks of the winding rivers. Light this halt of the pilgrims by the wild red flames of cressets and torches, streaming up at intervals from every part of the innumerable throng. Imagine the moonlight of the East, pouring in unclouded glory over all – and you will form some idea of the view that met me when I looked forth from the summit of the hill.

A strain of plaintive music, played on stringed instruments and flutes, recalled my attention to the hidden shrine.

I turned, and saw on the rocky platform, the figures of three men. In the central figure of the three I recognized the man to whom I had spoken in England, when the Indians appeared on the terrace at Lady

Verinder's house. The other two who had been his companions on that occasion, were no doubt his companions also on this.

One of the spectators, near whom I was standing, saw me start. In a whisper, he explained to me the apparition of the three figures on the platform of rock.

They were Brahmins (he said) who had forfeited their caste, in the service of the god. The god had commanded that their purification should be the purification by pilgrimage. On that night, the three men were to part. In three separate directions, they were to set forth as pilgrims to the shrines of India. Never more were they to look on each other's faces. Never more were they to rest on their wanderings, from the day which witnessed their separation, to the day which witnessed their death.

As those words were whispered to me, the plaintive music ceased. The three men prostrated themselves on the rock, before the curtain which hid the shrine. They rose – they looked on one another – they embraced. Then they descended separately among the people. The people made way for them in dead silence. In three different directions, I saw the crowd part, at one and the same moment. Slowly the grand white mass of the people closed together again. The track of the doomed men through the ranks of their fellow mortals was obliterated. We saw them no more.

A new strain of music, loud and jubilant, rose from the hidden shrine. The crowd around me shuddered, and pressed together.

The curtain between the trees was drawn aside, and the shrine was disclosed to view.

There, raised high on a throne – seated on his typical antelope, with his four arms stretching towards the four corners of the earth – there, soared above us, dark and awful in the mystic light of heaven, the god of the Moon. And there, in the forehead of the deity, gleamed the yellow Diamond, whose splendour had last shone on me in England, from the bosom of a woman's dress!

Yes! after the lapse of eight centuries, the Moonstone looks forth once more, over the walls of the sacred city in which its story first began. How it has found its way back to its wild native land – by what accident, or by what crime, the Indians regained possession of their sacred gem, may be in your knowledge, but is not in mine. You have lost sight of it in England, and (if I know anything of this people) you have lost sight of it for ever.

So the years pass, and repeat each other; so the same events revolve in the cycles of time. What will be the next adventures of the Moonstone? Who can tell!

THE HAUNTED HOTEL

To

Mr & Mrs Sebastian Schlesinger

in remembrance of much kindness

and of many happy days

THE FIRST PART

❧ ONE ❧

IN THE YEAR 1860, THE REPUTATION of Doctor Wybrow as a London physician reached its highest point. It was reported on good authority that he was in receipt of one of the largest incomes derived from the practice of medicine in modern times.

One afternoon, towards the close of the London season, the Doctor had just taken his luncheon after a specially hard morning's work in his consulting-room, and with a formidable list of visits to patients at their own houses to fill up the rest of his day – when the servant announced that a lady wished to speak to him.

'Who is she?' the Doctor asked. 'A stranger?'

'Yes, sir.'

'I see no strangers out of consulting-hours. Tell her what the hours are, and send her away.'

'I have told her, sir.'

'Well?'

'And she won't go.'

'Won't go?' The Doctor smiled as he repeated the words. He was a humourist in his way; and there was an absurd side to the situation which rather amused him. 'Has this obstinate lady given you her name?' he inquired.

'No, sir. She refused to give any name – she said she wouldn't keep you five minutes, and the matter was too important to wait till to-morrow. There she is in the consulting-room; and how to get her out again is more than I know.'

Doctor Wybrow considered for a moment. His knowledge of women (professionally speaking) rested on the ripe experience of more than thirty years; he had met with them in all their varieties – especially the variety which knows nothing of the value of time, and never hesitates at sheltering itself behind the privileges of its sex. A glance at his watch informed him that he must soon begin his rounds among the patients who were waiting for him at their own houses. He decided forthwith on taking the only wise course that was open under the circumstances. In other words, he decided on taking to flight.

'Is the carriage at the door?' he asked.

'Yes, sir.'

'Very well. Open the house-door for me without making any noise, and leave the lady in undisturbed possession of the consulting-room. When she gets tired of waiting, you know what to tell her. If she asks when I am expected to return, say that I dine at my club, and spend the evening at the theatre. Now then, softly, Thomas! If your shoes creak, I am a lost man.'

He noiselessly led the way into the hall, followed by the servant on tip-toe.

Did the lady in the consulting-room suspect him? or did Thomas's shoes creak, and was her sense of hearing unusually keen? Whatever the explanation may be, the event that actually happened was beyond all doubt. Exactly as Doctor Wybrow passed his consulting-room, the door opened – the lady appeared on the threshold – and laid her hand on his arm.

'I entreat you, sir, not to go away without letting me speak to you first.'

The accent was foreign; the tone was low and firm. Her fingers closed gently, and yet resolutely, on the Doctor's arm.

Neither her language nor her action had the slightest effect in inclining him to grant her request. The influence that instantly stopped him, on the way to his carriage, was the silent influence of her face. The startling contrast between the corpse-like pallor of her complexion and the over-powering life and light, the glittering metallic brightness in her large black eyes, held him literally spell-bound. She was dressed in dark colours, with perfect taste; she was of middle height, and (apparently) of middle age – say a year or two over thirty. Her lower features – the nose, mouth, and chin – possessed the fineness and delicacy of form which is oftener seen among women of foreign races than among women of English birth. She was unquestionably a handsome person – with the one serious drawback of her ghastly complexion, and with the less noticeable defect of a total want of tenderness in the expression of her eyes. Apart from his first emotion of surprise, the feeling she produced in the Doctor may be described as an overpowering feeling of professional curiosity. The case might prove to be something entirely new in his professional experience. 'It looks like it,' he thought; 'and it's worth waiting for.'

She perceived that she had produced a strong impression of some kind upon him, and dropped her hold on his arm.

'You have comforted many miserable women in your time,' she said. 'Comfort one more, to-day.'

Without waiting to be answered, she led the way back into the room. The Doctor followed her, and closed the door. He placed her in the patients' chair, opposite the windows. Even in London the sun, on that summer afternoon, was dazzlingly bright. The radiant light flowed in on her. Her eyes met it unflinchingly, with the steely steadiness of the eyes of an eagle. The smooth pallor of her unwrinkled skin looked more fearfully white than ever. For the first time, for many a long year past, the Doctor felt his pulse quicken its beat in the presence of a patient.

Having possessed herself of his attention, she appeared, strangely enough, to have nothing to say to him. A curious apathy seemed to have taken possession of this resolute woman. Forced to speak first, the Doctor merely inquired, in the conventional phrase, what he could do for her.

The sound of his voice seemed to rouse her. Still looking straight at the light, she said abruptly: 'I have a painful question to ask.'

'What is it?'

Her eyes travelled slowly from the window to the Doctor's face. Without the slightest outward appearance of agitation, she put the 'painful question' in these extraordinary words:

'I want to know, if you please, whether I am in danger of going mad?'

Some men might have been amused, and some might have been alarmed. Doctor Wybrow was only conscious of a sense of disappointment. Was this the rare case that he had anticipated, judging rashly by appearances? Was the new patient only a hypochondriacal woman, whose malady was a disordered stomach and whose misfortune was a weak brain? 'Why do you come to *me*?' he asked sharply. 'Why don't you consult a doctor whose special employment is the treatment of the insane?'

She had her answer ready on the instant.

'I don't go to a doctor of that sort,' she said, 'for the very reason that he *is* a specialist: he has the fatal habit of judging everybody by lines and rules of his own laying down. I come to *you*, because my case is outside of all lines and rules, and because you are famous in your profession for the discovery of mysteries in disease. Are you satisfied?'

He was more than satisfied – his first idea had been the right idea, after all. Besides, she was correctly informed as to his professional position. The capacity which had raised him to fame and fortune was his capacity (unrivalled among his brethren) for the discovery of remote disease.

'I am at your disposal,' he answered. 'Let me try if I can find out what is the matter with you.'

He put his medical questions. They were promptly and plainly answered; and they led to no other conclusion than that the strange lady was, mentally and physically, in excellent health. Not satisfied with questions, he carefully examined the great organs of life. Neither his hand nor his stethoscope could discover anything that was amiss. With the admirable patience and devotion to his art, which had distinguished him from the time when he was a student, he still subjected her to one test after another. The result was always the same. Not only was there no tendency to brain disease – there was not even a perceptible derangement of the nervous system. 'I can find nothing the matter with you,' he said. 'I can't even account for the extraordinary pallor of your complexion. You completely puzzle me.'

'The pallor of my complexion is nothing,' she answered a little impatiently. 'In my early life I had a narrow escape from death by poisoning. I have never had a complexion since – and my skin is so delicate, I cannot paint without producing a hideous rash. But that is of no importance. I wanted your opinion given positively. I believed in you, and you have disappointed me.' Her head dropped on her breast. 'And so it ends!' she said to herself bitterly.

The Doctor's sympathies were touched. Perhaps it might be more correct to say that his professional pride was a little hurt. 'It may end in the right way yet,' he remarked, 'if you choose to help me.'

She looked up again with flashing eyes, 'Speak plainly,' she said. 'How can I help you?'

'Plainly, madam, you come to me as an enigma, and you leave me to make the right guess by the unaided efforts of my art. My art will do much, but not all. For example, something must have occurred – something quite unconnected with the state of your bodily health – to frighten you about yourself, or you would never have come here to consult me. Is that true?'

She clasped her hands in her lap. 'That is true!' she said eagerly. 'I begin to believe in you again.'

'Very well. You can't expect me to find out the moral cause which has alarmed you. I can positively discover that there is no physical cause of alarm; and (unless you admit me to your confidence) I can do no more.'

She rose, and took a turn in the room. 'Suppose I tell you?' she said. 'But, mind, I shall mention no names!'

'There is no need to mention names. The facts are all I want.'

'The facts are nothing,' she rejoined, 'I have only my own impressions to confess – and you will very likely think me a fanciful fool when you hear what they are. No matter. I will do my best to content you – I will begin with the facts that you want. Take my word for it, *they* won't do much to help you.'

She sat down again. In the plainest possible words, she began the strangest and wildest confession that had ever reached the Doctor's ears.

∾ TWO ∾

'IT IS ONE FACT, SIR, THAT I am a widow,' she said. 'It is another fact, that I am going to be married again.'

There she paused, and smiled at some thought that occurred to her. Doctor Wybrow was not favourably impressed by her smile – there was something at once sad and cruel in it. It came slowly, and it went away suddenly. He began to doubt whether he had been wise in acting on his first impression. His mind reverted to the commonplace patients and the discoverable maladies that were waiting for him, with a certain tender regret.

The lady went on.

'My approaching marriage,' she said, 'has one embarrassing circumstance connected with it. The gentleman whose wife I am to be, was engaged to another lady when he happened to meet with me, abroad: that lady, mind, being of his own blood and family, related to him as his cousin. I have innocently robbed her of her lover, and destroyed her prospects in life. Innocently, I say – because he told me nothing of his engagement, until after I had accepted him. When we next met in England – and when there was danger, no doubt, of the affair coming to my knowledge – he told me the truth. I was naturally indignant. He had his excuse ready; he showed me a letter from the lady herself, releasing him from his engagement. A more noble, a more high-minded letter, I never read in my life. I cried over it – I who have no tears in me for sorrows of my own! If the letter had left him any hope of being forgiven, I would have positively refused to marry him. But the firmness of it – without anger, without a word of reproach, with heartfelt wishes even for his happiness – the firmness of it, I say, left him no hope. He appealed to my compassion; he applied to his love for me. You know what women are. I too was soft-hearted – I said, Very well; yes! In a week more (I tremble as I think of it) we are to be married.'

She did really tremble – she was obliged to pause and compose herself, before she could go on. The Doctor, waiting for more facts, began to fear that he stood committed to a long story.

'Forgive me for reminding you that I have suffering persons waiting to see me,' he said. 'The sooner you can come to the point, the better for my patients and for me.'

The strange smile – at once so sad and so cruel – showed itself again on the lady's lips. 'Every word I have said is to the point,' she answered. 'You will see it yourself in a moment more.'

She resumed her narrative.

'Yesterday – you need fear no long story, sir; only yesterday – I was among the visitors at one of your English luncheon parties. A lady, a perfect stranger to me, came in late – after we had left the table, and had retired to the drawing-room. She happened to take a chair near me; and we were presented to each other. I knew her by name, as she knew me; It was the woman whom I had robbed of her lover, the woman who had written the noble letter. Now listen! You were impatient with me for not interesting you in what I said just now. I said it to satisfy your mind that I had no enmity of feeling towards the lady, on my side. I admired her, I felt for her – I had no cause to reproach myself. This is very important, as you will presently see. On her side, I have reason to be assured that the circumstances had been truly explained to her, and that she understood I was in no way to blame. Now, knowing all these necessary things as you do, explain to me, if you can, why, when I rose and met that woman's eyes looking at me, I turned cold from head to foot, and shuddered, and shivered, and knew what a deadly panic of fear was, for the first time in my life.'

The Doctor began to feel interested at last.

'Was there anything remarkable in the lady's personal appearance?' he asked.

'Nothing whatever!' was the vehement reply. 'Here is the true description of her: – The ordinary English lady; the clear cold blue eyes, the fine rosy complexion, the inanimately polite manner, the large good-humoured mouth, the too plump cheeks and chin: these, and nothing more.'

'Was there anything in her expression, when you first looked at her, that took you by surprise?'

'There was natural curiosity to see the woman who had been preferred to her; and perhaps some astonishment also, not to see a more engaging and more beautiful person; both those feelings restrained within the limits of good breeding, and both not lasting for more than a few moments – so far as I could see. I say, "so far", because the horrible agitation that she communicated to me disturbed my judgment. If I could have got to the door, I would have run out of the room, she frightened me so! I was not even able to stand up – I sank back in my chair; I stared horror-struck at the calm blue eyes that were only looking at me with a gentle surprise. To say they affected me like the eyes of a serpent is to say nothing. I felt her soul in them, looking into mine – looking, if such a thing can be, unconsciously to her own mortal self. I tell you my impression, in all its horror and in all its folly! That woman is destined (without knowing it herself) to be the evil genius of my life. Her innocent eyes saw hidden capabilities of wickedness in me that I was not aware of myself, until I felt them stirring under her look. If I commit faults in my life to come – if I am even guilty of crimes – she will bring the retribution, without (as I firmly believe) any conscious exercise of her own will. In one indescribable moment I felt all this – and I suppose my face showed it. The good artless creature was inspired by a sort of gentle alarm for me. "I am afraid the heat of the room is too much for you; will you try my smelling-bottle?" ' I heard her say those kind words; and I remember nothing else – I fainted. When I recovered my senses, the company had all gone; only the lady of the house was with me. For the moment I could say nothing to her; the dreadful impression that I have tried to describe to you came back to me with the coming back of my life. As soon as I could speak, I implored her to tell me the whole truth about the woman whom I had supplanted. You see, I had a faint hope that her good character might not really be deserved, that her noble letter was a skilful piece of hypocrisy – in short, that she secretly hated me, and was cunning enough to hide it. No! the lady had been her friend from her girlhood, was as familiar with her as if they had been sisters – knew her positively to be as good, as innocent, as incapable of hating anybody, as the greatest saint that ever lived. My one last hope, that I had only felt an ordinary forewarning of danger in the presence of an ordinary enemy, was a hope destroyed for ever. There was one more effort I could make, and I made it. I went next to the man whom I am to marry. I implored him to release me from my promise. He refused. I declared I would break my engagement. He showed me letters from his sisters, letters from his brothers, and his dear friends – all entreating him to think again before he made me his wife; all repeating reports of me in Paris, Vienna, and London, which are so many vile lies. 'If you refuse to marry me,' he said, 'you admit that these reports are true – you admit that you are afraid to face society in the character of my wife.' What could I answer? There was no contradicting him – he was plainly right: if I persisted in my refusal, the utter destruction of my reputation would be the result. I consented to let the wedding take place as we had arranged it – and left him. The night has passed. I am here, with my fixed conviction – that innocent woman is ordained to have a fatal influence over my life. I am here with my one question to put, to the one man who can answer it. For the last time, sir, what am I – a demon who has seen the avenging angel? or only a poor mad woman, misled by the delusion of a deranged mind?'

Doctor Wybrow rose from his chair, determined to close the interview. He was strongly and painfully impressed by what he had heard. The longer he had listened to her, the more irresistibly the conviction of the woman's wickedness had forced itself on him. He tried vainly to think of her as a person to be pitied – a person with a morbidly sensitive imagination, conscious of the capacities for evil which lie dormant in us all, and striving earnestly to open her heart to the counter-influence of her own better nature; the effort was beyond him. A perverse instinct in him said, as if in words, Beware how you believe in her!

'I have already given you my opinion,' he said. 'There is no sign of your intellect being deranged, or being likely to be deranged, that medical science can discover – as *I* understand it. As for the impressions you have confided to me, I can only say that yours is a case (as I venture to think) for spiritual rather than for medical advice. Of one thing be assured: what you have said to me in this room shall not pass out of it. Your confession is safe in my keeping.'

She heard him, with a certain dogged resignation, to the end.

'Is that all?' she asked.

'That is all,' he answered.

She put a little paper packet of money on the table. 'Thank you, sir. There is your fee.'

With those words she rose. Her wild black eyes looked upwards, with an expression of despair so defiant and so horrible in its silent agony that the Doctor turned away his head, unable to endure the sight of it. The bare idea of taking anything from her – not money only, but anything even that she had touched – suddenly revolted him. Still without looking at her, he said, 'Take it back; I don't want any fee.'

She neither heeded nor heard him. Still looking upward, she said slowly to herself, 'Let the end come. I have done with the struggle; I submit.'

She drew her veil over her face, bowed to the Doctor, and left the room.

He rang the bell, and followed her into the hall. As the servant closed the door on her, a sudden impulse of curiosity – utterly unworthy of him, and at the same time utterly irresistible – sprang up in the Doctor's mind. Blushing like a boy, he said to the servant, 'Follow her home, and find out her name.' For one moment the man looked at his master, doubting if his own ears had not deceived him. Doctor Wybrow looked back at him in silence. The submissive servant knew what that silence meant – he took his hat and hurried into the street.

The Doctor went back to the consulting-room. A sudden revulsion of feeling swept over his mind. Had the woman left an infection of wickedness in the house, and had he caught it? What devil had possessed him to degrade himself in the eyes of his own servant? He had behaved infamously – he had asked an honest man, a man who had served him faithfully for years, to turn spy! Stung by the bare thought of it, he ran out into the hall again, and opened the door. The servant had disappeared; it was too late to call him back. But one refuge from his contempt for himself was now open to him – the refuge of work. He got into his carriage and went his rounds among his patients.

If the famous physician could have shaken his own reputation, he would have done it that afternoon. Never before had he made himself so little welcome at the bedside. Never before had he put off until to-morrow the prescription which ought to have been written, the opinion which ought to have been given, to-day. He went home earlier than usual – unutterably dissatisfied with himself.

The servant had returned. Dr Wybrow was ashamed to question him. The man reported the result of his errand, without waiting to be asked.

'The lady's name is the Countess Narona. She lives at—'

Without waiting to hear where she lived, the Doctor acknowledged the all-important discovery of her name by a silent bend of the head, and entered his consulting-room. The fee that he had vainly refused still lay in its little white paper covering on the table. He sealed it up in an envelope; addressed it to the 'Poor-box' of the nearest police-court; and, calling the servant in, directed him to take it to the magistrate the next morning. Faithful to his duties, the servant waited to ask the customary question, 'Do you dine at home to-day, sir?'

After a moment's hesitation he said, 'No: I shall dine at the club.'

The most easily deteriorated of all the moral qualities is the quality called 'conscience'. In one state of a man's mind, his conscience is the severest judge that can pass sentence on him. In another state, he and his conscience are on the best possible terms with each other in the comfortable capacity of accomplices. When Doctor Wybrow left his house for the second time, he did not even attempt to conceal from himself that his sole object, in dining at the club, was to hear what the world said of the Countess Narona.

❧ THREE ❧

THERE WAS A TIME WHEN A MAN in search of the pleasures of gossip sought the society of ladies. The man knows better now. He goes to the smoking-room of his club.

Doctor Wybrow lit his cigar, and looked round him at his brethren in social conclave assembled. The room was well filled; but the flow of talk was still languid. The Doctor innocently applied the stimulant that was wanted. When he inquired if anybody knew the Countess Narona, he was answered by something like a shout of astonishment. Never (the conclave agreed) had such an absurd question been asked before! Every human creature, with the slightest claim to a place in society, knew the Countess Narona. An adventuress with a European reputation of the blackest possible colour – such was the general description of the woman with the death-like complexion and the glittering eyes.

Descending to particulars, each member of the club contributed his own little stock of scandal to the memoirs of the Countess. It was doubtful whether she was really, what she called herself, a Dalmatian lady. It was doubtful whether she had ever been married to the Count whose widow she assumed to be. It was doubtful whether the man who accompanied her in her travels (under the name of Baron Rivar, and in the character of her brother) was her brother at all. Report pointed to the Baron as a gambler at every 'table' on the Continent. Report whispered that his so-called sister had narrowly escaped being implicated in a famous trial for poisoning at Vienna – that she had been known at Milan as a spy in the interests of Austria – that her 'apartment' in Paris had been denounced to the police as nothing less than a private gambling-house – and that her present appearance in England was the natural result of the discovery. Only one member of the assembly in the smoking-room took the part of this much-abused woman and declared that her character had been most cruelly and most unjustly assailed. But as the man was a lawyer, his interference went for nothing: it was naturally attributed to the spirit of contradiction inherent in his profession. He was asked derisively what he thought of the circumstances under which the Countess had become engaged to be married; and he made the characteristic answer, that he thought the circumstances highly creditable to both parties, and that he looked on the lady's future husband as a most enviable man.

Hearing this, the Doctor raised another shout of astonishment by inquiring the name of the gentleman whom the Countess was about to marry.

His friends in the smoking-room decided unanimously that the celebrated physician must be a second 'Rip-van-Winkle', and that he had just awakened from a supernatural sleep of twenty years. It was all very well to say that he was devoted to his profession, and that he had neither time nor inclination to pick up fragments of gossip at dinner-parties and balls. A man who did not know that the Countess Narona had borrowed money at Homberg of no less a person than Lord Montbarry, and had then deluded him into making her a proposal of marriage, was a man who had probably never heard of Lord Montbarry himself. The younger members of the club, humouring the joke, sent a waiter for the 'Peerage'; and read aloud the memoir of the nobleman in question, for the Doctor's benefit – with illustrative morsels of information interpolated by themselves.

'Herbert John Westwick. First Baron Montbarry, of Montbarry, King's County, Ireland. Created a Peer for distinguished military services in India. Born, 1812. Forty-eight years old, Doctor, at the present time. Not married. Will be married next week, Doctor, to the delightful creature we have been talking about. Heir presumptive, his lordship's next brother, Stephen Robert, married to Ella, youngest daughter of the Reverend Silas Marden, Rector of Runnigate, and has issue, three daughters. Younger brothers of his lordship, Francis and Henry, unmarried. Sisters of his lordship, Lady Barville, married to Sir Theodore Barville, Bart.; and Anne, widow of the late Peter Norbury, Esq., of Norbury Cross. Bear his lordship's relations well in mind, Doctor. Three brothers Westwick, Stephen, Francis, and Henry; and two sisters, Lady Barville and Mrs Norbury. Not one of the five will be present at the marriage; and not one of the five will leave a stone unturned to stop it, if the Countess will only give them a chance. Add to these hostile members of the family another offended relative not mentioned in the 'Peerage', a young lady——'

A sudden outburst of protest in more than one part of the room stopped the coming disclosure, and released the Doctor from further persecution.

'Don't mention the poor girl's name; it's too bad to make a joke of that part of the business; she has behaved nobly under shameful provocation; there is but one excuse for Montbarry – he is either a madman or a fool.' In these terms the protest expressed itself on all sides. Speaking confidentially to his next neighbour, the Doctor discovered that the lady referred to was already known to him (through the Countess's confession) as the lady deserted by Lord Montbarry. Her name was Agnes Lockwood. She was described as being the superior of the Countess in personal attraction, and as being also by some years the younger woman of the two. Making all allowance for the follies that men committed every day in their relations with women, Montbarry's delusion was still the most monstrous delusion on record. In this expression of opinion every man present agreed – the lawyer even included. Not one of them could call to mind the innumerable instances in which the sexual influence has proved irresistible in the persons of women without even the pretension to beauty. The very members of the club whom the Countess (in spite of her personal disadvantages) could have most easily fascinated, if she had thought it worth her while, were the members who wondered most loudly at Montbarry's choice of a wife.

While the topic of the Countess's marriage was still the one topic of conversation, a member of the club entered the smoking-room whose appearance instantly produced a dead silence. Doctor Wybrow's next neighbour whispered to him, 'Montbarry's brother – Henry Westwick!'

The new-comer looked round him slowly, with a bitter smile.

'You are all talking of my brother,' he said. 'Don't mind me. Not one of you can despise him more heartily than I do. Go on, gentlemen – go on!'

But one man present took the speaker at his word. That man was the lawyer who had already undertaken the defence of the Countess.

'I stand alone in my opinion,' he said, 'and I am not ashamed of repeating it in anybody's hearing. I consider the Countess Narona to be a cruelly-treated woman. Why shouldn't she be Lord Montbarry's wife? Who can say she has a mercenary motive in marrying him?'

Montbarry's brother turned sharply on the speaker. '*I* say it!' he answered.

The reply might have shaken some men. The lawyer stood on his ground as firmly as ever.

'I believe I am right,' he rejoined, 'in stating that his lordship's income is not more than sufficient to support his station in life; also that it is an income derived almost entirely from landed property in Ireland, every acre of which is entailed.'

Montbarry's brother made a sign, admitting that he had no objection to offer so far.

'If his lordship dies first,' the lawyer proceeded, 'I have been informed that the only provision he can make for his widow consists in a rent-charge on the property of no more than four hundred a year. His retiring pension and allowances, it is well known, die with him. Four hundred a year is therefore all that he can leave to the Countess, if he leaves her a widow.'

'Four hundred a year is *not* all,' was the reply to this. 'My brother has insured his life for ten thousand pounds; and he has settled the whole of it on the Countess, in the event of his death.'

This announcement produced a strong sensation. Men looked at each other, and repeated the three startling words, 'Ten thousand pounds!' Driven fairly to the wall, the lawyer made a last effort to defend his position.

'May I ask who made that settlement a condition of the marriage?' he said. 'Surely it was not the Countess herself?'

Henry Westwick answered, 'It was the Countess's brother;' and added, 'which comes to the same thing.'

After that, there was no more to be said – so long, at least, as Montbarry's brother was present. The talk flowed into other channels; and the Doctor went home.

But his morbid curiosity about the Countess was not set at rest yet. In his leisure moments he found himself wondering whether Lord Mont-barry's family would succeed in stopping the marriage after all. And more than this, he was conscious of a growing desire to see the infatuated man himself. Every day during the brief interval before the wedding, he looked in at the club, on the chance of hearing some news. Nothing had happened, so far as the club knew. The Countess's position was secure; Montbarry's resolution to be her husband was unshaken. They were both Roman Catholics, and they were to be married at the chapel in Spanish Place. So much the Doctor discovered about them – and no more.

On the day of the wedding, after a feeble struggle with himself, he actually sacrificed his patients and their guineas, and slipped away secretly to see the marriage. To the end of his life, he was angry with anybody who reminded him of what he had done on that day!

The wedding was strictly private. A close carriage stood at the church door; a few people, mostly of the lower class, and mostly old women, were scattered about the interior of the building. Here and there Doctor Wybrow detected the faces of some of his brethren of the club, attracted by curiosity, like himself. Four persons only stood before the altar – the bride and bridegroom and their two witnesses. One of these last was an elderly woman, who might have been the Countess's companion or maid; the other was undoubtedly her brother, Baron Rivar. The bridal party (the bride herself included) wore their ordinary morning costume. Lord Montbarry, personally viewed, was a middle-aged military man of the ordinary type: nothing in the least remarkable distinguished him either in face or figure. Baron Rivar, again, in his way was another conventional representative of another well-known type. One sees his finely-pointed moustache, his bold eyes, his crisply curling hair, and his dashing carriage of the head, repeated hundreds of times over on the Boulevards of Paris. The only noteworthy point about him was of the negative sort – he was not in the least like his sister. Even the officiating priest was only a harmless, humble-looking old man, who went through his duties resignedly, and felt visible rheumatic difficulties every time he bent his knees. The one remarkable person, the Countess herself, only raised her veil at the beginning of the ceremony, and pre-sented nothing in her plain dress that was worth a second look. Never, on the face of it, was there a less interesting and less romantic marriage than this. From time to time the Doctor glanced round at the door or up at the galleries, vaguely anticipating the appearance of some protesting stranger, in possession of some terrible secret, commissioned to forbid the progress of the service. Nothing in the shape of an event occurred – nothing extraordinary, nothing dramatic. Bound fast together as man and wife, the two disappeared, followed by their witnesses, to sign the registers; and still Doctor Wybrow waited, and still he cherished the obstinate hope that something worth seeing must certainly happen yet.

The interval passed, and the married couple, returning to the church, walked together down the nave to the door. Doctor Wybrow drew back as they approached. To his confusion and surprise, the Countess discovered him. He heard her say to her husband, 'One moment; I see a friend.' Lord Montbarry bowed and waited. She stepped up to the Doctor, took his hand, and wrung it hard. He felt her overpowering black eyes looking at him through her veil. 'One step more, you see, on the way to the end!' She whispered those strange words, and returned to her husband. Before the Doctor could recover himself and follow her, Lord and Lady Montbarry had stepped into their carriage, and had driven away.

Outside the church door stood the three or four members of the club who, like Doctor Wybrow, had watched the ceremony out of curiosity. Near them was the bride's brother, waiting alone. He was evidently bent on seeing the man whom his sister had spoken to, in broad daylight. His bold eyes rested on the Doctor's face, with a momentary flash of suspicion in them. The cloud suddenly cleared away; the Baron smiled with charming courtesy, lifted his hat to his sister's friend, and walked off.

The members constituted themselves into a club conclave on the church steps. They began with the Baron. 'Damned ill-looking rascal!' They went on with Montbarry. 'Is he going to take that horrid woman with him to Ireland?' 'Not he! he can't face the tenantry; they know about Agnes Lockwood.' 'Well, but where *is* he going?' 'To Scotland.' 'Does *she* like that?' 'It's only for a fortnight; they come back to London, and go abroad.' 'And they will never return to England, eh?' 'Who can tell? Did you see how she looked at Montbarry, when she had to lift her veil at the beginning of the service? In his place, I should have bolted. Did *you* see her, Doctor?' By this time, Doctor Wybrow had remembered his patients, and had heard enough of the club gossip. He followed the example of Baron Rivar, and walked off.

'One step more, you see, on the way to the end,' he repeated to himself, on his way home. 'What end?'

❧ FOUR ❦

ON THE DAY OF THE MARRIAGE, Agnes Lockwood sat alone in the little drawing-room of her London lodgings, burning the letters which had been written to her by Montbarry in the byegone time.

The Countess's maliciously smart description of her, addressed to

Doctor Wybrow, had not even hinted at the charm that most distinguished Agnes – the artless expression of goodness and purity which
instantly attracted everyone who approached her. She looked by many
years younger than she really was. With her fair complexion and her shy
manner, it seemed only natural to speak of her as 'a girl', although she
was now really advancing towards thirty years of age. She lived alone
with an old nurse devoted to her, on a modest little income, which was
just enough to support the two. There were none of the ordinary signs
of grief in her face, as she slowly tore the letters of her false lover in
two, and threw the pieces into the small fire which had been lit to
consume them. Unhappily for herself, she was one of those women who
feel too deeply to find relief in tears. Pale and quiet, with cold trembling
fingers, she destroyed the letters one by one without daring to read them
again. She had torn the last of the series, and was still shrinking from
throwing it after the rest into the swiftly destroying flame, when the old
nurse came in, and asked if she would see 'Master Henry', – meaning
that youngest member of the Westwick family, who had publicly declared
his contempt for his brother in the smoking-room of the club.

Agnes hesitated. A faint tinge of colour stole over her face.

There had been a long past time when Henry Westwick had owned
that he loved her. She had made her confession to him, acknowledging
that her heart was given to his eldest brother. He had submitted to his
disappointment; and they had met thenceforth as cousins and friends.
Never before had she associated the idea of him with embarrassing
recollection. But now, on the very day when his brother's marriage to
another woman had consummated his brother's treason towards her,
there was something vaguely repellent in the prospect of seeing him.
The old nurse (who remembered them both in their cradles) observed
her hesitation; and sympathizing of course with the man, put in a timely
word for Henry. 'He says he's going away, my dear; and he only wants
to shake hands, and say good-bye.' This plain statement of the case had
its effect. Agnes decided on receiving her cousin.

He entered the room so rapidly that he surprised her in the act of
throwing the fragments of Montbarry's last letter into the fire. She hurriedly spoke first.

'You are leaving London very suddenly, Henry. Is it business? or
pleasure?'

Instead of answering her, he pointed to the flaming letter, and to some
black ashes of burnt paper lying lightly in the lower part of the fireplace.

'Are you burning letters?'

'Yes.'

'His letters?'

'Yes.'

He took her hand gently. 'I had no idea I was intruding on you, at a time when you must wish to be alone. Forgive me, Agnes – I shall see you when I return.'

She signed to him, with a faint smile, to take a chair.

'We have known one another since we were children,' she said. 'Why should I feel a foolish pride about myself in your presence? why should I have any secrets from you? I sent back all your brother's gifts to me some time ago. I have been advised to do more, to keep nothing that can remind me of him – in short, to burn his letters. I have taken the advice; but I own I shrank a little from destroying the last of the letters. No – not because it was the last, but because it had this in it.' She opened her hand, and showed him a lock of Montbarry's hair, tied with a morsel of golden cord. 'Well! well! let it go with the rest.'

She dropped it into the flame. For a while, she stood with her back to Henry, leaning on the mantel-piece, and looking into the fire. He took the chair to which she had pointed, with a strange contradiction of expression in his face: the tears were in his eyes, while the brows above were knit close in an angry frown. He muttered to himself, 'Damn him!'

She rallied her courage, and looked at him again when she spoke. 'Well, Henry, and why are you going away?'

'I am out of spirits, Agnes, and I want a change.'

She paused before she spoke again. His face told her plainly that he was thinking of *her* when he made that reply. She was grateful to him, but her mind was not with him: her mind was still with the man who had deserted her. She turned round again to the fire.

'Is it true,' she asked, after a long silence, 'that they have been married to-day?'

He answered ungraciously in the one necessary word: – 'Yes.'

'Did you go to the church?'

He resented the question with an expression of indignant surprise. 'Go to the church?' he repeated. 'I would as soon go to—' He checked himself there. 'How can you ask?' he added in lower tones. 'I have never spoken to Montbarry, I have not even seen him, since he treated you like the scoundrel and the fool that he is.'

She looked at him suddenly, without saying a word. He understood her, and begged her pardon. But he was still angry. 'The reckoning comes to some men,' he said, 'even in this world. He will live to rue the day when he married that woman!'

Agnes took a chair by his side, and looked at him with a gentle surprise.

'Is it quite reasonable to be so angry with her, because your brother preferred her to me?' she asked.

Henry turned on her sharply. 'Do you defend the Countess, of all the people in the world?'

'Why not?' Agnes answered. 'I know nothing against her. On the only occassion when we met, she appeared to be a singularly timid, nervous person, looking dreadfully ill; and *being* indeed so ill that she fainted under the heat of the room. Why should we not do her justice? We know that she was innocent of any intention to wrong me; we know that she was not aware of my engagement—'

Henry lifted his hand impatiently, and stopped her. 'There is such a thing as being *too* just and *too* forgiving!' he interposed. 'I can't bear to hear you talk in that patient way, after the scandalously cruel manner in which you have been treated. Try to forget them both, Agnes. I wish to God I could help you to do it!'

Agnes laid her hand on his arm. 'You are very good to me, Henry; but you don't quite understand me. I was thinking of myself and my trouble in quite a different way, when you came in. I was wondering whether anything which has so entirely filled my heart, and so absorbed all that is best and truest in me, as my feeling for your brother, can really pass away as if it had never existed. I have destroyed the last visible things that remind me of him. In this world, I shall see him no more. But is the tie that once bound us, completely broken? Am I as entirely parted from the good and evil fortune of his life, as if we had never met and never loved? What do *you* think, Henry? I can hardly believe it.'

'If you could bring the retribution on him that he has deserved,' Henry Westwick answered sternly, 'I might be inclined to agree with you.'

As that reply passed his lips, the old nurse appeared again at the door, announcing another visitor.

'I'm sorry to disturb you, my dear. But here is little Mrs Ferrari wanting to know when she may say a few words to you.'

Agnes turned to Henry, before she replied. 'You remember Emily Bidwell, my favourite pupil years ago at the village school, and afterwards my maid? She left me, to marry an Italian courier, named Ferrari – and I am afraid it has not turned out very well. Do you mind my having her in here, for a minute or two?'

Henry rose to take his leave. 'I should be glad to see Emily again at any other time,' he said. 'But it is best that I should go now. My mind is disturbed, Agnes; I might say things to you, if I stayed here any longer, which – which are better not said now. I shall cross the Channel by the mail to-night, and see how a few weeks' change will help me.' He took her hand. 'Is there anything in the world that I can do for you?' he asked very earnestly. She thanked him, and tried to release her hand. He held it with a tremulous lingering grasp. 'God bless you, Agnes!' he said in faltering tones, with his eyes on the ground. Her face flushed again, and the next instant turned paler than ever; she knew his heart as well as he knew it himself – she was too distressed to speak. He lifted her hand to his lips, kissed it fervently, and, without looking at her again, left the room. The nurse hobbled after him to the head of the stairs; she had not forgotten the time when the younger brother had been the unsuccessful rival of the elder for the hand of Agnes. 'Don't be down-hearted, Master Henry,' whispered the old woman, with the unscrupulous common sense of persons in the lower rank of life. 'Try her again, when you come back!'

Left alone for a few moments, Agnes took a turn in the room trying to compose herself. She paused before a little water-colour drawing on the wall, which had belonged to her mother: it was her own portrait when she was a child. 'How much happier we should be,' she thought to herself sadly, 'if we never grew up!'

The courier's wife was shown in – a little meek melancholy woman, with white eyelashes, and watery eyes, who curtseyed deferentially and was troubled with a small chronic cough. Agnes shook hands with her kindly. 'Well, Emily, what can I do for you?'

The courier's wife made rather a strange answer: 'I'm afraid to tell you, Miss.'

'Is it such a very difficult favour to grant? Sit down, and let me hear how you are going on. Perhaps the petition will slip out while we are talking. How does your husband behave to you?'

Emily's light grey eyes looked more watery than ever. She shook her head and sighed resignedly. 'I have no positive complaint to make against him, Miss. But I'm afraid he doesn't care about me; and he seems to take no interest in his home – I may almost say he's tired of his home. It might be better for both of us, Miss, if he went travelling for a while – not to mention the money, which is beginning to be wanted sadly.' She put her handkerchief to her eyes, and sighed again more resignedly than ever.

'I don't quite understand,' said Agnes. 'I thought your husband had an engagement to take some ladies to Switzerland and Italy?'

'That was his ill-luck, Miss. One of the ladies fell ill – and the others wouldn't go without her. They paid him a month's salary as compensation. But they had engaged him for the autumn and winter – and the loss is serious.'

'I am sorry to hear it, Emily. Let us hope he will soon have another chance.'

'It's not his turn, Miss, to be recommended when the next applications come to the couriers' office. You see, there are so many of them out of employment just now. If he could be privately recommended——' She stopped, and left the unfinished sentence to speak for itself.

442

Agnes understood her directly. 'You want my recommendation,' she rejoined. 'Why couldn't you say so at once?'

Emily blushed. 'It would be such a chance for my husband,' she answered confusedly. 'A letter, inquiring for a good courier (a six months' engagement, Miss!) came to the office this morning. It's another man's turn to be chosen – and the secretary will recommend him. If my husband could only send his testimonials by the same post – with just a word in your name, Miss – it might turn the scale, as they say. A private recommendation between gentlefolks goes so far.' She stopped again, and sighed again, and looked down at the carpet, as if she had some private reason for feeling a little ashamed of herself.

Agnes began to be rather weary of the persistent tone of mystery in which her visitor spoke. 'If you want my interest with any friend of mine,' she said, 'why can't you tell me the name?'

The courier's wife began to cry. 'I'm ashamed to tell you, Miss.' For the first time, Agnes spoke sharply. 'Nonsense, Emily! Tell me the name directly – or drop the subject – whichever you like best.'

Emily made a last desperate effort. She wrung her handkerchief hard in her lap, and let off the name as if she had been letting off a loaded gun: – 'Lord Montbarry!'

Agnes rose and looked at her.

'You have disappointed me,' she said very quietly, but with a look which the courier's wife had never seen in her face before. 'Knowing what you know, you ought to be aware that it is impossible for me to communicate with Lord Montbarry. I always supposed you had some delicacy of feeling. I am sorry to find that I have been mistaken.'

Weak as she was, Emily had spirit enough to feel the reproof. She walked in her meek noiseless way to the door. 'I beg your pardon, Miss. I am not quite so bad as you think me. But I beg your pardon, all the same.'

She opened the door. Agnes called her back. There was something in the woman's apology that appealed irresistibly to her just and generous nature. 'Come,' she said; 'we must not part in this way. Let me not misunderstand you. What *is* it that you expected me to do?'

Emily was wise enough to answer this time without any reserve. 'My husband will send his testimonials, Miss, to Lord Montbarry in Scotland. I only wanted you to let him say in his letter that his wife has been known to you since she was a child, and that you feel some little interest in his welfare on that account. I don't ask it now, Miss. You have made me understand that I was wrong.'

Had she really been wrong? Past remembrances, as well as present troubles, pleaded powerfully with Agnes for the courier's wife. 'It seems only a small favour to ask,' she said, speaking under the impulse of kindness which was the strongest impulse in her nature. 'But I am not sure that I ought to allow my name to be mentioned in your husband's letter. Let me hear again exactly what he wishes to say.' Emily repeated the words – and then offered one of those suggestions, which have a special value of their own to persons unaccustomed to the use of their pens. 'Suppose you try, Miss, how it looks in writing?' Childish as the idea was, Agnes tried the experiment. 'If I let you mention me,' she said, 'we must at least decide what you are to say.' She wrote the words in the briefest and plainest form: – 'I venture to state that my wife has been known from her childhood to Miss Agnes Lockwood, who feels some little interest in my welfare on that account.' Reduced to this one sentence, there was surely nothing in the reference to her name which implied that Agnes had permitted it, or that she was even aware of it. After a last struggle with herself, she handed the written paper to Emily. 'Your husband must copy it exactly, without altering anything,' she stipulated. 'On that condition, I grant your request.' Emily was not only thankful – she was really touched. Agnes hurried the little woman out of the room. 'Don't give me time to repent and take it back again,' she said. Emily vanished.

'Is the tie that once bound us completely broken? Am I as entirely parted from the good and evil fortune of his life as if we had never met and never loved?' Agnes looked at the clock on the mantel-piece. Not ten minutes since, those serious questions had been on her lips. It almost shocked her to think of the common place manner in which they had already met with their reply. The mail of that night would appeal once more to Montbarry's remembrance of her – in the choice of a servant.

Two days later, the post brought a few grateful lines from Emily. Her husband had got the place. Ferrari was engaged, for six months certain, as Lord Montbarry's courier.

THE SECOND PART

✎ FIVE ✎

AFTER ONLY ONE WEEK OF TRAVELLING in Scotland, my lord and my lady returned unexpectedly to London. Introduced to the mountains and lakes of the Highlands, her ladyship positively declined to improve her acquaintance with them. When she was asked for her reason, she answered with a Roman brevity, 'I have seen Switzerland.'

For a week more, the newly-married couple remained in London, in the strictest retirement. On one day in that week the nurse returned in a state of most uncustomary excitement from an errand on which Agnes had sent her. Passing the door of a fashionable dentist, she had met Lord Montbarry himself just leaving the house. The good woman's report described him, with malicious pleasure, as looking wretchedly ill. 'His cheeks are getting hollow, my dear, and his beard is turning grey. I hope the dentist hurt him!'

Knowing how heartily her faithful old servant hated the man who had deserted her. Agnes made due allowance for a large infusion of exaggeration in the picture presented to her. The main impression produced on her mind was an impression of nervous uneasiness. If she trusted herself in the streets by daylight while Lord Montbarry remained in London, how could she be sure that his next chance-meeting might not be a meeting with herself? She waited at home, privately ashamed of her own undignified conduct, for the next two days. On the third day the fashionable intelligence of the newspapers announced the departures of Lord and Lady Montbarry for Paris, on their way to Italy.

Mrs Ferrari, calling the same evening, informed Agnes that her husband had left her with all reasonable expression of conjugal kindness; his temper being improved by the prospect of going abroad. But one other servant accompanied the travellers – Lady Montbarry's maid, rather a silent, unsociable woman, so far as Emily had heard. Her ladyship's brother, Baron Rivar, was already on the Continent. It had been arranged that he was to meet his sister and her husband at Rome.

One by one the dull weeks succeeded each other in the life of Agnes. She faced her position with admirable courage, seeing her friends, keeping herself occupied in her leisure hours with reading and drawing, leaving no means untried of diverting her mind from the melancholy remembrance of the past. But she had loved too faithfully, she had been wounded too deeply, to feel in any adequate degree the influence of the moral remedies which she employed. Persons who met with her in the ordinary relations of life, deceived by her outward serenity of manner, agreed that 'Miss Lockwood seemed to be getting over her disappointment.' But an old friend and school companion who happened to see her during a brief visit to London, was inexpressibly distressed by the change that she detected in Agnes. This lady was Mrs Westwick, the wife of that brother of Lord Montbarry who came next to him in age, and who was described in the 'Peerage' as presumptive heir to the title. He was then away, looking after his interests in some mining property which he possessed in America. Mrs Westwick insisted on taking Agnes back with her to her home in Ireland. 'Come and keep me company while my husband is away. My three little girls will make you their playfellow, and the only stranger you will meet is the governess, whom I answer for your liking beforehand. Pack up your things, and I will call for you to-morrow on my way to the train.' In those hearty terms the invitation was given. Agnes thankfully accepted it. For three happy months she lived under the roof of her friend. The girls hung round her in tears at her departure; the youngest of them wanted to go back with Agnes to London. Half in jest, half in earnest, she said to her old friend at parting, 'If your governess leaves you, keep the place open for me.' Mrs Westwick laughed. The wiser children took it seriously, and promised to let Agnes know.

On the very day when Miss Lockwood returned to London, she was recalled to those associations with the past which she was most anxious to forget. After the first kissings and greetings were over, the old nurse (who had been left in charge at the lodgings) had some startling information to communicate, derived from the courier's wife.

'Here has been little Mrs Ferrari, my dear, in a dreadful state of mind, inquiring when you would be back. Her husband has left Lord Montbarry, without a word of warning – and nobody knows what has become of him.'

Agnes looked at her in astonishment. 'Are you sure of what you are saying?' she asked.

The nurse was quite sure. 'Why, Lord bless you! the news comes from the couriers' office in Golden Square – from the secretary, Miss Agnes, the secretary himself!' Hearing this, Agnes began to feel alarmed as well as surprised. It was still early in the evening. She at once sent a message to Mrs Ferrari, to say that she had returned.

In an hour more the courier's wife appeared, in a state of agitation which it was not easy to control. Her narrative, when she was at last able to speak connectedly, entirely confirmed the nurse's report of it.

After hearing from her husband with tolerable regularity from Paris, Rome, and Venice, Emily had twice written to him afterwards – and had received no reply. Feeling uneasy, she had gone to the office in Golden Square, to inquire if he had been heard of there. The post of the morning had brought a letter to the secretary from a courier then at Venice. It contained startling news of Ferrari. His wife had been allowed to take a copy of it, which she now handed to Agnes to read.

The writer stated that he had recently arrived in Venice. He had previously heard that Ferrari was with Lord and Lady Montbarry, at one of the old Venetian palaces which they had hired for a term. Being a friend of Ferrari, he had gone to pay him a visit. Ringing at the door that opened on the canal, and failing to make anyone hear him, he had gone round to a side entrance opening on one of the narrow lanes of Venice. Here, standing at the door (as if she were waiting for him to try that way next), he found a pale woman with magnificent dark eyes, who proved to be no other than Lady Montbarry herself.

She asked, in Italian, what he wanted. He answered that he wanted to see the courier Ferrari, if it was quite convenient. She at once informed him that Ferrari had left the palace, without assigning any reason, and without even leaving an address at which his monthly salary (then due to him) could be paid. Amazed at this reply, the courier inquired if any person had offended Ferrari, or quarrelled with him. The lady answered, 'To my knowledge, certainly not. I am Lady Montbarry; and I can positively assure you that Ferrari was treated with the greatest kindness in this house. We are as much astonished as you are at his extraordinary disappearance. If you should hear of him, pray let us know, so that we may at least pay him the money which is due.'

After one or two more questions (quite readily answered) relating to the date and the time of day at which Ferrari had left the palace, the courier took his leave.

He at once entered on the necessary investigations – without the slightest result so far as Ferrari was concerned. Nobody had seen him. Nobody appeared to have been taken into his confidence. Nobody knew anything (that is to say, anything of the slightest importance) even about persons so distinguished as Lord and Lady Montbarry. It was reported that her ladyship's English maid had left her, before the disappearance of Ferrari, to return to her relatives in her own country, and that Lady Montbarry had taken no steps to supply her place. His lordship was described as being in delicate health. He lived in the strictest retirement – nobody was admitted to him, even his own countrymen. A stupid old woman was discovered who did the housework at the palace, arriving in the morning and going away at night. She had never seen the lost courier – she had never even seen Lord Montbarry, who was then confined to his room. Her ladyship, 'a most gracious and adorable mistress', was in constant attendance on her noble husband. There was no other servant then in the house (so far as the old woman knew) but herself. The meals were sent in from a restaurant. My lord, it was said, disliked strangers. My lord's brother-in-law, the Baron, was generally shut up in a remote part of the palace, occupied (the gracious mistress said) with experiments in chemistry. The experiments sometimes made a nasty smell. A doctor had latterly been called in to his lordship – an Italian doctor, long resident in Venice. Inquiries being addressed to this gentleman (a physician of undoubted capacity and respectability), it turned out that he also had never seen Ferrari, having been summoned to the palace (as his memorandum book showed) at a date subsequent to the courier's disappearance. The doctor described Lord Montbarry's malady as bronchitis. So far, there was no reason to feel any anxiety, though the attack was a sharp one. If alarming symptoms should appear, he had arranged with her ladyship to call in another physician. For the rest, it was impossible to speak too highly of my lady; night and day, she was at her lord's bedside.

With these particulars began and ended the discoveries made by Ferrari's courier-friend. The police were on the look-out for the lost man – and that was the only hope which could be held forth for the present, to Ferrari's wife.

'What do you think of it, Miss?' the poor woman asked eagerly. 'What would you advise me to do?'

Agnes was at a loss how to answer her; it was an effort even to listen to what Emily was saying. The references in the courier's letter to Montbarry – the report of his illness, the melancholy picture of his secluded life – had reopened the old wound. She was not even thinking of the lost Ferrari; her mind was at Venice, by the sick man's bedside.

'I hardly know what to say,' she answered. 'I have had no experience in serious matters of this kind.'

'Do you think it would help you, Miss, if you read my husband's letters to me? There are only three of them – they won't take long to read.'

Agnes compassionately read the letters.

They were not written in a very tender tone. 'Dear Emily,' and 'Yours affectionately' – these conventional phrases, were the only phrases of endearment which they contained. In the first letter, Lord Montbarry was not very favourably spoken of: – 'We leave Paris to-morrow. I don't much like my lord. He is proud and cold, and, between ourselves, stingy in money matters. I have had to dispute such trifles as a few centimes in the hotel bill; and twice already, some sharp remarks have passed between the newly-married couple, in consequence of her ladyship's freedom in purchasing pretty tempting things at the shops in Paris. "I can't afford it; you must keep to your allowance." She has had to hear those words already. For my part, I like her. She has the nice, easy foreign manners – *she* talks to me as if I was a human being like herself.'

The second letter was dated from Rome.

'My lord's caprices' (Ferrari wrote) 'have kept us perpetually on the move. He is becoming incurably restless. I suspect he is uneasy in his mind. Painful recollections, I should say – I find him constantly reading old letters, when her ladyship is not present. We were to have stopped at Genoa, but he hurried us on. The same thing at Florence. Here, at Rome, my lady insists on resting. Her brother has met us at this place. There has been a quarrel already (the lady's maid tells me) between my lord and the Baron. The latter wanted to borrow money of the former. His lordship refused in language which offended Baron Rivar. My lady pacified them, and made them shake hands.'

The third, and last letter, was from Venice.

'More of my lord's economy! Instead of staying at the hotel, we have hired a damp, mouldy, rambling old palace. My lady insists on having the best suites of rooms wherever we go – and the palace comes cheaper for a two month's term. My lord tried to get it for longer; he says the quiet of Venice is good for his nerves. But a foreign speculator has secured the palace, and is going to turn it into an hotel. The Baron is still with us, and there have been more disagreements about money matters. I don't like the Baron – and I don't find the attractions of my lady grow on me. She was much nicer before the Baron joined us. My lord is a punctual paymaster; it's a matter of honour with him; he hates parting with his money, but he does it because he has given his word. I receive my salary regularly at the end of each month – not a franc extra, though I have done many things which are not part of a courier's proper work. Fancy the Baron trying to borrow money of *me*! He is an inveterate gambler. I didn't believe it when my lady's maid first told me so – but I have seen enough since to satisfy me that she was right. I have seen other things besides, which – well! which don't increase my respect for my lady and the Baron. The maid says she means to give warning to leave. She is a respectable British female, and doesn't take things quite so easily as I do. It is a dull life here. No going into company – no company at home – not a creature sees my lord – not even the consul, or the banker. When he goes out, he goes alone, and generally towards nightfall. Indoors, he shuts himself up in his own room with his books, and sees as little of his wife and the Baron as possible. I fancy things are coming to a crisis here. If my lord's suspicions are once awakened, the consequences will be terrible. Under certain provocations, the noble Montbarry is a man who would stick at nothing. However, the pay is good – and I can't afford to talk of leaving the place, like my lady's maid.'

Agnes handed back the letters – so suggestive of the penalty paid already for his own infatuation by the man who had deserted her! – with feelings of shame and distress, which made her no fit counsellor for the helpless woman who depended on her advice.

'The one thing I can suggest,' she said, after first speaking some kind words of comfort and hope, 'is that we should consult a person of greater experience than ours. Suppose I write and ask my lawyer (who is also my friend and trustee) to come and advise us to-morrow after his business hours?'

Emily eagerly and gratefully accepted the suggestion. An hour was arranged for the meeting on the next day; the correspondence was left under the care of Agnes; and the courier's wife took her leave.

Weary and heartsick, Agnes lay down on the sofa, to rest and compose herself. The careful nurse brought in a reviving cup of tea. Her quaint gossip about herself and her occupations while Agnes had been away, acted as a relief to her mistress's overburdened mind. They were still talking quietly, when they were startled by a loud knock at the house door. Hurried footsteps ascended the stairs. The door of the sitting-room was thrown open violently; the courier's wife rushed in like a mad woman. 'He's dead! they've murdered him!' Those wild words were all she could say. She dropped on her knees at the foot of the sofa – held out her hand with something clasped in it – and fell back in a swoon.

The nurse, signing to Agnes to open the window, took the necessary measures to restore the fainting woman. 'What's this?' she exclaimed. 'Here's a letter in her hand. See what it is, Miss.'

The open envelope was addressed (evidently in a feigned handwriting) to 'Mrs Ferrari'. The post-mark was 'Venice'. The contents of the envelope were a sheet of foreign note-paper, and a folded enclosure.

On the note-paper, one line only was written. It was again in a feigned handwriting, and it contained these words:

'*To console you for the loss of your husband.*'

Agnes opened the enclosure next.

It was a Bank of England note for a thousand pounds.

⊱ SIX ⊰

THE NEXT DAY, THE FRIEND and legal adviser of Agnes Lockwood, Mr
Troy, called on her by appointment in the evening.

Mrs Ferrari – still persisting in the conviction of her husband's death
– had sufficiently recovered to be present at the consultation. Assisted
by Agnes, she told the lawyer the little that was known relating to
Ferrari's disappearance, and then produced the correspondence connected with that event. Mr Troy read (first) the three letters addressed by
Ferrari to his wife; (secondly) the letter written by Ferrari's courier-
friend, describing his visit to the palace and his interview with Lady
Montbarry; and (thirdly) the one line of anonymous writing which had
accompanied the extraordinary gift of a thousand pounds to Ferrari's
wife.

Well known, at a later period, as the lawyer who acted for Lady
Lydiard, in the case of theft, generally described as the case of 'My Lady's
Money', Mr Troy was not only a man of learning and experience in his
profession – he was also a man who had seen something of society at
home and abroad. He possessed a keen eye for character, a quaint
humour, and a kindly nature which had not been deteriorated even by
a lawyer's professional experience of mankind. With all these personal
advantages, it is a question, nevertheless, whether he was the fittest
adviser whom Agnes could have chosen under the circumstances. Little
Mrs Ferrari, with many domestic merits, was an essentially commonplace
woman. Mr Troy was the last person living who was likely to attract her
sympathies – he was the exact opposite of a commonplace man.

'She looks very ill, poor thing!' In these words the lawyer opened the
business of the evening, referring to Mrs Ferrari as unceremoniously as
if she had been out of the room.

'She has suffered a terrible shock,' Agnes answered.

Mr Troy turned to Mrs Ferrari, and looked at her again, with the
interest due to the victim of a shock. He drummed absently with his
fingers on the table. At last he spoke to her.

'My good lady, you don't really believe that your husband is dead?'

Mrs Ferrari put her handkerchief to her eyes. The word 'dead' was
ineffectual to express her feelings. 'Murdered!' she said sternly, behind
her handkerchief.

'Why? And by whom?' Mr Troy asked.

Mrs Ferrari seemed to have some difficulty in answering. 'You have

read my husband's letters, sir,' she began. 'I believe he discovered——'
She got as far as that, and there she stopped.

'What did he discover?'

There are limits to human patience – even the patience of a bereaved wife. This cool question irritated Mrs Ferrari into expressing herself plainly at last.

'He discovered Lady Montbarry and the Baron!' she answered, with a burst of hysterical vehemence. 'The Baron is no more that vile woman's brother than I am. The wickedness of those two wretches came to my poor dear husband's knowledge. The lady's maid left her place on account of it. If Ferrari had gone away too, he would have been alive at this moment. They have killed him. I say they have killed him, to prevent it from getting to Lord Montbarry's ears.' So, in short sharp sentences, and in louder and louder accents, Mrs Ferrari stated *her* opinion of the case.

Still keeping his own view in reserve, Mr Troy listened with an expression of satirical approval.

'Very strongly stated, Mrs Ferrari,' he said. 'You build up your sentences well; you clinch your conclusions in a work-manlike manner. If you had been a man, you would have made a good lawyer – you would have taken juries by the scruff of their necks. Complete the case, my good lady – complete the case. Tell us next who sent you this letter, enclosing the bank-note. The "two wretches" who murdered Mr Ferrari would hardly put their hands in their pockets and send you a thousand pounds. Who is it – eh? I see the post-mark on the letter is "Venice". Have you any friend in that interesting city, with a large heart, and a purse to correspond, who has been let into the secret and who wishes to console you anonymously?'

It was not easy to reply to this. Mrs Ferrari began to feel the first inward approaches of something like hatred towards Mr Troy. 'I don't understand you, sir,' she answered. 'I don't think this is a joking matter.'

Agnes interfered, for the first time. She drew her chair a little nearer to her legal counsellor and friend.

'What is the most probable explanation, in your opinion?' she asked.

'I shall offend Mrs Ferrari if I tell you,' Mr Troy answered.

'No, sir, you won't!' cried Mrs Ferrari, hating Mr Troy undisguisedly by this time.

The lawyer leaned back in his chair. 'Very well,' he said, in his most good-humoured manner. 'Let's have it out. Observe, madam, I don't dispute your view of the position of affairs at the palace in Venice. You have your husband's letters to justify you; and you have also the significant fact that Lady Montbarry's maid did really leave the house. We will say, then, that Lord Montbarry has presumably been made the victim of a foul wrong – that Mr Ferrari was the first to find it out – and that the guilty persons had reason to fear, not only that he would acquaint Lord Montbarry with his discovery, but that he would be a principal witness against them if the scandal was made public in a court of law. Now mark! Admitting all this, I draw a totally different conclusion from the conclusion at which you have arrived. Here is your husband left in the miserable household of three, under very awkward circumstances for *him*. What does he do? But for the bank-note and the written message sent to you with it, I should say that he had wisely withdrawn himself from association with a disgraceful discovery and exposure, by taking secretly to flight. The money modifies this view – unfavourably so far as Mr Ferrari is concerned. I still believe he is keeping out of the way. But I now say he is *paid* for keeping out of the way – and that bank-note there on the table is the price of his absence, sent by the guilty persons to his wife.'

Mrs Ferrari's watery grey eyes brightened suddenly; Mrs Ferrari's dull drab-coloured complexion became enlivened by a glow of brilliant red.

'It's false!' she cried. 'It's a burning shame to speak of my husband in that way!'

'I told you I should offend you!' said Mr Troy.

Agnes interposed once more – in the interests of peace. She took the offended wife's hand; she appealed to the lawyer to reconsider that side of his theory which reflected harshly on Ferrari. While she was still speaking, the servant interrupted her by entering the room with a visiting-card. It was the card of Henry Westwick; and there was an ominous request written on it in pencil. 'I bring bad news. Let me see you for a minute downstairs.' Agnes immediately left the room.

Alone with Mrs Ferrari, Mr Troy permitted his natural kindness of heart to show itself on the surface at last. He tried to make his peace with the courier's wife.

'You have every claim, my good soul, to resent a reflection cast upon your husband,' he began. 'I may even say that I respect you for speaking so warmly in his defence. At the same time, remember, that I am bound, in such a serious matter as this, to tell you what is really in my mind. I can have no intention of offending you, seeing that I am a total stranger to you and to Mr Ferrari. A thousand pounds is a large sum of money; and a poor man may excusably be tempted by it to do nothing worse than to keep out of the way for a while. My only interest, acting on your behalf, is to get at the truth. If you will give me time, I see no reason to despair of finding your husband yet.'

Ferrari's wife listened, without being convinced: her narrow little mind, filled to its extreme capacity by her unfavourable opinon of Mr Troy, had no room left for the process of correcting its first impression. 'I am much obliged to you, sir,' was all she said. Her eyes were more communicative – her eyes added, in *their* language, 'You may say what you please; I will never forgive you to my dying day.'

Mr Troy gave it up. He composedly wheeled his chair round, put his hands in his pockets, and looked out of the window.

After an interval of silence, the drawing-room door was opened.

Mr Troy wheeled round again briskly to the table, expecting to see Agnes. To his surprise there appeared, in her place, a perfect stranger to him – a gentleman, in the prime of life, with a marked expression of pain and embarrassment on his handsome face. He looked at Mr Troy, and bowed gravely.

'I am so unfortunate as to have brought news to Miss Agnes Lockwood which has greatly distressed her,' he said. 'She has retired to her room. I am requested to make her excuses, and to speak to you in her place.'

Having introduced himself in those terms, he noticed Mrs Ferrari, and held out his hand to her kindly. 'It is some years since we last met, Emily,' he said. 'I am afraid you have almost forgotten the "Master Henry" of old times.' Emily, in some little confusion, made her acknowledgments, and begged to know if she could be of any use to Miss Lockwood. 'The old nurse is with her,' Henry answered; 'they will be better left together.' He turned once more to Mr Troy. 'I ought to tell you,' he said, 'that my name is Henry Westwick. I am the younger brother of the late Lord Montbarry.'

'The *late* Lord Montbarry!' Mr Troy exclaimed.

'My brother died at Venice, yesterday evening. There is the telegram.' With that startling answer, he handed the paper to Mr Troy.

The message was in these words:

'Lady Montbarry, Venice. To Stephen Robert Westwick, Newbury's Hotel, London. It is useless to take the journey. Lord Montbarry died of bronchitis, at 8.40 this evening. All needful details by post.'

'Was this expected, sir?' the lawyer asked.

'I cannot say that it has taken us entirely by surprise,' Henry answered. 'My brother Stephen (who is now the head of the family) received a telegram three days since, informing him that alarming symptoms had declared themselves, and that a second physician had been called in. He telegraphed back to say that he had left Ireland for London, on his way to Venice, and to direct that any further message might be sent to his hotel. The reply came in a second telegram. It announced that Lord Montbarry was in a state of insensibility, and that, in his brief intervals of consciousness, he recognized nobody. My brother was advised to wait in London for later information. The third telegram is now in your hands. That is all I know, up to the present time.'

Happening to look at the courier's wife, Mr Troy was struck by the expression of blank fear which showed itself in the woman's face.

'Mrs Ferrari,' he said, 'have you heard what Mr Westwick has just told me?'

'Every word of it, sir.'

'Have you any questions to ask?'

'No, sir.'

'You seem to be alarmed,' the lawyer persisted. 'Is it still about your husband?'

'I shall never see my husband again, sir. I have thought so all along, as you know. I feel sure of it now.'

'Sure of it, after what you have just heard?'

'Yes, sir.'

'Can you tell me why?'

'No, sir. It's a feeling I have. I can't tell why.'

'Oh, a feeling?' Mr Troy repeated, in a tone of compassionate contempt. 'When it comes to feelings, my good soul—!' He left the sentence unfinished, and rose to take his leave of Mr Westwick. The truth is, he began to feel puzzled himself, and he did not choose to let Mrs Ferrari see it. 'Accept the expression of my sympathy, sir,' he said to Mr Westwick politely. 'I wish you good evening.'

Henry turned to Mrs Ferrari as the lawyer closed the door. 'I have heard of your trouble, Emily, from Miss Lockwood. Is there anything I can do to help you?'

'Nothing, sir, thank you. Perhaps, I had better go home after what has happened? I will call to-morrow, and see if I can be of any use to Miss Agnes. I am very sorry for her.' She stole away, with her formal curtsey, her noiseless step, and her obstinate resolution to take the gloomiest view of her husband's case.

Henry Westwick looked round him in the solitude of the little drawing-room. There was nothing to keep him in the house, and yet he lingered in it. It was something to be even near Agnes – to see the things belonging to her that were scattered about the room. There, in one corner, was her chair, with her embroidery on the work-table by its side. On the little easel near the window was her last drawing, not quite finished yet. The book she had been reading lay on the sofa, with her tiny pencil-case in it to mark the place at which she had left off. One after another, he looked at the objects that reminded him of the woman whom he loved – took them up tenderly – and laid them down again with a sigh. Ah, how far, how unattainably far from him, she was still! 'She will never forget Montbarry,' he thought to himself as he took up his hat to go. 'Not one of us feels his death as she feels it. Miserable, miserable wretch – how she loved him!'

In the street, as Henry closed the house-door, he was stopped by a passing acquaintance – a wearisome inquisitive man – doubly unwelcome to him, at that moment. 'Sad news, Westwick, this about your brother. Rather an unexpected death, wasn't it? We never heard at the club that Montbarry's lungs were weak. What will the insurance offices do?'

Henry started; he had never thought of his brother's life insurance. What could the offices do but pay? A death by bronchitis, certified by two physicians, was surely the least disputable of all deaths. 'I wish you hadn't put that question into my head!' he broke out irritably. 'Ah!' said his friend, 'you think the widow will get the money? So do I! so do I!'

❧ SEVEN ❧

SOME DAYS LATER, THE INSURANCE offices (two in number) received the formal announcement of Lord Montbarry's death, from her ladyship's London solicitors. The sum insured in each office was five thousand pounds – on which one year's premium only had been paid. In the face of such a pecuniary emergency as this, the Directors thought it desirable to consider their position. The medical advisers of the two offices, who had recommended the insurance of Lord Montbarry's life, were called into council over their own reports. The result excited some interest among persons connected with the business of life insurance. Without absolutely declining to pay the money, the two offices (acting in concert) decided on sending a commission of inquiry to Venice, 'for the purpose of obtaining further information.'

Mr Troy received the earliest intelligence of what was going on. He wrote at once to communicate his news to Agnes; adding, what he considered to be a valuable hint, in these words:

'You are intimately acquainted, I know, with Lady Barville, the late Lord Montbarry's eldest sister. The solicitors employed by her husband, are also the solicitors to one of the two insurance offices. There may possibly be something in the Report of the commission of inquiry touching on Ferrari's disappearance. Ordinary persons would not be permitted, of course, to see such a document. But a sister of the late lord is so near a relative as to be an exception to general rules. If Sir Theodore Barville puts it on that footing, the lawyers, even if they do not allow his wife to look at the Report, will at least answer any discreet questions she may ask referring to it. Let me hear what you think of this suggestion, at your earliest convenience.'

The reply was received by return of post. Agnes declined to avail herself of Mr Troy's proposal.

'My interference, innocent as it was,' she wrote, 'has already been productive of such deplorable results, that I cannot and dare not stir any further in the case of Ferrari. If I had not consented to let that unfortunate man refer to me by name, the late Lord Montbarry would never have engaged him, and his wife would have been spared the misery and suspense from which she is suffering now. I would not even look at the Report to which you allude if it was placed in my hands – I have heard more than enough already of that hideous life in the palace at Venice. If Mrs Ferrari chooses to address herself to Lady Barville (with your assistance), that is of course quite another thing. But, even in this case, I must make it a positive condition that my name shall not be mentioned. Forgive me, dear Mr Troy! I am very unhappy, and very unreasonable – but I am only a woman, and you must not expect too much from me.'

Foiled in this direction, the lawyer next advised making the attempt to discover the present address of Lady Montbarry's English maid. This excellent suggestion had one drawback: it could only be carried out by spending money – and there was no money to spend. Mrs Ferrari shrank from the bare idea of making any use of the thousand-pound note. It had been deposited in the safe keeping of a bank. If it was even mentioned in her hearing, she shuddered and referred to it, with melodramatic fervour, as 'my husband's blood-money!'

So, under stress of circumstances, the attempt to solve the mystery of Ferrari's disappearance was suspended for a while.

It was the last month of the year 1860. The commission of inquiry was already at work; having begun its investigations on December 6. On the 10th, the term for which the late Lord Montbarry had hired the Venetian palace expired. News by telegram reached the insurance offices that Lady Montbarry had been advised by her lawyers to leave for London with as little delay as possible. Baron Rivar, it was believed, would accompany her to England, but would not remain in that country, unless his services were absolutely required by her ladyship. The Baron, 'well known as an enthusiastic student of chemistry', had heard of certain recent discoveries in connection with that science, in the United States, and was anxious to investigate them personally.

These items of news, collected by Mr Troy, were duly communicated to Mrs Ferrari, whose anxiety about her husband made her a frequent, a too frequent, visitor at the lawyer's office. She attempted to relate what she had heard to her good friend and protectress. Agnes steadily refused to listen, and positively forbade any further conversation relating to Lord Montbarry's wife, now that Lord Montbarry was no more. 'You have Mr

Troy to advise you,' she said; 'and you are welcome to what little money I can spare, if money is wanted. All I ask in return is that you will not distress me. I am trying to separate myself from remembrances——' her voice faltered; she paused to control herself – 'from remembrances,' she resumed, 'which are sadder than ever since I have heard of Lord Montbarry's death. Help me by your silence to recover my spirits, if I can. Let me hear nothing more, until I can rejoice with you that your husband is found.'

Time advanced to the 13th of the month; and more information of the interesting sort reached Mr Troy. The labours of the insurance commission had come to an end – the Report had been received from Venice on that day.

❧ EIGHT ❧

ON THE 14TH THE DIRECTORS and their legal advisers met for the reading of the Report, with closed doors. These were the terms in which the Commissioners related the results of their inquiry:

'Private and confidential.

'We have the honour to inform our Directors that we arrived in Venice on December 6, 1860. On the same day we proceeded to the palace inhabited by Lord Montbarry at the time of his last illness and death.

'We were received with all possible courtesy by Lady Montbarry's brother, Baron Rivar. "My sister was her husband's only attendant throughout his illness," the Baron informed us. "She is overwhelmed by grief and fatigue – or she would have been here to receive you personally. What are your wishes, gentlemen? and what can I do for you, in her ladyship's place?"

'In accordance with our instructions, we answered that the death and burial of Lord Montbarry abroad made it desirable to obtain more complete information relating to his illness, and to the circumstances which had attended it, than could be conveyed in writing. We explained that the law provided for the lapse of a certain interval of time before the payment of the sum assured, and we expressed our wish to conduct the inquiry with the most respectful consideration for her ladyship's feelings, and for the convenience of any other members of the family inhabiting the house.

'To this the Baron replied, "I am the only member of the family living here, and I and the palace are entirely at your disposal." From first to last we found this gentleman perfectly straightforward, and most amiably willing to assist us.

'With the one exception of her ladyship's room, we went over the whole of the palace the same day. It is an immense place, only partially furnished. The first floor and part of the second floor were the portions of it that had been inhabited by Lord Montbarry and the members of the household. We saw the bedchamber, at one extremity of the palace, in which his lordship died, and the small room communicating with it, which he used as a study. Next to this was a large apartment or hall, the doors of which he habitually kept locked, his object being (as we were informed) to pursue his studies uninterruptedly in perfect solitude. On the other side of the large hall were the bedchamber occupied by her ladyship, and the dressing-room in which the maid slept previous to her departure for England. Beyond these were the dining and reception rooms, opening into an antechamber, which gave access to the grand staircase of the palace.

'The only inhabited rooms on the second floor were the sitting-room and bed-room occupied by Baron Rivar, and another room at some distance from it, which had been the bed-room of the courier Ferrari.

'The rooms on the third floor and on the basement were completely unfurnished, and in a condition of great neglect. We inquired if there was anything to be seen below the basement – and we were at once informed that there were vaults beneath, which we were at perfect liberty to visit.

'We went down, so as to leave no part of the palace unexplored. The vaults were, it was believed, used as dungeons in the old times – say, some centuries since. Air and light were only partially admitted to these dismal places by two long shafts of winding construction, which communicated with the back yard of the palace, and the openings of which, high above the ground, were protected by iron gratings. The stone stairs leading down into the vaults could be closed at will by a heavy trap-door in the back hall, which we found open. The Baron himself led the way down the stairs. We remarked that it might be awkward if that trap-door fell down and closed the opening behind us. The Baron smiled at the idea. "Don't be alarmed, gentlemen," he said; "the door is safe. I had an interest in seeing to it myself, when we first inhabited the palace. My favourite study is the study of experimental chemistry – and my work-shop, since we have been in Venice, is down here."

'These last words explained a curious smell in the vaults, which we noticed the moment we entered them. We can only describe the smell by saying that it was of a twofold sort – faintly aromatic, as it were, in its first effect, but with some after-odour very sickening in our nostrils.

The Baron's furnaces and retorts, and other things, were all there to speak for themselves, together with some packages of chemicals, having the name and address of the person who had supplied them plainly visible on their labels. "Not a pleasant place for study," Baron Rivar observed, "but my sister is timid. She has a horror of chemical smells and explosions – and she has banished me to these lower regions, so that my experiments may neither be smelt or heard." He held out his hands, on which we had noticed that he wore gloves in the house. "Accidents will happen sometimes," he said, "no matter how careful a man may be. I burnt my hands severely in trying a new combination the other day, and they are only recovering now."

'We mention these otherwise unimportant incidents, in order to show that our exploration of the palace was not impeded by any attempt at concealment. We were even admitted to her ladyship's own room – on a subsequent occasion, when she went out to take the air. Our instructions recommended us to examine his lordship's residence, because the extreme privacy of his life at Venice, and the remarkable departure of the only two servants in the house, might have some suspicious connection with the nature of his death. We found nothing to justify suspicion.

'As to his lordship's retired way of life, we have conversed on the subject with the consul and the banker – the only two strangers who held any communication with him. He called once at the bank to obtain money on his letter of credit, and excused himself from accepting an invitation to visit the banker at his private residence, on the ground of delicate health. His lordship wrote to the same effect on sending his card to the consul, to excuse himself from personally returning that gentleman's visit to the palace. We have seen the letter, and we beg to offer the following copy of it. "Many years passed in India have injured my constitution. I have ceased to go into society; the one occupation of my life now is the study of Oriental literature. The air of Italy is better for me than the air of England, or I should never have left home. Pray accept the apologies of a student and an invalid. The active part of my life is at an end." The self-seclusion of his lordship seems to us to be explained in these brief lines. We have not, however, on that account spared our inquiries in other directions. Nothing to excite a suspicion of anything wrong has come to our knowledge.

'As to the departure of the lady's maid, we have seen the woman's receipt for her wages, in which it is expressly stated that she left Lady Montbarry's service because she disliked the Continent, and wished to get back to her own country. This is not an uncommon result of taking English servants to foreign parts. Lady Montbarry has informed us that she abstained from engaging another maid, in consequence of the extreme dislike which his lordship expressed to having strangers in the house, in the state of his health at that time.

'The disappearance of the courier Ferrari is, in itself, unquestionably a suspicious circumstance. Neither her ladyship nor the Baron can explain it; and no investigation that we could make has thrown the smallest light on this event, or has justified us in associating it, directly or indirectly, with the object of our inquiry. We have even gone the length of examining the portmanteau which Ferrari left behind him. It contains nothing but clothes and linen – no money, and not even a scrap of paper in the pockets of the clothes. The portmanteau remains in charge of the police.

'We have also found opportunities of speaking privately to the old woman who attends to the rooms occupied by her ladyship and the Baron. She was recommended to fill this situation by the keeper of the restaurant who has supplied the meals to the family throughout the period of their residence at the palace. Her character is most favourably spoken of. Unfortunately, her limited intelligence makes her of no value as a witness. We were patient and careful in questioning her, and we found her perfectly willing to answer us; but we could elicit nothing which is worth including in the present Report.

'On the second day of our inquiries, we had the honour of an interview with Lady Montbarry. Her ladyship looked miserably worn and ill, and seemed to be quite at a loss to understand what we wanted with her. Baron Rivar, who introduced us, explained the nature of our errand in Venice, and took pains to assure her that it was a purely formal duty on which we were engaged. Having satisfied her ladyship on this point, he discreetly left the room.

'The questions which we addressed to Lady Montbarry related mainly, of course, to his lordship's illness. The answers, given with great nervousness of manner, but without the slightest appearance of reserve, informed us of the facts that follow:

'Lord Montbarry had been out of order for some time past – nervous and irritable. He first complained of having taken cold on November 13 last; he passed a wakeful and feverish night, and remained in bed the next day. Her ladyship proposed sending for medical advice. He refused to allow her to do this, saying that he could quite easily be his own doctor in such a trifling matter as a cold. Some hot lemonade was made at his request, with a view to producing perspiration. Lady Montbarry's maid having left her at that time, the courier Ferrari (then the only servant in the house) went out to buy the lemons. Her ladyship made the drink with her own hands. It was successful in producing perspiration – and Lord Montbarry had some hours of sleep afterwards. Later in the day, having need of Ferrari's services, Lady Montbarry rang for him. The bell was not answered. Baron Rivar searched for the man, in the palace and out of it, in vain. From that time forth, not a trace of Ferrari could be discovered. This happened on November 14.

'On the night of the 14th, the feverish symptoms accompanying his lordship's cold returned. They were in part perhaps attributable to the annoyance and alarm caused by Ferrari's mysterious disappearance. It had been impossible to conceal the circumstance, as his lordship rang repeatedly for the courier; insisting that the man should relieve Lady Montbarry and the Baron by taking their places during the night at his bedside.

'On the 15th (the day on which the old woman first came to do the housework), his lordship complained of a sore throat, and of a feeling of oppression on the chest. On this day, and again on the 16th, her ladyship and the Baron entreated him to see a doctor. He still refused. "I don't want strange faces about me; my cold will run its course, in spite of the doctor," – that was his answer. On the 17th he was so much worse, that it was decided to send for medical help whether he liked it or not. Baron Rivar, after inquiry at the consul's, secured the services of Doctor Bruno, well known as an eminent physician in Venice; with the additional recommendation of having resided in England, and having made himself acquainted with English forms of medical practice.'

Thus far, our account of his lordship's illness has been derived from statements made by Lady Montbarry. The narrative will now be most fitly continued in the language of the doctor's own report, herewith subjoined.

' "My medical diary informs me that I first saw the English Lord Montbarry, on November 17. He was suffering from a sharp attack of bronchitis. Some previous time had been lost, through his obstinate objection to the presence of a medical man at his bedside. Generally speaking, he appeared to be in a delicate state of health. His nervous system was out of order – he was at once timid and contradictory. When I spoke to him in English, he answered in Italian; and when I tried him in Italian, he went back to English. It mattered little – the malady had already made such progress that he could only speak a few words at a time, and those in a whisper.

' "I at once applied the necessary remedies. Copies of my prescriptions (with translation into English) accompany the present statement, and are left to speak for themselves.

' "For the next three days I was in constant attendance on my patient. He answered to the remedies employed – improving slowly, but decidedly. I could conscientiously assure Lady Montbarry that no danger was to be apprehended thus far. She was indeed a most devoted wife. I vainly endeavoured to induce her to accept the services of a competent nurse; she would allow nobody to attend on her husband but herself. Night and day this estimable woman was at his bedside. In her brief intervals of repose, her brother watched the sick man in her place. This brother was, I must say, very good company, in the intervals when we had time for a little talk. He dabbled in chemistry, down in the horrid under-water vaults of the palace; and he wanted to show me some of his experiments. I have enough of chemistry in writing prescriptions – and I declined. He took it quite good-humouredly.

'"I am straying away from my subject. Let me return to the sick lord.

'"Up to the 20th, then, things went well enough. I was quite unpre-pared for the disastrous change that showed itself, when I paid Lord Montbarry my morning visit on the 21st. He had relapsed, and seriously relapsed. Examining him to discover the cause, I found symptoms of pneumonia – that is to say, in unmedical language, inflammation of the substance of the lungs. He breathed with difficulty, and was only partially able to relieve himself by coughing. I made the strictest inquiries, and was assured that his medicine had been administered as carefully as usual, and that he had not been exposed to any changes of temperature. It was with great reluctance that I added to Lady Montbarry's distress; but I felt bound, when she suggested a consultation with another phys-ician, to own that I too thought there was really need for it.

'"Her ladyship instructed me to spare no expense, and to get the best medical opinion in Italy. The best opinion was happily within our reach. The first and foremost of Italian physicians, is Torello of Padua. I sent a special messenger for the great man. He arrived on the evening of the 21st, and confirmed my opinion that pneumonia had set in, and that our patient's life was in danger. I told him what my treatment of the case had been, and he approved of it in every particular. He made some valuable suggestions, and (at Lady Montbarry's express request) he con-sented to defer his return to Padua until the following morning.

'"We both saw the patient at intervals in the course of the night. The disease, steadily advancing, set our utmost resistance at defiance. In the morning Doctor Torello took his leave. 'I can be of no further use,' he said to me. 'The man is past all help – and he ought to know it.'

'"Later in the day I warned my lord, gently as I could, that his time had come. I am informed that there are serious reasons for my stating what passed between us on this occasion, in detail, and without any reserve. I comply with the request.

'"Lord Montbarry received the intelligence of his approaching death with becoming composure, but with a certain doubt. He signed to me to put my ear to his mouth. He whispered faintly, 'Are you sure?' It was no time to deceive him; I said, 'Positively sure.' He waited a little, gasping for breath, and then he whispered again, 'Feel under my pillow.' I found under his pillow a letter, sealed and stamped, ready for the post. His next words were just audible and no more – 'Post it yourself.' I answered, of course, that I would do so – and I did post the letter with my own hand. I looked at the address. It was directed to a lady in London. The street I cannot remember. The name I can perfectly recall: it was an Italian name – 'Mrs Ferrari.'

' "That night my lord nearly died of asphyxia. I got him through it for the time; and his eyes showed that he understood me when I told him, the next morning, that I had posted the letter. This was his last effort of consciousness. When I saw him again he was sunk in apathy. He lingered in a state of insensibility, supported by stimulants, until the 25th, and died (unconscious to the last) on the evening of that day.

' "As to the cause of his death, it seems (if I may be excused for saying so) simply absurd to ask the question. Bronchitis, terminating in pneumonia – there is no more doubt that this, and this only, was the malady of which he expired, than that two and two make four. Doctor Torello's own note of the case is added here to a duplicate of my certificate, in order (as I am informed) to satisfy some English offices in which his lordship's life was insured. The English offices must have been founded by the celebrated saint and doubter, mentioned in the New Testament, whose name was Thomas!" '

'Doctor Bruno's evidence ends here.

'Reverting for a moment to our inquiries addressed to Lady Montbarry, we have to report that she can give us no information on the subject of the letter which the doctor posted at Lord Montbarry's request. When his lordship wrote it? what it contained? why he kept it a secret from Lady Montbarry (and from the Baron also); and why he should write at all to the wife of his courier? these are questions to which we find it simply impossible to obtain any replies. It seems even useless to say that the matter is open to suspicion. Suspicion implies conjecture of some kind – and the letter under my lord's pillow baffles all conjecture. Application to Mrs Ferrari may perhaps clear up the mystery. Her residence in London will be easily discovered at the Italian Couriers' Office, Golden Square.

'Having arrived at the close of the present Report, we have now to draw your attention to the conclusion which is justified by the results of our investigation.

'The plain question before our Directors and ourselves appears to be this: Has the inquiry revealed any extraordinary circumstances which render the death of Lord Montbarry open to suspicion? The inquiry has revealed extraordinary circumstances beyond all doubt – such as the disappearance of Ferrari, the remarkable absence of the customary establishment of servants in the house, and the mysterious letter which his lordship asked the doctor to post. But where is the proof that any one of these circumstances is associated – suspiciously and directly associated – with the only event which concerns us, the event of Lord Montbarry's death? In the absence of any such proof, and in the face of the evidence of two eminent physicians, it is impossible to dispute the statement on the certificate that his lordship died a natural death. We are bound, therefore, to report, that there are no valid grounds for refusing the payment of the sum for which the late Lord Montbarry's life was assured.

'We shall send these lines to you by the post of to-morrow, December 10; leaving time to receive your further instructions (if any), in reply to our telegram of this evening announcing the conclusion of the inquiry.'

NINE

'Now, MY GOOD CREATURE, WHATEVER you have to say to me, out with it at once! I don't want to hurry you needlessly; but these are business hours, and I have other people's affairs to attend to besides yours.'

Addressing Ferrari's wife, with his usual blunt good-humour, in these terms, Mr Troy registered the lapse of time by a glance at the watch on his desk, and then waited to hear what his client had to say to him.

'It's something more, sir, about the letter with the thousand-pound note,' Mrs Ferrari began. 'I have found out who sent it to me.'

Mr Troy started. 'This is news indeed!' he said. 'Who sent you the letter?'

'Lord Montbarry sent it, sir.'

It was not easy to take Mr Troy by surprise. But Mrs Ferrari threw him completely off his balance. For a while he could only look at her in silent surprise. 'Nonsense!' he said, as soon as he had recovered himself. 'There is some mistake – it can't be!'

'There is no mistake,' Mrs Ferrari rejoined, in her most positive manner. 'Two gentlemen from the insurance offices called on me this morning, to see the letter. They were completely puzzled – especially when they heard of the bank-note inside. But they know who sent the letter. His lordship's doctor in Venice posted it at his lordship's request. Go to the gentlemen yourself, sir, if you don't believe me. They were polite enough to ask if I could account for Lord Montbarry writing to me and sending me the money. I gave them my opinion directly – I said it was like his lordship's kindness.'

'Like his lordship's kindness?' Mr Troy repeated, in blank amazement.

'Yes, sir! Lord Montbarry knew me, like all the other members of the family, when I was at school on the estate in Ireland. If he could have done it, he would have protected my poor dear husband. But he was helpless himself in the hands of my lady and the Baron – and the only kind thing he could do was to provide for me in my widowhood, like the true nobleman he was!'

'A very pretty explanation!' said Mr Troy. 'What did your visitors from the insurance offices think of it?'

'They asked if I had any proof of my husband's death.'

'And what did you say?'

'I said, "I give you better than proof, gentlemen; I give you my positive opinion." '

'That satisfied them, of course?'

'They didn't say so in words, sir. They looked at each other – and wished me good-morning.'

'Well, Mrs Ferrari, unless you have some more extraordinary news for me, I think I shall wish you good-morning too. I can take a note of your information (very startling information, I own); and, in the absence of proof, I can do no more.'

'I can provide you with proof, sir – if that is all you want,' said Mrs Ferrari, with great dignity. 'I only wish to know, first, whether the law justifies me in doing it. You may have seen in the fashionable intelligence of the newspapers, that Lady Montbarry has arrived in London, at New-bury's Hotel. I propose to go and see her.'

'The deuce you do! May I ask for what purpose?'

Mrs Ferrari answered in a mysterious whisper. 'For the purpose of catching her in a trap! I shan't send in my name – I shall announce myself as a person on business, and the first words I say to her will be these: "I come, my lady, to acknowledge the receipt of the money sent to Ferrari's widow." Ah! you may well start, Mr Troy! It almost takes *you* off your guard, doesn't it? Make your mind easy, sir; I shall find the proof that everybody asks me for in her guilty face. Let her only change colour by the shadow of a shade – let her eyes only drop for half an instant – I shall discover her! The one thing I want to know is, does the law permit it?'

'The law permits it,' Mr Troy answered gravely; 'but whether her ladyship will permit it, is quite another question.

'Have you really courage enough, Mrs Ferrari, to carry out this notable scheme of yours? You have been described to me, by Miss Lockwood, as rather a nervous, timid sort of person – and, if I may trust my own observation, I should say you justify the description.'

'If you had lived in the country, sir, instead of living in London,' Mrs

Ferrari replied, 'you would sometimes have seen even a sheep turn on a dog. I am far from saying that I am a bold woman – quite the reverse. But when I stand in that wretch's presence, and think of my murdered husband, the one of us two who is likely to be frightened is not *me*. I am going there now, sir. You shall hear how it ends. I wish you good-morning.'

With those brave words the courier's wife gathered her mantle about her, and walked out of the room.

Mr Troy smiled – not satirically, but compassionately. 'The little simpleton!' he thought to himself. 'If half of what they say of Lady Montbarry is true, Mrs Ferrari and her trap have but a poor prospect before them. I wonder how it will end?'

All Mr Troy's experience failed to forewarn him of how it *did* end.

❧ TEN ❧

IN THE MEAN TIME, MRS Ferrari held to her resolution. She went straight from Mr Troy's office to Newbury's Hotel.

Lady Montbarry was at home, and alone. But the authorities of the hotel hesitated to disturb her when they found that the visitor declined to mention her name. Her ladyship's new maid happened to cross the hall while the matter was still in debate. She was a Frenchwoman, and, on being appealed to, she settled the question in the swift, easy, rational French way. 'Madame's appearance was perfectly respectable. Madame might have reasons for not mentioning her name which Miladi might approve. In any case, there being no orders forbidding the introduction of a strange lady, the matter clearly rested between Madame and Miladi. Would Madame, therefore, be good enough to follow Miladi's maid up the stairs?'

In spite of her resolution, Mrs Ferrari's heart beat as if it would burst out of her bosom, when her conductress led her into an ante-room, and knocked at a door opening into a room beyond. But it is remarkable that persons of sensitively-nervous organization are the very persons who are capable of forcing themselves (apparently by the exercise of a spasmodic effort of will) into the performance of acts of the most audacious courage. A low, grave voice from the inner room said, 'Come in.' The maid, opening the door, announced, 'A person to see you, Miladi, on business,' and immediately retired. In the one instant while these events passed, timid little Mrs Ferrari mastered her own throbbing heart; stepped over the threshold, conscious of her clammy hands, dry lips, and burning head; and stood in the presence of Lord Montbarry's widow, to all outward appearance as supremely self-possessed as her ladyship herself.

It was still early in the afternoon, but the light in the room was dim. The blinds were drawn down. Lady Montbarry sat with her back to the windows, as if even the subdued daylight were disagreeable to her. She had altered sadly for the worse in her personal appearance, since the memorable day when Doctor Wybrow had seen her in his consulting-room. Her beauty was gone – her face had fallen away to mere skin and bone; the contrast between her ghastly complexion and her steely glittering black eyes was more startling than ever. Robed in dismal black, relieved only by the brilliant whiteness of her widow's cap – reclining in a panther-like suppleness of attitude on a little green sofa – she looked at the stranger who had intruded on her, with a moment's languid curiosity, then dropped her eyes again to the hand-screen which she held between her face and the fire. 'I don't know you,' she said. 'What do you want with me?'

Mrs Ferrari tried to answer. Her first burst of courage had already worn itself out. The bold words that she had determined to speak were living words still in her mind, but they died on her lips.

There was a moment of silence. Lady Montbarry looked round again at the speechless stranger. 'Are you deaf?' she asked. There was another pause. Lady Montbarry quietly looked back again at the screen, and put another question. 'Do you want money?'

'Money!' That one word roused the sinking spirit of the courier's wife. She recovered her courage; she found her voice. 'Look at me, my lady, if you please,' she said, with a sudden outbreak of audacity.

Lady Montbarry looked round for the third time. The fatal words passed Mrs Ferrari's lips.

'I come, my lady, to acknowledge the receipt of the money sent to Ferrari's widow.'

Lady Montbarry's glittering black eyes rested with steady attention on the woman who had addressed her in those terms. Not the faintest expression of confusion or alarm, not even a momentary flutter of interest stirred the deadly stillness of her face. She reposed as quietly, she held the screen as composedly, as ever. The test had been tried, and had utterly failed.

There was another silence. Lady Montbarry considered with herself. The smile that came slowly and went away suddenly – the smile at once so sad and so cruel – showed itself on her thin lips. She lifted her screen, and pointed with it to a seat at the farther end of the room. 'Be so good as to take that chair,' she said.

Helpless under her first bewildering sense of failure – not knowing what to say or what to do next – Mrs Ferrari mechanically obeyed. Lady Montbarry, rising on the sofa for the first time, watched her with undisguised scrutiny as she crossed the room – then sank back into a reclining position once more. 'No,' she said to herself, 'the woman walks steadily; she is not intoxicated – the only other possibility is that she may be mad.'

She had spoken loud enough to be heard. Stung by the insult, Mrs Ferrari instantly answered her: 'I am no more drunk or mad than you are.'

'No?' said Lady Montbarry. 'Then you are only insolent? The ignorant English mind (I have observed) is apt to be insolent in the exercise of unrestrained English liberty. This is very noticeable to us foreigners among you people in the streets. Of course I can't be insolent to you, in return. I hardly know what to say to you. My maid was imprudent in admitting you so easily to my room. I suppose your respectable appearance misled her. I wonder who you are? You mentioned the name of a courier who left us very strangely. Was he married by any chance? Are you his wife? And do you know where he is?'

Mrs Ferrari's indignation burst its way through all restraints. She advanced to the sofa; she feared nothing, in the fervour and rage of her reply.

'I am his widow – and you know it, you wicked woman! Ah! it was an evil hour when Miss Lockwood recommended my husband to be his lordship's courier—!'

Before she could add another word, Lady Montbarry sprang from the sofa with the stealthy suddenness of a cat – seized her by both shoulders – and shook her with the strength and frenzy of a madwoman. 'You lie! you lie! you lie!' She dropped her hold at the third repetition of the accusation, and threw up her hands wildly with a gesture of despair. 'Oh, Jesu Maria! is it possible?' she cried. '*Can* the courier have come to me through that woman?' She turned like lightning on Mrs Ferrari, and stopped her as she was escaping from the room. 'Stay here, you fool – stay here, and answer me! If you cry out, as sure as the heavens are above you, I'll strangle you with my own hands. Sit down again – and fear nothing. Wretch! It is I who am frightened – frightened out of my senses. Confess that you lied, when you used Miss Lockwood's name just now! No! I don't believe you on your oath; I will believe nobody but Miss Lockwood herself. Where does she live? Tell me that, you noxious stinging little insect – and you may go.' Terrified as she was, Mrs Ferrari hesitated. Lady Montbarry lifted her hands threateningly, with the long, lean, yellow-white fingers outspread and crooked at the tips. Mrs Ferrari shrank at the sight of them, and gave the address. Lady Montbarry pointed contemptuously to the door – then changed her mind.

'No! not yet! you will tell Miss Lockwood what has happened, and she may refuse to see me. I will go there at once, and you shall go with me. As far as the house – not inside of it. Sit down again. I am going to ring for my maid. Turn your back to the door – your cowardly face is not fit to be seen!'

She rang the bell. The maid appeared.

'My cloak and bonnet – instantly!'

The maid produced the cloak and bonnet from the bedroom.

'A cab at the door – before I can count ten!'

The maid vanished. Lady Montbarry surveyed herself in the glass, and wheeled round again, with her cat-like suddenness, to Mrs Ferrari.

'I look more than half dead already, don't I?' she said with a grim outburst of irony. 'Give me your arm.'

She took Mrs Ferrari's arm, and left the room. 'You have nothing to fear, so long as you obey,' she whispered, on the way downstairs. 'You leave me at Miss Lockwood's door, and never see me again.'

In the hall, they were met by the landlady of the hotel. Lady Montbarry graciously presented her companion. 'My good friend Mrs Ferrari; I am so glad to have seen her.' The landlady accompanied them to the door. The cab was waiting. 'Get in first, good Mrs Ferrari,' said her ladyship; 'and tell the man where to go.'

They were driven away. Lady Montbarry's variable humour changed again. With a low groan of misery, she threw herself back in the cab. Lost in her own dark thoughts, as careless of the woman whom she had bent to her iron will as if no such person sat by her side, she preserved a sinister silence, until they reached the house where Miss Lockwood lodged. In an instant, she roused herself to action. She opened the door of the cab, and closed it again on Mrs Ferrari, before the driver could get off his box.

'Take that lady a mile farther on her way home!' she said, as she paid the man his fare. The next moment she had knocked at the house-door. 'Is Miss Lockwood at home?' 'Yes, ma'am.' She stepped over the threshold – the door closed on her.

'Which way, ma'am?' asked the driver of the cab.

Mrs Ferrari put her hand to her head, and tried to collect her thoughts. Could she leave her friend and benefactress helpless at Lady Montbarry's mercy? She was still vainly endeavouring to decide on the course that she ought to follow – when a gentleman, stopping at Miss Lockwood's door, happened to look towards the cab-window, and saw her.

'Are you going to call on Miss Agnes too?' he asked.

It was Henry Westwick. Mrs Ferrari clasped her hands in gratitude as she recognized him.

470

'Go in, sir!' she cried. 'Go in, directly. That dreadful woman is with Miss Agnes. Go and protect her!'

'What woman?' Henry asked.

The answer literally struck him speechless. With amazement and indignation in his face, he looked at Mrs Ferrari as she pronounced the hated name of 'Lady Montbarry'. 'I'll see to it,' was all he said. He knocked at the house-door; and he too, in his turn, was let in.

❧ ELEVEN ❧

'LADY MONTBARRY, MISS.'

Agnes was writing a letter, when the servant astonished her by announcing the visitor's name. Her first impulse was to refuse to see the woman who had intruded on her. But Lady Montbarry had taken care to follow close on the servant's heels. Before Agnes could speak, she had entered the room.

'I beg to apologize for my intrusion, Miss Lockwood. I have a question to ask you, in which I am very much interested. No one can answer me but yourself.' In low hesitating tones, with her glittering black eyes bent modestly on the ground, Lady Montbarry opened the interview in those words.

Without answering, Agnes pointed to a chair. She could do this, and, for the time, she could do no more. All that she had read of the hidden and sinister life in the palace at Venice; all that she had heard of Montbarry's melancholy death and burial in a foreign land; all that she knew of the mystery of Ferrari's disappearance, rushed into her mind, when the black-robed figure confronted her, standing just inside the door. The strange conduct of Lady Montbarry added a new perplexity to the doubts and misgivings that troubled her. There stood the adventuress whose character had left its mark on society all over Europe – the Fury who had terrified Mrs Ferrari at the hotel – inconceivably transformed into a timid, shrinking woman! Lady Montbarry had not once ventured to look at Agnes, since she had made her way into the room. Advancing to take the chair that had been pointed out to her, she hesitated, put her hand on the rail to support herself, and still remained standing. 'Please give me a moment to compose myself,' she said faintly. Her head sank on her bosom: she stood before Agnes like a conscious culprit before a merciless judge.

The silence that followed was, literally, the silence of fear on both sides. In the midst of it, the door was opened once more – and Henry Westwick appeared.

He looked at Lady Montbarry with a moment's steady attention – bowed to her with formal politeness – and passed on in silence. At the sight of her husband's brother, the sinking spirit of the woman sprang to life again. Her drooping figure became erect. Her eyes met Westwick's look, brightly defiant. She returned his bow with an icy smile of contempt.

Henry crossed the room to Agnes.

'Is Lady Montbarry here by your invitation?' he asked quietly.

'No.'

'Do you wish to see her?'

'It is very painful to me to see her.'

He turned and looked at his sister-in-law. 'Do you hear that?' he asked coldly.

'I hear it,' she answered, more coldly still.

'Your visit is, to say the least of it, ill-timed.'

'Your interference is, to say the least of it, out of place.'

With that retort, Lady Montbarry approached Agnes. The presence of Henry Westwick seemed at once to relieve and embolden her. 'Permit me to ask my question, Miss Lockwood,' she said, with graceful courtesy. 'It is nothing to embarrass you. When the courier Ferrari applied to my late husband for employment, did you—' Her resolution failed her, before she could say more. She sank trembling into the nearest chair, and, after a moment's struggle, composed herself again. 'Did you permit Ferrari,' she resumed, 'to make sure of being chosen for our courier, by using your name?'

Agnes did not reply with her customary directness. Trifling as it was, the reference to Montbarry, proceeding from *that* woman of all others, confused and agitated her.

'I have known Ferrari's wife for many years,' she began. 'And I take an interest—'

Lady Montbarry abruptly lifted her hands with a gesture of entreaty. 'Ah, Miss Lockwood, don't waste time by talking of his wife! Answer my plain question, plainly!'

'Let me answer her,' Henry whispered. 'I will undertake to speak plainly enough.'

Agnes refused by a gesture. Lady Montbarry's interruption had roused her sense of what was due to herself. She resumed her reply in plainer terms.

'When Ferrari wrote to the late Lord Montbarry,' she said, 'he did certainly mention my name.'

Even now, she had innocently failed to see the object which her visitor had in view. Lady Montbarry's impatience became ungovernable. She started to her feet, and advanced to Agnes.

'Was it with your knowledge and permission that Ferrari used your name?' she asked. 'The whole soul of my question is in *that*. For God's sake answer me – Yes, or No!'

'Yes.'

That one word struck Lady Montbarry as a blow might have struck her. The fierce life that had animated her face the instant before, faded out of it suddenly, and left her like a woman turned to stone. She stood, mechanically confronting Agnes, with a stillness so wrapt and perfect that not even the breath she drew was perceptible to the two persons who were looking at her.

Henry spoke to her roughly. 'Rouse yourself,' he said. 'You have received your answer.'

She looked round at him. 'I have received my Sentence,' she rejoined – and turned slowly to leave the room.

To Henry's astonishment, Agnes stopped her. 'Wait a moment, Lady Montbarry. I have something to ask on my side. You have spoken of Ferrari. I wish to speak of him too.'

Lady Montbarry bent her head in silence. Her hand trembled as she took out her handkerchief, and passed it over her forehead. Agnes detected the trembling, and shrank back a step. 'Is the subject painful to you?' she asked timidly.

Still silent, Lady Montbarry invited her by a wave of the hand to go on. Henry approached, attentively watching his sister-in-law. Agnes went on.

'No trace of Ferrari has been discovered in England,' she said. 'Have you any news of him? And will you tell me (if you have heard anything), in mercy to his wife?'

Lady Montbarry's thin lips suddenly relaxed into their sad and cruel smile.

'Why do you ask *me* about the lost courier?' she said. 'You will know what has become of him, Miss Lockwood, when the time is ripe for it.'

Agnes started. 'I don't understand you,' she said. 'How shall I know? Will some one tell me?'

'Some one will tell you.'

Henry could keep silence no longer. 'Perhaps, your ladyship may be the person?' he interrupted with ironical politeness.

She answered him with contemptuous ease. 'You may be right, Mr Westwick. One day or another, I may be the person who tells Miss Lockwood what has become of Ferrari, if—' She stopped; with her eyes fixed on Agnes.

'If what?' Henry asked.

'If Miss Lockwood forces me to it.'

Agnes listened in astonishment. 'Force you to it?' she repeated. 'How can I do that? Do you mean to say my will is stronger than yours?'

'Do *you* mean to say that the candle doesn't burn the moth, when the moth flies into it?' Lady Montbarry rejoined. 'Have you ever heard of such a thing as the fascination of terror? I am drawn to you by a fascination of terror. I have no right to visit you, I have no wish to visit you: you are my enemy. For the first time in my life, against my own will, I submit to my enemy. See! I am waiting because you told me to wait – and the fear of you (I swear it!) creeps through me while I stand here. Oh, don't let me excite your curiosity or your pity! Follow the example of Mr Westwick. Be hard and brutal and unforgiving, like him. Grant me my release. Tell me to go.'

The frank and simple nature of Agnes could discover but one intelligible meaning in this strange outbreak.

'You are mistaken in thinking me your enemy,' she said. 'The wrong you did me when you gave your hand to Lord Montbarry was not intentionally done. I forgave you my sufferings in his lifetime. I forgive you even more freely now that he has gone.'

Henry heard her with mingled emotions of admiration and distress. 'Say no more!' he exclaimed. 'You are too good to her; she is not worthy of it.'

The interruption passed unheeded by Lady Montbarry. The simple words in which Agnes had replied seemed to have absorbed the whole attention of this strangely-changeable woman. As she listened, her face settled slowly into an expression of hard and tearless sorrow. There was a marked change in her voice when she spoke next. It expressed that last worst resignation which has done with hope.

'You good innocent creature,' she said, 'what does your amiable forgiveness matter? What are your poor little wrongs, in the reckoning for greater wrongs which is demanded of me? I am not trying to frighten you; I am only miserable about myself. Do you know what it is to have a firm presentiment of calamity that is coming to you – and yet to hope that your own positive conviction will not prove true? When I first met you, before my marriage, and first felt your influence over me, I had that hope. It was a starveling sort of hope that lived a lingering life in me until to-day. *You* struck it dead, when you answered my question about Ferrari.'

'How have I destroyed your hopes?' Agnes asked. 'What connection is there between my permitting Ferrari to use my name to Lord Montbarry, and the strange and dreadful things you are saying to me now?'

'The time is near, Miss Lockwood, when you will discover that for yourself. In the mean while, you shall know what my fear of you is, in the plainest words I can find. On the day when I took your hero from you and blighted your life – I am firmly persuaded of it! – you were made the instrument of the retribution that my sins of many years had deserved. Oh, such things have happened before to-day! One person has, before now, been the means of innocently ripening the growth of evil in another. You have done that already – and you have more to do yet. You have still to bring me to the day of discovery, and to the punishment that is my doom. We shall meet again – here in England, or there in Venice where my husband died – and meet for the last time.'

In spite of her better sense, in spite of her natural superiority to superstitions of all kinds, Agnes was impressed by the terrible earnestness with which those words were spoken. She turned pale as she looked at Henry. 'Do *you* understand her?' she asked.

'Nothing is easier than to understand her,' he replied contemptuously. 'She knows what has become of Ferrari; and she is confusing you in a cloud of nonsense, because she daren't own the truth. Let her go!'

If a dog had been under one of the chairs, and had barked, Lady Montbarry could not have proceeded more impenetrably with the last words she had to say to Agnes.

'Advise your interesting Mrs Ferrari to wait a little longer,' she said. '*You* will know what has become of her husband, and you will tell her. There will be nothing to alarm you. Some trifling event will bring us together the next time – as trifling, I dare say, as the engagement of Ferrari. Sad nonsense, Mr Westwick, is it not? But you make allowances for women; we all talk nonsense. Good morning, Miss Lockwood.'

She opened the door – suddenly, as if she was afraid of being called back for the second time – and left them.

🕮 TWELVE 🕮

'Do you think she is mad?' Agnes asked.

'I think she is simply wicked. False, superstitious, inveterately cruel – but not mad. I believe her main motive in coming here was to enjoy the luxury of frightening you.'

'She *has* frightened me. I am ashamed to own it – but so it is.'

Henry looked at her, hesitated for a moment, and seated himself on the sofa by her side.

'I am very anxious about you, Agnes,' he said. 'But for the fortunate chance which led me to call here to-day – who knows what that vile woman might not have said or done, if she found you alone? My dear, you are leading a sadly unprotected solitary life. I don't like to think of it; I want to see it changed – especially after what has happened to-day. No! no! it is useless to tell me that you have your old nurse. She is too old; she is not in your rank of life – there is no sufficient protection in the companionship of such a person for a lady in your position. Don't mistake me, Agnes! what I say, I say in the sincerity of my devotion to you.' He paused, and took her hand. She made a feeble effort to withdraw it – and yielded. 'Will the day never come,' he pleaded, 'when the privilege of protecting you may be mine? when you will be the pride and joy of my life, as long as my life lasts?' He pressed her hand gently. She made no reply. The colour came and went on her face; her eyes were turned away from him. 'Have I been so unhappy as to offend you?' he asked.

She answered that – she said, almost in a whisper, 'No.'

'Have I distressed you?'

'You have made me think of the sad days that are gone.' She said no more; she only tried to withdraw her hand from his for the second time. He still held it; he lifted it to his lips.

'Can I never make you think of other days than those – of the happier days to come? Or, if you must think of the time that is passed, can you not look back to the time when I first loved you?'

She sighed as he put the question. 'Spare me Henry,' she answered sadly. 'Say no more!'

The colour again rose in her cheeks; her hand trembled in his. She looked lovely, with her eyes cast down and her bosom heaving gently. At that moment he would have given everything he had in the world to take her in his arms and kiss her. Some mysterious sympathy, passing from his hand to hers, seemed to tell her what was in his mind. She snatched her hand away, and suddenly looked up at him. The tears were in her eyes. She said nothing; she let her eyes speak for her. They warned him – without anger, without unkindness – but still they warned him to press her no further that day.

'Only tell me that I am forgiven,' he said, as he rose from the sofa.

'Yes,' she answered quietly, 'you are forgiven.'

'I have not lowered myself in your estimation, Agnes?'

'Oh, no!'

'Do you wish me to leave you?'

She rose, in her turn, from the sofa, and walked to her writing-table before she replied. The unfinished letter which she had been writing when Lady Montbarry interrupted her, lay open on the blotting-book. As she looked at the letter, and then looked at Henry, the smile that charmed everybody showed itself in her face.

'You must not go just yet,' she said: 'I have something to tell you. I hardly know how to express it. The shortest way perhaps will be to let you find it out for yourself. You have been speaking of my lonely unprotected life here. It is not a very happy life, Henry – I own that.' She paused, observing the growing anxiety of his expression as he looked at her, with a shy satisfaction that perplexed him. 'Do you know that I have anticipated your idea?' she went on. 'I am going to make a great change in my life – if your brother Stephen and his wife will only consent to it.' She opened the desk of the writing-table while she spoke, took a letter out, and handed it to Henry.

He received it from her mechanically. Vague doubts, which he hardly understood himself, kept him silent. It was impossible that the 'change in her life' of which she had spoken could mean that she was about to be married – and yet he was conscious of a perfectly unreasonable reluctance to open the letter. Their eyes met; she smiled again. 'Look at the address,' she said. 'You ought to know the handwriting – but I dare say you don't.'

He looked at the address. It was in the large, irregular, uncertain writing of a child. He opened the letter instantly.

'Dear Aunt Agnes, – Our governess is going away. She has had money left to her, and a house of her own. We have had cake and wine to drink her health. You promised to be our governess if we wanted another. We want you. Mamma knows nothing about this. Please come before Mamma can get another governess. Your loving Lucy, who writes this. Clara and Blanche have tried to write too. But they are too young to do it. They blot the paper.'

'Your eldest niece,' Agnes explained, as Henry looked at her in amazement. 'The children used to call me aunt when I was staying with their mother in Ireland, in the autumn. The three girls were my inseparable companions – they are the most charming children I know. It is quite true that I offered to be their governess, if they ever wanted one, on the day when I left them to return to London. I was writing to propose it to their mother, just before you came.'

'Not seriously!' Henry exclaimed.

Agnes placed her unfinished letter in his hand. Enough of it had been written to show that she did seriously propose to enter the household of Mr and Mrs Stephen Westwick as governess to their children! Henry's bewilderment was not to be expressed in words.

'They won't believe you are in earnest,' he said.

'Why not?' Agnes asked quietly.

'You are my brother Stephen's cousin; you are his wife's old friend.'

'All the more reason, Henry, for trusting me with the charge of their children.'

'But you are their equal; you are not obliged to get your living by teaching. There is something absurd in your entering their service as a governess!'

'What is there absurd in it? The children love me; the mother loves me; the father has shown me innumerable instances of his true friendship and regard. I am the very woman for the place – and, as to my education, I must have completely forgotten it indeed, if I am not fit to teach three children the eldest of whom is only eleven years old. You say I am their equal. Are there no other women who serve as governesses, and who are the equals of the persons whom they serve? Besides, I don't know that I *am* their equal. Have I not heard that your brother Stephen was the next heir to the title? Will he not be the new lord? Never mind answering me! We won't dispute whether I am right or wrong in turning governess – we will wait the event. I am weary of my lonely useless existence here, and eager to make my life more happy and more useful, in the household of all others in which I should like most to have a place. If you will look again, you will see that I have these personal considerations still to urge before I finish my letter. You don't know your brother and his wife as well I do, if you doubt their answer. I believe they have courage enough and heart enough to say Yes.'

Henry submitted without being convinced.

He was a man who disliked all eccentric departures from custom and routine; and he felt especially suspicious of the change proposed in the life of Agnes. With new interests to occupy her mind, she might be less favourably disposed to listen to him, on the next occasion when he urged his suit. The influence of the 'lonely useless existence' of which she complained, was distinctly an influence in his favour. While her heart was empty, her heart was accessible. But with his nieces in full possession of it, the clouds of doubt overshadowed his prospects. He knew the sex well enough to keep these purely selfish perplexities to himself. The waiting policy was especially the policy to pursue with a woman as sensitive as Agnes. If he once offended her delicacy he was lost. For the moment he wisely controlled himself and changed the subject.

'My little niece's letter has had an effect,' he said, 'which the child never contemplated in writing it. She has just reminded me of one of the objects that I had in calling on you to-day.'

Agnes looked at the child's letter. 'How does Lucy do that?' she asked.

'Lucy's governess is not the only lucky person who has had money left her,' Henry answered. 'Is your old nurse in the house?'

'You don't mean to say that nurse has got a legacy?'

'She has got a hundred pounds. Send for her, Agnes, while I show you the letter.'

He took a handful of letters from his pocket, and looked through them, while Agnes rang the bell. Returning to him, she noticed a printed letter among the rest, which lay open on the table. It was a 'prospectus', and the title of it was 'Palace Hotel Company of Venice (Limited)'. The two words, 'Palace' and 'Venice', instantly recalled her mind to the unwelcome visit of Lady Montbarry. 'What is that?' she asked, pointing to the title.

Henry suspended his search, and glanced at the prospectus. 'A really promising speculation,' he said. 'Large hotels always pay well, if they are well managed. I know the man who is appointed to be manager of this hotel when it is opened to the public; and I have such entire confidence in him that I have become one of the shareholders of the Company.'

The reply did not appear to satisfy Agnes. 'Why is the hotel called the "Palace Hotel"?' she inquired.

Henry looked at her, and at once penetrated her motive for asking the question. 'Yes,' he said, 'it *is* the palace that Montbarry hired at Venice; and it has been purchased by the Company to be changed into an hotel.'

Agnes turned away in silence, and took a chair at the farther end of the room. Henry had disappointed her. His income as a younger son stood in need, as she well knew, of all the additions that he could make to it by successful speculation. But she was unreasonable enough, nevertheless, to disprove of his attempting to make money already out of the house in which his brother had died. Incapable of understanding this purely sentimental view of a plain matter of business, Henry returned to his papers, in some perplexity at the sudden change in the manner of Agnes towards him. Just as he found the letter of which he was in search, the nurse made her appearance. He glanced at Agnes, expecting that she would speak first. She never even looked up when the nurse came in. It was left to Henry to tell the old woman why the bell had summoned her to the drawing-room.

'Well, nurse,' he said, 'you have had a windfall of luck. You have had a legacy left you of a hundred pounds.'

The nurse showed no outward signs of exultation. She waited a little to get the announcement of the legacy well settled into her mind – and then she said quietly, 'Master Henry, who gives me that money, if you please?'

'My late brother, Lord Montbarry, gives it to you.' (Agnes instantly looked up, interested in the matter for the first time. Henry went on.) 'His will leaves legacies to the surviving old servants of the family. There is a letter from his lawyers, authorizing you to apply to them for the money.'

In every class of society, gratitude is the rarest of all human virtues. In the nurse's class it is extremely rare. Her opinion of the man who had deceived and deserted her mistress remained the same opinion still, perfectly undisturbed by the passing circumstance of the legacy.

'I wonder who reminded my lord of the old servants?' she said. 'He would never have heart enough to remember them himself!'

Agnes suddenly interposed. Nature, always abhorring monotony, institutes reserves of temper as elements in the composition of the gentlest women living. Even Agnes could, on rare occasions, be angry. The nurse's view of Montbarry's character seemed to have provoked her beyond endurance.

'If you have any sense of shame in you,' she broke out, 'you ought to be ashamed of what you have just said! Your ingratitude disgusts me. I leave you to speak with her, Henry – *you* won't mind it!' With this significant intimation that he too had dropped out of his customary place in her good opinion, she left the room.

The nurse received the smart reproof administered to her with every appearance of feeling rather amused by it than not. When the door had closed, this female philosopher winked at Henry.

'There's a power of obstinacy in young women,' she remarked. 'Miss Agnes wouldn't give my lord up as a bad one, even when he jilted her. And now she's sweet on him after he's dead. Say a word against him, and she fires up as you see. All obstinacy! It will wear out with time. Stick to her, Master Henry – stick to her!'

'She doesn't seem to have offended you,' said Henry.

'*She*?' the nurse repeated in amazement – 'she offend me? I like her in her tantrums; it reminds me of her when she was a baby. Lord bless you! when I go to bid her good night, she'll give me a big kiss, poor dear – and say, Nurse, I didn't mean it! About this money, Master Henry? If I was younger I should spend it in dress and jewelry. But I'm too old for that. What shall I do with my legacy when I have got it?'

'Put it out at interest,' Henry suggested. 'Get so much a year for it, you know.'

'How much shall I get?' the nurse asked.

'If you put your hundred pounds into the Funds, you will get between three and four pounds a year.'

The nurse shook her head. 'Three or four pounds a year? That won't do! I want more than that. Look here, Master Henry. I don't care about this bit of money – I never did like the man who has left it to me, though he *was* your brother. If I lost it all to-morrow, I shouldn't break my heart; I'm well enough off, as it is, for the rest of my days. They say you're a speculator. Put me in for a good thing, there's a dear! Neck-or-nothing – and *that* for the Funds!' She snapped her fingers to express her contempt for security of investment at three per cent.

Henry produced the prospectus of the Venetian Hotel Company.

'You're a funny old woman,' he said. 'There, you dashing speculator – there is neck-or-nothing for you! You must keep it a secret from Miss Agnes, mind. I'm not at all sure that she would approve of my helping you to this investment.'

The nurse took out her spectacles. 'Six per cent. guaranteed,' she read; 'and the Directors have every reason to believe that ten per cent., or more will be ultimately realized to the shareholders by the hotel. Put me into that, Master Henry! And, wherever you go, for Heaven's sake recommend the hotel to your friends!'

So the nurse, following Henry's mercenary example, had *her* pecuniary interest, too, in the house in which Lord Montbarry had died.

Three days passed before Henry was able to visit Agnes again. In that time, the little cloud between them had entirely passed away. Agnes received him with even more than her customary kindness. She was in better spirits than usual. Her letter to Mrs Stephen Westwick had been answered by return of post; and her proposal had been joyfully accepted, with one modification. She was to visit the Westwicks for a month – and, if she really liked teaching the children, she was then to be governess, aunt, and cousin, all in one – and was only to go away in an event which her friends in Ireland persisted in contemplating, the event of her marriage.

'You see I was right,' she said to Henry.

He was still incredulous. 'Are you really going?' he asked.

'I am going next week.'

'When shall I see you again?'

'You know you are always welcome at your brother's house. You can see me when you like.' She held out her hand. 'Pardon me for leaving you – I am beginning to pack up already.'

Henry tried to kiss her at parting. She drew back directly.

'Why not? I am your cousin,' he said.

'I don't like it,' she answered.

Henry looked at her, and submitted. Her refusal to grant him his privilege as a cousin was a good sign – it was indirectly an act of encouragement to him in the character of her lover.

On the first day in the new week, Agnes left London on her way to Ireland. As the event proved, this was not destined to be the end of her journey. The way to Ireland was only the first stage on a roundabout road – the road that led to the palace at Venice.

THE THIRD PART

❧ THIRTEEN ❧

IN THE SPRING OF THE YEAR 1861, Agnes was established at the country-seat of her two friends – now promoted (on the death of the first lord, without offspring) to be the new Lord and Lady Montbarry. The old nurse was not separated from her mistress. A place, suited to her time of life, had been found for her in the pleasant Irish household. She was perfectly happy in her new sphere; and she spent her first half-year's dividend from the Venice Hotel Company, with characteristic prodigality, in presents for the children.

Early in the year, also, the Directors of the life insurance offices sub-mitted to circumstances, and paid the ten thousand pounds. Immediately afterwards, the widow of the first Lord Montbarry (otherwise, the dowa-ger Lady Montbarry) left England, with Baron Rivar, for the United States. The Baron's object was announced, in the scientific columns of the newspapers, to be investigation into the present state of experimental chemistry in the great American republic. His sister informed inquiring friends that she accompanied him, in the hope of finding consolation in change of scene after the bereavement that had fallen on her. Hearing this news from Henry Westwick (then paying a visit at his brother's house), Agnes was conscious of a certain sense of relief. 'With the Atlantic between us,' she said, 'surely I have done with that terrible woman now!'

Barely a week passed after those words had been spoken, before an event happened which reminded Agnes of 'the terrible woman' once more.

On that day, Henry's engagements had obliged him to return to London. He had ventured, on the morning of his departure, to press his suit once more on Agnes; and the children, as he had anticipated, proved to be innocent obstacles in the way of his success. On the other hand, he had privately secured a firm ally in his sister-in-law. 'Have a little patience,' the new Lady Montbarry had said; 'and leave me to turn the influence of the children in the right direction. If they can persuade her to listen to you – they shall!'

The two ladies had accompanied Henry, and some other guests who went away at the same time, to the railway station, and had just driven back to the house, when the servant announced that 'a person of the name of Rolland was waiting to see her ladyship'.

'Is it a woman?'

'Yes, my lady.'

Young Lady Montbarry turned to Agnes.

'This is the very person,' she said, 'whom your lawyer thought likely to help him, when he was trying to trace the lost courier.'

'You don't mean the English maid who was with Lady Montbarry at Venice?'

'My dear! don't speak of Montbarry's horrid widow by the name which is *my* name now. Stephen and I have arranged to call her by her foreign title, before she was married. I am "Lady Montbarry", and she is "the Countess". In that way there will be no confusion. – Yes, Mrs Rolland was in my service before she became the Countess's maid. She was a perfectly trustworthy person, with one defect that obliged me to send her away – a sullen temper which led to perpetual complaints of her in the servants' hall. Would you like to see her?'

Agnes accepted the proposal, in the faint hope of getting some information for the courier's wife. The complete defeat of every attempt to trace the lost man had been accepted as final by Mrs Ferrari. She had deliberately arrayed herself in widow's mourning; and was earning her livelihood in an employment which the unwearied kindness of Agnes had procured for her in London. The last chance of penetrating the mystery of Ferrari's disappearance seemed to rest now on what Ferrari's former fellow-servant might be able to tell. With highly-wrought expectations, Agnes followed her friend into the room in which Mrs Rolland was waiting.

A tall bony woman, in the autumn of life, with sunken eyes and iron-grey hair, rose stiffly from her chair, and saluted the ladies with stern submission as they opened the door. A person of unblemished character, evidently – but not without visible drawbacks. Big bushy eyebrows, an awfully deep and solemn voice, a harsh unbending manner, a complete absence in her figure of the undulating lines characteristic of the sex, presented Virtue in this excellent person under its least alluring aspect. Strangers, on a first introduction to her, were accustomed to wonder why she was not a man.

'Are you pretty well, Mrs Rolland?'

'I am as well as I can expect to be, my lady, at my time of life.'

'Is there anything I can do for you?'

'Your ladyship can do me a great favour, if you will please speak to my character while I was in your service. I am offered a place, to wait on an invalid lady who has lately come to live in this neighbourhood.'

'Ah, yes – I have heard of her. A Mrs Carbury, with a very pretty niece I am told. But, Mrs Rolland, you left my service some time ago. Mrs

Carbury will surely expect you to refer to the last mistress by whom you were employed.'

A flash of virtuous indignation irradiated Mrs Rolland's sunken eyes. She coughed before she answered, as if her 'last mistress' stuck in her throat.

'I have explained to Mrs Carbury, my lady, that the person I last served – I really cannot give her her title in your ladyship's presence! – has left England for America. Mrs Carbury knows that I quitted the person of my own free will, and knows why, and approves of my conduct so far. A word from your ladyship will be amply sufficient to get me the situation.'

'Very well, Mrs Rolland, I have no objection to be your reference, under the circumstances. Mrs Carbury will find me at home to-morrow until two o'clock.'

'Mrs Carbury is not well enough to leave the house, my lady. Her niece, Miss Haldane, will call and make the inquiries, if your ladyship has no objections.'

'I have not the least objection. The pretty niece carries her own welcome with her. Wait a minute, Mrs Rolland. This lady is Miss Lockwood – my husband's cousin, and my friend. She is anxious to speak to you about the courier who was in the late Lord Montbarry's service at Venice.'

Mrs Rolland's bushy eyebrows frowned in stern disapproval of the new topic of conversation. 'I regret to hear it, my lady,' was all she said.

'Perhaps, you have not been informed of what happened after you left Venice?' Agnes ventured to add. 'Ferarri left the palace secretly; and he has never been heard of since.'

Mrs Rolland mysteriously closed her eyes – as if to exclude some vision of the lost courier which was of a nature to disturb a respectable woman. 'Nothing that Mr Ferrari could do would surprise me,' she replied in her deepest bass tones.

'You speak rather harshly of him,' said Agnes.

Mrs Rolland suddenly opened her eyes again. 'I speak harshly of nobody without reason,' she said. 'Mr Ferrari behaved to me, Miss Lockwood, as no man living has ever behaved – before or since.'

'What did he do?'

Mrs Rolland answered, with a stony stare of horror: –

'He took liberties with me.'

Young Lady Montbarry suddenly turned aside, and put her handkerchief over her mouth in convulsions of suppressed laughter.

Mrs Rolland went on, with a grim enjoyment of the bewilderment which her reply had produced in Agnes: 'And when I insisted on an apology, Miss, he had the audacity to say that the life at the palace was dull, and he didn't know how else to amuse himself!'

'I am afraid I have hardly made myself understood,' said Agnes. 'I am not speaking to you out of any interest in Ferrari. Are you aware that he is married?'

'I pity his wife,' said Mrs Rolland.

'She is naturally in great grief about him,' Agnes proceeded.

'She ought to thank God she is rid of him,' Mrs Rolland interposed.

Agnes still persisted. 'I have known Mrs Ferrari from her childhood, and I am sincerely anxious to help her in this matter. Did you notice anything, while you were at Venice, that would account for her husband's extraordinary disappearance? On what sort of terms, for instance, did he live with his master and mistress?'

'On terms of familiarity with his mistress,' said Mrs Rolland, 'which were simply sickening to a respectable English servant. She used to encourage him to talk to her about all his affairs – how he got on with his wife, and how pressed he was for money, and such like – just as if they were equals. Contemptible – that's what I call it:'

'And his master?' Agnes continued. 'How did Ferrari get on with Lord Montbarry?'

'My lord used to live shut up with his studies and his sorrows,' Mrs Rolland answered, with a hard solemnity expressive of respect for his lordship's memory. 'Mr Ferrari got his money when it was due; and he cared for nothing else. "If I could afford it, I would leave the place too; but I can't afford it." Those were the last words he said to me, on the morning when I left the palace. I made no reply. After what had happened (on that other occasion) I was naturally not on speaking terms with Mr Ferrari.'

'Can you really tell me nothing which will throw any light on this matter?'

'Nothing,' said Mrs Rolland, with an undisguised relish of the disappointment that she was inflicting. ˉ

'There was another member of the family at Venice,' Agnes resumed, determined to sift the question to the bottom while she had the chance. 'There was Baron Rivar.'

Mrs Rolland lifted her large hands, covered with rusty black gloves, in mute protest against the introduction of Baron Rivar as a subject of inquiry. 'Are you aware, Miss,' she began, 'that I left my place in consequence of what I observed—?'

Agnes stopped her there. 'I only wanted to ask,' she explained, 'if anything was said or done by Baron Rivar which might account for Ferrari's strange conduct.'

'Nothing that I know of,' said Mrs Rolland. 'The Baron and Mr Ferrari (if I may use such an expression) were "birds of a feather", so far as I could see – I mean, one was as unprincipled as the other. I am a just woman; and I will give you an example. Only the day before I left, I heard the Baron say (through the open door of his room while I was passing along the corridor), "Ferrari, I want a thousand pounds. What would you do for a thousand pounds?" And I heard Mr Ferrari answer, "Anything, sir, as long as I was not found out." And then they both burst out laughing. I heard no more than that. Judge for yourself, Miss.'

Agnes reflected for a moment. A thousand pounds was the sum that had been sent to Mrs Ferrari in the anonymous letter. Was that enclosure in any way connected, as a result, with the conversation between the Baron and Ferrari? It was useless to press any more inquiries on Mrs Rolland. She could give no further information which was of the slightest importance to the object in view. There was no alternative but to grant her her dismissal. One more effort had been made to find a trace of the lost man, and once again the effort had failed.

They were a family party at the dinner-table that day. The only guest left in the house was a nephew of the new Lord Montbarry – the eldest son of his sister, Lady Barville. Lady Montbarry could not resist telling the story of the first (and last) attack made on the virtue of Mrs Rolland, with a comically-exact imitation of Mrs Rolland's deep and dismal voice. Being asked by her husband what was the object which had brought that formidable person to the house, she naturally mentioned the expected visit of Miss Haldane. Arthur Barville, unusually silent and pre-occupied so far, suddenly struck into the conversation with a burst of enthusiasm. 'Miss Haldane is the most charming girl in all Ireland!' he said. 'I caught sight of her yesterday, over the wall of her garden, as I was riding by. What time is she coming to-morrow? Before two? I'll look into the drawing-room by accident – I am dying to be introduced to her!'

Agnes was amused by his enthusiasm. 'Are you in love with Miss Haldane already?' she asked.

Arthur answered gravely, 'It's no joking matter. I have been all day at the garden wall, waiting to see her again! It depends on Miss Haldane to make me the happiest or the wretchedest man living.'

'You foolish boy! How can you talk such nonsense?'

He was talking nonsense undoubtedly. But, if Agnes had only known it, he was doing something more than that. He was innocently leading her another stage nearer on the way to Venice.

❧ FOURTEEN ❧

As THE SUMMER MONTHS ADVANCED, the transformation of the Venetian palace into the modern hotel proceeded rapidly towards completion.

The outside of the building, with its fine Palladian front looking on the canal, was wisely left unaltered. Inside, as a matter of necessity, the rooms were almost rebuilt – so far at least as the size and the arrangement of them were concerned. The vast saloons were partitioned off into 'apartments' containing three or four rooms each. The broad corridors in the upper regions afforded spare space enough for rows of little bedchambers, devoted to servants and to travellers with limited means. Nothing was spared but the solid floors and the finely-carved ceilings. These last, in excellent preservation as to workmanship, merely required cleaning, and regilding here and there, to add greatly to the beauty and importance of the best rooms in the hotel. The only exception to the complete re-organization of the interior was at one extremity of the edifice, on the first and second floors. Here there happened, in each case, to be rooms of such comparatively moderate size, and so attractively decorated, that the architect suggested leaving them as they were. It was afterwards discovered that these were no other than the apartments formerly occupied by Lord Montbarry (on the first floor), and by Baron Rivar (on the second). The room in which Montbarry had died was still fitted up as a bed-room, and was now distinguished as Number Fourteen. The room above it, in which the Baron had slept, took its place on the hotel-register as Number Thirty-eight. With the ornaments on the walls and ceilings cleaned and brightened up, and with the heavy old-fashioned beds, chairs, and tables replaced by bright, pretty, and luxurious modern furniture, these two promised to be at once the most attractive and the most comfortable bedchambers in the hotel. As for the once-desolate and disused ground floor of the building, it was now transformed, by means of splendid dining-rooms, reception-rooms, billiard-rooms, and smoking-rooms, into a palace by itself. Even the dungeon-like vaults beneath, now lighted and ventilated on the most approved modern plan, had been turned as if by magic into kitchens, servants' offices, ice-rooms, and wine cellars, worthy of the splendour of the grandest hotel in Italy, in the now bygone period of seventeen years since.

Passing from the lapse of the summer months at Venice, to the lapse of the summer months in Ireland, it is next to be recorded that Mrs

Rolland obtained the situation of attendant on the invalid Mrs Carbury; and that the fair Miss Haldane, like a female Caesar, came, saw, and conquered, on her first day's visit to the new Lord Montbarry's house.

The ladies were as loud in her praises as Arthur Barville himself. Lord Montbarry declared that she was the only perfectly pretty woman he had ever seen, who was really unconscious of her own attractions. The old nurse said she looked as if she had just stepped out of a picture, and wanted nothing but a gilt frame round her to make her complete. Miss Haldane, on her side, returned from her first visit to the Montbarrys charmed with her new acquaintances. Later on the same day, Arthur called with an offering of fruit and flowers for Mrs Carbury, and with instructions to ask if she was well enough to receive Lord and Lady Montbarry and Miss Lockwood on the morrow. In a week's time, the two households were on the friendliest terms. Mrs Carbury, confined to the sofa by a spinal malady, had been hitherto dependent on her niece for one of the few pleasures she could enjoy, the pleasure of having the best new novels read to her as they came out. Discovering this, Arthur volunteered to relieve Miss Haldane, at intervals, in the office of reader. He was clever at mechanical contrivances of all sorts, and he introduced improvements in Mrs Carbury's couch, and in the means of conveying her from the bedchamber to the drawing-room, which alleviated the poor lady's sufferings and brightened her gloomy life. With these claims on the gratitude of the aunt, aided by the personal advantages which he unquestionably possessed, Arthur advanced rapidly in the favour of the charming niece. She was, it is needless to say, perfectly well aware that he was in love with her, while he was himself modestly reticent on the subject – so far as words went. But she was not equally quick in penetrating the nature of her own feelings towards Arthur. Watching the two young people with keen powers of observation, necessarily concentrated on them by the complete seclusion of her life, the invalid lady discovered signs of roused sensibility in Miss Haldane, when Arthur was present, which had never yet shown themselves in her social relations with other admirers eager to pay their addresses to her. Having drawn her own conclusions in private, Mrs Carbury took the first favourable opportunity (in Arthur's interests) of putting them to the test.

'I don't know what I shall do,' she said one day, 'when Arthur goes away.'

Miss Haldane looked up quickly from her work. 'Surely he is not going to leave us!' she exclaimed.

'My dear! he has already stayed at his uncle's house a month longer than he intended. His father and mother naturally expect to see him at home again'

Miss Haldane met this difficulty with a suggestion, which could only have proceeded from a judgment already disturbed by the ravages of the tender passion. 'Why can't his father and mother go and see him at Lord Montbarry's?' she asked. 'Sir Theodore's place is only thirty miles away, and Lady Barville is Lord Montbarry's sister. They needn't stand on ceremony.'

'They may have other engagements,' Mrs Carbury remarked.

'My dear aunt, we don't know that! Suppose you ask Arthur?'

'Suppose *you* ask him?'

Miss Haldane bent her head again over her work. Suddenly as it was done, her aunt had seen her face – and her face betrayed her.

When Arthur came the next day, Mrs Carbury said a word to him in private, while her niece was in the garden. The last new novel lay neglected on the table. Arthur followed Miss Haldane into the garden. The next day he wrote home, enclosing in his letter a photograph of Miss Haldane. Before the end of the week, Sir Theodore and Lady Barville arrived at Lord Montbarry's, and formed their own judgment of the fidelity of the portrait. They had themselves married early in life – and, strange to say, they did not object on principle to the early marriages of other people. The question of age being thus disposed of, the course of true love had no other obstacles to encounter. Miss Haldane was an only child, and was possessed of an ample fortune. Arthur's career at the university had been creditable, but certainly not brilliant enough to present his withdrawal in the light of a disaster. As Sir Theodore's eldest son, his position was already made for him. He was two-and-twenty years of age; and the young lady was eighteen. There was really no producible reason for keeping the lovers waiting, and no excuse for deferring the wedding-day beyond the first week in September. In the interval while the bride and bridegroom would be necessarily absent on the inevitable tour abroad, a sister of Mrs Carbury volunteered to stay with her during the temporary separation from her niece. On the conclusion of the honeymoon, the young couple were to return to Ireland, and were to establish themselves in Mrs Carbury's spacious and comfortable house.

These arrangements were decided upon early in the month of August. About the same date, the last alterations in the old palace at Venice were completed. The rooms were dried by steam; the cellars were stocked; the manager collected round him his army of skilled servants; and the new hotel was advertised all over Europe to open in October.

❧ FIFTEEN ❧

(MISS AGNES LOCKWOOD TO MRS FERRARI)

'I PROMISED TO GIVE YOU some account, dear Emily, of the marriage of Mr Arthur Barville and Miss Haldane. It took place ten days since. But I have had so many things to look after in the absence of the master and mistress of this house, that I am only able to write to you to-day.

'The invitations to the wedding were limited to members of the families, on either side, in consideration of the ill health of Miss Haldane's aunt. On the side of the Montbarry family, there were present, besides Lord and Lady Montbarry, Sir Theodore and Lady Barville; Mrs Norbury (whom you may remember as his lordship's second sister); and Mr Francis Westwick, and Mr Henry Westwick. The three children and I attended the ceremony as bridesmaids. We were joined by two young ladies, cousins of the bride and very agreeable girls. Our dresses were white, trimmed with green in honour of Ireland; and we each had a handsome gold bracelet given to us as a present from the bridegroom. If you add to the persons whom I have already mentioned, the elder members of Mrs Carbury's family, and the old servants in both houses – privileged to drink the healths of the married pair at the lower end of the room – you will have the list of the company at the wedding-breakfast complete.

'The weather was perfect, and the ceremony (with music) was beautifully performed. As for the bride, no words can describe how lovely she looked, or how well she went through it all. We were very merry at the breakfast, and the speeches went off on the whole quite well enough. The last speech, before the party broke up, was made by Mr Henry Westwick, and was the best of all. He offered a happy suggestion, at the end, which has produced a very unexpected change in my life here.

'As well as I remember, he concluded in these words: – "On one point, we are all agreed – we are sorry that the parting hour is near, and we should be glad to meet again. Why should we not meet again? This is the autumn time of the year; we are most of us leaving home for the holidays. What do you say (if you have no engagements that will prevent it) to joining our young married friends before the close of their tour, and renewing the social success of this delightful breakfast by another festival in honour of the honeymoon? The bride and bridegroom are going to Germany and the Tyrol, on their way to Italy. I propose that we allow them a month to themselves, and that we arrange to meet them afterwards in the North of Italy – say at Venice."

'This proposal was received with great applause, which was changed into shouts of laughter by no less a person than my dear old nurse. The moment Mr Westwick pronounced the word "Venice", she started up among the servants at the lower end of the room, and called out at the top of her voice, "Go to our hotel, ladies and gentlemen! We get six per cent. on our money already; and if you will only crowd the place and call for the best of everything, it will be ten per cent. in our pockets in no time. Ask Master Henry!"

'Appealed to in this irresistible manner, Mr Westwick had no choice but to explain that he was concerned as a shareholder in a new Hotel Company at Venice, and that he had invested a small sum of money for the nurse (not very considerately, as I think) in the speculation. Hearing this, the company, by way of humouring the joke, drank a new toast: – Success to the nurse's hotel, and a speedy rise in the dividend!

'When the conversation returned in due time to the more serious question of the proposed meeting at Venice, difficulties began to present themselves, caused of course by invitations for the autumn which many of the guests had already accepted. Only two members of Mrs Carbury's family were at liberty to keep the proposed appointment. On our side we were more at leisure to do as we pleased. Mr Henry Westwick decided to go to Venice in advance of the rest, to test the accommodation of the new hotel on the opening day. Mrs Norbury and Mr Francis Westwick volunteered to follow him; and, after some persuasion, Lord and Lady Montbarry consented to a species of compromise. His lordship could not conveniently spare time enough for the journey to Venice, but he and Lady Montbarry arranged to accompany Mrs Norbury and Mr Francis Westwick as far on their way to Italy as Paris. Five days since, they took their departure to meet their travelling companions in London; leaving me here in charge of the three dear children. They begged hard, of course, to be taken with papa and mamma. But it was thought better not to interrupt the progress of their education, and not to expose them (especially the two younger girls) to the fatigues of travelling.

'I have had a charming letter from the bride, this morning, dated Cologne. You cannot think how artlessly and prettily she assures me of her happiness. Some people, as they say in Ireland, are born to good luck – and I think Arthur Barville is one of them.

'When you next write, I hope to hear that you are in better health and spirits, and that you continue to like your employment. Believe me, sincerely your friend, – A. L.'

Agnes had just closed and directed her letter, when the eldest of her three pupils entered the room with the startling announcement that Lord Montbarry's travelling-servant had arrived from Paris! Alarmed by the idea that some misfortune had happened, she ran out to meet the man in the hall. Her face told him how seriously he had frightened her, before she could speak. 'There's nothing wrong, Miss,' he hastened to say. 'My lord and my lady are enjoying themselves at Paris. They only want you and the young ladies to be with them.' Saying these amazing words, he handed to Agnes a letter from Lady Montbarry.

'Dearest Agnes,' (she read) 'I am so charmed with the delightful change in my life – it is six years, remember, since I last travelled on the Continent – that I have exerted all my fascinations to persuade Lord Montbarry to go on to Venice. And, what is more to the purpose, I have actually succeeded! He has just gone to his room to write the necessary letters of excuse in time for the post to England. May you have as good a husband, my dear, when your time comes! In the mean while, the one thing wanting now to make my happiness complete, is to have you and the darling children with us. Montbarry is just as miserable without them as I am – though he doesn't confess it so freely. You will have no difficulties to trouble you. Louis will deliver these hurried lines, and will take care of you on the journey to Paris. Kiss the children for me a thousand times – and never mind their education for the present! Pack up instantly, my dear, and I will be fonder of you than ever. Your affectionate friend, Ella Montbarry.'

Agnes folded up the letter; and feeling the need of composing herself, took refuge for a few minutes in her own room.

Her first natural sensations of surprise and excitement at the prospect of going to Venice were succeeded by impressions of a less agreeable kind. With the recovery of her customary composure came the unwelcome remembrance of the parting words spoken to her by Montbarry's widow: – 'We shall meet again – here in England, or there in Venice where my husband died – and meet for the last time.'

It was an odd coincidence, to say the least of it, that the march of events should be unexpectedly taking Agnes to Venice, after those words had been spoken! Was the woman of the mysterious warnings and the wild black eyes, still thousands of miles away in America? Or was the march of events taking *her* unexpectedly, too, on the journey to Venice? Agnes started out of her chair, ashamed of even the momentary concession to superstition which was implied by the mere presence of such questions as these in her mind.

She rang the bell, and sent for her little pupils, and announced their approaching departure to the household. The noisy delight of the children, the inspiriting effort of packing up in a hurry, roused all her energies. She dismissed her own absurd misgivings from consideration, with the contempt that they deserved. She worked as only women *can* work, when their hearts are in what they do. The travellers reached Dublin that day, in time for the boat to England. Two days later, they were with Lord and Lady Montbarry at Paris.

THE FOURTH PART

❧ SIXTEEN ❧

IT WAS ONLY THE TWENTIETH OF SEPTEMBER, when Agnes and the children reached Paris. Mrs Norbury and her brother Francis had then already started on their journey to Italy – at least three weeks before the date at which they new hotel was to open for the reception of travellers.

The person answerable for this premature departure was Francis Westwick.

Like his younger brother Henry, he had increased his pecuniary resources by his own enterprise and ingenuity; with this difference, that his speculations were connected with the Arts. He had made money, in the first instance, by a weekly newspaper; and he had then invested his profits in a London Theatre. This latter enterprise, admirably conducted, had been rewarded by the public with steady and liberal encouragement. Pondering over a new form of theatrical attraction for the coming winter season, Francis had determined to revive the languid public taste for the 'ballet' by means of an entertainment of his own invention, combining dramatic interest with dancing. He was now, accordingly, in search of the best dancer (possessed of the indispensable personal attractions) who was to be found in the theatres of the Continent. Hearing from his foreign correspondents of two women who had made successful first appearances, one at Milan and one at Florence, he had arranged to visit those cities, and to judge of the merits of the dancers for himself, before he joined the bride and bridegroom. His widowed sister, having friends at Florence whom she was anxious to see, readily accompanied him. The Montbarrys remained at Paris, until it was time to present themselves at the family meeting in Venice. Henry found them still in the French capital, when he arrived from London on his way to the opening of the new hotel.

Against Lady Montbarry's advice, he took the opportunity of renewing his addresses to Agnes. He could hardly have chosen a more unpropitious time for pleading his cause with her. The gaieties of Paris (quite incomprehensibly to herself as well as to everyone about her) had a depressing effect on her spirits. She had no illness to complain of; she shared willingly in the ever-varying succession of amusements offered to strangers by the ingenuity of the liveliest people in the world – but nothing roused her: she remained persistently dull and weary through it all. In this frame of mind and body, she was in no humour to receive Henry's ill-timed addresses with favour, or even with patience: she plainly and positively refused to listen to him. 'Why do you remind me of what I have suffered?' she asked petulantly. 'Don't you see that it has left its mark on me for life?'

'I thought I knew something of women by this time,' Henry said, appealing privately to Lady Montbarry for consolation. 'But Agnes completely puzzles me. It is a year since Montbarry's death; and she remains as devoted to his memory as if he had died faithful to her – she still feels the loss of him, as none of *us* feel it!'

'She is the truest woman that ever breathed the breath of life,' Lady Montbarry answered. 'Remember that, and you will understand her. Can such a woman as Agnes give her love or refuse it, according to circumstances? Because the man was unworthy of her, was he less the man of her choice? The truest and best friend to him (little as he deserved it) in his lifetime, she naturally remains the truest and best friend to his memory now. If you really love her, wait; and trust to your two best friends – to time and to me. There is my advice; let your own experience decide whether it is not the best advice that I can offer. Resume your journey to Venice to-morrow; and when you take leave of Agnes, speak to her as cordially as if nothing had happened.'

Henry wisely followed this advice. Thoroughly understanding him, Agnes made the leave-taking friendly and pleasant on her side. When he stopped at the door for a last look at her, she hurriedly turned her head so that her face was hidden from him. Was that a good sign? Lady Montbarry, accompanying Henry down the stairs, said, 'Yes, decidedly! Write when you get to Venice. We shall wait here to receive letters from Arthur and his wife, and we shall time our departure for Italy accordingly.'

A week passed, and no letter came from Henry. Some days later, a telegram was received from him. It was despatched from Milan, instead of from Venice; and it brought this strange message: – 'I have left the hotel. Will return on the arrival of Arthur and his wife. Address, meanwhile, Albergo Reale, Milan.'

Preferring Venice before all other cities of Europe, and having arranged to remain there until the family meeting took place, what unexpected event had led Henry to alter his plans? and why did he state the bare fact, without adding a word of explanation? Let the narrative follow him – and find the answer to those questions at Venice.

❧ SEVENTEEN ❧

The Palace Hotel, appealing for encouragement mainly to English and American travellers, celebrated the opening of its doors, as a matter of course, by the giving of a grand banquet, and the delivery of a long succession of speeches.

Delayed on his journey, Henry Westwick only reached Venice in time to join the guests over their coffee and cigars. Observing the splendour of the reception rooms, and taking note especially of the artful mixture of comfort and luxury in the bedchambers, he began to share the old nurse's view of the future, and to contemplate seriously the coming dividend of ten per cent. The hotel was beginning well, at all events. So much interest in the enterprise had been aroused, at home and abroad, by profuse advertising, that the whole accommodation of the building had been secured by travellers of all nations for the opening night. Henry only obtained one of the small rooms on the upper floor, by a lucky accident – the absence of the gentlemen who had written to engage it. He was quite satisfied, and was on his way to bed, when another accident altered his prospects for the night, and moved him into another and a better room.

Ascending on his way to the higher regions as far as the first floor of the hotel, Henry's attention was attracted by an angry voice protesting, in a strong New England accent, against one of the greatest hardships that can be inflicted on a citizen of the United States – the hardship of sending him to bed without gas in his room.

The Americans are not only the most hospitable people to be found on the face of the earth – they are (under certain conditions) the most patient and good-tempered people as well. But they are human; and the limit of American endurance is found in the obsolete institution of a bedroom candle. The American traveller, in the present case, declined to believe that his bedroom was in a completely finished state without a gas-burner. The manager pointed to the fine antique decorations (renewed and regilt) on the walls and the ceiling, and explained that the emanations of burning gas-light would certainly spoil them in the course of a few months. To this the traveller replied that it was possible, but that he did not understand decorations. A bed-room with gas in it was what he was used to, was what he wanted, and was what he was determined to have. The compliant manager volunteered to ask some other gentleman, housed on the inferior upper story (which was lit throughout with gas), to change rooms. Hearing this, and being quite willing to exchange a small bedchamber for a large one, Henry volunteered to be the other gentleman. The excellent American shook hands with him on the spot. 'You are a cultured person, sir,' he said; 'and *you* will no doubt understand the decorations.'

Henry looked at the number of the room on the door as he opened it. The number was Fourteen.

Tired and sleepy, he naturally anticipated a good night's rest. In the thoroughly healthy state of his nervous system, he slept as well in a bed abroad as in a bed at home. Without the slightest assignable reason, however, his just expectations were disappointed. The luxurious bed, the well-ventilated room, the delicious tranquillity of Venice by night, all were in favour of his sleeping well. He never slept at all. An indescribable sense of depression and discomfort kept him waking through darkness and daylight alike. He went down to the coffee-room as soon as the hotel was astir, and ordered some breakfast. Another unaccountable change in himself appeared with the appearance of the meal. He was absolutely without appetite. An excellent omelette, and cutlets cooked to perfection, he sent away untasted – he, whose appetite never failed him, whose digestion was still equal to any demands on it!

The day was bright and fine. He sent for a gondola, and was rowed to the Lido.

Out on the airy Lagoon, he felt like a new man. He had not left the hotel ten minutes before he was fast asleep in the gondola. Waking, on reaching the landing-place, he crossed the Lido, and enjoyed a morning's swim in the Adriatic. There was only a poor restaurant on the island, in those days; but his appetite was now ready for anything; he ate whatever was offered to him, like a famished man. He could hardly believe, when he reflected on it, that he had sent away untasted his excellent breakfast at the hotel.

Returning to Venice, he spent the rest of the day in the picture-galleries and the churches. Towards six o'clock his gondola took him back, with another fine appetite, to meet some travelling acquaintances with whom he had engaged to dine at the table d'hôte.

The dinner was deservedly rewarded with the highest approval by every guest in the hotel but one. To Henry's astonishment, the appetite with which he had entered the house mysteriously and completely left him when he sat down to table. He could drink some wine, but he could literally eat nothing. 'What in the world is the matter with you?' his travelling acquaintances asked. He could honestly answer, 'I know no more than you do.'

When night came, he gave his comfortable and beautiful bedroom another trial. The result of the second experiment was a repetition of the result of the first. Again he felt the all-pervading sense of depression and discomfort. Again he passed a sleepless night. And once more, when he tried to eat his breakfast, his appetite completely failed him!

This personal experience of the new hotel was too extraordinary to be passed over in silence. Henry mentioned it to his friends in the public room, in the hearing of the manager. The manager, naturally zealous in defence of the hotel, was a little hurt at the implied reflection cast on Number Fourteen. He invited the travellers present to judge for themselves whether Mr Westwick's bedroom was to blame for Mr Westwick's sleepless nights; and he especially appealed to a grey-headed gentleman, a guest at the breakfast-table of an English traveller, to take the lead in the investigation. 'This is Doctor Bruno, our first physician in Venice,' he explained. 'I appeal to him to say if there are any unhealthy influences in Mr Westwick's room.'

Introduced to Number Fourteen, the doctor looked round him with a certain appearance of interest which was noticed by everyone present. 'The last time I was in this room,' he said, 'was on a melancholy occasion. It was before the palace was changed into an hotel. I was in professional attendance on an English nobleman who died here.' One of the persons present inquired the name of the nobleman. Doctor Bruno answered (without the slightest suspicion that he was speaking before a brother of the dead man), 'Lord Montbarry.'

Henry quietly left the room, without saying a word to anybody.

He was not, in any sense of the term, a superstitious man. But he felt, nevertheless, an insurmountable reluctance to remaining in the hotel. He decided on leaving Venice. To ask for another room would be, as he could plainly see, an offence in the eyes of the manager. To remove to another hotel, would be to openly abandon an establishment in the success of which he had a pecuniary interest. Leaving a note for Arthur Barville, on his arrival in Venice, in which he merely mentioned that he had gone to look at the Italian lakes, and that a line addressed to his hotel at Milan would bring him back again, he took the afternoon train to Padua – and dined with his usual appetite, and slept as well as ever that night.

The next day, a gentleman and his wife (perfect strangers to the Montbarry family), returning to England by way of Venice, arrived at the hotel and occupied Number Fourteen.

Still mindful of the slur that had been cast on one of his best bed-chambers, the manager took occasion to ask the travellers the next morning how they liked their room. They left him to judge for himself how well they were satisfied, by remaining a day longer in Venice than they had originally planned to do, solely for the purpose of enjoying the excellent accommodation offered to them by the new hotel. 'We have met with nothing like it in Italy,' they said; 'you may rely on our recommending you to all our friends.'

On the day when Number Fourteen was again vacant, an English lady travelling alone with her maid arrived at the hotel, saw the room, and at once engaged it.

The lady was Mrs Norbury. She had left Francis Westwick at Milan, occupied in negotiating for the appearance at his theatre of the new dancer at the Scala. Not having heard to the contrary, Mrs Norbury supposed that Arthur Barville and his wife had already arrived at Venice. She was more interested in meeting the young married couple than in awaiting the result of the hard bargaining which delayed the engagement of the new dancer; and she volunteered to make her brother's apologies, if his theatrical business caused him to be late in keeping his appointment at the honeymoon festival.

Mrs Norbury's experience of Number Fourteen differed entirely from her brother Henry's experience of the room.

Falling asleep as readily as usual, her repose was disturbed by a succession of frightful dreams; the central figure in everyone of them being the figure of her dead brother, the first Lord Montbarry. She saw him starving in a loathsome prison; she saw him pursued by assassins, and dying under their knives; she saw him drowning in immeasurable depths of dark water; she saw him in a bed on fire, burning to death in the flames; she saw him tempted by a shadowy creature to drink, and dying of the poisonous draught. The reiterated horror of these dreams had such an effect on her that she rose with the dawn of day, afraid to trust herself again in bed. In the old times, she had been noted in the family as the one member of it who lived on affectionate terms with Montbarry. His other sister and his brothers were constantly quarrelling with him. Even his mother owned that her eldest son was of all her children the child whom she least liked. Sensible and resolute woman as she was, Mrs Norbury shuddered with terror as she sat at the window of her room, watching the sunrise, and thinking of her dreams.

She made the first excuse that occurred to her, when her maid came in at the usual hour, and noticed how ill she looked. The woman was of so superstitious a temperament that it would have been in the last degree indiscreet to trust her with the truth. Mrs Norbury merely remarked that she had not found the bed quite to her liking, on account of the large size of it. She was accustomed at home, as her maid knew, to sleep in a small bed. Informed of this objection later in the day, the manager regretted that he could only offer to the lady the choice of one other bedchamber, numbered Thirty-eight, and situated immediately over the bedchamber which she desired to leave. Mrs Norbury accepted the proposed change of quarters. She was now about to pass her second night in the room occupied in the old days of the palace by Baron Rivar.

Once more, she fell asleep as usual. And, once more, the frightful dreams of the first night terrified her; following each other in the same succession. This time her nerves, already shaken, were not equal to the renewed torture of terror inflicted on them. She threw on her dressing-gown, and rushed out of her room in the middle of the night. The porter, alarmed by the banging of the door, met her hurrying headlong down the stairs, in search of the first human being she could find to keep her company. Considerably surprised at this last new manifestation of the famous 'English eccentricity', the man looked at the hotel register, and led the lady upstairs again to the room occupied by her maid. The maid was not asleep, and, more wonderful still, was not even undressed. She received her mistress quietly. When they were alone, and when Mrs Norbury had, as a matter of necessity, taken her attendant into her confidence, the woman made a very strange reply.

'I have been asking about the hotel, at the servants' supper to-night,' she said. 'The valet of one of the gentlemen staying here has heard that the late Lord Montbarry was the last person who lived in the palace, before it was made into an hotel. The room he died in, ma'am, was the room you slept in last night. Your room to-night is the room just above it. I said nothing for fear of frightening you. For my own part, I have passed the night as you see, keeping my light in, and reading my Bible. In my opinion, no member of your family can hope to be happy or comfortable in this house.'

'What do you mean?'

'Please to let me explain myself, ma'am. When Mr Henry Westwick was here (I have this from the valet, too) he occupied the room his brother died in (without knowing it), like you. For two nights he never closed his eyes. Without any reason for it (the valet heard him tell the gentlemen in the coffee-room) he could *not* sleep; he felt so low and so wretched in himself. And what is more, when daytime came, he couldn't eat while he was under this roof. You may laugh at me, ma'am – but even a servant may draw her own conclusions. It's my conclusion that something happened to my lord, which we none of us know about, when he died in this house. His ghost walks in torment until he can tell it – and the living persons related to him are the persons who feel he is near them. Those persons may yet see him in the time to come. Don't, pray don't stay any longer in this dreadful place! I wouldn't stay another night here myself – no, not for anything that could be offered me!'

Mrs Norbury at once set her servant's mind at ease on this last point.

'I don't think about it as you do,' she said gravely. 'But I should like to speak to my brother of what has happened. We will go back to Milan.'

Some hours necessarily elapsed before they could leave the hotel, by the first train in the forenoon.

In that interval, Mrs Norbury's maid found an opportunity of confidentially informing the valet of what had passed between her mistress and herself. The valet had other friends to whom he related the circumstances in his turn. In due course of time, the narrative, passing from mouth to mouth, reached the ears of the manager. He instantly saw that the credit of the hotel was in danger, unless something was done to retrieve the character of the room numbered Fourteen. English travellers, well acquainted with the peerage of their native country, informed him that Henry Westwick and Mrs Norbury were by no means the only members of the Montbarry family. Curiosity might bring more of them to the hotel, after hearing what had happened. The manager's ingenuity easily hit on the obvious means of misleading them, in this case. The numbers of the rooms were enamelled in blue, on white china plates, screwed to the doors. He ordered a new plate to be prepared bearing the number, '13A'; and he kept the room empty, after its tenant for the time being had gone away, until the plate was ready. He then re-numbered the room; placing the removed Number Fourteen on the door of his own room (on the second floor), which, not being to let had not previously been numbered at all. By this device, Number Fourteen disappeared at once and for ever from the books of the hotel, as the number of a bedroom to let.

Having warned the servants to beware of gossiping with travellers, on the subject of the changed numbers, under penalty of being dismissed, the manager composed his mind with the reflection that he had done his duty to his employers. 'Now,' he thought to himself, with an excusable sense of triumph, 'let the whole family come here if they like! The hotel is a match for them.'

⊷ EIGHTEEN ⊷

BEFORE THE END OF THE week, the manager found himself in relations with 'the family' once more. A telegram from Milan announced that Mr Francis Westwick would arrive in Venice on the next day; and would be obliged if Number Fourteen, on the first floor, could be reserved for him, in the event of its being vacant at the time.

The manager paused to consider, before he issued his directions.

The re-numbered room had been last let to a French gentleman. It would be occupied on the day of Mr Francis Westwick's arrival, but it would be empty again on the day after. Would it be well to reserve the room for the special occupation of Mr Francis? and when he had passed the night unsuspiciously and comfortably in 'No 13 A', to ask him in the presence of witnesses how he liked his bedchamber? In this case, if the reputation of the room happened to be called in question again, the answer would vindicate it, on the evidence of a member of the very family which had first given Number Fourteen a bad name. After a little reflection, the manager decided on trying the experiment, and directed that '13 A' should be reserved accordingly.

On the next day, Francis Westwick arrived in excellent spirits.

He had signed agreements with the most popular dancer in Italy; he had transferred the charge of Mrs Norbury to his brother Henry, who had joined him in Milan; and he was now at full liberty to amuse himself by testing in every possible way the extraordinary influence exercised over his relatives by the new hotel. When his brother and sister first told him what their experience had been, he instantly declared that he would go to Venice in the interest of his theatre. The circumstances related to him contained invaluable hints for a ghost-drama. The title occurred to him in the railway: 'The Haunted Hotel.' Post that in red letters six feet high, on a black ground, all over London – and trust the excitable public to crowd into the theatre!

Received with the politest attention by the manager, Francis met with a disappointment on entering the hotel. 'Some mistake, sir. No such room on the first floor as Number Fourteen. The room bearing that number is on the second floor, and has been occupied by me, from the day when the hotel opened. Perhaps you meant number 13 A, on the first floor? It will be at your service to-morrow – a charming room. In the mean time, we will do the best we can for you, to-night.'

A man who is the successful manager of a theatre is probably the last man in the civilized universe who is capable of being impressed with favourable opinions of his fellow-creatures. Francis privately set the manager down as a humbug, and the story about the numbering of the rooms as a lie.

On the day of his arrival, he dined by himself in the restaurant, before the hour of the table d'hôte, for the express purpose of questioning the waiter, without being overheard by anybody. The answer led him to the conclusion that '13 A' occupied the situation in the hotel which had been described by his brother and sister as the situation of '14'. He asked next for the Visitors' List; and found that the French gentleman who then occupied '13 A', was the proprietor of a theatre in Paris, personally well known to him. Was the gentleman then in the hotel? He had gone out, but would certainly return for the table d'hôte. When the public dinner was over, Francis entered the room, and was welcomed by his Parisian colleague, literally, with open arms. 'Come and have a cigar in my room,' said the friendly Frenchman. 'I want to hear whether you have really engaged that woman at Milan or not.' In this easy way, Francis found his opportunity of comparing the interior of the room with the description which he had heard of it at Milan.

Arriving at the door, the Frenchman bethought himself of his travelling companion. 'My scene-painter is here with me,' he said, 'on the look-out for materials. An excellent fellow, who will take it as a kindness if we ask him to join us. I'll tell the porter to send him up when he comes in.' He handed the key of his room to Francis. 'I will be back in a minute. It's at the end of the corridor – 13 A.'

Francis entered the room alone. There were the decorations on the walls and the ceiling, exactly as they had been described to him! He had just time to perceive this at a glance, before his attention was diverted to himself and his own sensations, by a grotesquely disagreeable occurrence which took him completely by surprise.

He became conscious of a mysteriously offensive odour in the room, entirely new in his experience of revolting smells. It was composed (if such a thing could be) of two mingling exhalations, which were separately-discoverable exhalations nevertheless. This strange blending of odours consisted of something faintly and unpleasantly aromatic, mixed with another underlying smell, so unutterably sickening that he threw open the window, and put his head out into the fresh air, unable to endure the horribly infected atmosphere for a moment longer.

The French proprietor joined his English friend, with his cigar already lit. He started back in dismay at a sight terrible to his countrymen in general – the sight of an open window. 'You English people are perfectly mad on the subject of fresh air!' he exclaimed. 'We shall catch our deaths of cold.'

Francis turned, and looked at him in astonishment. 'Are you really not aware of the smell there is in the room?' he asked.

'Smell!' repeated his brother-manager. 'I smell my own good cigar. Try one yourself. And for Heaven's sake shut the window!'

Francis declined the cigar by a sign. 'Forgive me,' he said. 'I will leave you to close the window. I feel faint and giddy – I had better go out.' He put his handkerchief over his nose and mouth, and crossed the room to the door.

The Frenchman followed the movements of Francis, in such a state of bewilderment that he actually forgot to seize the opportunity of shutting out the fresh air. 'Is it so nasty as that?' he asked, with a broad stare of amazement.

'Horrible!' Francis muttered behind his handkerchief. 'I never smelt anything like it in my life!'

There was a knock at the door. The scene-painter appeared. His employer instantly asked him if he smelt anything.

'I smell your cigar. Delicious! Give me one directly!'

'Wait a minute. Besides my cigar, do you smell anything else – vile, abominable, overpowering, indescribable, never-never-never-smelt before?'

The scene-painter appeared to be puzzled by the vehement energy of the language addressed to him. 'The room is as fresh and sweet as a room can be,' he answered. As he spoke, he looked back with astonishment at Francis Westwick, standing outside in the corridor, and eyeing the interior of the bedchamber with an expression of undisguised disgust.

The Parisian director approached his English colleague, and looked at him with grave and anxious scrutiny.

'You see, my friend, here are two of us, with as good noses as yours, who smell nothing. If you want evidence from more noses, look there!' He pointed to two little English girls, at play in the corridor. 'The door of my room is wide open – and you know how fast a smell can travel. Now listen, while I appeal to these innocent noses, in the language of their own dismal island. My little loves, do you sniff a nasty smell here – ha?' The children burst out laughing, and answered emphatically, 'No.' 'My good Westwick,' the Frenchman resumed, in his own language, 'the conclusion is surely plain? There is something wrong, very wrong, with your own nose. I recommend you to see a medical man.'

Having given that advice, he returned to his room, and shut out the horrid fresh air with a loud exclamation of relief. Francis left the hotel, by the lanes that led to the Square of St Mark. The night-breeze soon revived him. He was able to light a cigar, and to think quietly over what had happened.

❧ NINETEEN ❧

AVOIDING THE CROWD UNDER THE colonnades, Francis walked slowly up and down the noble open space of the square, bathed in the light of the rising moon.

Without being aware of it himself, he was a thorough materialist. The strange effect produced on him by the room – following on the other strange effects produced on the other relatives of his dead brother – exercised no perplexing influence over the mind of this sensible man. 'Perhaps,' he reflected, 'my temperament is more imaginative than I supposed it to be – and this is a trick played on me by my own fancy?

Or, perhaps, my friend is right; something is physically amiss with me? I don't feel ill, certainly. But that is no safe criterion sometimes. I am not going to sleep in that abominable room to-night – I can well wait till to-morrow to decide whether I shall speak to a doctor or not. In the mean time, the hotel doesn't seem likely to supply me with the subject of a piece. A terrible smell from an invisible ghost is a perfectly new idea. But it has one drawback. If I realize it on the stage, I shall drive the audience out of the theatre.'

As his strong common sense arrived at this facetious conclusion, he became aware of a lady, dressed entirely in black, who was observing him with marked attention. 'Am I right in supposing you to be Mr Francis Westwick?' the lady asked, at the moment when he looked at her.

'That is my name, madam. May I inquire to whom I have the honour of speaking?'

'We have only met once,' she answered a little evasively, 'when your late brother introduced me to the members of his family. I wonder if you have quite forgotten my big black eyes and my hideous complexion?' She lifted her veil as she spoke, and turned so that the moonlight rested on her face.

Francis recognized at a glance the woman of all others whom he most cordially disliked – the widow of his dead brother, the first Lord Montbarry. He frowned as he looked at her. His experience on the stage, gathered at innumerable rehearsals with actresses who had sorely tried his temper, had accustomed him to speak roughly to women who were distasteful to him. 'I remember you,' he said. 'I thought you were in America!'

She took no notice of his ungracious tone and manner; she simply stopped him when he lifted his hat, and turned to leave her.

'Let me walk with you for a few minutes,' she quietly replied. 'I have something to say to you.'

He showed her his cigar. 'I am smoking,' he said.

'I don't mind smoking.'

After that, there was nothing to be done (short of downright brutality) but to yield. He did it with the worst possible grace. 'Well?' he resumed. 'What do you want of me?'

'You shall hear directly, Mr Westwick. Let me first tell you what my position is. I am alone in the world. To the loss of my husband has now been added another bereavement, the loss of my companion in America, my brother – Baron Rivar.'

The reputation of the Baron, and the doubt which scandal had thrown on his assumed relationship to the Countess, were well known to Francis. 'Shot in a gambling-saloon?' he asked brutally.

'The question is a perfectly natural one on your part,' she said, with the impenetrably ironical manner which she could assume on certain occasions. 'As a native of horse-racing England, you belong to a nation of gamblers. My brother died no extraordinary death, Mr Westwick. He sank, with many other unfortunate people, under a fever prevalent in a Western city which we happened to visit. The calamity of his loss made the United States unendurable to me. I left by the first steamer that sailed from New York – a French vessel which brought me to Havre. I continued my lonely journey to the South of France. And then I went on to Venice.'

'What does all this matter to me?' Francis thought to himself. She paused, evidently expecting him to say something. 'So you have come to Venice?' he said carelessly. 'Why?'

'Because I couldn't help it,' she answered.

Francis looked at her with cynical curiosity. 'That sounds odd,' he remarked. 'Why couldn't you help it?'

'Women are accustomed to act on impulse,' she explained. 'Suppose we say that an impulse had directed my journey? And yet, this is the last place in the world that I wish to find myself in. Associations that I detest are connected with it in my mind. If I had a will of my own, I would never see it again. I hate Venice. As you see, however, I am here. When did you meet with such an unreasonable woman before? Never, I am sure!' She stopped, eyed him for a moment, and suddenly altered her tone. 'When is Miss Agnes Lockwood expected to be in Venice?' she asked.

It was not easy to throw Francis off his balance, but that extraordinary question did it. 'How the devil did you know that Miss Lockwood was coming to Venice?' he exclaimed.

She laughed – a bitter mocking laugh. 'Say I guessed it!'

Something in her tone, or perhaps something in the audacious defiance of her eyes as they rested on him, roused the quick temper that was in Francis Westwick. 'Lady Montbarry—!' he began.

'Stop there!' she interposed. 'Your brother Stephen's wife calls herself Lady Montbarry now. I share my title with no woman. Call me by my name before I committed the fatal mistake of marrying your brother. Address me, if you please, as Countess Narona.'

'Countess Narona,' Francis resumed, 'if your object in claiming my acquaintance is to mystify me, you have come to the wrong man. Speak plainly, or permit me to wish you good evening.'

'If your object is to keep Miss Lockwood's arrival in Venice a secret,' she retorted, 'speak plainly, Mr Westwick, on *your* side, and say so.'

Her intention was evidently to irritate him; and she succeeded. 'Nonsense!' he broke out petulantly. 'My brother's travelling arrangements are secret to nobody. He brings Miss Lockwood here, with Lady

Montbarry and the children. As you seem so well informed, perhaps you know why she is coming to Venice?'

The Countess had suddenly become grave and thoughtful. She made no reply. The two strangely associated companions, having reached one extremity of the square, were now standing before the church of St Mark. The moonlight was bright enough to show the architecture of the grand cathedral in its wonderful variety of detail. Even the pigeons of St Mark were visible, in dark closely packed rows, roosting in the archways of the great entrance doors.

'I never saw the old church look so beautiful by moonlight,' the Countess said quietly; speaking, not to Francis, but to herself. 'Good-bye, St Mark's by moonlight! I shall not see you again.'

She turned away from the church, and saw Francis listening to her with wondering looks. 'No,' she resumed, placidly picking up the lost thread of the conversation, 'I don't know why Miss Lockwood is coming here, I only know that we are to meet in Venice.'

'By previous appointment?'

'By Destiny,' she answered, with her head on her breast, and her eyes on the ground. Francis burst out laughing. 'Or if you like it better,' she instantly resumed, 'by what fools call Chance.'

Francis answered easily, out of the depths of his strong common sense. 'Chance seems to be taking a queer way of bringing the meeting about,' he said. 'We have all arranged to meet at the Palace Hotel. How is it that your name is not on the Visitors' List? Destiny ought to have brought you to the Palace Hotel too.'

She abruptly pulled down her veil. 'Destiny may do that yet!' she said. 'The Palace Hotel?' she repeated, speaking once more to herself. 'The old hell, transformed into the new purgatory. The place itself! Jesu Maria! the place itself!' She paused and laid her hand on her companion's arm. 'Perhaps Miss Lockwood is not going there with the rest of you?' she burst out with sudden eagerness. 'Are you positively sure she will be at the hotel?'

'Positively! Haven't I told you that Miss Lockwood travels with Lord and Lady Montbarry? and don't you know that she is a member of the family? You will have to move, Countess, to our hotel.'

She was perfectly impenetrable to the bantering tone in which he spoke. 'Yes,' she said faintly, 'I shall have to move to your hotel.' Her hand was still on his arm – he could feel her shivering from head to foot while she spoke. Heartily as he disliked and distrusted her, the common instinct of humanity obliged him to ask if she felt cold.

'Yes,' she said. 'Cold and faint.'

'Cold and faint, Countess, on such a night as this?'

'The night has nothing to do with it, Mr Westwick. How do you suppose the criminal feels on the scaffold, while the hangman is putting the rope round his neck? Cold and faint, too, I should think. Excuse my grim fancy. You see, Destiny has got the rope round *my* neck – and *I* feel it.'

She looked about her. They were at that moment close to the famous café known as 'Florian's'. 'Take me in there,' she said; 'I must have something to revive me. You had better not hesitate. You are interested in reviving me. I have not said what I wanted to say to you yet. It's business, and it's connected with your theatre.'

Wondering inwardly what she could possibly want with his theatre, Francis reluctantly yielded to the necessities of the situation, and took her into the café. He found a quiet corner in which they could take their place without attracting notice. 'What will you have?' he inquired resignedly. She gave her own orders to the waiter, without troubling him to speak for her.

'Maraschino. And a pot of tea.'

The waiter stared; Francis stared. The tea was a novelty (in connection with maraschino) to both of them. Careless whether she surprised them or not, she instructed the waiter, when her directions had been complied with, to pour a large wine-glass-full of the liqueur into a tumbler, and to fill it up from the teapot. 'I can't do it for myself,' she remarked, 'my hand trembles so.' She drank the strange mixture eagerly, hot as it was. 'Maraschino punch – will you taste some of it?' she said. 'I inherit the discovery of this drink. When your English Queen Caroline was on the Continent, my mother was attached to her court. That much injured Royal Person invented, in her happier hours, maraschino punch. Fondly attached to her gracious mistress, my mother shared her tastes. And I, in my turn, learnt from my mother. Now, Mr Westwick, suppose I tell you what my business is. You are manager of a theatre. Do you want a new play?'

'I always want a new play – provided it's a good one.'

'And you pay, if it's a good one?'

'I pay liberally – in my own interests.'

'If *I* write the play, will you read it?'

Francis hesitated. 'What has put writing a play into your head?' he asked.

'Mere accident,' she answered. 'I had once occasion to tell my late brother of a visit which I paid to Miss Lockwood, when I was last in England. He took no interest in what happened at the interview, but something struck him in my way of relating it. He said, "You describe what passed between you and the lady with the point and contrast of good stage dialogue. You have the dramatic instinct – try if you can write a play. You might make money." *That* put it into my head.'

Those last words seemed to startle Francis. 'Surely you don't want money!' he exclaimed.

'I always want money. My tastes are expensive. I have nothing but my poor little four hundred a year – and the wreck that is left of the other money: about two hundred pounds in circular notes – no more.'

Francis knew that she was referring to the ten thousand pounds paid by the insurance offices. 'All those thousands gone already!' he exclaimed.

She blew a little puff of air over her fingers. 'Gone like that!' she answered coolly.

'Baron Rivar?'

She looked at him with a flash of anger in her hard black eyes.

'My affairs are my own secret, Mr Westwick. I have made you a proposal – and you have not answered me yet. Don't say No, without thinking first. Remember what a life mine has been. I have seen more of the world than most people, playwrights included. I have had strange adventures; I have heard remarkable stories; I have observed; I have remembered. Are there no materials, here in my head, for writing a play – if the opportunity is granted to me?' She waited a moment, and suddenly repeated her strange question about Agnes. 'When is Miss Lockwood expected to be in Venice?'

'What has that to do with your new play, Countess?'

The Countess appeared to feel some difficulty in giving that question its fit reply. She mixed another tumbler full of the maraschino punch, and drank one good half of it before she spoke again.

'It has everything to do with my new play,' was all she said. 'Answer me.' Francis answered her.

'Miss Lockwood may be here in a week. Or, for all I know to the contrary, sooner than that.'

'Very well. If I am a living woman and a free woman in a week's time – or if I am in possession of my senses in a week's time (don't interrupt me; I know what I am talking about) – I shall have a sketch or outline of my play ready, as a specimen of what I can do. Once again, will you read it?'

'I will certainly read it. But, Countess, I don't understand—'

She held up her hand for silence, and finished the second tumbler of maraschino punch.

'I am a living enigma – and you want to know the right reading of me,' she said. 'Here is the reading, as your English phrase goes, in a nutshell. There is a foolish idea in the minds of many persons that the natives of the warm climates are imaginative people. There never was a greater mistake. You will find no such unimaginative people anywhere as you find in Italy, Spain, Greece, and the other Southern countries. To anything fanciful, to anything spiritual, their minds are deaf and blind by nature. Now and then, in the course of centuries, a great genius springs up among them; and he is the exception which proves the rule. Now see! I, though I am no genius – I am, in my little way (as I suppose), an exception too. To my sorrow, I have some of that imagination which is so common among the English and the Germans – so rare among the Italians, the Spaniards, and the rest of them! And what is the result? I think it has become a disease in me. I am filled with presentiments which make this wicked life of mine one long terror to me. It doesn't matter, just now, what they are. Enough that they absolutely govern me – they drive me over land and sea at their own horrible will; they are in me, and torturing me, at this moment! Why don't I resist them? Ha! but I do resist them. I am trying (with the help of the good punch) to resist them now. At intervals I cultivate the difficult virtue of sound sense. Sometimes, sound sense makes a hopeful woman of me. At one time, I had the hope that what seemed reality to me was only mad delusion, after all – I even asked the question of an English doctor! At other times, other sensible doubts of myself beset me. Never mind dwelling on them now – it always ends in the old terrors and superstitions taking possession of me again. In a week's time, I shall know whether Destiny does indeed decide my future for me, or whether I decide it for myself. In the last case, my resolution is to absorb this self-tormenting fancy of mine in the occupation that I have told you of already. Do you understand me a little better now? And, our business being settled, dear Mr Westwick, shall we get out of this hot room into the nice cool air again?'

They rose to leave the café. Francis privately concluded that the maraschino punch offered the only discoverable explanation of what the Countess had said to him.

❧ TWENTY ❧

'SHALL I SEE YOU AGAIN?' she asked, as she held out her hand to take leave. 'It is quite understood between us, I suppose, about the play?'

Francis recalled his extraordinary experience of that evening in the renumbered room. 'My stay in Venice is uncertain,' he replied. 'If you have anything more to say about this dramatic venture of yours, it may be as well to say it now. Have you decided on a subject already? I know the public taste in England better than you do – I might save you some waste of time and trouble, if you have not chosen your subject wisely.'

'I don't care what subject I write about, so long as I write,' she answered carelessly. 'If *you* have got a subject in your head, give it to me. I answer for the characters and the dialogue.'

'You answer for the characters and the dialogue,' Francis repeated. 'That's a bold way of speaking for a beginner! I wonder if I should shake your sublime confidence in yourself, if I suggested the most ticklish subject to handle which is known to the stage? What do you say, Countess, to entering the lists with Shakespeare, and trying a drama with a ghost in it? A true story, mind! founded on events in this very city in which you and I are interested.'

She caught him by the arm, and drew him away from the crowded colonnade into the solitary middle space of the square. 'Now tell me!' she said eagerly. 'Here, where nobody is near us. How am I interested in it? How? how?'

Still holding his arm, she shook him in her impatience to hear the coming disclosure. For a moment he hesitated. Thus far, amused by her ignorant belief in herself, he had merely spoken in jest. Now, for the first time, impressed by her irresistible earnestness, he began to consider what he was about from a more serious point of view. With her knowledge of all that had passed in the old palace, before its transformation into an hotel, it was surely possible that she might suggest some explanation of what had happened to his brother, and sister, and himself. Or, failing to do this, she might accidentally reveal some event in her own experience which, acting as a hint to a competent dramatist, might prove to be the making of a play. The prosperity of his theatre was his one serious object in life. 'I may be on the trace of another "Corsican Brothers",' he thought. 'A new piece of that sort would be ten thousand pounds in my pocket, at least.'

With these motives (worthy of the single-hearted devotion to dramatic business which made Francis a successful manager) he related, without further hesitation, what his own experience had been, and what the experience of his relatives had been, in the haunted hotel. He even described the outbreak of superstitious terror which had escaped Mrs Norbury's ignorant mind. 'Sad stuff, if you look at it reasonably,' he remarked. 'But there is something dramatic in the notion of the ghostly influence making itself felt by the relations in succession, as they one after another enter the fatal room – until the one chosen relative comes who will see the Unearthly Creature, and know the terrible truth. Material for a play, Countess – first-rate material for a play!'

There he paused. She neither moved nor spoke. He stooped and looked closer at her.

What impression had he produced? It was an impression which his utmost ingenuity had failed to anticipate. She stood by his side – just as she had stood before Agnes when her question about Ferrari was plainly answered at last – like a woman turned to stone. Her eyes were vacant and rigid; all the life in her face had faded out of it. Francis took her by the hand. Her hand was as cold as the pavement that they were standing on. He asked her if she was ill.

Not a muscle in her moved. He might as well have spoken to the dead.

'Surely,' he said, 'you are not foolish enough to take what I have been telling you seriously?'

Her lips moved slowly. As it seemed, she was making an effort to speak to him.

'Louder,' he said. 'I can't hear you.'

She struggled to recover possession of herself. A faint light began to soften the dull cold stare of her eyes. In a moment more she spoke so that he could hear her.

'I never thought of the other world,' she murmured, in low dull tones, like a woman talking in her sleep.

Her mind had gone back to the day of her last memorable interview with Agnes; she was slowly recalling the confession that had escaped her, the warning words which she had spoken at that past time. Necessarily incapable of understanding this, Francis looked at her in perplexity. She went on in the same dull vacant tone, steadily following out her own train of thought, with her heedless eyes on his face, and her wandering mind far away from him.

'I said some trifling event would bring us together the next time. I was wrong. No trifling event will bring us together. I said I might be the person who told her what had become of Ferrari, if she forced me to it. Shall I feel some other influence than hers? Will he force me to it? When she sees him, shall I see him too?'

Her head sank a little; her heavy eyelids dropped slowly; she heaved a long low weary sigh. Francis put her arm in his, and made an attempt to rouse her.

'Come, Countess, you are weary and over-wrought. We have had enough talking to-night. Let me see you safe back to your hotel. Is it far from here?'

She started when he moved, and obliged her to move with him, as if he had suddenly awakened her out of a deep sleep.

'Not far,' she said faintly. 'The old hotel on the quay. My mind's in a strange state; I have forgotten the name.'

'Danieli's?'

'Yes!'

He led her on slowly. She accompanied him in silence as far as the end of the Piazzetta. There, when the full view of the moonlit Lagoon revealed itself, she stopped him as he turned towards the Riva degli Schiavoni. 'I have something to ask you. I want to wait and think.'

She recovered her lost idea, after a long pause.

'Are you going to sleep in the room to-night?' she asked.

He told her that another traveller was in possession of the room that night. 'But the manager has reserved it for me to-morrow,' he added, 'if I wish to have it.'

'No,' she said. 'You must give it up.'

'To whom?'

'To me!'

He started. 'After what I have told you, do you really wish to sleep in that room to-morrow night?'

'I *must* sleep in it.'

'Are you not afraid?'

'I am horribly afraid.'

'So I should have thought, after what I have observed in you to-night. Why should you take the room? You are not obliged to occupy it, unless you like.'

'I was not obliged to go to Venice, when I left America,' she answered. 'And yet I came here. I must take the room, and keep the room, until—' She broke off at those words. 'Never mind the rest,' she said. 'It doesn't interest you.'

It was useless to dispute with her. Francis changed the subject. 'We can do nothing to-night,' he said. 'I will call on you to-morrow morning and hear what you think of it then.'

They moved on again to the hotel. As they approached the door, Francis asked if she was staying in Venice under her own name.

She shook her head. 'As your brother's widow, I am known here. As Countess Narona, I am known here. I want to be unknown, this time, to strangers in Venice; I am travelling under a common English name.' She hesitated, and stood still. 'What has come to me?' she muttered to herself. 'Some things I remember; and some I forget. I forgot Danieli's – and now I forget my English name.' She drew him hurriedly into the hall of the hotel, on the wall of which hung a list of visitor's names. Running her finger slowly down the list, she pointed to the English name that she has assumed: – 'Mrs James.'

'Remember that when you call to-morrow,' she said. 'My head is heavy. Good night.'

Francis went back to his own hotel, wondering what the events of the next day would bring forth. A new turn in his affairs had taken place in his absence. As he crossed the hall, he was requested by one of the servants to walk into the private office. The manager was waiting there with a gravely preoccupied manner, as if he had something serious to say.

He regretted to hear that Mr Francis Westwick had, like other members of his family, discovered mysterious sources of discomfort in the new hotel. He had been informed in strict confidence of Mr Westwick's extraordinary objection to the atmosphere of the bedroom upstairs. Without presuming to discuss the matter, he must beg to be excused from reserving the room for Mr Westwick after what had happened.

Francis answered sharply, a little ruffled by the tone in which the manager had spoken to him. 'I might, very possibly, have declined to sleep in the room, if you *had* reserved it,' he said. 'Do you wish me to leave the hotel?'

The manager saw the error that he had committed, and hastened to repair it. 'Certainly not, sir! We will do our best to make you comfortable while you stay with us. I beg your pardon, if I have said anything to offend you. The reputation of an establishment like this is a matter of very serious importance. May I hope that you will do us the great favour to say nothing about what has happened upstairs? The two French gentlemen have kindly promised to keep it a secret.'

This apology left Francis no polite alternative but to grant the manager's request. 'There is an end to the Countess's wild scheme,' he thought to himself, as he retired for the night. 'So much the better for the Countess!'

He rose late the next morning. Inquiring for his Parisian friends, he was informed that both the French gentlemen had left for Milan. As he crossed the hall, on his way to the restaurant, he noticed the head porter chalking the numbers of the rooms on some articles of luggage which were waiting to go upstairs. One trunk attracted his attention by the extraordinary number of old travelling labels left on it. The porter was marking it at the moment – and the number was, '13 A'. Francis instantly looked at the card fastened on the lid. It bore the common English name, 'Mrs James'! He at once inquired about the lady. She had arrived early that morning, and she was then in the Reading Room. Looking into the room, he discovered a lady in it alone. Advancing a little nearer, he found himself face to face with the Countess.

She was seated in a dark corner, with her head down and her arms crossed over her bosom. 'Yes,' she said, in a tone of weary impatience, before Francis could speak to her. 'I thought it best not to wait for you – I determined to get here before anybody else could take the room.'

'Have you taken it for long?' Francis asked.

'You told me Miss Lockwood would be here in a week's time. I have taken it for a week.'

'What has Miss Lockwood to do with it?'

'She has everything to do with it – she must sleep in the room. I shall give the room up to her when she comes here.'

Francis began to understand the superstitious purpose that she had in view. 'Are you (an educated woman) really of the same opinion as my sister's maid!' he exclaimed. 'Assuming your absurd superstition to be a serious thing, you are taking the wrong means to prove it true. If I and my brother and sister have seen nothing, how should Agnes Lockwood discover what was not revealed to us? She is only distantly related to the Montbarrys – she is only our cousin.'

'She was nearer to the heart of the Montbarry who is dead than any of you,' the Countess answered sternly. 'To the last day of his life, my miserable husband repented his desertion of her. She will see what none of you have seen – she shall have the room.'

Francis listened, utterly at a loss to account for the motives that animated her. 'I don't see what interest *you* have in trying this extraordinary experiment,' he said.

'It is my interest *not* to try it! It is my interest to fly from Venice, and never set eyes on Agnes Lockwood or any of your family again!'

'What prevents you from doing that?'

She started to her feet and looked at him wildly. 'I know no more what prevents me than you do!' she burst out. 'Some will that is stronger than mine drives me on to my destruction, in spite of my own self!' She suddenly sat down again, and waved her hand for him to go. 'Leave me,' she said. 'Leave me to my thoughts.'

Francis left her, firmly persuaded by this time that she was out of her senses. For the rest of the day, he saw nothing of her. The night, so far as he knew, passed quietly. The next morning he breakfasted early, determining to wait in the restaurant for the appearance of the Countess. She came in and ordered her breakfast quietly, looking dull and worn and self-absorbed, as she had looked when he last saw her. He hastened to her table, and asked if anything had happened in the night.

'Nothing,' she answered.

'You have rested as well as usual?'

'Quite as well as usual. Have you had any letters this morning? Have you heard when she is coming?'

'I have had no letters. Are you really going to stay here? Has your experience of last night not altered the opinion which you expressed to me yesterday?'

'Not in the least.'

The momentary gleam of animation which had crossed her face when she questioned him about Agnes, died out of it again when he answered her. She looked, she spoke, she ate her breakfast, with a vacant resignation, like a woman who had done with hopes, done with interests, done with everything but the mechanical movements and instincts of life.

Francis went out, on the customary travellers' pilgrimage to the shrines of Titian and Tintoret. After some hours of absence, he found a letter waiting for him when he got back to the hotel. It was written by his brother Henry, and it recommended him to return to Milan immediately. The proprietor of a French theatre, recently arrived from Venice, was trying to induce the famous dancer whom Francis had engaged to break faith with him and accept a higher salary.

Having made this startling announcement, Henry proceeded to inform his brother that Lord and Lady Montbarry, with Agnes and the children, would arrive in Venice in three days more. 'They know nothing of our adventures at the hotel,' Henry wrote; 'and they have telegraphed to the manager for the accommodation that they want. There would be something absurdly superstitious in our giving them a warning which would frighten the ladies and children out of the best hotel in Venice. We shall be a strong party this time – too strong a party for ghosts! I shall meet the travellers on their arrival, of course, and try my luck again at what you call the Haunted Hotel. Arthur Barville and his wife have already got as far on their way as Trent; and two of the lady's relations have arranged to accompany them on the journey to Venice.'

Naturally indignant at the conduct of his Parisian colleague, Francis made his preparations for returning to Milan by the train of that day.

On his way out, he asked the manager if his brother's telegram had been received. The telegram had arrived, and, to the surprise of Francis, the rooms were already reserved. 'I thought you would refuse to let any more of the family into the house,' he said satirically. The manager answered (with the due dash of respect) in the same tone. 'Number 13 A is safe, sir, in the occupation of a stranger. I am the servant of the Company; and I dare not turn money out of the hotel.'

Hearing this, Francis said good-bye – and said nothing more. He was ashamed to acknowledge it to himself, but he felt an irresistible curiosity to know what would happen when Agnes arrived at the hotel. Besides, 'Mrs James' had reposed a confidence in him. He got into his gondola, respecting the confidence of 'Mrs James'.

Towards evening on the third day, Lord Montbarry and his travelling companions arrived, punctual to their appointment.

'Mrs James', sitting at the window of her room watching for them, saw the new Lord land from the gondola first. He handed his wife to the steps. The three children were next committed to his care. Last of all, Agnes appeared in the little black doorway of the gondola cabin, and, taking Lord Montbarry's hand, passed in her turn to the steps. She wore no veil. As she ascended to the door of the hotel, the Countess (eyeing her through an opera-glass) noticed that she paused to look at the outside of the building, and that her face was very pale.

❧ TWENTY-ONE ❧

LORD AND LADY MONTBARRY were received by the housekeeper; the manager being absent for a day or two on business connected with the affairs of the hotel.

The rooms reserved for the travellers on the first floor were three in number; consisting of two bedrooms opening into each other, and communicating on the left with a drawing-room. Complete so far, the arrangements proved to be less satisfactory in reference to the third bedroom required for Agnes and for the eldest daughter of Lord Montbarry, who usually slept with her on their travels. The bed-chamber on the right of the drawing-room was already occupied by an English widow lady. Other bed-chambers at the other end of the corridor were also let in every case. There was accordingly no alternative but to place at the disposal of Agnes a comfortable room on the second floor. Lady Montbarry vainly complained of this separation of one of the members of her travelling party from the rest. The housekeeper politely hinted that it was impossible for her to ask other travellers to give up their rooms. She could only express her regret, and assure Miss Lockwood that her bed-chamber on the second floor was one of the best rooms in that part of the hotel.

On the retirement of the housekeeper, Lady Montbarry noticed that Agnes had seated herself apart, feeling apparently no interest in the question of the bedrooms. Was she ill? No; she felt a little unnerved by the railway journey, and that was all. Hearing this, Lord Montbarry proposed that she should go out with him, and try the experiment of half an hour's walk in the cool evening air. Agnes gladly accepted the suggestion. They directed their steps towards the square of St Mark, so as to enjoy the breeze blowing over the lagoon. It was the first visit of Agnes to Venice. The fascination of the wonderful city of the waters exerted its full influence over her sensitive nature. The proposed half-hour of the walk had passed away, and was fast expanding to half an hour more, before Lord Montbarry could persuade his companion to remember that dinner was waiting for them. As they returned, passing under the colonnade, neither of them noticed a lady in deep mourning, loitering in the open space of the square. She started as she recognized Agnes walking with the new Lord Montbarry – hesitated for a moment – and then followed them, at a discreet distance, back to the hotel.

Lady Montbarry received Agnes in high spirits – with news of an event which had happened in her absence.

She had not left the hotel more than ten minutes, before a little note in pencil was brought to Lady Montbarry by the housekeeper. The writer proved to be no less a person than the widow lady who occupied the room on the other side of the drawing-room, which her ladyship had vainly hoped to secure for Agnes. Writing under the name of Mrs James, the polite widow explained that she had heard from the housekeeper of the disappointment experienced by Lady Montbarry in the matter of the rooms. Mrs James was quite alone; and as long as her bed-chamber was airy and comfortable, it mattered nothing to her whether she slept on the first or the second floor of the house. She had accordingly much pleasure in proposing to change rooms with Miss Lockwood. Her luggage had already been removed, and Miss Lockwood had only to take possession of the room (Number 13 A), which was now entirely at her disposal.

'I immediately proposed to see Mrs James,' Lady Montbarry continued, 'and to thank her personally for her extreme kindness. But I was informed that she had gone out, without leaving word at what hour she might be expected to return. I have written a little note of thanks, saying that we hope to have the pleasure of personally expressing our sense of Mrs James's, courtesy to-morrow. In the mean time, Agnes, I have ordered your boxes to be removed downstairs. Go! – and judge for yourself, my dear, if that good lady has not given up to you the prettiest room in the house!'

With those words, Lady Montbarry left Miss Lockwood to make a hasty toilet for dinner.

The new room at once produced a favourable impression on Agnes. The large window, opening into a balcony, commanded an admirable view of the canal. The decorations on the walls and ceiling were skillfully copied from the exquisitely graceful designs of Raphael in the Vatican. The massive wardrobe possessed compartments of unusual size, in which double the number of dresses that Agnes possessed might have been conveniently hung at full length. In the inner corner of the room, near the head of the bedstead, there was a recess which had been turned into a little dressing-room, and which opened by a second door on the inferior staircase of the hotel, commonly used by the servants. Noticing these aspects of the room at a glance, Agnes made the necessary change in her dress, as quickly as possible. On her way back to the drawing-room she was addressed by a chambermaid in the corridor who asked for her key.

'I will put your room tidy for the night, Miss,' the woman said, 'and I will then bring the key back to you in the drawing-room.'

While the chambermaid was at her work, a solitary lady, loitering about the corridor of the second storey, was watching her over the banisters. After a while, the maid appeared, with her pail in her hand, leaving the room by way of the dressing-room and the back stairs. As she passed out of sight, the lady on the second floor (no other, it is needless to add, than the Countess herself) ran swiftly down the stairs, entered the bed-chamber by the principal door, and hid herself in the empty side compartment of the wardrobe. The chambermaid returned, completed her work, locked the door of the dressing-room on the inner side, locked the principal entrance-door on leaving the room, and returned the key to Agnes in the drawing-room.

The travellers were just sitting down to their late dinner, when one of the children noticed that Agnes was not wearing her watch. Had she left it in her bed-chamber in the hurry of changing her dress? She rose from the table at once in search of her watch; Lady Montbarry advising her, as she went out, to see to the security of her bed-chamber, in the event of there being thieves in the house. Agnes found her watch, forgotten on the toilet table, as she had anticipated. Before leaving the room again she acted on Lady Montbarry's advice, and tried the key in the lock of the dressing-room door. It was properly secured. She left the bed-chamber, locking the main door behind her.

Immediately on her departure, the Countess, oppressed by the confined air in the wardrobe, ventured on stepping out of her hiding place into the empty room.

Entering the dressing-room, she listened at the door, until the silence outside informed her that the corridor was empty. Upon this, she unlocked the door, and, passing out, closed it again softly; leaving it to all appearance (when viewed on the inner side) as carefully secured as Agnes had seen it when she tried the key in the lock with her own hand.

While the Montbarrys were still at dinner, Henry Westwick joined them, arriving from Milan.

When he entered the room, and again when he advanced to shake hands with her, Agnes was conscious of a latent feeling which secretly reciprocated Henry's unconcealed pleasure on meeting her again. For a moment only, she returned his look; and in that moment her own observation told her that she had silently encouraged him to hope. She saw it in the sudden glow of happiness which overspread his face; and she confusedly took refuge in the usual conventional inquiries relating to the relatives whom he had left at Milan.

Taking his place at the table, Henry gave a most amusing account of the position of his brother Francis between the mercenary opera-dancer on one side, and the unscrupulous manager of the French theatre on the other. Matters had proceeded to such extremities, that the law had been called on to interfere, and had decided the dispute in favour of Francis. On winning the victory the English manager had at once left Milan, recalled to London by the affairs of his theatre. He was accompanied on the journey back, as he had been accompanied on the journey out, by his sister. Resolved, after passing two nights of terror in the Venetian hotel, never to enter it again, Mrs Norbury asked to be excused from appearing at the family festival, on the ground of ill-health. At her age, travelling fatigued her, and she was glad to take advantage of her brother's escort to return to England.

While the talk at the dinner-table flowed easily onward, the evening-time advanced to night – and it became necessary to think of sending the children to bed.

As Agnes rose to leave the room, accompanied by the eldest girl, she observed with surprise that Henry's manner suddenly changed. He looked serious and pre-occupied; and when his niece wished him good night, he abruptly said to her, 'Lucy, I want to know what part of the hotel you sleep in?' Lucy, puzzled by the question, answered that she was going to sleep, as usual, with 'Aunt Agnes'. Not satisfied with that reply, Henry next inquired whether the bedroom was near the rooms occupied by the other members of the travelling party. Answering for the child, and wondering what Henry's object could possibly be, Agnes mentioned the polite sacrifice made to her convenience by Mrs James. 'Thanks to that lady's kindness,' she said, 'Lucy and I are only on the other side of the drawing-room.' Henry made no remark; he looked incomprehensibly discontented as he opened the door for Agnes and her companion to pass out. After wishing them good night, he waited in the corridor until he saw them enter the fatal corner-room – and then he called abruptly to his brother, 'Come out, Stephen, and let us smoke!'

As soon as the two brothers were at liberty to speak together privately, Henry explained the motive which had led his strange inquiries about the bed-rooms. Francis had informed him of the meeting with the Countess at Venice, and of all that had followed it; and Henry now carefully repeated the narrative to his brother in all its details. 'I am not satisfied,' he added, 'about that woman's purpose in giving up her room. Without alarming the ladies by telling them what I have just told you, can you not warn Agnes to be careful in securing her door?'

Lord Montbarry replied, that the warning had been already given by his wife, and that Agnes might be trusted to take good care of herself and her little bedfellow. For the rest, he looked upon the story of the Countess and her superstitions as a piece of theatrical exaggeration, amusing enough in itself, but unworthy of a moment's serious attention.

While the gentlemen were absent from the hotel, the room which had been already associated with so many startling circumstances, became the scene of another strange event in which Lady Montbarry's eldest child was concerned.

Little Lucy had been got ready for bed as usual, and had (so far) taken hardly any notice of the new room. As she knelt down to say her prayers, she happened to look up at that part of the ceiling above her which was just over the head of the bed. The next instant she alarmed Agnes, by starting to her feet with a cry of terror, and pointing to a small brown spot on one of the white panelled spaces of the carved ceiling. 'It's a spot of blood!' the child exclaimed. 'Take me away! I won't sleep here!'

Seeing plainly that it would be useless to reason with her while she was in the room, Agnes hurriedly wrapped Lucy in a dressing-gown, and carried her back to her mother in the drawing-room. Here, the ladies did their best to soothe and reassure the trembling girl. The effort proved to be useless; the impression that had been produced on the young and sensitive mind was not to be removed by persuasion. Lucy could give no explanation of the panic of terror that had seized her. She was quite unable to say why the spot on the ceiling looked like the colour of a spot of blood. She only knew that she should die of terror if she saw it again. Under these circumstances, but one alternative was left. It was arranged that the child should pass the night in the room occupied by her two younger sisters and the nurse.

In half an hour more, Lucy was peacefully asleep with her arm round her sister's neck. Lady Montbarry went back with Agnes to her room to see the spot on the ceiling which had so strangely frightened the child. It was so small as to be only just perceptible, and it had in all probability been caused by the carelessness of a workman, or by a dripping from water accidentally spilt on the floor of the room above.

'I really cannot understand why Lucy should place such a shocking interpretation on such a trifling thing,' Lady Montbarry remarked.

'I suspect the nurse is in some way answerable for what has happened,' Agnes suggested. 'She may quite possibly have been telling Lucy some tragic nursery story which has left its mischievous impression behind it. Persons in her position are sadly ignorant of the danger of exciting a child's imagination. You had better caution the nurse to-morrow.'

Lady Montbarry looked round the room with admiration. 'Is it not prettily decorated?' she said. 'I suppose, Agnes, you don't mind sleeping here by yourself?'

Agnes laughed. 'I feel so tired,' she replied, 'that I was thinking of bidding you good-night, instead of going back to the drawing-room.'

Lady Montbarry turned towards the door. 'I see your jewel-case on the table,' she resumed. 'Don't forget to lock the other door there, in the dressing-room.'

'I have already seen to it, and tried the key myself,' said Agnes. 'Can I be of any use to you before I go to bed?'

'No, my dear, thank you; I feel sleepy enough to follow your example. Good night, Agnes – and pleasant dreams on your first night in Venice.'

❧ TWENTY-TWO ❦

HAVING CLOSED AND SECURED THE door on Lady Montbarry's departure, Agnes put on her dressing-gown, and, turning to her open boxes, began the business of unpacking. In the hurry of making her toilet for dinner, she had taken the first dress that lay uppermost in the trunk, and had thrown her travelling costume on the bed. She now opened the doors of the wardrobe for the first time, and began to hang her dresses on the hooks in the large compartment on one side.

After a few minutes only of this occupation, she grew weary of it, and decided on leaving the trunks as they were, until the next morning. The oppressive south wind, which had blown throughout the day, still prevailed at night. The atmosphere of the room felt close; Agnes threw a shawl over her head and shoulders, and, opening the window, stepped into the balcony to look at the view.

The night was heavy and overcast: nothing could be distinctly seen. The canal beneath the window looked like a black gulf; the opposite houses were barely visible as a row of shadows, dimly relieved against the starless and moonless sky. At long intervals, the warning cry of a belated gondolier was just audible, as he turned the corner of a distant canal, and called to invisible boats which might be approaching him in the darkness. Now and then, the nearer dip of an oar in the water told of the viewless passage of other gondolas bringing guests back to the hotel. Excepting these rare sounds, the mysterious night-silence of Venice was literally the silence of the grave.

Leaning on the parapet of the balcony, Agnes looked vacantly into the black void beneath. Her thoughts reverted to the miserable man who had broken his pledged faith to her, and who had died in that house. Some change seemed to have come over her, since her arrival in Venice; some new influence appeared to be at work. For the first time in her experience of herself, compassion and regret were not the only emotions aroused in her by the remembrance of the dead Montbarry. A keen sense of the wrong that she had suffered, never yet felt by that gentle and forgiving nature, was felt by it now. She found herself thinking of the bygone days of her humiliation almost as harshly as Henry Westwick had thought of them – she who had rebuked him the last time he had spoken slightingly of his brother in her presence! A sudden fear and doubt of herself, startled her physically as well as morally. She turned from the shadowy abyss of the dark water as if the mystery and the gloom of it had been answerable for the emotions which had taken her by surprise. Abruptly closing the window, she threw aside her shawl, and lit the candles on the mantelpiece, impelled by a sudden craving for light in the solitude of her room.

The cheering brightness round her, contrasting with the black gloom outside, restored her spirits. She felt herself enjoying the light like a child!

Would it be well (she asked herself) to get ready for bed? No! The sense of drowsy fatigue that she had felt half an hour since was gone. She returned to the dull employment of unpacking her boxes. After a few minutes only, the occupation became irksome to her once more. She sat down by the table, and took up a guide-book. 'Suppose I inform myself,' she thought, 'on the subject of Venice?'

Her attention wandered from the book, before she had turned the first page of it.

The image of Henry Westwick was the presiding image in her memory now. Recalling the minutest incidents and details of the evening, she could think of nothing which presented him under other than a favourable and interesting aspect. She smiled to herself softly, her colour rose by fine gradations, as she felt the full luxury of dwelling on the perfect truth and modesty of his devotion to her. Was the depression of spirits from which she had suffered so persistently on her travels attributable, by any chance, to their long separation from each other – embittered perhaps by her own vain regret when she remembered her harsh reception of him in Paris? Suddenly conscious of this bold question, and of the self-abandonment which it implied, she returned mechanically to her book, distrusting the unrestrained liberty of her own thoughts. What lurking temptations to forbidden tenderness find their hiding places in a woman's dressing-gown, when she is alone in her room at night! With her heart in the tomb of the dead Montbarry, could Agnes even think of another man, and think of love? How shameful! how unworthy of her! For the second time, she tried to interest herself in the guide-book – and once more she tried in vain. Throwing the book aside, she turned desperately to the one resource that was left, to her luggage – resolved to fatigue herself without mercy, until she was weary enough and sleepy enough to find a safe refuge in bed.

For some little time, she persisted in the monotonous occupation of transferring her clothes from her trunk to the wardrobe. The large clock in the hall, striking midnight, reminded her that it was getting late. She sat down for a moment in an arm-chair by the bedside, to rest.

The silence in the house now caught her attention, and held it – held it disagreeably. Was everybody in bed and asleep but herself? Surely it was time for her to follow the general example? With a certain irritable nervous haste, she rose again and undressed herself. 'I have lost two hours of rest,' she thought, frowning at the reflection of herself in the glass, as she arranged her hair for the night. 'I shall be good for nothing to-morrow!'

She lit the night-light, and extinguished the candles – with one exception, which she removed to a little table, placed on the side of the bed opposite to the side occupied by the arm-chair. Having put her travelling-box of matches and the guide-book near the candle, in case she might be sleepless and might want to read, she blew out the light, and laid her head on the pillow.

The curtains of the bed were looped back to let the air pass freely over her. Lying on her left side, with her face turned away from the table, she could see the arm-chair by the dim night-light. It had a chintz covering – representing large bunches of roses scattered over a pale green ground. She tried to weary herself into drowsiness by counting over and over again the bunches of roses that were visible from her point of view. Twice her attention was distracted from the counting, by sounds outside – by the clock chiming the half-hour past twelve; and then again, by the fall of a pair of boots on the upper floor, thrown out to be cleaned, with that barbarous disregard of the comfort of others which is observable in humanity when it inhabits an hotel. In the silence that followed these passing disturbances, Agnes went on counting the roses on the arm-chair, more and more slowly. Before long, she confused herself in the figures – tried to begin counting again – thought she would wait a little first – felt her eyelids drooping, and her head reclining lower and lower on the pillow – sighed faintly – and sank into sleep.

How long that first sleep lasted, she never knew. She could only remember, in the after-time, that she woke instantly.

Every faculty and perception in her passed the boundary line between insensibility and consciousness, so to speak, at a leap. Without knowing why, she sat up suddenly in the bed, listening for she knew not what. Her head was in a whirl; her heart beat furiously, without any assignable cause. But one trivial event had happened during the interval while she had been asleep. The night-light had gone out; and the room, as a matter of course, was in total darkness.

She felt for the match-box, and paused after finding it. A vague sense of confusion was still in her mind. She was in no hurry to light the match. The pause in the darkness was, for the moment, agreeable to her.

In the quieter flow of her thoughts during this interval, she could ask herself the natural question: – What cause had awakened her so suddenly, and had so strangely shaken her nerves? Had it been the influence of a dream? She had not dreamed at all – or, to speak more correctly, she had no waking remembrance of having dreamed. The mystery was beyond her fathoming: the darkness began to oppress her. She struck the match on the box, and lit her candle.

As the welcome light diffused itself over the room, she turned from the table and looked towards the other side of the bed.

In the moment when she turned, the chill of a sudden terror gripped her round the heart, as with the clasp of an icy hand.

She was not alone in her room!

There – in the chair at the bedside – there, suddenly revealed under the flow of light from the candle, was the figure of a woman, reclining. Her head lay back over the chair. Her face, turned up to the ceiling, had the eyes closed, as if she was wrapped in a deep sleep.

The shock of the discovery held Agnes speechless and helpless. Her first conscious action, when she was in some degree mistress of herself again, was to lean over the bed, and to look closer at the woman who had so incomprehensibly stolen into her room in the dead of night. One glance was enough: she started back with a cry of amazement. The person in the chair was no other than the widow of the dead Montbarry – the woman who had warned her that they were to meet again, and that the place might be Venice!

Her courage returned to her, stung into action by the natural sense of indignation which the presence of the Countess provoked.

'Wake up!' she called out. 'How dare you come here? How did you get in? Leave the room – or I will call for help!'

She raised her voice at the last words. It produced no effect. Leaning farther over the bed, she boldly took the Countess by the shoulder and shook her. Not even this effort succeeded in rousing the sleeping woman. She still lay back in the chair, possessed by a torpor like the torpor of death – insensible to sound, insensible to touch. Was she really sleeping? Or had she fainted?

Agnes looked closer at her. She had not fainted. Her breathing was audible, rising and falling in deep heavy gaps. At intervals she ground her teeth savagely. Beads of perspiration stood thickly on her forehead. Her clenched hands rose and fell slowly from time to time on her lap. Was she in the agony of a dream? or was she spiritually conscious of something hidden in the room?

The doubt involved in that last question was unendurable. Agnes determined to rouse the servants who kept watch in the hotel at night.

The bell-handle was fixed to the wall, on the side of the bed by which the table stood.

She raised herself from the crouching position which she had assumed in looking close at the Countess; and, turning towards the other side of the bed, stretched out her hand to the bell. At the same instant, she stopped and looked upward. Her hand fell helplessly at her side. She shuddered, and sank back on the pillow.

What had she seen?

She had seen another intruder in her room.

Midway between her face and the ceiling, there hovered a human head – severed at the neck, like a head struck from the body by the guillotine.

Nothing visible, nothing audible, had given her any intelligible warning of its appearance. Silently and suddenly, the head had taken its place above her. No supernatural change had passed over the room, or was perceptible in it now. The dumbly-tortured figure in the chair; the broad window opposite the foot of the bed, with the black night beyond it; the candle burning on the table – these, and all other objects in the room, remained unaltered. One object more, unutterably horrid, had been added to the rest. That was the only change – no more, no less.

By the yellow candlelight she saw the head distinctly, hovering in mid-air above her. She looked at it steadfastly, spellbound by the terror that held her.

The flesh of the face was gone. The shrivelled skin was darkened in hue, like the skin of an Egyptian mummy – except at the neck. There it was of a lighter colour; there it showed spots and splashes of the hue of the brown spot on the ceiling, which the child's fanciful terror had distorted into the likeness of a spot of blood. Thin remains of a discoloured moustache and whiskers, hanging over the upper lip, and over the hollows where the cheeks had once been, made the head just recognizable as the head of a man. Over all the features death and time had done their obliterating work. The eyelids were closed. The hair on the skull, discoloured like the hair on the face, had been burnt away in places. The bluish lips, parted in a fixed grin, showed the double row of teeth. By slow degrees, the hovering head (perfectly still when she first saw it) began to descend towards Agnes as she lay beneath. By slow degrees, that strange doubly-blended odour, which the Commissioners had discovered in the vaults of the old palace – which had sickened Francis Westwick in the bed-chamber of the new hotel – spread its fetid exhalations over the room. Downward and downward the hideous apparition made its slow progress, until it stopped close over Agnes –

stopped, and turned slowly, so that the face of it confronted the upturned face of the woman in the chair.

There was a pause. Then, a supernatural movement disturbed the rigid repose of the dead face.

The closed eyelids opened slowly. The eyes revealed themselves, bright with the glassy film of death – and fixed their dreadful look on the woman in the chair.

Agnes saw that look; saw the eyelids of the living woman open slowly like the eyelids of the dead; saw her rise, as if in obedience to some silent command – and saw no more.

Her next conscious impression was of the sunlight pouring in at the window; of the friendly presence of Lady Montbarry at the bedside; and of the children's wondering faces peeping in at the door.

❧ TWENTY-THREE ❧

' . . . You have some influence over Agnes. Try what you can do, Henry, to make her take a sensible view of the matter. There is really nothing to make a fuss about. My wife's maid knocked at her door early in the morning, with the customary cup of tea. Getting no answer, she went round to the dressing-room – found the door on that side unlocked – and discovered Agnes on the bed in a fainting fit. With my wife's help, they brought her to herself again; and she told the extraordinary story which I have just repeated to you. You must have seen for yourself that she has been over-fatigued, poor thing, by our long railway journeys; her nerves are out of order – and she is just the person to be easily terrified by a dream. She obstinately refuses, however, to accept this rational view. Don't suppose that I have been severe with her! All that a man can do to humour her I have done. I have written to the Countess (in her assumed name) offering to restore the room to her. She writes back, positively declining to return to it. I have accordingly arranged (so as not to have the thing known in the hotel) to occupy the room for one or two nights, and to leave Agnes to recover her spirits under my wife's care. Is there anything more that I can do? Whatever questions Agnes has asked of me I have answered to the best of my ability; she knows all that you told me about Francis and the Countess last night. But try as I may I can't quiet her mind. I have given up the attempt in despair, and left her in the drawing-room. Go, like a good fellow, and try what you can do to compose her.'

In those words, Lord Montbarry stated the case to his brother from the rational point of view. Henry made no remark, he went straight to the drawing-room.

He found Agnes walking rapidly backwards and forwards, flushed and excited. 'If you come here to say what your brother has been saying to me,' she broke out, before he could speak, 'spare yourself the trouble. I don't want common sense – I want a true friend who will believe in me.'

'I am that friend, Agnes,' Henry answered quietly, 'and you know it.'

'You really believe that I am not deluded by a dream?'

'I know that you are not deluded – in one particular, at least.'

'In what particular?'

'In what you have said of the Countess. It is perfectly true――'

Agnes stopped him there. 'Why do I only hear this morning that the Countess and Mrs James are one and the same person?' she asked distrustfully. 'Why was I not told of it last night?'

'You forget that you had accepted the exchange of rooms before I reached Venice,' Henry replied. 'I felt strongly tempted to tell you, even then – but your sleeping arrangements for the night were all made; I should only have inconvenienced and alarmed you. I waited till the morning, after hearing from my brother that you had yourself seen to your security from any intrusion. How that intrusion was accomplished it is impossible to say. I can only declare that the Countess's presence by your bedside last night was no dream of yours. On her own authority I can testify that it was a reality.'

'On her own authority?' Agnes repeated eagerly. 'Have you seen her this morning?'

'I have seen her not ten minutes since.'

'What was she doing?'

'She was busily engaged in writing. I could not even get her to look at me until I thought of mentioning your name.'

'She remembered me, of course?'

'She remembered you with some difficulty. Finding that she wouldn't answer me on any other terms, I questioned her as if I had come direct from you. Then she spoke. She not only admitted that she had the same superstitious motive for placing you in that room which she had acknowledged to Francis – she even owned that she had been by your bedside, watching through the night, "to see what you saw", as she expressed it. Hearing this, I tried to persuade her to tell me how she got into the room. Unluckily, her manuscript on the table caught her eye; she returned to her writing. "The Baron wants money," she said; "I must get on with my play." What she saw or dreamed, while she was in your room last night, it is at present impossible to discover. But judging by my brother's account of her, as well as by what I remember of her myself, some recent influence has been at work which has produced a marked change in this wretched woman for the worse. Her mind (since last night, perhaps) is partially deranged. One proof of it is that she spoke to me of the Baron as if he were still a living man. When Francis saw her, she declared that the Baron was dead, which is the truth. The United States Consul at Milan showed us the announcement of the death in an American newspaper. So far as I can see, such sense as she still possesses seems to be entirely absorbed in one absurd idea – the idea of writing a play for Francis to bring out at his theatre. He admits that he encouraged her to hope she might get money in this way. I think he did wrong. Don't you agree with me?'

Without heeding the question, Agnes rose abruptly from her chair.

'Do me one more kindness, Henry,' she said. 'Take me to the Countess at once.'

Henry hesitated. 'Are you composed enough to see her, after the shock that you have suffered?' he asked.

She trembled, the flush on her face died away, and left it deadly pale. But she held to her resolution. 'You have heard of what I saw last night?' she said faintly.

'Don't speak of it!' Henry interposed. 'Don't uselessly agitate yourself.'

'I must speak! My mind is full of horrid questions about it. I know I can't identify it – and yet I ask myself over and over again, in whose likeness did it appear? Was it in the likeness of Ferrari? or was it——?' she stopped, shuddering. 'The Countess knows, I must see the Countess!' she resumed vehemently. 'Whether my courage fails me or not, I must make the attempt. Take me to her before I have time to feel afraid of it!'

Henry looked at her anxiously. 'If you are really sure of your own resolution,' he said, 'I agree with you – the sooner you see her the better. You remember how strangely she talked of your influence over her, when she forced her way into your room in London?'

'I remember it perfectly. Why do you ask?'

'For this reason. In the present state of her mind, I doubt if she will be much longer capable of realizing her wild idea of you as the avenging angel who is to bring her to a reckoning for her evil deeds. It may be well to try what your influence can do while she is still capable of feeling it.'

He waited to hear what Agnes would say. She took his arm and led him in silence to the door.

They ascended to the second floor, and, after knocking, entered the Countess's room.

She was still busily engaged in writing. When she looked up from the paper, and saw Agnes, a vacant expression of doubt was the only expression in her wild black eyes. After a few moments, the lost remembrances and associations appeared to return slowly to her mind. The pen dropped from her hand. Haggard and trembling, she looked closer at Agnes, and recognized her at last. 'Has the time come already?' she said in low awe-struck tones. 'Give me a little longer respite, I haven't done my writing yet!'

She dropped on her knees, and held out her clasped hands entreatingly. Agnes was far from having recovered, after the shock that she had suffered in the night: her nerves were far from being equal to the strain that was now laid on them. She was so startled by the change in the Countess, that she was at a loss what to say or to do next. Henry was obliged to speak to her. 'Put your questions while you have the chance,' he said, lowering his voice. 'See! the vacant look is coming over her face again.'

Agnes tried to rally her courage. 'You were in my room last night—' she began. Before she could add a word more, the Countess lifted her hands, and wrung them above her head with a low moan of horror. Agnes shrank back, and turned as if to leave the room. Henry stopped her, and whispered to her to try again. She obeyed him after an effort. 'I slept last night in the room that you gave up to me,' she resumed. 'I saw—'

The Countess suddenly rose to her feet. 'No more of that,' she cried. 'Oh, Jesu Maria! do you think I want to be told what you saw? Do you think I don't know what it means for you and for me? Decide for yourself, Miss. Examine your own mind. Are you well assured that the day of reckoning has come at last? Are you ready to follow me back, through the crimes of the past, to the secrets of the dead?'

She turned again to the writing-table, without waiting to be answered. Her eyes flashed; she looked like her old self once more as she spoke. It was only for a moment. The old ardour and impetuosity were nearly worn out. Her head sank; she sighed heavily as she unlocked a desk which stood on the table. Opening a drawer in the desk, she took out a leaf of vellum, covered with faded writing. Some ragged ends of silken thread were still attached to the leaf, as if it had been torn out of a book.

'Can you read Italian?' she asked, handing the leaf to Agnes.

Agnes answered silently by an inclination of her head.

'The leaf,' the Countess proceeded, 'once belonged to a book in the old library of the palace, while this building was still a palace. By whom it was torn out you have no need to know. For what purpose it was torn out you may discover for yourself, if you will. Read it first – at the fifth line from the top of the page.'

Agnes felt the serious necessity of composing herself. 'Give me a chair,' she said to Henry; 'and I will do my best.' He placed himself behind her chair so that he could look over her shoulder and help her to understand the writing on the leaf. Rendered into English, it ran as follows:-

'I have now completed my literary survey of the first floor of the palace. At the desire of my noble and gracious patron, the lord of this glorious edifice, I next ascend to the second floor, and continue my catalogue or description of the pictures, decorations, and other treasures of art therein contained. Let me begin with the corner room at the western extremity of the palace, called the Room of the Caryatides, from the statues which support the mantel-piece. This work is of comparatively recent execution: it dates from the eighteenth century only, and reveals the corrupt taste of the period in every part of it. Still, there is a certain interest which attaches to the mantel-piece: it conceals a cleverly constructed hiding-place, between the floor of the room and the ceiling of the room beneath, which was made during the last evil days of the Inquisition in Venice, and which is reported to have saved an ancestor of my gracious lord pursued by that terrible tribunal. The machinery of this curious place of concealment has been kept in good order by the present lord, as a species of curiosity. He condescended to show me the method of working it. Approaching the two Caryatides, rest your hand on the forehead (midway between the eyebrows) of the figure which is on your left as you stand opposite to the fireplace, then press the head inwards as if you were pushing it against the wall behind. By doing this, you set in motion the hidden machinery in the wall which turns the hearthstone on a pivot, and discloses the hollow place below. There is room enough in it for a man to lie easily at full length. The method of closing the cavity again is equally simple. Place both your hands on the temples of the figure; pull as if you were pulling it towards you – and the hearthstone will revolve into its proper position again.'

'You need read no further,' said the Countess. 'Be careful to remember what you have read.'

She put back the page of vellum in her writing-desk, locked it, and led the way to the door.

'Come!' she said; 'and see what the mocking Frenchman called "The beginning of the end." '

Agnes was barely able to rise from her chair; she trembled from head to foot. Henry gave her his arm to support her. 'Fear nothing,' he whispered; 'I shall be with you.'

The Countess proceeded along the westward corridor, and stopped at the door numbered Thirty-eight. This was the room which had been inhabited by Baron Rivar in the old days of the palace; it was situated immediately over the bedchamber in which Agnes had passed the night. For the last two days the room had been empty. The absence of luggage in it, when they opened the door, showed that it had not yet been let.

'You see?' said the Countess, pointing to the carved figure at the fire-place; 'and you know what to do. Have I deserved that you should temper justice with mercy?' she went on in lower tones. 'Give me a few hours more to myself. The Baron wants money – I must get on with my play.'

She smiled vacantly, and imitated the action of writing with her right hand as she pronounced the last words. The effort of concentrating her weakened mind on other and less familiar topics than the constant want of money in the Baron's lifetime, and the vague prospect of gain from the still unfinished play, had evidently exhausted her poor reserves of strength. When her request had been granted, she addressed no expressions of gratitude to Agnes; she only said, 'Feel no fear, miss, of my attempting to escape you. Where you are, there I must be till the end comes.'

Her eyes wandered round the room with a last weary and stupefied look. She returned to her writing with slow and feeble steps, like the steps of an old woman.

❧ TWENTY-FOUR ❧

HENRY AND AGNES WERE LEFT ALONE in the Room of the Caryatides.

The person who had written the description of the palace – probably a poor author or artist – had correctly pointed out the defects of the mantel-piece. Bad taste, exhibiting itself on the most costly and splendid scale, was visible in every part of the work. It was nevertheless greatly admired by ignorant travellers of all classes; partly on account of its imposing size, and partly on account of the number of variously-coloured marbles which the sculptor had contrived to introduce into his design. Photographs of the mantel-piece were exhibited in the public rooms, and found a ready sale among English and American visitors to the hotel.

Henry led Agnes to the figure on the left, as they stood facing the empty fire-place. 'Shall I try the experiment,' he asked, 'or will you?' She abruptly drew her arm away from him, and turned back to the door. 'I can't even look at it,' she said. 'That merciless marble face frightens me!'

Henry put his hand on the forehead of the figure. 'What is there to alarm you, my dear, in this conventionally classical face?' he asked jestingly. Before he could press the head inwards, Agnes hurriedly opened the door. 'Wait till I am out of the room!' she cried. 'The bare idea of what you may find there horrifies me!' She looked back into the room as she crossed the threshold. 'I won't leave you altogether,' she said, 'I will wait outside.'

She closed the door. Left by himself, Henry lifted his hand once more to the marble forehead of the figure.

For the second time, he was checked on the point of setting the machinery of the hiding-place in motion. On this occasion, the interruption came from an outbreak of friendly voices in the corridor. A woman's voice exclaimed, 'Dearest Agnes, how glad I am to see you again!' A man's voice followed, offering to introduce some friend to 'Miss Lockwood'. A third voice (which Henry recognized as the voice of the manager of the hotel) became audible next, directing the housekeeper to show the ladies and gentlemen the vacant apartments at the other end of the corridor. 'If more accommodation is wanted,' the manager went on, 'I have a charming room to let here.' He opened the door as he spoke, and found himself face to face with Henry Westwick.

'This is indeed an agreeable surprise, sir!' said the manager cheerfully. 'You are admiring our famous chimney-piece, I see. May I ask, Mr Westwick, how you find yourself in the hotel, this time? Have the supernatural influences affected your appetite again?'

'The supernatural influences have spared me, this time,' Henry answered. 'Perhaps you may yet find that they have affected some other member of the family.' He spoke gravely, resenting the familiar tone in which the manager had referred to his previous visit to the hotel. 'Have you just returned?' he asked, by way of changing the topic.

'Just this minute, sir. I had the honour of travelling in the same train with friends of yours who have arrived at the hotel – Mr and Mrs Arthur Barville, and their travelling companions. Miss Lockwood is with them, looking at the rooms. They will be here before long, if they find it convenient to have an extra room at their disposal.'

This announcement decided Henry on exploring the hiding-place, before the interruption occurred. It had crossed his mind, when Agnes left him, that he ought perhaps to have a witness, in the not very probable event of some alarming discovery taking place. The too-familiar manager, suspecting nothing, was there at his disposal. He turned again to the Caryan figure, maliciously resolving to make the manager his witness.

'I am delighted to hear that our friends have arrived at last,' he said. 'Before I shake hands with them, let me ask you a question about this queer work of art here. I see photographs of it downstairs. Are they for sale?'

'Certainly, Mr Westwick!'

'Do you think the chimney-piece is as solid as it looks?' Henry proceeded. 'When you came in, I was just wondering whether this figure here had not accidentally got loosened from the wall behind it.' He laid his hand on the marble forehead, for the third time. 'To my eye, it looks a little out of the perpendicular. I almost fancied I could jog the head just now, when I touched it.' He pressed the head inwards as he said those words.

A sound of jarring iron was instantly audible behind the wall. The solid hearthstone in front of the fire-place turned slowly at the feet of the two men, and disclosed a dark cavity below. At the same moment, the strange and sickening combination of odours, hitherto associated with the vaults of the old palace and with the bedchamber beneath, now floated up from the open recess, and filled the room.

The manager started back. 'Good God, Mr Westwick!' he exclaimed, 'what does this mean?'

Remembering, not only what his brother Francis had felt in the room beneath, but what the experience of Agnes had been on the previous night, Henry was determined to be on his guard. 'I am as much surprised as you are,' was his only reply.

'Wait for me one moment, sir,' said the manager. 'I must stop the ladies and gentlemen outside from coming in.'

He hurried away – not forgetting to close the door after him. Henry opened the window, and waited there breathing the purer air. Vague apprehensions of the next discovery to come, filled his mind for the first time. He was doubly resolved, now, not to stir a step in the investigation without a witness.

The manager returned with a wax taper in his hand, which he lighted as soon as he entered the room.

'We need fear no interruption now,' he said. 'Be so kind, Mr Westwick, as to hold the light. It is *my* business to find out what this extraordinary discovery means.'

Henry held the taper. Looking into the cavity, by the dim and flickering light, they both detected a dark object at the bottom of it. 'I think I can reach the thing,' the manager remarked, 'if I lie down, and put my hand into the hole.'

He knelt on the floor – and hesitated. 'Might I ask you, sir, to give me my gloves?' he said. 'They are in my hat, on the chair behind you.'

Henry gave him the gloves. 'I don't know what I may be going to take hold of,' the manager explained, smiling rather uneasily as he put on his right glove.

He stretched himself at full length on the floor, and passed his right arm into the cavity. 'I can't say exactly what I have got hold of,' he said. 'But I have got it.'

Half raising himself, he drew his hand out.

The next instant, he started to his feet with a shriek of terror. A human head dropped from his nerveless grasp on the floor, and rolled to Henry's feet. It was the hideous head that Agnes had seen hovering above her, in the vision of the night!

The two men looked at each other, both struck speechless by the same emotion of horror. The manager was the first to control himself. 'See to the door, for God's sake!' he said. 'Some of the people outside may have heard me.'

Henry moved mechanically to the door.

Even when he had his hand on the key, ready to turn it in the lock in case of necessity, he still looked back at the appalling object on the floor. There was no possibility of identifying those decayed and distorted features with any living creature whom he had seen – and yet, he was conscious of feeling a vague and awful doubt which shook him to the soul. The questions which had tortured the mind of Agnes, were now *his* questions too. *He* asked himself, 'In whose likeness might I have recognized it before the decay set in? The likeness of Ferrari? or the likeness of—?' He paused trembling, as Agnes had paused trembling before him. Agnes! The name, of all women's names the dearest to him, was a terror to him now! What was he to say to her? What might be the consequence if he trusted her with the terrible truth?

No footsteps approached the door; no voices were audible outside. The travellers were still occupied in the rooms at the eastern end of the corridor.

In the brief interval that had passed, the manager had sufficiently recovered himself to be able to think once more of the first and foremost interests of his life – the interests of the hotel. He approached Henry anxiously.

'If this frightful discovery becomes known,' he said, 'the closing of the hotel and the ruin of the Company will be the inevitable results. I feel sure that I can trust your discretion, sir, so far?'

'You can certainly trust me,' Henry answered. 'But surely discretion has its limits,' he added, 'after such a discovery as we have made?'

The manager understood that the duty which they owed to the community, as honest and law-abiding men, was the duty to which Henry now referred. 'I will at once find the means,' he said, 'of conveying the remains privately out of the house, and I will myself place them in the care of the police authorities. Will you leave the room with me? or do you not object to keep watch here, and help me when I return?'

While he was speaking, the voices of the travellers made themselves heard again at the end of the corridor. Henry instantly consented to wait in the room. He shrank from facing the inevitable meeting with Agnes if he showed himself in the corridor at that moment.

The manager hastened his departure, in the hope of escaping notice. He was discovered by his guests before he could reach the head of the stairs. Henry heard the voices plainly as he turned the key. While the terrible drama of discovery was in progress on one side of the door, trivial questions about the amusements of Venice, and facetious discussions on the relative merits of French and Italian cookery, were proceeding on the other. Little by little, the sound of the talking grew fainter. The visitors, having arranged their plans of amusement for the day, were on their way out of the hotel. In a minute or two, there was silence once more.

Henry turned to the window, thinking to relieve his mind by looking at the bright view over the canal. He soon grew wearied of the familiar scene. The morbid fascination which seems to be exercised by all horrible sights, drew him back again to the ghastly object on the floor.

Dream or reality, how had Agnes survived the sight of it? As the question passed through his mind, he noticed for the first time something lying on the floor near the head. Looking closer, he perceived a thin little plate of gold, with three false teeth attached to it, which had apparently dropped out (loosened by the shock) when the manager let the head fall on the floor.

The importance of this discovery, and the necessity of not too readily communicating it to others, instantly struck Henry. Here surely was a chance – if any chance remained – of identifying the shocking relic of humanity which lay before him, the dumb witness of a crime! Acting on this idea, he took possession of the teeth, purposing to use them as a last means of inquiry when other attempts at investigation had been tried and had failed.

He went back to the window: the solitude of the room began to weigh on his spirits. As he looked out again at the view, there was a soft knock at the door. He hastened to open it – and checked himself in the act. A doubt occurred to him. Was it the manager who had knocked? He called out, 'Who is there?'

The voice of Agnes answered him. 'Have you anything to tell me, Henry?'

He was hardly able to reply, 'Not just now,' he said, confusedly. 'Forgive me if I don't open the door. I will speak to you a little later.'

The sweet voice made itself heard again, pleading with him piteously. 'Don't leave me alone, Henry! I can't go back to the happy people downstairs.'

How could he resist that appeal? He heard her sigh – he heard the rustling of her dress as she moved away in despair. The very thing that he had shrunk from doing but a few minutes since was the thing that he did now! He joined Agnes in the corridor. She turned as she heard him, and pointed, trembling, in the direction of the closed room. 'Is it so terrible as that?' she asked faintly.

He put his arm round her to support her. A thought came to him as he looked at her, waiting in doubt and fear for his reply. 'You shall know what I have discovered,' he said, 'if you will first put on your hat and cloak, and come out with me.'

She was naturally surprised. 'Can you tell me your object in going out?' she asked.

He owned what his object was unreservedly. 'I want, before all things,' he said, 'to satisfy your mind and mine, on the subject of Montbarry's death. I am going to take you to the doctor who attended him in his illness, and to the consul who followed him to the grave.'

Her eyes rested on Henry gratefully. 'Oh, how well you understand me!' she said. The manager joined them at the same moment, on his way up the stairs. Henry gave him the key of the room, and then called to the servants in the hall to have a gondola ready at the steps. 'Are you leaving the hotel?' the manager asked. 'In search of evidence,' Henry whispered, pointing to the key. 'If the authorities want me, I shall be back in an hour.'

❧ TWENTY-FIVE ❦

THE DAY HAD ADVANCED TO evening. Lord Montbarry and the bridal party had gone to the Opera. Agnes alone, pleading the excuse of fatigue, remained at the hotel. Having kept up appearances by accompanying his friends to the theatre, Henry Westwick slipped away after the first act, and joined Agnes in the drawing-room.

'Have you thought of what I said to you earlier in the day?' he asked, taking a chair at her side. 'Do you agree with me that the one dreadful doubt which oppressed us both is at least set at rest?'

Agnes shook her head sadly. 'I wish I could agree with you, Henry – I wish I could honestly say that my mind is at ease.'

The answer would have discouraged most men. Henry's patience (where Agnes was concerned) was equal to any demands on it.

'If you will only look back at the events of the day,' he said, 'you must surely admit that we have not been completely baffled. Remember how Dr Bruno disposed of our doubts: – "After thirty years of medical practice, do you think I am likely to mistake the symptoms of death by bronchitis?" If ever there was an unanswerable question, there it is! Was the consul's testimony doubtful in any part of it? He called at the palace to offer his services, after hearing of Lord Montbarry's death; he arrived at the time when the coffin was in the house; he himself saw the corpse placed in it, and the lid screwed down. The evidence of the priest is equally beyond dispute. He remained in the room with the coffin, reciting the prayers for the dead, until the funeral left the palace. Bear all these statements in mind, Agnes; and how can you deny that the question of Montbarry's death and burial is a question set at rest? We have really but one doubt left: we have still to ask ourselves whether the remains which I discovered are the remains of the lost courier, or not. There is the case, as I understand it. Have I stated it fairly?'

Agnes could not deny that he had stated it fairly.

'Then what prevents you from experiencing the same sense of relief that I feel?' Henry asked.

'What I saw last night prevents me,' Agnes answered. 'When we spoke of this subject, after our inquiries were over, you reproached me with taking what you called the superstitious view. I don't quite admit that – but I do acknowledge that I should find the superstitious view intelligible if I heard it expressed by some other person. Remembering what your brother and I once were to each other in the bygone time, I can understand the apparition making itself visible to Me, to claim the mercy of Christian burial, and the vengeance due to a crime. I can even perceive some faint possibility of truth in the explanation which you described as the mesmeric theory – that what I saw might be the result of magnetic influence communicated to me, as I lay between the remains of the murdered husband above me and the guilty wife suffering the tortures of remorse at my bedside. But what I do *not* understand is, that I should have passed through that dreadful ordeal; having no previous knowledge of the murdered man in his lifetime, or only knowing him (if you suppose that I saw the apparition of Ferrari) through the interest which I took in his wife. I can't dispute your reasoning, Henry. But I feel in my heart of hearts that you are deceived. Nothing will shake my belief that we are still as far from having discovered the dreadful truth as ever.'

Henry made no further attempt to dispute with her. She had impressed him with a certain reluctant respect for her own opinion, in spite of himself.

'Have you thought of any better way of arriving at the truth?' he asked. 'Who is to help us? No doubt there is the Countess, who has the clue to the mystery in her own hands. But, in the present state of her mind, is her testimony to be trusted – even if she were willing to speak? Judging by my own experience, I should say decidedly not.'

'You don't mean that you have seen her again?' Agnes eagerly interposed.

'Yes. I disturbed her once more over her endless writing; and I insisted on her speaking out plainly.'

'Then you told her what you found when you opened the hiding-place?'

'Of course I did!' Henry replied. 'I said that I held her responsible for the discovery, though I had not mentioned her connection with it to the authorities as yet. She went on with her writing as if I had spoken in an unknown tongue! I was equally obstinate, on my side. I told her plainly that the head had been placed under the care of the police, and that the manager and I had signed our declarations and given our evidence. She paid not the slightest heed to me. By way of tempting her to speak, I added that the whole investigation was to be kept a secret, and that she might depend on my discretion. For the moment I thought I had succeeded. She looked up from her writing with a passing flash of curiosity, and said, "What are they going to do with it?" – meaning, I suppose, the head, I answered that it was to be privately buried, after the photographs of it had first been taken. I even went the length of communicating the opinion of the surgeon consulted, that some chemical means of arresting decomposition had been used, and had only partially succeeded – and I asked her point-blank if the surgeon was right? The trap was not a bad one – but it completely failed. She said in the coolest manner, "Now you are here, I should like to consult you about my play; I am at a loss for some new incidents." Mind! there was nothing satirical in this. She was really eager to read her wonderful work to me – evidently supposing that I took a special interest in such things, because my brother is the manager of a theatre! I left her, making the first excuse that occurred to me. So far as I am concerned, I can do nothing with her. But it is possible that *your* influence may succeed with her again, as it has succeeded already. Will you make the attempt, to satisfy your own mind? She is still upstairs; and I am quite ready to accompany you.'

Agnes shuddered at the bare suggestion of another interview with the Countess.

'I can't! I daren't!' she exclaimed. 'After what has happened in that horrible room, she is more repellent to me than ever. Don't ask me to do it, Henry! Feel my hand – you have turned me as cold as death only with talking of it!'

She was not exaggerating the terror that possessed her. Henry hastened to change the subject.

'Let us talk of something more interesting,' he said. 'I have a question to ask you about yourself. Am I right in believing that the sooner you get away from Venice the happier you will be?'

'Right?' she repeated excitedly. 'You are more than right! No words can say how I long to be away from this horrible place. But you know how I am situated – you heard what Lord Montbarry said at dinner-time?'

'Suppose he has altered his plans, since dinner-time?' Henry suggested.

Agnes looked surprised. 'I thought he had received letters from England which obliged him to leave Venice to-morrow,' she said.

'Quite true,' Henry admitted. 'He had arranged to start for England to-morrow, and to leave you and Lady Montbarry and the children to enjoy your holiday in Venice, under my care. Circumstances have occurred, however, which have forced him to alter his plans. He must take you all back with him to-morrow, because I am not able to assume the charge of you. I am obliged to give up my holiday in Italy, and return to England too.'

Agnes looked at him in some little perplexity: she was not quite sure whether she understood him or not. 'Are you really obliged to go back?' she asked.

Henry smiled as he answered her. 'Keep the secret,' he said, 'or Montbarry will never forgive me!'

She read the rest in his face. 'Oh!' she exclaimed, blushing brightly, 'you have not given up your pleasant holiday in Italy on my account?'

'I shall go back with you to England, Agnes. That will be holiday enough for *me*.'

She took his hand in an irrepressible outburst of gratitude. 'How good you are to me!' she murmured tenderly. 'What should I have done in the troubles that have come to me, without your sympathy? I can't tell you, Henry, how I feel your kindness.'

She tried impulsively to lift his hand to her lips. He gently stopped her. 'Agnes,' he said, 'are you beginning to understand how truly I love you?'

That simple question found its own way to her heart. She owned the whole truth, without saying a word. She looked at him – and then looked away again.

He drew her nearer to him. 'My own darling!' he whispered – and kissed her. Softly and tremulously, the sweet lips lingered, and touched his lips in return. Then her head dropped. She put her arms round his neck, and hid her face on his bosom. They spoke no more.

The charmed silence had lasted but a little while, when it was mercilessly broken by a knock at the door.

Agnes started to her feet. She placed herself at the piano; the instrument being opposite to the door, it was impossible, when she seated herself on the music-stool, for any person entering the room to see her face. Henry called out irritably, 'Come in.'

The door was not opened. The person on the other side of it asked a strange question.

'Is Mr Henry Westwick alone?'

Agnes instantly recognized the voice of the Countess. She hurried to a second door, which communicated with one of the bed-rooms. 'Don't let her come near me!' she whispered nervously. 'Good night, Henry! good night!'

If Henry could, by an effort of will, have transported the Countess to the uttermost ends of the earth, he would have made the effort without remorse. As it was, he only repeated, more irritably than ever, 'Come in!'

She entered the room slowly with her everlasting manuscript in her hand. Her step was unsteady; a dark flush appeared on her face, in place of its customary pallor; her eyes were bloodshot and widely dilated. In approaching Henry, she showed a strange incapability of calculating her distances – she struck against the table near which he happened to be sitting. When she spoke, her articulation was confused, and her pronunciation of some of the longer words was hardly intelligible. Most men would have suspected her of being under the influence of some intoxicating liquor. Henry took a truer view – he said, as he placed a chair for her, 'Countess, I am afraid you have been working too hard: you look as if you wanted rest.'

She put her hand to head. 'My invention has gone,' she said. 'I can't write my fourth act. It's all a blank – all a blank!'

Henry advised her to wait till the next day. 'Go to bed,' he suggested; 'and try to sleep.'

She waved her hand impatiently. 'I must finish the play,' she answered. 'I only want a hint from you. You must know something about plays. Your brother has got a theatre. You must often have heard him talk about fourth and fifth acts – you must have seen rehearsals, and all the rest of it.' She abruptly thrust the manuscript into Henry's hand. 'I can't read it to you,' she said; 'I feel giddy when I look at my own writing. Just run your eye over it, there's a good fellow – and give me a hint.'

Henry glanced at the manuscript. He happened to look at the list of the persons of the drama. As he read the list he started and turned abruptly to the Countess, intending to ask her for some explanation. The words were suspended on his lips. It was but too plainly useless to speak to her. Her head lay back on the rail of the chair. She seemed to be half asleep already. The flush on her face had deepened: she looked like a woman who was in danger of having a fit.

He rang the bell, and directed the man who answered it to send one of the chambermaids upstairs. His voice seemed to partially rouse the

Countess; she opened her eyes in a slow drowsy way. 'Have you read it?' she asked.

It was necessary as a mere act of humanity to humour her. 'I will read it willingly,' said Henry, 'if you will go upstairs to bed. You shall hear what I think of it to-morrow morning. Our heads will be clearer, we shall be better able to make the fourth act in the morning.'

The chambermaid came in while he was speaking. 'I am afraid the lady is ill,' Henry whispered. 'Take her up to her room.' The woman looked at the Countess and whispered back, 'Shall we send for a doctor, sir?'

Henry advised taking her upstairs first, and then asking the manager's opinion. There was great difficulty in persuading her to rise, and accept the support of the chambermaid's arm. It was only by reiterated promises to read the play that night, and to make the fourth act in the morning, that Henry prevailed on the Countess to return to her room.

Left to himself, he began to feel a certain languid curiosity in relation to the manuscript. He looked over the pages, reading a line here and a line there. Suddenly he changed colour as he read – and looked up from the manuscript like a man bewildered. 'Good God! what does this mean?' he said to himself.

His eyes turned nervously to the door by which Agnes had left him. She might return to the drawing-room; she might want to see what the Countess had written. He looked back again at the passage which had startled him – considered with himself for a moment – and, snatching up the unfinished play, suddenly and softly left the room.

⟡ TWENTY-SIX ⟡

ENTERING HIS OWN ROOM ON the upper floor, Henry placed the manuscript on his table, open at the first leaf. His nerves were unquestionably shaken; his hand trembled as he turned the pages, he started at chance noises on the staircase of the hotel.

The scenario, or outline, of the Countess's play began with no formal prefatory phrases. She presented herself and her work with the easy familiarity of an old friend.

'Allow me, dear Mr Francis Westwick, to introduce to you the persons in my proposed Play. Behold them, arranged symmetrically in a line.

'My Lord. The Baron. The Courier. The Doctor. The Countess.

'I don't trouble myself, you see, to invent fictitious family names. My characters are sufficiently distinguished by their social titles, and by the striking contrast which they present one with another.

'The First Act opens—

'No! Before I open the First Act, I must announce, in justice to myself, that this Play is entirely the work of my own invention. I scorn to borrow from actual events; and, what is more extraordinary still, I have not stolen one of my ideas from the Modern French drama. As the manager of an English theatre, you will naturally refuse to believe this. It doesn't matter. Nothing matters – except the opening of my first act.

'We are at Homburg, in the famous Salon d'Or, at the height of the season. The Countess (exquisitely dressed) is seated at the green table. Strangers of all nations are standing behind the players, venturing their money or only looking on. My Lord is among the strangers. He is struck by the Countess's personal appearance, in which beauties and defects are fantastically mingled in the most attractive manner. He watches the Countess's game, and places his money where he sees her deposit her own little stake. She looks round at him, and says, "Don't trust to my colour; I have been unlucky the whole evening. Place your stake on the other colour, and you may have a chance of winning." My Lord (a true Englishman) blushes, bows, and obeys. The Countess proves to be a prophet. She loses again. My Lord wins twice the sum that he has risked.

'The Countess rises from the table. She has no more money, and she offers my Lord her chair.

'Instead of taking it, he politely places his winnings in her hand, and begs her to accept the loan as a favour to himself. The Countess stakes again, and loses again. My Lord smiles superbly, and presses a second loan on her. From that moment her luck turns. She wins, and wins largely. Her brother, the Baron, trying his fortune in another room, hears of what is going on, and joins my Lord and the Countess.

'Pay attention, if you please, to the Baron. He is delineated as a remarkable and interesting character.

'This noble person has begun life with a single-minded devotion to the science of experimental chemistry, very surprising in a young and handsome man with a brilliant future before him. A profound knowledge of the occult sciences has persuaded the Baron that it is possible to solve the famous problem called the "Philosopher's Stone". His own pecuniary resources have long since been exhausted by his costly experiments. His sister has next supplied him with the small fortune at her disposal: reserving only the family jewels, placed in the charge of her banker and friend at Frankfort. The Countess's fortune also being swallowed up, the Baron has in a fatal moment sought for new supplies at the gaming table. He proves, at starting on his perilous career, to be a favourite of fortune;

wins largely, and, alas! profanes his noble enthusiasm for science by yielding his soul to the all-debasing passion of the gamester.

'At the period of the Play, the Baron's good fortune has deserted him. He sees his way to a crowning experiment in the fatal search after the secret of transmuting the baser metals into gold. But how is he to pay the preliminary expenses? Destiny like a mocking echo answers, How?

'Will his sister's winnings (with my Lord's money) prove large enough to help him? Eager for this result, he gives the Countess his advice on how to play. From that disastrous moment the infection of his own adverse fortune spreads to his sister. She loses again, and again – loses to the last farthing.

'The amiable and wealthy Lord offers a third loan; but the scrupulous Countess positively refuses to take it. On leaving the table, she presents her brother to my Lord. The gentlemen fall into pleasant talk. My Lord asks leave to pay his respects to the Countess, the next morning, at her hotel. The Baron hospitably invites him to breakfast. My Lord accepts, with a last admiring glance at the Countess which does not escape her brother's observation, and takes his leave for the night.

'Alone with his sister, the Baron speaks out plainly. "Our affairs," he says, "are in a desperate condition, and must find a desperate remedy. Wait for me here, while I make inquiries about my Lord. You have evidently produced a strong impression on him. If we can turn that impression into money, no matter at what sacrifice, the thing must be done."

'The Countess now occupies the stage alone, and indulges in a soliloquy which develops her character.

'It is at once a dangerous and attractive character. Immense capacities for good are implanted in her nature, side by side with equally remarkable capacities for evil. It rests with circumstances to develop either the one or the other. Being a person who produces a sensation wherever she goes, this noble lady is naturally made the subject of all sorts of scandalous reports. To one of these reports (which falsely and abominably points to the Baron as her lover instead of her brother) she now refers with just indignation. She has just expressed her desire to leave Homburg, as the place in which the vile calumny first took its rise, when the Baron returns, overhears her last words, and says to her, 'Yes, leave Homburg by all means; provided you leave it in the character of my Lord's betrothed wife!'

'The Countess is startled and shocked. She protests that she does not reciprocate my Lord's admiration for her. She even goes the length of refusing to see him again. The Baron answers, "I must positively have command of money. Take your choice, between marrying my Lord's income, in the interest of my grand discovery – or leave me to sell myself and my title to the first rich woman of low degree who is ready to buy me."

'The Countess listens in surprise and dismay. Is it possible that the Baron is in earnest? He is horribly in earnest. "The woman who will buy me," he says, "is in the next room to us at this moment. She is the wealthy widow of a Jewish usurer. She has the money I want to reach the solution of the great problem. I have only to be that woman's husband, and to make myself master of untold millions of gold. Take five minutes to consider what I have said to you, and tell me on my return which of us is to marry for the money I want, you or I."

'As he turns away, the Countess stops him.

'All the noblest sentiments in her nature are exalted to the highest pitch. "Where is the true woman," she exclaims, "who wants time to consummate the sacrifice of herself, when the man to whom she is devoted demands it? She does not want five minutes – she does not want five seconds – she holds out her hand to him, and she says, Sacrifice me on the altar of your glory! Take as stepping-stones on the way to your triumph, my love, my liberty, and my life!"

'On this grand situation the curtain falls. Judging by my first act, Mr Westwick, tell me truly, and don't be afraid of turning my head: – Am I not capable of writing a good play?'

Henry paused between the First and Second Acts; reflecting, not on the merits of the Play, but on the strange resemblance which the incidents so far presented to the incidents that had attended the disastrous marriage of the first Lord Montbarry.

Was it possible that the Countess, in the present condition of her mind, supposed herself to be exercising her invention when she was only exercising her memory?

The question involved considerations too serious to be made the subject of a hasty decision. Reserving his opinion, Henry turned the page, and devoted himself to the reading of the next act. The manuscript proceeded as follows:–

'The Second Act opens at Venice. An interval of four months has elapsed since the date of the scene at the gambling table. The action now takes place in the reception-room of one of the Venetian palaces.

'The Baron is discovered, alone, on the stage. He reverts to the events which have happened since the close of the First Act. The Countess has sacrificed herself; the mercenary marriage has taken place – but not without obstacles, caused by difference of opinion on the question of marriage settlements.

'Private inquiries, instituted in England, have informed the Baron that my Lord's income is derived chiefly from what is called entailed property. In case of accidents, he is surely bound to do something for his bride?

544

Let him, for example, insure his life, for a sum proposed by the Baron, and let him so settle the money that his widow shall have it, if he dies first.

'My Lord hesitates. The Baron wastes no time in useless discussion. "Let us by all means" (he says) "consider the marriage as broken off." My Lord shifts his ground, and pleads for a smaller sum than the sum proposed. The Baron briefly replies, "I never bargain." My lord is in love; the natural result follows – he gives way.

'So far, the Baron has no cause to complain. But my Lord's turn comes, when the marriage has been celebrated, and when the honeymoon is over. The Baron has joined the married pair at a palace which they have hired in Venice. He is still bent on solving the problem of the "Philosopher's Stone". His laboratory is set up in the vaults beneath the palace – so that smells from chemical experiments may not incommode the Countess, in the higher regions of the house. The one obstacle in the way of his grand discovery is, as usual, the want of money. His position at the present time has become truly critical. He owes debts of honour to gentlemen in his own rank of life, which must positively be paid; and he proposes, in his own friendly manner, to borrow the money of my Lord. My Lord positively refuses, in the rudest terms. The Baron applies to his sister to exercise her conjugal influence. She can only answer that her noble husband (being no longer distractedly in love with her) now appears in his true character, as one of the meanest men living. The sacrifice of the marriage has been made, and has already proved useless.

'Such is the state of affairs at the opening of the second act.

'The entrance of the Countess suddenly disturbs the Baron's reflections. She is in a state bordering on frenzy. Incoherent expressions of rage burst from her lips: it is some time before she can sufficiently control herself to speak plainly. She has been doubly insulted – first, by a menial person in her employment; secondly, by her husband. Her maid, an Englishwoman, has declared that she will serve the Countess no longer. She will give up her wages, and return at once to England. Being asked her reason for this strange proceeding, she insolently hints that the Countess's service is no service for an honest woman, since the Baron has entered the house. The Countess does, what any lady in her position would do; she indignantly dismisses the wretch on the spot.

'My Lord, hearing his wife's voice raised in anger, leaves the study in which he is accustomed to shut himself up over his books, and asks what this disturbance means. The Countess informs him of the outrageous language and conduct of her maid. My Lord not only declares his entire approval of the woman's conduct, but expresses his own abominable doubts of his wife's fidelity in language of such horrible brutality that no lady could pollute her lips by repeating it. "If I had been a man," the Countess says, "and if I had had a weapon in my hand, I would have struck him dead at my feet!"

'The Baron, listening silently so far, now speaks. "Permit me to finish the sentence for you," he says. "You would have struck your husband dead at your feet; and by that rash act, you would have deprived yourself of the insurance money settled on the widow – the very money which is wanted to relieve your brother from the unendurable pecuniary position which he now occupies!"

'The Countess gravely reminds the Baron that this is no joking matter. After what my Lord has said to her, she has little doubt that he will communicate his infamous suspicions to his lawyers in England. If nothing is done to prevent it, she may be divorced and disgraced, and thrown on the world, with no resource but the sale of her jewels to keep her from starving.

'At this moment, the Courier who has been engaged to travel with my Lord from England crosses the stage with a letter to take to the post. The Countess stops him, and asks to look at the address on the letter. She takes it from him for a moment, and shows it to her brother. The handwriting is my Lord's; and the letter is directed to his lawyers in London.

'The Courier proceeds to the post-office. The Baron and the Countess look at each other in silence. No words are needed. They thoroughly understand the position in which they are placed; they clearly see the terrible remedy for it. What is the plain alternative before them? Disgrace and ruin – or, my Lord's death and the insurance money!

'The Baron walks backwards and forwards in great agitation, talking to himself. The Countess hears fragments of what he is saying. He speaks of my Lord's constitution, probably weakened in India – of a cold which my Lord has caught two or three days since – of the remarkable manner in which such slight things as colds sometimes end in serious illness and death.

'He observes that the Countess is listening to him, and asks if she has anything to propose. She is a woman who, with many defects, has the great merit of speaking out. "Is there no such thing as a serious illness," she asks, "corked up in one of those bottles of yours in the vaults downstairs?"

'The Baron answers by gravely shaking his head. What is he afraid of? – a possible examination of the body after death? No: he can set any post-mortem examination at defiance. It is the process of administering the poison that he dreads. A man so distinguished as my Lord cannot ube taken seriously ill without medical attendance. Where there is a Doctor there is always danger of discovery. Then, again, there is the Courier, faithful to my Lord as long as my Lord pays him. Even if the Doctor sees nothing suspicious, the Courier may discover something.

The poison, to do its work with the necessary secrecy, must be repeatedly administered in graduated doses. One trifling miscalculation or mistake may rouse suspicion. The insurance offices may hear of it, and may refuse to pay the money. As things are, the Baron will not risk it, and will not allow his sister to risk it in his place.

'My Lord himself is the next character who appears. He has repeatedly rung for the Courier, and the bell has not been answered. "What does this insolence mean?"

'The Countess (speaking with quiet dignity – for why should her infamous husband have the satisfaction of knowing how deeply he has wounded her?) reminds my Lord that the Courier has gone to the post. My Lord asks suspiciously if she has looked at the letter. The Countess informs him coldly that she has no curiosity about his letters. Referring to the cold from which he is suffering, she inquires if he thinks of consulting a medical man. My Lord answers roughly that he is quite old enough to be capable of doctoring himself.

'As he makes this reply, the Courier appears, returning from the post. My Lord gives him orders to go out again and buy some lemons. He proposes to try hot lemonade as a means of inducing perspiration in bed. In that way he has formerly cured colds, and in that way he will cure the cold from which he is suffering now.

'The Courier obeys in silence. Judging by appearances, he goes very reluctantly on this second errand.

'My Lord turns to the Baron (who has thus far taken no part in the conversation) and asks him, in a sneering tone, how much longer he proposes to prolong his stay in Venice. The Baron answers quietly, "Let us speak plainly to one another, my Lord. If you wish me to leave your house, you have only to say the word, and I go." My Lord turns to his wife, and asks if she can support the calamity of her brother's absence – laying a grossly insulting emphasis on the word "brother". The Countess preserves her impenetrable composure; nothing in her betrays the deadly hatred with which she regards the titled ruffian who has insulted her. "You are master in this house, my Lord," is all she says. "Do as you please."

'My Lord looks at his wife; looks at the Baron – and suddenly alters his tone. Does he perceive in the composure of the Countess and her brother something lurking under the surface that threatens him? This is at least certain, he makes a clumsy apology for the language that he has used. (Abject wretch!)

'My Lord's excuses are interrupted by the return of the Courier with the lemons and hot water.

'The Countess observes for the first time that the man looks ill. His hands tremble as he places the tray on the table. My Lord orders his

Courier to follow him, and make the lemonade in the bedroom. The Countess remarks that the Courier seems hardly capable of obeying his orders. Hearing this, the man admits that he is ill. He, too, is suffering from a cold; he has been kept waiting in a draught at the shop where he bought the lemons; he feels alternately hot and cold, and he begs permission to lie down for a little while on his bed.

'Feeling her humanity appealed to, the Countess volunteers to make the lemonade herself. My Lord takes the Courier by the arm, leads him aside, and whispers these words to him: "Watch her, and see that she puts nothing into the lemonade; then bring it to me with your own hands; and, then, go to bed, if you like."

'Without a word more to his wife, or to the Baron, my Lord leaves the room.

'The Countess makes the lemonade, and the Courier takes it to his master.

'Returning, on the way to his own room, he is so weak, and feels, he says, so giddy, that he is obliged to support himself by the backs of the chairs as he passes them. The Baron, always considerate to persons of low degree, offers his arm. "I am afraid, my poor fellow," he says, "that you are really ill." The Courier makes this extraordinary answer: "It's all over with me, Sir: I have caught my death."

'The Countess is naturally startled. "You are not an old man," she says, trying to rouse the Courier's spirits. "At your age, catching cold doesn't surely mean catching your death?" The Courier fixes his eyes despairingly on the Countess.

' "My lungs are weak, my Lady," he says; "I have already had two attacks of bronchitis. The second time, a great physician joined my own doctor in attendance on me. He considered my recovery almost in the light of a miracle. Take care of yourself," he said. "If you have a third attack of bronchitis, as certainly as two and two make four, you will be a dead man. I feel the same inward shivering, my Lady, that I felt on those two former occasions – and I tell you again, I have caught my death in Venice."

'Speaking some comforting words, the Baron leads him to his room. The Countess is left alone on the stage.

'She seats herself, and looks towards the door by which the Courier has been led out. "Ah! my poor fellow," she says, "if you could only change constitutions with my Lord, what a happy result would follow for the Baron and for me! If *you* could only get cured of a trumpery cold with a little hot lemonade, and if *he* could only catch his death in your place—!"

'She suddenly pauses – considers for a while – and springs to her feet, with a cry of triumphant surprise: the wonderful, the unparalleled idea has crossed her mind like a flash of lightning. Make the two men change names and places – and the deed is done! Where are the obstacles? Remove my Lord (by fair means or foul) from his room; and keep him secretly prisoner in the palace, to live or die as future necessity may determine. Place the Courier in the vacant bed, and call in the doctor to see him – ill, in my Lord's character, and (if he dies) dying under my Lord's name.'

The manuscript dropped from Henry's hands. A sickening sense of horror overpowered him. The question which had occurred to his mind at the close of the First Act of the Play assumed a new and terrible interest now. As far as the scene of the Countess's soliloquy, the incidents of the Second Act had reflected the events of his late brother's life as faithfully as the incidents of the First Act. Was the monstrous plot, revealed in the lines which he had just read, the offspring of the Countess's morbid imagination? or had she, in this case also, deluded herself with the idea that she was inventing when she was really writing under the influence of her own guilty remembrances of the past? If the latter interpretation were the true one, he had just read the narrative of the contemplated murder of his brother, planned in cold blood by a woman who was at that moment inhabiting the same house with him. While, to make the fatality complete, Agnes herself had innocently provided the conspirators with the one man who was fitted to be the passive agent of their crime.

Even the bare doubt that it might be so was more than he could endure. He left his room; resolved to force the truth out of the Countess, or to denounce her before the authorities as a murderess at large.

Arrived at her door, he was met by a person just leaving the room. The person was the manager. He was hardly recognizable; he looked and spoke like a man in a state of desperation.

'Oh, go in if you like!' he said to Henry. 'Mark this, sir! I am not a superstitious man; but I do begin to believe that crimes carry their own curse with them. This hotel is under a curse. What happens in the morning? We discover a crime committed in the old days of the palace. The night comes, and brings another dreadful event with it – a death; a sudden and shocking death, in the house. Go in, and see for yourself! I shall resign my situation, Mr Westwick: I can't contend with the fatalities that pursue me here!'

Henry entered the room.

The Countess was stretched on her bed. The doctor on one side, and the chambermaid on the other, were standing looking at her. From time to time, she drew a heavy stertorous breath, like a person oppressed in sleeping. 'Is she likely to die?' Henry asked.

'She is dead,' the doctor answered. 'Dead of the rupture of a blood-vessel on the brain. Those sounds that you hear are purely mechanical – they may go on for hours.'

Henry looked at the chambermaid. She had little to tell. The Countess had refused to go to bed, and had placed herself at her desk to proceed with her writing. Finding it useless to remonstrate with her, the maid had left the room to speak to the manager. In the shortest possible time, the doctor was summoned to the hotel, and found the Countess dead on the floor. There was this to tell – and no more.

Looking at the writing-table as he went out, Henry saw the sheet of paper on which the Countess had traced her last lines of writing. The characters were almost illegible. Henry could just distinguish the words, 'First Act', and Persons of the Drama'. The lost wretch had been thinking of her Play to the last, and had begun it all over again!

❧ TWENTY-SEVEN ❧

HENRY RETURNED TO HIS ROOM.

His first impulse was to throw aside the manuscript, and never to look at it again. The one chance of relieving his mind from the dreadful uncertainty that oppressed it, by obtaining positive evidence of the truth, was a chance annihilated by the Countess's death. What good purpose could be served, what relief could he anticipate, if he read more?

He walked up and down the room. After an interval, his thoughts took a new direction; the question of the manuscript presented itself under another point of view. Thus far, his reading had only informed him that the conspiracy had been planned. How did he know that the plan had been put in execution?

The manuscript lay just before him on the floor. He hesitated – then picked it up; and, returning to the table, read on as follows, from the point at which he had left off.

'While the Countess is still absorbed in the bold yet simple combination of circumstances which she has discovered, the Baron returns. He takes a serious view of the case of the Courier; it may be necessary, he thinks, to send for medical advice. No servant is left in the palace, now the English maid has taken her departure. The Baron himself must fetch the doctor, if the doctor is really needed.

' "Let us have medical help, by all means," his sister replies. "But wait and hear something that I have to say to you first." She then electrifies the Baron by communicating her idea to him. What danger of discovery have they to dread? My Lord's life in Venice has been a life of absolute seclusion: nobody but his banker knows him, even by personal appearance. He has presented his letter of credit as a perfect stranger; and he and his banker have never seen each other since that first visit. He has given no parties, and gone to no parties. On the few occasions when he has hired a gondola or taken a walk, he has always been alone. Thanks to the atrocious suspicion which makes him ashamed of being seen with his wife, he has led the very life which makes the proposed enterprise easy of accomplishment.

'The cautious Baron listens – but gives no positive opinion, as yet. "See what you can do with the Courier," he says; "and I will decide when I hear the result. One valuable hint I may give you before you go. Your man is easily tempted by money – if you only offer him enough. The other day, I asked him, in jest, what he would do for a thousand pounds. He answered, 'Anything.' Bear that in mind; and offer your highest bid without bargaining."

'The scene changes to the Courier's room, and shows the poor wretch with a photographic portrait of his wife in his hand, crying. The Countess enters.

'She wisely begins by sympathizing with her contemplated accomplice. He is duly grateful; he confides his sorrows to his gracious mistress. Now that he believes himself to be on his death-bed, he feels remorse for his neglectful treatment of his wife. He could resign himself to die; but despair overpowers him when he remembers that he has saved no money, and that he will leave his widow, without resources, to the mercy of the world.

'On this hint, the Countess speaks. "Suppose you were asked to do a perfectly easy thing," she says; "and suppose you were rewarded for doing it by a present of a thousand pounds, as a legacy for your widow?"

'The Courier raises himself on his pillow, and looks at the Countess with an expression of incredulous surprise. She can hardly be cruel enough (he thinks) to joke with a man in his miserable plight. Will she say plainly what this perfectly easy thing is, the doing of which will meet with such a magnificent reward?

'The Countess answers that question by confiding her project to the Courier, without the slightest reserve.

'Some minutes of silence follow when she had done. The Courier is not weak enough yet to speak without stopping to think first. Still keeping his eyes on the Countess, he makes a quaintly-insolent remark on what he has just heard. "I have not hitherto been a religious man; but I feel myself on the way to it. Since your ladyship has spoken to me, I believe in the Devil." It is the Countess's interest to see the humorous side of this confession of faith. She takes no offence. She only says, "I will give you half an hour by yourself, to think over my proposal. You are in danger of death. Decide, in your wife's interests, whether you will die worth nothing, or die worth a thousand pounds."

'Left alone, the Courier seriously considers his position – and decides. He rises with difficulty; writes a few lines on a leaf taken from his pocket-book; and with slow and faltering steps leaves the room.

'The Countess, returning at the expiration of the half-hour's interval, finds the room empty. While she is wondering, the Courier opens the door. What has he been doing out of his bed? He answers, "I have been protecting my own life, my lady, on the bare chance that I may recover from the bronchitis for the third time. If you or the Baron attempts to hurry me out of this world, or to deprive me of my thousand pounds reward, I shall tell the doctor where he will find a few lines of writing, which describe your ladyship's plot. I may not have strength enough, in the case supposed, to betray you by making a complete confession with my own lips; but I can employ my last breath to speak the half-dozen words which will tell the doctor where he is to look. Those words, it is needless to add, will be addressed to your Ladyship, if I find your engagements towards me faithfully kept."

'With this audacious preface, he proceeds to state the conditions on which he will play his part in the conspiracy, and die (if he does die) worth a thousand pounds.

'Either the Countess or the Baron are to taste the food and drink brought to his bedside, in his presence, and even the medicines which the doctor may prescribe for him. As for the promised sum of money, it is to be produced in one bank-note, folded in a sheet of paper, on which a line is to be written, dictated by the Courier. The two enclosures are then to be sealed up in an envelope, addressed to his wife, and stamped ready for the post. This done, the letter is to be placed under his pillow; the Baron or the Countess being at liberty to satisfy themselves, day by day, at their own time, that the letter remains in its place, with the seal unbroken, as long as the doctor has any hope of his patient's recovery. The last stipulation follows. The Courier has a conscience; and with a view to keeping it easy, insists that he shall be left in ignorance of that part of the plot which relates to the sequestration of my Lord. Not that he cares particularly what becomes of his miserly master – but he does dislike taking other people's responsibilities on his own shoulders.

'These conditions being agreed to, the Countess calls in the Baron, who has been waiting events in the next room.

'He is informed that the Courier has yielded to temptation; but he is still too cautious to make any compromising remarks. Keeping his back turned on the bed, he shows a bottle to the Countess. It is labelled "Chloroform". She understands that my Lord is to be removed from his room in a convenient state of insensibility. In what part of the palace is he to be hidden? As they open the door to go out, the Countess whispers that question to the Baron. The Baron whispers back, "In the vaults!" The curtain falls.'

🙂 **TWENTY-EIGHT** 🙂

So the Second Act ended.

Turning to the Third Act, Henry looked wearily at the pages as he let them slip through his fingers. Both in mind and body, he began to feel the need of repose.

In one important respect, the later portion of the manuscript differed from the pages which he had just been reading. Signs of an overwrought brain showed themselves, here and there, as the outline of the Play approached its end. The handwriting grew worse and worse. Some of the longer sentences were left unfinished. In the exchange of dialogue, questions and answers were not always attributed respectively to the right speaker. At certain intervals the writer's failing intelligence seemed to recover itself for a while; only to relapse again, and to lose the thread of the narrative more hopelessly than ever.

After reading one or two of the more coherent passages, Henry recoiled from the ever-darkening horror of the story. He closed the manuscript, heartsick and exhausted, and threw himself on his bed to rest. The door opened almost at the same moment. Lord Montbarry entered the room.

'We have just returned from the Opera,' he said; 'and we have heard the news of that miserable woman's death. They say you spoke to her in her last moments; and I want to hear how it happened.'

'You shall hear how it happened,' Henry answered; 'and more than that. You are now the head of the family, Stephen; and I feel bound, in the position which oppresses me, to leave you to decide what ought to be done.'

With those introductory words, he told his brother how the Countess's Play had come into his hands. 'Read the first few pages,' he said. 'I am anxious to know whether the same impression is produced on both of us.'

Before Lord Montbarry had got half-way through the First Act, he stopped, and looked at his brother. 'What does she mean by boasting of this as her own invention?' he asked. 'Was she too crazy to remember that these things really happened?'

This was enough for Henry: the same impression had been produced on both of them. 'You will do as you please,' he said. 'But if you will be guided by me, spare yourself the reading of those pages to come, which describe our brother's terrible expiation of his heartless marriage.'

'Have you read it all, Henry?'

'Not all. I shrank from reading some of the latter part of it. Neither you nor I saw much of our elder brother after we left school; and, for my part, I felt, and never scrupled to express my feeling, that he behaved infamously to Agnes. But when I read that unconscious confession of the murderous conspiracy to which he fell a victim, I remembered, with something like remorse, that the same mother bore us. I have felt for him to-night, what I am ashamed to think I never felt for him before.'

Lord Montbarry took his brother's hand.

'You are a good fellow, Henry,' he said; 'but are you quite sure that you have not been needlessly distressing yourself? Because some of this crazy creature's writing accidentally tells what we know to be the truth, does it follow that all the rest is to be relied on to the end?'

'There is no possible doubt of it,' Henry replied.

'No possible doubt?' his brother repeated. 'I shall go on with my reading, Henry – and see what justification there may be for that confident conclusion of yours.'

He read on steadily, until he had reached the end of the Second Act. Then he looked up.

'Do you really believe that the mutilated remains which you discovered this morning are the remains of our brother?' he asked. 'And do you believe it on such evidence as this?'

Henry answered silently by a sign in the affirmative.

Lord Montbarry checked himself – evidently on the point of entering an indignant protest.

'You acknowledge that you have not read the later scenes of the piece,' he said. 'Don't be childish, Henry! If you persist in pinning your faith on such stuff as this, the least you can do is to make yourself thoroughly acquainted with it. Will you read the Third Act? No? Then I shall read it to you.'

He turned to the Third Act, and ran over those fragmentary passages which were clearly enough written and expressed to be intelligible to the mind of a stranger.

'Here is a scene in the vaults of the palace,' he began. 'The victim of the conspiracy is sleeping on his miserable bed; and the Baron and the Countess are considering the position in which they stand. The Countess (as well as I can make it out) has raised the money that is wanted by borrowing on the security of her jewels at Frankfort; and the Courier upstairs is still declared by the Doctor to have a chance of recovery. What are the conspirators to do, if the man does recover? The cautious Baron suggests setting the prisoner free. If he ventures to appeal to the law, it is easy to declare that he is subject to insane delusion, and to call his own wife as witness. On the other hand, if the Courier dies, how is the sequestrated and unknown nobleman to be put out of the way? Passively, by letting him starve in his prison? No: the Baron is a man of refined tastes; he dislikes needless cruelty. The active policy remains – say, assassination by the knife of a hired bravo? The Baron objects to trusting an accomplice; also to spending money on anyone but himself. Shall they drop their prisoner into the canal? The Baron declines to trust water; water will show him on the surface. Shall they set his bed on fire? An excellent idea; but the smoke might be seen. No: the circumstances being now entirely altered, poisoning him presents the easiest way out of it. He has become simply a superfluous person. The cheapest poison will do. – Is it possible, Henry, that you believe this consultation really took place?'

Henry made no reply. The succession of the questions that had just been read to him, exactly followed the succession of the dreams that had terrified Mrs Norbury, on the two nights which she had passed in the hotel. It was useless to point out this coincidence to his brother. He only said, 'Go on.'

Lord Montbarry turned the pages until he came to the next intelligible passage.

'Here,' he proceeded, 'is a double scene on the stage – so far as I can understand the sketch of it. The doctor is upstairs, innocently writing his certificate of my Lord's decease, by the dead Courier's bedside. Down in the vaults, the Baron stands by the corpse of the poisoned lord, preparing the strong chemical acids which are to reduce it to a heap of ashes – Surely, it is not worth while to trouble ourselves with deciphering such melodramatic horrors as these? Let us get on! let us get on!'

He turned the leaves again; attempting vainly to discover the meaning of the confused scenes that followed. On the last page but one, he found the last intelligible sentences.

'The Third Act seems to be divided,' he said, 'into two Parts or Tableaux. I think I can read the writing at the beginning of the Second Part. The Baron and the Countess open the scene. The Baron's hands are mysteriously concealed by gloves. He has reduced the body to ashes by his own system of cremation, with the exception of the head——'

Henry interrupted his brother there. 'Don't read any more!' he exclaimed.

'Let us do the Countess justice,' Lord Montbarry persisted. 'There are not half a dozen lines more that I can make out! The accidental breaking of his jar of acid has burnt the Baron's hands severely. He is still unable to proceed to the destruction of the head – and the Countess is woman enough (with all her wickedness) to shrink from attempting to take his place – when the first news is received of the coming arrival of the commission of inquiry despatched by the insurance offices. The Baron feels no alarm. Inquire as the commission may, it is the natural death of the Courier (in my Lord's character) that they are blindly investigating. The head not being destroyed, the obvious alternative is to hide it – and the Baron is equal to the occasion. His studies in the old library have informed him of a safe place of concealment in the palace. The Countess may recoil from handling the acids and watching the process of cremation; but she can surely sprinkle a little disinfecting powder——'

'No more!' Henry reiterated. 'No more!'

'There is no more that can be read, my dear fellow. The last page looks like sheer delirium. She may well have told you that her invention had failed her!'

'Face the truth honestly, Stephen, and say her memory.'

Lord Montbarry rose from the table at which he had been sitting, and looked at his brother with pitying eyes.

'Your nerves are out of order, Henry,' he said. 'And no wonder, after that frightful discovery under the hearthstone. We won't dispute about it; we will wait a day or two until you are quite yourself again. In the mean time, let us understand each other on one point at least. You leave the question of what is to be done with these pages of writing to me, as the head of the family?'

'I do.'

Lord Montbarry quietly took up the manuscript, and threw it into the fire. 'Let this rubbish be of some use,' he said, holding the pages down with the poker. 'The room is getting chilly – the Countess's Play will set some of these charred logs flaming again.' He waited a little at the fireplace, and returned to his brother. 'Now, Henry, I have a last word to say, and then I have done. I am ready to admit that you have stumbled, by an unlucky chance, on the proof of a crime committed in the old days of the palace, nobody knows how long ago. With that one concession, I dispute everything else. Rather than agree in the opinion you have formed, I won't believe anything that has happened. The supernatural influences that some of us felt when we first slept in this hotel – your loss of appetite, our sister's dreadful dreams, the smell that overpowered Francis, and the head that appeared to Agnes – I declare them all to be sheer delusions! I believe in nothing, nothing, nothing!' He opened the door to go out, and looked back into the room. 'Yes,' he resumed, 'there is one thing I believe in. My wife has committed a breach of confidence – I believe Agnes will marry you. Good night, Henry. We leave Venice the first thing to-morrow morning.'

So Lord Montbarry disposed of the mystery of The Haunted Hotel.

POSTSCRIPT

A LAST CHANCE OF DECIDING THE DIFFERENCE of opinion between the two brothers remained in Henry's possession. He had his own idea of the use to which he might put the false teeth as a means of inquiry when he and his fellow-travellers returned to England.

The only surviving depository of the domestic history of the family in past years, was Agnes Lockwood's old nurse. Henry took his first opportunity of trying to revive her personal recollections of the deceased Lord Montbarry. But the nurse had never forgiven the great man of the family for his desertion of Agnes; she flatly refused to consult her memory. 'Even the bare sight of my lord, when I last saw him in London,' said the old woman,' made my finger-nails itch to set their mark on his face. I was sent on an errand by Miss Agnes; and I met him coming out of his dentist's door – and, thank God, that's the last I ever saw of him!'

Thanks to the nurse's quick temper and quaint way of expressing herself, the object of Henry's inquiries was gained already! He ventured on asking if she had noticed the situation of the house. She had noticed, and still remembered the situation – did Master Henry suppose she had lost the use of her senses, because she happened to be nigh on eighty years old? The same day, he took the false teeth to the dentist, and set all further doubt (if doubt had still been possible) at rest for ever. The teeth had been made for the first Lord Montbarry.

Henry never revealed the existence of this last link in the chain of discovery to any living creature, his brother Stephen included. He carried his terrible secret with him to the grave.

There was one other event in the memorable past on which he preserved the same compassionate silence. Little Mrs Ferrari never knew that her husband had been – not, as she supposed, the Countess's victim – but the Countess's accomplice. She still believed that the late Lord Montbarry had sent her the thousand-pound note, and still recoiled from making use of a present which she persisted in declaring had 'the stain of her husband's blood on it'. Agnes, with the widow's entire approval, took the money to the Children's Hospital; and spent it on adding to the number of the beds.

In the spring of the new year, the marriage took place. At the special request of Agnes, the members of the family were the only persons present at the ceremony. There was no wedding breakfast – and the honeymoon was spent in the retirement of a cottage on the banks of the Thames.

During the last few days of the residence of the newly-married couple by the riverside, Lady Montbarry's children were invited to enjoy a day's play in the garden. The eldest girl overheard (and reported to her mother) a little conjugal dialogue which touched on the topic of the haunted hotel.

'Henry, I want you to give me a kiss.'

'There it is, my dear.'

'Now I am your wife, may I speak to you about something?'

'What is it?'

'Something that happened the day before we left Venice. You saw the Countess, during the last hours of her life. Won't you tell me whether she made any confession to you?'

'No conscious confession, Agnes – and therefore no confession that I need distress you by repeating.'

'Did she say nothing about what she saw or heard, on that dreadful night in my room?'

'Nothing. We only know that her mind never recovered the terror of it.'

Agnes was not quite satisfied. The subject troubled her. Even her own brief intercourse with her miserable rival of other days suggested questions that perplexed her. She remembered the Countess's prediction. 'You have to bring me to the day of discovery, and to the punishment that is my doom.' Had the prediction simply failed, like the other mortal prophecies? or had it been fulfilled on the terrible night when she had seen the apparition, and when she had innocently tempted the Countess to watch her in her room?

Let it, however, be recorded, among the other virtues of Mrs Henry Westwick, that she never again attempted to persuade her husband into betraying his secrets. Other men's wives, hearing of this extraordinary conduct (and being trained in the modern school of morals and manners), naturally regarded her with compassionate contempt. They spoke of Agnes, from that time forth, as 'rather an old-fashioned person'.

Is that all?

That is all.

Is there no explanation of the mystery of The Haunted Hotel?

Ask yourself if there is any explanation of the mystery of your own life and death. – Farewell.

MY LADY'S
MONEY

PERSONS OF THE STORY

WOMEN

LADY LYDIARD (*Widow of Lord Lydiard*)
ISABEL MILLER (*her Adopted Daughter*)
MISS PINK (*of South Morden*)
THE HON. MRS DRUMBLADE (*Sister to the Hon. A. Hardyman*)

MEN

THE HON. ALFRED HARDYMAN (*of the Stud Farm*)
MR FELIX SWEETSIR (*Lady Lydiard's Nephew*)
ROBERT MOODY (*Lady Lydiard's Footman*)
MR TROY (*Lady Lydiard's Lawyer*)
OLD SHARON (*in the Byeways of Legal Bohemia*)

ANIMAL

TOMMIE (*Lady Lydiard's Dog*)

PART THE FIRST

The Disappearance

❧ ONE ❧

OLD LADY LYDIARD SAT MEDITATING by the fireside, with three letters lying open on her lap.

Time had discoloured the paper, and had turned the ink to a brownish hue. The letters were all addressed to the same person – 'THE RIGHT HON. LORD LYDIARD' – and were all signed in the same way – 'Your affectionate cousin, James Tollmidge.' Judged by these specimens of his correspondence, Mr Tollmidge must have possessed one great merit as a letter-writer – the merit of brevity. He will weary nobody's patience, if he is allowed to have a hearing. Let him, therefore, be permitted, in his own high-flown way, to speak for himself.

First Letter. – 'My statement, as your Lordship requests, shall be short and to the point. I was doing very well as a portrait-painter in the country; and I had a wife and children to consider. Under the circumstances, if I had been left to decide for myself, I should certainly have waited until I had saved a little money before I ventured on the serious expense of taking a house and studio at the west end of London. Your Lordship, I positively declare, encouraged me to try the experiment without waiting. And here I am, unknown and unemployed, a helpless artist lost in London – with a sick wife and hungry children, and bankruptcy staring me in the face. On whose shoulders does this dreadful responsibility rest? On your Lordship's!'

Second Letter. – 'After a week's delay, you favour me, my Lord, with a curt reply. I can be equally curt on my side. I indignantly deny that I or my wife ever presumed to see your Lordship's name as a means of recommendation to sitters without your permission. Some enemy has slandered us. I claim as my right to know the name of that enemy.'

Third (and last) Letter. – 'Another week has passed – and not a word of answer has reached me from your Lordship. It matters little. I have employed the interval in making inquiries, and I have at last discovered the hostile influence which has estranged you from me. I have been, it seems, so unfortunate as to offend Lady Lydiard (how, I cannot imagine); and the all-powerful influence of this noble lady is now used against the struggling artist who is united to you by the sacred ties of kindred. Be it so. I can fight my way upwards, my Lord, as other men have done before me. A day may yet come when the throng of carriages waiting at the door of the fashionable portrait-painter will include her Ladyship's vehicle, and bring me the tardy expression of her Ladyship's regret. I refer you, my Lord Lydiard, to that day!'

Having read Mr Tollmidge's formidable assertions relating to herself for the second time, Lady Lydiard's meditations came to an abrupt end. She rose, took the letters in both hands to tear them up, hesitated, and threw them back in the cabinet drawer in which she had discovered them, among other papers that had not been arranged since Lord Lydiard's death.

'The idiot!' said her Ladyship, thinking of Mr Tollmidge, 'I never even heard of him, in my husband's lifetime; I never even knew that he was really related to Lord Lydiard, till I found his letters. What is to be done next?'

She looked, as she put that question to herself, at an open newspaper thrown on the table, which announced the death of 'that accomplished artist Mr Tollmidge, related, it is said, to the late well-known connoisseur, Lord Lydiard'. In the next sentence the writer of the obituary notice deplored the destitute condition of Mrs Tollmidge and her children, 'thrown helpless on the mercy of the world'. Lady Lydiard stood by the table with her eyes on those lines, and saw but too plainly the direction in which they pointed – the direction of her cheque-book.

Turning towards the fireplace, she rang the bell. 'I can do nothing in this matter,' she thought to herself, 'until I know whether the report about Mrs Tollmidge and her family is to be depended on. Has Moody come back?' she asked, when the servant appeared at the door. 'Moody' (otherwise her Ladyship's steward) had not come back. Lady Lydiard dismissed the subject of the artist's widow from further consideration until the steward returned, and gave her mind to a question of domestic interest which lay nearer to her heart. Her favourite dog had been ailing for some time past, and no report of him had reached her that morning. She opened a door near the fireplace, which led, through a little corridor hung with rare prints, to her own boudoir. 'Isabel!' she called out, 'how is Tommie?'

A fresh young voice answered from behind the curtain which closed the further end of the corridor, 'No better, my Lady.'

A low growl followed the fresh young voice, and added (in dog's language), 'Much worse, my Lady – much worse!'

Lady Lydiard closed the door again, with a compassionate sigh for Tommie, and walked slowly to and fro in her spacious drawing-room, waiting for the steward's return.

Accurately described, Lord Lydiard's widow was short and fat, and, in the matter of age, perilously near her sixtieth birthday. But it may be said, without paying a compliment, that she looked younger than her age by ten years at least. Her complexion was of that delicate pink tinge which is sometimes seen in old women with well-preserved constitutions. Her eyes (equally well preserved) were of that hard light blue colour which wears well, and does not wash out when tried by the test of tears. Add to this her short nose, her plump cheeks that set wrinkles at defiance, her white hair dressed in stiff little curls; and, if a doll could grow old, Lady Lydiard, at sixty, would have been the living image of that doll, taking life easily on its journey downwards to the prettiest of tombs, in a burial-ground where the myrtles and roses grew all the year round!

These being her Ladyship's personal merits, impartial history must acknowledge, on the list of her defects, a total want of tact and taste in her attire. The lapse of time since Lord Lydiard's death had left her at liberty to dress as she pleased. She arrayed her short, clumsy figure in colours that were far too bright for a woman of her age. Her dresses, badly chosen as to their hues, were perhaps not badly made, but were certainly badly worn. Morally, as well as physically, it must be said of Lady Lydiard that her outward side was her worst side. The anomalies of her dress were matched by the anomalies of her character. There were moments when she felt and spoke as became a lady of rank; and there were other moments when she felt and spoke as might have become the cook in the kitchen. Beneath these superficial inconsistencies, the great heart, the essentially true and generous nature of the woman, only waited the sufficient occasion to assert themselves. In the trivial intercourse of society she was open to ridicule on every side of her. But when a serious emergency tried the metal of which she was really made, the people who were loudest in laughing at her stood aghast, and wondered what had become of the familiar companion of their everyday lives.

Her Ladyship's promenade had lasted but a little while, when a man in black clothing presented himself noiselessly at the great door which opened on the staircase. Lady Lydiard signed to him impatiently to enter the room.

'I have been expecting you for some time, Moody,' she said. 'You look tired. Take a chair.'

The man in black bowed respectfully, and took his seat.

❧ TWO ❧

ROBERT MOODY WAS AT THIS time nearly forty years of age. He was a shy, quiet, dark person, with a pale, closely-shaven face, agreeably animated by large black eyes, set deep in their orbits. His mouth was perhaps his best feature; he had firm, well-shaped lips, which softened on rare occasions into a particularly winning smile. The whole look of the man, in spite of his habitual reserve, declared him to be eminently trustworthy. His position in Lady Lydiard's household was in no sense of the menial sort. He acted as her almoner and secretary as well as her steward – distributed her charities, wrote her letters on business, paid her bills, engaged her servants, stocked her wine-cellar, was authorized to borrow books from her library, and was served with his meals in his own room. His parentage gave him claims to these special favours; he was by birth entitled to rank as a gentleman. His father had failed at a time of commercial panic as a country banker, had paid a good dividend, and had died in exile abroad a broken-hearted man. Robert had tried to hold his place in the world, but adverse fortune kept him down. Undeserved disaster followed him from one employment to another, until he abandoned the struggle, bade a last farewell to the pride of other days, and accepted the position considerately and delicately offered to him in Lady Lydiard's house. He had now no near relations living, and he had never made many friends. In the intervals of occupation he led a lonely life in his little room. It was a matter of secret wonder among the women in the servants' hall, considering his personal advantages and the opportunities which must surely have been thrown in his way, that he had never tempted fortune in the character of a married man. Robert Moody entered into no explanations on that subject. In his own sad and quiet way he continued to lead his own sad and quiet life. The women all failing, from the handsome housekeeper downwards, to make the smallest impression on him, consoled themselves by prophetic visions of his future relations with the sex, and predicted vindictively that 'his time would come'.

'Well,' said Lady Lydiard, 'and what have you done?'

'Your Ladyship seemed to be anxious about the dog,' Moody answered, in the low tone which was habitual to him. 'I went first to the veterinary surgeon. He had been called away into the country; and—'

Lady Lydiard waved away the conclusion of the sentence with her hand. 'Never mind the surgeon. We must find somebody else. Where did you go next?'

'To your Ladyship's lawyer. Mr Troy wished me to say that he will have the honour of waiting on you—'

'Pass over the lawyer, Moody. I want to know about the painter's widow. Is it true that Mrs Tollmidge and her family are left in helpless poverty?'

'Not quite true, my Lady. I have seen the clergyman of the parish, who takes an interest in the case—'

Lady Lydiard interrupted her steward for the third time. 'Did you mention my name?' she asked sharply.

'Certainly not, my Lady. I followed my instructions, and described you as a benevolent person in search of cases of real distress. It is quite true that Mr Tollmidge has died, leaving nothing to his family. But the widow has a little income of seventy pounds in her own right.'

'Is that enough to live on, Moody?' her Ladyship asked.

'Enough, in this case, for the widow and her daughter,' Moody answered. 'The difficulty is to pay the few debts left standing, and to start the two sons in life. They are reported to be steady lads; and the family is much respected in the neighbourhood. The clergyman proposes to get a few influential names to begin with, and to start a subscription.'

'No subscription!' protested Lady Lydiard. 'Mr Tollmidge was Lord Lydiard's cousin; and Mrs Tollmidge is related to his Lordship by marriage. It would be degrading to my husband's memory to have the begging-box sent round for his relations, no matter how distant they may be. Cousins!' exclaimed her Ladyship, suddenly descending from the lofty ranges of sentiment to the low. 'I hate the very name of them! A person who is near enough to me to be my relation and far enough off from me to be my sweetheart, is a double-faced sort of person that I don't like. Let's get back to the widow and her sons. How much do they want?'

'A subscription of five hundred pounds, my Lady, would provide for everything – if it could only be collected.'

'It *shall* be collected, Moody! I will pay the subscription out of my own purse.' Having asserted herself in those noble terms, she spoilt the effect of her own outburst of generosity by dropping to the sordid view of the subject in her next sentence. 'Five hundred pounds is a good bit of money, though; isn't it, Moody?'

'It is, indeed, my Lady.' Rich and generous as he knew his mistress to be, her proposal to pay the whole subscription took the steward by surprise. Lady Lydiard's quick perception instantly detected what was passing in his mind.

'You don't quite understand my position in this matter,' she said. 'When I read the newspaper notice of Mr Tollmidge's death, I searched among his Lordship's papers to see if they really were related. I discovered some letters from Mr Tollmidge, which showed me that he and Lord Lydiard were cousins. One of those letters contains some very painful statements, reflecting most untruly and unjustly on my conduct; lies, in short,' her Ladyship burst out, losing her dignity, as usual. 'Lies, Moody, for which Mr Tollmidge deserved to be horsewhipped. I would have done it myself if his Lordship had told me at the time. No matter; it's useless to dwell on the thing now,' she continued, ascending again to the forms of expression which became a lady of rank. 'This unhappy man has done me a gross injustice; my motives may be seriously misjudged, if I appear personally in communicating with his family. If I relieve them anonymously in their present trouble, I spare them the exposure of a public subscription, and I do what I believe his Lordship would have done himself if he had lived. My desk is on the other table. Bring it here, Moody; and let me return good for evil, while I'm in the humour for it!'

Moody obeyed in silence. Lady Lydiard wrote a cheque.

'Take that to the banker's, and bring back a five-hundred pound note,' she said. 'I'll enclose it to the clergyman as coming from "an unknown friend". And be quick about it. I am only a fallible mortal, Moody. Don't leave me time enough to take the stingy view of five hundred pounds.'

Moody went out with the cheque. No delay was to be apprehended in obtaining the money; the banking-house was hard by, in St James's Street. Left alone, Lady Lydiard decided on occupying her mind in the generous direction by composing her anonymous letter to the clergyman. She had just taken a sheet of note-paper from her desk, when a servant appeared at the door announcing a visitor—

'Mr Felix Sweetsir!'

❧   THREE   ❧

'MY NEPHEW!' LADY LYDIARD EXCLAIMED, in a tone which expressed astonishment, but certainly not pleasure as well. 'How many years is it since you and I last met?' she asked, in her abruptly straightforward way, as Mr Felix Sweetsir approached her writing-table.

The visitor was not a person easily discouraged. He took Lady

Lydiard's hand, and kissed it with easy grace. A shade of irony was in his manner, agreeably relieved by a playful flash of tenderness.

'Years, my dear aunt?' he said. 'Look in your glass and you will see that time has stood still since we met last. How wonderfully well you wear! When shall we celebrate the appearance of your first wrinkle? I am too old; I shall never live to see it.'

He took an easy-chair, uninvited; placed himself close at his aunt's side, and ran his eye over her ill-chosen dress with an air of satirical admiration. 'How perfectly successful!' he said, with his well-bred insolence. 'What a chaste gaiety of colour!'

'What do you want?' asked her Ladyship, not in the least softened by the compliment.

'I want to pay my respects to my dear aunt,' Felix answered, perfectly impenetrable to his ungracious reception, and perfectly comfortable in a spacious arm-chair.

No pen-and-ink portrait need surely be drawn of Felix Sweetsir – he is too well-known a picture in society. The little lithe man, with his bright, restless eyes, and his long iron-grey hair falling in curls to his shoulders; his airy step and his cordial manner; his uncertain age, his innumerable accomplishments, and his unbounded popularity – is he not familiar everywhere, and welcome everywhere? How gratefully he receives, how prodigally he repays, the cordial appreciation of an admiring world! Every man he knows is 'a charming fellow'. Every woman he sees is 'sweetly pretty'. What picnics he gives on the banks of the Thames in the summer season! What a well-earned little income he derives from the whist-table! What an inestimable actor he is at private theatricals of all sorts (weddings included)! Did you never read Sweetsir's novel, dashed off in the intervals of curative perspiration at a German bath? Then you don't know what brilliant fiction really is. He has never written a second work; he does everything, and only does it once. One song – the despair of professional composers. One picture – just to show how easily a gentleman can take up an art and drop it again. A really multiform man, with all the graces and all the accomplishments scintillating perpetually at his fingers' ends. If these poor pages have achieved nothing else, they have done a service to persons not in society by presenting them to Sweetsir. In his gracious company the narrative brightens; and writer and reader (catching reflected brilliancy) understand each other at last, thanks to Sweetsir.

'Well,' said Lady Lydiard, 'now you are here, what have you got to say for yourself? You have been abroad, of course! Where?'

'Principally at Paris, my dear aunt. The only place that is fit to live in – for this excellent reason, that the French are the only people who know how to make the most of life. One has relations and friends in England; and every now and then one returns to London—'

'When one has spent all one's money in Paris,' her Ladyship interposed. 'That's what you were going to say, isn't it?'

Felix submitted to the interruption with his delightful good-humour.

'What a bright creature you are!' he exclaimed. 'What would I not give for your flow of spirits! Yes – one does spend money in Paris, as you say. The clubs, the stock exchange, the race-course: you try your luck here, there, and everywhere; and you lose and win, win and lose – and you haven't a dull day to complain of.' He paused, his smile died away, he looked inquiringly at Lady Lydiard. 'What a wonderful existence yours must be,' he resumed. 'The everlasting question with your needy fellow-creatures, "Where am I to get money?" is a question that has never passed your lips. Enviable woman!' He paused once more – surprised and puzzled this time. 'What is the matter, my dear aunt? You seem to be suffering under some uneasiness.'

'I am suffering under your conversation,' her Ladyship answered sharply. 'Money is a sore subject with me just now,' she went on, with her eyes on her nephew, watching the effect of what she said. 'I have spent five hundred pounds this morning with a scrape of my pen. And, only a week since, I yielded to temptation and made an addition to my picture-gallery.' She looked, as she said those words, towards an archway at the farther end of the room, closed by curtains of purple velvet. 'I really tremble when I think of what that one picture cost me before I could call it mine. A landscape by Hobbema; and the National Gallery bidding against me. Never mind!' she concluded, consoling herself, as usual, with considerations that were beneath her. 'Hobbema will sell at my death for a bigger price than I gave for him – that's one comfort!' She looked again at Felix; a smile of mischievous satisfaction began to show itself in her face. 'Anything wrong with your watch-chain?' she asked.

Felix, absently playing with his watch-chain, started as if his aunt had suddenly awakened him. While Lady Lydiard had been speaking, his vivacity had subsided little by little, and had left him looking so serious and so old that his most intimate friend would hardly have known him again. Roused by the sudden question that had been put to him, he seemed to be casting about in his mind in search of the first excuse for his silence that might turn up.

'I was wondering,' he began, 'why I miss something when I look round this beautiful room; something familiar, you know, that I fully expected to find here.'

'Tommie?' suggested Lady Lydiard, still watching her nephew as maliciously as ever.

'That's it!' cried Felix, seizing his excuse, and rallying his spirits. 'Why don't I hear Tommie snarling behind me; why don't I feel Tommie's teeth in my trousers?'

The smile vanished from Lady Lydiard's face; the tone taken by her nephew in speaking of her dog was disrespectful in the extreme. She showed him plainly that she disapproved of it. Felix went on, nevertheless, impenetrable to reproof of the silent sort. 'Dear little Tommie! So delightfully fat; and such an infernal temper! I don't know whether I hate him or love him. Where is he?'

'Ill in bed,' answered her ladyship, with a gravity which startled even Felix himself. 'I wish to speak to you about Tommie. You know everybody. Do you know of a good dog-doctor? The person I have employed so far doesn't at all satisfy me.'

'Professional person?' inquired Felix.

'Yes.'

'All humbugs, my dear aunt. The worse the dog gets the bigger the bill grows, don't you see? I have got the man for you – a gentleman. Knows more about horses and dogs than all the veterinary surgeons put together. We met in the boat yesterday crossing the Channel. You know him by name, of course? Lord Rotherfield's youngest son, Alfred Hardyman.'

'The owner of the stud farm? The man who has bred the famous race-horses?' cried Lady Lydiard. 'My dear Felix, how can I presume to trouble such a great personage about my dog?'

Felix burst into his genial laugh. 'Never was modesty more woefully out of place,' he rejoined. 'Hardyman is dying to be presented to your Ladyship. He has heard, like everybody, of the magnificent decorations of this house, and he is longing to see them. His chambers are close by, in Pall-Mall. If he is at home we will have him here in five minutes. Perhaps I had better see the dog first?'

Lady Lydiard shook her head. 'Isabel says he had better not be disturbed,' she answered. 'Isabel understands him better than anybody.'

Felix lifted his lively eyebrows with a mixed expression of curiosity and surprise. 'Who is Isabel?'

Lady Lydiard was vexed with herself for carelessly mentioning Isabel's name in her nephew's presence. Felix was not the sort of person whom she was desirous of admitting to her confidence in domestic matters. 'Isabel is an addition to my household since you were here last,' she answered shortly.

'Young and pretty?' inquired Felix. 'Ah! you look serious, and you don't answer me. Young and pretty, evidently. Which may I see first, the addition to your household or the addition to your picture-gallery? You look at the picture-gallery – I am answered again.' He rose to approach the archway, and stopped at his first step forward. 'A sweet girl is a dreadful responsibility, aunt,' he resumed, with an ironical assumption of gravity. 'Do you know, I shouldn't be surprised if Isabel, in the long run, cost you more than Hobbema. Who is this at the door?'

The person at the door was Robert Moody, returned from the bank. Mr Felix Sweetsir, being near-sighted, was obliged to fit his eye-glass in position before he could recognize the prime minister of Lady Lydiard's household.

'Ha! our worthy Moody. How well he wears! Not a grey hair on his head – and look at mine! What dye do you use, Moody? If he had my open disposition he would tell. As it is, he looks unutterable things, and holds his tongue. Ah! if I could only have held *my* tongue – when I was in the diplomatic service, you know – what a position I might have occupied by this time! Don't let me interrupt you, Moody, if you have anything to say to Lady Lydiard.'

Having acknowledged Mr Sweetsir's lively greeting by a formal bow, and a grave look of wonder which respectfully repelled that vivacious gentleman's flow of humour, Moody turned towards his mistress.

'Have you got the bank-note?' asked her Ladyship.

Moody laid the bank-note on the table.

'Am I in the way?' inquired Felix.

'No,' said his aunt. 'I have a letter to write; it won't occupy me for more than a few minutes. You can stay here, or go and look at the Hobbema, which you please.'

Felix made a second sauntering attempt to reach the picture-gallery. Arrived within a few steps of the entrance, he stopped again, attracted by an open cabinet of Italian workmanship, filled with rare old china. Being nothing if not a cultivated amateur, Mr Sweetsir paused to pay his passing tribute of admiration before the contents of the cabinet. 'Charming! charming!' he said to himself, with his head twisted appreciatively a little on one side. Lady Lydiard and Moody left him in undisturbed enjoyment of the china, and went on with the business of the bank-note.

'Ought we to take the number of the note, in case of accident?' asked her Ladyship.

Moody produced a slip of paper from his waistcoat pocket. 'I took the number, my Lady, at the bank.'

'Very well. You keep it. While I am writing my letter, suppose you direct the envelope. What is the clergyman's name?'

Moody mentioned the name and directed the envelope. Felix, happening to look round at Lady Lydiard and the steward while they were both engaged in writing, returned suddenly to the table as if he had been struck by a new idea.

'Is there a third pen?' he asked. 'Why shouldn't I write a line at once to Hardyman, aunt? The sooner you have his opinion about Tommie the better – don't you think so?'

Lady Lydiard pointed to the pen tray, with a smile. To show consideration for her dog was to seize irresistibly on the high-road to her favour. Felix set to work on his letter, in a large scrambling hand-writing, with plenty of ink and a noisy pen. 'I declare we are like clerks in an office,' he remarked, in his cheery way. 'All with our noses to the paper, writing as if we lived by it! Here, Moody, let one of the servants take this at once to Mr Hardyman's.'

The messenger was despatched. Robert returned, and waited near his mistress, with the directed envelope in his hand. Felix sauntered back slowly towards the picture-gallery, for the third time. In a moment more Lady Lydiard finished her letter, and folded up the bank-note in it. She had just taken the directed envelope from Moody, and had just placed the letter inside it, when a scream from the inner room, in which Isabel was nursing the sick dog, startled everybody. 'My Lady! my Lady!' cried the girl, distractedly, 'Tommie is in a fit? Tommie is dying!'

Lady Lydiard dropped the unclosed envelope on the table, and ran – yes, short as she was and fat as she was, ran – into the inner room. The two men, left together, looked at each other.

'Moody,' said Felix, in his lazily-cynical way, 'do you think if you or I were in a fit that her Ladyship would run? Bah! these are the things that shake one's faith in human nature. I feel infernally seedy. That cursed Channel passage – I tremble in my inmost stomach when I think of it. Get me something, Moody.'

'What shall I send you, sir?' Moody asked coldly.

'Some dry curaçoa and a biscuit. And let it be brought to me in the picture-gallery. Damn the dog! I'll go and look at Hobbema.'

This time he succeeded in reaching the archway, and disappeared behind the curtains of the picture-gallery.

❧ FOUR ❧

LEFT ALONE IN THE DRAWING-ROOM, Moody looked at the unfastened envelope on the table.

Considering the value of the inclosure, might he feel justified in wetting the gum and securing the envelope for safety's sake? After thinking it over, Moody decided that he was not justified in meddling with the letter. On reflection, her Ladyship might have changes to make in it – or might have a postscript to add to what she had already written. Apart, too, from these considerations, was it reasonable to act as if Lady Lydiard's house was an hotel, perpetually open to the intrusion of strangers? Objects worth twice five hundred pounds in the aggregate were scattered about on the tables and in the unlocked cabinets all round him. Moody withdrew, without further hesitation, to order the light restorative prescribed for himself by Mr Sweetsir.

The footman who took the curaçoa into the picture-gallery found Felix recumbent on a sofa, admiring the famous Hobbema.

'Don't interrupt me,' he said peevishly, catching the servant in the act of staring at him. 'Put down the bottle and go!' Forbidden to look at Mr Sweetsir, the man's eyes as he left the gallery turned wonderingly towards the famous landscape. And what did he see? He saw one towering big cloud in the sky that threatened rain, two withered mahogany-coloured trees sorely in want of rain, a muddy road greatly the worse for rain, and a vagabond boy running home who was afraid of the rain. That was the picture, to the footman's eye. He took a gloomy view of the state of Mr Sweetsir's brains on his return to the servants' hall. 'A slate loose, poor devil!' That was the footman's report of the brilliant Felix.

Immediately on the servant's departure, the silence in the picture-gallery was broken by voices penetrating into it from the drawing-room. Felix rose to a sitting position on the sofa. He had recognized the voice of Alfred Hardyman saying, 'Don't disturb Lady Lydiard,' and the voice of Moody answering, 'I will just knock at the door of her Ladyship's room, sir; you will find Mr Sweetsir in the picture-gallery.'

The curtains over the archway parted, and disclosed the figure of a tall man, with a closely cropped head set a little stiffly on his shoulders. The immovable gravity of face and manner which every Englishman seems to acquire who lives constantly in the society of horses, was the gravity which this gentleman displayed as he entered the picture-gallery. He was a finely made, sinewy man, with clearly cut, regular features. If he had not been affected with horses on the brain he would doubtless have been personally popular with the women. As it was, the serene and hippic gloom of the handsome horse-breeder daunted the daughters of Eve, and they failed to make up their minds about the exact value of him, socially considered. Alfred Hardyman was nevertheless a remarkable man in his way. He had been offered the customary alternatives submitted to the younger sons of the nobility – the Church or the diplomatic service – and had refused the one and the other. 'I like horses,' he said, 'and I mean to get my living out of them. Don't talk to me about my position in the world. Talk to my eldest brother, who gets the money and the title.' Starting in life with these sensible views, and with a small capital of five thousand pounds, Hardyman took his own place in the sphere that was fitted for him. At the period of this narrative he was already a rich man, and one of the greatest authorities on horse-breeding in England. His prosperity made no change in him. He was always the same grave, quiet, obstinately resolute man – true to the few friends whom he admitted to his intimacy, and sincere to a fault in the expression of his feelings among persons whom he distrusted or disliked. As he entered the picture-gallery and paused for a moment looking at Felix on the sofa, his large, cold, steady grey eyes rested on the little man with an indifference that just verged on contempt. Felix, on the other hand, sprang to his feet with alert politeness and greeted his friend with exuberant cordiality.

'Dear old boy! This is so good of you,' he began. 'I feel it – I do assure you I feel it!'

'You needn't trouble yourself to feel it,' was the quietly-ungracious answer. 'Lady Lydiard brings me here. I come to see the house – and the dog.' He looked round the gallery in his gravely attentive way. 'I don't understand pictures,' he remarked resignedly. 'I shall go back to the drawing-room.'

After a moment's consideration, Felix followed him into the drawing-room, with the air of a man who was determined not to be repelled.

'Well?' asked Hardyman. 'What is it?'

'About that matter?' Felix said, inquiringly.

'What matter?'

'Oh, you know. Will next week do?'

'Next week *won't* do.'

Mr Felix Sweetsir cast one look at his friend. His friend was too intently occupied with the decorations of the drawing-room to notice the look.

'Will to-morrow do?' Felix resumed, after an interval.

'Yes.'

'At what time?'

'Between twelve and one in the afternoon.'

'Between twelve and one in the afternoon,' Felix repeated. He looked again at Hardyman and took his hat. 'Make my apologies to my aunt,' he said. 'You must introduce yourself to her Ladyship. I can't wait here any longer.' He walked out of the room, having deliberately returned the contemptuous indifference of Hardyman by a similar indifference on his own side, at parting.

Left by himself, Hardyman took a chair and glanced at the door which led into the boudoir. The steward had knocked at that door, had disappeared through it, and had not appeared again. How much longer was Lady Lydiard's visitor to be left unnoticed in Lady Lydiard's house?

As the question passed through his mind the boudoir door opened. For once in his life, Alfred Hardyman's composure deserted him. He started to his feet, like an ordinary mortal taken completely by suprise.

Instead of Mr Moody, instead of Lady Lydiard, there appeared in the open doorway a young woman in a state of embarrassment, who actually quickened the beat of Mr Hardyman's heart the moment he set eyes on her. Was the person who produced this amazing impression at first sight a person of importance? Nothing of the sort. She was only 'Isabel', surnamed 'Miller'. Even her name had nothing in it. Only 'Isabel Miller'!

Had she any pretensions to distinction in virtue of her personal appearance?

It is not easy to answer the question. The women (let us put the worst judges first) had long since discovered that she wanted that indispensable elegance of figure which is derived from slimness of waist and length of limb. The men (who were better acquainted with the subject) looked at her figure from their point of view; and, finding it essentially embraceable, asked for nothing more. It might have been her bright complexion, or it might have been the bold lustre of her eyes (as the women considered it), that dazzled the lords of creation generally, and made them all alike incompetent to discover her faults. Still, she had compensating attractions which no severity of criticism could dispute. Her smile, beginning at her lips, flowed brightly and instantly over her whole face. A delicious atmosphere of health, freshness, and good humour seemed to radiate from her wherever she went and whatever she did. For the rest, her brown hair grew low over her broad white forehead, and was topped by a neat little lace cap with ribbons of a violet colour. A plain collar and plain cuffs encircled her smooth, round neck, and her plump dimpled hands. Her merino dress, covering but not hiding the charming outline of her bosom, matched the colour of the cap-ribbons, and was brightened by a white muslin apron coquettishly trimmed about the pockets, a gift from Lady Lydiard. Blushing and smiling, she let the door fall to behind her, and, shyly approaching the stranger, said to him, in her small, clear voice, 'If you please, sir, are you Mr Hardyman?'

The gravity of the great horsebreeder deserted him at her first question. He smiled as he acknowledged that he was 'Mr Hardyman' – he smiled as he offered her a chair.

'No, thank you, sir,' she said, with a quaintly pretty inclination of her head. 'I am only sent here to make her Ladyship's apologies. She has put the poor dear dog into a warm bath, and she can't leave him. And Mr Moody can't come instead of me, because I was too frightened to be of any use, and so he had to hold the dog. That's all. We are very anxious, sir, to know if the warm bath is the right thing. Please come into the room and tell us.'

She led the way back to the door. Hardyman, naturally enough, was
slow to follow her. When a man is fascinated by the charm of youth and
beauty, he is in no hurry to transfer his attention to a sick animal in a
bath. Hardyman seized on the first excuse that he could devise for
keeping Isabel to himself – that is to say, for keeping her in the drawing-
room.

'I think I shall be better able to help you,' he said, 'if you will tell me
something about the dog first.'

Even his accent in speaking had altered to a certain degree. The quiet,
dreary monotone in which he habitually spoke quickened a little under
his present excitement. As for Isabel, she was too deeply interested in
Tommie's welfare to suspect that she was being made the victim of a
stratagem. She left the door and returned to Hardyman with eager eyes.
'What can I tell you, sir?' she asked innocently.

Hardyman pressed his advantage without mercy.

'You can tell me what sort of dog he is?'

'Yes, sir.'

'How old he is?'

'Yes, sir.'

'What his name is? – what his temper is? – what his illness is? what
diseases his father and mother had? – what——'

Isabel's head began to turn giddy. 'One thing at a time, sir!' she
interposed, with a gesture of entreaty. 'The dog sleeps on my bed, and I
had a bad night with him, he disturbed me so, and I am afraid I am
very stupid this morning. His name is Tommie. We are obliged to call
him by it, because he won't answer to any other than the name he had
when my Lady bought him. But we spell it with an 'i e' at the end,
which makes it less vulgar than Tommy with a 'y'. I am very sorry, sir
– I forget what else you wanted to know. Please to come in here and my
Lady will tell you everything.'

She tried to get back to the door of the boudoir. Hardyman, feasting
his eyes on the pretty, changeful face that looked up at him with such
innocent confidence in his authority, drew her away from the door by the
one means at his disposal. He returned to his questions about Tommie.

'Wait a little, please. What sort of dog is he?'

Isabel turned back again from the door. To describe Tommie was a
labour of love. 'He is the most beautiful dog in the world!' the girl began,
with kindling eyes. 'He has the most exquisite white curly hair and two
light brown patches on his back – and, oh! *such* lovely dark eyes! They
call him a Scotch terrier. When he is well his appetite is truly wonderful
– nothing comes amiss to him, sir, from pâté de foie gras to potatoes. He
has his enemies, poor dear, though you wouldn't think it. People who
won't put up with being bitten by him (what shocking tempers one does

meet with, to be sure!) call him a mongrel. Isn't it a shame? Please come in and see him, sir; my Lady will be tired of waiting.'

Another journey to the door followed those words, checked instantly by a serious objection.

'Stop a minute! You must tell me what his temper is, or I can do nothing for him.'

Isabel returned once more, feeling that it was really serious this time. Her gravity was even more charming than her gaiety. As she lifted her face to him, with large solemn eyes, expressive of her sense of responsibility, Hardyman would have given every horse in his stables to have had the privilege of taking her in his arms and kissing her.

'Tommie has the temper of an angel with the people he likes,' she said. 'When he bites, it generally means that he objects to strangers. He loves my Lady, and he loves Mr Moody, and he loves me, and – and I think that's all. This way, sir, if you please, I am sure I heard my Lady call.'

'No,' said Hardyman, in his immovably obstinate way. 'Nobody called. About this dog's temper? Doesn't he take to any strangers? What sort of people does he bite in general?'

Isabel's pretty lips began to curl upward at the corners in a quaint smile. Hardyman's last imbecile question had opened her eyes to the true state of the case. Still, Tommie's future was in this strange gentleman's hands; she felt bound to consider that. And, moreover, it was no everyday event, in Isabel's experience, to fascinate a famous personage, who was also a magnificent and perfectly dressed man. She ran the risk of wasting another minute or two, and went on with the memoirs of Tommie.

'I must own, sir,' she resumed, 'that he behaves a little ungratefully – even to strangers who take an interest in him. When he gets lost in the streets (which is very often), he sits down on the pavement and howls till he collects a pitying crowd round him; and when they try to read his name and address on his collar he snaps at them. The servants generally find him and bring him back; and as soon as he gets home he turns round on the doorstep and snaps at the servants. I think it must be his fun. You should see him sitting up in his chair at dinner-time, waiting to be helped, with his fore paws on the edge of the table, like the hands of a gentleman at a public dinner making a speech. But, oh!' cried Isabel, checking herself, with the tears in her eyes, 'how can I talk of him in this way when he is so dreadfully ill! Some of them say it's bronchitis, and some say it's his liver. Only yesterday I took him to the front door to give him a little air, and he stood still on the pavement, quite stupefied. For the first time in his life, he snapped at nobody who went by; and, oh, dear, he hadn't even the heart to smell a lamp-post!'

Isabel had barely stated this last afflicting circumstance when the memoirs of Tommie were suddenly cut short by the voice of Lady Lydiard – really calling this time – from the inner room.

'Isabel! Isabel!' cried her Ladyship, 'what are you about?'

Isabel ran to the door of the boudoir and threw it open. 'Go in, sir! Pray go in!' she said.

'Without you?' Hardyman asked.

'I will follow you, sir. I have something to do for her Ladyship first.'

She still held the door open, and pointed entreatingly to the passage which led to the boudoir. 'I shall be blamed, sir,' she said, 'if you don't go in.'

This statement of the case left Hardyman no alternative. He presented himself to Lady Lydiard without another moment of delay.

Having closed the drawing-room door on him, Isabel waited a little, absorbed in her own thoughts.

She was now perfectly well aware of the effect which she had produced on Hardyman. Her vanity, it is not to be denied, was flattered by his admiration – he was so grand and so tall, and he had such fine large eyes. The girl looked prettier than ever as she stood with her head down and her colour heightened, smiling to herself. A clock on the chimneypiece striking the half-hour roused her. She cast one look at the glass, as she passed it, and went to the table at which Lady Lydiard had been writing.

Methodical Mr Moody, in submitting to be employed as bath-attendant upon Tommie, had not forgotten the interests of his mistress. He reminded her Ladyship that she had left her letter, with a bank-note inclosed in it, unsealed. Absorbed in the dog, Lady Lydiard answered, 'Isabel is doing nothing, let Isabel seal it. Show Mr Hardyman in here,' she continued, turning to Isabel, 'and then seal a letter of mine which you will find on the table.' 'And when you have sealed it,' careful Mr Moody added, 'put it back on the table; I will take charge of it when her Ladyship has done with me.'

Such were the special instructions which now detained Isabel in the drawing-room. She lit the taper, and closed and sealed the open envelope, without feeling curiosity enough even to look at the address. Mr Hardyman was the uppermost subject in her thoughts. Leaving the sealed letter on the table, she returned to the fireplace, and studied her own charming face attentively in the looking-glass. The time passed – and Isabel's reflection was still the subject of Isabel's contemplation. 'He must see many beautiful ladies,' she thought, veering backwards and forwards between pride and humility. 'I wonder what he sees in Me?'

The clock struck the hour. Almost at the same moment the boudoir-door opened, and Robert Moody, released at last from attendance on Tommie, entered the drawing-room.

∞ FIVE ∞

'WELL?' ASKED ISABEL EAGERLY, 'what does Mr Hardyman say? Does he think he can cure Tommie?'

Moody answered a little coldly and stiffly. His dark, deeply set eyes rested on Isabel with an uneasy look.

'Mr Hardyman seems to understand animals,' he said. 'He lifted the dog's eyelid and looked at his eyes, and then he told us the bath was useless.'

'Go on!' said Isabel impatiently. 'He did something, I suppose, besides telling you that the bath was useless?'

'He took a knife out of his pocket, with a lancet in it.'

Isabel clasped her hands with a faint cry of horror. 'Oh, Mr Moody! did he hurt Tommie?'

'Hurt him?' Moody repeated, indignant at the interest which she felt in the animal, and the indifference which she exhibited towards the man (as represented by himself). 'Hurt him, indeed! Mr Hardyman bled the brute – '

'Brute?' Isabel reiterated, with flashing eyes. 'I know some people, Mr Moody, who really deserve to be called by that horrid word. If you can't say "Tommie" when you speak of him in my presence, be so good as to say "the dog".'

Moody yielded with the worst possible grace. 'Oh, very well! Mr Hardyman bled the dog, and brought him to his senses directly. I am charged to tell you—' He stopped, as if the message which he was instructed to deliver was in the last degree distasteful to him.

'Well, what were you charged to tell me?'

'I was to say that Mr Hardyman will give you instructions how to treat the dog for the future.'

Isabel hastened to the door, eager to receive her instructions. Moody stopped her before she could open it.

'You are in a great hurry to get to Mr Hardyman,' he remarked.

Isabel looked back at him in surprise. 'You said just now that Mr Hardyman was waiting to tell me how to nurse Tommie.'

'Let him wait,' Moody rejoined sternly. 'When I left him, he was sufficiently occupied in expressing his favourable opinion of you to her Ladyship.'

The steward's pale face turned paler still as he said those words. With the arrival of Isabel in Lady Lydiard's house 'his time had come' – exactly as the women in the servants' hall had predicted. At last the impenetrable man felt the influence of the sex; at last he knew the passion of love – misplaced, ill-starred, hopeless love, for a woman who was young enough to be his child. He had already spoken to Isabel more than once in terms which told his secret plainly enough. But the smouldering fire of jealousy in the man, fanned into flame by Hardyman, now showed itself for the first time. His looks, even more than his words, would have warned a woman with any knowledge of the natures of men to be careful how she answered him. Young, giddy, and inexperienced, Isabel followed the flippant impulse of the moment, without a thought of the consequences. 'I'm sure it's very kind of Mr Hardyman to speak favourably of me,' she said, with a pert little laugh. 'I hope you are not jealous of him, Mr Moody?'

Moody was in no humour to make allowances for the unbridled gaiety of youth and good spirits. 'I hate any man who admires you,' he burst out passionately, 'let him be who he may!'

Isabel looked at her strange lover with unaffected astonishment. How unlike Mr Hardyman, who had treated her as a lady from first to last! 'What an odd man you are!' she said. 'You can't take a joke. I'm sure I didn't mean to offend you.'

'You don't offend me – you do worse, you distress me.'

Isabel's colour began to rise. The merriment died out of her face; she looked at Moody gravely. 'I don't like to be accused of distressing people when I don't deserve it,' she said. 'I had better leave you. Let me by, if you please.'

Having committed one error in offending her, Moody committed another in attempting to make his peace with her. Acting under the fear that she would really leave him, he took her roughly by the arm.

'You are always trying to get away from me,' he said. 'I wish I knew how to make you like me, Isabel.'

'I don't allow you to call me Isabel!' she retorted, struggling to free herself from his hold. 'Let go of my arm. You hurt me.'

Moody dropped her arm with a bitter sigh. 'I don't know how to deal with you,' he said simply. 'Have some pity on me!'

If the steward had known anything of women (at Isabel's age) he would never have appealed to her mercy in those plain terms, and at the unpropitious moment. 'Pity you?' she repeated contemptuously. 'Is that all you have to say to me after hurting my arm? What a bear you are!' She shrugged her shoulders and put her hands coquettishly into the pockets of her apron. That was how she pitied him! His face turned paler and paler – he writhed under it.

'For God's sake, don't turn everything I say to you into ridicule!' he cried. 'You know I love you with all my heart and soul. Again and again I have asked you to be my wife – and you laugh at me as if it was a joke. I haven't deserved to be treated in that cruel way. It maddens me – I can't endure it!'

Isabel looked down on the floor, and followed the lines in the pattern of the carpet with the end of her smart little shoe. She could hardly have been farther away from really understanding Moody if he had spoken in Hebrew. She was partly startled, partly puzzled, by the strong emotions which she had unconsciously called into being. 'Oh dear me!' she said, 'why can't you talk of something else? Why can't we be friends? Excuse me for mentioning it,' she went on, looking up at him with a saucy smile, 'you are old enough to be my father.'

Moody's head sank on his breast. 'I own it,' he answered humbly. 'But there is something to be said for me. Men as old as I am have made good husbands before now. I would devote my whole life to make you happy. There isn't a wish you could form which I wouldn't be proud to obey. You mustn't reckon me by years. My youth has not been wasted in a profligate life; I can be truer to you and fonder of you than many a younger man. Surely my heart is not quite unworthy of you, when it is all yours. I have lived such a lonely, miserable life – and you might so easily brighten it. You are kind to everybody else, Isabel. Tell me, dear, why are you so hard on *me*?'

His voice trembled as he appealed to her in those simple words. He had taken the right way at last to produce an impression on her. She really felt for him. All that was true and tender in her nature began to rise in her and take his part. Unhappily, he felt too deeply and too strongly to be patient, and give her time. He completely misinterpreted her silence – completely mistook the motive that made her turn aside for a moment, to gather composure enough to speak to him. 'Ah!' he burst out bitterly, turning away on his side, 'you have no heart.'

She instantly resented those unjust words. At that moment they wounded her to the quick.

'You know best,' she said. 'I have no doubt you are right. Remember one thing, however, though I have no heart, I have never encouraged you, Mr Moody. I have declared over and over again that I could only be your friend. Understand that for the future, if you please. There are plenty of nice women who will be glad to marry you, I have no doubt. You will always have my best wishes for your welfare. Good morning. Her Ladyship will wonder what has become of me. Be so kind as to let me pass.'

Tortured by the passion that consumed him, Moody obstinately kept his place between Isabel and the door. The unworthy suspicion of her, which had been in his mind all through the interview, now forced its way outwards to expression at last.

'No woman ever used a man as you use me without some reason for it,' he said. 'You have kept your secret wonderfully well – but sooner or later all secrets get found out. I know what is in your mind as well as you know it yourself. You are in love with some other man.'

Isabel's face flushed deeply; the defensive pride of her sex was up in arms in an instant. She cast one disdainful look at Moody, without troubling herself to express her contempt in words. 'Stand out of my way, sir!' – that was all she said to him.

'You are in love with some other man,' he reiterated passionately. 'Deny it if you can!'

'Deny it?' she repeated with flashing eyes. 'What right have you to ask the question? Am I not free to do as I please?'

He stood looking at her, meditating his next words with a sudden and sinister change to self-restraint. Suppressed rage was in his rigidly set eyes, suppressed rage was in his trembling hand as he raised it emphatically while he spoke his next words.

'I have one thing more to say,' he answered, 'and then I have done. If I am not your husband, no other man shall be. Look well to it, Isabel Miller. If there *is* another man between us, I can tell him this – he shall find it no easy matter to rob me of you!'

She started, and turned pale – but it was only for a moment. The high spirit that was in her rose brightly in her eyes, and faced him without shrinking.

'Threats?' she said with quiet contempt. 'When you make love, Mr Moody, you take strange ways of doing it. My conscience is easy. You may try to frighten me, but you will not succeed. When you have recovered your temper I will accept your excuses.' She paused, and pointed to the table. 'There is the letter that you told me to leave for you when I had sealed it,' she went on. 'I suppose you have her Ladyship's orders. Isn't it time you began to think of obeying them?'

The contemptuous composure of her tone and manner seemed to act on Moody with crushing effect. Without a word of answer, the unfortunate steward took up the letter from the table. Without a word of answer, he walked mechanically to the great door which opened on the staircase – turned on the threshold to look at Isabel – waited a moment, pale and still – and suddenly left the room.

That silent departure, that hopeless submission, impressed Isabel in spite of herself. The sustaining sense of injury and insult sank, as it were, from under her the moment she was alone. He had not been gone a minute before she began to be sorry for him once more. The interview had taught her nothing. She was neither old enough nor experienced enough to understand the overwhelming revolution produced in a man's character when he feels the passion of love for the first time in the maturity of his life. If Moody had stolen a kiss at the first opportunity, she would have resented the liberty he had taken with her; but she would have thoroughly understood him. His terrible earnestness, his overpowering agitation, his abrupt violence – all these evidences of a passion that was a mystery to himself – simply puzzled her. 'I'm sure I didn't wish to hurt his feelings' (such was the form that her reflections took, in her present penitent frame of mind); 'but why did he provoke me? It is a shame to tell me that I love some other man – when there is no other man. I declare I begin to hate the men, if they are all like Mr Moody. I wonder whether he will forgive me when he sees me again? I'm sure I'm willing to forget and forgive on my side – especially if he won't insist on my being fond of him because he is fond of me. Oh, dear! I wish he would come back and shake hands. It's enough to try the patience of a saint to be treated in this way. I wish I was ugly! The ugly ones have a quiet time of it – the men let them be. Mr Moody! Mr Moody!' She went out to the landing and called to him softly. There was no answer. He was no longer in the house. She stood still for a moment in silent vexation. 'I'll go to Tommie!' she decided. 'I'm sure he's the more agreeable company of the two. And – oh, good gracious! there's Mr Hardyman waiting to give me my instructions! How do I look, I wonder?'

She consulted the glass once more – gave one or two corrective touches to her hair and her cap – and hastened into the boudoir.

⮠ SIX ⮐

For a quarter of an hour the drawing-room remained empty. At the end of that time the council in the boudoir broke up. Lady Lydiard led the way back into the drawing-room, followed by Hardyman, Isabel being left to look after the dog. Before the door closed behind him, Hardyman turned round to reiterate his last medical directions – or, in plainer words, to take a last look at Isabel.

'Plenty of water, Miss Isabel, for the dog to lap, and a little bread or biscuit, if he wants something to eat. Nothing more, if you please, till I see him to-morrow.'

'Thank you, sir. I will take the greatest care—'

At that point Lady Lydiard cut short the interchange of instructions and civilities. 'Shut the door, if you please, Mr Hardyman. I feel the draught. Many thanks! I am really at a loss to tell you how gratefully I feel your kindness. But for you my poor little dog might be dead by this time.'

Hardyman answered, in the quiet melancholy monotone which was habitual with him, 'Your Ladyship need feel no further anxiety about the dog. Only be careful not to overfeed him. He will do very well under Miss Isabel's care. By the bye, her family name is Miller – is it not? Is she related to the Warwickshire Millers of Duxborough House?'

Lady Lydiard looked at him with an expression of satirical surprise. 'Mr Hardyman,' she said, 'this makes the fourth time you have questioned me about Isabel. You seem to take a great interest in my little companion. Don't make any apologies, pray! You pay Isabel a compliment; and, as I am very fond of her, I am naturally gratified when I find her admired. At the same time,' she added, with one of her abrupt transitions of language, 'I had my eye on you, and I had my eye on her, when you were talking in the next room; and I don't mean to let you make a fool of the girl. She is not in your line of life, and the sooner you know it the better. You make me laugh when you ask if she is related to gentlefolks. She is the orphan daughter of a chemist in the country. Her relations haven't a penny to bless themselves with; except an old aunt, who lives in a village on two or three hundred a year. I heard of the girl by accident. When she lost her father and mother, her aunt offered to take her. Isabel said, "No, thank you; I will not be a burden on a relation who has only enough for herself. A girl can earn an honest living if she tries; and I mean to try" – that's what she said. I admired her independence,' her Ladyship proceeded, ascending again to the higher regions of thought and expression. 'My niece's marriage, just at that time, had left me alone in this great house. I proposed to Isabel to come to me as companion and reader for a few weeks, and to decide for herself whether she liked the life or not. We have never been separated since that time. I could hardly be fonder of her if she were my own daughter; and she returns my affection with all her heart. She has excellent qualities – prudent, cheerful, sweet-tempered; with good sense enough to understand what her place is in the world, as distinguished from her place in my regard. I have taken care, for her own sake, never to leave that part of the question in any doubt. It would be cruel kindness to deceive her as to her future position when she marries. I shall take good care that the man who pays his addresses to her is a man in her rank of life. I know but too well, in the case of one of my own relatives, what miseries unequal marriages bring with them. Excuse me for troubling you at this length on domestic matters. I am very fond of Isabel; and a girl's head is so easily turned. Now you know what her position really is, you will also know what limits there must be to the expression of your interest in her. I am sure we understand each other; and I say no more.'

Hardyman listened to this long harangue with the immovable gravity which was part of his character – except when Isabel had taken him by surprise. When her Ladyship gave him the opportunity of speaking on his side, he had very little to say, and that little did not suggest that he had greatly profited by what he had heard. His mind had been full of Isabel when Lady Lydiard began, and it remained just as full of her, in just the same way, when Lady Lydiard had done.

'Yes,' he remarked quietly, 'Miss Isabel is an uncommonly nice girl, as you say. Very pretty, and such frank, unaffected manners. I don't deny that I feel an interest in her. The young ladies one meets in society are not much to my taste. Miss Isabel is my taste.'

Lady Lydiard's face assumed a look of blank dismay. 'I am afraid I have failed to convey my exact meaning to you,' she said.

Hardyman gravely declared that he understood her perfectly. 'Perfectly!' he repeated, with his impenetrable obstinacy. 'Your Ladyship exactly expresses my opinion of Miss Isabel. Prudent, and cheerful, and sweet-tempered, as you say – all the qualities in a woman that I admire. With good looks, too – of course, with good looks. She will be a perfect treasure (as you remarked just now) to the man who marries her. I may claim to know something about it. I have twice narrowly escaped being married myself; and, though I can't exactly explain it, I'm all the harder to please in consequence. Miss Isabel pleases me. I think I have said that before? Pardon me for saying it again. I'll call again to-morrow morning and look at the dog, as early as eleven o'clock, if you will allow me. Later in the day I must be off to France to attend a sale of horses. Glad to have been of any use to your Ladyship, I am sure. Good morning.'

Lady Lydiard let him go, wisely resigning any further attempt to establish an understanding between her visitor and herself.

'He is either a person of very limited intelligence when he is away from his stables,' she thought, 'or he deliberately declines to take a plain hint when it is given to him. I can't drop his acquaintance, on Tommie's account. The only other alternative is to keep Isabel out of his way. My good little girl shall not drift into a false position while I am living to look after her. When Mr Hardyman calls to-morrow she shall be out on an errand. When he calls the next time she shall be upstairs with a headache. And if he tries it again she shall be away at my house in the country. If he makes any remarks on her absence – well, he will find that I can be just as dull of understanding as he is when the occasion calls for it.'

Having arrived at this satisfactory solution of the difficulty, Lady

Lydiard became conscious of an irresistible impulse to summon Isabel to her presence and caress her. In the nature of a warm-hearted woman, this was only the inevitable reaction which followed the subsidence of anxiety about the girl, after her own resolution had set that anxiety at rest. She threw open the door and made one of her sudden appearances at the boudoir. Even in the fervent outpouring of her affection, there was still the inherent abruptness of manner which so strongly marked Lady Lydiard's character in all the relations of life.

'Did I give you a kiss, this morning?' she asked, when Isabel rose to receive her.

'Yes, my Lady,' said the girl, with her charming smile.

'Come, then, and give me a kiss in return. Do you love me? Very well, then, treat me like your mother. Never mind "my Lady" this time. Give me a good hug!'

Something in those homely words, or something perhaps in the look that accompanied them, touched sympathies in Isabel which seldom showed themselves on the surface. Her smiling lips trembled, the bright tears rose in her eyes. 'You are too good to me,' she murmured, with her head on Lady Lydiard's bosom. 'How can I ever love you enough in return?'

Lady Lydiard patted the pretty head that rested on her with such filial tenderness. 'There! there!' she said, 'Go back and play with Tommie, my dear. We may be as fond of each other as we like; but we mustn't cry. God bless you! Go away – go away!'

She turned aside quickly; her own eyes were moistening, and it was part of her character to be reluctant to let Isabel see it. 'Why have I made a fool of myself?' she wondered, as she approached the drawing-room door. 'It doesn't matter. I am all the better for it. Odd, that Mr Hardyman should have made me feel fonder of Isabel than ever!'

With those reflections she re-entered the drawing-room – and suddenly checked herself with a start. 'Good Heavens!' she exclaimed irritably, 'how you frightened me! Why was I not told you were here?'

Having left the drawing-room in a state of solitude, Lady Lydiard on her return found herself suddenly confronted with a gentleman, mysteriously planted on the hearth-rug in her absence. The new visitor may be rightly described as a grey man. He had grey hair, eyebrows, and whiskers; he wore a grey coat, waistcoat, and trousers, and grey gloves. For the rest, his appearance was eminently suggestive of wealth and respectability – and, in this case, appearances were really to be trusted. The grey man was no other than Lady Lydiard's legal adviser, Mr Troy.

'I regret, my Lady, that I should have been so unfortunate as to startle you,' he said, with a certain underlying embarrassment in his manner. 'I had the honour of sending word by Mr Moody that I would call at this hour, on some matters of business connected with your Ladyship's house property. I presumed that you expected to find me here, waiting your pleasure—'

Thus far Lady Lydiard had listened to her legal adviser, fixing her eyes on his face in her usually frank, straightforward way. She now stopped him in the middle of a sentence, with a change of expression in her own face which was undisguisedly a change to alarm.

'Don't apologise, Mr Troy,' she said. 'I am to blame for forgetting your appointment, and for not keeping my nerves under proper control.' She paused for a moment, and took a seat before she said her next words. 'May I ask,' she resumed, 'if there is something unpleasant in the business that brings you here?'

'Nothing whatever, my Lady; mere formalities, which can wait till to-morrow or next day, if you wish it.'

Lady Lydiard's fingers drummed impatiently on the table. 'You have known me long enough, Mr Troy, to know that I cannot endure suspense. You *have* something unpleasant to tell me.'

The lawyer respectfully remonstrated. 'Really, Lady Lydiard!— he began.

'It won't do, Mr Troy! I know how you look at me on ordinary occasions, and I see how you look at me now. You are a very clever lawyer; but, happily for the interests that I commit to your charge, you are also a thoroughly honest man. After twenty years' experience of you, you can't deceive *me*. You bring me bad news. Speak at once, sir, and speak plainly.'

Mr Troy yielded – inch by inch, as it were. 'I bring news which, I fear, may annoy your Ladyship.' He paused, and advanced another inch. 'It is news which I only became acquainted with myself on entering this house.' He waited again, and made another advance. 'I happened to meet your Ladyship's steward, Mr Moody, in the hall—'

'Where is he?' Lady Lydiard interposed angrily. 'I can make *him* speak out, and I will. Send him here instantly.'

The lawyer made a last effort to hold off the coming disclosure a little longer. 'Mr Moody will be here directly,' he said. 'Mr Moody requested me to prepare your Ladyship—'

'Will you ring the bell, Mr Troy, or must I?'

Moody had evidently been waiting outside while the lawyer spoke for him. He saved Mr Troy the trouble of ringing the bell by presenting himself in the drawing-room. Lady Lydiard's eyes searched his face as he approached. Her bright complexion faded suddenly. Not a word more passed her lips. She looked, and waited.

In silence on his part, Moody laid an open sheet of paper on the table. The paper quivered in his trembling hand.

Lady Lydiard recovered herself first. 'Is that for me?' she asked.

'Yes, my Lady.'

She took up the paper without an instant's hesitation. Both the men watched her anxiously as she read it.

The handwriting was strange to her. The words were these:

'I hearby certify that the bearer of these lines, Robert Moody by name, has presented to me the letter with which he was charged, addressed to myself, with the seal intact. I regret to add that there is, to say the least of it, some mistake. The inclosure referred to by the anonymous writer of the letter, who signs "a friend in need", has not reached me. No five hundred pound bank-note was in the letter when I opened it. My wife was present when I broke the seal, and can certify to this statement if necessary. Not knowing who my charitable correspondent is (Mr Moody being forbidden to give me any information), I can only take this means of stating the case exactly as it stands, and hold myself at the disposal of the writer of the letter. My private address is at the head of the page. – Samuel Bradstock, Rector, St Anne's, Deansbury, London.'

Lady Lydiard dropped the paper on the table. For the moment, plainly as the Rector's statement was expressed, she appeared to be incapable of understanding it. 'What, in God's name, does this mean?' she asked.

The lawyer and the steward looked at each other. Which of the two was entitled to speak first? Lady Lydiard gave them no time to decide. 'Moody,' she said sternly, 'you took charge of the letter – I look to you for an explanation.'

Moody's dark eyes flashed. He answered Lady Lydiard without caring to conceal that he resented the tone in which she had spoken to him.

'I undertook to deliver the letter at its address,' he said. 'I found it, sealed, on the table. Your Ladyship has the clergyman's written testimony that I handed it to him with the seal unbroken. I have done my duty; and I have no explanation to offer.'

Before Lady Lydiard could speak again, Mr Troy discreetly interfered. He saw plainly that his experience was required to lead the investigation in the right direction.

'Pardon me, my Lady,' he said, with that happy mixture of the positive and the polite in his manner, of which lawyers alone possess the secret. 'There is only one way of arriving at the truth in painful matters of this sort. We must begin at the beginning. May I venture to ask your Ladyship a question?'

Lady Lydiard felt the composing influence of Mr Troy. 'I am at your disposal, sir,' she said quietly.

'Are you absolutely certain that you enclosed the bank-note in the letter?' the lawyer asked.

'I certainly believe I enclosed it,' Lady Lydiard answered. 'But I was so alarmed at the time by the sudden illness of my dog, that I do not feel justified in speaking positively.'

'Was anybody in the room with your Ladyship when you put the inclosure in the letter – as you believe?'

'*I* was in the room,' said Moody. 'I can swear that I saw her Ladyship put the bank-note in the letter, and the letter in the envelope.'

'And seal the envelope?' asked Mr Troy.

'No, sir. Her Ladyship was called away into the next room to the dog, before she could seal the envelope.'

Mr Troy addressed himself once more to Lady Lydiard. 'Did your Ladyship take the letter into the next room with you?'

'I was too much alarmed to think of it, Mr Troy. I left it here, on the table.'

'With the envelope open?'

'Yes.'

'How long were you absent in the other room?'

'Half an hour or more.'

'Ha!' said Mr Troy to himself. 'This complicates it a little.' He reflected for a while, and then turned again to Moody. 'Did any of the servants know of this bank-note being in her Ladyship's possession?'

'Not one of them,' Moody answered.

'Do you suspect any of the servants?'

'Certainly not, sir.'

'Are there any workmen employed in the house?'

'No, sir.'

'Do you know of any persons who had access to the room while Lady Lydiard was absent from it?'

'Two visitors called, sir.'

'Who were they?'

'Her Ladyship's nephew, Mr Felix Sweetsir, and the Honourable Alfred Hardyman.'

Mr Troy shook his head irritably. 'I am not speaking of gentlemen of high position and repute,' he said. 'It's absurd even to mention Mr Sweetsir and Mr Hardyman. My question related to strangers who might have obtained access to the drawing-room – people calling, with her Ladyship's sanction, for subscriptions, for instance; or people calling with articles of dress or ornament to be submitted to her Ladyship's inspection.'

'No such persons came to the house with my knowledge,' Moody answered.

Mr Troy suspended the investigation, and took a turn thoughtfully in the room. The theory on which his inquiries had proceeded thus far had failed to produce any results. His experience warned him to waste no more time on it, and to return to the starting-point of the investigation – in other words, to the letter. Shifting his point of view, he turned again to Lady Lydiard, and tried his questions in a new direction.

'Mr Moody mentioned just now,' he said, 'that your Ladyship was called into the next room before you could seal your letter. On your return to this room, did you seal the letter?'

'I was busy with the dog,' Lady Lydiard answered. 'Isabel Miller was of no use in the boudoir, and I told her to seal it for me.'

Mr Troy started. The new direction in which he was pushing his inquiries began to look like the right direction already. 'Miss Isabel Miller,' he proceeded, 'has been a resident under your Ladyship's roof for some little time, I believe?'

'For nearly two years, Mr Troy.'

'As your Ladyship's companion and reader?'

'As my adopted daughter,' her Ladyship answered, with marked emphasis.

Wise Mr Troy rightly interpreted the emphasis as a warning to him to suspend the examination of her Ladyship, and to address to Mr Moody the far more serious questions which were now to come.

'Did anyone give you the letter before you left the house with it?' he said to the steward. 'Or did you take it yourself?'

'I took it myself, from the table here.'

'Was it sealed?'

'Yes.'

'Was anybody present when you took the letter from the table?'

'Miss Isabel was present.'

'Did you find her alone in the room?'

'Yes, sir.'

Lady Lydiard opened her lips to speak, and checked herself. Mr Troy, having cleared the ground before him, put the fatal question.

'Mr Moody,' he said, 'when Miss Isabel was instructed to seal the letter, did she know that a bank-note was inclosed in it?'

Instead of replying, Robert drew back from the lawyer with a look of horror. Lady Lydiard started to her feet – and checked herself again, on the point of speaking.

'Answer him, Moody,' she said, putting a strong constraint on herself.

Robert answered very unwillingly. 'I took the liberty of reminding her ladyship that she had left her letter unsealed,' he said. 'And I mentioned as my excuse for speaking' – he stopped, and corrected himself – 'I *believe* I mentioned that a valuable inclosure was in the letter.'

'You believe?' Mr Troy repeated. 'Can't you speak more positively than that?'

'*I* can speak positively,' said Lady Lydiard, with her eyes on the lawyer. 'Moody did mention the inclosure in the letter – in Isabel Miller's hearing as well as in mine.' She paused, steadily controlling herself. 'And what of that, Mr Troy?' she added, very quietly and firmly.

Mr Troy answered quietly and firmly, on his side. 'I am surprised that your Ladyship should ask the question,' he said.

'I persist in repeating the question,' Lady Lydiard rejoined. 'I say that Isabel Miller knew of the inclosure in my letter – and I ask, What of that?'

'And I answer,' retorted the impenetrable lawyer, 'that the suspicion of theft rests on your Ladyship's adopted daughter, and on nobody else.'

'It's false!' cried Robert, with a burst of honest indignation. 'I wish to God I had never said a word to you about the loss of the bank-note! Oh, my Lady! my Lady! don't let him distress you! What does *he* know about it?'

'Hush!' said Lady Lydiard. 'Control yourself, and hear what he has to say.' She rested her hand on Moody's shoulder, partly to encourage him, partly to support herself; and, fixing her eyes again on Mr Troy, repeated his last words, ' "Suspicion rests on my adopted daughter, and on nobody else." Why on nobody else?'

'Is your Ladyship prepared to suspect the Rector of St Anne's of embezzlement, or your own relatives and equals of theft?' Mr Troy asked. 'Does a shadow of doubt rest on the servants? Not if Mr Moody's evidence is to be believed. Who, to our own certain knowledge, had access to the letter while it was unsealed? Who was alone in the room with it? And who knew of the inclosure in it? I leave the answer to your Ladyship.'

'Isabel Miller is as incapable of an act of theft as I am. There is my answer, Mr Troy.'

The lawyer bowed resignedly, and advanced to the door.

'Am I to take your Ladyship's generous assertion as finally disposing of the question of the lost bank-note?' he inquired.

Lady Lydiard met the challenge without shrinking from it.

'No!' she said. 'The loss of the bank-note is known out of my house. Other persons may suspect this innocent girl as you suspect her. It is due to Isabel's reputation – her unstained reputation, Mr Troy! – that she should know what has happened, and should have an opportunity of defending herself. She is in the next room, Moody. Bring her here.'

Robert's courage failed him: he trembled at the bare idea of exposing Isabel to the terrible ordeal that awaited her. 'Oh, my Lady!' he pleaded, 'think again before you tell the poor girl that she is suspected of theft. Keep it a secret from her – the shame of it will break her heart!'

'Keep it a secret,' said Lady Lydiard, 'when the Rector and the Rector's wife both know of it! Do you think they will let the matter rest where it is, even if I could consent to hush it up? I must write to them; and I can't write anonymously after what has happened. Put yourself in Isabel's place, and tell me if you would thank the person who knew you to be innocently exposed to a disgraceful suspicion, and who concealed it from you? Go, Moody! The longer you delay, the harder it will be.'

With his head sunk on his breast, with anguish written in every line of his face, Moody obeyed. Passing slowly down the short passage which connected the two rooms, and still shrinking from the duty that had been imposed on him, he paused, looking through the curtains which hung over the entrance to the boudoir.

❧ SEVEN ❧

THE SIGHT THAT MET MOODY'S view wrung him to the heart.

Isabel and the dog were at play together. Among the varied accomplishments possessed by Tommie, the capacity to take his part at a game of hide-and-seek was one. His playfellow for the time being put a shawl or a handkerchief over his head, so as to prevent him from seeing, and then hid among the furniture a pocket-book, or a cigar-case, or a purse, or anything else that happened to be at hand, leaving the dog to find it, with his keen sense of smell to guide him. Doubly relieved by the fit and the bleeding, Tommie's spirits had revived; and he and Isabel had just begun their game when Moody looked into the room, charged with his terrible errand. 'You're burning, Tommie, you're burning!' cried the girl, laughing and clapping her hands. The next moment she happened to look round and saw Moody through the parted curtains. His face warned her instantly that something serious had happened. She advanced a few steps, her eyes resting on him in silent alarm. He was himself too painfully agitated to speak. Not a word was exchanged between Lady Lydiard and Mr Troy in the next room. In the complete stillness that prevailed, the dog was heard sniffing and fidgeting about the furniture. Robert took Isabel by the hand and led her into the drawing-room. 'For God's sake, spare her, my Lady!' he whispered. The lawyer heard him. 'No,' said Mr Troy. 'Be merciful, and tell her the truth!'

He spoke to a woman who stood in no need of his advice. The inherent nobility in Lady Lydiard's nature was aroused: her great heart offered itself patiently to any sorrow, to any sacrifice.

Putting her arm round Isabel – half caressing her, half supporting her – Lady Lydiard accepted the whole responsibility and told the whole truth.

Reeling under the first shock, the poor girl recovered herself with admirable courage. She raised her head, and eyed the lawyer without uttering a word. In its artless consciousness of innocence the look was nothing less than sublime. Addressing herself to Mr Troy, Lady Lydiard pointed to Isabel. 'Do you see guilt there?' she asked.

Mr Troy made no answer. In the melancholy experience of humanity to which his profession condemned him, he had seen conscious guilt assume the face of innocence, and helpless innocence admit the disguise of guilt: the keenest observation, in either case, failing completely to detect the truth. Lady Lydiard misinterpreted his silence as expressing the sullen self-assertion of a heartless man. She turned from him, in contempt, and held out her hand to Isabel.

'Mr Troy is not satisfied yet,' she said bitterly. 'My love, take my hand, and look me in the face as your equal; I know no difference of rank at such a time as this. Before God, who hears you, are you innocent of the theft of the bank-note?'

'Before God, who hears me,' Isabel answered, 'I am innocent.'

Lady Lydiard looked once more at the lawyer, and waited to hear if he believed *that*.

Mr Troy took refuge in dumb diplomacy – he made a low bow. It might have meant that he believed Isabel, or it might have meant that he modestly withdrew his own opinion into the background. Lady Lydiard did not condescend to inquire what it meant.

'The sooner we bring this painful scene to an end the better,' she said. 'I shall be glad to avail myself of your professional assistance, Mr Troy, within certain limits. Outside of my house, I beg that you will spare no trouble in tracing the lost money to the person who has really stolen it. Inside of my house, I must positively request that the disappearance of the note may never be alluded to, in any way whatever, until your inquiries have been successful in discovering the thief. In the meanwhile, Mrs Tollmidge and her family must not be sufferers by my loss: I shall pay the money again.' She paused, and pressed Isabel's hand with affectionate fervour. 'My child,' she said, 'one last word to you, and I have done. You remain here, with my trust in you, and my love for you, absolutely unshaken. When you think of what has been said here to-day, never forget that.'

Isabel bent her head, and kissed the kind hand that still held hers. The high spirit that was in her, inspired by Lady Lydiard's example, rose equal to the dreadful situation in which she was placed.

'No, my Lady,' she said calmly and sadly; 'it cannot be. What this gentleman has said of me is not to be denied – the appearances are against me. The letter was open, and I was alone in the room with it, and Mr Moody told me that a valuable inclosure was inside it. Dear and kind mistress! I am not fit to be a member of your household, I am not worthy to live with the honest people who serve you, while my innocence is in doubt. It is enough for me now that *you* don't doubt it. I can wait patiently, after that, for the day that gives me back my good name. Oh, my Lady, don't cry about it! Pray, pray don't cry!'

Lady Lydiard's self-control failed her for the first time. Isabel's courage had made Isabel dearer to her than ever. She sank into a chair, and covered her face with her handkerchief. Mr Troy turned aside abruptly, and examined a Japanese vase, without any idea in his mind of what he was looking at. Lady Lydiard had gravely misjudged him in believing him to be a heartless man.

Isabel followed the lawyer, and touched him gently on the arm to rouse his attention.

'I have one relation living, sir – an aunt – who will receive me if I go to her,' she said simply. 'Is there any harm in my going? Lady Lydiard will give you the address when you want me. Spare her Ladyship, sir, all the pain and trouble that you can.'

At last the heart that was in Mr Troy asserted itself. 'You are a fine creature!' he said, with a burst of enthusiasm. 'I agree with Lady Lydiard – I believe you are innocent, too; and I will leave no effort untried to find the proof of it' He turned aside again, and had another look at the Japanese vase.

As the lawyer withdrew himself from observation, Moody approached Isabel.

Thus far he had stood apart, watching her and listening to her in silence. Not a look that had crossed her face, not a word that had fallen from her, had escaped him. Unconsciously on her side, unconsciously on his side, she now wrought on his nature with a purifying and ennobling influence which animated it with a new life. All that had been selfish and violent in his passion for her left him to return no more. The immeasurable devotion which he laid at her feet, in the days that were yet to come – the unyielding courage which cheerfully accepted the sacrifice of himself when events demanded it at a later period of his life – struck root in him now. Without attempting to conceal the tears that were falling fast over his cheeks – striving vainly to express those new thoughts in him that were beyond the reach of words – he stood before her the truest friend and servant that ever woman had. 'Oh, my dear!

my heart is heavy for you. Take me to serve you and help you. Her Ladyship's kindness will permit it, I am sure.'

He could say no more. In those simple words the cry of his heart reached her. 'Forgive me, Robert,' she answered, gratefully, 'if I said anything to pain you when we spoke together a little while since. I didn't mean it.' She gave him her hand, and looked timidly over her shoulder at Lady Lydiard. 'Let me go!' she said, in low, broken tones, 'Let me go!'

Mr Troy heard her, and stepped forward to interfere before Lady Lydiard could speak. The man had recovered his self-control; the lawyer took his place again on the scene.

'You must not leave us, my dear,' he said to Isabel, 'until I have put a question to Mr Moody in which you are interested. Do you happen to have the number of the lost bank-note?' he asked, turning to the steward.

Moody produced his slip of paper with the number on it. Mr Troy made two copies of it before he returned the paper. One copy he put in his pocket, the other he handed to Isabel.

'Keep it carefully,' he said. 'Neither you nor I know how soon it may be of use to you.'

Receiving the copy from him, she felt mechanically in her apron for her pocket-book. She had used it, in playing with the dog, as an object to hide from him; but she had suffered, and was still suffering, too keenly to be capable of the effort of remembrance. Moody, eager to help her even in the most trifling thing, guessed what had happened. 'You were playing with Tommie,' he said; 'is it in the next room?'

The dog heard his name pronounced through the open door. The next moment he trotted into the drawing-room with Isabel's pocket-book in his mouth. He was a strong, well-grown Scotch terrier of the largest size, with bright, intelligent eyes, and a coat of thick curling white hair, diversified by two light brown patches on his back. As he reached the middle of the room, and looked from one to another of the persons present, the fine sympathy of his race told him that there was trouble among his human friends. His tail dropped; he whined softly as he approached Isabel, and laid her pocket-book at her feet.

She knelt as she picked up the pocket-book, and raised her play-fellow of happier days to take her leave of him. As the dog put his paws on her shoulders, returning her caress, her first tears fell. 'Foolish of me,' she said, faintly, 'to cry over a dog. I can't help it. Good-by, Tommie!'

Putting him away from her gently, she walked towards the door. The dog instantly followed. She put him away from her, for the second time, and left him. He was not to be denied; he followed her again, and took the skirt of her dress in his teeth, as if to hold her back. Robert forced the dog, growling and resisting with all his might, to let go of the dress. 'Don't be rough with him,' said Isabel. 'Put him on her ladyship's lap;

he will be quieter there.' Robert obeyed. He whispered to Lady Lydiard as she received the dog: she seemed to be still incapable of speaking – she bowed her head in silent assent. Robert hurried back to Isabel before she had passed the door. 'Not alone!' he said entreatingly. 'Her Ladyship permits it, Isabel. Let me see you safe to your aunt's house.'

Isabel looked at him, felt for him, and yielded.

'Yes,' she answered softly; 'to make amends for what I said to you when I was thoughtless and happy!' She waited a little to compose herself before she spoke her farewell words to Lady Lydiard. 'Good-bye, my Lady. Your kindness has not been thrown away on an ungrateful girl. I love you, and thank you, with all my heart.'

Lady Lydiard rose, placing the dog on the chair as she left it. She seemed to have grown older by years, instead of by minutes, in the short interval that had passed since she had hidden her face from view. 'I can't bear it!' she cried, in husky, broken tones. 'Isabel! Isabel! I forbid you to leave me!'

But one person could venture to resist her. That person was Mr Troy – and Mr Troy knew it.

'Control yourself,' he said to her in a whisper. 'The girl is doing what is best and most becoming in her position – and is doing it with a patience and courage wonderful to see. She places herself under the protection of her nearest relative, until her character is vindicated and her position in your house is once more beyond a doubt. Is this a time to throw obstacles in her way? Be worthy of yourself, Lady Lydiard – and think of the day when she will return to you without the breath of a suspicion to rest on her!'

There was no disputing with him – he was too plainly in the right. Lady Lydiard submitted; she concealed the torture that her own resolution inflicted on her with an endurance which was, indeed, worthy of herself. Taking Isabel in her arms she kissed her in a passion of sorrow and love. 'My poor dear! My own sweet girl! don't suppose that this is a parting kiss! I shall see you again – often and often I shall see you again at your aunt's!' At a sign from Mr Troy, Robert took Isabel's arm in his and led her away. Tommie, watching her from his chair, lifted his little white muzzle as his play-fellow looked back on passing the doorway. The long, melancholy, farewell howl of the dog was the last sound Isabel Miller heard as she left the house.

PART THE SECOND
The Discovery

❧ EIGHT ❧

ON THE DAY AFTER ISABEL's departure, diligent Mr Troy set forth for the Head Office in Whitehall to consult the police on the question of the missing money. He had previously sent information of the robbery to the Bank of England, and had also advertised the loss in the daily newspapers.

The air was so pleasant, and the sun was so bright, that he determined on proceeding to his destination on foot. He was hardly out of sight of his own offices when he was overtaken by a friend, who was also walking in the direction of Whitehall. This gentleman was a person of considerable worldly wisdom and experience; he had been officially associated with cases of striking and notorious crime, in which Government had lent its assistance to discover and punish the criminals. The opinion of a person in this position might be of the greatest value to Mr Troy, whose practice as a solicitor had thus far never brought him into collision with thieves and mysteries. He accordingly decided, in Isabel's interests, on confiding to his friend the nature of his errand to the police. Concealing the name, but concealing nothing else, he described what had happened on the previous day at Lady Lydiard's house, and then put the question plainly to his companion.

'What would you do in my place?'

'In your place,' his friend answered quietly, 'I should not waste time and money in consulting the police.'

'Not consult the police!' exclaimed Mr Troy in amazement. 'Surely, I have not made myself understood? I am going to the Head Office; and I have got a letter of introduction to the chief inspector in the detective department. I am afraid I omitted to mention that?'

'It doesn't make any difference,' proceeded the other, as coolly as ever. 'You have asked for my advice, and I give you my advice. Tear up your letter of introduction, and don't stir a step farther in the direction of Whitehall.'

Mr Troy began to understand. 'You don't believe in the detective police?' he said.

'Who *can* believe in them, who reads his newspaper and remembers what he reads?' his friend rejoined. 'Fortunately for the detective department, the public in general forgets what it reads. Go to your club, and look at the criminal history of our own time, recorded in the newspapers. Every crime is more or less a mystery. You will see that the mysteries which the police discover are, almost without exception, mysteries made penetrable by the commonest capacity, through the extraordinary stupidity exhibited in the means taken to hide the crime. On the other hand, let the guilty man or woman be a resolute and intelligent person, capable of setting his (or her) wits fairly against the wits of the police – in other words, let the mystery really *be* a mystery – and cite me a case if you can (a really difficult and perplexing case) in which the criminal has not escaped. Mind! I don't charge the police with neglecting their work. No doubt they do their best, and take the greatest pains in following the routine to which they have been trained. It is their misfortune, not their fault, that there is no man of superior intelligence among them – I mean no man who is capable, in great emergencies, of placing himself above conventional methods, and following a new way of his own. There have been such men in the police – men naturally endowed with that faculty of mental analysis which can decompose a mystery, resolve it into its component parts, and find the clue at the bottom, no matter how remote from ordinary observation it may be. But those men have died, or have retired. One of them would have been invaluable to you in the case you have just mentioned to me. As things are, unless you are wrong in believing in the young lady's innocence, the person who has stolen that bank-note will be no easy person to find. In my opinion, there is only one man now in London who is likely to be of the slightest assistance to you – and he is not in the police.'

'Who is he?' asked Mr Troy.

'An old rogue, who was once in your branch of the legal profession,' the friend answered. 'You may, perhaps, remember the name: they call him "Old Sharon".'

'What! The scoundrel who was struck off the Roll of Attorneys, years since? Is he still alive?'

'Alive and prospering. He lives in a court or lane running out of Long-acre, and he offers advice to persons interested in recovering missing objects of any sort. Whether you have lost your wife, or lost your cigar-case, Old Sharon is equally useful to you. He has an inbred capacity for reading the riddle the right way in cases of mystery, great or small. In short, he possesses exactly that analytical faculty to which I alluded just now. I have his address at my office, if you think it worth while to try him.'

'Who can trust such a man?' Mr Troy objected. 'He would be sure to deceive me.'

'You are entirely mistaken. Since he was struck off the Rolls Old Sharon has discovered that the straight way is, on the whole, the best way, even in a man's own interests. His consultation fee is a guinea; and he gives a signed estimate beforehand for any supplementary expenses that may follow. I can tell you (this is, of course, strictly between ourselves) that the authorities at my office took his advice in a Government case that puzzled the police. We approached him, of course, through persons who were to be trusted to represent us, without betraying the source from which their instructions were derived; and we found the old rascal's advice well worth paying for. It is quite likely that he may not succeed so well in your case. Try the police, by all means; and, if they fail, why, there is Sharon as a last resort.'

This arrangement commended itself to Mr Troy's professional caution. He went on to Whitehall, and he tried the detective police. They at once adopted the obvious conclusion to persons of ordinary capacity – the conclusion that Isabel was the thief.

Acting on this conviction, the authorities sent an experienced woman from the office to Lady Lydiard's house, to examine the poor girl's clothes and ornaments before they were packed up and sent after her to her aunt's. The search led to nothing. The only objects of any value that were discovered had been presents from Lady Lydiard. No jewellers' or milliners' bills were among the papers found in her desk. Not a sign of secret extravagance in dress was to be seen anywhere. Defeated so far, the police proposed next to have Isabel privately watched. There might be a prodigal lover somewhere in the background, with ruin staring him in the face unless he could raise five hundred pounds. Lady Lydiard (who had only consented to the search under stress of persuasive argument from Mr Troy) resented this ingenious idea as an insult. She declared that if Isabel was watched the girl should know of it instantly from her own lips. The police listened with perfect resignation and decorum, and politely shifted their ground. A certain suspicion (they remarked) always rested in cases of this sort on the servants. Would her Ladyship object to private inquiries into the characters and proceedings of the servants? Her Ladyship instantly objected, in the most positive terms. Thereupon the 'Inspector' asked for a minute's private conversation with Mr Troy. 'The thief is certainly a member of Lady Lydiard's household,' this functionary remarked, in his politely-positive way. 'If her Ladyship persists in refusing to let us make the necessary inquiries, our hands are tied, and the case comes to an end through no fault of ours. If her Ladyship changes her mind, perhaps you will drop me a line, sir, to that effect. Good morning.'

So the experiment of consulting the police came to an untimely end. The one result obtained was the expression of purblind opinion by the authorities of the detective department, which pointed to Isabel, or to one of the servants, as the undiscovered thief. Thinking the matter over in the retirement of his own office – and not forgetting his promise to Isabel to leave no means untried of establishing her innocence – Mr Troy could see but one alternative left to him. He took up his pen, and wrote to his friend at the Government office. There was nothing for it now but to run the risk, and try Old Sharon.

NINE

THE NEXT DAY, MR TROY (taking Robert Moody with him as a valuable witness) rang the bell at the mean and dirty lodging-house in which Old Sharon received the clients who stood in need of his advice.

They were led up stairs to a back room on the second floor of the house. Entering the room, they discovered through a thick cloud of tobacco smoke, a small, fat, baldheaded, dirty, old man, in an arm-chair, robed in a tattered flannel dressing-gown, with a short pipe in his mouth, a pug-dog on his lap, and a French novel in his hands.

'Is it business?' asked Old Sharon, speaking in a hoarse, asthmatical voice, and fixing a pair of bright, shameless, black eyes attentively on the two visitors.

'It *is* business,' Mr Troy answered, looking at the old rogue who had disgraced an honourable profession, as he might have looked at a reptile which had just risen rampant at his feet. 'What is your fee for a consultation?'

'You give me a guinea, and I'll give you half an hour.' With this reply Old Sharon held out his unwashed hand across the rickety ink-splashed table at which he was sitting.

Mr Troy would not have touched him with the tips of his own fingers for a thousand pounds. He laid the guinea on the table.

Old Sharon burst into a fierce laugh – a laugh strangely accompanied by a frowning contraction of his eyebrows, and a frightful exhibition of the whole inside of his mouth. 'I'm not clean enough for you – eh?' he said, with an appearance of being very much amused. 'There's a dirty old man described in this book that is a little like me.' He held up his French novel. 'Have you read it? A capital story – well put together. Ah, you haven't read it? You have got a pleasure to come. I say, do you mind tobacco-smoke? I think faster while I smoke – that's all.'

Mr Troy's respectable hand waved a silent permission to smoke, given under dignified protest.

'All right,' said Old Sharon. 'Now, get on.'

He laid himself back in his chair, and puffed out his smoke, with eyes lazily half closed, like the eyes of the pug-dog on his lap. At that moment, indeed, there was a curious resemblance between the two. They both seemed to be preparing themselves, in the same idle way, for the same comfortable nap.

Mr Troy stated the circumstances under which the five-hundred-pound note had disappeared, in clear and consecutive narrative. When he had done, Old Sharon suddenly opened his eyes. The pug-dog suddenly opened his eyes. Old Sharon looked hard at Mr Troy. The pug looked hard at Mr Troy. Old Sharon spoke. The pug growled.

'I know who you are – you're a lawyer. Don't be alarmed! I never saw you before; and I don't know your name. What I do know is a lawyer's statement of facts when I hear it. Who's this?' Old Sharon looked inquisitively at Moody as he put the question.

Mr Troy introduced Moody as a competent witness, thoroughly acquainted with the circumstances, and ready and willing to answer any questions relating to them. Old Sharon waited a little, smoking hard and thinking hard. 'Now, then!' he burst out in his fiercely sudden way. 'I'm going to get to the root of the matter.'

He leaned forward with his elbows on the table, and began his examination of Moody. Heartily as Mr Troy despised and disliked the old rogue, he listened with astonishment and admiration – literally extorted from him by the marvellous ability with which the questions were adapted to the end in view. In a quarter of an hour Old Sharon had extracted from the witness everything, literally everything down to the smallest detail, that Moody could tell him. Having now, in his own phrase, 'got to the root of the matter', he relit his pipe with a grunt of satisfaction, and laid himself back in his old arm-chair.

'Well?' said Mr Troy. 'Have you formed your opinion?'

'Yes; I've formed my opinion.'

'What is it?'

Instead of replying, Old Sharon winked confidentially at Mr Troy, and put a question on his side.

'I say! is a ten-pound note much of an object to you?'

'It depends on what the money is wanted for,' answered Mr Troy.

'Look here,' said Old Sharon; 'I give you an opinion for your guinea; but, mind this, it's an opinion founded on hearsay – and you know as a lawyer what that is worth. Venture your ten pounds – in plain English, pay me for my time and trouble in a baffling and difficult case – and I'll give you an opinion founded on my own experience.'

'Explain yourself a little more clearly,' said Mr Troy. 'What do you guarantee to tell us if we venture the ten pounds?'

'I guarantee to name the person, or the persons, on whom the suspicion really rests. And if you employ me after that, I guarantee (before you pay me a halfpenny more) to prove that I am right by laying my hand on the thief.'

'Let us have the guinea opinion first,' said Mr Troy.

Old Sharon made another frightful exhibition of the whole inside of his mouth; his laugh was louder and fiercer than ever. 'I like you!' he said to Mr Troy, 'you are so devilish fond of your money. Lord! how rich you must be! Now listen. Here's the guinea opinion: – Suspect, in this case, the very last person on whom suspicion could possibly fall.'

Moody, listening attentively, started, and changed colour at those last words. Mr Troy looked thoroughly disappointed and made no attempt to conceal it.

'Is that all?' he asked.

'All?' retorted the cynical vagabond. 'You're a pretty lawyer! What more can I say, when I don't know for certain whether the witness who has given me my information has misled me or not? Have I spoken to the girl and formed my own opinion? No! Have I been introduced among the servants (as errand-boy, or to clean the boots and shoes, or what not), and have I formed my own judgement of *them*? No! I take your opinions for granted, and I tell you how I should set to work myself if they were *my* opinions too – and that's a guinea's-worth, a devilish good guinea's-worth to a rich man like you!'

Old Sharon's logic produced a certain effect on Mr Troy, in spite of himself. It was smartly put from his point of view – there was no denying that.

'Even if I consented to your proposal,' he said, 'I should object to your annoying the young lady with impertinent questions, or to your being introduced as a spy into a respectable house.'

Old Sharon doubled his dirty fists and drummed with them on the rickety table in a comical frenzy of impatience while Mr Troy was speaking.

'What the devil do you know about my way of doing my business?' he burst out when the lawyer had done. 'One of us two is talking like a born idiot – and (mind this) it isn't me. Look here! Your young lady goes out for a walk, and she meets with a dirty, shabby old beggar – I look like a shabby old beggar already, don't I? Very good. This dirty old wretch whines and whimpers and tells a long story, and gets sixpence out of the girl – and knows her by that time, inside and out, as well as if he had made her – and, mark! hasn't asked her a single question, and, instead of annoying her, has made her happy in the performance of a charitable action. Stop a bit! I haven't done with you yet. Who blacks your boots and shoes? Look here!' He pushed his pug-dog off his lap, dived under the table, appeared again with an old boot and a bottle of blackening, and set to work with tigerish activity. 'I'm going out for a walk, you know, and I may as well make myself smart.' With that announcement, he began to sing over his work – a song of sentiment, popular in England in the early part of the present century – 'She's all my fancy painted her; she's lovely, she's divine; but her heart it is another's; and it never can be mine! Too-ral-loo-ral-loo. I like a love song. Brush away! brush away! till I see my own pretty face in the blacking. Hey! Here's a nice, harmless, jolly old man! sings and jokes over his work, and makes the kitchen quite cheerful. What's that you say? He's a stranger, and don't talk to him too freely. You ought to be ashamed of yourself to speak in that way of a poor old fellow with one foot in the grave. Mrs-cook will give him a nice bit of dinner in the scullery; and John-footman will look out an old coat for him. And when he's heard everything he wants to hear, and doesn't come back again the next day to his work – what do they think of it in the servants' hall? Do they say, "We've had a spy among us!" Yah! you know better than that, by this time. The cheerful old man has been run over in the street, or is down with the fever, or has turned up his toes in the parish dead-house – that's what they say in the servants' hall. Try me in your own kitchen, and see if your servants take me for a spy. Come, come, Mr Lawyer! out with your ten pounds, and don't waste any more precious time about it!'

'I will consider and let you know,' said Mr Troy.

Old Sharon laughed more ferociously than ever, and hobbled round the table in a great hurry to the place at which Moody was sitting. He laid one hand on the steward's shoulder, and pointed derisively with the other to Mr Troy.

'I say, Mr Silent-man! Bet you five pounds I never hear of that lawyer again!'

Silently attentive all through the interview (except when he was answering questions), Moody only replied in the fewest words. 'I don't bet,' was all he said. He showed no resentment at Sharon's familiarity, and he appeared to find no amusement in Sharon's extraordinary talk. The old vagabond seemed actually to produce a serious impression on him! When Mr Troy set the example of rising to go, he still kept his seat, and looked at the lawyer as if he regretted leaving the atmosphere of tobacco-smoke reeking in the dirty room.

'Have you anything to say before we go?' Mr Troy asked.

Moody rose slowly and looked at Old Sharon. 'Not just now, sir, ' he replied, looking away again, after a moment's reflection.

Old Sharon interpreted Moody's look and Moody's reply from his own peculiar point of view. He suddenly drew the steward away into a corner of the room.

'I say!' he began, in a whisper. 'Upon your solemn word of honour, you know – are you as rich as the lawyer there?'

'Certainly not.'

'Look here! It's half price to a poor man. If you feel like coming back, on your own account – five pounds will do from *you*. There! there! Think of it! – think of it!'

'Now, then!' said Mr Troy, waiting for his companion, with the door open in his hand. He looked back at Sharon when Moody joined him. The old vagabond was settled again in his arm-chair, with his dog in his lap; his pipe in his mouth, and his French novel in his hand; exhibiting exactly the picture of frowsy comfort which he had presented when his visitors first entered the room.

'Good-day,' said Mr Troy, with haughty condescension.

'Don't interrupt me!' rejoined Old Sharon, absorbed in his novel. 'You've had your guinea's worth. Lord! what a lovely book this is! Don't interrupt me!'

'Impudent scoundrel!' said Mr Troy, when he and Moody were in the street again. 'What could my friend mean by recommending him? Fancy his expecting me to trust him with ten pounds! I consider even the guinea completely thrown away.'

'Begging your pardon, sir,' said Moody, 'I don't quite agree with you there.'

'What! you don't mean to tell me you understand that oracular sentence of his – "Suspect the very last person on whom suspicion could possibly fall." Rubbish!'

'I don't say I understand it, sir. I only say it has set me thinking.'

'Thinking of what? Do your suspicions point to the thief?'

'If you will please to excuse me, Mr Troy, I should like to wait a while before I answer that.'

Mr Troy suddenly stood still, and eyed his companion a little distrustfully.

'Are you going to turn detective policeman on your own account?' he asked.

'There's nothing I won't turn to, and try, to help Miss Isabel in this matter,' Moody answered firmly. 'I have saved a few hundred pounds in Lady Lydiard's service, and I am ready to spend every farthing of it, if I can only discover the thief.'

Mr Troy walked on again. 'Miss Isabel seems to have a good friend in you,' he said. He was (perhaps unconsciously) a little offended by the independent tone in which the steward spoke, after he had himself engaged to take the vindication of the girl's innocence into his own hands.

'Miss Isabel has a devoted servant and slave in me!' Moody answered, with passionate enthusiasm.

'Very creditable; I haven't a word to say against it,' Mr Troy rejoined. 'But don't forget that the young lady has other devoted friends besides you. I am her devoted friend, for instance – I have promised to serve her, and I mean to keep my word. You will excuse me for adding that my experience and discretion are quite as likely to be useful to her as your enthusiasm. I know the world well enough to be careful in trusting strangers. It will do you no harm, Mr Moody, to follow my example.'

Moody accepted his reproof with becoming patience and resignation. 'If you have anything to propose, sir, that will be of service to Miss Isabel,' he said, 'I shall be happy if I can assist you in the humblest capacity.'

'And if not?' Mr Troy inquired, conscious of having nothing to propose as he asked the question.

'In that case, sir, I must take my own course, and blame nobody but myself if it leads me astray.'

Mr Troy said no more: he parted from Moody at the next turning.

Pursuing the subject privately in his own mind, he decided on taking the earliest opportunity of visiting Isabel at her aunt's house, and on warning her, in her future intercouse with Moody, not to trust too much to the steward's discretion. 'I haven't a doubt,' thought the lawyer, 'of what he means to do next. The infatuated fool is going back to Old Sharon!'

⊛ TEN ⊛

RETURNING TO HIS OFFICE, MR TROY DISCOVERED, among the correspondence that was waiting for him, a letter from the very person whose welfare was still the uppermost subject in his mind. Isabel Miller wrote in these terms:

'Dear Sir, – My aunt, Miss Pink, is very desirous of consulting you professionally at the earliest opportunity. Although South Morden is within little more than half an hour's railway ride from London, Miss Pink does not presume to ask you to visit her, being well aware of the value of your time. Will you, therefore, be so kind as to let me know when it will be convenient to you to receive my aunt at your office in London? Believe me, dear Sir, respectfully yours, ISABEL MILLER P.S. – I am further instructed to say that the regrettable event at Lady Lydiard's house is the proposed subject of the consultation. The Lawn, South Morden. Thursday.'

Mr Troy smiled as he read the letter. 'Too formal for a young girl!' he said to himself. 'Every word of it has been dictated by Miss Pink.' He was not long in deciding what course he should take. There was a pressing necessity for cautioning Isabel, and here was his opportunity. He sent for his head clerk, and looked at his list of engagements for the day. There was nothing set down in the book which the clerk was not quite as well able to do as the master. Mr Troy consulted his railway-guide, ordered his cab, and caught the next train to South Morden.

South Morden was then (and remains to this day) one of those primitive agricultural villages, passed over by the march of modern progress, which are still to be found in the near neighbourhood of London. Only the slow trains stopped at the station; and there was so little to do that the station-master and his porter grew flowers on the embankment, and trained creepers over the waiting-room window. Turning your back on the railway, and walking along the one street of South Morden, you found yourself in the old England of two centuries since. Gabled cottages, with fast-closed windows; pigs and poultry in quiet possession of the road; the venerable church surrounded by its shady burial-ground; the grocer's shop which sold everything, and the butcher's shop which sold nothing; the scarce inhabitants who liked a good look at a stranger, and the unwashed children who were pictures of dirty health; the clash of the iron-chained bucket in the public well, and the thump of the falling ninepins in the skittle-ground behind the public-house; the horse-pond on the one bit of open ground, and the old elm-tree with the wooden seat round it on the other – these were some of the objects that you saw, and some of the noises that you heard in South Morden, as you passed from one end of the village to the other.

About half a mile beyond the last of the old cottages, modern England met you again under the form of a row of little villas, set up by an adventurous London builder who had bought the land a bargain. Each villa stood in its own little garden, and looked across a stony road at the meadow lands and softly-rising wooded hills beyond. Each villa faced you in the sunshine with the horrid glare of new red brick, and forced its nonsensical name on your attention, traced in bright paint on the posts of its entrance gate. Consulting the posts as he advanced, Mr Troy arrived in due course of time at the villa called The Lawn, which derived its name apparently from a circular patch of grass in front of the house. The gate resisting his efforts to open it, he rang the bell.

Admitted by a trim, clean, shy little maid-servant, Mr Troy looked about him in amazement. Turn which way he might, he found himself silently confronted by posted and painted instructions to visitors, which forbade him to do this, and commanded him to do that, at every step of his progress from the gate to the house. On the side of the lawn a label informed him that he was not to walk on the grass. On the other side a painted hand pointed along a boundary-wall to an inscription which warned him to go that way if he had business in the kitchen. On the gravel walk at the foot of the house-steps words, neatly traced in little white shells, reminded him not to 'forget the scraper'. On the door-step he was informed, in letters of lead, that he was 'Welcome!'. On the mat in the passage bristly black words burst on his attention, commanding him to 'wipe his shoes'. Even the hat-stand in the hall was not allowed to speak for itself: it had 'Hats and Cloaks' inscribed on it, and it issued its directions imperatively in the matter of your wet umbrella – 'Put it here!'

Giving the trim little servant his card, Mr Troy was introduced to a reception-room on the lower floor. Before he had time to look round him the door was opened again from without, and Isabel stole into the room on tiptoe. She looked worn and anxious. When she shook hands with the old lawyer the charming smile that he remembered so well was gone.

'Don't say you have seen me,' she whispered. 'I am not to come into the room till my aunt sends for me. Tell me two things before I run away again. How is Lady Lydiard? And have you discovered the thief?'

'Lady Lydiard was well when I last saw her; and we have not yet succeeded in discovering the thief.' Having answered the questions in those terms, Mr Troy decided on cautioning Isabel on the subject of the steward while he had the chance. 'One question on my side,' he said, holding her back from the door by the arm. 'Do you expect Moody to visit you here?'

'I am *sure* he will visit me,' Isabel answered warmly. 'He has promised to come here at my request. I never knew what a kind heart Robert Moody had till this misfortune fell on me. My aunt, who is not easily taken with strangers, respects and admires him. I can't tell you how good he was to me on the journey here – and how kindly, how nobly, he spoke to me when we parted.' She paused, and turned her head away. The tears were rising in her eyes. 'In my situation,' she said faintly, 'kindness is very keenly felt. Don't notice me, Mr Troy.'

The lawyer waited a moment to let her recover herself.

'I agree entirely, my dear, in your opinion of Moody,' he said. 'At the same time, I think it right to warn you that his zeal in your service

611

may possibly outrun his discretion. He may feel too confidently about penetrating the mystery of the missing money; and, unless you are on your guard, he may raise false hopes in you when you next see him. Listen to any advice that he may give you, by all means. But, before you decide on being guided by his opinion, consult my older experience, and hear what I have to say on the subject. Don't suppose that I am attempting to make you distrust this good friend,' he added, noticing the look of uneasy surprise which Isabel fixed on him. 'No such idea is in my mind. I only warn you that Moody's eagerness to be of service to you may mislead him. You understand me.'

'Yes, sir,' replied Isabel coldly; 'I understand you. Please let me go now. My aunt will be down directly; and she must not find me here.' She curtseyed with distant respect, and left the room.

'So much for trying to put two ideas together into a girl's mind!' thought Mr Troy, when he was alone again. 'The little fool evidently thinks I am jealous of Moody's place in her estimation. Well! I have done my duty – and I can do no more.'

He looked round the room. Not a chair was out of its place, not a speck of dust was to be seen. The brightly-perfect polish of the table made your eyes ache; the ornaments on it looked as if they had never been touched by mortal hand; the piano was an object for distant admiration, not an instrument to be played on; the carpet made Mr Troy look nervously at the soles of his shoes; and the sofa (protected by layers of white crochet-work) said as plainly as if in words, 'Sit on me if you dare!' Mr Troy retreated to a bookcase at the farther end of the room. The books fitted the shelves to such absolute perfection that he had some difficulty in taking one of them out. When he had succeeded, he found himself in possession of a volume of the History of England. On the fly-leaf he encountered another written warning: – 'This book belongs to Miss Pink's Academy for Young Ladies, and is not to be removed from the library.' The date, which was added, referred to a period of ten years since. Miss Pink now stood revealed as a retired schoolmistress; and Mr Troy began to understand some of the characteristic peculiarities of that lady's establishment which had puzzled him up to the present time.

He had just succeeded in putting the book back again when the door opened once more, and Isabel's aunt entered the room.

If Miss Pink could, by any possible conjuncture of circumstances, have disappeared mysteriously from her house and her friends, the police would have found the greatest difficulty in composing the necessary description of the missing lady. The acutest observer could have discovered nothing that was noticeable or characteristic in her personal appearance. The pen of the present writer portrays her in despair by a series of negatives. She was not young, she was not old; she was neither tall nor short, nor stout nor thin; nobody could call her features attractive, and nobody could call them ugly; there was nothing in her voice, her expression, her manner, or her dress that differed in any appreciable degree from the voice, expression, manner, and dress of five hundred thousand other single ladies of her age and position in the world. If you had asked her to describe herself, she would have answered, 'I am a gentlewoman'; and if you had further inquired which of her numerous accomplishments took highest rank in her own esteem, she would have replied, 'My powers of conversation'. For the rest, she was Miss Pink, of South Morden; and, when that has been said, all has been said.

'Pray be seated, sir. We have had a beautiful day, after the long-continued wet weather. I am told that the season is very unfavourable for wall-fruit. May I offer you some refreshment after your journey?' In these terms and in the smoothest of voices, Miss Pink opened the interview.

Mr Troy made a polite reply, and added a few strictly conventional remarks on the beauty of the neighbourhood. Not even a lawyer could sit in Miss Pink's presence, and hear Miss Pink's conversation, without feeling himself called upon (in the nursery phrase) to 'be on his best behaviour'.

'It is extremely kind of you, Mr Troy, to favour me with this visit,' Miss Pink resumed. 'I am well aware that the time of professional gentlemen is of especial value to them; and I will therefore ask you to excuse me if I proceed abruptly to the subject on which I desire to consult your experience.'

Here the lady modestly smoothed out her dress over her knees, and the lawyer made a bow. Miss Pink's highly-trained conversation had perhaps one fault – it was not, strictly speaking, conversation at all. In its effect on her hearers it rather resembled the contents of a fluently conventional letter, read aloud.

'The circumstances under which my niece Isabel has left Lady Lydiard's house,' Miss Pink proceeded, 'are so indescribably painful – I will go further, I will say so deeply humiliating – that I have forbidden her to refer to them again in my presence, or to mention them in the future to any living creature besides myself. You are acquainted with those circumstances, Mr Troy; and you will understand my indignation when I first learnt that my sister's child had been suspected of theft. I have not the honour of being acquainted with Lady Lydiard. She is not a Countess, I believe? Just so! Her husband was only a Baron. I am not acquainted with Lady Lydiard; and I will not trust myself to say what I think of her conduct to my niece.'

'Pardon me, madam,' Mr Troy interposed. 'Before you say any more about Lady Lydiard, I really must beg leave to observe——'

'Pardon *me*,' Miss Pink rejoined. 'I never form a hasty judgment. Lady Lydiard's conduct is beyond the reach of any defence, no matter how ingenious it may be. You may not be aware, sir, that in receiving my niece under her roof her Ladyship was receiving a gentlewoman by birth as well as by education. My late lamented sister was the daughter of a clergyman of the Church of England. I need hardly remind you that, as such, she was a born lady. Under favouring circumstances, Isabel's maternal grandfather might have been Archbishop of Canterbury, and have taken precedence of the whole House of Peers, the Princes of the blood Royal alone excepted. I am not prepared to say that my niece is equally well connected on her father's side. My sister surprised – I will not add shocked – us when she married a chemist. At the same time, a chemist is not a tradesman. He is a gentleman at one end of the profession of Medicine, and a titled physician is a gentleman at the other end. That is all. In inviting Isabel to reside with her, Lady Lydiard, I repeat, was bound to remember that she was associating herself with a young gentlewoman. She has *not* remembered this, which is one insult; and she had suspected my niece of theft, which is another.'

Miss Pink paused to take breath. Mr Troy made a second attempt to get a hearing.

'Will you kindly permit me, madam, to say a few words?'

'No!' said Miss Pink, asserting the most immovable obstinacy under the blandest politeness of manner. 'Your time, Mr Troy, is really too valuable! Not even your trained intellect can excuse conduct which is manifestly *in*excusable on the face of it. Now you know my opinion of Lady Lydiard, you will not be surprised to hear that I decline to trust her Ladyship. She may, or she may not, cause the necessary inquiries to be made for the vindication of my niece's character. In a matter so serious as this – I may say, in a duty which I owe to the memories of my sister and my parents – I will not leave the responsibility to Lady Lydiard. I will take it on myself. Let me add that I am able to pay the necessary expenses. The earlier years of my life, Mr Troy, have been passed in the tuition of young ladies. I have been happy in meriting the confidence of parents; and I have been strict in observing the golden rules of economy. On my retirement, I have been able to invest a modest, a very modest, little fortune in the Funds. A portion of it is at the service of my niece for the recovery of her good name; and I desire to place the necessary investigation confidentially in your hands. You are acquainted with the case, and the case naturally goes to you. I could not prevail on myself – I really could not prevail on myself to mention it to a stranger. That is the business on which I wished to consult you. Please say nothing more about Lady Lydiard – the subject is inexpressibly disagreeable to me. I will only trespass on your kindness to tell me if I have succeeded in making myself understood.'

Miss Pink leaned back in her chair, at the exact angle permitted by the laws of propriety; rested her left elbow on the palm of her right hand, and lightly supported her cheek with her fore finger and thumb. In this position she waited Mr Troy's answer – the living picture of human obstinacy in its most respectable form.

If Mr Troy had not been a lawyer – in other words, if he had not been professionally capable of persisting in his own course, in the face of every conceivable difficulty and discouragement – Miss Pink might have remained in undisturbed possession of her own opinions. As it was, Mr Troy had got his hearing at last; and no matter how obstinately she might close her eyes to it, Miss Pink was now destined to have the other side of the case presented to her view.

'I am sincerely obliged to you, madam, for the expression of your confidence in me,' Mr Troy began; 'at the same time, I must beg you to excuse me if I decline to accept your proposal.'

Miss Pink had not expected to receive such an answer as this. The lawyer's brief refusal surprised and annoyed her.

'Why do you decline to assist me?' she asked.

'Because,' answered Mr Troy, 'my services are already engaged, in Miss Isabel's interest, by a client whom I have served for more than twenty years. My client is——'

Miss Pink anticipated the coming disclosure. 'You need not trouble yourself, sir, to mention your client's name,' she said.

'My client,' persisted Mr Troy, 'loves Miss Isabel dearly——'

'That is a matter of opinion,' Miss Pink interposed.

'And believes in Miss Isabel's innocence,' proceeded the irrepressible lawyer, 'as firmly as you believe in it yourself.'

Miss Pink (being human) had a temper; and Mr Troy had found his way to it.

'If Lady Lydiard believes in my niece's innocence,' said Miss Pink, suddenly sitting bolt upright in her chair, 'why has my niece been compelled, in justice to herself, to leave Lady Lydiard's house?'

'You will admit, madam,' Mr Troy answered cautiously, 'that we are all of us liable, in this wicked world, to be the victims of appearances. Your niece is a victim – an innocent victim. She wisely withdraws from Lady Lydiard's house until appearances are proved to be false and her position is cleared up.'

Miss Pink had her reply ready. 'That is simply acknowledging, in other words, that my niece is suspected. I am only a woman, Mr Troy – but it is not quite so easy to mislead me as you seem to suppose.'

Mr Troy's temper was admirably trained. But it began to acknowledge that Miss Pink's powers of irritation could sting to some purpose.

'No intention of misleading you, madam, has ever crossed my mind,' he rejoined warmly. 'As for your niece, I can tell you this. In all my experience of Lady Lydiard, I never saw her so distressed as she was when Miss Isabel left the house!'

'Indeed!' said Miss Pink, with an incredulous smile. 'In my rank of life, when we feel distressed about a person, we do our best to comfort that person by a kind letter or an early visit. But then I am not a lady of title.'

'Lady Lydiard engaged herself to call on Miss Isabel in my hearing,' said Mr Troy. 'Lady Lydiard is the most generous woman living!'

'Lady Lydiard is here!' cried a joyful voice on the other side of the door.

At the same moment, Isabel burst into the room in a state of excitement which actually ignored the formidable presence of Miss Pink. 'I beg your pardon, aunt! I was upstairs at the window, and I saw the carriage stop at the gate. And Tommie has come, too! The darling saw me at the window!' cried the poor girl, her eyes sparkling with delight as a perfect explosion of barking made itself heard over the tramp of horses' feet and the crash of carriage wheels outside.

Miss Pink rose slowly, with a dignity that looked capable of adequately receiving – not one noble lady only, but the whole peerage of England.

'Control yourself, dear Isabel,' she said. 'No well-bred young lady permits herself to become unduly excited. Stand by my side – a little behind me.'

Isabel obeyed. Mr Troy kept his place, and privately enjoyed his triumph over Miss Pink. If Lady Lydiard had been actually in league with him, she could not have chosen a more opportune time for her visit. A momentary interval passed. The carriage drew up at the door; the horses trampled on the gravel; the bell rung madly; the uproar of Tommie, released from the carriage and clamouring to be let in, redoubled its fury. Never before had such an unruly burst of noises invaded the tranquillity of Miss Pink's villa!

❧ ELEVEN ❧

THE TRIM LITTLE MAID-SERVANT RAN UP stairs from the modest little kitchen, trembling at the terrible prospect of having to open the door. Miss Pink, deafened by the barking, had just time to say, 'What a very ill-behaved dog!' when a sound of small objects overthrown in the hall, and a scurrying of furious claws across the oil-cloth, announced that Tommie had invaded the house. As the servant appeared, introducing Lady Lydiard, the dog ran in. He made one frantic leap at Isabel, which would certainly have knocked her down but for the chair that happened to be standing behind her. Received on her lap, the faithful creature half-smothered her with his caresses. He barked, he shrieked, in his joy at seeing her again. He jumped off her lap and tore round and round the room at the top of his speed; and every time he passed Miss Pink he showed the whole range of his teeth and snarled ferociously at her ankles. Having at last exhausted his superfluous energy, he leapt back again on Isabel's lap, with his tongue quivering in his open mouth – his tail wagging softly, and his eye on Miss Pink, inquiring how she liked a dog in her drawing-room!

'I hope my dog has not disturbed you, ma'am?' said Lady Lydiard, advancing from the mat at the doorway, on which she had patiently waited until the raptures of Tommie subsided into repose.

Miss Pink, trembling between terror and indignation, acknowledged Lady Lydiard's polite inquiry by a ceremonious bow, and an answer which administered by implication a dignified reproof. 'Your Ladyship's dog does not appear to be a very well-trained animal,' the ex-schoolmistress remarked.

'Well trained?' Lady Lydiard repeated, as if the expression was perfectly unintelligible to her. 'I don't think you have had much experience of dogs, ma'am.' She turned to Isabel, and embraced her tenderly. 'Give me a kiss, my dear – you don't know how wretched I have been since you left me.' She looked back again at Miss Pink. 'You are not, perhaps, aware, ma'am, that my dog is devotedly attached to your niece. A dog's love has been considered by many great men (whose names at the moment escape me) as the most touching and disinterested of all earthly affections.' She looked the other way, and discovered the lawyer. 'How do you do, Mr Troy? It's a pleasant surprise to find you here. The house was so dull without Isabel that I really couldn't put off seeing her any longer. When you are more used to Tommie, Miss Pink, you will understand and admire him. *You* understand and admire him, Isabel – don't you? My child! you are not looking well. I shall take you back with me, when the horses have had their rest. We shall never be happy away from each other.'

Having expressed her sentiments, distributed her greetings, and defended her dog – all, as it were, in one breath – Lady Lydiard sat down by Isabel's side, and opened a large green fan that hung at her girdle. 'You have no idea, Miss Pink, how fat people suffer in hot weather,' said the old lady, using her fan vigorously.

Miss Pink's eyes dropped modestly to the ground – 'fat' was such a coarse word to use, if a lady *must* speak of her own superfluous flesh! 'May I offer some refreshment?' Miss Pink asked, mincingly. 'A cup of tea?'

Lady Lydiard shook her head.

'A glass of water?'

Lady Lydiard declined this last hospitable proposal with an exclamation of disgust. 'Have you got any beer?' she inquired.

'I beg your Ladyship's pardon,' said Miss Pink, doubting the evidence of her own ears. 'Did you say – beer?'

Lady Lydiard gesticulated vehemently with her fan. 'Yes, to be sure! Beer! beer!'

Miss Pink rose, with a countenance expressive of genteel disgust, and rang the bell. 'I think you have beer down stairs, Susan?' she said, when the maid appeared at the door.

'Yes, Miss.'

'A glass of beer for Lady Lydiard,' said Miss Pink – under protest.

'Bring it in a jug,' shouted her Ladyship, as the maid left the room. 'I like to froth it up for myself,' she continued, addressing Miss Pink. 'Isabel sometimes does it for me, when she is at home – don't you, my dear?'

Miss Pink had been waiting her opportunity to assert her own claim to the possession of her own niece, from the time when Lady Lydiard had coolly declared her intention of taking Isabel back with her. The opportunity now presented itself.

'Your Ladyship will pardon me,' she said, 'if I remark that my niece's home is under my humble roof. I am properly sensible, I hope, of your kindness to Isabel; but while she remains the object of a disgraceful suspicion she remains with me.'

Lady Lydiard closed her fan with an angry snap.

'You are completely mistaken, Miss Pink. You may not mean it – but you speak most unjustly if you say that your niece is an object of suspicion to me, or to anybody in my house.'

Mr Troy, quietly listening up to this point, now interposed to stop the discussion before it could degenerate into a personal quarrel. His keen observation, aided by his accurate knowledge of his client's character, had plainly revealed to him what was passing in Lady Lydiard's mind. She had entered the house, feeling (perhaps unconsciously) a jealousy of Miss Pink, as her predecessor in Isabel's affections, and as the natural protectress of the girl under existing circumstances. Miss Pink's reception of her dog had additionally irritated the old lady. She had taken a malicious pleasure in shocking the schoolmistress's sense of propriety – and she was now only too ready to proceed to further extremities on the delicate question of Isabel's justification for leaving her house. For Isabel's own sake, therefore – to say nothing of other reasons – it was urgently desirable to keep the peace between the two ladies. With this excellent object in view, Mr Troy seized his opportunity of striking into the conversation for the first time.

'Pardon me, Lady Lydiard,' he said, 'you are speaking of a subject which has been already sufficiently discussed between Miss Pink and myself. I think we shall do better not to dwell uselessly on past events, but to direct our attention to the future. We are all equally satisfied of the complete rectitude of Miss Isabel's conduct, and we are all equally interested in the vindication of her good name.'

Whether these temperate words would of themselves have exercised the pacifying influence at which Mr Troy aimed may be doubtful. But, as he ceased speaking, a powerful auxiliary appeared in the shape of the beer. Lady Lydiard seized on the jug, and filled the tumbler for herself with an unsteady hand. Miss Pink, trembling for the integrity of her carpet, and scandalized at seeing a peeress drinking beer like a washerwoman, forgot the sharp answer that was just rising to her lips when the lawyer interfered. 'Small!' said Lady Lydiard, setting down the empty tumbler, and referring to the quality of the beer. 'But very pleasant and refreshing. What's the servant's name? Susan? Well, Susan, I was dying of thirst; and you have saved my life. You can leave the jug – I dare say I shall empty it before I go.'

Mr Troy, watching Miss Pink's face, saw that it was time to change the subject again.

'Did you notice the old village, Lady Lydiard, on your way here?' he asked. 'The artists consider it one of the most picturesque places in England.'

'I noticed that it was a very dirty village,' Lady Lydiard answered, still bent on making herself disagreeable to Miss Pink. 'The artists may say what they please; I see nothing to admire in rotten cottages, and bad drainage, and ignorant people. I suppose the neighbourhood has its advantages. It looks dull enough, to my mind.'

Isabel had hitherto modestly restricted her exertions to keeping Tommie quiet on her lap. Like Mr Troy, she occasionally looked at her aunt – and she now made a timid attempt to defend the neighbourhood, as a duty that she owed to Miss Pink.

'Oh, my Lady! don't say it's a dull neighbourhood,' she pleaded. 'There are such pretty walks all round us. And, when you get to the hills, the view is beautiful.'

Lady Lydiard's answer to this was a little masterpiece of good-humoured contempt. She patted Isabel's cheek, and said, 'Pooh! pooh!'

'Your Ladyship does not admire the beauties of Nature,' Miss Pink remarked, with a compassionate smile. 'As we get older, no doubt our sight begins to fail——'

'And we leave off canting about the beauties of Nature,' added Lady Lydiard. 'I hate the country. Give me London, and the pleasures of society.'

'Come! come! Do the country justice, Lady Lydiard!' put in peace-making Mr Troy. 'There is plenty of society to be found out of London – as good society as the world can show.'

'The sort of society,' added Miss Pink, 'which is to be found, for example, in this neighbourhood. Her Ladyship is evidently not aware that persons of distinction surround us, whichever way we turn. I may instance among others, the Honourable Mr Hardyman——'

Lady Lydiard, in the act of pouring out a second glassful of beer, suddenly set down the jug.

'Who is that you're talking of, Miss Pink?'

'I am talking of our neighbour, Lady Lydiard – the Honourable Mr Hardyman.'

'Do you mean Alfred Hardyman – the man who breeds the horses?'

'The distinguished gentleman who owns the famous studfarm,' said Miss Pink, correcting the bluntly-direct form in which Lady Lydiard had put her question.

'Is he in the habit of visiting here?' the old lady inquired, with a sudden appearance of anxiety. 'Do you know him?'

'I had the honour of being introduced to Mr Hardyman at our last flower show,' Miss Pink replied. 'He has not yet favoured me with a visit.'

Lady Lydiard's anxiety appeared to be to some extent relieved.

'I knew that Hardyman's farm was in this county,' she said; 'but I had no notion that it was in the neighbourhood of South Morden. How far away is he – ten or a dozen miles, eh?'

'Not more than three miles,' answered Miss Pink. 'We consider him quite a near neighbour of ours.'

Renewed anxiety showed itself in Lady Lydiard. She looked round sharply at Isabel. The girl's head was bent so low over the rough head of the dog that her face was almost entirely concealed from view. So far as appearances went, she seemed to be entirely absorbed in fondling Tommie. Lady Lydiard roused her with a tap of the green fan.

'Take Tommie out, Isabel, for a run in the garden,' she said. 'He won't sit still much longer – and he may annoy Miss Pink. Mr Troy, will you kindly help Isabel to keep my ill-trained dog in order?'

Mr Troy got on his feet, and, not very willingly, followed Isabel out of the room. 'They will quarrel now, to a dead certainty!' he thought to himself, as he closed the door. 'Have you any idea of what this means?' he said to his companion, as he joined her in the hall. 'What has Mr Hardyman done to excite all this interest in him?'

Isabel's guilty colour rose. She knew perfectly well that Hardyman's unconcealed admiration of her was the guiding motive of Lady Lydiard's inquiries. If she had told the truth, Mr Troy would have unquestionably returned to the drawing-room, with or without an acceptable excuse for intruding himself. But Isabel was a woman; and her answer, it is needless to say, was 'I don't know, I'm sure.'

In the mean time, the interview between the two ladies began in a manner which would have astonished Mr Troy – they were both silent. For once in her life Lady Lydiard was considering what she should say, before she said it. Miss Pink, on her side, naturally waited to hear what object her Ladyship had in view – waited, until her small reserve of patience gave way. Urged by irresistible curiosity, she spoke first.

'Have you anything to say to me in private?' she asked.

Lady Lydiard had not got to the end of her reflections. She said 'Yes!' – and she said no more.

'Is it anything relating to my niece?' persisted Miss Pink.

Still immersed in her reflections, Lady Lydiard suddenly rose to the surface, and spoke her mind, as usual.

'About your niece, ma'am. The other day Mr Hardyman called at my house, and saw Isabel.'

'Yes,' said Miss Pink, politely attentive, but not in the least interested, so far.

'That's not all, ma'am. Mr Hardyman admires Isabel; he owned it to me himself in so many words.'

Miss Pink listened, with a courteous inclination of her head. She looked mildly gratified, nothing more. Lady Lydiard proceeded:

'You and I think differently on many matters,' she said. 'But we are both agreed, I am sure, in feeling the sincerest interest in Isabel's welfare. I beg to suggest to you, Miss Pink, that Mr Hardyman, as a near neighbour of yours, is a very undesirable neighbour while Isabel remains in your house.'

Saying those words, under a strong conviction of the serious importance of the subject, Lady Lydiard insensibly recovered the manner and resumed the language which befitted a lady of her rank. Miss Pink, noticing the change, set it down to an expression of pride on the part of her visitor which, in referring to Isabel, assailed indirectly the social position of Isabel's aunt.

'I fail entirely to understand what your Ladyship means,' she said coldly.

Lady Lydiard, on her side, looked in undisguised amazement at Miss Pink.

'Haven't I told you already that Mr Hardyman admires your niece?' she asked.

'Naturally,' said Miss Pink. 'Isabel inherits her lamented mother's personal advantages. If Mr Hardyman admires her, Mr Hardyman shows his good taste.'

Lady Lydiard's eyes opened wider and wider in wonder. 'My good lady!' she exclaimed, 'is it possible you don't know that when a man admires a women he doesn't stop there? He falls in love with her (as the saying is) next.'

'So I have heard,' said Miss Pink.

'So you have *heard*?' repeated Lady Lydiard. 'If Mr Hardyman finds his way to Isabel I can tell you what you will *see*. Catch the two together, ma'am – and you will see Mr Hardyman making love to your niece.'

'Under due restrictions, Lady Lydiard, and with my permission first obtained, of course, I see no objection to Mr Hardyman paying his addresses to Isabel.'

'The woman is mad!' cried Lady Lydiard. 'Do you actually suppose, Miss Pink, that Alfred Hardyman could, by any earthly possibility, marry your niece!'

Not even Miss Pink's politeness could submit to such a question as this. She rose indignantly from her chair. 'Are you aware, Lady Lydiard, that the doubt you have just expressed is an insult to my niece, and an insult to Me?'

'Are *you* aware of who Mr Hardyman really is?' retorted her Ladyship. 'Or do you judge of his position by the vocation in life which he has perversely chosen to adopt? I can tell you, if you do, that Alfred Hardyman is the younger son of one of the oldest barons in the English Peerage, and that his mother is related by marriage to the Royal family of Wurtemberg.'

Miss Pink received the full shock of this information without receding from her position by a hair's breadth.

'An English gentlewoman offers a fit alliance to any man living who seeks her hand in marriage,' said Miss Pink. 'Isabel's mother (you may not be aware of it) was the daughter of an English clergyman—'

'And Isabel's father was a chemist in a country town,' added Lady Lydiard.

'Isabel's father,' rejoined Miss Pink, 'was attached in a most responsible capacity to the useful and honourable profession of Medicine. Isabel is, in the strictest sense of the word, a young gentlewoman. If you contradict that for a single instant, Lady Lydiard, you will oblige me to leave the room.'

Those last words produced a result which Miss Pink had not anticipated – they roused Lady Lydiard to assert herself. As usual in such cases, she rose superior to her own eccentricity. Confronting Miss Pink, she now spoke and looked with the gracious courtesy and the unpresuming self-confidence of the order to which she belonged.

'For Isabel's own sake, and for the quieting of my conscience,' she answered, 'I will say one word more, Miss Pink, before I relieve you of my presence. Considering my age and my opportunities, I may claim to know quite as much as you do of the laws and customs which regulate society in our time. Without contesting your niece's social position – and without the slightest intention of insulting you – I repeat that the rank which Mr Hardyman inherits makes it simply impossible for him even to think of marrying Isabel. You will do well not to give him any opportunities of meeting with her alone. And you will do better still (seeing that he is so near a neighbour of yours) if you permit Isabel to return to my protection, for a time at least. I will wait to hear from you when you have thought the matter over at your leisure. In the mean time, if I have inadvertently offended you, I ask your pardon – and I wish you good evening.'

She bowed, and walked to the door. Miss Pink, as resolute as ever in maintaining her pretensions, made an effort to match the great lady on her own ground.

'Before you go, Lady Lydiard, I beg to apologize if I have spoken too warmly on my side,' she said. 'Permit me to send for your carriage.'

'Thank you, Miss Pink. My carriage is only at the village inn. I shall enjoy a little walk in the cool evening air. Mr Troy, I have no doubt, will give me his arm.' She bowed once more, and quietly left the room.

Reaching the little back garden of the villa, through an open door at the farther end of the hall, Lady Lydiard found Tommie rolling luxuriously on Miss Pink's flower-beds, and Isabel and Mr Troy in close consultation on the gravel walk. She spoke to the lawyer first.

'They are baiting the horses at the inn,' she said. 'I want your arm, Mr Troy, as far as the village – and, in return, I will take you back to London with me. I have to ask your advice about one or two little matters, and this is a good opportunity.'

'With the greatest pleasure, Lady Lydiard. I suppose I must say good-bye to Miss Pink?'

'A word of advice to you, Mr Troy. Take care how you ruffle Miss Pink's sense of her own importance. Another word for your private ear. Miss Pink is a fool.'

On the lawyer's withdrawal, Lady Lydiard put her arm fondly round Isabel's waist. 'What were you and Mr Troy so busy in talking about?' she asked.

'We were talking, my Lady, about tracing the person who stole the money,' Isabel answered, rather sadly. 'It seems a far more difficult matter than I supposed it to be. I try not to lose patience and hope – but it is a little hard to feel that appearances are against me, and to wait day after day in vain for the discovery that is to set me right.'

'You are a dear good child,' said Lady Lydiard; 'and you are more precious to me than ever. Don't despair, Isabel. With Mr Troy's means of inquiring, and with my means of paying, the discovery of the thief cannot be much longer delayed. If you don't return to me soon, I shall come back and see you again. Your aunt hates the sight of me – but I don't care two straws for that,' remarked Lady Lydiard, showing the undignified side of her character once more. 'Listen to me, Isabel! I have no wish to lower your aunt in your estimation, but I feel far more confidence in your good sense than in hers. Mr Hardyman's business has taken him to France for the present. It is at least possible that you may meet with him on his return. If you do, keep him at a distance, my dear – politely, of course. There! there! you needn't turn red; I am not blaming you; I am only giving you a little good advice. In your position you cannot possibly be too careful. Here is Mr Troy! You must come to the gate with us, Isabel, or we shall never get Tommie away from you; I am only his second favourite; you have the first place in his affections. God bless and prosper you, my child! – I wish to Heaven you were going back to London with me! Well, Mr Troy, how have you done with Miss Pink? Have you offended that terrible 'gentlewoman' (hateful word!); or has it been all the other way, and has she given you a kiss at parting?'

Mr Troy smiled mysteriously, and changed the subject. His brief parting interview with the lady of the house was not of a nature to be rashly related. Miss Pink had not only positively assured him that her visitor was the most ill-bred woman she had ever met with, but had further accused Lady Lydiard of shaking her confidence in the aristocracy of her native country. 'For the first time in my life,' said Miss Pink, 'I feel that something is to be said for the Republican point of view; and

I am not indisposed to admit that the constitution of the United States *has* its advantages!'

⊷ TWELVE ⥱

THE CONFERENCE BETWEEN LADY LYDIARD AND MR TROY, on the way back to London, led to some practical results.

Hearing from her legal adviser that the inquiry after the missing money was for a moment at a standstill, Lady Lydiard made one of those bold suggestions with which she was accustomed to startle her friends in cases of emergency. She had heard favourable reports of the extraordinary ingenuity of the French police; and she now proposed sending to Paris for assistance, after first consulting her nephew, Mr Felix Sweetsir. 'Felix knows Paris as well as he knows London,' she remarked. 'He is an idle man, and it is quite likely that he will relieve us of all trouble by taking the matter into his own hands. In any case, he is sure to know who are the right people to address in our present necessity. What do you say?'

Mr Troy, in reply, expressed his doubts as to the wisdom of employing foreigners in a delicate investigation which required an accurate knowledge of English customs and English character. Waiving this objection, he approved of the idea of consulting her Ladyship's nephew. 'Mr Sweetsir is a man of the world,' he said. 'In putting the case before him, we are sure to have it presented to us from a new point of view.' Acting on this favourable expression of opinion, Lady Lydiard wrote to her nephew. On the day after the visit to Miss Pink, the proposed council of three was held at Lady Lydiard's house.

Felix, never punctual at keeping an appointment, was even later than usual on this occasion. He made his apologies with his hand pressed upon his forehead, and his voice expressive of the languor and discouragement of a suffering man.

'The beastly English climate is telling on my nerves,' said Mr Sweetsir – 'the horrid weight of the atmosphere, after the exhilarating air of Paris; the intolerable dirt and dullness of London, you know. I was in bed, my dear aunt, when I received your letter. You may imagine the completely demoralised state I was in, when I tell you of the effect which the news of the robbery produced on me. I fell back on my pillow, as if I had been shot. Your Ladyship should really be a little more careful in communicating these disagreeable surprises to a sensitively-organised man. Never mind – my valet is a perfect treasure; he brought me some drops of ether on a lump of sugar. I said, "Alfred" (his name is Alfred), "put me into my clothes!" Alfred put me in. I assure you it reminded me of my young days, when I was put into my first pair of trousers. Has Alfred forgotten anything? Have I got my braces on? Have I come out in my shirt-sleeves? Well, dear aunt; – well, Mr Troy! – what can I say? What can I do?'

Lady Lydiard, entirely without sympathy for nervous suffering, nodded to the lawyer. 'You tell him,' she said.

'I believe I speak for her Ladyship,' Mr Troy began, 'when I say that we should like to hear, in the first place, how the whole case strikes you, Mr Sweetsir?'

'Tell it me all over again,' said Felix.

Patient Mr Troy told it all over again – and waited for the result.

'Well?' said Felix.

'Well?' said Mr Troy. 'Where does the suspicion of robbery rest in your opinion? You look at the theft of the bank-note with a fresh eye.'

'You mentioned a clergyman just now,' said Felix. 'The man, you know, to whom the money was sent. What was his name?'

'The Reverend Samuel Bradstock.'

'You want me to name the person whom I suspect?'

'Yes, if you please,' said Mr Troy.

'I suspect the Reverend Samuel Bradstock,' said Felix.

'If you have come here to make stupid jokes,' interposed Lady Lydiard, 'you had better go back to your bed again. We want a serious opinion.'

'You *have* a serious opinion,' Felix coolly rejoined. 'I never was more in earnest in my life. Your Ladyship is not aware of the first principle to be adopted in cases of suspicion. One proceeds on what I will call the exhaustive system of reasoning. Thus: – Does suspicion point to the honest servants down stairs? No. To your Ladyship's adopted daughter? Appearances are against the poor girl; but you know her better than to trust to appearances. Are you suspicious of Moody? No. Of Hardyman – who was in the house at the time? Ridiculous! But I was in the house at the time, too. Do you suspect Me? Just so! That idea is ridiculous, too. Now let us sum up. Servants, adopted daughter, Moody, Hardyman, Sweetsir – all beyond suspicion. Who is left? The Reverend Samuel Bradstock.'

This ingenious exposition of 'the exhaustive system of reasoning', failed to produce any effect on Lady Lydiard. You are wasting our time,' she said sharply. 'You know as well as I do that you are talking nonsense.'

'I don't,' said Felix. 'Taking the gentlemanly professions all round, I know of no men who are so eager to get money, and who have so few scruples about how they get it, as the parsons. Where is there a man in any other profession who perpetually worries you for money? – who holds the bag under your nose for money? – who sends his clerk round from door to door to beg a few shillings of you, and calls it an "Easter offering"? The parson does all this. Bradstock is a parson. I put it logically. Bowl me over, if you can.'

Mr Troy attempted to 'bowl him over', nevertheless. Lady Lydiard wisely interposed.

'When a man persists in talking nonsense,' she said, 'silence is the best answer; anything else only encourages him.' She turned to Felix. 'I have a question to ask you,' she went on. 'You will either give me a serious reply, or wish me good morning.' With this brief preface, she made her inquiry as to the wisdom and possibility of engaging the services of the French police.

Felix took exactly the view of the matter which had been already expressed by Mr Troy. 'Superior in intelligence,' he said, 'but not superior in courage, to the English police. Capable of performing wonders on their own ground and among their own people. But, my dear aunt, the two most dissimilar nations on the face of the earth are the English and the French. The French police may speak our language – but they are incapable of understanding our national character and our national manners. Set them to work on a private inquiry in the city of Pekin – and they would get on in time with the Chinese people. Set them to work in the city of London – and the English people would remain, from first to last, the same impenetrable mystery to them. In my belief the London Sunday would be enough of itself to drive them back to Paris in despair. No balls, no concerts, no theatres, not even a museum or a picture-gallery open; every shop shut up but the gin-shop; and nothing moving but the church bells and the men who sell the penny ices. Hundreds of Frenchmen come to see me on their first arrival in England. Every man of them rushes back to Paris on the second Saturday of his visit; rather than confront the horrors of a second Sunday in London! However, you can try it if you like. Send me a written abstract of the case, and I will forward it to one of the official people in the Rue Jerusalem, who will do anything he can to oblige me. Of course,' said Felix, turning to Mr Troy, 'some of you have got the number of the lost bank-note? If the thief has tried to pass it in Paris, my man may be of some use to you.'

'Three of us have got the number of the note,' answered Mr Troy; 'Miss Isabel Miller, Mr Moody, and myself.'

'Very good,' said Felix. 'Send me the number, with the abstract of the case. Is there anything else I can do towards recovering the money?' he asked, turning to his aunt. 'There is one lucky circumstance in connection with this loss – isn't there? It has fallen on a person who is rich enough to take it easy. Good Heavens! suppose it had been *my* loss!'

'It has fallen doubly on me,' said Lady Lydiard; 'and I am certainly not rich enough to take it *that* easy. The money was destined to a charitable purpose; and I have felt it my duty to pay it again.'

Felix rose and approached his aunt's chair with faltering steps, as became a suffering man. He took Lady Lydiard's hand and kissed it with enthusiastic admiration.

'You excellent creature!' he said. 'You may not think it, but you reconcile me to human nature. How generous! how noble! I think I'll go to bed again, Mr Troy, if you really don't want any more of me. My head feels giddy and my legs tremble under me. It doesn't matter; I shall feel easier when Alfred has taken me out of my clothes again. God bless you, my dear aunt! I never felt so proud of being related to you as I do to-day. Good-morning Mr Troy! Don't forget the abstract of the case; and don't trouble yourself to see me to the door. I dare say I shan't tumble down stairs; and, if I do, there's the porter in the hall to pick me up again. Enviable porter! as fat as butter and as idle as a pig! *Au revoir! au revoir!*' He kissed his hand, and drifted feebly out of the room. Sweetsir, one might say, in a state of eclipse; but still the serviceable Sweetsir, who was never consulted in vain by the fortunate people privileged to call him friend!

'Is he really ill, do you think?' Mr Troy asked.

'My nephew has turned fifty,' Lady Lydiard answered, 'and he persists in living as if he was a young man. Every now and then Nature says to him, "Felix you are old!" And Felix goes to bed, and says it's his nerves.'

'I suppose he is to be trusted to keep his word about writing to Paris?' pursued the lawyer.

'Oh, yes! He may delay doing it; but he will do it. In spite of his lackadaisical manner, he has moments of energy that would surprise you. Talking of surprises, I have something to tell you about Moody. Within the last day or two there has been a marked change in him – a change for the worse.'

'You astonish me, Lady Lydiard! In what way has Moody deteriorated?'

'You shall hear. Yesterday was Friday. You took him out with you, on business, early in the morning.'

Mr Troy bowed, and said nothing. He had not thought it desirable to mention the interview at which Old Sharon had cheated him of his guinea.

'In the course of the afternoon,' pursued Lady Lydiard, 'I happened to want him, and I was informed that Moody had gone out again. Where had he gone? Nobody knew. Had he left word when he would be back?

He had left no message of any sort. Of course, he is not in the position of an ordinary servant. I don't expect him to ask permission to go out. But I do expect him to leave word downstairs of the time at which he is likely to return. When he did come back, after an absence of some hours, I naturally asked for an explanation. Would you believe it? he simply informed me that he had been away on business of his own; expressed no regret, and offered no explanation – in short, spoke as if he was an independent gentleman. You may not think it, but I kept my temper. I merely remarked that I hoped it would not happen again. He made me a bow, and he said, "My business is not completed yet, my Lady. I cannot guarantee that it may not call me away again at a moment's notice." What do you think of that? Nine people out of ten would have given him warning to leave their service. I begin to think I am a wonderful woman – I only pointed to the door. One does hear sometimes of men's brains softening in the most unexpected manner. I have my suspicions of Moody's brains, I can tell you.'

Mr Troy's suspicions took a different direction: they pointed along the line of streets which led to Old Sharon's lodgings. Discreetly silent as to the turn which his thoughts had taken, he merely expressed himself as feeling too much surprised to offer any opinion at all.

'Wait a little,' said Lady Lydiard, 'I haven't done surprising you yet. You have seen a boy here in a page's livery, I think? Well, he is a good boy; and he has gone home for a week's holiday with his friends. The proper person to supply his place with the boots and shoes and other small employments, is of course the youngest footman, a lad only a few years older than himself. What do you think Moody does? Engages a stranger, with the house full of idle men-servants already, to fill the page's place. At intervals this morning I heard them wonderfully merry in the servant's hall – *so* merry that the noise and laughter found its way up stairs to the breakfast-room. I like my servants to be in good spirits; but it certainly did strike me that they were getting beyond reasonable limits. I questioned my maid, and was informed that the noise was all due to the jokes of the strangest old man that ever was seen. In other words, to the person whom my steward had taken it on himself to engage in the page's absence. I spoke to Moody on the subject. He answered in an odd, confused way, that he had exercised his discretion to the best of his judgment, and that (if I wished it), he would tell the old man to keep his good spirits under better control. I asked him how he came to hear of the man. He only answered, "By accident, my Lady" – and not one more word could I get out of him, good or bad. Moody engages the servants, as you know; but on every other occasion he has invariably consulted me before an engagement was settled. I really don't feel at all sure about this person who has been so strangely introduced into the house – he may be a drunkard or a thief. I wish you would speak to Moody yourself, Mr Troy. Do you mind ringing the bell?'

Mr Troy rose, as a matter of course, and rang the bell.

He was by this time, it is needless to say, convinced that Moody had not only gone back to consult Old Sharon on his own responsibility, but, worse still, had taken the unwarrantable liberty of introducing him, as a spy, into the house. To communicate this explanation to Lady Lydiard would, in her present humour, be simply to produce the dismissal of the steward from her service. The only other alternative was to ask leave to interrogate Moody privately, and, after duly reproving him, to insist on the departure of Old Sharon as the one condition on which Mr Troy would consent to keep Lady Lydiard in ignorance of the truth.

'I think I shall manage better with Moody, if your Ladyship will permit me to see him in private,' the lawyer said. 'Shall I go downstairs and speak with him in his own room?'

'Why should you trouble yourself to do that?' said her Ladyship. 'See him here; and I will go into the boudoir.'

As she made that reply the footman appeared at the drawing-room door.

'Send Moody here,' said Lady Lydiard.

The footman's answer, delivered at that moment, assumed an importance which was not expressed in the footman's words. 'My Lady,' he said, 'Mr Moody has gone out.'

❧ THIRTEEN ❦

WHILE THE STRANGE PROCEEDINGS OF THE steward were the subject of conversation between Lady Lydiard and Mr Troy, Moody was alone in his room, occupied in writing to Isabel. Being unwilling that any eyes but his own should see the address, he had himself posted his letter; the time that he had chosen for leaving the house proving, unfortunately, to be also the time proposed by her Ladyship for his interview with the lawyer. In ten minutes after the footman had reported his absence, Moody returned. It was then too late to present himself in the drawing-room. In the interval, Mr Troy had taken his leave, and Moody's position had dropped a degree lower in Lady Lydiard's estimation.

Isabel received her letter by the next morning's post. If any justification of Mr Troy's suspicions had been needed, the terms in which Moody wrote would have amply supplied it.

'Dear Isabel (I hope I may call you 'Isabel' without offending you, in your present trouble?) – I have a proposal to make, which, whether you accept it or not, I beg you will keep a secret from every living creature but ourselves. You will understand my request, when I add that these lines relate to the matter of tracing the stolen bank-note.

'I have been privately in communication with a person in London, who is, as I believe, the one person competent to help us in gaining our end. He has already made many inquiries in private. With some of them I am acquainted; the rest he has thus far kept to himself. The person to whom I allude, particularly wishes to have half an hour's conversation with you – in my presence. I am bound to warn you that he is a very strange and very ugly old man; and I can only hope that you will look over his personal appearance in consideration of what he is likely to do for your future advantage.

'Can you conveniently meet us, at the farther end of the row of villas in which your aunt lives, the day after to-morrow, at four o'clock? Let me have a line to say if you will keep the appointment, and if the hour named will suit you. And believe me your devoted friend and servant,

'ROBERT MOODY.'

The lawyer's warning to her to be careful how she yielded too readily to any proposal of Moody's recurred to Isabel's mind while she read those lines. Being pledged to secrecy, she could not consult Mr Troy – she was left to decide for herself.

No obstacle stood in the way of her free choice of alternatives. After their early dinner at three o'clock, Miss Pink habitually retired to her own room 'to meditate', as she expressed it. Her 'meditations' inevitably ended in a sound sleep of some hours; and during that interval Isabel was at liberty to do as she pleased. After considerable hesitation, her implicit belief in Moody's truth and devotion, assisted by a strong feeling of curiosity to see the companion with whom the steward had associated himself, decided Isabel on consenting to keep the appointment.

Taking up her position beyond the houses, on the day and at the hour mentioned by Moody, she believed herself to be fully prepared for the most unfavourable impression which the most disagreeable of all possible strangers could produce.

But the first appearance of Old Sharon – as dirty as ever, clothed in a long, frowsy, grey overcoat, with his pug-dog at his heels, and his smoke-blackened pipe in his mouth, with a tall white hat on his head, which looked as if it had been picked up in a gutter, a hideous leer in his eyes, and a jaunty trip in his walk – took her so completely by surprise that she could only return Moody's friendly greeting by silently pressing his hand. As for Moody's companion, to look at him for a second time was more than she had resolution to do. She kept her eyes fixed on the pug-dog, and with good reason: as far as appearances went, he was indisputably the nobler animal of the two.

Under the circumstances, the interview threatened to begin in a very embarrassing manner. Moody, disheartened by Isabel's silence, made no attempt to set the conversation going; he looked as if he meditated a hasty retreat to the railway station which he had just left. Fortunately, he had at his side the right man (for once) in the right place. Old Sharon's effrontery was equal to any emergency.

'I am not a nice-looking old man, my dear, am I?' he said, leering at Isabel with cunning, half-closed eyes. 'Bless your heart! you'll soon get used to me! You see, I am the sort of colour, as they say at the linen-drapers', that doesn't wash well. It's all through love; upon my life it is! Early in the present century I had my young affections blighted; and I've neglected myself ever since. Disappointment takes different forms, Miss, in different men. I don't think I have had heart enough to brush my hair for the last fifty years. She was a magnificent woman, Mr Moody, and she dropped me like a hot potato. Dreadful! dreadful! Let us pursue this painful subject no further. Ha! here's a pretty country! Here's a nice blue sky! I admire the country, Miss; I see so little of it, you know. Have you any objection to walk along into the fields? The fields, my dear, bring out all the poetry of my nature. Where's the dog? Here, Puggy! Puggy! hunt about, my man, and find some dog-grass. Does his inside good, you know, after a meat diet in London. Lord! how I feel my spirits rising in this fine air! Does my complexion look any brighter, Miss? Will you run a race with me, Mr Moody, or will you oblige me with a back at leap-frog? I'm not mad, my dear young lady; I'm only merry. I live, you see, in the London stink; and the smell of the hedges and the wild flowers is too much for me at first. It gets into my head, it does. I'm drunk! As I live by bread, I'm drunk on fresh air! Oh! what a jolly day! Oh! how young and innocent I do feel!' Here his innocence got the better of him, and he began to sing, 'I wish I were a little fly, in my love's bosom for to lie!' 'Hullo! here we are on the nice soft grass! and, oh, my gracious! there's a bank running down into a hollow! I can't stand that, you know. Mr Moody, hold my hat, and take the greatest care of it. Here goes for a roll down the bank!'

He handed his horrible hat to the astonished Moody, laid himself flat on the top of the bank, and deliberately rolled down it, exactly as he might have done when he was a boy. The tails of his long grey coat flew madly in the wind: the dog pursued him, jumping over him, and barking with delight; he shouted and screamed in answer to the dog, as he rolled over and over faster and faster; and, when he got up, on the level ground, and called out cheerfully to his companions standing above him, 'I say, you two, I feel twenty years younger already!' – human gravity could hold out no longer. The sad and silent Moody smiled, and Isabel burst into fits of laughter.

'There,' he said, 'didn't I tell you you would get used to me, Miss? There's a deal of life left in the old man yet – isn't there? Shy me down, my hat, Mr Moody. And now we'll get to business!' He turned round to the dog still barking at his heels. 'Business, Puggy!' he called out sharply, and Puggy instantly shut up his mouth, and said no more.

'Well, now,' Old Sharon resumed when he had joined his friends and had got his breath again, 'let's have a little talk about yourself, Miss. Has Mr Moody told you who I am, and what I want with you? Very good. May I offer you my arm? No! You like to be independent, don't you? All right – I don't object. I am an amiable old man, I am. About this Lady Lydiard, now? Suppose you tell me how you first got acquainted with her?'

In some surprise at this question, Isabel told her little story. Observing Sharon's face while she was speaking, Moody saw that he was not paying the smallest attention to the narrative. His sharp shameless black eyes watched the girl's face absently; his gross lips curled upwards in a sardonic and self-satisfied smile. He was evidently setting a trap for her of some kind. Without a word of warning – while Isabel was in the middle of a sentence – the trap opened, with the opening of Old Sharon's lips.

'I say,' he burst out. 'How came *you* to seal her Ladyship's letter – eh?'

The question bore no sort of relation, direct or indirect, to what Isabel happened to be saying at the moment. In the sudden surprise of hearing it, she started and fixed her eyes in astonishment on Sharon's face. The old vagabond chuckled to himself. 'Did you see that?' he whispered to Moody. 'I beg your pardon, Miss,' he went on; 'I won't interrupt you again. Lord! how interesting it is! – ain't it, Mr Moody? Please to go on, Miss.'

But Isabel, though she spoke with perfect sweetness and temper, declined to go on. 'I had better tell you, sir, how I came to seal her Ladyship's letter,' she said. 'If I may venture on giving my opinion, *that* part of my story seems to be the only part of it which relates to your business with me to-day.'

Without further preface she described the circumstances which had led to her assuming the perilous responsibility of sealing the letter. Old Sharon's wandering attention began to wander again: he was evidently occupied in setting another trap. For the second time he interrupted

Isabel in the middle of a sentence. Suddenly stopping short, he pointed to some sheep, at the farther end of the field through which they happened to be passing at the moment.

'There's a pretty sight,' he said. 'There are the innocent sheep a-feeding – all following each other as usual. And there's the sly dog waiting behind the gate till the sheep wants his services. Reminds me of Old Sharon and the public!' He chuckled over the discovery of the remarkable similarity between the sheep-dog and himself, and the sheep and the public – and then burst upon Isabel with a second question. 'I say! didn't you look at the letter before you sealed it?'

'Certainly not!' Isabel answered.

'Not even at the address?'

'No!'

'Thinking of something else – eh?'

'Very likely,' said Isabel.

'Was it your new bonnet, my dear?'

Isabel laughed. 'Women are not always thinking of their new bonnets,' she answered.

Old Sharon, to all appearance, dropped the subject there. He lifted his lean brown forefinger and pointed again – this time to a house at a short distance from them. 'That's a farm-house, surely?' he said. 'I'm thirsty, after my roll down the hill. Do you think, Miss, they would give me a drink of milk?'

'I am sure they would,' said Isabel. 'I know the people. Shall I go and ask them?'

'Thank you, my dear. One word more before you go. About the sealing of that letter? What *could* you have been thinking of while you were doing it?' He looked hard at her, and took her suddenly by the arm. 'Was it your sweetheart?' he asked, in a whisper.

The question instantly reminded Isabel that she had been thinking of Hardyman while she sealed the letter. She blushed as the remembrance crossed her mind. Robert, noticing the embarrassment, spoke sharply to Old Sharon. 'You have no right to put such a question to a young lady,' he said. 'Be a little more careful for the future.'

'There! there! don't be hard on me,' pleaded the old rogue. 'An ugly old man like me may make his innocent little joke – eh, Miss? I'm sure you're too sweet-tempered to be angry when I meant no offence. Show me that you bear no malice. Go, like a forgiving young angel, and ask for the milk.'

Nobody appealed to Isabel's sweetness of temper in vain. 'I will do it with pleasure,' she said – and hastened away to the farm-house.

❧ FOURTEEN ❧

THE INSTANT ISABEL WAS OUT OF hearing, Old Sharon slapped Moody on the shoulder to rouse his attention. 'I've got her out of the way,' he said, 'now listen to me. My business with the young angel is done – I may go back to London.'

Moody looked at him with astonishment.

'Lord! how little you know of thieves!' exclaimed Old Sharon. 'Why, man alive, I have tried her with two plain tests! If you wanted a proof of her innocence, there it was, as plain as the nose in your face. Did you hear me ask her how she came to seal the letter – just when her mind was running on something else?'

'I heard you,' said Moody.

'Did you see how she started and stared at me?'

'I did.'

'Well, I can tell you this – if she *had* stolen the money she would neither have started nor stared. She would have had her answer ready beforehand in her own mind, in case of accidents. There's only one thing in my experience that you can never do with a thief, when a thief happens to be a woman – you can never take her by surprise. Put that remark by in your mind; one day you may find a use for remembering it. Did you see her blush, and look quite hurt in her feelings, pretty dear, when I asked about her sweetheart? Do you think a thief, in her place, would have shown such a face as that? Not she! The thief would have been relieved. The thief would have said to herself, "All right! the more the old fool talks about sweethearts the further he is from tracing the robbery to Me!" Yes! yes! the ground's cleared now, Master Moody. I've reckoned up the servants; I've questioned Miss Isabel; I've made my inquiries in all the other quarters that may be useful to us – and what's the result? The advice I gave, when you and the lawyer first came to me – I hate that fellow! – remains as sound and good advice as ever. I have got the thief in my mind,' said Old Sharon, closing his cunning eyes and then opening them again, 'as plain as I've got you in my eye at this minute. No more of that now,' he went on, looking round sharply at the path that led to the farm-house. 'I've something particular to say to you – and there's barely time to say it before that nice girl comes back. Look here! Do you happen to be acquainted with Mr-Honourable-Hardyman's valet?'

Moody's eyes rested on Old Sharon with a searching and doubtful look.

'Mr Hardyman's valet?' he repeated. 'I wasn't prepared to hear Mr Hardyman's name.'

Old Sharon looked at Moody, in his turn, with a flash of sardonic triumph.

'Oho!' he said. 'Has my good boy learnt his lesson? Do you see the thief through my spectacles, already?'

'I began to see him,' Moody answered, 'when you gave us the guinea opinion at your lodgings.'

'Will you whisper his name?' asked Old Sharon.

'Not yet. I distrust my own judgment. I wait till time proves that you are right.'

Old Sharon knitted his shaggy brows and shook his head. 'If you had only a little more dash and go in you,' he said, 'you would be a clever fellow. As it is——!' He finished the sentence by snapping his fingers with a grin of contempt. 'Let's get to business. Are you going back by the next train along with me? or are you going to stop with the young lady?'

'I will follow you by a later train,' Moody answered.

'Then I must give you my instructions at once,' Sharon continued. 'You get better acquainted with Hardyman's valet. Lend him money if he wants it – stick at nothing to make a bosom friend of him. I can't do that part of it; my appearance would be against me. *You* are the man – you are respectable from the top of your hat to the tips of your boots; nobody would suspect You. Don't make objections! Can you fix the valet? Or can't you?'

'I can try,' said Moody. 'And what then?'

Old Sharon put his gross lips disagreeably close to Moody's ear.

'Your friend the valet can tell you who his master's bankers are,' he said; 'and he can supply you with a specimen of his master's handwriting.'

Moody drew back, as suddenly as if his vagabond companion had put a knife to his throat. 'You old villain!' he said. 'Are you tempting me to forgery?'

'You infernal fool!' retorted Old Sharon. '*Will* you hold that long tongue of yours, and hear what I have to say. You go to Hardyman's bankers, with a note in Hardyman's handwriting (exactly imitated by me) to this effect: – "Mr H. presents his compliments to Messrs So-and-So, and is not quite certain whether a payment of five hundred pounds has been made within the last week to his account. He will be much obliged if

636

Messrs So-and-So will inform him by a line in reply, whether there is such an entry to his credit in their books, and by whom the payment has been made." You wait for the bankers' answer, and bring it to me. It's just possible that the name you're afraid to whisper may appear in the letter. If it does, we've caught our man. Is *that* forgery, Mr Muddlehead Moody? I'll tell you what – if I had lived to be your age, and knew no more of the world than you do, I'd go and hang myself. Steady! here's our charming friend with the milk. Remember your instructions, and don't lose heart if my notion of the payment to the bankers comes to nothing. I know what to do next, in that case – and, what's more, I'll take all the risk and trouble on my own shoulders. Oh, Lord! I'm afraid I shall be obliged to drink the milk, now it's come!'

With this apprehension in his mind, he advanced to relieve Isabel of the jug that she carried.

'Here's a treat!' he burst out, with an affectation of joy, which was completely belied by the expression of his dirty face. 'Here's a kind and dear young lady, to help an old man to a drink with her own pretty hands.' He paused, and looked at the milk very much as he might have looked at a dose of physic. 'Will anyone take a drink first?' he asked, offering the jug piteously to Isabel and Moody. 'You see, I'm not used to genuine milk; I'm used to chalk and water. I don't know what effect the unadulterated cow might have on my poor old inside.' He tasted the milk with the greatest caution. 'Upon my soul, this is too rich for me! The unadulterated cow is a deal too strong to be drunk alone. If you'll allow me, I'll qualify it with a drop of gin. Here, Puggy, Puggy!' He set the milk down before the dog; and, taking a flask out of his pocket, emptied it at a draught. 'That's something like!' he said, smacking his lips with an air of infinite relief. 'So sorry, Miss, to have given you all your trouble for nothing; it's my ignorance that's to blame, not me. I couldn't know I was unworthy of genuine milk till I tried – could I? And do you know,' he proceeded, with his eyes directed slyly on the way back to the station, 'I begin to think I'm not worthy of the fresh air, either. A kind of longing seems to come over me for the London stink. I'm home-sick already for the soot of my happy childhood and my own dear native mud. The air here is too thin for me, and the sky's too clean; and – oh, Lord! – when you're used to the roar of the traffic – the 'buses and the cabs and what not – the silence in these parts is downright awful. I'll wish you good evening, Miss; and get back to London.'

Isabel turned to Moody with disappointment plainly expressed in her face and manner.

'Is that all he has to say?' she asked. 'You told me he could help us. You led me to suppose he could find the guilty person.'

Sharon heard her. 'I could name the guilty person,' he answered, 'as easily, Miss, as I could name you.'

'Why don't you do it, then?' Isabel inquired, not very patiently.

'Because the time's not ripe for it yet, Miss – that's one reason. Because, if I mentioned the thief's name, as things are now, you, Miss Isabel, would think me mad; and you would tell Mr Moody I had cheated him out of his money – that's another reason. The matter's in train, if you will only wait a little longer.'

'So you say,' Isabel rejoined. 'If you really could name the thief, I believe you would do it now.'

She turned away with a frown on her pretty face. Old Sharon followed her. Even his coarse sensibilities appeared to feel the irresistible ascendancy of beauty and youth.

'I say!' he began, 'we must part friends, you know – or I shall break my heart over it. They have got milk at the farm-house. Do you think they have got pen, ink, and paper too?'

Isabel answered, without turning to look at him, 'Of course they have!'

'And a bit of sealing-wax?'

'I dare say!'

Old Sharon laid his dirty claws on her shoulder and forced her to face him as the best means of shaking them off.

'Come along!' he said. 'I am going to pacify you with some information in writing.'

'Why should you write it?' Isabel asked suspiciously.

'Because I mean to make my own conditions, my dear, before I let you into the secret.'

In ten minutes more they were all three in the farm-house parlour. Nobody but the farmer's wife was at home. The good woman trembled from head to foot at the sight of Old Sharon. In all her harmless life she had never yet seen humanity under the aspect in which it was now presented to her. 'Mercy preserve us, Miss!' she whispered to Isabel, 'how come you to be in such company as *that*?' Instructed by Isabel, she produced the necessary materials for writing and sealing – and, that done, she shrank away to the door. 'Please to excuse me, Miss,' she said with a last horrified look at her venerable visitor; 'I really can't stand the sight of such a blot of dirt as that in my nice clean parlour.' With those words she disappeared, and was seen no more.

Perfectly indifferent to his reception, Old Sharon wrote; inclosed what he had written in an envelope; and sealed it (in the absence of anything better fitted for his purpose) with the mouth-piece of his pipe.

'Now, Miss,' he said, 'you give me your word of honour' – he stopped and looked round at Moody with a grin – 'and you give me yours, that you won't either of you break the seal on this envelope till the expiration of one week from the present day. There are the conditions, Miss Isabel, on which I'll give you your information. If you stop to dispute with me, the candle's alight, and I'll burn it!'

It was useless to contend with him. Isabel and Moody gave him the promise that he required. He handed the sealed envelope to Isabel with a low bow. 'When the week's out,' he said, 'you will own I'm a cleverer fellow than you think me now. Wish you good evening, Miss. Come along, Puggy! Farewell to the horrid clean country, and back again to the nice London stink!'

He nodded to Moody – he leered at Isabel – he chuckled to himself – he left the farm-house.

⚘ FIFTEEN ⚘

ISABEL LOOKED DOWN AT THE LETTER in her hand – considered it in silence – and turned to Moody. 'I feel tempted to open it already,' she said.

'After giving your promise?' Moody gently remonstrated.

Isabel met that objection with a woman's logic.

'Does a promise matter?' she asked, 'when one gives it to a dirty, disreputable, presuming old wretch like Mr Sharon? It's a wonder to me that you trust such a creature. *I* wouldn't!'

'I doubted him just as you do,' Moody answered, 'when I first saw him in company with Mr Troy. But there was something in the advice he gave us at that first consultation which altered my opinion of him for the better. I dislike his appearance and his manners as much as you do – I may even say I felt ashamed of bringing such a person to see you. And yet I can't think that I have acted unwisely in employing Mr Sharon.'

Isabel listened absently. She had something more to say, and she was considering how she should say it. 'May I ask you a bold question?' she began.

'Any question you like.'

'Have you—' she hesitated and looked embarrassed. 'Have you paid Mr Sharon much money?' she resumed, suddenly rallying her courage. Instead of answering, Moody suggested that it was time to think of returning to Miss Pink's villa. 'Your aunt may be getting anxious about you.' he said.

Isabel led the way out of the farm-house in silence. She reverted to Mr

Sharon and the money, however, as they returned by the path across the fields.

'I am sure you will not be offended with me,' she said gently, 'if I own that I am uneasy about the expense. I am allowing you to use your purse as if it was mine – and I have hardly any savings of my own.'

Moody entreated her not to speak of it. 'How can I put my money to a better use than in serving your interests?' he asked. 'My one object in life is to relieve you of your present anxieties. I shall be the happiest man living if you only owe a moment's happiness to my exertions!'

Isabel took his hand, and looked at him with grateful tears in her eyes.

'How good you are to me, Mr Moody!' she said. 'I wish I could tell you how deeply I feel your kindness.'

'You can do it easily,' he answered, with a smile. 'Call me "Robert" – don't call me "Mr Moody".'

She took his arm with a sudden familiarity that charmed him.

'If you had been my brother I should have called you "Robert",' she said; 'and no brother could have been more devoted to me than you are.'

He looked eagerly at her bright face turned up to his. 'May I never hope to be something nearer and dearer to you than a brother?' he asked timidly.

She hung her head, and said nothing. Moody's memory recalled Sharon's coarse reference to her 'sweetheart'. She had blushed when he put the question? What had she done when Moody put *his* question? Her face answered for her – she had turned pale; she was looking more serious than usual. Ignorant as he was of the ways of women, his instinct told him that this was a bad sign. Surely her rising colour would have confessed it, if time and gratitude together were teaching her to love him? He sighed as the inevitable conclusion forced itself on his mind.

'I hope I have not offended you?' he said sadly.

'Oh, no.'

'I wish I had not spoken. Pray don't think that I am serving you with any selfish motive.'

'I don't think that, Robert. I never could think it of you.'

He was not quite satisfied yet. 'Even if you were to marry some other man,' he went on earnestly, 'it would make no difference in what I am trying to do for you. No matter what I might suffer, I should still go on – for your sake.'

'Why do you talk so?' she burst out passionately. 'No other man has such a claim as you to my gratitude and regard. How can you let such thoughts come to you? I have done nothing in secret. I have no friends who are not known to you. Be satisfied with that, Robert – and let us drop the subject.'

'Never to take it up again?' he asked, with the infatuated pertinacity of a man clinging to his last hope.

At other times and under other circumstances, Isabel might have answered him sharply. She spoke with perfect gentleness now.

'Not for the present,' she said. 'I don't know my own heart. Give me time.'

His gratitude caught at those words, as the drowning man is said to catch at the proverbial straw. He lifted her hand, and suddenly and fondly pressed his lips on it. She showed no confusion. Was she sorry for him, poor wretch! – and was that all?

They walked on, arm-in-arm, in silence.

Crossing the last field, they entered again on the high road leading to the row of villas in which Miss Pink lived. The minds of both were preoccupied. Neither of them noticed a gentleman approaching on horseback, followed by a mounted groom. He was advancing slowly, at the walking-pace of his horse, and he only observed the two foot-passengers when he was close to them.

'Miss Isabel!'

She started, looked up, and discovered – Alfred Hardyman.

He was dressed in a perfectly-made travelling suit of light brown, with a peaked felt hat of a darker shade of the same colour, which, in a picturesque sense, greatly improved his personal appearance. His pleasure at discovering Isabel gave the animation to his features which they wanted on ordinary occasions. He sat his horse, a superb hunter, easily and gracefully. His light amber-coloured gloves fitted him perfectly. His obedient servant, on another magnificent horse, waited behind him. He looked the impersonation of rank and breeding – of wealth and prosperity. What a contrast, in a woman's eyes, to the shy, pale, melancholy man, in the ill-fitting black clothes, with the wandering uneasy glances, who stood beneath him, and felt, and showed that he felt, his inferior position keenly! In spite of herself, the treacherous blush flew over Isabel's face, in Moody's presence, and with Moody's eyes distrustfully watching her.

'This is a piece of good fortune that I hardly hoped for,' said Hardyman, his cool, quiet, dreary way of speaking quickened, as usual, in Isabel's presence. 'I only got back from France this morning, and I called on Lady Lydiard in the hope of seeing you. She was not at home – and you were in the country – and the servants didn't know the address. I could get nothing out of them, except that you were on a visit to a relation.' He looked at Moody while he was speaking. 'Haven't I seen you before?' he said carelessly. 'Yes; at Lady Lydiard's. You're her steward, are you not? How d'ye do?' Moody, with his eyes on the ground, answered silently by a bow. Hardyman, perfectly indifferent whether Lady

Lydiard's steward spoke or not, turned on his saddle and looked admiringly at Isabel. 'I begin to think I am a lucky man at last,' he went on with a smile. 'I was jogging along to my farm, and despairing of ever seeing Miss Isabel again – and Miss Isabel herself meets me at the roadside! I wonder whether you are as glad to see me as I am to see you? You won't tell me – eh? May I ask you something else? Are you staying in our neighbourhood?'

There was no alternative before Isabel but to answer this last question. Hardyman had met her out walking, and had no doubt drawn the inevitable inference – although he was too polite to say so in plain words.

'Yes, sir,' she answered shyly, 'I am staying in this neighbourhood.'

'And who is your relation?' Hardyman proceeded, in his easy, matter-of-course way. 'Lady Lydiard told me, when I had the pleasure of meeting you at her house, that you had an aunt living in the country. I have a good memory, Miss Isabel, for anything that I hear about You! It's your aunt, isn't it? Yes? I know everybody about here. What is your aunt's name?'

Isabel, still resting her hand on Robert's arm, felt it tremble a little as Hardyman made this last inquiry. If she had been speaking to one of her equals she would have known how to dispose of the question without directly answering it. But what could she say to the magnificent gentleman on the stately horse? He had only to send his servant into the village to ask who the young lady from London was staying with, and the answer, in a dozen mouths at least, would direct him to her aunt. She cast one appealing look at Moody and pronounced the distinguished name of Miss Pink.

'Miss Pink?' Hardyman repeated. 'Surely I know Miss Pink?' (He had not the faintest remembrances of her.) 'Where did I meet her last?' (He ran over in his memory the different local festivals at which strangers had been introduced to him.) 'Was it at the archery meeting? or at the grammar-school when the prizes were given? No? It must have been at the flower show, then, surely?'

It *had* been at the flower show. Isabel had heard it from Miss Pink fifty times at least, and was obliged to admit it now.

'I am quite ashamed of never having called,' Hardyman proceeded. 'The fact is, I have so much to do. I am a bad one at paying visits. Are you on your way home? Let me follow you and make my apologies personally to Miss Pink.'

Moody looked at Isabel. It was only a momentary glance, but she perfectly understood it.

'I am afraid, sir, my aunt cannot have the honour of seeing you to-day,' she said.

Hardyman was all compliance. He smiled and patted his horse's neck.

'To-morrow, then,' he said. 'My compliments, and I will call in the afternoon. Let me see: Miss Pink lives at—?' He waited, as if he expected Isabel to assist his treacherous memory once more. She hesitated again. Hardyman looked round at his groom. The groom could find out the address, even if he did not happen to know it already. Besides, there was the little row of houses visible at the farther end of the road. Isabel pointed to the villas, as a necessary concession to good manners, before the groom could anticipate her. 'My aunt lives there, sir; at the house called The Lawn.'

'Ah! to be sure!' said Hardyman. 'I oughtn't to have wanted reminding; but I have so many things to think of at the farm. And I am afraid I must be getting old – my memory isn't as good as it was. I am so glad to have seen you, Miss Isabel. You and your aunt must come and look at my horses. Do you like horses? Are you fond of riding? I have a quiet roan mare that is used to carrying ladies; she would be just the thing for you. Did I beg you to give my best compliments to your aunt? Yes? How well you are looking! our air here agrees with you. I hope I haven't kept you standing too long? I didn't think of it in the pleasure of meeting you. Good-bye, Miss Isabel; good-bye, till to-morrow!'

He took off his hat to Isabel, nodded to Moody, and pursued his way to the farm.

Isabel looked at her companion. His eyes were still on the ground. Pale, silent, motionless, he waited by her like a dog, until she gave the signal of walking on again towards the house.

'You are not angry with me for speaking to Mr Hardyman?' she asked anxiously.

He lifted his head at the sound of her voice. 'Angry with you, my dear! why should I be angry?'

'You seem so changed, Robert, since we met Mr Hardyman. I couldn't help speaking to him – could I?'

'Certainly not.'

They moved on towards the villa. Isabel was still uneasy. There was something in Moody's silent submission to all that she said and all that she did which pained and humiliated her. 'You're not jealous?' she said, smiling timidly.

He tried to speak lightly on his side. 'I have no time to be jealous while I have your affairs to look after,' he answered.

She pressed his arm tenderly. 'Never fear, Robert, that new friends will make me forget the best and dearest friend who is now at my side.' She paused, and looked up at him with a compassionate fondness that was very pretty to see. 'I can keep out of the way to-morrow, when Mr Hardyman calls,' she said. 'It is my aunt he is coming to see – not me.'

It was generously meant. But while her mind was only occupied with the present time, Moody's mind was looking into the future. He was learning the hard lesson of self-sacrifice already. 'Do what you think is right,' he said quietly; 'don't think of me.'

They reached the gate of the villa. He held out his hand to say good-bye.

'Won't you come in?' she asked. 'Do come in!'

'Not now, my dear. I must get back to London as soon as I can. There is some more work to be done for you, and the sooner I do it the better.'

She heard his excuse without heeding it.

'You are not like yourself, Robert,' she said. 'Why is it? What are you thinking of?'

He was thinking of the bright blush that overspread her face when Hardyman first spoke to her; he was thinking of the invitation to her to see the stud-farm, and to ride the roan mare; he was thinking of the utterly powerless position in which he stood towards Isabel and towards the highly-born gentleman who admired her. But he kept his doubts and fears to himself. 'The train won't wait for me,' he said, and held out his hand once more.

She was not only perplexed; she was really distressed. 'Don't take leave of me in that cold way!' she pleaded. Her eyes dropped before his, and her lips trembled a little. 'Give me a kiss, Robert, at parting.' She said those bold words softly and sadly, out of the depth of her pity for him! He started; his face brightened suddenly; his sinking hope rose again. In another moment the change came; in another moment he under-stood her. As he touched her cheek with his lips, he turned pale again. 'Don't quite forget me,' he said, in low faltering tones – and left her.

Miss Pink met Isabel in the hall. Refreshed by unbroken repose, the ex-schoolmistress was in the happiest frame of mind for the reception of her niece's news.

Informed that Moody had travelled to South Morden to personally report the progress of the inquiries, Miss Pink highly approved of him as a substitute for Mr Troy. 'Mr Moody, as a banker's son, is a gentleman by birth,' she remarked; 'he has condescended, in becoming Lady Lydiard's steward. What I saw of him, when he came here with you, pre-possessed me in his favour. He has my confidence, Isabel, as well as yours – he is in every respect a superior person to Mr Troy. Did you meet any friends, my dear, when you were out walking?'

The answer to this question produced a species of transformation in Miss Pink. The rapturous rank-worship of her nation feasted, so to speak, on Hardyman's message. She looked taller and younger than usual – she was all smiles and sweetness. 'At last, Isabel, you have seen birth and breeding under their right aspect,' she said. 'In the society of Lady Lydiard, you cannot possibly have formed correct ideas of the English aristocracy. Observe Mr Hardyman when he does me the honour to call to-morrow – and you will see the difference.'

'Mr Hardyman is your visitor, aunt – not mine. I was going to ask you to let me remain upstairs in my room.'

Miss Pink was unaffectedly shocked. 'This is what you learn at Lady Lydiard's!' she observed. 'No, Isabel, your absence would be a breach of good manners – I cannot possibly permit it. You will be present to receive our distinguished friend with me. And mind this!' added Miss Pink, in her most impressive manner, 'If Mr Hardyman should by any chance ask why you have left Lady Lydiard, not one word about those disgraceful circumstances which connect you with the loss of the banknote! I should sink into the earth if the smallest hint of what has really happened should reach Mr Hardyman's ears. My child, I stand towards you in the place of your lamented mother; I have the right to command your silence on this horrible subject, and I do imperatively command it.'

In these words foolish Miss Pink sowed the seed for the harvest of trouble that was soon come.

❧ SIXTEEN ❦

PAYING HIS COURT TO THE EX-SCHOOLMISTRESS on the next day, Hardyman made such excellent use of his opportunities that the visit to the stud-farm took place on the day after. His own carriage was placed at the disposal of Isabel and her aunt; and his own sister was present to confer special distinction on the reception of Miss Pink.

In a country like England, which annually suspends the sitting of its Legislature in honour of a horse-race, it is only natural and proper that the comfort of the horses should be the first object of consideration at a stud-farm. Nine tenths of the land at Hardyman's farm was devoted, in one way or another, to the noble quadruped with the low forehead and the long nose. Poor humanity was satisfied with second-rate and third-rate accommodation. The ornamental grounds, very poorly laid out, were also very limited in extent – and, as for the dwelling-house, it was literally a cottage. A parlour and a kitchen, a smoking-room, a bed-room, and a spare chamber for a friend, all scantily furnished, sufficed for the modest wants of the owner of the property. If you wished to feast your eyes on luxury you went to the stables.

The stud-farm being described, the introduction to Hardyman's sister follows in due course.

The Honourable Lavinia Hardyman was, as all persons in society know, married rather late in life to General Drumblade. It is saying a great deal, but it is not saying too much, to describe Mrs Drumblade as the most mischievous woman of her age in all England. Scandal was the breath of her life; to place people in false positions, to divulge secrets and destroy characters, to undermine friendships, and aggravate enmities – these were the sources of enjoyment from which this dangerous woman drew the inexhaustible fund of good spirits that made her a brilliant light in the social sphere. She was one of the privileged sinners of modern society. The worst mischief that she could work was ascribed to her 'exuberant vitality'. She had that ready familiarity of manner which is (in *her* class) so rarely discovered to be insolence in disguise. Her power of easy self-assertion found people ready to accept her on her own terms wherever she went. She was one of those big, overpowering women, with blunt manners, voluble tongues, and goggle eyes, who carry everything before them. The highest society modestly considered itself in danger of being dull in the absence of Mrs Drumblade. Even Hardyman himself – who saw as little of her as possible, whose frankly straightforward nature recoiled by instinct from contact with his sister – could think of no fitter person to make Miss Pink's reception agreeable to her, while he was devoting his own attentions to her niece. Mrs Drumblade accepted the position thus offered with the most amiable readiness. In her own private mind she placed an interpretation on her brother's motives which did him the grossest injustice. She believed that Hardyman's designs on Isabel contemplated the most profligate result. To assist this purpose, while the girl's nearest relative was supposed to be taking care of her, was Mrs Drumblade's idea of 'fun'. Her worst enemies admitted that the Honourable Lavinia had redeeming qualities, and owned that a keen sense of humour was one of her merits.

Was Miss Pink a likely person to resist the fascinations of Mrs Drumblade? Alas, for the ex-schoolmistress! Before she had been five minutes at the farm, Hardyman's sister had fished for her, caught her, landed her. Poor Miss Pink!

Mrs Drumblade could assume a grave dignity of manner when the occasion called for it. She was grave, she was dignified, when Hardyman performed the ceremonies of introduction. She would not say she was charmed to meet Miss Pink – the ordinary slang of society was not for Miss Pink's ears – she would say she felt this introduction as a privilege. It was so seldom one met with persons of trained intellect in society. Mrs Drumblade was already informed of Miss Pink's earlier triumphs in the instruction of youth. Mrs Drumblade had not been blessed with children herself; but she had nephews and nieces, and she was anxious about their education, especially the nieces. What a sweet, modest girl Miss Isabel was! The fondest wish she could form for her nieces would be that they should resemble Miss Isabel when they grew up. The question was, as to the best method of education. She would own that she had selfish motives in becoming acquainted with Miss Pink. They were at the farm, no doubt, to see Alfred's horses. Mrs Drumblade did not understand horses; her interest was in the question of education. She might even confess that she had accepted Alfred's invitation in the hope of hearing Miss Pink's views. There would be opportunities, she trusted, for a little instructive conversation on that subject. It was, perhaps, ridiculous to talk, at her age, of feeling as if she was Miss Pink's pupil; and yet it exactly expressed the nature of the aspiration which was then in her mind. In these terms, feeling her way with the utmost nicety, Mrs Drumblade wound the net of flattery round and round Miss Pink until her hold on that innocent lady was, in every sense of the word, secure. Before half the horses had been passed under review, Hardyman and Isabel were out of sight, and Mrs Drumblade and Miss Pink were lost in the intricacies of the stables. 'Excessively stupid of me! We had better go back, and establish ourselves comfortably in the parlour. When my brother misses us, he and your charming niece will return to look for us in the cottage.' Under cover of this arrangement the separation became complete. Miss Pink held forth on education to Mrs Drumblade in the parlour; while Hardyman and Isabel were on their way to a paddock at the farthest limits of the property.

'I am afraid you are getting a little tired,' said Hardyman. 'Won't you take my arm?'

Isabel was on her guard: she had not forgotten what Lady Lydiard had said to her. 'No, thank you, Mr Hardyman; I am a better walker than you think.'

Hardyman continued the conversation in his blunt, resolute way. 'I wonder whether you will believe me,' he asked, 'if I tell you that this is one of the happiest days of my life.'

'I should think you were always happy,' Isabel cautiously replied, 'having such a pretty place to live in as this.'

Hardyman met that answer with one of his quietly-positive denials. 'A man is never happy by himself,' he said. 'He is happy with a companion. For instance, I am happy with you.'

Isabel stopped and looked back. Hardyman's language was becoming a little too explicit. 'Surely we have lost Mrs Drumblade and my aunt,' she said. 'I don't see them anywhere.'

'You will see them directly; they are only a long way behind.' With this assurance, he returned, in his own obstinate way, to his one object in view. 'Miss Isabel, I want to ask you a question. I'm not a ladies' man. I speak my mind plainly to everybody – women included. Do you like being here to-day?'

Isabel's gravity was not proof against this very downright question. 'I should be hard to please,' she said laughing, 'if I didn't enjoy my visit to the farm.'

Hardyman pushed steadily forward through the obstacle of the farm to the question of the farm's master. 'You like being here,' he repeated. 'Do you like Me?'

This was serious. Isabel drew back a little, and looked at him. He waited with the most impenetrable gravity for her reply.

'I think you can hardly expect me to answer that question,' she said.

'Why not?'

'Our acquaintance has been a very short one, Mr Hardyman. And, if *you* are so good as to forget the difference between us, I think *I* ought to remember it.'

'What difference?'

'The difference in rank.'

Hardyman suddenly stood still, and emphasized his next words by digging his stick into the grass.

'If anything I have said has vexed you,' he began, 'tell me so plainly, Miss Isabel, and I'll ask your pardon. But don't throw my rank in my face. I cut adrift from all that nonsense when I took this farm and got my living out of the horses. What has a man's rank to do with a man's feelings?' he went on, with another emphatic dig of his stick. 'I am quite serious in asking if you like me – for this good reason, that I like you. Yes, I do. You remember that day when I bled the old lady's dog – well, I have found out since then that there's a sort of incompleteness in my life which I never suspected before. It's you who have put that idea into my head. You didn't mean it, I dare say, but you have done it all the same. I sat alone here yesterday evening smoking my pipe – and I didn't enjoy it. I breakfasted alone this morning – and I didn't enjoy *that*. I said to myself, She's coming to lunch, that's one comfort – I shall enjoy lunch. That's what I feel, roughly described. I don't suppose I've been five minutes together without thinking of you, now in one way and now in another, since the day when I first saw you. When a man comes to my time of life, and has had any experience, he knows what that means. It means, in plain English, that his heart is set on a woman. You're the woman.'

Isabel had thus far made several attempts to interrupt him, without success. But, when Hardyman's confession attained its culminating point, she insisted on being heard.

'If you will excuse me, sir,' she interposed gravely, 'I think I had better go back to the cottage. My aunt is a stranger here, and she doesn't know where to look for us.'

'We don't want your aunt,' Hardyman remarked, in his most positive manner.

'We do want her,' Isabel rejoined. 'I won't venture to say it's wrong in you, Mr Hardyman, to talk to me as you have just done, but I am quite sure it's very wrong of me to listen.'

He looked at her with such unaffected surprise and distress that she stopped, on the point of leaving him, and tried to make herself better understood.

'I had no intention of offending you, sir,' she said, a little confusedly. 'I only wanted to remind you that there are some things which a gentleman in your position—' She stopped, tried to finish the sentence, failed, and began another. 'If I had been a young lady in your own rank of life,' she went on, 'I might have thanked you for paying me a compliment, and have given you a serious answer. As it is, I am afraid that I must say that you have surprised and disappointed me. I can claim very little for myself, I know. But I did imagine – so long as there was nothing unbecoming in my conduct – that I had some right to your respect.'

Listening more and more impatiently, Hardyman took her by the hand, and burst out with another of his abrupt questions.

'What can you possibly be thinking of?' he asked.

She gave him no answer; she only looked at him reproachfully, and tried to release herself.

Hardyman held her hand faster than ever.

'I believe you think me an infernal scoundrel!' he said. 'I can stand a good deal, Miss Isabel, but I can't stand *that*. How have I failed in respect toward you, if you please? I have told you you're the woman my heart is set on. Well? Isn't it plain what I want of you, when I say that? Isabel Miller, I want you to be my wife!'

Isabel's only reply to this extraordinary proposal of marriage was a faint cry of astonishment, followed by a sudden trembling that shook her from head to foot.

Hardyman put his arm round her with a gentleness which his oldest friend would have been surprised to see in him.

'Take your time to think of it,' he said, dropping back again into his usual quiet tone. 'If you had known me a little better you wouldn't have mistaken me, and you wouldn't be looking at me now as if you were afraid to believe your own ears. What is there so very wonderful in my wanting to marry you? I don't set up for being a saint. When I was a younger man I was no better (and no worse) than other young men. I'm getting on now to middle life. I don't want romances and adventures – I want an easy existence with a nice lovable woman who will make me a good wife. You're the woman, I tell you again. I know it by what I've seen of you myself, and by what I have heard of you from Lady Lydiard. She said you were prudent, and sweet-tempered, and affectionate; to which I wish to add that you have just the face and figure that I like, and the modest manners and the blessed absence of all slang in your talk, which I don't find in the young women I meet with in the present day. That's my view of it: I think for myself. What does it matter to me whether you're the daughter of a Duke or the daughter of a Dairyman? It isn't your father I want to marry – it's you. Listen to reason, there's a dear! We have only one question to settle before we go back to your aunt. You wouldn't answer me when I asked it a little while since. Will you answer now? *Do* you like me?'

Isabel looked up at him timidly.

'In my position, sir,' she asked, 'have I any right to like you? What would your relations and friends think, if I said Yes?'

Hardyman gave her waist a little admonitory squeeze with his arm.

'What? You're at it again? A nice way to answer a man, to call him "Sir", and to get behind his rank as if it was a place of refuge from him! I hate talking of myself, but you force me to it. Here is my position in the world – I have got an elder brother; he is married, and he has a son to succeed him in the title and the property. You understand, so far? Very well! Years ago I shifted my share of the rank (whatever it may be) on to my brother's shoulders. He is a thorough good fellow, and he has carried my dignity for me, without once dropping it, ever since. As for what people may say, they have said it already, from my father and mother downwards, in the time when I took to the horses and the farm. If they're the wise people I take them for, they won't be at the trouble of saying it all over again. No, no. Twist it how you may, Miss Isabel, whether I'm single or whether I'm married, I'm plain Alfred Hardyman; and everybody who knows me knows that I go on my way, and please myself. If you don't like me, it will be the bitterest disappointment I ever had in my life; but say so honestly, all the same.'

Where is the woman in Isabel's place whose capacity for resistance would not have yielded a little to such an appeal as this?

'I should be an insensible wretch,' she replied warmly, 'if I didn't feel the honour you have done me, and feel it gratefully.'

'Does that mean you will have me for a husband?' asked downright Hardyman.

She was fairly driven into a corner; but (being a woman) she tried to slip through his fingers at the last moment.

'Will you forgive me,' she said, 'if I ask you for a little more time? I am so bewildered. I hardly know what to say or do for the best. You see, Mr Hardyman, it would be a dreadful thing for me to be the cause of giving offence to your family. I am obliged to think of that. It would be so distressing for you (I will say nothing of myself) if your friends closed their doors on me. They might say I was a designing girl, who had taken advantage of your good opinion to raise herself in the world. Lady Lydiard warned me long since not to be ambitious about myself and not to forget my station in life, because she treated me like her adopted daughter. Indeed – indeed, I can't tell you how I feel your goodness, and the compliment – the very great compliment, you pay me! My heart is free; and if I followed my own inclinations——' She checked herself, conscious that she was on the brink of saying too much. 'Will you give me a few days,' she pleaded, 'to try if I can think composedly of all this? I am only a girl, and I feel quite dazzled by the prospect that you set before me.'

Hardyman seized on those words as offering all the encouragement that he desired to his suit.

'Have your own way in this thing and in everything!' he said, with an unaccustomed fervour of language and manner. 'I am so glad to hear that your heart is open to me, and that all your inclinations take my part.'

Isabel instantly protested against this misrepresentation of what she had really said, 'Oh, Mr Hardyman, you quite mistake me!'

He answered her very much as he had answered Lady Lydiard, when she had tried to make him understand his proper relations towards Isabel.

'No, no; I don't mistake you. I agree to every word you say. How can I expect you to marry me, as you very properly remark, unless I give you a day or two to make up your mind? It's quite enough for me that you like the prospect. If Lady Lydiard treated you as her daughter, why shouldn't you be my wife? It stands to reason that you're quite right to marry a man who can raise you in the world. I like you to be ambitious – though Heaven knows it isn't much I can do for you, except to love you with all my heart. Still, it's a great encouragement to hear that her Ladyship's views agree with mine——'

'They don't agree, Mr Hardyman!' protested poor Isabel. 'You are entirely misrepresenting——'

Hardyman cordially concurred in this view of the matter. 'Yes! yes! I can't pretend to represent her Ladyship's language, or yours either; I am obliged to take my words as they come to me. Don't disturb yourself: it's all right – I understand. You have made me the happiest man living. I shall ride over to-morrow to your aunt's house, and hear what you have to say to me. Mind you're at home! Not a day must pass now without my seeing you. I do love you, Isabel – I do indeed!' He stooped, and kissed her heartily. 'Only to reward me,' he explained, 'for giving you time to think.'

She drew herself away from him – resolutely, not angrily. Before she could make a third attempt to place the subject in its right light before him, the luncheon bell rang at the cottage – and a servant appeared, evidently sent to look for them.

'Don't forget to-morrow,' Hardyman whispered confidentially. 'I'll call early – and then go to London, and get the ring.'

⚜ SEVENTEEN ⚜

EVENTS SUCCEEDED EACH OTHER RAPIDLY, AFTER the memorable day to Isabel of the luncheon at the farm.

On the next day (the ninth of the month) Lady Lydiard sent for her steward, and requested him to explain his conduct in repeatedly leaving the house without assigning any reason for his absence. She did not dispute his claims to a freedom of action which would not be permitted to an ordinary servant. Her objection to his present course of proceeding related entirely to the mystery in which it was involved, and to the uncertainty in which the household was left as to the hour of his return. On those grounds, she thought herself entitled to an explanation. Moody's habitual reserve – strengthened, on this occasion, by his dread of ridicule, if his efforts to serve Isabel ended in failure – disinclined him to take Lady Lydiard into his confidence, while his inquiries were still beset with obstacles and doubts. He respectfully entreated her Ladyship to grant him a delay of a few weeks before he entered on his explanation. Lady Lydiard's quick temper resented his request. She told Moody plainly that he was guilty of an act of presumption in making his own conditions with his employer. He received the reproof with exemplary resignation; but he held to his conditions nevertheless. From that moment the result of the interview was no longer in doubt. Moody was directed to send in his accounts. The accounts having been examined, and found to be scrupulously correct, he declined accepting the balance of salary that was offered to him. The next day he left Lady Lydiard's service.

On the tenth of the month her Ladyship received a letter from her nephew.

The health of Felix had not improved. He had made up his mind to go abroad again towards the end of the month. In the meantime, he had written to his friend in Paris, and he had the pleasure of forwarding an answer. The letter inclosed announced that the lost five-hundred-pound note had been made the subject of careful inquiry in Paris. It had not been traced. The French police offered to send to London one of their best men, well acquainted with the English language, if Lady Lydiard was desirous of employing him. He would be perfectly willing to act with an English officer in conducting the investigation, should it be thought necessary. Mr Troy being consulted as to the expediency of accepting this proposal, objected to the pecuniary terms demanded as being extravagantly high. He suggested waiting a little before any reply was sent to Paris; and he engaged meanwhile to consult a London solicitor who had great experience in cases of theft, and whose advice might enable them to dispense entirely with the services of the French police.

Being now a free man again, Moody was able to follow his own inclinations in regard to the instructions which he had received from Old Sharon.

The course that had been recommended to him was repellent to the self-respect and the sense of delicacy which were among the inbred virtues of Moody's character. He shrank from forcing himself as a friend on Hardyman's valet: he recoiled from the idea of tempting the man to steal a specimen of his master's handwriting. After some consideration, he decided on applying to the agent who collected the rents at Hardyman's London chambers. Being an old acquaintance of Moody's, this person would certainly not hesitate to communicate the address of Hardyman's bankers, if he knew it. The experiment, tried under these favouring circumstances, proved perfectly successful. Moody proceeded to Sharon's lodgings the same day, with the address of the bankers in his pocket-book. The old vagabond, greatly amused by Moody's scruples, saw plainly enough that, so long as he wrote the supposed letter from Hardyman in the third person, it mattered little what handwriting was employed, seeing that no signature would be necessary. The letter was at once composed, on the model which Sharon had already suggested to Moody, and a respectable messenger (so far as outward appearances went) was employed to take it to the bank. In half an hour the answer came back. It added one more to the difficulties which beset the inquiry after the lost money. No such sum as five hundred pounds had been paid, within the dates mentioned, to the credit of Hardyman's account.

Old Sharon was not in the least discomposed by this fresh check. 'Give my love to the dear young lady,' he said with his customary impudence; 'and tell her we are one degree nearer to finding the thief.'

Moody looked at him, doubting whether he was in jest or in earnest.

'Must I squeeze a little more information into that thick head of yours?' asked Sharon. With this question he produced a weekly newspaper, and pointed to a paragraph which reported, among the items of sporting news, Hardyman's recent visit to a sale of horses at a town in the north of France. 'We know he didn't pay the bank-note in to his account,' Sharon remarked. 'What else did he do with it? Took it to pay for the horses that he bought in France! Do you see your way a little plainer now? Very good. Let's try next if your money holds out. Somebody must cross the Channel in search of the note. Which of us two is to sit in the steam-boat with a white basin on his lap? Old Sharon, of course!' He stopped to count the money still left, out of the sum deposited by Moody to defray the cost of the inquiry. 'All right!' he went on. 'I've got enough to pay my expenses there and back. Don't stir out of London till you hear from me. I can't tell how soon I may not want you. If there's any difficulty in tracing the note, your hand will have to go into your pocket again. Can't you get the lawyer to join you? Lord! how I should enjoy squandering *his* money! It's a downright disgrace to me to have only got one guinea out of him. I could tear my flesh off my bones when I think of it.'

The same night Old Sharon started for France, by way of Dover and Calais.

Two days elapsed, and brought no news from Moody's agent. On the third day, he received some information relating to Sharon – not from the man himself, but in a letter from Isabel Miller.

'For once, dear Robert,' she wrote, 'my judgment has turned out to be sounder than yours. That hateful old man has confirmed my worst opinion of him. Pray have him punished. Take him before a magistrate and charge him with cheating you out of your money. I enclose the sealed letter which he gave me at the farm-house. The week's time before I was to open it expired yesterday. Was there ever anything so impudent and so inhuman? I am too vexed and angry about the money you have wasted on this old wretch to write more. Yours, gratefully and affectionately, Isabel.'

The letter in which Old Sharon had undertaken (by way of pacifying Isabel) to write the name of the thief, contained these lines:

'You are a charming girl, my dear; but you still want one thing to make you perfect – and that is a lesson in patience. I am proud and happy to teach you. The name of the thief remains, for the present, Mr – (Blank).'

From Moody's point of view, there was but one thing to be said of this:

it was just like Old Sharon! Isabel's letter was of infinitely greater interest to him. He feasted his eyes on the words above the signature: she signed herself, 'Yours gratefully and affectionately.' Did the last words mean that she was really beginning to be fond of him? After kissing the word, he wrote a comforting letter to her, in which he pledged himself to keep a watchful eye on Sharon, and to trust him with no more money until he had honestly earned it first.

A week passed. Moody (longing to see Isabel) still waited in vain for news from France. He had just decided to delay his visit to South Morden no longer, when the errand-boy employed by Sharon brought him this message: – 'The old 'un's at home, and waitin' to see yer.'

⟡   EIGHTEEN   ⟡

Sharon's news was not of an encouraging character. He had met with serious difficulties, and had spent the last farthing of Moody's money in attempting to overcome them.

One discovery of importance he had certainly made. A horse withdrawn from the sale was the only horse that had met with Hardyman's approval. He had secured the animal at the high reserved price of twelve thousand francs – being four hundred and eighty pounds in English money; and he had paid with an English bank-note. The seller (a French horse-dealer resident in Brussels) had returned to Belgium immediately on completing the negotiations. Sharon had ascertained his address, and had written to him at Brussels, enclosing the number of the lost bank-note. In two days he had received an answer, informing him that the horse-dealer had been called to England by the illness of a relative, and that he had hitherto failed to send any address to which his letters could be forwarded. Hearing this, and having exhausted his funds, Sharon had returned to London. It now rested with Moody to decide whether the course of the inquiry should follow the horse-dealer next. Here was the cash account, showing how the money had been spent. And there was Sharon, with his pipe in his mouth and his dog on his lap, waiting for orders.

Moody wisely took time to consider before he committed himself to a decision. In the meanwhile, he ventured to recommend a new course of proceeding which Sharon's report had suggested to his mind.

'It seems to me,' he said, 'that we have taken the round-about way of getting to our end in view, when the straight road lay before us. If Mr Hardyman has passed the stolen note, you know, as well as I do, that he has passed it innocently. Instead of wasting time and money in trying to trace a stranger, why not tell Mr Hardyman what has happened, and ask him to give us the number of the note? You can't think of everything, I know; but it does seem strange that this idea didn't occur to you before you went to France.'

'Mr Moody,' said Old Sharon, 'I shall have to cut your acquaintance. You are a man without faith; I don't like you. As if I hadn't thought of Hardyman weeks since!' he exclaimed contemptuously. 'Are you really soft enough to suppose that a gentleman in his position would talk about his money affairs to me? You know mighty little of him if you do. A fortnight since I sent one of my men (most respectably dressed) to hang about his farm, and see what information he could pick up. My man became painfully acquainted with the toe of a boot. It was thick, sir; and it was Hardyman's.'

'I will run the risk of the boot,' Moody replied, in his quiet way.

'And put the question to Hardyman?'

'Yes.'

'Very good,' said Sharon. 'If you get your answer from his tongue, instead of his boot, the case is cleared up – unless I have made a complete mess of it. Look here, Moody! If you want to do me a good turn, tell the lawyer that the guinea-opinion was the right one. Let him know that *he* was the fool, not you, when he buttoned up his pockets and refused to trust me. And, I say,' pursued Old Sharon, relapsing into his customary impudence, 'you're in love, you know, with that nice girl. I like her myself. When you marry her invite me to the wedding. I'll make a sacrifice: I'll brush my hair and wash my face in honour of the occasion.'

Returning to his lodgings, Moody found two letters waiting on the table. One of them bore the South Morden postmark. He opened that letter first.

It was written by Miss Pink. The first lines contained an urgent entreaty to keep the circumstances connected with the loss of the five hundred pounds the strictest secret from everyone in general, and from Hardyman in particular. The reasons assigned for making the strange request were next expressed in these terms: – 'My niece Isabel is, I am happy to inform you, engaged to be married to Mr Hardyman. If the slightest hint reached him of her having been associated, no matter how cruelly and unjustly, with a suspicion of theft, the marriage would be broken off, and the result to herself and to everybody connected with her, would be disgrace for the rest of our lives.'

On the blank space at the foot of the page a few words were added in Isabel's writing: – 'Whatever changes there may be in my life, your place in my heart is one that no other person can fill: it is the place of my dearest friend. Pray write and tell me that you are not distressed and not angry. My one anxiety is that you should remember what I have always told you about the state of my own feelings. My one wish is that you will still let me love you and value you, as I might have loved and valued a brother.'

The letter dropped from Moody's hand. Not a word – not even a sigh – passed his lips. In tearless silence he submitted to the pang that wrung him. In tearless silence he contemplated the wreck of his life.

❧ NINETEEN ❧

THE NARRATIVE RETURNS TO SOUTH MORDEN, and follows the events which attended Isabel's marriage engagement.

To say that Miss Pink, inflated by the triumph, rose, morally speaking, from the earth and floated among the clouds, is to indicate faintly the effect produced on the ex-schoolmistress when her niece first informed her of what had happened at the farm. Attacked on one side by her aunt, and on the other by Hardyman, and feebly defended, at the best, by her own doubts and misgivings, Isabel ended by surrendering at discretion. Like thousands of other women in a similar position, she was in the last degree uncertain as to the state of her own heart. To what extent she was insensibly influenced by Hardyman's commanding position in believing herself to be sincerely attached to him, it was beyond her power of self-examination to discover. He doubly dazzled her by his birth and by his celebrity. Not in England only, but throughout Europe, he was a recognized authority on his own subject. How could she – how could any woman – resist the influence of his steady mind, his firmness of purpose, his manly resolution to owe everything to himself and nothing to his rank, set off as these attractive qualities were by the outward and personal advantages which exercise an ascendancy of their own? Isabel was fascinated, and yet Isabel was not at ease. In her lonely moments she was troubled by regretful thoughts of Moody, which perplexed and irritated her. She had always behaved honestly to him; she had never encouraged him to hope that his love for her had the faintest prospect of being returned. Yet, knowing, as she did, that her conduct was blameless so far, there were nevertheless perverse sympathies in her which took his part. In the wakeful hours of the night there were whispering voices in her which said, 'Think of Moody!' Had there been a growing kindness towards this good friend in her heart, of which she herself was not aware? She tried to detect it – to weigh it for what it was really worth. But it lay too deep to be discovered and estimated, if it did really exist – if it had any sounder origin than her own morbid fancy. In the broad light of day, in the little bustling duties of life, she forgot it again. She could think of what she ought to wear on the wedding day; she could even try privately how her new signature, 'Isabel Hardyman', would look when she had the right to use it. On the whole, it may be said that the time passed smoothly – with some occasional checks and drawbacks, which were the more easily endured seeing that they took their rise in Isabel's own conduct. Compliant as she was in general, there were two instances, among others, in which her resolution to take her own way was not to be overcome. She refused to write either to Moody or to Lady Lydiard informing them of her engagement; and she steadily disapproved of Miss Pink's policy of concealment, in the matter of the robbery at Lady Lydiard's house. Her aunt could only secure her as a passive accomplice by stating family considerations in the strongest possible terms. 'If the disgrace was confined to you, my dear, I might leave you to decide. But I am involved in it, as your nearest relative; and, what is more, even the sacred memories of your father and mother might feel the slur cast on them.' This exaggerated language – like all exaggerated language, a mischievous weapon in the arsenal of weakness and prejudice – had its effect on Isabel. Reluctantly and sadly, she consented to be silent.

Miss Pink wrote word of the engagement to Moody first; reserving to a later day the superior pleasure of informing Lady Lydiard of the very event which that audacious woman had declared to be impossible. To her aunt's surprise, just as she was about to close the envelope Isabel stepped forward, and inconsistently requested leave to add a postscript to the very letter which she had refused to write! Miss Pink was not even permitted to see the postscript. Isabel secured the envelope the moment she laid down her pen, and retired to her room with a headache (which was heartache in disguise) for the rest of the day.

While the question of marriage was still in debate, an event occurred which exercised a serious influence on Hardyman's future plans.

He received a letter from the Continent which claimed his immediate attention. One of the sovereigns of Europe had decided on making some radical changes in the mounting and equipment of a cavalry regiment; and he required the assistance of Hardyman in that important part of the contemplated reform which was connected with the choice and purchase of horses. Setting his own interests out of the question, Hardyman owed obligations to the kindness of his illustrious correspondent which made it impossible for him to send an excuse. In a fortnight's time, at the latest, it would be necessary for him to leave England; and a month or more might elapse before it would be possible for him to return.

Under these circumstances, he proposed, in his own precipitate way, to hasten the date of the marriage. The necessary legal delay would permit the ceremony to be performed on that day fortnight. Isabel might then accompany him on his journey, and spend a brilliant honeymoon at the foreign Court. She at once refused, not only to accept his proposal, but even to take it into consideration. While Miss Pink dwelt eloquently on the shortness of the notice, Miss Pink's niece based her resolution on far more important grounds. Hardyman had not yet announced the contemplated marriage to his parents and friends; and Isabel was determined not to become his wife until she could be first assured of a courteous and tolerant reception by the family – if she could hope for no warmer welcome at their hands.

Hardyman was not a man who yielded easily, even in trifles. In the present case, his dearest interests were concerned in inducing Isabel to reconsider her decision. He was still vainly trying to shake her resolution, when the afternoon post brought a letter for Miss Pink which introduced a new element of disturbance into the discussion. The letter was nothing less than Lady Lydiard's reply to the written announcement of Isabel's engagement, despatched on the previous day by Miss Pink.

Her Ladyship's answer was a surprisingly short one. It only contained these lines:

'Lady Lydiard begs to acknowledge the receipt of Miss Pink's letter requesting that she will say nothing to Mr Hardyman of the loss of a bank-note in her house, and, assigning as a reason that Miss Isabel Miller is engaged to be married to Mr Hardyman, and might be prejudiced in his estimation if the facts were made known. Miss Pink may make her mind easy. Lady Lydiard had not the slightest intention of taking Mr Hardyman into her confidence on the subject of her domestic affairs. With regard to the proposed marriage, Lady Lydiard casts no doubt on Miss Pink's perfect sincerity and good faith; but, at the same time, she positively declines to believe that Mr Hardyman means to make Miss Isabel Miller his wife. Lady L. will yield to the evidence of a properly-attested certificate – and to nothing else.'

A folded piece of paper, directed to Isabel, dropped out of this characteristic letter as Miss Pink turned from the first page to the second. Lady Lydiard addressed her adopted daughter in these words:

'I was on the point of leaving home to visit you again, when I received your aunt's letter. My poor deluded child, no words can tell how distressed I am about you. You are already sacrificed to the folly of the most foolish woman living. For God's sake, take care you do not fall a victim next to the designs of a profligate man. Come to me instantly, Isabel, and I promise to take care of you.'

Fortified by these letters, and aided by Miss Pink's indignation, Hardyman pressed his proposal on Isabel with renewed resolution. She made no attempt to combat his arguments – she only held firmly to her decision. Without some encouragement from Hardyman's father and mother she still steadily refused to become his wife. Irritated already by Lady Lydiard's letters, he lost the self-command which so eminently distinguished him in the ordinary affairs of life, and showed the domineering and despotic temper which was an inbred part of his disposition. Isabel's high spirit at once resented the harsh terms in which he spoke to her. In the plainest words, she released him from his engagement, and, without waiting for his excuses, quitted the room.

Left together, Hardyman and Miss Pink devised an arrangement which paid due respect to Isabel's scruples, and at the same time met Lady Lydiard's insulting assertion of disbelief in Hardyman's honour, by a formal and public announcement of the marriage.

It was proposed to give a garden party at the farm in a week's time, for the express purpose of introducing Isabel to Hardyman's family and friends in the character of his betrothed wife. If his father and mother accepted the invitation, Isabel's only objection to hastening the union would fall to the ground. Hardyman might, in that case, plead with his Imperial correspondent for a delay in his departure of a few days more; and the marriage might still take place before he left England. Isabel, at Miss Pink's intercession, was induced to accept her lover's excuses, and, in the event of her favourable reception by Hardyman's parents at the farm, to give her consent (not very willingly even yet) to hastening the ceremony which was to make her Hardyman's wife.

On the next morning the whole of the invitations were sent out, excepting the invitation to Hardyman's father and mother. Without mentioning it to Isabel, Hardyman decided on personally appealing to his mother before he ventured on taking the head of the family into his confidence.

The result of the interview was partially successful – and no more. Lord Rotherfield declined to see his youngest son; and he had engagements which would, under any circumstances, prevent his being present at the garden party. But, at the express request of Lady Rotherfield, he was willing to make certain concessions.

'I have always regarded Alfred as a barely sane person,' said his Lordship, 'since he turned his back on his prospects to become a horse-dealer. If we decline altogether to sanction this new act – I won't say, of insanity, I will say, of absurdity – on his part, it is impossible to predict to what discreditable extremities he may not proceed. We must temporise with Alfred. In the meantime I shall endeavour to obtain some information respecting this young person – named Miller, I think you said, and now resident at South Morden. If I am satisfied that she is a woman of reputable character, possessing an average education and presentable manners, we may as well let Alfred take his own way. He is out of the pale of Society, as it is; and Miss Miller has no father and mother to complicate matters, which is distinctly a merit on her part – and, in short, if the marriage is not absolutely disgraceful, the wisest way (as we have no power to prevent it) will be to submit. You will say nothing to Alfred about what I propose to do. I tell you plainly I don't trust him. You will simply inform him from me that I want time to consider, and that, unless he hears to the contrary in the interval, he may expect to have the sanction of your presence at his breakfast, or luncheon, or whatever it is. I must go to town in a day or two, and I shall ascertain what Alfred's friends know about this last of his many follies, if I meet any of them at the club.'

Returning to South Morden in no serene frame of mind, Hardyman found Isabel in a state of depression which perplexed and alarmed him.

The news that his mother might be expected to be present at the garden party failed entirely to raise her spirits. The only explanation she gave of the change in her was, that the dull heavy weather of the last few days made her feel a little languid and nervous. Naturally dissatisfied with this reply to his inquiries, Hardyman asked for Miss Pink. He was informed that Miss Pink could not see him. She was constitutionally subject to asthma, and, having warnings of the return of the malady, she was (by the doctor's advice) keeping her room. Hardyman returned to the farm in a temper which was felt by everybody in his employment, from the trainer to the stable-boys.

While the apology made for Miss Pink stated no more than the plain truth, it must be confessed that Hardyman was right in declining to be satisfied with Isabel's excuse for the melancholy that oppressed her. She had that morning received Moody's answer to the lines which she had addressed to him at the end of her aunt's letter; and she had not yet recovered from the effect which it had produced on her spirits.

'It is impossible for me to say honestly that I am not distressed (Moody wrote) by the news of your marriage engagement. The blow has fallen very heavily on me. When I look at the future now, I see only a dreary blank. This is not your fault – you are in no way to blame. I remember the time when I should have been too angry to own this – when I might have said or done things which I should have bitterly repented afterwards. That time is past. My temper has been softened, since I have befriended you in your troubles. That good at least has come out of my foolish hopes, and perhaps out of the true sympathy which I have felt for you. I can honestly ask you to accept my heart's dearest wishes for your happiness – and I can keep the rest to myself.

'Let me say a word now relating to the efforts that I have made to help you, since that sad day when you left Lady Lydiard's house.

'I had hoped (for reasons which it is needless to mention here) to interest Mr Hardyman himself in aiding our inquiry. But your aunt's wishes, as expressed in her letter to me, close my lips. I will only beg you, at some convenient time, to let me mention the last discoveries that we have made; leaving it to your discretion, when Mr Hardyman has become your husband, to ask him the questions which, under other circumstances, I should have put to him myself.

'It is, of course, possible that the view I take of Mr Hardyman's capacity to help us may be a mistaken one. In this case, if you still wish the investigation to be privately carried on, I entreat you to let me continue to direct it, as the greatest favour you can confer on your devoted old friend.

'You need be under no apprehension about the expense to which you are likely to put me. I have unexpectedly inherited what is to me a handsome fortune.

'The same post which brought your aunt's letter brought a line from a lawyer asking me to see him on the subject of my late father's affairs. I waited a day or two before I could summon heart enough to see him, or to see anybody; and then I went to his office. You have heard that my father's bank stopped payment, at a time of commercial panic. His failure was mainly attributable to the treachery of a friend to whom he had lent a large sum of money, and who paid him the yearly interest, without acknowledging that every farthing of it had been lost in unsuccessful speculations. The son of this man has prospered in business, and he has honourably devoted a part of his wealth to the payment of his father's creditors. Half the sum due to *my* father has thus passed into my hands as his next of kin; and the other half is to follow in course of time. If my hopes had been fulfilled, how gladly I should have shared my prosperity with you! As it is, I have far more than enough for my wants as a lonely man, and plenty left to spend in your service.

'God bless and prosper you, my dear. I shall ask you to accept a little present from me, among the other offerings that are made to you before the wedding day. – R.M.'

The studiously considerate and delicate tone in which these lines were written had an effect on Isabel which was exactly the opposite of the effect intended by the writer. She burst into a passionate fit of tears; and in the safe solitude of her own room, the despairing words escaped her, 'I wish I had died before I met with Alfred Hardyman!'

As the days wore on, disappointments and difficulties seemed by a kind of fatality to beset the contemplated announcement of the marriage. Miss Pink's asthma, developed by the unfavourable weather, set the doctor's art at defiance, and threatened to keep that unfortunate lady a prisoner in her room on the day of the party. Hardyman's invitations were in some cases refused; and in others accepted by husbands with excuses for the absence of their wives. His elder brother made an apology for himself as well as for his wife. Felix Sweetsir wrote, 'With pleasure, dear Alfred, if my health permits me to leave the house.' Lady Lydiard, invited at Miss Pink's special request, sent no reply. The one encouraging circumstance was the silence of Lady Rotherfield. So long as her son received no intimation to the contrary, it was a sign that Lord Rotherfield permitted his wife to sanction the marriage by her presence.

Hardyman wrote to his Imperial correspondent, engaging to leave England on the earliest possible day, and asking to be pardoned if he failed to express himself more definitely, in consideration of domestic affairs, which it was necessary to settle before he started for the Continent. If there should not be time enough to write again, he promised to send a telegraphic announcement of his departure. Long afterwards, Hardyman remembered the misgivings that had troubled him when he wrote that letter. In the rough draught of it, he had mentioned, as his excuse for not being yet certain of his own movements, that he expected to be immediately married. In the fair copy, the vague foreboding of some accident to come was so painfully present to his mind, that he struck out the words which referred to his marriage, and substituted the designedly indefinite phrase, 'domestic affairs'.

▫ TWENTY ▫

THE DAY OF THE GARDEN PARTY arrived. There was no rain; but the air was heavy, and the sky was overcast by lowering clouds.

Some hours before the guests were expected, Isabel arrived alone at the farm, bearing the apologies of unfortunate Miss Pink, still kept a prisoner in her bed-chamber by the asthma. In the confusion produced at the cottage by the preparations for entertaining the company, the one room in which Hardyman could receive Isabel with the certainty of not being interrupted was the smoking-room. To this haven of refuge he led her – still reserved and silent, still not restored to her customary spirits. 'If any visitors come before the time,' Hardyman said to his servant, 'tell them I am engaged at the stables. I must have an hour's quiet talk with you,' he continued, turning to Isabel, 'or I shall be in too bad a temper to receive my guests with common politeness. The worry of giving this party is not to be told in words. I almost wish I had been content with presenting you to my mother, and had let the rest of my acquaintances go to the devil.'

A quiet half hour passed; and the first visitor, a stranger to the servants, appeared at the cottage-gate. He was a middle-aged man, and he had no wish to disturb Mr Hardyman. 'I will wait in the grounds,' he said, 'and trouble nobody.' The middle-aged man, who expressed himself in these modest terms, was Robert Moody.

Five minutes later, a carriage drove up to the gate. An elderly lady got out of it, followed by a fat white Scotch terrier, who growled at every stranger within his reach. It is needless to introduce Lady Lydiard and Tommie.

Informed that Mr Hardyman was at the stables, Lady Lydiard gave the servant her card. 'Take that to your master, and say I won't detain him five minutes.' With these words, her Ladyship sauntered into the grounds. She looked about her with observant eyes; not only noticing the tent which had been set up on the grass to accommodate the expected guests, but entering it, and looking at the waiters who were engaged in placing the luncheon on the table. Returning to the outer world, she next remarked that Mr Hardyman's lawn was in very bad order. Barren sun-dried patches, and little holes and crevices opened here and there by the action of the summer heat, announced that the lawn, like everything else at the farm, had been neglected, in the exclusive attention paid to the claims of the horses. Reaching a shrubbery which bounded one side of the grounds next, her Ladyship became aware of a man slowly approaching her, to all appearance absorbed in thought. The man drew a little nearer. She lifted her glasses to her eyes and recognized – Moody.

No embarrassment was produced on either side by this unexpected meeting. Lady Lydiard had, not long since, sent to ask her former steward to visit her; regretting, in her warm-hearted way, the terms on which they had separated, and wishing to atone for the harsh language that had escaped her at their parting interview. In the friendly talk which followed the reconciliation, Lady Lydiard not only heard the news of Moody's pecuniary inheritance – but, noticing the change in his appearance for the worse, contrived to extract from him the confession of his ill-starred passion for Isabel. To discover him now, after all that he had acknowledged, walking about the grounds at Hardyman's farm, took her Ladyship completely by surprise. 'Good Heavens!' she exclaimed, in her loudest tones, 'what are you doing here?'

'You mentioned Mr Hardyman's garden party, my Lady, when I had the honour of waiting on you,' Moody answered. 'Thinking over it afterwards, it seemed the fittest occasion I could find for making a little wedding present to Miss Isabel. Is there any harm in my asking Mr Hardyman to let me put the present on her plate, so that she may see it when she sits down to luncheon? If your Ladyship thinks so, I will go away directly, and send the gift by post.'

Lady Lydiard looked at him attentively. 'You don't despise the girl,' she asked, 'for selling herself for rank and money? I do – I can tell you!'

Moody's worn white face flushed a little. 'No, my Lady,' he answered, 'I can't hear you say that! Isabel would not have engaged herself to Mr Hardyman unless she had been fond of him – as fond, I dare say, as I once hoped she might be of me. It's a hard thing to confess that; but I do confess it, in justice to her – God bless her!'

The generosity that spoke in those simple words touched the finest sympathies in Lady Lydiard's nature. 'Give me your hand,' she said, with her own generous spirit kindling in her eyes. 'You have a great heart, Moody. Isabel Miller is a fool for not marrying *you* – and one day she will know it!'

Before a word more could pass between them, Hardyman's voice was audible on the other side of the shrubbery, calling irritably to his servant to find Lady Lydiard.

Moody retired to the farther end of the walk, while Lady Lydiard advanced in the opposite direction, so as to meet Hardyman at the entrance to the shrubbery. He bowed stiffly, and begged to know why her Ladyship had honoured him with a visit.

Lady Lydiard replied without noticing the coldness of her reception. 'I have not been very well, Mr Hardyman, or you would have seen me before this. My only object in presenting myself here is to make my excuses personally for having written of you in terms which expressed a doubt of your honour. I have done you an injustice, and I beg you to forgive me.'

Hardyman acknowledged this frank apology as unreservedly as it had been offered to him. 'Say no more, Lady Lydiard. And let me hope, now you are here, that you will honour my little party with your presence.'

Lady Lydiard gravely stated her reasons for not accepting the invitation.

'I disapprove so strongly of unequal marriages,' she said, walking on slowly towards the cottage, 'that I cannot, in common consistency, become one of your guests. I shall always feel interested in Isabel Miller's welfare; and I can honestly say I shall be glad if your married life proves that my old-fashioned prejudices are without justification in your case. Accept my thanks for your invitation; and let me hope that my plain-speaking has not offended you.'

She bowed, and looked about her for Tommie before she advanced to the carriage waiting for her at the gate. In the surprise of seeing Moody she had forgotten to look back for the dog when she entered the shrubbery. She now called to him, and blew the whistle at her watch-chain. Not a sign of Tommie was to be seen. Hardyman instantly directed the servants to search in the cottage and out of the cottage for the dog. The order was obeyed with all needful activity and intelligence, and entirely without success. For the time being, at any rate, Tommie was lost.

Hardyman promised to have the dog looked for in every part of the farm, and to send him back in the care of one of his own men. With these polite assurances Lady Lydiard was obliged to be satisfied. She drove away in a very despondent frame of mind. 'First Isabel, and now Tommie,' thought her Ladyship. 'I am losing the only companions who made life tolerable to me.'

Returning from the garden gate, after taking leave of his visitor, Hardyman received from his servant a handful of letters which had just arrived for him. Walking slowly over the lawn as he opened them, he found nothing but excuses for the absence of guests who had already accepted their invitations. He had just thrust the letters into his pocket, when he heard footsteps behind him, and, looking round, found himself confronted by Moody.

'Hullo! have you come to lunch?' Hardyman asked roughly.

'I have come here, sir, with a little gift for Miss Isabel, in honour of her marriage,' Moody answered quietly. 'And I ask your permission to put it on the table, so that she may see it when your guests sit down to luncheon.'

He opened a jeweller's case as he spoke, containing a plain gold bracelet with an inscription engraved on the inner side: – 'To Miss Isabel Miller, with the sincere good wishes of Robert Moody.'

Plain as it was, the design of the bracelet was unusually beautiful. Hardyman had noticed Moody's agitation on the day when he had met Isabel near her aunt's house, and had drawn his own conclusions from it. His face darkened with a momentary jealousy as he looked at the bracelet. 'All right, old fellow!' he said, with contemptuous familiarity. 'Don't be modest. Wait and give it to her with your own hand.'

'No, sir,' said Moody 'I would rather leave it, if you please, to speak for itself.'

Hardyman understood the delicacy of feeling which dictated those words, and, without well knowing why, resented it. He was on the point of speaking, under the influence of this unworthy motive, when Isabel's voice reached his ears, calling to him from the cottage.

Moody's face contracted with a sudden expression of pain as he too recognised the voice. 'Don't let me detain you, sir,' he said sadly. 'Good morning!'

Hardyman left him without ceremony. Moody, slowly following, entered the tent. All the preparations for the luncheon had been completed; nobody was there. The places to be occupied by the guests were indicated by cards bearing their names. Moody found Isabel's card, and put his bracelet inside the folded napkin on her plate. For a while he stood with his hand on the table, thinking. The temptation to communicate once more with Isabel before he lost her for ever, was fast getting the better of his powers of resistance. 'If I could persuade her to write a word to say she liked her bracelet,' he thought, 'it would be a comfort when I go back to my solitary life.' He tore a leaf out of his pocket book and wrote on it, 'One line to say you accept my gift and my good wishes. Put it under the cushion of your chair, and I shall find it when the company have left the tent.' He slipped the paper into the case which held the bracelet, and instead of leaving the farm as he had intended, turned back to the shelter of the shrubbery.

❧ TWENTY-ONE ❦

HARDYMAN WENT ON TO THE COTTAGE. He found Isabel in some agitation. And there, by her side, with his tail wagging slowly, and his eye on Hardyman in expectation of a possible kick – there was the lost Tommie!

'Has Lady Lydiard gone?' Isabel asked eagerly.

'Yes,' said Hardyman. 'Where did you find the dog?'

As events had ordered it, the dog had found Isabel, under these circumstances.

The appearance of Lady Lydiard's card in the smoking-room had been an alarming event for Lady Lydiard's adopted daughter. She was guiltily conscious of not having answered her Ladyship's note, enclosed in Miss Pink's letter, and of not having taken her Ladyship's advice in regulating her conduct towards Hardyman. As he rose to leave the room and receive his visitor in the grounds, Isabel begged him to say nothing of her presence at the farm, unless Lady Lydiard exhibited a forgiving turn of mind by asking to see her. Left by herself in the smoking-room, she suddenly heard a bark in the passage which had a familiar sound in her ears. She opened the door – and in rushed Tommie, with one of his shrieks of delight! Curiosity had taken him into the house. He had heard the voices in the smoking-room; had recognized Isabel's voice; and had waited, with his customary cunning and his customary distrust of strangers, until Hardyman was out of the way. Isabel kissed and caressed him, and then drove him out again to the lawn, fearing that Lady Lydiard might return to look for him. Going back to the smoking-room, she stood at the window watching for Hardyman's return. When the servants came to look for the dog, she could only tell them that she had last seen him in the grounds, not far from the cottage. The useless search being abandoned, and the carriage having left the gate, who should crawl out from the back of a cupboard in which some empty hampers were placed but Tommie himself! How he had contrived to get back to the smoking-room (unless she had omitted to completely close the door on her return) it was impossible to say. But there he was, determined this time to stay with Isabel, and keeping in his hiding place until he heard the movement of the carriage-wheels, which informed him that his lawful mistress had left the cottage! Isabel had at once called Hardyman, on the chance that the carriage might yet be stopped. It was already out of sight, and nobody knew which of two roads it had taken, both leading to London. In this emergency, Isabel could only look at Hardyman and ask what was to be done.

'I can't spare a servant till after the party,' he answered. 'The dog must be tied up in the stables.'

Isabel shook her head. Tommie was not accustomed to be tied up. He would make a disturbance, and he would be beaten by the grooms. 'I will take care of him,' she said. 'He won't leave me.'

'There's something else to think of besides the dog,' Hardyman rejoined irritably. 'Look at these letters!' He pulled them out of his pocket as he spoke. 'Here are no less than seven men, all calling themselves my friends, who accepted my invitation, and who write to excuse themselves on the very day of the party. Do you know why? They're all afraid of my father – I forgot to tell you he's a Cabinet Minister as well as a Lord. Cowards and cads. They have heard he isn't coming, and they think to curry favour with the great man by stopping away. Come along, Isabel! Let's take their names off the luncheon table. Not a man of them shall ever darken my doors again!'

'I am to blame for what has happened,' Isabel answered sadly. 'I am estranging you from your friends. There is still time, Alfred, to alter your mind and let me go.'

He put his arm round her with rough fondness. 'I would sacrifice every friend I have in the world rather than lose you. Come along!'

They left the cottage. At the entrance to the tent, Hardyman noticed the dog at Isabel's heels, and vented his ill-temper, as usual with male humanity, on the nearest unoffending creature that he could find 'Be off, you mongrel brute!' he shouted. The tail of Tommie relaxed from its customary tight curve over the small of his back; and the legs of Tommie (with his tail between them) took him at full gallop to the friendly shelter of the cupboard in the smoking-room. It was one of those trifling circumstances which women notice seriously. Isabel said nothing; she only thought to herself, 'I wish he had shown his temper when I first knew him!'

They entered the tent.

'I'll read the names,' said Hardyman, 'and you find the cards and tear them up. Stop! I'll keep the cards. You're just the sort of woman my father likes. He'll be reconciled to me when he sees you, after we are married. If one of those men ever asks him for a place, I'll take care, if it's years hence, to put an obstacle in his way! Here; take my pencil, and make a mark on the cards to remind me; – the same mark I set against a horse in my book when I don't like him – a cross, enclosed in a circle.' He produced his pocket-book. His hands trembled with anger as he gave the pencil to Isabel and laid the book on the table. He had just read the name of the first false friend, and Isabel had just found the card, when a servant appeared with a message. 'Mrs Drumblade has arrived, sir, and wishes to see you on a matter of the greatest importance.'

Hardyman left the tent, not very willingly. 'Wait here,' he said to Isabel; 'I'll be back directly.'

She was standing near her own place at the table. Moody had left one end of the jeweller's case visible above the napkin, to attract her attention. In a minute more the bracelet and note were in her hands. She dropped on her chair, overwhelmed by the conflicting emotions that rose in her at the sight of the bracelet, at the reading of the note. Her head drooped, and the tears filled her eyes. 'Are all women as blind as I have been to what is good and noble in the men who love them?' she wondered, sadly. 'Better as it is,' she thought, with a bitter sigh; 'I am not worthy of him.'

As she took up the pencil to write her answer to Moody on the back of her dinner-card, the servant appeared again at the door of the tent.

'My master wants you at the cottage, Miss, immediately.'

Isabel rose, putting the bracelet and the note in the silver-mounted leather pocket (a present from Hardyman) which hung at her belt. In the hurry of passing round the table to get out, she never noticed that her dress touched Hardyman's pocket-book, placed close to the edge, and threw it down on the grass below. The book fell into one of the heatcracks which Lady Lydiard had noticed as evidence of the neglected condition of the cottage lawn.

'You ought to hear the pleasant news my sister has just brought me,' said Hardyman, when Isabel joined him in the parlour. 'Mrs Drumblade has been told, on the best authority, that my mother is not coming to the party.'

'There must be some reason, of course, dear Isabel,' added Mrs Drumblade. 'Have you any idea of what it can be? I haven't seen my mother myself; and all my inquiries have failed to find it out.'

She looked searchingly at Isabel as she spoke. The mask of sympathy on her face was admirably worn. Nobody who possessed only a superficial acquaintance with Mrs Drumblade's character would have suspected how thoroughly she was enjoying in secret the position of embarrassment in which her news had placed her brother. Instinctively doubting whether Mrs Drumblade's friendly behaviour was quite as sincere as it appeared to be, Isabel answered that she was a stranger to Lady Rotherfield, and was therefore quite at a loss to explain the cause of her ladyship's absence. As she spoke, the guests began to arrive in quick succession, and the subject was dropped as a matter of course.

It was not a merry party. Hardyman's approaching marriage had been made the topic of much malicious gossip; and Isabel's character had, as usual in such cases, become the object of all the false reports that scandal could invent. Lady Rotherfield's absence confirmed the general conviction that Hardyman was disgracing himself. The men were all more or less uneasy. The women resented the discovery that Isabel was – personally speaking, at least – beyond the reach of hostile criticism. Her beauty was viewed as a downright offence; her refined and modest manners were set down as perfect acting; 'really disgusting, my dear, in so young a girl.' General Drumblade, a large and mouldy veteran, in a state of chronic astonishment (after his own matrimonial experience) at Hardyman's folly in marrying at all, diffused a wide circle of gloom, wherever he went and whatever he did. His accomplished wife, forcing her high spirits on everybody's attention with a sort of kittenish playfulness, intensified the depressing effect of the general dullness by all the force of the strongest contrast. After waiting half an hour for his mother, and waiting in vain, Hardyman led the way to the tent in despair. 'The sooner I fill their stomachs and get rid of them,' he thought savagely, 'the better I shall be pleased!'

The luncheon was attacked by the company with a certain silent ferocity, which the waiters noticed as remarkable, even in their large experience. The men drank deeply, but with wonderfully little effect in raising their spirits; the women, with the exception of amiable Mrs Drumblade, kept Isabel deliberately out of the conversation that went on among them. General Drumblade, sitting next to her in one of the places of honour, discoursed to Isabel privately on 'my brother-in-law Hardyman's infernal temper'. A young marquis, on her other side – a mere lad, chosen to make the necessary speech in acknowledgment of his superior rank – rose, in a state of nervous trepidation, to propose Isabel's health as the chosen bride of their host. Pale and trembling, conscious of having forgotten the words which he had learnt before-hand, this unhappy young nobleman began, 'Ladies and gentlemen, I haven't an idea——' He stopped, put his hand to his head, stared wildly, and sat down again; having contrived to state his own case with masterly brevity and perfect truth, in a speech of seven words.

While the dismay, in some cases, and the amusement in others, was still at its height, Hardyman's valet made his appearance, and, approaching his master, said in a whisper, 'Could I speak to you, sir, for a moment outside?'

'What the devil do you want?' Hardyman asked irritably. 'Is that a letter in your hand? Give it to me.'

The valet was a Frenchman. In other words, he had a sense of what was due to himself. His master had forgotten this. He gave up the letter with a certain dignity of manner, and left the tent. Hardyman opened the letter. He turned pale as he read it; crumpled it in his hand, and threw it down on the table. 'By G——d! it's a lie!' he exclaimed furiously.

The guests rose in confusion. Mrs Drumblade, finding the letter within her reach, coolly possessed herself of it; recognized her mother's handwriting; and read these lines:

'I have only now succeeded in persuading your father to let me write to you. For God's sake, break off your marriage at any sacrifice. Your father has heard, on unanswerable authority, that Miss Isabel Miller left her situation in Lady Lydiard's house on suspicion of theft.'

While his sister was reading this letter, Hardyman had made his way to Isabel's chair. 'I must speak to you, directly,' he whispered. 'Come away with me!' He turned, as he took her arm, and looked at the table. 'Where is my letter?' he asked. Mrs Drumblade handed it to him, dexterously crumpled up again as she had found it. 'No bad news, dear Alfred, I hope?' she said, in her most affectionate manner. Hardyman snatched the letter from her, without answering, and led Isabel out of the tent.

'Read that!' he said, when they were alone. 'And tell me at once whether it's true or false.'

Isabel read the letter. For a moment the shock of the discovery held her speechless. She recovered herself, and returned the letter.

'It is true,' she answered.

671

Hardyman staggered back as if she had shot him.

'True that you are guilty?' he asked.

'No; I am innocent. Everybody who knows me believes in my innocence. It is true the appearances were against me. They are against me still.' Having said this, she waited, quietly and firmly, for his next words.

He passed his hand over his forehead with a sigh of relief. 'It's bad enough as it is,' he said, speaking quietly on his side. 'But the remedy for it is plain enough. Come back to the tent.'

She never moved. 'Why?' she asked.

'Do you suppose I don't believe in your innocence too?' he answered. 'The one way of setting you right with the world now is for me to make you my wife, in spite of the appearances that point to you. I'm too fond of you, Isabel, to give you up. Come back with me, and I will announce our marriage to my friends.'

She took his hand, and kissed it. 'It is generous and good of you,' she said; 'but it must not be.'

He took a step nearer to her. 'What do you mean?' he asked.

'It was against my will,' she pursued, 'that my aunt concealed the truth from you. I did wrong to consent to it; I will do wrong no more. Your mother is right, Alfred. After what has happened, I am not fit to be your wife until my innocence is proved. It is not proved yet.'

The angry colour began to rise in his face once more. 'Take care,' he said; 'I am not in a humour to be trifled with.'

'I am not trifling with you,' she answered, in low, sad tones.

'You really mean what you say?'

'I mean it.'

'Don't be obstinate, Isabel. Take time to consider.'

'You are very kind, Alfred. My duty is plain to me. I will marry you – if you still wish it – when my good name is restored to me. Not before.'

He laid one hand on her arm, and pointed with the other to the guests in the distance, all leaving the tent on the way to their carriages.

'Your good name will be restored to you,' he said, 'on the day when I make you my wife. The worst enemy you have cannot associate *my* name with a suspicion of theft. Remember that and think a little before you decide. You see those people there. If you don't change your mind by the time they have got to the cottage, it's good-bye between us, and good-bye for ever. I refuse to wait for you; I refuse to accept a conditional engagement. Wait, and think. They're walking slowly; you have got some minutes more.'

He still held her arm, watching the guests as they gradually receded from view. It was not until they had all collected in a group outside the cottage door that he spoke himself, or that he permitted Isabel to speak again.

'Now,' he said, 'you have had your time to get cool. Will you take my arm, and join those people with me? or will you say good-bye for ever?'

'Forgive me, Alfred!' she began, gently. 'I cannot consent, in justice to you, to shelter myself behind your name. It is the name of your family; and they have a right to expect that you will not degrade it—'

'I want a plain answer,' he interposed sternly. 'Which is it? Yes, or No?'

She looked at him with sad compassionate eyes. Her voice was firm as she answered him in one word as he had desired. The word was – 'No.'

Without speaking to her, without even looking at her, he turned and walked back to the cottage.

Making his way silently through the group of visitors – every one of whom had been informed of what had happened by his sister – with his head down and his lips fast closed, he entered the parlour, and rang the bell which communicated with his foreman's rooms at the stables.

'You know that I am going abroad on business?' he said, when the man appeared.

'Yes, sir.'

'I am going to-day – going by the night train to Dover. Order the horse to be put to instantly in the dog-cart. Is there anything wanted before I am off?'

The inexorable necessities of business asserted their claims through the obedient medium of the foreman. Chafing at the delay, Hardyman was obliged to sit at his desk, signing cheques and passing accounts, with the dog-cart waiting in the stable-yard.

A knock at the door startled him in the middle of his work. 'Come in,' he called out sharply.

He looked up, expecting to see one of the guests or one of the servants. It was Moody who entered the room. Hardyman laid down his pen, and fixed his eyes sternly on the man who had dared to interrupt him.

'What the devil do *you* want?' he asked.

'I have seen Miss Isabel, and spoken with her,' Moody replied. 'Mr Hardyman, I believe it is in your power to set this matter right. For the young lady's sake, sir, you must not leave England without doing it.'

Hardyman turned to his foreman. 'Is this fellow mad or drunk?' he asked.

Moody proceeded as calmly and as resolutely as if those words had not been spoken. 'I apologize for my intrusion, sir. I will trouble you with no explanations. I will only ask one question. Have you a memorandum of the number of that five-hundred pound note you paid away in France?'

Hardyman lost all control over himself.

'You scoundrel!' he cried, 'have you been prying into my private affairs? Is it *your* business to know what I did in France?'

'Is it *your* vengeance on a woman to refuse to tell her the number of a bank-note?' Moody rejoined, firmly.

That answer forced its way, through Hardyman's anger, to Hardyman's sense of honour. He rose and advanced to Moody. For a moment the two men faced each other in silence. 'You're a bold fellow,' said Hardyman, with a sudden change from anger to irony. 'I'll do the lady justice. I'll look at my pocket-book.'

He put his hand into the breast-pocket of his coat; he searched his other pockets; he turned over the objects on his writing-table. The book was gone.

Moody watched him with a feeling of despair. 'Oh! Mr Hardyman, don't say you have lost your pocket-book!'

He sat down again at his desk, with sullen submission to the new disaster. 'All I can say is you're at liberty to look for it,' he replied. 'I must have dropped it somewhere.' He turned impatiently to the foreman, 'Now then! What is the next cheque wanted? I shall go mad if I wait in this damned place much longer!'

Moody left him, and found his way to the servants' offices. 'Mr Hardyman has lost his pocket-book,' he said. 'Look for it, indoors and out – on the lawn, and in the tent. Ten pounds reward for the man who finds it!'

Servants and waiters instantly dispersed, eager for the promised reward. The men who pursued the search outside the cottage divided their forces. Some of them examined the lawn and the flower-beds. Others went straight to the empty tent. These last were too completely absorbed in pursuing the object in view to notice that they disturbed a dog, eating a stolen lunch of his own from the morsels left on the plates. The dog slunk away under the canvas when the men came in, waited in hiding until they had gone, then returned to the tent, and went on with his luncheon.

Moody hastened back to the part of the grounds (close to the shrubbery) in which Isabel was waiting his return.

She looked at him, while he was telling her of his interview with Hardyman, with an expression in her eyes which he had never seen in them before – an expression which set his heart beating wildly, and made him break off in his narrative before he had reached the end.

'I understand,' she said quietly, as he stopped in confusion. 'You have made one more sacrifice to my welfare. Robert! I believe you are the noblest man that ever breathed the breath of life!'

His eyes sank before hers; he blushed like a boy. 'I have done nothing for you yet,' he said. 'Don't despair of the future, if the pocket-book should not be found. I know who the man is who received the bank-

674

note; and I have only to find him to decide the question whether it *is* the stolen note or not.'

She smiled sadly as his enthusiasm. 'Are you going back to Mr Sharon to help you?' she asked. 'That trick he played me has destroyed *my* belief in him. He no more knows than I do who the thief really is.'

'You are mistaken, Isabel. He knows – and I know.' He stopped there, and made a sign to her to be silent. One of the servants was approaching them.

'Is the pocket-book found?' Moody asked.

'No, sir.'

'Has Mr Hardyman left the cottage?'

'He has just gone, sir. Have you any further instructions to give us?'

'No. There is my address in London, if the pocket-book should be found.'

The man took the card that was handed to him and retired. Moody offered his arm to Isabel. 'I am at your service,' he said, 'when you wish to return to your aunt.'

They had advanced nearly as far as the tent, on their way out of the grounds, when they were met by a gentleman walking towards them from the cottage. He was a stranger to Isabel. Moody immediately recognised him as Mr Felix Sweetsir.

'Ha! our good Moody!' cried Felix. 'Enviable man! you look younger than ever.' He took off his hat to Isabel; his bright restless eyes suddenly became quiet as they rested on her. 'Have I the honour of addressing the future Mrs Hardyman? May I offer my best congratulations? What has become of our friend Alfred?'

Moody answered for Isabel. 'If you will make inquiries at the cottage, sir,' he said, 'you will find that you are mistaken, to say the least of it, in addressing your questions to this young lady.'

Felix took off his hat again – with the most becoming appearance of surprise and distress.

'Something wrong, I fear?' he said, addressing Isabel. 'I am, indeed, ashamed if I have ignorantly given you a moment's pain. Pray accept my most sincere apologies. I have only this instant arrived; my health would not allow me to be present at the luncheon. Permit me to express the earnest hope that matters may be set right to the satisfaction of all parties. Good afternoon!'

He bowed with elaborate courtesy, and turned back to the cottage.

'Who is that?' Isabel asked.

'Lady Lydiard's nephew, Mr Felix Sweetsir,' Moody answered, with a sudden sternness of tone, and a sudden coldness of manner, which surprised Isabel.

'You don't like him?' she said.

As she spoke, Felix stopped to give audience to one of the grooms, who had apparently been sent with a message to him. He turned so that his face was once more visible to Isabel. Moody pressed her hand significantly as it rested on his arm.

'Look well at that man,' he whispered. 'It's time to warn you. Mr Felix Sweetsir is the worst enemy you have!'

Isabel heard him in speechless astonishment. He went on in tones that trembled with suppressed emotion.

'You doubt if Sharon knows the thief. You doubt if I know the thief. Isabel! as certainly as the heaven is above us, there stands the wretch who stole the bank-note!'

She drew her hand out of his arm with a cry of terror. She looked at him as if she doubted whether he was in his right mind.

He took her hand, and waited a moment trying to compose himself.

'Listen to me,' he said. 'At the first consultation I had with Sharon he gave this advice to Mr Troy and to me. He said, "Suspect the very last person on whom suspicion could possibly fall." Those words, taken with the questions he had asked before he pronounced his opinion, struck through me as if he had struck me with a knife. I instantly suspected Lady Lydiard's nephew. Wait! From that time to this I have said nothing of my suspicion to any living soul. I knew in my own heart that it took its rise in the inveterate dislike that I have always felt for Mr Sweetsir, and I distrusted it accordingly. But I went back to Sharon, for all that, and put the case into his hands. His investigations informed me that Mr Sweetsir owed "debts of honour" (as gentlemen call them), incurred through lost bets, to a large number of persons, and among them a bet of five hundred pounds lost to Mr Hardyman. Further inquiries showed that Mr Hardyman had taken the lead in declaring that he would post Mr Sweetsir as a defaulter, and have him turned out of his clubs, and turned out of the betting-ring. Ruin stared him in the face if he failed to pay his debt to Mr Hardyman on the last day left to him – the day after the note was lost. On that very morning, Lady Lydiard, speaking to me of her nephew's visit to her, said, "If I had given him an opportunity of speaking, Felix would have borrowed money of me; I saw it in his face." One moment more, Isabel. I am not only certain that Mr Sweetsir took the five-hundred pound note out of the open letter, I am firmly persuaded that he is the man who told Lord Rotherfield of the circumstances under which you left Lady Lydiard's house. Your marriage to Mr Hardyman might have put you in a position to detect the theft. You, not I, might, in that case, have discovered from your husband that the stolen note was the note with which Mr Sweetsir paid his debt. He came here, you may depend on it, to make sure that he had succeeded in destroying your prospects. A more depraved villain at heart than that man never swung from a gallows!'

He checked himself at those words. The shock of the disclosure, the passion and vehemence with which he spoke, overwhelmed Isabel. She trembled like a frightened child.

While he was still trying to soothe and reassure her, a low whining made itself heard at her feet. They looked down, and saw Tommie. Finding himself noticed at last, he expressed his sense of relief by a bark. Something dropped out of his mouth. As Moody stooped to pick it up, the dog ran to Isabel and pushed his head against her feet, as his way was when he expected to have the handkerchief thrown over him, preparatory to one of those games at hide-and-seek which have been already mentioned. Isabel put out her hand to caress him, when she was stopped by a cry from Moody. It was *his* turn to tremble now. His voice faltered as he said the words, 'The dog has found the pocket-book!'

He opened the book with shaking hands. A betting-book was bound up in it, with the customary calendar. He turned to the date of the day after the robbery.

There was the entry: – 'Felix Sweetsir. Paid £500. Note numbered, N 8, 70564; dated 15 May, 1875.'

Moody took from his waistcoat-pocket his own memorandum of the number of the lost bank-note. 'Read it, Isabel,' he said. 'I won't trust my memory.'

She read it. The number and date of the note entered in the pocket-book exactly corresponded with the number and date of the note that Lady Lydiard had placed in her letter.

Moody handed the pocket-book to Isabel. 'There is the proof of your innocence,' he said, 'thanks to the dog! Will you write and tell Mr Hardyman what has happened?' he asked, with his head down, and his eyes on the ground.

She answered him, with the bright colour suddenly flowing over her face.

'*You* shall write to him,' she said, 'when the time comes.'

'What time?' he asked.

She threw her arms round his neck, and hid her face on his bosom.

'The time,' she whispered, 'when I am your wife.'

A low growl from Tommie reminded them that he too had some claim to be noticed.

Isabel dropped on her knees, and saluted her old playfellow with the heartiest kisses she had ever given him since the day when their acquaintance began. 'You darling!' she said, as she put him down again, 'what can I do to reward you?'

Tommie rolled over on his back – more slowly than usual, in consequence of his luncheon in the tent. He elevated his four paws in the air, and looked lazily at Isabel out of his bright brown eyes. If ever a dog's look spoke yet, Tommie's look said, 'I have eaten too much; rub my stomach.'

❧ POSTSCRIPT ❧

Persons of a speculative turn of mind are informed that the following document is for sale, and are requested to mention what sum they will give for it.

'IOU, Lady Lydiard, five hundred pounds (£500), Felix Sweetsir.'

Her Ladyship became possessed of this pecuniary remittance under circumstances which surround it with a halo of romantic interest. It was the last communication she was destined to receive from her accomplished nephew. There was a Note attached to it, which cannot fail to enhance its value in the estimation of all right-minded persons who assist the circulation of paper money.

The lines that follow are strictly confidential:

'Note. – Our excellent Moody informs me, my dear aunt, that you have decided (against his advice) on "refusing to prosecute". I have not the slightest idea of what he means; but I am very much obliged to him, nevertheless, for reminding me of a circumstance which is of some interest to yourself personally.

'I am on the point of retiring to the Continent in search of health. One generally forgets something important when one starts on a journey. Before Moody called, I had entirely forgotten to mention that I had the pleasure of borrowing five hundred pounds of you some little time since.

'On the occasion to which I refer, your language and manner suggested that you would not lend me the money if I asked for it. Obviously, the only course left was to take it without asking. I took it while Moody was gone to get some curaçoa; and I returned to the picture-gallery in time to receive that delicious liqueur from the footman's hands.

'You will naturally ask why I found it necessary to supply myself (if I may borrow an expression from the language of State finance) with this "forced loan". I was actuated by motives which I think do

me honour. My position at the time was critical in the extreme. My credit with the money-lenders was at an end; my friends had all turned their backs on me. I must either take the money or disgrace my family. If there is a man living who is sincerely attached to his family, I am that man. I took the money.

'Conceive your position as my aunt (I say nothing of myself), if I had adopted the other alternative. Turned out of the Jockey Club, turned out of Tattersalls', turned out of the betting-ring; in short, posted publicly as a defaulter before the noblest institution in England, the Turf – and all for want of five hundred pounds to stop the mouth of the greatest brute I know of, Alfred Hardyman! Let me not harrow your feelings (and mine) by dwelling on it. Dear and admirable woman! To you belongs the honour of saving the credit of the family; I can claim nothing but the inferior merit of having offered you the opportunity.

'My IOU, it is needless to say, accompanies these lines. Can I do anything for you abroad? – F.S.'

To this it is only necessary to add (first) that Moody was perfectly right in believing F.S. to be the person who informed Hardyman's father of Isabel's position when she left Lady Lydiard's house; and (secondly) that Felix did really forward Mr Troy's narrative of the theft to the French police, altering nothing in it but the number of the lost bank-note.

What is there left to write about? Nothing is left – but to say good-bye (very sorrowfully on the writer's part) to the Persons of the Story.

Good-bye to Miss Pink – who will regret to her dying day that Isabel's answer to Hardyman was No.

Good-bye to Lady Lydiard – who differs with Miss Pink, and would have regretted it, to *her* dying day, if the answer had been Yes.

Good-bye to Moody and Isabel – whose history has closed with the closing of the clergyman's book on their wedding-day.

Good-bye to Hardyman – who has sold his farm and his horses, and has begun a new life among the famous fast trotters of America.

Good-bye to Old Sharon – who, a martyr to his promise, brushed his hair and washed his face in honour of Moody's marriage; and catching a severe cold as the necessary consequence, declared, in the intervals of sneezing, that he would 'never do it again'.

And last, not least, good-bye to Tommie? No. The writer gave Tommie his dinner not half an hour since, and is too fond of him to say good-bye.